Praise

THE ROGUES WHO ~~~~~~

"*Another absolutely fantastic book. The writing is always well thought out, character development is fantastic. I loved the first book and I loved this second book possibly more.*"

— **Laura Lawson**, *iReader*

"*Holy moly! I have not been that absorbed by a series in a long time. Thank you for sharing these stories with us and I cannot wait to see what the next books have in store!*"

— **Amber Doseck**, *iReader*

"*I just moved this author to the top of my must-read list. Absolutely fantastic!*"

— **Rebecca Barwig**, *iReader*

"*I've read many books and been struggling to say which one is the best of the best, now I can safely say this is it – the best of the best.*"

— **Jabuh Mzimela**, *GoodNovel*

"*This is an excellent book, with involved story, developed characters and depth far beyond just the surface.*"

— **Jenniffer Martin**, *GoodNovel*

"*Love this book. This and the one before it. Exceptional writing and delved into rejection, love, identity, self-worth, and community. It's an awesome book. Read it twice.*"

— **Obinna Anyadike**, *GoodNovel*

THE ROGUES WHO WENT ROGUE

Book Two
of Coalescence of the Five

STINA'S PEN

For those seeking second chances,
at times even creating some on their own

PROLOGUE

Drip.

Drop.

Drip.

Drop.

Stalactites along the gravelly, protruding and depressing ceiling guided droplets down their edges and into the puddle below the way melted ice cream meanders down a cone to its tip, the pool of water reflecting the next bead that was about to fall. The rhythm of each fall—normally negligible— now became the most distinct sound in the cave that was tucked in a forest not far from the White Blood Pack. The trees stood so close that darkness seemed to engulf the surroundings earlier than usual. The night silence blanketed the life of day, putting those sounds to rest.

But not everyone was resting.

One of the only two red wolves in existence, Margaret Rouge, had her fist clenched on a long-shaped boulder with the guise of a table. Her red hair only complemented her seething rage. Her followers sat around the boulder, each lost in their own thoughts while their leader's eyes pierced into the woman seated facing her.

They had just returned from scouring for three of their own, only calling it quits when—after three hours of relentless but cautious tracking—they learned that the scents of the ones they'd been looking for trailed to a highly guarded pack with an impenetrable border.

No one said a word, but their eyes spoke volumes: some remained optimistic and unjustifiably ambitious, wondering if there was a way into the White

Blood Pack; some—instead of thinking of a solution—resorted to blaming the one who was supposed to be watching the trio when they snuck out; and the last group simply looked out of the cave, into the gloom of the night, dark as their future was and dead as they felt at the moment.

A low, angered growl came from the red wolf. "You were supposed to be watching them."

All eyes fell on Kate, who had been momentarily distracted during pup-sitting. Her teeth let go of her bottom lip, and after swallowing a lump in her throat, the above-average-sized woman tried to walk around the problem. "We caught their scent trailing to White Blood, Margaret. We can get them back."

Another growl left the depths of Margaret's lungs. One of protest, condescension, and threat. "That is *the most idiotic* thing I've heard from you thus far, Kate. My daughter and her friends have, under your supposed supervision, found their way to one of the most guarded packs in the territory. You really think we can just show up and snatch them back?"

A sudden protrusion of her claws like a sword unsheathed from a scabbard made her followers flinch. In a voice as cold as the night air, Margaret warned, "For your own sake, Kate, you'd better hope I get my daughter back in one piece, or I'll rip out your throat myself."

Everyone agreed that it was reckless to enter the pack. Fortunately, rogues like them had been noticing lycan warriors coming a day after a rogue capture to escort rogues and board them onto jets, bringing them to Goddess knew where. The plan now was to take back her daughter and the other two with her after they were transported out of the pack but before they were brought onto the jet. It wasn't a foolproof plan, but it was the best one they had.

After putting together her best team for a rescue mission, Margaret went to bed and couldn't help but imagine her poor girl being locked in some filthy dungeon. Her eyes pooled in tears as she considered the possibility of her only pup getting raped.

Pack leaders of the strongest packs had no mercy, especially when it came to rogues. She simply hoped that this alpha was either gay or already had a luna who would be merciful enough to spare her daughter of any torment, at least until tomorrow.

CHAPTER 1

Queen Lucianne had just ended the link with Alpha Tate of the White Blood Pack, and his message befuddled and worried her.

She was perched on the edge of the bed, brows knitted and heart racing, even after the link. She considered every possibility of underage rogues running on their own. Some part of her wondered if it was a trap. After she reminded Tate and his people to exercise the highest level of caution, her mind still didn't rest. Couldn't rest. If she didn't give the order to kill and the rogues ended up harming anyone in White Blood, it'd be blood on her hands.

An attack occurred in the Forest Gloom Pack not long ago after a rogue feigned sickness to be released from her cell. Lucy gave permission for her transfer to more hygienic accommodations. The moment the captured impostor saw daylight, her claws went for the guards. A few pack members were injured, but the threat ended when Alpha Clement's claws plunged through the rogue's chest.

No one blamed Lucy for the attack, but the queen blamed herself. *Someone could have gotten hurt. Or died*, she had told her husband.

King Alexandar had to remind her, repeatedly, that wolves healed and no one died and she gave the green light in a situation where anyone in her position would. He would, without hesitation.

The mistake clung onto her mind like a leech. She never allowed rogues to be released for any reason, pending governmental extraction, after that.

In her mind-link with Tate—while considering the dangers of leniency—he reported that the ones he caught tonight were "rogues with no balls" who quivered and whimpered for mercy even before being cuffed. The dungeon and pack border were on full guard, and security cameras were monitored. Nothing out of the ordinary was happening. In fact, the prisoners looked like they'd given up. Although no express permission was sought or given, both Lucy and Tate were considering going easier on the youngest rogue: a thirteen-year-old red wolf.

Lucy's thoughts then went to this species in particular. Red wolves were thought to be extinct generations ago. These were clairvoyants, and—depending on their maturity and psychological stability—they could be either very accurate or inaccurate in telling the future. In the past, some of their precognition abilities were so inaccurate that their own clients had them slaughtered for poor fortune-telling.

Was this why the thirteen-year-old was running? Was she running away from her clients?

The bed dipped, and before Lucy registered the presence, a strong pair of hands wrapped her shoulders, massaging them in slow, affectionate strokes. A ghost of a smile lifted the corner of her lips as her head turned to the side, where her mate's lips trapped hers in a kiss. His large, rough hands trailed down the side of her body, feeling her perfect curves before his arms circled her waist, his thumb brushing her skin through the thin nightwear.

Xandar buried his face in her neck to take in her scent before his deep voice reverberated through her ears, "Who was it, baby?"

"Tate. He said hi," she answered simply, and immediately felt Xandar's grip around her waist tighten. Her hand reached to stroke his muscular arm, tracing its bulges as she continued, "One of the three rogues they caught today was a thirteen-year-old she-wolf. A red one."

His brows shot to his hair. "They still exist?" he asked, pulling away, and his wide eyes were met with his queen's nod.

Forehead creased, his lilac eyes matched the concern in his wife's own when she whispered, "We didn't find any minors in Wu Bi Corp, and none of the rogues behind bars said anything about pups. Where did this girl come from?"

A moment of silence passed between them, the kind that commanded an atmosphere when one was given a mind-boggling riddle. "Would a pack kick out a thirteen-year-old?" he ultimately asked.

"Never!" Lucy exclaimed, then paused, second-guessing. "Not to my knowledge, at least. Disloyal members are normally only cast out after turning eighteen."

"So it's safe to say this one has rogue parents."

"That's . . . possible. But why weren't they with her? Why would one let their teenage daughter run around foreign territory, knowing the risks of getting caught?"

Xandar heaved a heavy, frustrated sigh as his hands moved up to caress his mate's tense shoulders again. "I don't know, sweetheart. Maybe they're dead, already caught, or her parents didn't know what she was up to? Maybe she advertised herself as a precocious fortune-teller and the gig went sideways? Goddess, it could be anything."

"I know." Her small hand reached to stroke his large one. "I thought it was a ploy at first, but it doesn't seem like one. Minors aren't used in a ruse. They panic and shift too quickly." Considering her next move, she uttered, "Before bringing them to lycan territory, I want to meet the red wolf. She and her friends are already scared as it is. I'm going to White Blood with the lycan warriors tomorrow to collect the rogues, Xandar."

The king's animal turned alert. "And you're not thinking of dragging me there with you? Baby, we've been through this!"

Her brows crinkled at the obvious fact he was forgetting. "You and your second-in-command are scheduled to check out a suspected rogue supplier site with the police force tomorrow, my king."

"I could sit this one out. Those sites are always a bust anyway!"

"That doesn't guarantee that this would be a bust as well. You gave them your word, Xandar. You have to go with them," she insisted. She studied Xandar's expression more carefully, feeling his insecurity through their mate bond, seeing some fear in those lilac orbs she had fallen in love with.

Her hand reached for his cheek, bringing their faces closer so their foreheads touched. "Darling, we've marked each other. Tate is not a threat. No one is. I'm only in love with you." After pecking a kiss on his lips, she whispered, "I'm yours, my indecent beast. Only yours."

The largest animal in the kingdom cooed and wagged its tail like it was high on the drug that his mate's words had injected into his brain.

Xandar sighed, knowing nothing was going to change his queen's mind. Leaving a kiss on her head, he muttered, "Keep me posted, okay?"

"Okay," she responded in a shy whisper under his affectionate gaze, which turned flirtatious when he slowly pulled down the straps lining her shoulders. His lips traced her warm skin, then moved to her neck, pecking a trail of soft kisses. Lucy closed her eyes and tilted her head to the side, giving him full access, not caring that she was now topless as she sighed in bliss.

After Xandar's rough hands traced her smooth arms, he lowered Lucy flat on the bed and continued sucking on her neck, relishing in this brand of honey that only he could taste, enjoying the sound of her moans and the feeling of her beautiful breasts pressed against his hot skin.

His hands trailed down to her firm buttocks. Lucy's own palms traced his broad shoulders and hard torso as her feet skillfully pushed down his boxers to bring his erection into full view. In between her moans, her body moved in response to her mate's touch as their lips trapped each other in a deep kiss.

After parting her legs and revealing the glistening moisture, the king entered and began pumping in slow paces, focusing on connecting with the most beautiful and amazing creature in the kingdom now lying below him as he made love to her. The way they looked at each other whenever they started with slow, passionate sex always ignited feelings of love as deep and fiery as the earth's core, happiness as blissful as walking along the shoreline, and desire that made them crave for each other even more than they already were.

Xandar gradually increased his speed as his queen gasped, whimpered, and moaned his name. It didn't take long before he began moaning with her. When her core locked him in, they both came with irrepressible screams.

Their euphoric eyes met as they took quickened breaths like they had just completed a race. And without pulling out, Xandar pecked a loving kiss on Lucy's lips before he whispered, "I love you."

She knew. She knew because she felt it. Not just through those three words or through his eyes, but through their bond. He loved her.

Leaning in to touch her nose with his, she replied, "I know, Xandar. I love you too."

CHAPTER 2

The next morning, Xandar and Lucy kissed baby Reida goodbye and left her in the safe hands of the three hundred-year-old babysitter, Mrs. Parker. Lucy took Xandar's private jet with three lycan warriors, and they made their way to White Blood.

Tate came to pick them up from the open field where they landed. On the passenger's seat in the car, Lucy noticed that her friend was feeling uneasy, like he was hiding something. Since he was driving, she didn't think it was a good idea to bring it up.

As soon as Tate entered White Blood and parked outside the pack house, Lucy turned to the lycan warriors in the back seat. "Phelton, August, Fiona, could you give Alpha Tate and I a moment please?"

"Yes, my queen," they obliged, getting the cue to get out and wait.

The moment the door shut behind Phelton, Tate continued to stare at his windscreen as he blurted, "I let the red wolf sleep in my basement last night."

In essence, he had deliberately gone against her orders to leave the rogues in the dungeon.

The lilac shade in Lucy's eyes turned onyx in anger as she prompted, "And?"

Tate shrugged to get off some of the fire that he was feeling from his long-time friend, who was beginning to bubble like an active volcano. "And I offered her breakfast this morning."

"And after that?" Lucy cued, still simmering.

"I locked her in my basement again. Timmy said she only used the attached washroom once throughout the night. She didn't try to escape." Tate's brown eyes showed that he was visibly scared.

Even the lycan warriors outside saw this. Anxiety crawled their necks for the alpha as they prayed and waited.

"Was anyone hurt?" Lucy's voice of rage echoed, laced with undeniable worry.

"No, 'course not." Tate tried to sound carefree to cope with the inferno.

A relieved sigh left Lucy as she leaned back on the headrest. The building concern gradually evaporated as the lilac shade in her eyes returned.

Tate's head spun to her. "Wait, you're not mad at me anymore? I could have sworn you were going to kill me." He deliberately had disregarded her order for a stranger, and he had done so out of pure instinct.

Lucy smirked. "My concern was the safety of everyone in this pack, Tate. Since no one got hurt, you're safe from my wrath for now."

He chuckled as the atmosphere eased, and the lycan warriors outside relaxed.

Tate led them into the pack house, and Lucy insisted that only she and Tate go to the basement, letting the warriors wait in the living room.

The moment the red wolf heard the door being unlocked with a click, she closed the dusty photo album in her hands, put it back on the shelf in the exact position she had found it in, and dashed to the couch to wait.

Tate and Lucy descended the stairs and came to a stop in front of the girl. She stood at about five feet, with brown hair that reached her waist, and rosewood eyes that declared the type of wolf she was. Her bones were conspicuously wrapped by her skin. Freckles scattered on her nose and some on her cheeks.

She rose from her perched position on the couch, staring at Lucy with more curiosity than fear. The teenager could tell that this creature carried a lycan scent. She was brought up to fear—even hate—lycans, but why wasn't she able to channel any fear or hate now?

Tate's commanding voice rang cold through the space, "Bow before the qu—"

"That really isn't necessary, Tate." Lucy moved to sit at the far end of the couch before looking at the rogue with a welcoming smile. "Have a seat," she invited, gingerly patting on the cushion.

The rogue hesitated but obliged in the end, sitting somewhere in the middle of the couch instead of the far end, wanting to feel Lucy's warmth.

"What's your name?" Lucy began with a smile.

The rogue seemed hesitant. Her mouth opened and her lips quivered, not knowing whether to lie or tell the truth.

Noticing her predicament, Lucy changed tactics. "This isn't going to be on any official document, so you don't have to give me your real name yet if you don't want to, but I do need something to call you."

When her rosewood eyes met Lucy's sincere gaze, she found herself giving her real name. "Stella."

Lucy nodded. "Stella, do your parents know where you are?"

Stella bit her bottom lip. No? Not at first when she left. But now? "Maybe? I'm not sure."

Lucy's eyes flickered to Tate's for a moment. So she wasn't abandoned. "Are they close by?" Lucy ventured.

A long, piercing moment of silence passed before Stella spoke in a pleading whisper, "You can't ask me to do this."

"Do what?"

"Admit and expose everything and everyone," Stella muttered, though her wolf was telling her to tell Lucy everything. It was her human part that was fighting the urge to do just that.

Stella's loyalty to her family was eminent, and Lucy's heart ached from the undeniable fact that they were rogues. "Stella . . . were you and your parents cast out?"

Lucy saw and felt no menace or trickery from this teenager and wondered what her parents could have possibly done to disqualify them from seeking refuge in any other pack in existence.

Stella thought about whether her answer would give something away, before ultimately uttering, "My mother left her old pack and took me with her. We've been running with a few others ever since."

"Weren't there any packs to take you both in?" Blue Crescent—Lucy's birth pack—would've welcomed them. This was a single mother with a pup!

"Mom . . . didn't know who to trust. She said that it was better . . . safer to be on our own so that we don't get cast out again."

Taking one step forward, Tate's brows knitted when he questioned, "Cast out? You said you both left!"

Stella stiffened in realization. Regret and fear filled her eyes.

Lucy's own eyes narrowed at Tate, who raised his hands in surrender. "Sorry."

Stella stammered, "W-We didn't know wh-who to trust. Mom said t-that packs could be enemies one day and allies on another. W-We didn't know if . . . if . . ."

Seeing how she was struggling, with eyes darting from one part of the cement floor to the next, Lucy gently finished her sentence, "You both didn't know if the pack you later sought refuge from turned out to be an ally of your old pack, who would then send you and your mother back to your birth pack to be punished."

Sighing and shutting her eyes in embarrassment, Stella nodded.

The queen and alpha locked gazes, both wanting to know which pack Stella was referring to but doubting Stella would give up the location willingly and truthfully. She had already given more than they'd expected. Lucy then began wondering whether Stella's mother was even safe. Perhaps Stella and her friends were out hunting for food for her sickly mother?

"Stella, I'm going to bring you and your friends to lycan territory." Stella's eyes widened in horror. Leaning closer, Lucy added, "I'll make sure you're safe, but we need you to cooperate with the authorities when they ask questions. Your mother . . . might not be safe where she is. We can help her as we'll help you. We'll keep you both safe."

"No! Please, no! Don't do this to me. Please. Just let me go. I'll be fine, I promise," Stella pleaded, eyes forming a dam, the film of moisture turning into a puddle.

"Stella, there's nothing to worry about. You will be fine. Your mother will be safe soon."

Almost shuddering now, Stella blurted, "She's safe. She's completely safe where she is. Please, just let me go. Don't go after her, please." Tears trickled down her cheeks, and she continued begging as her voice lost strength.

Lucy and Tate threw each other perplexed glances. How could one ever expect to be safe as a rogue? Nothing about being a rogue was safe. They were practically shunned by everyone and now hunted down by everyone. Rogues, as far as they knew, didn't form alliances like packs did. If they worked together, it would be solely for commercial reasons. Cooperating solely for commercial reasons, with little to no trust and confidence in each other's loyalty, was *not* safe.

In any other position, Lucy would've considered letting this slide and letting Stella go, perhaps even wishing her well. But she was queen, entrusted by her king and the rest of the kingdom to abide by the laws and policies made by the governing body in which she was a member.

Watching this girl now, Lucy wondered why she hadn't considered making exceptions for pups. "I'm sorry, Stella. But I can't just let you go. I need you to come with me. But I'll make sure nothing bad happens to you, okay?"

"And my moth-er?" her voice croaked.

Walking on eggshells again, Lucy said, "If and when we find her, and she isn't guilty of any crimes, she'll walk away a free creature. We'll then provide you both with any aid you may need to start a life together again."

"And if she . . . isn't innocent?" Stella knew she had just let another cat out of the bag, but she couldn't help herself from asking.

Tate pinched the bridge of his nose, swallowing a frustrated sigh threatening to fully express how he really felt. He had let this particular pup sleep in his basement because—ever since the capture—he'd been getting an unexplainable instinct to protect her. He couldn't understand it, nor could his wolf. Some primal part of them simply felt there was a need to keep Stella safe. Tate tried to ignore the urge to have her transferred at first, but when the thought of her being in the dungeon kept him lying awake in bed, he gave up fighting and got Stella out of the dungeon and into his basement, offering her blankets and the couch, but left her with a warning to not even try to break free since it'd only make things more difficult for her. He half expected her to disobey and attempt an escape. When she didn't, he was relieved.

At this point, his wolf wanted to do everything to protect the teenager, but how was he going to protect her from the law when she had a mother who seemed to have ventured against it? He had already vouched to stand with the law when he took an oath as the newly elected deputy defense minister of the Wolf Division just several weeks ago. The whole situation with Stella now felt like a joke shoved in his face to taunt his newly minted power.

Lucy swallowed a lump in her throat and tried not to look too ominous when she delivered the truth. "If that's the case, then she has to be fined or . . . kept in custody."

Kept in custody was a nicer way of saying *jailed*. Stella obviously knew this. "NO! NO! PLEASE! YOU CAN'T! YOU CAN'T! PUT ME THERE INSTEAD! PLEASE!"

Lucy sat closer to her and wrapped her arms around the girl to comfort her. Stella's tears drenched a part of Lucy's cerulean-colored blouse, but the queen didn't mind it as she let the poor girl cry her eyes out until the weeping eventually reduced to sobs and sniffles.

Stella eventually came to terms with the fact that there wasn't a way to change the queen's mind. And it made her even more afraid. "You'll take care of us? You promise?" she questioned, reddened eyes glued to the queen's shoes.

Gently lifting the girl's chin, looking deep into her eyes, Lucy vouched, "I promise."

Tate got Xiera to lead the lycan warriors to the dungeons where the other two rogues had been held, and Xiera drove them back to the open space where the jet was.

Lucy sat with Stella in the back seat as Tate drove them. A large part of him felt that Stella shouldn't be going with Lucy, that she should remain in White Blood under his care. He glanced at the girl through the rearview mirror every few seconds, and the decision not to turn the car around felt increasingly erroneous by the second.

They said that, instinctively a creature would know when something was wrong, could sense if a plan was going sideways, could perceive when a particular move shouldn't be made even before reason hits the brain. That very instinct was a guide: a guide to change course, alter rules, avoid pitfalls, right the wrongs before the wrongs materialized.

This. *This* rogue extraction was hitting his instincts in *all* angles.

Tate stole glances at Lucy and saw that she wasn't enjoying any of this either. But what choice did they have? They had a duty to uphold. But why did upholding a duty have to go against their instincts and feel so . . . wrong?

The car reached the field, and the three reluctantly got out.

Xiera had just assisted the lycan warriors in securing the two other rogues in the jet. Xiera guarded Stella as Tate ushered Lucy to the side. With nothing but hesitance, he confessed in a murmur, "Lucy, I don't feel good about this."

She scoffed. "I guess it's comforting to know I'm not alone."

"Can't you do something?" Tate pressed in a dismayed whisper.

"I can. But I need to take her for now. You and I both know that, Tate. I'll talk to Xandar and Chief Dalloway. We probably have to call for a government meeting soon to discuss rogues beyond the Wu Bi Corp sphere, specifically when it comes to minors. I'll make sure she's okay."

Tate's anxiety eased a little. Lucy shook her head, then muttered helplessly, "Why her? Apart from her scent, she's nothing like the typical rogue we've been slaughtering for years."

Glancing at Stella, he added, "I wonder what's with her mother."

"Whatever it is, I hope it's not too grave. Parents have this instinct to do anything to make sure their pups are safe. We just don't know how many laws her mother had to violate to raise her."

A stretch of silence unreeled between them as a gentle gust of wind graced their skin. The corner of Tate's lips curled depressedly. "You know, I wished I wasn't elected all of a sudden. At least then I wouldn't be torn between duty and instinct."

Lucy's frown turned into a similar smile. "I'd say I wish I wasn't the queen so that I could ask Juan and Hale to take Stella into Blue Crescent, but it somehow feels irresponsible of me to deny the position I'm given now. The coronation ceremony cost taxpayers a lot of money."

"Not to mention your mate wouldn't like to hear you refusing the crown," Tate reminded, making light of the situation.

A broader smile graced Lucy's features at the mention of Xandar. "That's true. But I'm still more concerned about the taxpayers' expenditure in this case." Tate chuckled at her response, and they embraced like old friends.

Lucy then approached Stella and Xiera. Her mouth had barely opened when thunderous growls cut through the morning air. To their right, five wolves charged toward Lucy, Xiera, and Stella at lightning speed. One of them was a red wolf and about to pounce at Lucy before Lucy's eyes turned as blue as sapphires when she radiated the Queen's Authority. The power took control of the rogues' nerves, overriding their autonomy, and instead of running or attacking, they were compelled to stay rooted to their spot.

The lycan warriors on the jet heard the commotion and cursed when they realized they had left the queen unguarded. Phelton sprinted out of the plane and appeared by his queen's side, preparing to shift into his animal to defend her.

Lucy's eyes returned to their black-and-lilac color as she had Phelton stand down while she scrutinized the rogues, wondering why they were attacking in an open space, in broad daylight. Rogues normally attacked after dusk or before dawn to avoid capture and to ease escape.

Registering the red wolf, Lucy's mind was beginning to form the pertinent conclusion that would explain the unusual attack, when Stella exclaimed, "MOM!"

Oh no. Lucy thought to herself. A mere attempt to attack Lucy was a crime on its own since she was queen. It was already going to be difficult to convince the entire governing body to allow different standards for different sets of rogues. How was she going to persuade her overprotective husband to go easy on Stella's mother now that treason had entered into the mess?

And just when Lucy thought things couldn't get any more complicated, she noticed Tate's gaze lingering on the rogues like he was in a trance. Unlike with their usual encounters with these outcasts, Tate's eyes held no desire to kill. He simply stared at them for a good three seconds before approaching them in slow, careful steps. That was when Lucy realized the red wolf leading the other four had her rosewood eyes fixed on Tate as well.

Tate was following the delightful scent of hyacinths and morning dew, leading him to the red rogue wolf. When he got down on one knee, leveling himself with her, only one word left his lips—*mate*.

No one bothered to mask their widened eyes. Xiera even covered her mouth after gasping. Tate, the alpha of one of the strongest packs in existence, one of the kingdom's two deputy defense ministers, was bonded to a rogue?

The quiet, seemingly ordinary morning wasn't all that tranquil anymore. With one problem stacked on top of another with no feasible solution or tried-and-tested methods at hand, Lucy did the very thing she had come to do—extract all rogues and bring them with her back to lycan territory.

CHAPTER 3

L ucy mind-linked Xandar on the jet, breaking her dam of frustration and uncertainty and pouring every nitty gritty detail onto her husband, conveniently leaving out the part when the rogues almost pounced on her.

Pinching the bridge of his nose at his end at the mention of Tate's bonded mate, the king sighed to himself. When Xandar secretly prayed to the Moon Goddess to give Alpha Tate a mate, he didn't mean a rogue. Wasn't that an understood part of his prayer? *'Please be careful, Lucy,'* he reminded, undeniably worried since the rogues onboard outnumbered the warriors who had gone with her.

'We'll be fine, Xandar. If it comes down to it, I can always use the Authority on them.'

'Thank Goddess for that. So ... how's Tate taking this?' As much as Xandar didn't like Tate having feelings for Lucy long before the king had met her, he couldn't deny Tate was a good person and was one of the few creatures he and Lucy could trust without question.

'He seems genuinely interested in her, but they haven't said a word to each other since we got on the plane. He can't take his eyes off her though.'

A ripple of relief sent a pleasant intrusion to Xandar's concern. *'I guess it's good to know he doesn't mind that she's a rogue ... with a teenage pup.'*

'I wonder if she minds being with him.'

'What do you mean by that, sweetheart?'

'She's avoiding his gaze. That's why they haven't spoken to each other. I haven't even heard her voice yet. Her lips are sealed shut.'

Xandar scoffed and teased, *'Don't you think she and Tate are not interacting because you and Tate look like you're a couple?'* Now that Tate seemed to be falling for the one he was bonded to, Xandar felt more comfortable cracking jokes like this.

In annoyance, Lucy retorted, *'Your mark on my neck is exposed to all, Xandar! And Tate's neck is bare. Our scents don't even match. Even a child would know he and I are not together!'*

A smile graced the lycan king's face as his animal stood tall and grinned wide. A familiar warmth spread across his chest, one that made him feel at peace, in love. His fingers reached to his neck, gently tracing the mark his wife had made there, which sent a tingling sensation throughout his being, penetrating every cell in his body and firing every nerve.

Lucy felt it, too, despite being nowhere near him. *'You're doing it again, aren't you, Xandar?'*

Chuckling through their link, he admitted, *'I can't help it, my love.'*

Pink spread over her cheeks as her heart melted and every part of her softened, wondering how she had hit the jackpot for a mate. Before straying too far away from the issue at hand, she cleared her throat and linked, *'Darling, about these rogues . . . even if we have to put them behind bars before the interrogation, can we at least put Stella somewhere else? And maybe give her mother visitation rights even if she's charged and prosecuted later on?'*

'Lucy, you know that would depend on how grave her mother's crimes are.' He hated to deny her of anything but knew she was smart enough to understand this.

She sighed. *'Should her daughter be punished for this though? Denied of her mother through no fault of her own?'*

Biting the insides of his mouth, he replied, *'It's an unwanted side effect, but . . . if her mother acted out of necessity rather than malice, then any punishment imposed will be mitigated.'*

'For Stella's sake, I really hope it's that.' Looking out of the window and—for once—not registering the view, she turned her attention to his task. *'How's the site, by the way? Another bust?'*

'Yes.' Xandar's voice carried a light matter-of-fact element, the sign that he was about to deliver a complain. *'As king, I'm given fake leads with zero excitement and no results. But my queen leaves for* one *trip and brings back eight unusual rogues, two of whom are wolves thought to be extinct, along with a front-row seat to an ally finding his mate. The Moon Goddess clearly has her favorite.'*

His wife's chuckles were lighter than the gentle breeze of dawn, livelier than any sound of nature, more precious than the rarest of gems. The fact that he was the one who had elicited that wonderous melody made him all the more elated. *'Don't worry, my king,'* she said. *'After our daughter, you're my favorite.'*

'And you are mine, my little freesia. I'll see you when you land.'

After his wife ended their link, the king heaved a heavy sigh. That was a lot to take in.

Seated next to him on the jet was his second-in-command and maternal cousin, Christian Blackfur, whose furrowed brows were a reason to be worried. As Christian continued scrolling through an email on his phone, he asked in a low, monotonous voice, "Everything okay with the queen, Cuz?"

"She's safe. As are the others onboard. They're coming back with eight rogues, not three." His cousin's eyes snapped to his before the king filled him in on the rogue extraction.

The duke's eyes widened in shock at the mention of Tate's rogue mate. The second-in-command sighed. The word *why* was written all over his face. Slumped into his seat from the exhaustion of doing nothing more than listening, he tossed his phone onto his cousin's lap while he got some quick shuteye. "Then this will nicely add on to our list of problems."

With Christian's phone in hand, Xandar read the text on the lit screen:

It is with great urgency that we **insist** on an audience with King Alexandar Thomas Claw and Queen Lucianne Freesia Paw-Claw TONIGHT.

Time: 10:00 p.m.

Place: Polje

Kindly acknowledge receipt of this email along with confirmation of the rulers' attendance.

[Large, illegible digital signature]
Pellethia Gangnes
Empress of Vampires

What did we do? was the first thing that came to Xandar's mind. He had never gotten anything like this in his nineteen years on the throne. Come to think of it, his late father had never gotten such a thing during his reign either. The truce with vampires was 204 years ago, and that was the last anyone heard from them. Sure, they weren't at war anymore, but that didn't mean their species liked each other enough to communicate with one another, especially after what the lycans had had to give up to secure the peace.

When the war over two centuries ago was nearing its end, it was clear to any creature alive that the vampires were winning. Many lycan warriors lost their lives, and even more werewolves were sacrificed. Seeing that the vampires had the upper hand, the late Emperor Kosh offered an alternative to the continuous bloodshed: that King Lucas and Queen Vera, Xandar's late parents, admitted that vampires were the species of superior ruling status, meaning that the title "Your Majesty" could never be used by any lycan or werewolf ruler again.

The vampires had no intention to rule over the lycans and werewolves, which had been explicitly stated in their treaty. All they wanted was to be recognized as the species of higher status so that lycans and werewolves would think twice before pissing off a vampire by criticizing their abilities, culture, and habits. More importantly, it was to ensure that they weren't bullied in terms of business and economics anymore.

Since the vampires had a better chance of winning, a significant population of werewolves and lycans took part in demonstrations in many towns and streets, pushing for the lycan king and queen to swallow their pride and give in, threatening to turn against the rulers like many of their kind already had by going rogue if their demand was refused.

The lycans from noble families unanimously refused to give in at first, but after being informed that even the remaining lycan warriors were threatening to turn against them, those in the safe seats of power reluctantly gave in. The royal scepter wielded and brooches worn by every lycan ruler were surrendered to the vampires as part of the compromise.

This surrender of title, status, and crown jewels was a negligible issue to some, but a big deal to the rest of the world. It was a declaration. A surrender. An ongoing wave of a white flag that plagued their species. King Lucas vowed to earn the Majesty title back, promising to "perform to the best of my abilities" every Nouvelan—the celebration that marked the beginning of a new year in the lycan and werewolf calendar. In the Gregorian calendar, Nouvelan falls on the 29th of July.

However, as time went on, it became apparent that the annual vow was more wishful thinking than an achievable aspiration. There came a point when it became a laughable part of the late king's annual speech. Most wolves even joked about it amongst themselves, reciting this ludicrous line in games of Guess Who.

When Xandar rose as king after his parents' death, he very appropriately refused to listen to any old-timer's advice to include the embarrassing line in his Nouvelan speeches. And after a few years of relentlessly pestering him to add it back in, they eventually gave up. From the way Xandar saw things, his species very much asked for the war, thus deserved the demotion in their status.

Once upon a time, lycans encroached into vampire territory on numerous occasions without plausible reason, even sending wolves to do their bidding. The lycan government and monarchy even imposed irrational taxes and unconscionable conditions in business, which carried appalling penalties when breached. This double-standard treatment existed for no other reason than the fact that they were contracting with a vampire.

When Xandar voiced his perspective during a dinner hosted by his parents and attended by the most prestigious families and government ministers, he only had one supporter—Christian. The rest thought that he was "still young" and "didn't understand the gravity of the situation of a time that was prior to his birth."

After that dinner, Xandar had to endure a full-hour lecture from King Lucas, who felt embarrassed that his own heir was siding with "the enemy." Queen Vera, on the other hand, shrugged off Xandar's action as being a rebellious youngster, which baffled Xandar, since he was fifty-four years old.

As much as Xandar tried, he couldn't make his parents see how he saw things, how history actually recorded the affair. After constantly being told, "You don't understand. One day you will," Xandar gave up trying to explain, accepting his parents' adamance. But unlike the elders thought, his perspective never changed. In social events, he'd block out any baseless, negative assertions about the vampires, and left circles which ventured along these lines. His maternal grandfather and aunt advised him to be patient, assuring him that when he ascended the throne, he'd have that chance to affect the change he sought.

Of course, that day came. Xandar's status ended those insults to their foreign counterpart like paper thrown into fire.

When he was crowned king, an invitation was sent to the vampires in the name of diplomacy, but the vampires politely refused to attend his coronation. Xandar hadn't tried to reach out to them since. He didn't want them to think that he was trying to manipulate them into returning the scepter, brooches, and status, so he left things as they were, being content with the sliver of peace established.

Looking at the email now, Xandar wondered what could have possibly happened. If they were demanding a meeting on such short notice after 204 years of avoidance, whatever they wanted to discuss had to be abominable.

It was Christian's exhausted voice that interrupted Xandar's thoughts. "It's really weird to see the queen's name like that. Who in the kingdom has four words in their name anyway?"

Straightening in his seat, Xandar explained, "Well, Paw was who I fell for, and Lucy was stubborn in putting in Claw. Hyphenating our last names seemed to be the only way to make us both happy."

Adjusting himself to sit upright, Christian mused, "Annie says it's cute, but Toby agrees it's weird."

To be fair, Toby only said so to annoy his best friend, which worked. Lucy punched him in the gut but instantly apologized right after because she had forgotten about her enhanced strength as a lycan and exerted more force than she intended. Toby groaned and feigned anguish all the way out of the room. He only began sprinting when Lucy saw through his extended act and was barging over to deliver another punch for making her feel bad longer than necessary.

A modicum of happiness flashed through Xandar's mind at the memory but was quickly washed away the moment he reassessed the email. "What did we do, Christian? I don't recall interfering with any vampires."

Christian rubbed a hand down his face. "Cuz, we're always too busy to interfere with anything. But after the whole thing with the Kyltons and Wu Bi Corp, you have to admit that there are a lot of people with too much time on their hands to detonate a bomb of shit all over the place for us to clean up."

After Xandar sent a response confirming his and Lucy's attendance, Christian asked, "So how many of us are invited to that vampire rendezvous?"

Turning to his best friend, the king asked, "Can you come though? Wouldn't Annie need help with the twins?"

Christian scoffed. "Ianne will be fine with her mother and Mrs. Clifford. And Lewis *hates* me."

"C'mon, Christian. That's not true."

"It is true, Cuz. Remember when he was sick two weeks ago? He slept so well in Annie's arms. But once I took over, he pooped so much that the shit overflowed from his diaper and got onto my pants. You're saying he doesn't hate me?"

Xandar's lips pressed together, suppressing laughter and a smile with immense difficulty. "Well, I mean . . . it just shows that he feels . . . comfortable to share his . . . dirtiest secrets with you."

Christian threw his cousin a glare. "The shit stain won't come off."

"Give him a break, Christian. He's only a few weeks old. And Annie said Ianne loves you."

That made him soften and smile. He stared into space, picturing his daughter. "I love holding her and watching her sleep. But I think she only looks like she loves me because she feels sorry for me. There was once when I had just cleaned her up and put a clean diaper on her before she saw it fit to squirt urine right at my face." Despite the complaint, his voice gave away how happy he was.

The duke and duchess named their baby girl Lucianne after . . . well, Lucianne. And since everyone was already calling the queen Lucy, they decided to call their daughter by the second part of the name—Ianne.

Christian added, "I guess it's appropriate to name her after the queen. Ianne's ability to act like I'm her favorite parent is definitely convincing."

Xandar's brows furrowed. "Christian, how would your daughter know how to act? We're talking about a nine-week-old baby."

"They're both lucky they're only nine weeks old, or I'd be giving them a lecture on where half of their genes come from. Seriously, why doesn't Annie or Mrs. Clifford get baby poop on their pants, or pee in their faces? Why is it just me?" As Xandar tried his best to suppress his laughter again, Christian prompted, "So who should we inform about the date with the vampires, Cuz?"

CHAPTER 4

Every government minister, lycan warrior, and police officer was informed about the meeting with the vampires, and it was decided that only half of the ministers would attend, along with ten lycan warriors and the chief of the police force.

Lucy managed to persuade Xandar to let Margaret and the rest of the rogues be kept in holding units in the police station instead of a prison cell, for the sake of the teenager and her alpha friend. Stella appeared a little less worried, and Tate was immensely grateful.

As the policewoman brought Margaret into the holding unit, Tate trailed closely behind.

Stella was brought to another room to be questioned, and Lucy had to ensure her that everything was going to be okay before the girl reluctantly followed another smiling policewoman.

There was a one-way mirror in the room where Margaret was held, and Tate stood facing the mirror, close to the square table where his mate and the policewoman sat. The door was left open to make sure Margaret wasn't too intimidated by the confined space.

Outside, Lucy, Xandar, and Christian peered through the mirror.

"Your full name, ma'am?" the policewoman, Officer Laila, began.

Margaret's eyes were glued to the white table with scratches and scuffs, no doubt from the violent scraping of cuffs against the table. The little dents must have been made from interrogative torture. Despite these warnings, Margaret's lips sealed.

"Ma'am, can you give me your full name?"

Nothing.

Tate leveled himself with her and urged gently, "They won't hurt you or Stella. All you need to do is cooperate, please."

Her frosty rosewood eyes locked with Tate's soft brown orbs as she spat, "Don't tell me what to do."

Tate felt a knife plunged into his center, swift and deep.

Margaret then turned to Officer Laila and demanded, "I want to speak to my daughter. Alone."

Officer Laila and Tate exchanged glances, and Tate explained in the same gentle voice, "You'll see Stella soon, I promise. But for now . . ."

"*You* promise?" she scoffed darkly. "And who are you in all of this?" As sweet as her voice was to Tate, the tone felt like a blow to his gut. His lungs punctured and he felt like he was running out of air.

Seeing Tate tongue-tied, Officer Laila took over. "This is one of our two deputy ministers of defense. Apart from him, the queen herself has promised that your daughter will be allowed to see you after we've asked a few questions. This won't take long if you cooperate."

The raging anger and defiance behind Margaret's eyes flared. Leaning toward Officer Laila, she retorted, "Tell your queen that her word means *nothing*. She is still second to the king."

"That's not true," Tate rasped. "If you knew how they worked, you'd know that there's no second with them."

Margaret smirked in what seemed like bile—bitterness. "How about that? Another powerful man bending to the will of a vulnerable-looking woman capable of doing nothing more than putting on a good act. Kings. Alphas. You're all the same. What is it with your type? Is there always this need to boost your ego by showing the world that you're capable of sheltering a weak . . ."

Xandar's growl shook the walls of the police station, and he stormed into the room as Lucy frantically dashed after him. She stood before her husband, blocking his way. Tate simultaneously shielded his mate, blocking her from the king's view, begging to Goddess that Lucy had this under control.

Christian was between Tate and Lucy, acting as a second buffer after the queen, though he was contemplating helping his cousin after the rogue insulted her.

Lucy cupped Xandar's slightly furry face and gently guided their eyes to meet. His claws were out, his breathing shallow, his energy deathly. Bringing their foreheads to touch, her thumb drew circular strokes on his cheeks as she whispered, "Xandar, shh . . . everything's okay. Breathe. Just breathe, darling. Breathe. It's okay. We're okay."

The embers in his onyx eyes burned into her black-and-lilac orbs as his voice came in a low rumble, "Insulting you . . . is *not okay*."

Through their mate bond, she felt his internal volcano bubbling further, the earlier eruption just being the first cascade of a wave of outbursts.

Never taking her soft gaze off him, she nodded and whispered, "You're right, darling. It's not okay. It's wrong. You have every right to be angry. But just take deep breaths. Deep breaths. Okay? Deep breaths. That's it. In. And out. And in."

Validating his rage made his animal—who Lucy learned was the more hot-tempered one—start to really listen to her. As the bubbling slowed and subsided, Xandar buried his nose in her hair and closed his eyes, letting her scent cool the ember to a cinder.

The king's black fur gradually shortened and retreated, and his claws retracted from sight. Lucy was pressed into his chest, and relief washed over her when his erratic heart rate slowed down and steadied: a sign that his anger was under control.

The gentlest pressure fell on her head when Xandar planted a deep kiss, sending a shower of sparks down to her toes. With a small smile, she suggested, "How about you and Christian wait outside, dearest?"

His calm eyes turned defensive once more, and his grip on her arms tightened when his guttural reply came. "No."

"Darling, it—"

"Oh, give me a break," the rogue groaned, disgusted.

This time, both Xandar and Christian growled at her, but she merely rolled her eyes as Lucy pulled Christian back and now had to restrain two angry lycans.

Tate turned to his mate and hissed, "Just stop it!"

Did she have a death wish? Why was she trying to anger the three most powerful creatures in the kingdom? Sure, Lucy wouldn't do anything lethal yet, but Xandar and Christian could kill right then and there if they weren't restrained.

Margaret scoffed darkly, crossing her legs as she stared at the gray wall like it was just another day at the office.

Sternly, Lucy reminded the two cousins, "Tearing her to shreds is *not* going to serve anyone. I'll handle this. The two of you wait by the door. Now."

Registering the tone she used when it was an order, Christian groaned and reluctantly went to lean against the doorframe, refusing to go any further. Xandar—like he was in a trance—ran his thumb along Lucy's cheek and neck before letting her push him toward his cousin.

The queen turned back to Margaret, done playing nice. "If you want to see your daughter, you need to tell us everything we need to know. Stella's questioning is almost done. If she isn't allowed to see you because you're refusing to cooperate, don't blame anyone but yourself when I have to disappoint your little girl."

The rogue's chest rose and fell as she breathed in rage. "You can't make me talk."

"I can. But I don't want to do it that way." Tate was finding it impossible to continue defending her now. "Don't make me do it," Lucy warned.

Margaret simpered and remarked, "*Don't make me do it*. What a perfect line before exerting violence and then playing victim to gain the sympathy of everyone you tell the tale to. Typical."

Xandar and Christian lost it again and were about to bolt and pounce before Tate's strained voice rooted them to their spot when he said, "Just do it, Lucy."

Lucy's brows furrowed in uncertainty. "Are you sure, Tate?"

"WHY ARE YOU EVEN ASKING HIM? I'M NOT HIS! I'M NOT ANYONE'S! GIVE ME MY DAUGHTER! NOW!"

After another subtle nod from the alpha, Lucy sighed in despair. Her eyes turned sapphire blue, and Officer Laila went through the questions quickly, "Name?"

"Margaret Nyphea Rouge."

"Age?"

"Thirty-three."

"Birth pack?"

"Fleet Wood."

Lucy and Tate exchanged glances of shock and bewilderment. Fleet Wood was demolished by rogues years ago. The alpha and luna were killed, along with everyone else. No one survived. Margaret and Stella must have been cast out before then. Wait, were the rogues who destroyed Fleet Wood . . . Margaret's rogues?

"Husband's name?"

Margaret swallowed a lump in her throat before Lucy's Authority compelled her to answer, albeit in a small voice, "I have no husband."

"The name of your daughter's birth fa—"

Lucy interjected, "Skip that one please, Laila."

"As you wish, my queen. Uh . . . any other blood-related family members besides your daughter?"

"No."

"Daughter's name?"

"Estella Fort Rouge."

"Age?"

"Thirteen."

"Is her birth pack also Fleet Wood?"

Swallowing another lump, her answer came out in another whisper, "No."

"Where was she born?"

Margaret tried her best to fight the Authority, but it was no use. "In a forest by the River of Partager." Tears of anger filled her eyes as she kept her head low. Humiliation meandered through her like a coursing river. This wasn't supposed to happen. She wasn't supposed to feel so powerless. She had promised herself that her naivety would end the moment she stepped out of Fleet Wood and into the real world—the one where only the strong survived.

Officer Laila continued, "Where did you and your followers seek shelter before the arrest?"

"About ten miles south of White Blood," she murmured.

"How long have you been there?"

"Two days."

"Where was your group before that?"

"About eight miles from where Fleet Wood used to be."

"Thank you, Miss Rouge. That will be all for now. You'll see your daughter in five minutes."

With an arm across her chest, Officer Laila offered the royals a bow before leaving the room. When Lucy's eyes returned to normal and the compulsion from her Authority wore off, she looked at Margaret with sad eyes and muttered, "I'm sorry."

Her hand reached out to touch Tate's shoulder for a brief second to convey the same apology before her legs brought her out of the room in haste.

In the corner she sought refuge in, her eyes welled up in tears, replaying her inhumanity, unable to deny that she had just coerced a mother against her will, a mother who only asked to see her daughter.

Xandar caught up to his wife and peeled her from the wall to cement her to his warm chest, pecking kisses in her hair, trying his best to comfort her. "You didn't have a choice, Lucy."

In a chopped voice, she murmured, "We c-ould've waited. But then Stella…"

"Exactly. Stella wouldn't have been able to see her mother if you didn't make Margaret cooperate. You put Stella before her mother. It wasn't ideal. But it wasn't wrong, Lucy."

After some sniffles, she whispered, "I know I'm just shifting blame to think this, but . . . I wish Tate had stopped me somehow."

As his hand ran down her hair, he said, "Margaret may not see it now, but if she's smart, she'll come to see one day that Tate was only giving her what she wants: to see her pup, though not the way she would have preferred. You already did everything within your power to protect her, baby. The situation worked out. I didn't tear her to shreds, and she gets to see Stella."

A brief chuckle broke from his mate at the last line. His thumb reached to smoothen the creases on her beautiful forehead, then trailed down her cheek, where she leaned into his touch, taking a deep breath to calm herself while she let the sparks from his touch ease the nerves and soothe her soul.

The moment was only broken when they heard dragging feet exiting Margaret's holding room. Tate emerged and shut the door behind him gently, joining Christian. The alpha's exhaustion and sorrow were eminent. The duke wasn't even that close to him yet felt so bad for him that he offered him a pat on his shoulder, which Tate responded to with a meek smile.

'And I thought you were bad,' Xandar linked his wife. When their eyes met, he continued, *'I honestly didn't think anyone else could beat you in pushing their mate away upon the first meeting. Seeing Tate like that now, I have to say… I'm very grateful you didn't fire insults at me and shut the door in my face during our first encounter, sweetheart.'*

Her eyes narrowed. *'There wasn't even a door for me to shut in your face when we met at the dining hall, Xandar. And in Tate's situation, he was the one who shut the door.'*

'But why do you think he did? It can't be because he wanted to leave her there.'

'Why are we even talking about this?'

'There seems to be a vague similarity in how Tate and I met our mates. Mine was, fortunately for me, less aggressive. Probably equal in hostility, but much less aggressive.'

'Margaret is just hurt, Xandar. Very hurt.' The moment Margaret spoke, Lucy couldn't help but see some of her past self in the red wolf. The hate. The rage. The bitterness. Of life. Of the situation she was in. Of everyone and everything.

Xandar argued, *'That doesn't justify taking it out on people she hardly knows, especially not her bonded mate or her queen.'*

'It's more complicated than that, Xandar.' When she got his attention, she went on, *'She has a pup but no husband or partner. There was nothing but fear in her eyes when she was almost made to give the identity of Stella's birth father. It only points to two things: either she was impregnated by force, amounting to rape, and was shunned by the people around her because of that, thus forced to become a rogue; or the intercourse was consensual before a betrayal eventually broke things apart.'*

Xandar blinked and digested the two scenarios before asking in dismay, *'She was raped?'*

'I don't know. But it's definitely a possibility.'

A few silent moments passed before Xander asked, *'Why would people shun rape victims?'*

'Let's not call them victims, darling. These creatures, women and men alike, are very much survivors. As for why, let's just say many out there still blame the survivors for the rape. You know, things like, her skirt was too short, or she was wearing a thong so what did you expect, or she went out alone at a particular time when perpetrators are out hunting—those kinds of baseless reasonings to put the blame back on the survivors when it should be on the perpetrators.'

Xandar exhaled and ran his fingers through his hair. *'That's just inhumane. I thought we were done with vict— with blaming the survivors.'*

'In certain regions, maybe. But not in many parts of the kingdom, especially not among wolves. Hale has been working on this very issue these past few weeks. The last time I spoke to Juan, he said we should be ready for a very heavy topic of discussion at a government meeting soon.'

Luna Hale was now the minister of welfare, and this was among the many major issues that she had been researching on and questioning creatures about for months.

Xandar nodded, noting that. "Better to deal with it soon than to continue letting innocents pay for the consequences later."

"Cuz. My queen." Christian came to them with Deputy Chief Lauren by his side. The duke stretched out a hand with two earpieces and said, "Margaret Rouge is going to see her daughter now. Want to know what they'll be saying?"

Hesitance intruded Lucy. Yes, she knew about the hidden bugs in the room, but should they be used on this occasion? Tate put her doubt to rest when he admitted, "I'll be listening, too, Lucy. We all should. Let's just put the mate bond aside for now. We don't know what she's capable of as a rogue. We don't know if . . ." He paused, envisioning the worst.

They knew what he was going to say: who'd know if Margaret and her people were the cause of some of the rogue attacks they'd been fighting off for years. Seeing that it was painful to let him finish, Lucy took the earpiece and uttered, "Let's hope she's not."

They stood with Deputy Chief Lauren outside the holding unit and looked through the one-way mirror after Officer Laila brought Stella in, reminding the teenager that she only had fifteen minutes.

After the door closed behind Officer Laila, Margaret began with a straight face, "Stella, whatever you do, show as little emotion as possible. They're watching us through that mirror. Now, what did they ask you and what did you tell them?"

CHAPTER 5

Stella's hair curtained the side of her face. Her eyes darted away from the woman who had raised her when she spoke to the table. "They asked for my name and age, your name and age, where our pack was, and about my birth father."

"And what did you tell them about your birth father?"

Stella took a moment, cleared her throat, and muttered, "What you told me to say, that he died before I was born and you've never told me anything about him."

"Good girl. And did they believe you?"

"I don't think so," she confessed.

Despite Margaret's poker face, those pair of eyes sent a meteor of angered disappointment. "You could lie with a straight face before running through pack territories, but you can't lie to protect your own mother?"

The teenager's chin finally lifted. "Mom, these people aren't like whatever you say they are. They're different. The alpha didn't even lock me in the dungeon with Milo and Chase. And that woman . . ."

Margaret's eyes slammed shut as she exhaled hard. "Don't tell me. The queen?"

"Yes! She's different, Mom. If you spoke to her . . ."

"I have spoken to her, Stella."

Stella's eyes widened in enthusiasm, a modicum of hope graced her lips. "And? She's different, isn't she? She doesn't want to hurt us."

Margaret scoffed, head swiveling left and right, disappointed and upset by her daughter's ignorance of creatures from the real world. "She used her

Authority on me. Forced me to answer questions, questions I'd rather not answer because there are things that every creature has a right to keep private. Worship that woman all you want, but at the end of the day, the queen is no different from your father—prone to manipulation and power abuse, especially when it comes to using their Authorities."

Stella was taken aback, and so were the others eavesdropping outside, albeit for different reasons.

The teenager's surprised eyes went blank for a moment before her thought process kicked in. "What did you do?" she demanded in a whisper.

"Excuse me?" Margaret questioned defensively in return. It was a warning, either to watch her tone or take back the question.

But Stella didn't back down. "What did you do to make her use her Authority on you?"

"I was exercising my right to remain silent," her mother countered.

"You told me rogues didn't have the right to remain silent. Has our status changed already? Have you accepted the alpha as your mate?" Stella knew her mother wouldn't have accepted the mate bond, at least not yet.

Seeing that her teenager was winning the argument, Margaret invoked her mother privilege, retorting, "I'm your mother, Stella. Watch how you're talking to me."

"It's just a question, Mom. I only want answers. And you're not giving me anything. How else do you expect me to ask?"

"I would prefer it if you didn't ask at all."

Lucy was finding it harder to watch. Her eyes glistened at the strained relationship. Lucy didn't remember much about her birth mother, but her adoptive mother was never this cold to her. Strict and firm, yes, definitely. But never this . . . frosty and dismissive. Registering her sadness, Xandar's arm went around her waist and pulled her close.

Stella asked, "Then what am I even doing here? Answering all your questions until you dismiss me?"

"Since you and your friends are the reason that we're all here, yes. Only I get to ask the questions." Stella's eyes began alternating shades, which was when Margaret warned, "Control your emotions, Stella. Don't give yourself away. Never show what you're feeling. It's the first thing they'll use against you."

Speaking through gritted teeth, she spat "They . . . are NOT like that."

"And how would you know?" her mother challenged, raising her voice. "You have been shielded from hypocrites your whole life. You won't even know one when you see one. You're too young and immature to tell the difference. For all we know, that queen you're so smitten with is only earning your trust to turn you against us! All of us! Do you want to be personally responsible for the decimation of our pack, of everyone you know? You'd best pray the others we left behind are okay right now."

Stella took another moment before her answer came out in an adamant whisper, "The queen is not like that. I trust her. My wolf trusts her. You and the others have told me that our wolf instinct is hardly ever wrong."

A gentle warmth snaked into Lucy's heart, and Tate gave her shoulder a grateful squeeze.

Margaret continued to argue, "Well my wolf doesn't. And mine is clearly older than yours."

"Older wolves are not always right. At least that's what you told our elders before you took the mantle. Are you saying that's wrong now?" This was a very different side of Stella that neither Tate nor Lucy had seen back in White Blood. Teenagers of any species are known to be rebellious, but this one was gutsy on an exponential level.

Margaret's neck stiffened for a brief second. "Fine. If you think that your wolf is right, then ask the queen to release us without charge."

Lucy's eyes widened as her posture stiffened. Xandar's thumb that was stroking her waist paused as well, waiting for the ball to drop.

Inside, Stella blinked before questioning, "How did you even connect . . . me trusting her to . . . demanding that she release us from prison?"

"It's simple. If you trust her and she trusts you, she'll believe you when you tell her that we acted in self-defense on the field."

"How was that self-defense? They weren't even attacking. You and the others just appeared out of nowhere and almost attacked HER!" Stella exclaimed.

"To save YOU!"

The ears of Xandar's animal perked up. In Lucy's head, her lycan smacked her forehead and pulled her ears forward to cover her eyes. Whatever Stella had just said was not supposed to be brought up in front of their mate this soon.

The king turned his wife, angling her to face him. His stern eyes demanded a confirmation or contradiction from his beautiful but guilty-looking mate. Unlike her animal, who had already given up, Lucy still tried to use her doe eyes in hopes that Xandar would go easy on her when she explained meekly, "I was going to tell you after we got home. I didn't want them to be refused requests to speak to each other today. Besides, I stopped them with the Queen's Authority, so they couldn't do anything, really."

His animal was not pleased. It took some heavy breaths, internalizing her reasoning. Xandar tried very hard to swallow an angered and hurt snarl, but a faint part of it got through their mind-link, which Lucy and her animal easily caught. Seeing that they were in public, the king decided to use their link to remind his queen in a tone that left no room for argument, *'Next time when I say keep me posted, I mean keep me posted on EVERYTHING, Lucy. Alright?'*

Nodding dotingly, she replied almost inaudibly, *'I'm sorry.'*

Her small voice vaporized her mate's anger. Xandar sighed. He never intended to make her feel bad. Holding her in his arms, he left a kiss on her hair. *'I love you, my little freesia. I just . . . want to know everything. And I really need you to be safe.'*

'I know. I love you, too, Xandar. It won't happen again, I promise.'

The answer brought a satisfied smile to his lips. "Thank you, baby."

Their attention was brought back to the room when Margaret's demanding voice rang through. "If you're not comfortable with self-defense, then use something else. Just make sure everyone gets out of here. This is your chance to prove your loyalty."

"Prove my loyalty? When did we have to prove our loyalty in our rogue pack?"

"When I say so."

Stella looked at her mother blankly before stating the obvious, "I'm your daughter, Mom."

"After that stunt you pulled with your friends, after the risks you three took without considering the repercussions, trust is not something you're entitled to anymore, not until you've proven yourselves worthy of that trust."

"We didn't mean to get caught, Mom. It was an accident!"

"Which is why I told you to never run anywhere you liked! We are rogues! We don't have that privilege!" It was only when Stella was backed further and further into her chair that Margaret realized her voice was raised. She cursed under her breath for losing her composure before continuing to speak to her daughter, "Anyway, what's done is done. There's no use wishing that things were different. I don't care what you say to the queen or to anyone she listens to. Lie as convincingly as you can to get your family out of here, because we know who got us in here."

Before Stella could retort, Officer Laila knocked on the door twice to indicate that their fifteen minutes were up. Without looking at her mother or waiting for her permission, Stella rose from her chair like she couldn't wait to escape her mother's wrath, trotting to the door.

The moment her hand fell on the doorknob, she turned back to her mother. "You were wrong about me being shielded from hypocrites my whole life, Mom. From the way I see it, I've been brought up by the best one."

Lucy's hand flew to her gaped mouth.

Margaret was finding it harder to maintain a straight face now. "I'm nothing like them."

"You're right about that. They're real. You're not. You've been holding onto your past for so long that you've forgotten what being real feels like. *You're* the hypocrite, Mom. That's why you haven't rejected the alpha. You used to tell me that if you ever had a second-chance mate, you'd reject him without giving it a second thought, especially if it was an alpha. Now, you can't even bring yourself to look at Alpha Tate or say the words. And do you know why? It's because your wolf is telling you NOT to! It's because your wolf is telling you that he's not my birth father, that he's different! Yet you're so stubborn to not listen to it!"

Margaret's mouth opened, but Stella was already out the door. The four outside hastily took out the earpieces and hid them in their hands.

CHAPTER 6

Stella shut the door behind her, resisting the urge to slam it. Hanging her head low, her hands reached to wipe away her stray tears. Then she felt something warm: a foreign body, arms wrapping her. She was shocked at first, but when Stella noted Lucy's scent, her human and wolf let themselves cry in her embrace.

"We'll take care of you and your mother, Stella. Don't worry, okay?" Lucy assured.

Stella nodded in obedience and managed a meek smile.

In a soft voice, Lucy said, "Why don't you follow Officer Laila and get some water and something to eat. We'll discuss where you'll stay for the time being to make it easier for you to visit your mother, and I'll let you know."

Nodding again, Stella saw Officer Laila ready to lead her away when the teenager hesitated, "Um . . ."

The four eavesdroppers stiffened in response. Everyone was silently praying that Stella wasn't going to lie like her mother asked her to do. Lying to authoritative figures carried a sentence for both adults and minors above the age of twelve. Needless to say, lying to the royal family carried an even heavier sentence. Lucy was even considering taking a few steps back and pushing Tate forward instead so that if Stella lied, she'd technically be lying to Tate, not to Lucy herself.

Fumbling over her words, Stella admitted, "Before . . . I didn't . . . wh-when Officer Katie a-asked about my dad—birth father's identity . . . I lied. Can I get a do-over on that part?"

Christian sighed aloud. Tate's tensed shoulders fell. His wolf felt . . . proud of her honesty. It took a certain degree of bravery, he could see.

Lucy smiled radiantly as she gave Stella a brief hug. "Thank you for owning up, Stella. You can tell Officer Laila on the way, okay?"

"Yeah, okay. Thank you, uh . . . Queen . . . Your Highness."

"It's just Lucy, Stella. Go on, now."

After Officer Laila took Stella to the cafeteria, Lucy's composure melted when she slumped against the wall and muttered, "Thank Goddess."

"True that, My Queen. True that," Christian said with a satisfied smile.

At their side, Deputy Chief Lauren asked whether they should deploy troops to collect the rest of the rogues in Margaret's pack. After being granted permission and receiving explicit instructions to only kill for self-defense, Lauren left their circle to round up her folks.

When the atmosphere eased, Christian asked, "So who's taking the teenager?"

"What?" Tate replied, brows shooting to his hair.

Christian explained the problem, "Well, I doubt she can go back and forth with you to and from White Blood, Alpha. It's too far from her mother. Annie and I could take her in for now, if you don't mind."

After some thinking, Lucy suggested, "Maybe it's better if she stayed with us, Xandar." When her husband's eyes met hers, she elaborated, "Her wolf trusts us."

Christian snorted. "No. No, no, no, no, no, my queen. You must have heard the teenager wrong. Her wolf trusts *you*, not my cousin." With a hand on his best friend's shoulder, the duke continued, "It's hard to trust him. I mean, look at him, especially after you marked him. Bigger. Scarier. Deathlier. Angr—oof!" The duke groaned when Xandar hit the back of his head, eliciting Lucy's giggles.

Her laughter—as always—made the bigger, scarier, and deathlier animal coo in tenderness. "We can take her in for the time being. We have a few extra rooms at home anyway."

"Great!" Lucy exclaimed, then turned her attention to her friend. "So how often are you dropping by, Tate?"

Tate scratched the back of his head, sheepishly admitting, "Well, I'm thinking of staying, actually. I'll handle pack business from here. Beta Mannon will take care of the face-to-face things back in White Blood. I think there's a hotel not far down the street."

"You could stay with us. You'll get to know Stella better too," Lucy offered, hoping that he'd accept.

"Oh no, Lucy. I couldn't impose."

Xandar insisted, "You won't be. It'll be fine."

Tate looked at the king, and he asked like he once did before, "Are you sure, Your Highness?"

Christian chuckled at a memory they all shared. Xandar patted Tate on his shoulder as he repeated the same words from the previous time, "I trust you."

Nodding to express his gratitude for his understanding, Tate accepted, "Well then, who am I to refuse? Thank you, Xandar. And you, too, Lucy."

Xandar continued, "Don't worry about it. The only thing that's off-limits in the house is the chocolate bars in the fridge. I *will* know if even one goes missing."

Tate and Christian laughed, but Lucy could only try to suppress a guilty smile when her mate's loving and knowing gaze fixed on her because she was the one who stole his chocolate bar last time . . . or the last few times, not that he minded anyway.

Relief abraded Stella's fear and anxiety when Lucy informed her that she was going to stay with her. The teenager thought she was going to be thrown into one of the cleaner cells in prison at worst, and put into a temporary room before being sent to a juvenile institution at best. She'd never expected to be able to live in the queen's home.

After leaving the police station, Xandar and Lucy brought Tate and Stella to a mall to pick out some clothes before returning to the villa. They let Stella pick her room, and she chose the smallest one with the smallest window. Tate opted for the room next to hers in case she needed anything.

With that settled and a few hours to kill before the vampire rendezvous, Lucy breastfed Reida with Xandar by her side, enjoying the private moment with their pup. The couple watched their child's bright lilac eyes looking up at them as her tiny hands wrapped tightly around Xandar's pinky finger, holding it close to her small chest, making the fiercest animal in the kingdom melt in blissful happiness.

When Reida dozed off with her mother's nipple in her mouth, Lucy carefully detached herself from her daughter before Xandar helped pull down her shirt. Leaving a sweet kiss on her cheek, he uttered, "You're amazing."

A red tinge appeared on her cheeks like it always did whenever Xandar said those words. Lucy carried Reida to the nursery, gently placing her into the cot. The happy parents stood there and just watched their child sleep, listening to her breathing that sounded as gentle as the morning breeze.

When it was time to get ready, they reluctantly left Reida to Mrs. Parker. Half an hour to the rendezvous appointment, they bid Tate goodbye and made sure Stella was well settled in before making their way to Polje.

CHAPTER 7

At 9:58 p.m., Xandar, Lucy, Christian, Toby, Phelton, Weaver, Yarrington, Lovelace, Chief Dalloway, General Langford, and ten lycan warriors stepped onto the large open space beneath the full moon. They waited for the vampires to appear.

At 10:00 p.m., they did.

Around twenty pale-skinned creatures emerged from the thick forest, their teal-green eyes glimmering in the darkness. A vampire, unlike a lycan or werewolf, was born with one of four distinct abilities: speed as quick as lycans, called a velox (plural: veloces); strength superior to werewolves but inferior to lycans, called a fortis (plural: fortes); invisibility, called a discretus (plural: discreti); or the most-feared—mind-manipulation, called a decipio (plural: dicipimus).

Only a ruler and his rightful heir was a velox, fortis, discretus, and decipio all at once. Apart from a vampire's general scent, the only thing they all had in common with each other was venomous fangs that could weaken their prey or enemy long enough for the predators to drain them of their blood. Only vampires themselves and their mates were immune to the venom.

The woman in the middle, with strawberry-blonde hair that touched her shoulders, stepped forward with a grim expression. Her eyes were not teal green like the rest, but were as bright as polished emeralds. A black leather pantsuit accentuated her triangle figure. Her frown and furrowed brows showed that she was only there because she had to be.

When the emerald-eyed vampire came closer into view, the lycans and werewolves noticed the copper-colored streaks in her blonde hair. Five streaks, to be exact.

Lucy took a lungful of air, bracing herself. This was her first encounter with the species that the lycans and werewolves declared a truce with more than two centuries ago. In fact, this was everyone's first encounter with them. The oldest among them was Chief Dalloway, and even he had never met a vampire. Territorial lines are strictly drawn between their species not only for the purpose of preserving peace. It was also an open secret that it was a way to practice avoidance from a species that could very well drain them of their blood and their lives with it.

The tension in the atmosphere rose despite its silence. Xandar reached for Lucy's hand, leading their people forward together, approaching the middle of the field. The cold gust of wind was needles poking at their faces, but no one flinched, their vigilance increasing with each step.

As they got closer, Lucy felt her anxiety diminish little by little, which was confusing for her and her lycan. What she didn't realize was that the emerald-eyed vampire felt a sudden change of mood as well when she neared Lucy.

When the species came face-to-face, they offered each other slight bows, both sides wondering if they did it right since they didn't recall the last vampire and lycan or werewolf offering each other this kind of gesture.

"Your Imperial Majesty," Xandar greeted, and for once was grateful that he liked history enough to know this basic formality. This emerald-eyed vampire was definitely the empress, Pellethia Gangnes. Her aura spoke for her position. The pixie-haired brunette by her side looked particularly protective of her, so odds were this was the consort.

To everyone's surprise, Pellethia didn't respond to Xandar's greeting and chose to study Lucy instead. Lucy felt an unexplained pull toward the empress, and she saw from Pellethia's inquisitive eyes that she felt it too. Pellethia touched the pixie-haired woman's arm gently before approaching the queen at small paces.

Those by Lucy's side were getting ready to charge at the first sign of attack. Toby's hands were hidden behind his back, and his claws were slowly protruding. Xandar's arm instinctively reached out to shield his wife, but Lucy gently placed her hand over his arm, uttering, "It's okay, Xandar."

Her voice made Pellethia's brows knit deeper. She found it . . . familiar. But that wasn't possible. The empress doubted she had met Lucy before tonight. Although the queen's facial features were foreign, her energy felt like déjà vu. When it hit her, Pellethia's eyes widened in recognition before they glistened in happiness. A huge smile tamed her face when she whispered in a soft, hopeful voice, "Aunt Rosie?"

Oddly enough, Lucy found Pellethia's voice familiar. Despite her ongoing perplexity, she said, "I'm sorry, Your Imperial Majesty. You must be mistaking me for someone else. I'm Lucianne, but everyone calls me Lucy." Thrusting her hand out of a handshaking habit, her instinctive gesture was immediately met with threatening snarls from the vampires, making her retract her hand in haste.

Xandar's arm came forward to push his wife behind him. Toby and the others stood closer to the king, creating a barricade as they took their stance, ready to defend their queen at all costs.

Pellethia's tamed eyes reverted to their homicidal state as she glowered at her own people and yelled with protruded fangs, "Shut up, all of you! We are NOT at war! Watch your behavior before the king and queen!"

Toby blinked, then exchanged a surprised glance with his best friend, who was properly hidden behind her mate, whose grasp was refusing to let her move. Lucy didn't know how to react either. One minute the empress was cold and distant, then she looked warm and welcoming, now she was telling her own people off for snarling in her defense?

Xandar was getting befuddled as well and cracked his head on an instance in history where a vampire ruler told off his or her own people for another species. Despite being well versed in the historical relationship between their species, the king could think of no such situation.

The vampires offered bows in unison as a sign of apology. The lycans and werewolves continued exchanging baffled looks. Should they return the gesture or do nothing? No one knew.

Pellethia retracted her fangs and offered a bow as well before regaining her position. "Please accept my most heartfelt apologies for that, Your Highnesses. I can assure you," her head turned to the side and her voice projected in her people's direction when she continued, "if that happens again on my watch, I'll personally push my hand down their throats, extract their voice boxes, and break their kneecaps to make them kneel until they beg to be killed." A few vampires shuddered, from the empress's warning or from the cold wind . . . or both.

Pellethia's demeanor turned warm again as she looked at Lucy, who stepped out from behind her husband, but his grip still held her back.

Pellethia's hand cautiously stretched out like she was waiting for something to be put into her pale palm, asking politely, "May I, Lucy?"

Xandar was hesitant. Toby, Christian, and Phelton were defensive. Dalloway had already linked for backup. They wondered if this was a trick. But Lucy felt an unexplainable sureness that Pellethia wasn't going to hurt her. Gently moving away her mate's arm, she placed her hand in Pellethia's palm.

Xandar prayed to the Moon Goddess that this wasn't going to be a mistake. He would never forgive himself if his mate got hurt when he was right next to her.

The empress placed her cold thumb on Lucy's wrist to feel her pulse, closing her eyes and concentrating on the rhythm of her blood flow.

It took less than a minute, and when those emerald eyes came into view once more, they welled up again as a soft chuckle left the empress's lips, which then curled into a smile—the type of smile one wears when they see a loved one they haven't been in touch with for a long time, when one is reunited with a close friend after years or decades of separation, when one replays happy memories made with loved ones who have now passed on. It was the type of smile that screamed *I missed you . . . so much.*

Without warning, Pellethia pulled Lucy into a tight embrace. Xandar instinctively removed his hand just in time for the hug to happen then began wondering why he was sure that the empress wasn't going to hurt his queen. Lucy didn't know what was going on either, but her arms developed a mind of their own when they squeezed the empress in return.

Jealousy crept into Toby's center. Pellethia held Lucy like they were best friends. Eh, wrong! Lucy was *his* best friend! No one else's! Toby wouldn't share that status with anyone!

Christian blinked again and shook himself out of his daze before announcing his surrendered, "Okay, I give up. I'm quite sure this is a dream. I must have accidentally fallen asleep instead of heading to the actual inter-species rendezvous." A vampire pointed at Christian, nodding to his friend, conveying his agreement with the duke.

When Lucy and Pellethia finally let go of each other, Lucy said, "Your presence and energy are so familiar, but I don't know why. I'm quite sure we've never met."

Pellethia chuckled again. "We have met, actually. Well, in a different time, of course. Your name in that lifetime was Rosalie. I used to call you Aunt Rosie as a child."

That name hit Lucy and Xandar at the same time. Their suspicions from their date at the museum about a year ago were true. They were both mates and lovers in a different lifetime.

Pellethia excitedly pulled the pixie-haired vampire closer and introduced her, "This is my wife and consort, Octavia."

Lucy thrust out her hand, slowly this time, eyes instinctively darting across the field before falling on the consort. "It's a pleasure to meet you, Octavia."

Octavia's slightly deeper voice was firm and welcoming when she shook her hand with a warm smile. "Likewise, Lucy. Pellethia has spoken a lot about you . . . well, Rosalie, that is. Unfortunately, we never had the chance to meet. I didn't expect to have such an opportunity to meet you, to be honest."

Without even asking, Pellethia reached for Xandar's hand. As she started listening to the rhythm of his pulse, she confessed, "I wasn't very close to Uncle Reagan. I only met him a few times before the . . . well, before the murders. But I might still remember his rhythm. It's unique to each soul anyway."

Her brows furrowed as she concentrated. When she heard what she was hoping to hear, a smirk crawled up her lips as she noted pointedly, "You still owe me that doll, Uncle Reagan."

The vampires were throwing their hands in the air and exchanging glances like they were saying, "What did Her Imperial Majesty just say?" The more conventional ones were even pressing their finger pads to their foreheads as they shielded their faces, utterly embarrassed. The empress was asking for a doll? She wasn't 5! She was 1,578 years old! Less than 500 years to go and she'd be dead, since the oldest-living vampire only made it to 2,000 years of age.

Unlike Lucy, Xandar only felt a slight pull toward the empress now that he focused on his senses. It was the same pull when he was with Russell or Liam, both children who were extremely close to Lucy. This had to be right. "I didn't forget. I just thought it would've been better to . . . wait for better dolls to hit the market."

Narrowing her eyes, Pellethia declared, "Excuses."

After some chuckles, Toby coughed to remind Lucy of why they were there, at which time Lucy began, "Pellethia . . ."

"Oh, you used to call me Pelly, Aunt Ros—Lucy. Aunt Lucy."

Lucy couldn't believe she felt the warmth of a girl from a woman that was more than a millennium old. "Pelly, your email sounded urgent. What happened? And how can we help?"

The empress's smile faltered in an instant, as did Octavia's. The warm and welcoming atmosphere turned heavy and serious as Pellethia disclosed, "Last night, one of our villages, Falling Vines, was invaded. Every living vampire was abducted. The scents left in most homes confirmed that lycans and werewolves had been there."

The king and queen stared at each other in wide-eyed horror.

"Rogues," Toby muttered the word running through everyone's minds. The defense minister matched Lucy's look of dismay when he sighed in defeat. "Looks like we haven't gotten all of them yet, Lucy. This is definitely on us."

Octavia immediately said, "No, we're not blaming any authoritative figure in particular, but we were hoping for . . . a high degree of assistance in this matter. Our people are terrified. We don't know if another village is going to face the same thing."

Pellethia added, "The worst part is that the village had children. Not one or two, but six."

This was a mammoth of a problem because—by some divine law—the vampire population was fixed. There were only exactly 2,022,117 vampires in existence, no more and no less. A death of one would mean the birth of another, hence it was impermissible to congratulate a couple when a child was born, and it was very rude to celebrate birth because the child was the result of someone else's death. What one was allowed to say when they saw the newborn baby would be, "Good that it's healthy." That was it.

With the divine law of fixed population and long life, childbirth was scarce, and children, in turn, were sacred. Even those with little knowledge of vampires knew this, so everyone understood how dire the situation was.

Pellethia proceeded to explain, "We stationed guards around small villages and residential areas near Falling Vines, but we fear that they, too, will be vulnerable to the abduction. We don't know what the lycans and werewolves have with them to manage such a feat. It's extremely disturbing that they managed to get every single one without bloodshed. Not a drop of blood was found. It's like our people didn't even try to attack and defend themselves, which is very strange. We have no leads. The abductors' scents lead to nowhere. They just circle within the village itself. We don't know how to start tracking them down to get our people back."

The helplessness in her voice was evident. The vampires had tried everything, considered every possible option, and looked under every rock, and they came to a dead end, hence the demand for an immediate meeting with the species who took the lost vampires.

Toby then hissed under his breath as he thought out loud, "How are the rogues still so resourceful? We took down the major one less than a year ago!"

Xandar noted, "The last rogue supplier hasn't been found yet. So rogues are still operating, albeit more discreetly it seems, but . . . our rogues have never stepped foot into vampire territory before, have they?" he asked Pellethia and Octavia.

Pellethia affirmed, "Our borders have kept most lycans out. We've never had a werewolf trespassing since the declaration of peace. The few lycans who did trespass did so by mistake and were thrown back out of the border without question or exception. We don't even feed on them anymore. We haven't since the truce! Why are they taking us?"

Some lycans stood closer to each other at the mention of feeding. Everyone thought hard, but they couldn't come up with anything. Margaret, Stella, and their rogue pack came to mind, but they were near White Blood at the time being. White Blood was nowhere near any part of vampire territory. Plus, if they had rogue lycans on their side, they would've brought them along when they tried to take Stella back.

Even if Margaret's pack did abduct the vampires from miles away, there was no way they could trespass, abduct, and leave on a flight. They wouldn't even get past the custom officers with bags or suitcases of vampires. Were suitcases even large enough to fit a regular-sized vampire? They doubted it.

It couldn't be Margaret and her pack. Their timelines didn't match up.

Like the vampires, no lycan or wolf knew where to begin. In the bleak air of the night, Lucy's clear voice resonated through everyone's ears. "We don't know why this is happening or who may have taken them, but we know someone who might have such knowledge."

Her eyes locked with her husband's. It took Xandar a moment before realization hit him like a ton of bricks. "NO! No way! Sweetheart, we put him there for a reason!" Their followers and the vampires were exchanging puzzled but curious glances. Who were the king and queen referring to?

Lucy asked Xandar, "Do you happen to have an alternative solution?"

"I don't, but he can't be our only source to get the vampires back." Her brows raised, questioning his response. Xandar groaned, "Alright, fine. He could be our only source for now, but how do we know he didn't orchestrate this whole thing just to bargain for a reduced sentence he's now serving?"

"Why would he orchestrate this to get a reduced sentence when he could have done this earlier to avoid sentencing altogether?"

Toby and the others were catching up, and their expressions looked like they were saying, "Oh no!"

When Xandar couldn't give his wife an answer, she said, "We have to, Xandar. We don't know anyone else with that kind of knowledge or network. And we're short on time."

Xandar's animal slammed its head against an imaginary wall, and the king shook his head, muttering to himself, "Goddess, why must it be him?"

CHAPTER 8

At 2:00 a.m., Alissa cautiously removed the ceiling panel of a prison corridor after checking the outline of the place three times with Hailey. There was no room for error. They had a stringent timeline to stick to or they would all get caught. Hailey stayed in the space between the roof and ceiling as Alissa climbed down the rope she had just let loose, skillfully landing with an almost inaudible thud on the cement floor.

From her side pocket, Alissa extracted a few melatoxins—mothball-like objects that vaporized into the air to make everyone in the room drowsy—and rolled one into every prisoner's cell, making sure that the flicking of each ball made it to the far corner of each unit where their beds were. If one was already asleep, then the chemicals would induce deeper slumber.

At the end of the eight-cell prison corridor was the creature she came to see, one who lay in bed with a hand over his eyes, who—before Alissa said a word—muttered sleepily in his deep voice, "Is the queen in danger?"

In a cautious whisper, Alissa replied, "Well, not exactly, Your Grace. Ivory is watching her for now. But we need to get you out of here. There's w—"

"Are our sites compromised?" Greg asked.

"No, but . . ."

"Are any of our people taken?"

"No, Your Grace, but . . ."

"Then I don't have to leave yet, Alissa. Get out of here. Go join the others."

Turning to face the wall, Greg's eyelids fell, eager to continue his sleep that was unjustifiably interrupted when his sharp hearing caught Alissa's landing.

Alissa heaved a sharp, frustrated sigh and whispered a little louder, "Someone is in the midst of concocting a substance to challenge the Queen's Authority, Your Grace."

Greg's eyes snapped wide open. His body shot up from bed as he exclaimed a little too loudly, "What?"

The duke was hoping to find traces of humor on Alissa's face, but all he saw was anger and worry. In a frantic whisper, she continued, "This began as a joke, but it's turning serious, Your Grace. The boastful rumors are not dying off. It was cemented just recently, in fact. Certain groups are talking about other groups having a new source of ingredients for their experiments. We need to get you out to help us fix this!"

"Any names of the ones involved?"

"So far, Dr. Tanish and Madame Psych."

"The mad duo," muttered Greg.

Alissa nodded, and her leg fidgeted in impatience as she awaited instructions. Greg's heart was beating faster by the second as he questioned, "Anyone else?"

"Not that we're sure of yet."

"Who are the current suspects?"

Alissa bit back her tongue, hating it when Greg asked her or any member of the team to make guesses like this. They didn't like giving less-than-accurate information. After a moment, she admitted, "Desmond and Hailey are placing bets on J.J. and Bundy because they've gotten less chatty. Ivory and I think that Dormant Little Red might not be very dormant anymore. It's the first time in decades anyone has seen him sober up."

After a few seconds that felt like an eternity to Alissa, the duke muttered, "Deploy a team to study the movements of everyone you just named. Study only. Take no other action. And send a message to the queen. Tell her I'm requesting an immediate audience."

"And if she refuses?" Alissa challenged.

"I doubt she will."

"The king might stop her."

"My cousin . . . is powerless when it comes to the queen. He gives her anything she wants. The only thing stopping her from seeing me is herself, and I doubt she'd say no. I haven't given her a reason to mistrust me. If I go with you tonight, it won't just be me who'll be in trouble. It'll be all of us. She won't be able to help us out of this even if she wants to. As much as I dread wasting time, this is time that we must give. We have to do this by the book. Their book. Tell the queen I need to speak to her at her earliest convenience."

Alissa knew she couldn't convince Greg to do otherwise, and she was running out of time. "As you wish, Your Grace." After muttering in dissatisfaction, her feet pattered down the corridor before she climbed up the rope.

Greg and his animal couldn't sleep for the rest of the night. The duke thought he had already protected the queen from every possible danger. Who the fuck was trying to hurt her now?

Dr. Tanish and Madame Psych were self-proclaimed mad. But their madness never helped them accomplish much as far as Greg could recall. The only thing they succeeded in doing thus far was synthesizing silver with as little silver ore as possible. Silver ore was not only difficult to extract and steal, but also it was getting scarcer and scarcer each passing year. The mad duo's "revolutionary" breakthrough was coming up with a chemical formula that made silver manufacturing possible with the most minute amount of ore, which, to Greg, was not great, seeing that silver didn't affect lycans, and before Lucy, the duke didn't give a damn about werewolves.

He mentally pinned the duo in the "Small Achievers" category, and because of that, he almost forgot about them. That was a mistake. Sure, the duo didn't have the brains to create something that would harm or kill lycans, but that didn't mean they were incapable of replicating the formula of other scientists to synthesize deadly substances like oleander or the shell.

J.J. and Bundy were two loud-talking female lycans who spun more illogical tales of their purported heroism than they actually experienced. Once, the two entered Greg's casino, and the duke got his men to throw them out after he was done enduring their blabbering when he was in the midst of pondering a security plan. The best part of that night was, once the two were thrown out, the rest of the customers applauded and cheered at Greg's order. As it turns out, J.J. and Bundy's inconsiderately blaring chatter made players lose concentration, and thus lose games. The pair frequented other bars and recreation locations that were not owned by Greg, but one thing was for sure: they never stopped speaking loudly. If Alissa was right, if they were quieting down, something was wrong.

Dormant Little Red. Greg gave him that nickname because the smaller than average lycan went everywhere with an old red cap. Dormant, because apart from drinking with whatever he earned from the small drug trafficking cases, he never did anything else. He didn't talk, didn't mingle, didn't even look like he was interested in his surroundings. He just downed alcohol until he passed out on the table. Compared to everyone around him who was either having fun or throwing a fit, Dormant Little Red was literally dormant.

Two habitual tale spinners were no longer tale spinning at the top of their lungs. Dormant Little Red was sobering up. This was not a coincidence. And these were only the preliminary observations. Imagine what Alissa and the others would find when they looked further.

After Alissa covered the ceiling, she and Hailey stealthily left the prison grounds without being detected. Hailey, who hacked into the prison's security system, got the CCTVs back on their original track, removing traces of her cyber-intrusion to avoid detection.

In their escape van disguised to look like a transportation vehicle, Alissa got out a plain card and envelope she kept in the glove compartment. When the van had to stop at the traffic lights, she scribbled Greg's message to the queen while Hailey hacked into the postal system to reschedule the time when mail was due to be delivered to the king and queen's residence. They needed to get this message to them as early as possible.

The third member of the gang—the driver, Desmond—casually suggested, "Can't we all just, I dunno, bust into their place and go, 'Hey, Queen. Listen, y'all gonna be in a lot of trouble. See, some a-holes are gettin' jealous of that superpower ya have and uh . . . they're doin somethin' to make it second place, and we think ya need to chill and let our boss out, ya know? 'Cause he'd know how to clean this up for ya.'"

As Alissa chewed on gum while rereading her scribbled message, she asked, "Are you going to do it?"

"That depends. Will you two help me?"

The ladies responded. "No."

Desmond groaned. "Why's the boss like that? Why he like waitin' around when we can just bust in there?

As Hailey furiously swiped across her tablet to make sure nothing could be traced back to any of them. She answered, "Because the boss balances long-term safety and the goal. Quit whining like a baby, Des."

"Huh! We ain't know how big this shit is against us. It'd be dumb to not whine. Met Jackson last night. He said people are leaping."

"Leaping?" Alissa's eyes snapped to him. "As in, leaping sides? Switching sides?"

"Yeah! Ain't you worried? After the boss went all soft . . ."

"The boss doesn't go soft," Hailey retorted monotonously.

"With the queen he did. That what everyone sayin'. Listen, y'all. We know the boss good to us. But outside our people, they sayin' boss betrayin' us, and a lot of people ain't sure about boss's potential no more."

Taking out the gum and downing the rest of her espresso, Alissa spat, "They can think all they want. We know the duke. He won't do that to us."

"Yeah, I know. I know. We all know that. But those new members, those who didn't get a chance to know the boss long enough, they might be leapin' faster than if a cop come bangin' on their door. Y'all know what I'm sayin'?"

In a disturbingly casual tone, Alissa mused, "Then they'd best pray that we don't get orders to track them down and burn them when we get to the bottom of this shit."

Desmond parked not far from the king and queen's residence. It was going to be an ordeal waiting until seven in the morning. Just when the three of them thought they could take turns napping, Ivory's link came through. When he reported that the queen and many other high-ranking lycan and werewolf officials had met with vampires, Alissa's drowsiness wore off. *'Why the hell didn't you tell me this earlier? You knew I was meeting the boss TODAY!'*

'Ali, get real. Would telling the boss this make a difference?' Ivory retorted.

Knowing that she'd lost this verbal battle, Alissa sighed in defeat and responded, *'Fine. Thanks for the update. I'll take the next shift in an hour.'*

At five minutes to seven, Alissa got out of the van and stretched out her limbs before jogging in the direction leading to the royal residence. The courier truck came, and a mailman emerged with the usual mail. Alissa "accidentally" knocked into him, helped him pick up the letters scattered on the ground, and slipped in her own envelope, silently praying to Goddess that it got to the queen soon. *Desmond was right: they don't know who or what they are up against.*

CHAPTER 9

t 6:30 a.m., everyone was already in the dining room having breakfast. It wasn't that they had a habit of getting up early, but that everyone had something on their minds to get them out of bed. For one, Tate got a message from Mannon and Xiera that Margaret's rogue pack, which was purportedly ten miles south of White Blood, was no longer there. When the lycan warriors arrived and investigated the location together with the wolves, they discovered that the rogues had just left. Their scents led the authorities to a nearby stream and then just stopped.

The news wasn't a good start to anyone's morning. Even Stella looked a little worried. With another frustrating bust, Xandar tried to find some comfort in the sight before him. Lucy was trying extremely hard to get Reida to open her mouth as Xandar held their little girl on his lap, but the stubborn baby kept her lips sealed as her head shifted from side to side, avoiding the baby food that her mother was desperately trying to get into her mouth.

In the midst of their struggle, Vernon—one of their two house guards— came in with the morning mail and placed it next to Xandar. The king and queen thanked him before he left with a smile and a small wave to the baby, who returned the gesture like she was trained to.

Xandar's free hand pushed through the letters until he came across one faded red envelope that read: Queen Lucianne Freesia Paw. "Fuck," Xandar muttered without thinking.

Even Tate and Stella stopped chewing.

Lucy's attention went to her husband. "What is it?"

"Fuck," said little Reida, and it was her first word.

Lucy's widened eyes fell on her daughter. And as Tate pressed back a smile, trying to hide his amusement by sipping on his coffee, the lycan queen glared at her husband and exclaimed, "Xandar!"

"Fuck!" Reida repeated with a cute giggle that filled the room.

Tate praised in a hushed whisper, "Good girl, Reida."

This elicited more of the pup's giggles and earned a glare from his friend. Lucy was okay with cursing when one reached a particular age, but her daughter was nowhere near that age yet!

Xandar didn't need to look into his wife's eyes or feel her inferno through their bond to know that he'd messed up. Avoiding Lucy's glower, he whispered to Reida slowly, "Cupcake, it's fart. Fart. Okay? You're saying it wrong. Fart."

"Should that even be her first word?" Lucy complained.

"Fuck. F—" Reida's attempts were cut short by Lucy's swift stuffing of baby food into her mouth, making Stella chuckle.

Braving himself to meet Lucy's gaze, Xandar tried to explain, "This doesn't even make any sense. That was the first time I said that word around her, sweetheart, I swear."

Tate moved away, the mug hiding his smile, and offered an unhelpful suggestion, "Oh, you swore alright. Maybe the F-word is just easier to say than mama or dada." He and Stella laughed when Lucy threw her friend another murderous glare.

To change the subject, Xandar pushed the red envelope toward his wife. "I have a good guess who this is from."

Yeah, so did Tate. Smiles faltered and laughter died down. The atmosphere in the room turned dense. They only knew of one creature who'd send handwritten letters without a stamp. Stella didn't know what was going on, but judging by the looks on the adults' faces, this wasn't good news. Instinctively, she sidled up to Tate to feel safe.

Lucy almost cursed when she read and reread her name on the envelope, but her hand quickly reached to her mouth to stop the word from spilling out. Placing the baby spoon back into the bowl, she tore open the envelope.

In it was a white note with black handwriting that wasn't Greg's:

My queen, it is with great regret and urgency that I request an immediate audience with you. There may be new, dangerous players that you need to know about. Please allow me a few minutes of your time at your earliest convenience.

Greg

Sliding the note to her husband, who then passed it to Tate after skimming through it, Lucy held her mug to her lips and mused, "Looks like this meetup is a mutually intended one."

CHAPTER 10

The prisoners were jolted awake, given an hour to run around the treeless, electrically fenced-up prison track before hitting the cold showers.

Greg was surprised when a guard told him to rush through breakfast and get ready because he was summoned by the king and queen and the meeting was at 8:30 a.m. Greg knew Alissa and the others were efficient, but this was efficiency on a record-breaking level. He didn't expect the meeting to be any sooner than noon. The duke made a mental note to reward the team later.

Breezing through breakfast and putting on the short-sleeve shirt and trousers the policeman left on his bed, he was then escorted to a car. The three policemen assigned to accompany him remained silent throughout the hour's drive to the station, each trying their best to avoid making eye contact with the duke.

Greg didn't mind. He liked the silence. These weren't the kind of creatures he liked to make conversation with anyway.

At the station, Greg was placed in an interrogation room with a policeman at the corner. Diving into his own thoughts, rummaging through his mind on how best to tell the queen about Alissa's report, the big question became, how was he going to protect his people from the law while helping the queen and the law at the same time? When he considered *not* helping her altogether, a shot of guilt surged through his heart, making him abort the plan in an instant. Even so, he couldn't and wouldn't give his people up. They counted on him to survive.

The back of his head tingled at the intensity of his thoughts while his crafty mind went back and forth considering various options, building up from those before he eventually hit a mental dead end. Every. Single. Time. When he and his animal came to the only plausible plan, which was flimsy with too many variables to begin with, he muttered, "This isn't going to work."

Even his animal had to agree. They just hoped that Alissa and the others would have enough time to run if and when Greg's plan backfired and the queen used her Authority on him to hunt his people down.

The door opened, and Greg stood. He caught a three-second glimpse of the queen handing a baby girl to the cousin he hated before she pushed the king toward the one-way mirror and entered the interrogation room. Greg could've sworn his cousin threw him a warning glare, making his animal roll its eyes. If the duke wanted to challenge the king and claim the queen, he would've done it months ago. As for their child, Greg only had one complaint: why did it have to look so much like a Blackfur? The brown hair, the almond-shaped eyes, the thin lips. Seriously, was it so hard to copy Lucy's raven hair, round orbs, and plump lips? Shouldn't her genes be dominant over his dim cousin's? Why give the heir to the throne the less attractive set of features?

Well, Greg supposed he could appreciate that the child's nose and brows seemed to match the queen's.

"Thank you, Cedric," Lucy's voice prompted the policeman at the corner to leave, and he did so with a bow and smile.

Greg approached her and got down on one knee before pecking a polite kiss on her small hand. "My queen, thank you for granting me an audience on such short notice."

"You really don't have to do that every time we meet, Your Grace. Please stand."

He obeyed, and they sat in the only two chairs, separated by a square table. Their side profiles faced the one-way mirror, which Greg was dead certain that his cousin was looking through right now—a gaze that could burn through the mirror if it had the ability to set things ablaze.

Lucy began, "Just so you know, Your Grace, we asked the police to bring you here this morning before your letter arrived in the post."

Ah. So it wasn't his people's efficiency after all. Wait, she asked to see him? What had happened?

She proceeded to say, "Before we get into the details about how you were able to send word from where you were held, let's get to the more pressing issue at hand." Her eyebrows furrowed. "Who are these new players you mentioned?"

Greg cleared his throat, and the creases on his forehead spoke for his internal conflict. "My queen, before I . . . make full and frank disclosure, I need to ask that . . . I'm pleading with you to . . . offer pardons for past crimes."

He couldn't even meet her gaze, ashamed to ask for something like this when he should have been granting her everything she asked for as his queen.

Lucy was confused. She had never seen Greg this uncomfortable, and his request was . . . odd. "Your Grace, I'm not following. Why didn't you ask for this before you were tried and sentenced?"

The duke realized his plea was badly framed. "My apologies, my queen. What I meant was, I'm pleading for you . . . and the king to pardon . . . certain creatures who can help eradicate this new threat."

A moment of silence unreeled before she pressed, "And the new threat is?"

Greg was thinking of sealing his lips and aborting this whole plan, but it was too late for that now, and it wasn't as if his animal was going to let him get away with not telling her what she wanted to know. With nothing but troubled eyes, Greg muttered, "I received word that someone is coming up with a concoction to challenge the Queen's Authority."

The queen slowly leaned back into her seat, her brows pulled together, and pleated her glabella. Connecting the vampire abduction to the current threat Greg was telling her about, she finally muttered, "That makes sense."

"What makes sense, my queen?" Greg asked, relieved that something finally had come out from her delicate, pink lips. He was getting worried seeing her just sitting there without a word.

Meeting his gaze, she responded in a manner that was already agreed with Xandar and the other ministers the previous night. "There was an abduction in the vampire community. Six children were taken along with twenty-one adults."

That became a moment when the duke's thoughts synchronized with his queen's. "To create the concoction," he uttered.

Lucy continued, "The scent the abductors' left behind was that of werewolves and lycans. In your . . . experience, do you have any idea who could manage such a feat without bloodshed?"

Greg's brows rose to his hairline at the last words before he asked in disbelief, "Are the vampires certain that it was our kind who were there, my queen? Did they see any?"

Lucy blinked before admitting, "Well, there weren't any eyewitnesses to begin with, but I doubt they can be wrong about scents, Your Grace."

"Right. About that, there's something called *scent sprays*—illegal substances, but they do exist. One can essentially hide their scents by leaving an entirely different scent behind."

"You're saying that there are sprays with the scents of lycans and werewolves in your world?"

"Werewolves. Lycans. Vampires. Humans. Rogues . . ."

"Why would one need a scent spray of a rogue?"

"To throw the authorities off track, my queen."

"Ah. That makes sense." She nodded in understanding, looking more like a curious learner than an angered authority figure.

In fact, Greg sensed no anger at all despite just telling her about something that practically went against the system she was defending. Her bright, curious eyes encouraged him to give more than he was asked, so he did, "Human scents are the worst, by the way. Their general scent is very varied, unlike ours, which is quite standard. And because of that, scent sprays for humans are normally tailored to a specific region or group. And there'll be different scents when they sweat. It really is a hassle. If I ever started a business selling scent sprays, I would *never* take human scents into my inventory. Most of them would expire before they were bought off the shelf."

Lucy's light chuckling at Greg's candid admission warmed the duke's heart, but it pissed off the king. Registering her husband's raging jealousy through their bond, she quickly moved on, "So what you're saying is that it couldn't be werewolves or lycans who abducted the vampires?"

"Well, I'm not saying that it's impossible but . . . it would be very, very . . . very difficult without bloodshed. Am I allowed to know how deep in vampire territory this village was?"

"About an hour's run to the closest wolf pack."

"Any footprints?" Greg asked.

"That's where things get odd, Your Grace." The crease on her head returned. "It seems the lycan and wolf prints just go round and round the village. It leads to nowhere beyond that."

"Are those real prints or fake ones, my queen?"

Her shoulders fell. "Your kind has gadgets to fake those too?"

"Well, I wouldn't call them gadgets per se. But they have this rubber mold that can make similar prints on the gr—."

"Oh, Goddess," Lucy muttered in dismay as her fingers pressed her forehead, elbow now anchored on the table.

"There is some good news, my queen," Greg began. "That rubber mold doesn't make an exact print. If you compare a real print with a fake one, you can see that the way a fake print is pushed to the ground is fairly different from how an actual lycan or werewolf would leave a print. You've seen real prints in your time on the battlegrounds, so you'd be able to tell the difference, I'm sure. Perhaps you could request to see those in the village to conclude whether they're real."

Huh. She didn't think of that. She didn't think prints could be faked. Period.

Greg added, "And about scent sprays, I must inform you that the best sprays only leave a synthetic scent for up to forty hours at most. They fade faster than natural odor, which lingers up to forty-eight hours, give or take. If one were to investigate again after the forty-hour timeframe, they might pick up something other than werewolves or lycans."

"That's good to know," she mused, then asked, "So in your view, who could've abducted the vampires? The vampires themselves?"

"That would be my best guess with whatever I'm told as of now, Your Highness. But with new developments, I might come to a different conclusion."

"Okay." Straightening her back, she moved on to the next issue, "Now it's your turn, Your Grace. You were asking for a . . . conditional pardon for certain creatures: they assist us, and we relieve them of all legal consequences from past crimes. I'm a little reluctant to ask, but does this include the creature who sent me the message on your behalf."

Greg bit his lip, nodded once, and answered simply, "Yes, my queen."

"Alright," Lucy mouthed inaudibly, digesting the fact that Greg was admitting to someone breaking into prison just to get one message from her cousin-in-law before leaving without a trace. "I can't give you an answer yet, Your Grace. I must speak to the king and the rest of the ministers. But regarding the concoction to challenge the Queen's Authority . . . do you think it will succeed?"

From Greg's ominous look, she already had her answer. His next words only confirmed a fact that she didn't want to be true. "When I still had my freedom, I heard insane things like this all the time. Most were scams, out to get money in the name of investment. But some weren't just big talk. There are very ambitious creatures down there, and a notable handful are quite determined to succeed. The word I received about the concoction doesn't sound like fluff. Fluff doesn't create a seismic shift in our world. It normally just dies off without making any visible impact. But . . . this has turned the wheels of our system, and it's not stopping. In fact, from whatever I've been told recently . . . it seems like the momentum is only gaining speed. Creatures and systems don't change unless something is motivating them to change. Whatever that something is, it must have made a big promise, and the concoction fits the bill."

"So it will happen. Any idea how long we have?"

"Five to six months, I suppose. But it really is better to get this cleaned up sooner than that. With advancing technologies and new substances within reach every day, it is possible that they can get lucky and achieve it within three months."

"Three months," Lucy noted. Her chair scraped the floor as she got up from her seat, and Greg followed suit. "I'll get back to you on your request for the conditional pardon. For clarification purposes, how many people are we talking about here, those who can help?"

Greg cleared his throat and confessed, "Ninety-eight. Rogues. Lycans."

As composed as she had trained herself to be, Lucy failed to keep her eyes from widening in shock. Taking a moment to absorb those three simple words, she kept her voice steady and responded, "Okay. I'll get back to you on that. Thank you for your time, Your Grace." Thrusting her hand for a handshake, her stern eyes bore into Greg's when he was beginning to kneel again. "Don't, Your Grace. Just remain standing and shake my hand."

Greg was used to offering her nothing but the highest form of respect, not just because she was his queen, but because—to him—she was the only creature deserving of that form of respect. The duke was tempted to disregard her demand and kneel anyway, but her eyes insisted he give in, so he did, albeit reluctantly, shaking her hand awkwardly.

His discomfort sent a trace of humor into Lucy's eyes. "You're a lot like Christian when it comes to heeding formalities, aren't you, Your Grace?"

Greg went completely speechless, and the corner of Lucy's lips tilted up a little when she turned to leave. After the door closed behind her, Greg and his animal wondered if this was karma for what he had done to Blackfur's duchess, that a Blackfur trait somehow infected Greg himself. The thought made his animal shudder and gag.

No. No way. He couldn't be like his distant cousin. That guy was lame and slow and naive. Lucy had to be joking.

Right?

CHAPTER 11

After emailing Pelly and Octavia, requesting permission to help investigate Falling Vines, their reply that came within five minutes enabled Xandar, Christian, and Lucy to round up a few policemen, board Xandar's jet, and head to the vampire village.

Lucy linked Toby and Phelton to meet them there. Xandar persuaded her to stay on the jet with Reida. After giving thought to the fact that they'd be in a territory where the Queen's Authority would have no effect on its local species, she agreed.

When they landed, Pelly, Octavia, and a few others from the previous night were there to greet them: some with warm smiles, some not. Only high-born vampires—who had evolved to not feel the burn from sunlight—were there. Octavia wasn't high-born, but mating and marking Pelly gave her the evolved trait. Every vampire still hated the sun, but the light rays couldn't scar or kill them like it would their less-evolved counterparts. Those susceptible to burns remained indoors, and thus were absent.

Disappointment permeated through Pelly when Xandar said Lucy wasn't joining them, but with his permission and Octavia's green light, the empress boarded Xandar's jet to meet the queen and left her consort to lead the lycans and werewolf to Falling Vines.

Xandar noticed Toby's eyes darkened and forehead pleated as he watched Pelly dashing to the jet in excitement, so the king asked, "Toby, you're not jealous, are you?"

The defense minister's eyes narrowed. "I'm proud to say that I am, Xandar."

Christian burst out laughing. Phelton and the policemen were pressing back amused smiles.

As Xandar tried his best to ignore his cousin, he patted Toby on the shoulder and assured, "Don't worry, Toby. Lucy's relationship with Pelly is like the one with her nephews and nieces. You're on a different level with her as her best friend."

"And I *will* stay there," Toby proclaimed a little too seriously, then complained, "And why is Lucy the one who has to stay on the jet? If you stayed there with little Reida, I would at least get to keep an eye on my best friend so my position isn't compromised."

Christian's chuckles came out louder, and it was making some of the vampires loosen up. Many had begun eavesdropping, even Octavia, who reassured Toby, "I really wouldn't worry about Pelly being Lucy's best friend, Minister. Rafael over there is my wife's best friend. I doubt she'd replace him."

Their heads turned, and a male vampire with blonde hair combed to the back offered a brief wave with a wide smile and a knowing glint in his eye. As they continued striding forward, Toby waved back meekly and muttered in embarrassment, "That's good to know."

Some of the vampires chuckled at Toby's reaction, further easing the atmosphere between their species. The tension and awkwardness reduced considerably. Xandar felt it, as did Octavia. They exchanged a brief glance, and both rulers knew that it would be in the foreseeable future when their respective species no longer had to live within the territorial limits drawn by their ancestors.

Within a few minutes, they reached the village that was so quiet that it was eerie. Most homes had doors or windows left wide open, but there wasn't a soul in sight. Xandar told the vampires about Greg's suspicions, that the abductors had used scent sprays whose effects would have faded by now. They split into groups of three and started sniffing around the village again.

Lycans and werewolves had better noses for scents due to their more animalistic nature compared to vampires. Even so, it didn't take long for the vampires to conclude that the previously strong odor of lycans was now very, very faint. The lycans and Toby concluded that they smelled no wolves. At all. So lycans were involved, but there were only three. They couldn't have taken everyone in the village all on their own.

When the sniffing was done, Toby delved further into his gamma mode, studying the prints like he, Lucy, and many of their allies did when they found such prints in wiped-out wolf packs in the past. What they never had to do was tell a real print from a fake one. After silently scrutinizing a few prints here and there, the minister muttered, "Greg Claw was right."

"How can you tell?" Xandar asked. Those looked quite real to him.

Toby got Phelton to take off his shoe and make a footprint right next to one of the fake ones before he lowered himself into a squatting position. "If you looked here, Xandar, you'd see that the fake one went too deep at the second and third toe while leaving the first, fourth, and fifth toe print in unequal depth. It isn't possible to assert one's weight only on two toes when one is walking, much less when one is running. That's the problem with this print. That one . . ." Toby walked a few steps to another print, looking at it like a dissatisfied professor. "Okay, the one who made this print wasn't even trying. I mean, look at it."

Octavia had no idea what she was looking at, and neither did most of the others with furrowed brows.

Xandar looked hard and finally muttered, "The heel . . . it went too deep in comparison to the toe prints."

"Exactly. When a creature sprints, force is exerted on the front part of the foot, not the back. In other words, not the heel. Whoever did this was probably a newbie in this trade. Looks like the other duke was right. These prints are faked to throw us off. These weren't made by our animals."

"Are you suggesting that one of our own did this?" one of the vampires exclaimed in insult.

"Well, actually . . ."

Toby wanted to offer an alternative explanation, but he was immediately interrupted by the same offended vampire, "From the way this is going, it looks as if your species seek to wash your hands of this entire affair a—"

Octavia's snarl cut off the old man's words. "Watch your tone and attitude, Maddock."

On behalf of his species, Xandar uttered, "We're not dismissing this issue at our end until it's fully resolved at yours as well, Maddock."

"Hmph. So you say," Maddock muttered.

In a tone that sent a bone-deep shiver down everyone's spines, Octavia sneered, "Should I have your tongue cut or your title stripped, Viscount?"

Upon hearing that, Maddock pressed his lips shut.

Octavia conveyed an embarrassed apology to Xandar, who shrugged the matter off with a smile. A loss this huge would make anyone panic and short-tempered, so the king gathered that the viscount was just under a lot of pressure and plagued with worry.

Toby decided to get the ball rolling again to ease the increasingly tense atmosphere, "Wokay. Anyway, I was going to say that these prints weren't made by our animals, but it doesn't mean that there weren't any of our kind here. We smelled three lycans, so they had to be here."

Rafael spoke for the first time, "So now what?"

Toby said, "Now, we have to find out whether the three lycans came alone or with another set of vampires."

Maddock rolled his eyes. "And how on earth do you propose we do that? Need I remind you that unlike your species, we and the proditors don't smell any different." Vampires termed their version of a rogue as a proditor, whose indistinguishable general scent made it next to impossible to tell them apart from those loyal to the empire. Thus one could be standing right next to a proditor and not know it.

Xandar suggested, "If you and Octavia would allow it, Maddock, we could enter these houses to get a whiff of their belongings and the cumulated scents in the houses themselves. If we detect a scent in the house that's not found in a wardrobe or on the shelves, we'd know there was an intruder."

That logic sent a wave of realization among the vampires. Why didn't they think of it?

Octavia couldn't mask her smile. "Xandar, if and when you choose to retire, I hope you'll consider joining the Defense Department in our empire since it is clear that," her berating eyes went to Maddock, and she continued, "help is in dire need here."

Xandar tried to not increase the tension when he responded lightly, "Lucy would kill me if I dumped the kingdom on her and left, Octavia. My tenure in your empire would probably be the shortest one in history once my wife ordered for my assassination. But thank you for the offer. It's nice to know I have a safety net to fall back on should I need it." Christian patted his cousin's back as a chortle of laughter left him.

The mere mention of Lucy got Xandar thinking about her. As they made their way to one of the houses, his animal asked his human to link their mate, already missing her and their little girl. Xandar didn't need any more persuading since he felt the same, so he linked her.

When Pelly left her people under Octavia's supervision and stepped onto the jet, the three policemen who had stayed behind to guard Lucy and Reida growled in defensiveness and ferocity, claws protruding in a swift motion.

"Guys. Guys. It's okay. This is the empress," Lucy immediately said with Reida in her arms, her pup crying not long after they landed.

The embarrassed policemen retracted their claws and bowed low in apology before acknowledging Pelly, "Your Imperial Majesty."

"Sorry about that, Pelly. They really meant no harm."

The policemen still held their heads low, and as Pelly moseyed past them, she said, "It's alright. Heads up, gentlemen. You were simply defending your queen."

As she sank into the seat close to Lucy, who was walking along the aisle with a still-wailing Reida, Pelly mentioned in passing, "It's good to see you're being protected in this lifetime. The blatant disrespect you had to deal with in your last life was horrifying, unbefitting for a princess and future queen. Not that Uncle Reagan didn't do everything he could to give you the best."

"You know, Pelly, I'd really love to know more about Reagan and Rosalie. Their history isn't in the kingdom's archives. There there, Reida. Shh . . ."

"No surprise there." Pelly murmured at the memory as she watched the red-faced baby girl. "Can I hold her?" the empress asked with hopeful eyes.

Pausing, Lucy asked, "Are you sure, Pelly?" Normally, people would want to hold Reida if she *wasn't* crying and would return her daughter when the crying started. Pelly was doing the exact opposite.

"Only if you don't mind, Aunt Lucy." Pelly smiled meekly, looking disappointed because she thought Lucy was going to refuse.

As Lucy placed Reida into Pelly's arms, she teased, "Good luck."

Pelly chuckled lightly and held Reida close to her chest. The child screamed louder at first with the loss of her mother's scent, but as the seconds went by and the pup detected that her mother was still near, Reida's screams and cries subsided as she leaned into Pelly. Within a few short moments, Reida stretched her chubby arms and yawned in the most adorable way before her eyelids fell.

Lucy plopped into the seat next to Pelly, whispering with a smile of disbelief, "How did you do that?"

"I think it's because of my cold skin. This is one of the warmest regions in our territory. Reida here was probably protesting about the heat." It was only then Lucy realized that the surrounding temperature was indeed warmer than usual even though the air-conditioner was already set to the minimum.

Lucy began, "You left Octavia in charge?"

"Mm-hm. She'll be fine. She's led things like this a million times. Born an ironmonger's daughter but destined to be a leader."

"I can tell. You're both really lucky."

Pelly's grateful eyes met Lucy's sincere orbs as the empress said, "Thank you, Aunt Lucy. I'm glad you and Uncle Xandar got lucky this time too. What happened to you both last time was . . ." She shook her head in dismay, staring into space like the horrors of the past were in front of her in full display. "It was so unfair." Her emerald eyes returned to the sleeping baby as she continued her tale, "We had the tea party planned for weeks. Uncle Regan was getting me a new doll. But the party never happened. Aunt Rosie never canceled on me, so I knew something was up, despite just being eight. Father was an even-tempered man, and his mood that day when he told me that Aunt Rosie wasn't coming was nothing short of suppressed rage. I wrote to her every day, asking my governess to mail each one."

The empress's eyes pooled like two puddles, glistening against the light. "There were never any replies, not just because she was dead but because my letters were never sent. Only when I turned ten and tried to sneak out of the house to go look for her did Father tell me the truth, that she was poisoned. I'll never forget the day when he broke it to me that Aunt Rosie wasn't coming back. It was so surreal. I didn't believe it. I couldn't speak for a whole minute, just sitting next to him at the dining table, staring at him, praying that he was going to tell me he was joking, but he didn't."

Wiping away some stray tears, Pelly chuckled briefly and said, "The first question that came out of my mouth was, 'Did Uncle Reagan do it?'" She laughed again at the memory. "Father was undeniably shocked at my question and—of course—told me that it wasn't him, that he'd never do such a thing to her. He told me that it was the king and queen who plotted the whole thing, so I've hated lycans ever since. They took away my playmate like she was nothing, like they didn't just end the life of someone I held close to my heart."

Lucy's warm hand reached for Pelly's cold one as she gave it a gentle squeeze. The empress smiled. "I only told Octavia this, but . . . I just get so scared that *this* is all a dream, that I'll wake up and find that you're not really alive again."

"I'm alive, Pelly. I'm right here. I'm right here with you. I just wish I remembered you."

Pelly chuckled again. "I only want the same thing if the memory package doesn't come with the horrors that Aunt Rosie had to endure in her lifetime. Uncle Reagan was good to her, but literally everyone else attacked her left, right, and center, all because she wasn't born a noblewoman and was rejected twice. Shallow idiots." After a moment of silence, she asked, "Does your animal still have a striped tail, Aunt Lucy?"

Lucy exclaimed, "Yes! Rosalie had that too? What does it do? What do the stripes mean?"

"Shh . . . Aunt Lucy, you're going to wake Reida!" Pelly reprimanded. Lucy's hand flew to her mouth as Pelly continued to whisper, "I never got to know why Aunt Rosie's tail was like that. Being a child, I was only excited to sit on her animal's shoulders when she took me for a run in the evenings if she could make the time. We'd stop by a river not far from my place, and I would play with her tail while she rested. I liked furry things at that age. There was once when Aunt Rosie told me that we might share a sort of special connection."

Lucy's head tilted. "What special connection?"

"Did you notice these?" Pelly swayed her head to show Lucy the five copper-colored streaks in her blonde hair. "I was born with these streaks. It's not some stylish trend that I'm following. Aunt Rosie mentioned that because she had five stripes on her tail and I have five streaks in my hair, we're a special team, though I don't know how. I wished I was older when I met her. I would've asked a lot more useful questions."

"She never mentioned anything else?" Lucy asked in disappointment. She thought she was finally getting some answers.

"No, unfortunately. My parents got worried about these streaks at first, but the doctors said there was nothing wrong with me biologically, so none of us ever found out why I'm like this. None of the medical experts know either."

Staring at her streaks again, Lucy ventured, "Were you ever able to do anything . . . extra with the streaks?"

"Like what?"

"About a year ago, Xandar made me realize that my tail had an unusual amount of strength. Maybe yours isn't strength but something . . . different, something that sets you apart from the other vampires."

"Hm," Pelly's thumb continued to stroke Reida's small arm as she pondered. "Apart from the shade of my eyes and the oddity of my hair, I honestly don't know how else I'm different from my kind. I'm not even cloaked with the Emperor's Authority."

Lucy blinked in disbelief. "Are you sure? Isn't the Authority hereditary?"

"It is, but women don't inherit it. There was only one empress before me, and she never wielded that power in her years on the throne. It's probably only bestowed on males."

"That doesn't seem fair," Lucy mused.

Smiling sadly, Pelly confided, "That's what Octavia says too. Our Lord probably didn't want women on equal standing as men."

Taking one more look at the copper streaks, Lucy whispered, "Maybe we'll find out how we're a special team one day. Together."

"I'd like that."

Then, Lucy's eyes glazed over, and she excused herself to receive a link from her husband. *'Hey, baby. Everything alright?'*

'Yes. How are things on your side?'

'So far, so good. Greg was right. The scents here only point to three lycans. No wolves. We're now going to check if there were any proditors. Are you alright on the jet?'

'Since my overprotective husband left three policemen with me and our daughter, even sending the empress who clearly has the potential to be deadly if provoked, I really can't see how I'm not alright.'

He chuckled. After a moment, Xandar realized he had nothing to say, so he simply uttered, *'I love you.'*

A familiar heat crept up Lucy's cheeks. *'I love you, too, Xandar. Stay focused, alright? They need our help.'*

'We are helping them, sweetheart. What's wrong with me speaking to my wife during the investigation?'

'Oh, I don't know. Maybe it's that this conversation is steering away from the problem at hand?'

Xandar's voice turned deeper when he linked in mock ignorance, *'And which direction is our conversation headed toward, my love?'*

Lucy bit her bottom lip to hide a smile. *'There's a time to focus and a time to flirt, darling. This is not the time to flirt.'*

'I disagree. My animal is certain that I'm picking the right time.'

'That's because it's my INDECENT beast!'

As his lycan laughed hard, Xandar teased, *'The one you marked and married. What were you thinking?'*

She chuckled in a way that made his heart flutter and admitted, *'With hindsight, I'd say I was thinking too much. The human part of this beast has a way with words. He always knows what to say and what to do to make me feel . . . worthier than I thought I was, and sometimes even . . . beautiful. His animal has a protective streak that feels so . . . reliable. It's amazing that, despite his protectiveness, he gives me just enough space to move about in my life so that I don't feel caged.'* Her finger drew circles on the armrest as she continued with the same shy smile, *'The way he and his animal hold and touch me is more comforting and assuring than anything I can ever imagine. Had I known how much I meant to them both, how far they would go to keep me safe and make me feel loved, I would've given in much sooner.'*

The lycan king's heart softened with each word and melted in tenderness at the end of her speech. His animal lay on its back and cooed in bliss. The warmth in Xandar's heart made his eyes glisten in pure happiness. Being lost for words, all he could link back at that moment was, *'I love you, my little freesia.'*

'I know. I love you too.' Her voice turned stern when she reminded, *'Stay focused, my king.'*

After a short laugh, Xandar promised, *'As you wish, my queen.'*

Right after ending the link, Xandar walked through the entrance of a half-brick, half-wooden house with a few others, and he didn't realize that Rafael and the red-headed woman next to him, Amber, were looking at him, question marks floating above their heads.

CHAPTER 12

Seeing the vampires' discombobulation, Christian announced, "Oh, don't mind the king. He always gets all smiley and mushy like this after speaking to the queen. Even spending two seconds with her makes him look all soft and lovey-dovey. It really beats what he was like before he met her. Goddess, let me tell you, h—"

Xandar interrupted, "Let's just put our minds and noses into finding foreign scents, Christian."

With a wide grin, Rafael said, "I'm sure the duke meant no harm, Your Highness. He was merely sharing tales to enhance the diplomatic relationship between our species. Now," inching toward Christian conspiratorially, he asked, "what was the king like before he met the queen, Your Grace?"

Christian's eyes lit up, and as he lifted up a shirt from a stack of unfolded laundry on the living room couch, the duke explained, "He was only an approachable creature to a very select few. No one else in their right minds would've dared come near him, especially not the werewolves. Honestly, he just looked like a deadly beast waiti—"

Xandar pushed a pair of shorts at his cousin's face. "Smell more and talk less, Christian."

Toby had just sniffed through a few cushions before joining the conversation, "You get the idea, Rafael."

Shooting Xandar a taunting glance, Rafael said, "Good thing he didn't scare away the queen then."

After sniffing a folded handkerchief on the coffee table, Toby noted, "Oh, that five-foot thing isn't scared of anyone. Lucy's instinct to protect and defend somehow malfunctioned the fear switch in her. You should see her in battle. If you ask me, I'd say it's a good thing *she* didn't scare away the king."

Christian's laughter filled the space at how accurately Toby put things. Lucy was small, but she had proven to be more lethal than any creature on the battlefield. Every werewolf and lycan who had fought alongside her knew this. The king flushed as his animal wagged its tail, elated that its mate was being shown off despite her absence. It made staying away from her a little less difficult.

When they were done in the living room, they made their way upstairs when Toby casually asked, "So what do you two do? In terms of abilities, I mean."

As they entered the master bedroom, Amber said, "Rafael here is the most powerful decipio . . ."

Rafael stopped at the open wardrobe and interjected, "Skillful, Amber. The right word is *skillful*. Mental manipulation is a power given to a quarter of our population in equal proportion. No single decipio is more powerful than the other."

Exhaling hard, Amber turned to Toby and continued, "Rafael is the annoyingly humble vampire and the most powerful decipio of our time, even better than our empress herself. Pelly still practices with him weekly to sharpen her skills. That's how good he is. I, myself, am a . . ."

Rafael cut in, "A misleading, small-sized insect who relishes in making us larger-build creatures feel small and powerless when it comes to strength." Amber threw the pillow she was about to sniff at him, and he caught it with ease, a smile of amusement playing on his lips.

Xandar inferred, "So . . . you're a fortis? Your innate ability is your physical strength?"

"Yes! I can lift more than twice the weight that Rafael can," Amber uttered with pride.

Rafael protested, "Why am I always the one you use as a comparison? And did you have to bring that up, Am?"

"That both Pelly and I can lift more than you can? Yes."

Rafael put back a towel he just sniffed. "I'm immensely grateful Octavia is with us now. You two are brutal. Mostly you, Am."

Amber chuckled when Christian asked, "The consort's ability is invisibility, right?"

Rafael nodded. "Yes. Anyone without a fortis's ability for a consort was fine by me."

Taking note of the four different scents from the wardrobes, they then walked around the house, sniffing the kitchen, dining room, basement, attic, and garage before concluding that there were six foreign scents. Rafael took down the details on his phone, and they moved on to the next house, repeating the entire process.

An hour later, they joined the others, and everyone agreed that there were foreign scents in every house they entered. The next step would be to get trackers on it. Toby offered to send ten wolves he knew.

Maddock's posture turned rigid, crossing his arms with an air of a person who didn't want any help. "I'm sure we'll do just fine, Minister. There's no need to send wolves into our territory and cause more panic than there already is. Can you imagine the chaos if a child saw a wolf, or Lord forbid, a lycan? Unacceptable."

Toby's brows knitted. "What is your problem, Viscount?"

Xandar had had enough of the old-timer as well. "A simple refusal would have sufficed, Maddock. There's no need to berate my minister or any of my people. We are simply here to assist."

Octavia's nostrils flared as she ordered, "Apologize at once, Viscount."

"Whatever for, Your Majesty? Lycans were here as well! If anything, their kind aided in this abduction. How do we know this isn't some grand scheme to overthrow the empire we've defended for millennia?"

Rafael rubbed his forehead. "Viscount, I sincerely hope you can hear the ludicrousness of your suggestion. A sliver, if not the whole of it. The lycans who were here were clearly rogues, if you could smell them, that is. The last time I checked, the creatures before us are not within that category."

"The fact remains that it's their kind! They failed to hunt them down!"

"You're right. We did fail," Toby admitted with a glare that could kill, fury sizzling through his veins. "About nine months ago, the monarchy, government, warriors, and policemen from the kingdom brought down an entire corporation housing thousands of rogues. We snuffed out two out of three suppliers of illegal substances, hunted down hundreds of runaway rogues, and killed so many that we lost count, all to ensure the safety of the kingdom and its people. That venture came with huge success but also the undeniable failure that we didn't manage to find every single rogue out there. So if you think that's a failure, then I'm not going to deny it. But get the flip side of that coin into your skull: we *also* succeeded."

A pocket of silence welcomed a gust of wind that couldn't do anything to blow away the hostile atmosphere, nor could it mask the embarrassment crawling up the vampires' backs, many of whom were praying to the Lord that the unpleasant moment would end soon. Those who were loyal to Maddock found Toby's manner abhorrent and disrespectful. Admittedly, Maddock wasn't polite, but that didn't give Toby the right to speak to one of their most senior ministers like the werewolf minister was superior.

The king placed a hand on Toby's shoulder as a sign of support when his lilac eyes locked with Maddock's, declaring, "If the general safety of vampires is within your jurisdiction, Viscount, then we won't intervene if you don't want us to." Shifting his attention to Octavia, he said, "In the name of diplomacy, our offer to help remains open should your species seek it. Do let us know if it's required."

"Thank you, Alexandar," Octavia nodded with a hard smile. As the vampires walked them back to the jet, Xandar's sharp hearing caught Octavia hissing at the viscount, "The empress and I will deal with you later."

After bidding each other goodbye, Pelly embraced Lucy and reluctantly got off the jet after fist-bumping Xandar like she used to do with Uncle Reagan. She was all smiles until her wife whispered into her ear about Maddock. Her emerald eyes darkened, and anger seethed and heated her cold being, making her turn so slowly that it was hauntingly terrifying.

Her ministers knew exactly who their ruler wanted to kill with that glare she had inherited from her late father, and they instinctively stepped aside to bring the viscount into full view.

Maddock was afraid, but he didn't show it. *What's the worst that could happen?* he thought. He'd served for centuries and was a trusted member during her father's reign. Surely that would count as something to mitigate whatever damage he had caused, wouldn't it?

CHAPTER 13

Toby ranted about Maddock to Lucy for a good ten minutes through their mind-link before finally calming down and opting to take a nap on his jet. Xandar was agitated, too, but the sight of his wife on his lap and their daughter in her arms soothed his internal fury. The scent he greedily took from Lucy's hair further eased the internal storm as he held her close. As Reida slept, she hugged one of her father's pinky fingers tightly to her chest, and any remaining anger in the lycan king vaporized into a memory.

When they got home, it was late evening. Mrs. Parker got Reida to bed after Lucy was done bathing and breastfeeding her. Lucy and Xandar then had dinner with Tate and Stella, where they got Stella to talk more about herself and learned that she liked scenery viewing, especially during the night, "when the whole place just calms down and nature is seemingly asleep. It's so peaceful."

For Tate, Lucy, and almost any other non-rogue wolf who had a duty to defend their packs, night was anything but peaceful. It was a constant source of anxiety because rogues normally attacked anywhere between after dusk and before dawn. Not having to worry about rogue attacks was probably the only advantage of being a rogue.

The teenager's eyes sparkled when the adults asked if she had any specific scenery she enjoyed looking at at night. Getting out her phone with an excited grin, she showed them pictures from her photo gallery. The adults immediately noticed the no-service icon and concluded that this was one of the precautions rogues took to avoid being detected.

The first photo was a tree bark with a cricket perching on it; the second, a calm river with silver linings where the moonlight hit the water; the third was a picture taken from sitting under a tree, where the sun shone right through the faint gaps between the autumn leaves. The calming pictures went on and on, mostly taken when night fell.

Lucy had never known that nights could look this beautiful. In her days as gamma, she'd only look hard at a specific part of nature at night if she heard a sound where there should be silence, never pausing to simply appreciate the beauty of her surroundings.

Handing back Stella's phone, Lucy said, "It's amazing how you can take these on any normal night. The angle is impeccable, and the subtle lighting brings out the fine details in a view that just makes one feel . . . something, a sense of peace."

Stella's grin morphed into a softened smile, touched. "No one's ever said anything close to that about my pictures before." Swiping through her own pictures, now with more pride for her work, she missed Tate and Lucy exchanging sympathetic glances.

Clearing his throat, Tate began, "So you like photography. There are lots of scenic views in this city. I can take you around if you like."

"Really?" Stella exclaimed with starry eyes.

"Of course." Tate smiled wider and got up. "But not tonight. It's late."

"It's 9:30," Stella argued.

"Exactly. It's late and . . ." Tate was forced to stop when Lucy scoffed. As the queen covered her mouth and tried her best to swallow the chuckles, the alpha told the teenager, "You're seeing your mother tomorrow morning. You'll need your strength. Go to bed."

"At 9:30?" Stella asked in disbelief.

"What time do you normally go to sleep?"

"I don't know, 11:00? Sometimes midnight or after that? I once went to bed a little after 3:00."

"Fine. Go sit on your bed until it's time to sleep."

When Tate finished, Stella exclaimed in a hushed protest, "What?"

Lucy couldn't hold back anymore and burst out laughing, mouthing, "I'm sorry," to the slightly irritated alpha as she leaned into her husband for support. After wiping away the tears, she said, "That was quite the show, Tate. Uh . . ." she chuckled briefly before turning to the teen ". . . Stella, if you like, you can go around this compound and take whatever pictures you want. There's a . . ."

"Really? Thank you! I've seen lots of great spots around here, but I didn't know if I was allowed to take pictures. I'll start at that waterfall feature next to the garden." Jumping off her seat, she patted Tate on his arm and shouted, "Bye!" and sped out the door so quickly that it left a gust of wind in her wake.

As soon as the door shut with an excited thud, Lucy taunted, "A-plus for fatherhood, Tate." His eyes narrowed and she continued, "What teenager goes to bed at 9:30? Did you go to bed that early at that age?"

Xandar's arm wrapped around her abdomen from behind, speaking in Tate's defense, "Come on, Lucy. Give him a break. He just wants what's best for his future daughter."

Turning to face him, she uttered, "Well, that would surely pull at the protective mother's heartstrings." They spoke as if Tate wasn't right in front of them.

Seriousness took over the alpha when he murmured, "That's what I wanted to talk to you both about."

The couple dropped all humor. Tate peeped into the corridor to make sure Stella was really out of the house before whispering, "I need advice . . . about Margaret."

"What happened?" Lucy asked as Tate dropped back into his chair.

"That's the thing—*nothing* is happening." With his fingers laced tightly together as his forearms pressed onto the dining table, he explained, "Stella and I went to see her today. Margaret spoke to her. Briefly. Still asking her to lie or do something to get them out. Stella fought back. As usual. Came out drained after that, so I bought her a soda before I went in. Margaret . . . is still not talking to me. And I tried everything I know: I asked her if she needed anything, I asked if she wanted to eat something in particular, I asked if she'd like me to take her out for a walk for an hour or so." Sweeping a hand through his light brown hair, he heaved a sad but frustrated sigh before exclaiming as softly as he could, "She's not talking to me! She doesn't even want to look at me!"

Lucy's eyes watered with each word, and Xandar's thumb drew small circles on her shoulder to try to comfort her as he, too, empathized with their friend. Tate held back tears and cleared his throat again. "Lucy, I really didn't want to ask you this, but I'm out of options, so I really hope you won't mind me asking: is Margaret's behavior . . . normal for a rejected wolf? I mean, we only met after your third rejection, and you seemed . . . okay. No, okay isn't the right word. You looked a hundred percent like someone who had never been rejected before in her life. Were you anything like Margaret after your first two rejections?"

On a normal day, Xandar would have thrown a fit at anyone who brought up Lucy's rejections. But Tate's situation with Margaret made this a very unusual day. The king was even beginning to mentally apologize to the Moon Goddess for thinking that he had it hard with love.

With an unsmiling face and a deadpan voice, Lucy chose her words carefully. "It differs with each creature, each experience, and each reason leading to the rejection. After my first rejection, I was more . . . closed off. For a while, I became insecure about walking into the world with my size, which could be seen as unbefitting for a werewolf. After the second rejection, I wondered if fighting was even . . . my thing."

"WHAT?" Tate exclaimed at the absurdity. She was the best warrior even before she was a lycan. Every wolf knew that.

As Lucy stroked Xandar's arm that rigidified around her abdomen, she told Tate, "Like I said, it's different with each experience. But you must know that . . . it's different for everyone. After each rejection, I had Juan and my pack, and later on, I had you and Toby and so many others to . . . encourage me as I pulled myself back up again. I don't know if Margaret had that kind of support. And, Tate, if I'm being honest, I must tell you that you can't compare what I was to what she is now. We are on a completely different spectrum because I was never . . . impregnated by any of my rejected mates."

Xandar's grip around her constricted even further as he closed his eyes and buried his nose in her hair; the mere hypothetical suggestion turned on his defenses. In the silent dining room, Lucy continued in a pained whisper, "Margaret is not just hurt, Tate. Odds are, she was almost destroyed. If she wasn't raped, imagine what she felt when, after mating, she had to come to terms with the fact that she was betrayed by the person to whom she entrusted her heart, her soul, and her body. She trusted someone to love and protect her but he used his Authority to get her to leave after putting his seed in her like she was just another woman he'd sleep with on a regular night."

Tate scoffed sadly. "She thinks I'm like him, doesn't she? Guess this is karma for sleeping around."

"I wouldn't say that. I think it's more likely that she closed off all thinking in that department."

Confusion filled his eyes. "What does that mean?"

"After that . . . experience, she may have given up on the possibility of love and intimacy entirely. Remember what Stella said, that Margaret swore to reject her second-chance mate if she ever got one? Those words are only said by those who have given up."

Xandar tossed in a gentle, encouraging reminder, "But she didn't recite the rejection when she saw you, Tate. This is a good sign. Maybe she's thinking about giving it a chance."

Tate's eyes went to Xandar. "How did you get Lucy to give you a chance?"

It was on the tip of Xandar's tongue to say that he got lucky, but this was not the time for jokes or inapplicable solutions, so he scratched the back of his head before recalling the facts, "Well, I exploded when Lucy brought up . . . rejecting each other on our first meeting. I followed her and stuck around her at every chance I got. And I kept trying to get her to talk about herself. I made sure she knew I wanted to get to know her more than anything in the world, that I wasn't messing around and I wanted her for the long haul, for forever."

Tate was lost. Their situations were so different. Lucy was never a rogue who attacked a royal and was now subjected to prison custody. How was Tate going to follow her around and stick to her or explode into a room to show Margaret he was different? At least Lucy *talked* to Xandar. Margaret wasn't even looking at Tate, let alone talking to him.

Lucy saw his hurdle too. "You don't have to do what Xandar did, Tate. Besides, it was more about how he made me feel when he did those things. When he exploded, I was surprised—surprised that he was the first creature I was bonded to that was so sure that our bond wasn't a mistake. When he stuck around me even before knowing what I'd accomplished with the rest of you, I felt . . . seen and . . . wanted, not for my skills or reputation but for just . . . me. When he kept asking questions about my past, especially the most difficult parts, it made me feel heard and . . . special." Her hand reached out to give Tate's a gentle squeeze. "What worked for Xandar may not be suitable for you. But there's still a way to let Margaret know that you're different, to make her feel those things that Xandar made me feel. Taking care of her daughter is a great start. Only someone who's serious about starting a family with her would think of doing that."

"I'm not taking care of Stella because I want to get to Margaret. I'm doing it because I want to. My wolf wants to."

Lucy gave a nod of understanding. "Well, that's even better. It means our Goddess trusts the girl with you. As for Margaret, you just need to know more about her as a person for now. Maybe try talking to Stella?"

"I have," Tate murmured as he checked to make sure the corridor was still empty. "She didn't give me much, and I didn't want to go too far. Stella said that Margaret likes taking long walks, skipping stones, and anything green in nature, even weeds. She hates the rain, brick roads, and roses."

Taking a moment, Lucy then noted, "That's a very specific list."

Xandar went on, "Probably specific enough to know that her first mate used to give her roses, and the day she was forced to leave was a rainy one."

Tate rasped, "I thought so too. I didn't get the one with the brick road though. Do you remember any packs with brick roads, Lucy? Did Fleet Wood have that?"

Her head cocked to the side, eyes wandering. "Not the parts of the pack I walked through when I visited. But I do remember it being very green. There were trees, bushes, and plants everywhere, even on their roofs. It was like they wanted to live in a greenhouse."

Tate connected that information to Margaret's love for all things green, muttering sadly, "She misses home."

Lucy added, "And she misses the simpler times when she was home."

When Xandar felt sorrow engulfing her being, he pecked a kiss on her temple, whispering, "She can have those things again, baby. Once she opens up, she'll have Tate and the rest of us."

"If the law doesn't put her behind bars first," Lucy reminded ominously.

Right. Xandar had forgotten about that.

Suddenly, Tate asked, "Lucy, I was wondering. Could you talk to her?"

She blinked in disbelief. The only time she and Margaret "talked" and got actual answers was when she used the Queen's Authority. With furrowed brows, she leaned toward him and asked in a whisper like they were up to no good, "You want me to use the Queen's Authority on your mate again?"

"No! That's not where I was going. But you know you don't have the best past when it comes to mates, so maybe this common ground would somehow . . . make her listen?"

"Tate." Biting her bottom lip, she already felt bad for having to disappoint him. "I can't talk to her. No one can. At least not yet. She's not ready."

Not making sense of anything she'd just said, Tate asked, "When will she be ready?"

Bearing with the heaviness in her chest, Lucy admitted, "When she wants to be." Silence unfurled, leaving both men confused before she continued, "Margaret is not just hurt. She is in great pain. She has been since the rejection. Over the years, she buried that pain deep under the layers of hatred for everything and everyone. The bitterness is not something that any one of us can just . . . tear down. This is her fight, Tate. Until she decides to feel the pain and practice letting go, she won't improve from her current state. We can be there for her during her healing process, but the work—the bulk of the healing—is a lone journey, and Margaret will only embark on it when she chooses to."

In a coarser voice, on the verge of breaking down, he asked, "And if she doesn't?" Meeting her gaze, he pressed, "What happens if my mate never decides to heal? Or decides that she doesn't need to be healed in the first place? What then?"

Lucy reluctantly murmured, "Externally, she'll be pretty much the same. Internally . . . it just gets worse. When she speaks, it'll only be to defend herself in the most offensive way to avoid losing the smallest arguments to the biggest fights; she'll avoid expressing vulnerabilities at all costs, not wanting her insecurities to be used against her; she might even have more suicidal thoughts when she's alone. It varies depending on the severity of the experience that brought that pain."

Seeing his teary eyes facing the dining table, she offered him another gentle squeeze on his wrist. "We can make her feel safe to start healing, but beyond that . . . it's Margaret who has to admit she needs to heal. I know you want to do everything you can to help her, Tate, but when it comes to a battle within oneself, it's ultimately that person who has to choose to fight, accept, and make peace with the internal turmoil. We can't do anything more than to support them, make them feel safe, and love them."

Tate couldn't deny the tightness in his chest when he felt how powerless he was. There was no way he could connect to his mate until she wanted to lower her walls and let him in. She couldn't heal until she wanted to. Telling her directly wouldn't do much good. Margaret would just slap him or Lucy back with something cruel.

Lucy firmly assured, "As soon as Margaret opens up and lets us in, we go in and move at her pace. We're with you, Tate. I'm with you. Every step of the way. Okay?"

A smile—though drained—appeared when he gratefully uttered, "Thank you, Lucy."

The front door opened, and the adults immediately got up as Xandar casually reminded Tate about the government meeting the following morning. Tate played along, and they looked through Stella's pictures before returning to their rooms to hit the hay.

CHAPTER 14

In the walk-in closet of the master bedroom, Lucy undressed while saying, "A vast improvement in your acting abilities, my king. I don't think Stella suspected a thing."

Xandar's eyes lingered on the back of his mate's beautiful bare body, letting the last of his clothes fall when his arousal began circulating in the air, approaching her in slow steps like a predator would near its prey, muttering in a daze, "Well, I have a really good teacher."

Lucy scoffed, putting on one of Xandar's shirts that reached her upper thigh. As soon as she got her hair out of the oversized shirt, her mate's muscular arms came from behind, sliding across the fabric and feeling the softness of her skin hidden underneath. His lips came from the side to trap hers in a deep kiss. When his lips freed hers, he gazed deeply into her eyes and muttered in a deep voice, "Stealing my clothes again, sweetheart?"

His erect shaft pressed against her back, and her reply came in a shy whisper, "I like the material and the scent."

"Mm." Taking in a greedy whiff from her neck and squeezing her butt, relishing in the cute moan that escaped her lips, Xandar then asked, "If I told you I wanted to wear this shirt for the night, what would you do?"

"*Not* give it to you," Lucy replied meekly. Her arousal was starting to fill the space between them, and Xandar's own had long filled the entire closet.

"Is that so?" His fingers on her butt sneakily pulled up the shirt before his large hands gave her bare bottom a rough squeeze that made her gasp and moan louder. Her nipples hardened, and her body arched in a way that drew Xandar's attention to them. One hand continued his efforts on her bum while the other went for her clit, massaging it in slow, gentle motions as her entire body heated up and crumpled into his chest. When Xandar started planting soft kisses around her mark, she whimpered. And the way her lower body moved in response to his touch was a plea for Xandar to free her from her agony.

"Do you still want this shirt tonight, my love?" he whispered, his breath tickling her ear.

She whimpered. "No."

"What do you want?" Xandar asked, after which he gave her butt another rough squeeze.

Breathlessly, she surrendered, "You."

A triumphant smirk spread across his lips as he growled in that deep and alluring manner that intensified his wife's arousal. "As you wish, my queen."

The king spun her around and pressed her back against the wall. His tongue plunged into her mouth and reached for her throat. Xandar had been pinning her to walls more often after discovering that her animal got excited when he did it. Without breaking their kiss, he swiftly lifted her legs and crossed them around his waist. When Lucy had to break free for air, he pulled the shirt over her head and let it fall on the floor before gobbling her breasts.

His tongue teased her nipples as his stiffened shaft that was pressed against her sensitive region felt the increasing wetness. When her breasts had been properly worshipped, he positioned her legs on his broad shoulders before his tongue attacked the most delicious part of his mate. As Lucy's hand in his hair pulled his thick locks, her husband moaned in appreciation.

The pleasurable build-up intensified with each hungry stroke, and the reins of control no longer belonged to her body as Xandar took charge of every nerve that begged him to bring them to the high that ignited a synchronized explosion.

Not long later, a yelp left Lucy as her body arched away from the wall when her juices dispensed into her hungry beast's mouth. Xandar's ready hand gently pushed her body back against the wall, holding her in place as he drank from her while she took heavy breaths. After licking every last drop, he repositioned her legs back around his waist. She was getting impatient, pouting and whimpering as her bottom grazed the part of him she wanted in her at that second.

With a cocky smirk, he thrust right into her, making her gasp. She relished in the fullness, circling her bum against him and eliciting his moan before he began pumping. Their scorching skin felt like they were emanating heat into the room. Xandar's well-built body, moans, and the way he looked at Lucy were making her experience heightened levels of arousal. And the way she whispered his name and surrendered her beautiful body to him made him crave her so much that he'd give anything to stay in this moment forever.

When Lucy was close to release, Xandar increased his speed before his mouth covered her mark and sucked on it with such need that her body convulsed in shock and her core locked him. She gently bit his mark as his body stiffened and he emptied into her.

After taking a few breaths, Xandar's forehead touched hers. Their euphoric eyes fused when he whispered in a satisfied, husky voice, "Oh, my queen."

Pecking a kiss on his lips, she declared in a whisper, "You can have the shirt tonight, my king. I think I'll sleep just fine without it."

He smirked. "I'll make sure you will, baby."

Nuzzling her cheek and jawline to elicit her soft chuckles, he then carried her to bed, where he pulled her into his chest. She snuggled into his warm embrace before her eyelids fell in the darkness.

CHAPTER 15

In government headquarters the next morning, no one was pleased that Greg was "demanding" pardon for his ninety-eight people in exchange for cooperation to track down and annihilate whoever was in on challenging the Queen's Authority.

"Lucy," Toby began, trying to get a hold of his temper, "you *know* you can just use your Authority and make him and his people comply." He tried not to sound condescending. And he didn't. He just sounded angered. He couldn't understand why she wasn't just taking the shortcut. The Moon Goddess gave her the damn shortcut. It was meant to be used!

Lucy had known this was coming. She was surprised that whatever Toby said didn't come from her mate first. She had been cracking her head for a plausible argument ever since Greg asked for the pardon, and she only came to one mental block after another.

"It doesn't feel right," Lucy confessed. Although her voice was softer than usual, she still held the attention of the room. "He is willing to cooperate. He just needs those people safe. He didn't even ask to be pardoned himself. Don't you find it . . . not malicious, and maybe even a little noble? He's asking for a chance for his people to redeem themselves by helping the kingdom."

Christian had his lips pressed together since the meeting commenced and was suppressing his rage at Greg's demand in the police station from the moment the other duke made it. Who the hell did he think he was? He was behind bars! After what he'd done, he was the last creature to have any right to negotiate anything!

"My queen—" the usually cheerful duke took a deep breath to avoid losing his cool "—Greg may have helped us once. But what he did in the past is a thousand wrongs that cannot be corrected by a single right. We are not at his mercy in terms of information. You and the king can make him do whatever you both want. You both have the power."

"But should we use it, is the question," Xandar uttered, which shocked everyone, his own mate included. Lucy thought she was the only one on board with granting the conditional pardon. This was probably the first time Xandar and Christian weren't on the same page when it came to Greg. On the table, the king took his queen's hand as his thumb stroked it affectionately while he continued, "We're gifted this power because we're entrusted to use it only when necessary."

Christian took a moment before questioning, "And you think it isn't necessary to use it now?"

"It's hard to say. That's why we're here," Xandar responded simply.

"He's been housing rogues for Goddess knows how long, Cuz. When he gave up those from Wu Bi Corp, he conveniently omitted mentioning his own. We can't just grant a pardon, conditional or not, to rogues to hunt down another set of rogues. And how do we know we're not being played here? When was the last time anyone has heard that rogues . . . went rogue to help the government or monarchy? I'll tell you, *never*. Rogues don't go against their own kind, especially not to help law enforcement."

"Greg did."

"Greg was never a rogue, Cuz. For some unknown reason, his scent was never that of a rogue."

"He's been hiding ninety-eight of them, Christian. If you put the mystery of his scent aside, are you really not seeing him as one of them?"

"If he was a rogue who went against his kind, he would've given up his own people's names and location."

"Christian, we can't forget he gave us Kylton's rogues."

"I'm not saying that we should. All I'm saying is . . ." heaving another sigh, he cut the long explanation short ". . . they aren't innocent. Greg isn't innocent."

Xandar cast more doubt in the room when he said, "I'm not saying that he's a decent creature by normal standards either, Christian. But we need to balance what we know him to be, what he became recently, and the threat at hand. I agree that Greg isn't innocent, but are he and the rest of his followers guilty? Completely guilty?"

Christian scoffed darkly. "Yeah, I'd say they are! Why would one hide from authorities if they weren't up to no good? As for Greg, you don't need me to recite the long list of things he did to the monarchy and to you and me personally in the years before he decided to help in that *one case* after falling for the queen." Lucy bit her bottom lip at the rising voice and tension as Christian continued to argue with Xandar. "Greg is bound by law to divulge any information pertaining to national security. Everyone is. There is *zero* reason for us to give in to his demands. He's caused more damage than he's helped."

Xandar refused to return his cousin's angered, onyx glare that was beseeching him to give in. As he laced his fingers with his mate's, his lilac orbs held an assurance when he responded in an even voice, "I don't disagree. But if we continue closing opportunities for him and others like him to help, how are they expected to offset the damage?"

Christian threw his hands in the air as Annie mind-linked him, asking him to calm down and behave as professionally as possible.

Lucy's neck stiffened. A solid weight seemed to have formed at the pit of her stomach for dragging Xandar into a difficult situation—one that made her husband turn against his best friend. Debilitating guilt in her chest grew, coiling around her lungs and heart.

Xandar tore his eyes away from his cousin and turned to her, blind to everyone else in the room as he demanded firmly, "Baby, look at me." Her teeth reluctantly released her bottom lip before meeting her husband's lilac eyes. "Deep down, you know there's a solution, or you wouldn't have asked for a meeting to be called in the first place. You would've used your Authority without consulting anyone if you didn't think there was another way. You would've used it if you knew, without a doubt, that it was right to use it. You didn't use it, which means it isn't right and there could be another way. We'll find out if there is another way. Together. Alright?"

The denseness lifted, slowly subsiding as his words of assurance took the guilt away, allowing her to form a smile and offer a doting nod.

It was Toby's turn to feel bad for blocking out reason. "Lucy . . . help us understand why you don't think it's right. You've got to give us more than what you just did, because I still can't see the flip side here. Most of us can't." Nods of agreement went around the table. Only Tate's and Annie's heads remained still.

As Xandar's thumb stroked her hand, he reminded, "Don't hold back, baby."

Lucy cleared her throat. "It doesn't feel right because Greg didn't do anything to give rise to the present threat. When I spoke to him, he seemed so . . .

vulnerable. It was as if he was conflicted and torn between two sides. He was spilling the beans like he was throwing dice, not knowing whether he was making the right move. When he mentioned the ninety-eight rogues he sought the pardon for, there was . . . fear in his eyes—" her black-and-lilac orbs met her husband's as she went on "—the type of fear one has when someone he cares about is going to be in danger."

Yarrington spoke for the first time, sounding more worried than angered, "My queen, how sure are you that the other duke didn't do anything to give rise to the present threat?"

"A hundred percent sure," Toby muttered, more to himself than to anyone else, then speaking up, "If Greg Claw was behind the present threat, he would have let it happen. He would have wanted to see it succeed without being a suspect. And what better way *not* to be a suspect than to remain in jail? If he's trying to get out of jail, this threat . . . it stands to harm him too. I don't know how. Maybe it's being concocted by a rival rogue group or something. The fact is," Toby deduced, "the other duke has been doing things behind the kingdom's back for more than a decade, maybe even longer. If this scheme—this concoction—was a plan to set his people free, then . . ."

Lovelace finished for him, "Then he would have supported the threat because a successful concoction keeps even his own people safe from the highest power in the kingdom. He wouldn't need to ask for the rogues under his care to be pardoned."

The defense minister sighed in defeat, knowing that the queen had convinced him to go against his initial stance.

Everyone in the room took a moment before Weaver's voice permeated through the silence. "Although this sounds . . . plausible, I must say that it doesn't appear safe. We don't know the extent of the other duke's network and weaponry. I'm just concerned that if he decides to . . . turn against us halfway through the venture . . ." his head swung slowly and in dismay ". . . we might not be able to reverse the damage that could be done. We need a safety net to fall back on, for every creature in the kingdom, if not for ourselves."

Annie mused, "I have to agree with that." As the duchess continued stroking her mate's clenched fist, she uttered, "Lucy, if we choose to trust him, we need leverage. It's the best way to make sure both sides get what we're after and both sides come out safe."

Nodding in agreement, Lucy asked, "Any suggestions?"

Annie offered, "A longer jail sentence if things went sideways, maybe?"

"That would work," Luna Lovelace muttered in agreement.

Luna Hale, the minister of welfare, said, "Perhaps even a heftier fine."

Christian mumbled, "Or torture before invoking the death penalty."

Annie mouthed a fierce, inaudible "no" at her husband. Even then, the queen didn't sweep the duke's recommendation off the table. If it came down to it, if the betrayal was serious enough, death would be justified.

Looking around the table, Xandar prompted, "Anyone else?"

Vanessa, the minister of law, suggested, "I suggest he offer full and frank disclosure of *all* rogue suppliers and hideouts in exchange for the pardon of so many, Your Highnesses."

With furrowed brows, Phelton noted, "I'm not sure if that would be of value when we intend to use it, Vanessa. The last two suppliers that were captured essentially alarmed the third one quickly enough that they could run and disappear. We're still unable to hunt them down. If we do decide to press the other duke for information later, how sure are we that his knowledge wouldn't be outdated and useless?"

An idea came to Toby, but it was a horrible one. He decided to listen to the others while contemplating whether he should share his thoughts, because once they were laid on the table, he couldn't take them back, and he didn't want to regret his decision later.

The other recommendations were glaringly flimsy: strip him of his dukedom, increase sentencing, banishment, etcetera. Honestly, what would stripping the dukedom do? It wouldn't reverse any damage or bring back any lives that may be lost. Increased sentencing? Greg wouldn't care less if he stayed longer in prison. If he did, he wouldn't have gone in in the first place. And banishment? Really? Before Lucy showed up in Xandar's life, Greg practically self-banished when he disappeared from the kingdom for sixteen years. These weren't going to work as leverage. Everyone went back and forth with no satisfactory or agreeable idea in sight.

When Toby came to terms that there was no other way but the sinister one he had in mind, he cleared his throat and raised his hand. The whole room quieted down as they waited for the defense minister to speak. "Personally, I don't agree that granting conditional pardon for ninety-eight of them is the right thing to do. Not all crimes are created equal. Murder, for one, has to be . . . treated differently, as it was with the Kyltons. It's fairer to the victims and their families that way. If any of the ninety-eight has killed, they should be dealt with in the same way we're dealing with the rogues we've caught."

"Finally!" Christian exclaimed in a hushed tone of enthusiasm.

Phelton prompted, "And apart from murder?"

Toby continued, "Apart from murder—" his eyes locked with Lucy when he sighed "—I'm for granting pardon, as long as they cooperate in helping us hunt down and eliminate creatures challenging the Queen's Authority."

Christian's short-lived relief was replaced with strong objection when he whisper-yelled, "What the f—" Annie gently hit her husband's arm to stop the curse from dropping.

Lucy wasn't celebrating yet. "The issue on murderers . . . if that's our course of action, is there's no way they'd let themselves be caught. I doubt Greg would hand them over. We could compel him to, but if there's already a plan of escape—one that Greg may have not been privy to for his people's safety— then we'd lose the murderers along with any help Greg could offer. Maybe . . ." Leaning back, she uttered, "I wonder if there's some middle ground where . . . even if we can't win the whole battle, we'll win half of it, so it won't be a complete gain but not a complete loss either."

Thinking along those lines, Xandar offered, "A balanced solution, then." All eyes on him, he explained, "If any one of the rogue lycans under Greg has killed another, their case would be brought to court, like the others we've caught. The difference is that their punishments would be mitigated depending on how much blame they should take from their crime and how cooperative they'll be in helping us with the current threat."

Toby murmured, "That's actually . . . alright."

Yarrington prompted, "And what about the other duke? How do we hold him and make sure he understands the repercussions of conspiracy?"

Xandar uttered, "If he has murder on his hands as well, the same rule should apply. If murder isn't in the equation, then we could . . . perhaps use Greg as leverage." This line even made Christian's animal listen, really listen. His onyx eyes that held nothing but anger welcomed a shade of contemplation as he waited for his cousin to continue with his proposition. The king elaborated, "Greg has committed more crimes than he has admitted to. Hiding rogues is already one that we didn't know about. If the cooperation with his people goes sideways, we could make his people testify on every wrong that Greg committed and increase his sentencing with each one. We'll use our Authorities if it comes down to it. No more leeway will be given at that stage."

Lucy added, "In that situation, his people will be tried, too, but their own sentencing will be mitigated if and when they testify against Greg. In essence, if Greg turns against us, we turn against him *and* the creatures he seeks to protect."

Christian challenged, "And if they run or refuse to testify against him?"

Meeting Christian's hard gaze, Lucy declared, "After meeting them and listening to their voices, I'll be able to track down any and every one of them by hacking their mind-links, and I'll use my Authority to make each of them spit everything out myself." Christian blinked in surprise, his undivided attention poured on her as she continued, "I gave Greg a chance to drop his attitude after he pissed me off during the collaboration, Christian, and he made good on that chance. We should give his people that same chance. If we have a reason to question their loyalty, if there's the slightest reason to be suspicious, if they screw up when we try to find the creatures behind inventing the concoction, I'll personally break them, slowly, until I'm satisfied."

Sure, that sent a shudder down everyone's spines that may have crawled into their bones, but it was also assuring. Both the king and queen assured them that there was a line, that they wouldn't let their want to help get in the way of doing what was fair and safe for the rest of the kingdom.

Christian came out of his shock and seemed a little calmer. "Okay. That seems . . . balanced. I'm in." So was everyone else.

Just when Xandar thought he could dismiss everyone, Tate spoke, "I need to ask . . . can we offer the same pardon to Margaret and her rogues?"

Lucy questioned, "Are we talking about only those behind bars or . . ."

"All of them in her pack, Lucy, even those we haven't caught yet. We both know Margaret. Being their leader, she most likely knows where they ran to next. She just didn't tell us."

There was short silence—some were shocked, some were getting judgmental—before Lovelace snapped, "And you didn't think of mentioning this earlier? If you said something sooner, Lucy could've at least made Margaret spit it out."

Tate fired back, "The Authority isn't the answer to everything, Lovelace. If we can offer the rogues hidden by the other duke conditional pardon, why not these rogues? What's the difference? Both groups are hiding from us anyway!"

"I agree," Xandar said firmly. "Instead of wasting more resources and time to hunt them down, maybe it's better to give them a chance to come forward. If these rogues are trouble, it will show during the cooperation, and we'll have enough justification to compel them to be punished in any way we deem fit."

Lovelace clarified, "The consequences *will* be the same as the rogue lycans, my king?"

Xandar nodded. Lovelace's eyes went to Lucy next, who said, "I don't see why not." The queen's voice took a worried turn when she reminded, "Tate, if Margaret or any of her people screw up—"

Tate completed her sentence ominously, "You'll personally break them, slowly, until you're satisfied."

Nodding grudgingly, Lucy added, "But if it's Margaret herself, I could . . ."

"No, Lucy. You can't." Tate knew she was suggesting showing his mate mercy if Margaret eventually screwed up, so he didn't even let her finish. "It jeopardizes your credibility and reputation as our queen. If my mate remains stubborn and refuses to cooperate and make good on the chance we're giving her, which is essentially a way out, it's better to subject her to the same punishment and . . . let her go."

Toby blinked so many times and went completely speechless as he slowly sat upright from his laid-back position. Instinctively, the best friends' set of eyes met before Lucy linked Tate, *'She's your mate, Tate, your future luna.'* It was essentially a plea for him to reconsider.

Tate scoffed aloud. A pained smile made him look years older when he announced, "I want to help her. I want to get close to her. I want to know her. I'm willing to beg. I've already begged. I've just begged the third time this morning when I went to see her. I'm willing to give her the benefit of the doubt. But if she continues to keep me hanging, leaving me . . . guessing whether she feels the same way or wants the same thing by not saying one fucking word to me . . ."

A slit cut through his heart, the incision creating a crack, making his chest throb as his wolf howled in anguish when Tate continued, "I have to let her go. I'm not going to keep knocking on a closed door like an idiot. White Blood deserves a luna who can contribute in some way, or someone who's at least interested in what happens in and out of the pack. Margaret can be that. But if she refuses to be that, I can't make her. If she refuses to nurture our bond, it's better for the both of us if we just let each other go. I just hope she'll be okay after that."

Toby snapped, "You're giving up already? It's only been two days!"

Tate swallowed a lump in his throat. "And in those two days, it seems like she's pushing me further away with each visit, with each word I say. She's not playing hard to get. She's really shutting me out. The hurt just stacks. In me and my animal. Margaret is not interested in giving us a chance. But she's not severing the bond either. I have no idea what she wants. She's not talking."

Toby turned to Lucy. "Is the Queen's Authority off-limits?"

With a disapproving glare, Lucy spat, "Yes."

"But this is an emergency!" Toby argued meekly, motioning at Tate.

"Not the type of emergency that requires me to choke something out of someone, Toby," she insisted, turning back to the heartbroken alpha. "Talk to her, Tate. Tell her about our offer. Tell her how you feel, like how you've just told us, so that she sees your side. She might still be confused about what to do. You lay your cards on the table and let her decide what she wants to do with them. She might have a clearer idea of where to go from there. If this final attempt doesn't get to her, then . . . by all means, do what's best for yourself and White Blood." The last line was basically a fancier way of saying, "Reject her and find someone better." Everyone knew it.

Tate held her gaze, then asked with a smile, "You're with me, right?"

With the same firm gaze she offered him years ago when they declared their alliance, Lucy promised, "Every step of the way."

"And I've suddenly become invisible," Toby complained, crossing his arms and slumping back into his seat, sulking.

Tate turned to Toby. "You're my gamma, Minister. You're bound to stand with your alpha."

Toby smirked when everyone chuckled. "Unless you stand against the queen, in which case, you're on your own. The most humiliating thing to have written on my tombstone would be *slaughtered by a five-foot creature*."

Christian snorted, and his bark of laughter filled the room, as did Weaver's.

For some reason, Xandar had the urge to correct Toby, "Lucy is actually five-foot-three after being marked, Toby." The laughter from his cousin grew even louder as a few others began slamming the table at the hilarity.

Narrowing his eyes, Toby asked in mock anger, "Oh, and that's any better, my king?"

"Just saying," Xandar murmured with raised hands as the chuckles around the table continued.

When the meeting was officially over, Xandar left a kiss on Lucy's hair before going over to his cousin and wrapping him in a brotherly hug. Christian hugged him back, patting him on the back. Although Xandar didn't say a word, Christian proudly proclaimed, "I know. I know. I'm still your favorite cousin no matter what."

A mischievous smile danced across Toby's lips. "Yeah, we all know that. He doesn't have much to choose from anyway."

Christian lightly punched Toby in his gut, and Toby mocked an anguished reaction before they fist-bumped. After the duke and the queen embraced next, effectively clearing any hard feelings from their earlier disagreement, everyone left the meeting room in better spirits.

The king and queen walked out hand-in-hand when she linked her husband, *'Thank you for what you did in there. I didn't think you'd get on board with granting the conditional pardon.'*

Xandar's brows arched in a tease. *'Did you really think I was going in there to stand with my ministers and against my wife, sweetheart?'*

Lucy shrugged. *'If your wife is wrong, I don't see why not.'*

Xandar scoffed, letting go of her hand and reaching for her waist, pulling her closer. *'Would you have done it to me? Ambush me in a meeting room by standing with the majority?'*

'Well, I wouldn't ambush you per se. But I will stand against you if I don't think you're right . . . Come to think of it, I've already done it several times.'

'And in those times, did I know you were going to stand against me before we entered the meeting room?'

Her eyes narrowed in mock suspicion. *'I like to think that you did; otherwise it just means you weren't listening when I was talking to you.'*

Xandar chuckled and pecked a kiss on her temple. *'I was listening, sweetheart, so I did know you were dead set on taking a different approach all those times, and that's my point.'* Their footsteps slowed. *'I wouldn't just . . . skip the hard talk with you in private and then go all out against you in public. Baby, that's not how we work. And I'm proud to say that was never how we worked, even before we were married. We've always talked things through with each other first, even when it was hard. If I don't say anything beforehand, it's only because I'm on your side. Besides, I need a strong line of reasoning before even attempting to change your mind.'*

'Winning an argument against your wife is that hard, huh?' she teased.

Upon reaching the car, Xandar pinned her waist to the door, peering into her playful eyes as he uttered affectionately, "You don't know the half of it, my love. For comparison purposes, I'll have you know that it's tougher than writing a PhD dissertation."

She chuckled lightly as her hands instinctively reached for his chest, sliding up his shoulders. "So is it safe to say that you weren't able to produce a dissertation to refuse granting pardon, darling?"

Closing their distance, he confessed, "I was able to, actually, but submitting it was suicidal and potentially embarrassing. If I could come up with counterarguments against my own reasoning, imagine the ammunition you or Toby would have."

Her eyes softened at how much faith he had in her, and she felt like she was letting him down. "I wasn't sure if granting pardon was right though. I really went in on a hunch this time. You heard me in there. There was so little evidence and solidity in what I suggested. Maybe I was always sure in the past, but today . . . I wasn't."

"Oh, you were sure, Lucy," Xandar insisted, then added with a knowing smile, "You have a different look if you're unsure, which was not what I saw on your face after you spoke to Greg." Cupping her cheek and looking intensely into her eyes, he continued, "Whenever you weren't speaking to anyone yesterday, you looked like you were miles away. Those gears in your head looked like they were being pushed into overdrive. There were even a few times I felt your mental fatigue."

"Sorry," she muttered, her facial features cringed in guilt. She didn't know that, but it explained the extra kisses Xandar had planted on her head and temple the previous day.

Xandar chuckled. "I don't mind, Lucy. I love knowing how you feel, feeling how you feel. The thing is, even during those mental gymnastics, I didn't feel any uncertainty from you. You were so sure that granting pardon was the best way forward. What you weren't sure of was probably how you were going to convince an entire room of ministers who hate Greg to get onboard."

His response made her completely lost for words. He read her so well, not just from the mate bond but also from her face. Her heart melted, and her eyes glistened before her thumb traced his cheek when she whispered, "I love you."

"I love you too, baby." Xandar kissed her forehead, then gently nudged the tip of her nose and took a quick whiff of her scent from her hair. Only then did he open the door and usher her into the car.

Tate watched their entire exchange from his car. He started the engine and was about to drive off when the sight of the couple from across the parking lot made him pause. Despite not knowing what they were saying, he could see how they looked at each other when they spoke. The alpha couldn't help but feel envious. Why couldn't he have that? As he tore his eyes away, thinking about how he was going to break things down for Margaret when he saw her in the evening, he only hoped he wouldn't have to resort to doing what was best for himself and White Blood.

CHAPTER 16

The policewoman informed Margaret about Tate's visit, as usual. She groaned in annoyance, pushing herself off her bed, and followed the officer to the interrogation room, wondering why there wasn't a limit to the number of times Tate could visit her in a day when her own daughter was only allowed fifteen minutes.

Tate was already there, leaning against the wall behind his chair. Margaret's eyes stuck to the floor like they did the last few times. But unlike the last few times, she didn't feel his gaze on her. Curiosity got the better of her, and her downcast eyes rose a little just to take a peek.

Tate had his hands in his pockets, his gaze stuck to the floor. The creases on his forehead only added charm to his pensive look. Something in Margaret was eager to close their distance, dying to reach out to smoothen those lines, wanting to feel what the lines and grooves were like beneath her finger pads. And that something was the mate bond. And her wolf. Both of which she should not be listening to, let alone heeding. Margaret couldn't deny that Tate was one hell of a looker with his diamond-shaped face, hazelnut hair, and sinewy build, and there was something about his eyes that just drew her in. Sharp, bright, and determined.

As soon as his face moved an inch, she averted her gaze and chose to inspect the table instead.

"Thank you, Laila," Tate uttered. His deep voice was so good to hear, the baritone melody sent a pleasurable tingle through her animal right up to its tail, which wagged in happiness. *Damn it! Damn the mate bond!* Margaret thought.

She reminded her animal about their past, how they were both betrayed, but her wolf growled fiercely and defended their present bond. *Stubborn, naive wolf.*

"You're most welcome, Minister. I hope it won't be too much trouble to tell the queen that Hannah and Heather said hi."

"Who?" Tate asked, bewildered.

"My daughters, Minister. Four and five years old. I brought them to work one day, and coincidentally, it was the day the queen came to see our chief. My kids have been enchanted by her ever since."

Tate chuckled, charging defensiveness through the red wolf, making her growl ferociously when her mate was laughing because another woman made him laugh. She was only brought out of her rage when Tate replied, "I'll let her know, Laila. Thank you."

"I'll leave you to it. Let me know if you need anything."

"Will do," Tate responded simply, and the red wolf was brought back into bliss seeing that Laila was headed for the door.

Tate took his seat opposite Margaret. The door shut behind Officer Laila, and a deafening pocket of silence confined itself within the four walls. Margaret's wolf kept prompting her human to look at their mate, but Margaret adamantly kept her eyes down. What was unusual was that Tate had not initiated conversation. He'd normally say something by now. Anything.

When she finally decided that the silence wasn't normal, her brows wrinkled as she looked up. Tate's gorgeous brown eyes held her captive almost immediately. There was hurt, disappointment, and even some anger, but he wasn't any less attractive, despite the taut muscles of his jaw.

"So you do know that I'm here," Tate began with a sardonic smirk. Her wolf whimpered, pestering its human part to talk to their mate, to ask him what was wrong. He wasn't like this earlier this morning. This morning, he was soft, gentle, and patient. Now he just looked defensive and upset. What had happened?

"Still have nothing to say, mate?" Tate asked. His abrasive tone instantly dropped a stone of guilt into his abdomen, and it made Margaret's wolf whimper harder. Margaret remained stubborn and pressed her lips tighter to seal it up, choosing to look at the wall at the side.

"Fine," he muttered, then continued tersely, "You'll be happy to know that this is not entirely about the mate bond. I came on behalf of the government with an offer." Despite her averted gaze, her ears perked up, a detail that was hard to miss, so Tate continued, "We're willing to grant you and your people pardon over any crimes committed in the past on one condition." He dropped the silent bomb again. He was not going to let Margaret get away with getting full information without at least looking at him like he was one of her mindless goons. If Tate had learned anything about Lucy and her rejections, it was that she had enough self-respect to walk away from anyone who didn't see her value, who didn't give her the basic level of respect that any decent creature was entitled to receive.

Margaret would have loved to keep her eyes on the gray wall, but she was intrigued by the offer. She had been trying to get Stella to find a way out for all of them for days, but that useless daughter of hers had been more troublesome than helpful. This only confirmed what Margaret already knew when she became a rogue: if you want something done, you have to do it yourself.

Tate's offer seemed too good to be true. But what was the condition?

When she finally admitted defeat in the look-away contest and met Tate's hard gaze that had been waiting for her, Tate succinctly explained, "On the condition that you and your people work with us and another rogue group to track down a third group of rogues we're trying to find and eliminate."

Silence. This was getting ridiculous.

"I can't read your mind, Margaret. Is that a yes or a no? If you're afraid to speak because I can somehow steal your voice, at least give your head a nod or a shake."

His hostility made Margaret feel like she was being . . . pushed away, the same feeling she had been experiencing with Stella recently. It was familiar, but it still hurt.

Margaret gave a firm nod and began mentally planning an escape route when they let her and her people out.

Relief cascaded through Tate and his wolf at her acceptance. "Good. After this, I'll send in Officer Laila. You'll give us the location of your followers, and we'll bring them here to cooperate."

Her rosewood eyes widened in shock.

Tate's own brows rose. "I still can't read your mind, Margaret. But if this is your way of asking whether I meant the whole pack when I spelled out the offer, then, yes. This includes your *entire* pack—every last rogue under your protection and supervision. You know where they've run. If you continue to hide them, I can't promise you that our allies won't kill them when they hunt them down. You know how this works: all rogues are the same to us. It's safer to bring your people here and give them a shot at earning a safe future for themselves."

That warning put a halt on her escape plan. She was going to lie about her people's location, but Tate was right. If they were hunted down, there wouldn't be a way out. The past few months had been more hectic than ever before, with her pack having to move more frequently than they usually did because the wolves started tracking them down when they used to only stand guard at their own packs and attack rogues if the rogues chose to enter. The moves were tiring and angering her people and her.

This offer seemed like a ticket to freedom for all of them. No more constant running, moving, and hiding, and finally ridding of the anxiety of being found, caught, and slaughtered.

The thread of patience in Tate wore thin when he bluntly declared, "The offer doesn't get better than this, Margaret. This is already the best one on the table, hence the best one I could ask for."

Her wolf's ears perked up in attention once more. *He* asked for her and her people to be pardoned? It made her animal coo that he was being so protective of them.

Again, no response.

Tate heaved a frustrated sigh like he just wanted to get this part over with now when he said, "Anyway, it's not without a . . . penalty for breach." His eyes held hers when he warned in a low voice, "If at any point in time during the cooperation you or any of your people decide to do anything that goes against our purpose, be it betraying us, trying to escape, or hurting anyone on the team, the queen will personally end you or anyone else involved. And trust me when I say you don't want to get on the queen's bad side. She will break you. And she will make you feel it until you can't anymore."

Margaret shuddered, which hadn't happened in more than a decade. She'd trained herself to be dauntless and, at times, reckless. Her survival had only been possible because *she* was normally the one throwing out these threats. It hadn't been the other way around for a long time. Fear seeped through the surface of her skin and invaded her bloodstream, marking her cells and sinking into her bones because she already had an unwanted demonstration of what the queen could do to her by simply changing the color of her eyes.

Her wolf, on the other hand, was more intrigued than fearful. When they first met Lucy, they sensed that she was unusual. Her aura declared her power and status, but her energy amplified an unusual warmth that felt . . . trustworthy. Now, hearing that Lucy would end her, Margaret's wolf growled and scratched the invisible walls in her human's mind, angered that she had behaved so recklessly with the queen. It was so strange to Margaret that her wolf was not the slightest bit offended after Lucy used her Authority on them both. *Stupid, stupid wolf.*

"Do you understand everything I've just said?" Tate's voice held a balance of anger and concern.

Margaret nodded.

"Good. Now, about the mate bond. Let's just be frank: do you want it?"

The rosewood eyes widened in shock, but not at Margaret's own accord. It was her wolf. Her animal was trying to push forward despite the silver bracelet fastened around Margaret's wrist. The red wolf was done persuading her human. She just wanted to leap at Tate and bury herself in his chest to beg him to stay. The animal continued pushing even though it was pointless since they weren't immune to silver.

As Margaret continued enduring being pushed forward by her own animal and pushed back by the bracelet, varying levels of frustration continued piling up in her at the naivety of her animal that was essentially wasting her energy fighting a losing battle. *Why can't animals possess some basic human logic?* she thought.

Tate watched her look away as her chest rose and fell. Her head turned side to side like she was on the verge of going insane. Leaning forward with worry lining his head, Tate frantically asked, "Margaret, what is it? What's wrong?"

His worried voice sent the red wolf further to the edge. Margaret raised a finger. "Just . . . give me a minute." And she continued battling with her animal.

"Uh . . . alright," Tate muttered in uncertainty. He thought when she finally decided to speak to him with less hostility, he would feel like the luckiest wolf alive, but now, he was just distressed. After another few more seconds, Tate and his animal couldn't stand it anymore. His chair scraped the floor as he got up and dashed to Margaret's side, squatting and taking her forearms when he demanded, "Margaret, what is it? Why are you shaking?" When he saw the shade of her eyes alternating between light and dark, he understood.

His hands trailed to her wrists, and he planted a slow, deep kiss on her clenched fists, sending a burst of sparks throughout Margaret's being. His lips lingered on her knuckles, feeling the hardness, the pure strength in them. Only then did his mouth pull away.

Margaret fidgeted less, but her animal was still pushing, albeit less aggressively now. Tate's thumbs then stroked her fists in slow, soothing motions as he coaxed, "Shh . . . it's alright. You're safe. You're safe. No one is going to hurt you, alright? You're safe. Stay calm. You're good."

The red wolf's whimpering and tears subsided as she halted her struggle, finally calming down. His voice and touch became a drug. She wanted more, but the silver bracelet trapped her from making decisions. She cooed and begged her human to hug him, feel him, but Margaret didn't budge, reining back the primitive urge. Still, she felt . . . grateful that Tate had cooled down the monster living in her. Exhaling a relieved sigh, Margaret slowly slid her hands out of his grip before uttering, "Thank you. She can get really . . . emotional at times."

"That's good to know," Tate rasped. The upward curl of his lips was only overshadowed by the spark of hope in his eyes. His softness drew a small, sincere smile out of Margaret, a smile that Tate took full advantage of admiring, memorizing the barest upward bend of her chapped lips on the flawless face hooded only by some sweaty red streaks.

He meant what he said before—about feeling good that her wolf could get emotional. He had been wanting to know her and her animal since the moment they met but never got anything, so it felt good to finally know . . . something. Despite his urge to touch her cheek and wipe the beads of sweat on her forehead and temple, he held back and slowly stood, returning to his seat, much to his wolf's dismay. They lapsed into silence again, this time because Margaret didn't know what to say as opposed to not wanting to say anything.

Choosing his words with care, Tate noted, "Your wolf wants the bond, but you . . . both aren't on the same page."

Her dry lips curled into a sad smile. "You could say that." She was dead certain she didn't want a second-chance mate, but now that she had met Tate, she wasn't sure anymore.

"Margaret," he began. Her head inched slightly toward where he sat, but her eyes fixed on the table.

Tate decided to make do with this now. At least her body language showed she was listening. "I want the bond too. I admit I don't know you, but I want to. I want to give us a shot. But I can't if you won't let me. What happened to you in the past wasn't right, and I wish I could go back there and do something about it, but . . ." he sighed in dismay ". . . but I hope you understand that I can't. I can only be here for you now and help you get through this."

Margaret's eyes glistened with each word, and she had to press her lips together to control the tears from spilling out. It had been so long since someone wanted to be there for her and help her get through her past. If anything, she was implicitly taught to never bring it up, to suck it up and put on a strong face and a brave front. But at the end of the day, she knew that was all it was—

a front, an act. And that the truth was that she was breaking inside, shattering piece by piece every single day since the betrayal. She never healed. There was never time. Survival came first. As a rogue, there was never the luxury of time to heal. Time was spent on self-teaching through trial and error about which territories belonged to other rogues, which rivers were shared and which were not, and most importantly, how to run past packs in large numbers without being detected. It was a cold, dark world.

Tate was offering an assurance that she hadn't felt since before she was cast out, which held a life that she could no longer envision herself living. That life belonged to a girl who lived safely and predictably, a girl who had such innocuous optimism for the future. That was a girl that Margaret no longer recognized. That girl died long ago, along with a piece of Margaret's soul.

Pinching her left thigh to stop her grieving tears from spilling, she whispered, "I need . . . time . . . to decide." She felt so ashamed of saying that, so ashamed of not knowing what she wanted.

She knew what she wanted! Tate just had to be so different and ruin her well-thought-out plan!

Her words sent warmth into Tate's heart. He leaned across the table, meeting her gaze with smiling eyes. "Thank you."

Margaret's self-deprecating thoughts were put to an abrupt stop. "What?" she asked without thinking.

His perfect smile broadened at the sound of her voice, at her beauty despite her discombobulation. "Thank you for letting me know what you need. I've been trying to guess it for days. It's good to finally know what's on your mind." He carefully reached for her hand on the table, and when she didn't stop him, he lifted it to his lips, kissing the back.

After giving her hand an assuring squeeze, he said, "I'll let Officer Laila take over from here. Just give her the location and get a good night's sleep. I'll come get you tomorrow. Let me know if you need anything, alright?"

Unaccustomed to his gesture, Margaret could merely offer a nod.

Tate reluctantly let go of her hand and made his way out the door, but not before turning back to take another glimpse of her, and his face lit up like a lantern when he noticed that she, too, was looking at him before averting her eyes when he caught her doing it.

As Tate closed the door behind him after Officer Laila entered, he leaned against the wall, grinning to himself like he was swimming in a sea of love. It wasn't that she didn't want him. She just wasn't sure. The hopelessness he felt faded away, replaced by a strong determination to win his mate's heart.

CHAPTER 17

Simultaneously, in another interrogation room, Lucy met with Greg, who shook her hand less awkwardly this time. Taking note of the faint creases on her forehead, he prepared for the worst.

She began, "Your Grace, the monarchy and the government have agreed to provide the ninety-eight creatures under your care conditional pardon for all crimes, *except* murder."

Greg was internally grateful that he always preferred torture to death, and he never allowed his people to kill. The long-term goal of keeping these tortured creatures alive was for them to heal and live on to spread tales about how no one should mess with Greg Claw.

The queen continued, "The pardon comes with two caveats. One, we expect you and your people to make room for a few more rogues, who we've offered the same opportunity as your people to work on the case in exchange for their own pardon, should they accept the offer, that is."

Greg had a problem working with other creatures, which was why creatures worked *for* him, not with him. "And the second caveat, my queen?" he prompted.

Her eyes darted to the table as she harrumphed, then met his eyes again as she disclosed, "If at any point in time you or your people conspire against us, your followers will be compelled to testify against you for any and every past crime that they know about. They will be charged for their own crimes as well, but sentencing will be mitigated in accordance with the information they'll be able to provide to commit you to the highest levels of punishment. For clarity's sake, I should mention that any compulsion that . . . has to be exerted . . . won't be done by the king. It'll be by me."

Greg waited for her to go on, and when she didn't, his brows raised in disbelief. "That's it?" When he received nothing but the confused crumpling of Lucy's beautiful brows in return, he said, "My queen, if you wanted to know about my criminal past, all you had to do was ask. I genuinely thought you knew this. My people won't know the full extent of what I've done. It was a precaution I took. Individually, they'll know bits here and there, but I can tell you that it'll be quite difficult, tedious, and costly to piece any crime together. I'll happily provide full and frank disclosure right now if—"

"No!" Lucy exclaimed, and even she was surprised by her own outburst. Taking a moment to compose herself, she rephrased, "No, Your Grace. That is not necessary."

"Are you sure?" Greg asked, his concern temporarily clouding his ability to see the way Lucy was now battling with Xandar's jealousy through the mate bond.

Her curt reply finally came, "I'm quite certain, Your Grace. Anyway, that's the offer. Do you accept it?"

Greg didn't even take a second to think when he waved a hand. "That goes without saying, my queen, but do you need time to come up with more leverage?" There was no arrogance or sneer in his tone. He genuinely wanted to know whether she needed more time.

Lucy studied her cousin-in-law. His eyes held no malice. His confession was devoid of elusiveness and prevarication. Those lilac orbs had a different look before he turned over a new leaf. At that time, it was always clear that he was up to something, hiding something. Now, the only thing swimming in those lilac orbs was concern. She thought about how coming up with something else was going to waste time that they didn't have. If they didn't speed things up while the experiment for the concoction moved ahead, there'd be more test runs than there would be at present. More test runs meant more new ingredients would be required. Which would mean more abductions. Lives were at stake. At present, it was only vampires. Who knew if those behind the concoction would go after werewolves and lycans next? Her people might be used as lab mice to test the concoction to challenge her Authority.

With that in mind, she answered, "That won't be necessary, Your Grace. We'll just . . . come up with something along the way."

Greg's mouth opened, intending to ask her to reconsider her decision since he knew procedure meant the world to governing members. But the duke curbed his tongue when he noticed her taking slow, deep breaths as her arm went across her chest, probably without her being consciously aware of the movement. The duke put two and two together and concluded that she was most likely trying to cope with his idiotic cousin's jealousy. Guilt engulfed him, burying him deep and swallowing him whole. He never intended to put her in a situation where she had to fight through things alone. Aborting his earlier plan that was only going to make the mate bond harder on her, he diverted and chose to ask something else. "I do have one question about the offer, my queen—these new creatures we have to work with, who are they?"

Despite his straight face, Greg was relieved to see her breathing returning to normal when she answered, "Rogue wolves who've been running under the radar. None of them are lycans, so for Goddess sake, Your Grace, play nice."

"I'll try my best. And what could their connection to the crown be, if I may ask?" Greg was internally worried that she may have made a deal with rogues that could be more dangerous than useful. He didn't doubt she was smart, but knowing who to trust in the rogue world was not a matter of intelligence. It was about having the right network and connections.

Biting her bottom lip, Lucy disclosed who Margaret was, how she was connected to them through Tate.

Greg crossed his arms and slowly leaned back into his seat. The gears in his head turned like they'd never gotten rusty from the time behind bars. "Well, that will either simplify or complicate matters."

"Or both," Lucy mused, which Greg easily caught.

He let out a light chuckle, nodding in agreement with a wide smile when he repeated, "Or both." This was his first authentic laugh in a long time.

Seeing that there was nothing more to discuss, Lucy offered a small smile, saying, "Well, I should get going. Chief Dalloway and his task force will sort out the paperwork, and we should be able to get you out by tomorrow morning."

The word *paperwork* made his animal roll its eyes, but the thought of being able to get out of the boring shithole and work with Lucy made his lycan stretch in enthusiasm. As usual, Greg stood when the queen did. "Thank you for your time, Your Grace."

"It's a duty and an honor to serve, my queen," Greg responded with a slight bow and an arm across his chest.

Lucy tried not to look too hasty to leave the room to calm her still-agitated husband. The moment she opened the door, Xandar, who was waiting right outside, pulled her into a tight, possessive embrace as he pecked a statement kiss in her hair and shot Greg a warning glare before the door closed to block their views of each other.

A tightness formed in the duke's his chest at their sudden embrace, but he still managed to mutter, "Mated, marked, and married, and he's still looking at me like I have any shot at stealing her. How did this kingdom get a queen who ticked all the boxes and more but is forced to settle with a dumbass for a king? Hopeless idiot." Even his animal was shaking its head at their pathetic cousin.

But if Greg was being honest with himself, he'd admit that if it were him in his cousin's shoes, he would've reacted equally defensively, if not worse. Heck, he might not even let Lucy speak to another male who showed interest in her in the first place, despite already marking her.

CHAPTER 18

O utside the interrogation room, Lucy let the pair of large, warm arms cage her, a hand on the back of her head bringing her as close to his heart as feasibly possible. Her own hands circled his neck, thumb stroking his heated nape in slow, soothing motions as Xandar continued inhaling her scent, focusing on her animal's comforting coo through their mind-link. The erratic rhythm of his heart gradually returned to normal with each breath taken of his little flower. And when he was ready, his lips trailed to her forehead, where he pressed an open-mouthed kiss. Bringing their eyes to meet, he asked, "So what should we do if Greg does stray, my love?"

Seeing that their private moment was over, Christian came over to join the discussion.

Lucy took another hard look at Greg, who was now being escorted out through the second door that opened up on the other side of the room as she muttered, "If prison walls can't hold him . . . I don't think we're left with any other option."

Christian bluntly asked, "So death?"

In a reluctant whisper, she replied, "Yes."

Sensing the heaviness in her heart, Xandar brought her back to his embrace. "Lucy, if this isn't a game he's playing, we won't have to resort to that. Okay?" She forced a smile and nodded. Now that that was out of the way, Xandar brought up the second thing that bothered him, "You and Greg mentioned Tate and Margaret's bond would either simplify or complicate matters, or do both. What did you mean by that?"

She registered his sudden impatience and explained, "Well, if Margaret respects the bond and wouldn't let anything come between her and Tate, it would simplify matters for us because she'll be cooperative, and her followers will, hopefully, follow suit. But if she sees the bond as . . ." groping for the right word, she finally settled on ". . . a mistake . . ." she sighed in despair and proceeded in a troubled voice ". . . then things can get complicated. We don't know if we can trust her or any of the rogues she leads. If one of them turns against us, disclosing our plans to the creatures coming up with the concoction, our efforts to stop them will be in vain. Punishment and sentencing will be another complex element if such a betrayal does occur, because the big question would be whether Margaret knew or should have known what her people were up to."

Christian prompted, "And the third possibility, my queen, where it can become both a simplification *and* a complication?"

"Say, hypothetically speaking," Lucy articulated, "Margaret cooperates in the initial stages of our venture and she and Tate fall in love, simplifying things. But in the course of executing the plan, she changes her mind and chooses to . . . stray, after they both are already in love—"

"Oh, Goddess," Christian muttered in dismay.

Xandar thought aloud, "Tate might change his mind. Even if his mate conspires against us, he might ask for mercy."

Christian continued in a whisper, "Or even fight for it. I just hope he won't blackmail anyone to do it."

Xandar's brows knitted. "Christian, come on. It's Tate. He wouldn't do that to us. Right, baby?"

Meeting the line of worry on Christian's face, Lucy reassured, "For as long as I have known Tate, he's always been able to separate temporary urges from long-held principles, choosing the latter without fail. That's why White Blood has thrived in such a short span of time. I'm confident he'll do the right thing if such a time comes. I'm just not sure whether the right thing for us would also be the right thing for him, because his urge to give into the bond may not be temporary."

Xandar asked in a disbelieving whisper, "Lucy, you can't be suggesting that he'd resort to something illegal to free her?"

"He wouldn't. But that's not to say he wouldn't resort to finding some sort of . . . middle ground? Meaning to say he might help Margaret escape and disappear without hurting anyone, and then *he'd* stay back and suffer the consequences on her behalf."

Christian questioned, "But doesn't that seem a little extreme? Trading one's life and liberty for someone who just leaves him here and runs away?"

"Not if love is part of the equation, Christian," Lucy uttered. "Deep, intimate interest can make creatures do . . . unexpected things, even if it's one-sided."

Xandar pinned her to his side, muttering, "That, I have to agree."

Christian caught his cousin glancing at the one-way mirror where they watched Greg. An exhausted sigh left the duke before he asked, "But this is hypothetical, my queen? We don't know if that's what Alpha Tate would really do?"

She nodded without hesitation. "Yes, it's completely hypothetical, Christian. It's just about considering all possibilities. We are not saying that it will happen but that it *could* happen."

Xandar stiffened at the word *we* since it meant her and Greg, instead of her and him. It bothered the king that his wife and crooked cousin came to the same hypotheses without saying more than a few words to each other. Greg only took a few seconds to catch up to her thoughts, whereas Xandar needed her to spell the whole thing out for him.

"Darling, are you okay? What is it?" her angelic voice of concern rang through his ears, bringing him back to the present. Christian knew exactly what it was and decided to step away to join Tate instead, who had just come out of the interrogation room after speaking to Margaret, looking particularly sunshiny.

Xandar loosened his tightening grip on Lucy's waist, peering into her eyes. "I do try to be better every day. I love you, and I'll do anything for you. You know that, don't you?"

"I do. What is this about?" she asked, closing their distance.

"I just . . ." his hand threaded through her hair, running down the length, tracing the curls at the end ". . . wished I knew how you think . . . like how Greg knew."

Her body tensed up at the mention of the other duke. "Xandar, Greg didn't . . . know how I thought per se. We just came to the same conclusions with the available facts. It's just analysis and strategic thinking. He could do it because he has practice in committing crimes without ever getting caught. I have practice as a gamma when I needed to keep Blue Crescent and our allies safe. It's not about being able to . . . read one's thought process, darling. It's just . . . individual yet similar . . . thinking."

His fingers thread through her dark, luscious hair again, and he murmured, "I wish I could do that."

The simple sentence gnawed at her heart, threatening to make it bleed. Xandar was already so much and was still trying to be so much more than he already was. She couldn't have dreamt of a better mate, nor could the kingdom ask for a better king. How could he wish that he was different, that—of all creatures—he wished he was like Greg in any aspect?

Her hands reached to his shoulders, then slowly closed in on his neck, her thumb tracing the faint lines she'd kissed so many times before. In a whisper, she explained, "Strategy is a skill, darling. And all skills can be acquired and improved. You'll get there in no time once we work on this case." Pulling herself up and pecking a kiss on his cheek, she reminded, "You're more than what you think of yourself, Alexandar. Don't ever wish that you were different. I love you—all of you."

The caress of her words embraced his heart. He wasn't more, but she always made him feel more, be it as her mate, as king, or as the father to their pup. Leaving a kiss on her temple, his breath tickled her ear when he whispered, "Thank you, baby. I love you too."

Setting her free, he nuzzled her nose and elicited her soft chuckles before a cheeky glint entered Lucy's eyes when she began, "Honestly, my king, did you really think I'd favor anyone else over my history geek? Nerds are very hard to come by, and to this day, I've only met one who can make my heart flutter and has the ability to make me feel safe and loved with his presence."

Smirking at the label, he declared, "And I'm determined to keep it that way, my queen."

They joined Christian and Tate, who were both speaking to Chief Dalloway about extracting Margaret's pack.

Christian suggested, "Maybe the queen should go."

Tate's head swung left and right. "No. Using the Authority at this stage won't do any good, Your Grace. It'll just drive the rogues away. The compulsion might even make them consider turning against us. Besides, Lucy might be needed here when the other duke's people are rounded up. I can go with you, Chief."

Chief Dalloway replied, "As much as I appreciate that, Minister, I'm afraid it won't alleviate the problem."

"What problem?" Lucy asked.

Dalloway greeted the rulers and explained, "It's about extracting the rogues without bloodshed, Your Highnesses. I was telling the duke and the minister about how rogues are inclined to resort to violence in the presence of authorities. It's worse now because they know we're holding their leader."

"So," Lucy considered, "you're asking for permission to bring Margaret along to reduce the likelihood of any possible attack?"

The men around her turned wide-eyed before the chief muttered to himself, "That seems to be a workable solution." He then proceeded to ask, "Do we have the crown's permission to do this, Your Highnesses?"

Lucy looked up at her mate with her signature doe eyes, beseeching him to say yes. *'We have Stella. Margaret wouldn't run and leave her here, not after how much she risked to get her back. Let her go with them?'*

Xandar's heart always melted whenever she looked at him like that, and malfunctioned any ability he had to say no. Weaving his fingers through her hair in a way that made her animal purr, he linked, *'It's definitely better to bring her along. We should let Tate go too. Give them time to bond. Margaret might even open up.'*

Lucy's eyes twinkled at the unexpected bonus. "That's great!" The queen's hand flew to cover her mouth, realizing that her excitement made her respond to the king's link out loud.

Christian, Tate, and Dalloway jerked a little, but Xandar found her reaction to be so endearing that he couldn't resist pecking a sweet kiss on her head.

It was decided that Tate would accompany Margaret, Dalloway, and his task force to collect the rogues under her supervision. All that was left to do was hope that Margaret's and Greg's followers would get along.

CHAPTER 19

On Tate's jet, he took the seat next to Margaret. Twenty policemen and thirty lycan warriors around them chatted casually with one another like they weren't about to face a pack of rogues. Then again, the months of training under the queen's and defense minister's direct supervision had built not only their strength and skill set, but also confidence in their abilities.

Only Phelton was wary. When he heard that the king and queen had authorized extracting the rogue pack, he didn't think twice before volunteering to come keep his eye on Margaret. After what she and her wolves almost did to Lucy last time, Phelton kept his guard up. No one knew if they were walking into a trap. The queen may have been forgiving and open to the fact that creatures could change for the better, but Phelton wasn't. He had a solemn duty to protect her and the rest of the royal family as a warrior and minister. It really bothered him that Tate didn't seem the least bit suspicious or skeptical about Margaret. She was the *leader*. Of a *rogue* pack. Those two words together should say enough. There was every reason to be suspicious. Then again, the mate bond had been known to overturn all reasonableness.

Margaret was cuffed as a precaution, and Tate's animal whimpered at the sight of the silver accessory designed for prisoners. There wasn't anything he could do since it was to make sure Margaret didn't try to escape or attempt to mind-link her people to trap the authorities upon their arrival.

Margaret was at a window seat, but the view didn't interest her. Her eyes were fixed on the armrest, but her mind was miles away. She wondered who she was asked to work with and whether it was a group that her pack had already met. It would create quite a stir if the enmity of the past was brought to light, either forcing a temporary reconciliation or pushing for a deeper animosity between both sides.

"Hey," Tate's voice brought her out of her thoughts. "You okay?"

"Yes, thank you." Margaret's polite reply came in a mere whisper, without meeting his gaze.

Tate took comfort in the fact that she responded this time without being coerced. Without scorn. At least she wasn't shutting him out anymore. He wanted to get to know her. But her reluctance to face him made Tate feel that it may still be too early for that. The alpha cracked his head for a topic that she would be more open to talking about, and he casually asked, "About Stella . . . apart from photography, what does she like?"

That question worked like a charm. Margaret's eyes snapped to him. "She likes what?"

Tate's brows raised. "Photography. You know, taking pho—"

"No, I know what photography is. I mean," the creases on her forehead layered when she asked, "since when did she enjoy that?"

"Uh . . . I . . . don't know?" Tate didn't have a better answer, and when Margaret's eyes dimmed, he added, "But I could ask her the next time I see her. Or you could. Or we could ask her together."

Margaret smirked lightly as she started staring into space again, and Tate groaned internally. How could they be mates when he didn't even know what to say to her? Tate was convinced this was karma getting back at him for sleeping around with random she-wolves in his years as alpha and alpha-to-be. As he continued watching her, he couldn't help but admire her stunning side profile. Despite her eyebags and the few gray hairs, her feminine features would make heads turn in any pack. He wanted to talk to her. He didn't care if they had an empty conversation. He just wanted to talk to her.

As he continued pushing his mental gears for a safe—not insensitive—conversation topic, Margaret muttered grimly, "I'm a failure as a mother."

Tate's pondering halted from shock. "Margaret, don't say that. Stella's a good kid. You raised her well."

Margaret scoffed and shook her head; a self-deprecating smile stretched across her face. "If she were good, she wouldn't have run off with her friends like that right after I specifically told her *not* to." Sighing in frustration, she proceeded to say, "Stella used to be good—used to do as I say. Then one day she turned thirteen and . . ." she snapped her fingers ". . . it was like the genes of obedience had been flushed out of her system and all that came out of that teen-ager was nothing but a whole line of questions she doesn't need answers to."

"Like what?" Tate asked, engrossed in the tale.

Margaret picked the item on the top of her head. "Her all-time favorite question is, does she have a family, apart from me. I told her that she doesn't, but there's something in this teenager's brain that will process anything a parent says before it goes, 'Mom is definitely lying.'"

"Were you?"

"NO!" Margaret exclaimed at a volume that made Tate flinch a little in his seat. The noisy crowd fell into dead silence at her sudden high-pitched voice. The rogue leader closed her eyes and flushed crimson, muttering, "Oh, Goddess."

Tate smiled awkwardly at everyone, saying, "We're good, guys. Just . . . go back to whatever you were doing. Sorry about that."

The indistinct chatter started again, but most of their postures straight-ened, and their eyes darted in Margaret's direction more often than before. Some of them stole glances at her because of her beauty; others were just being careful as they reminded themselves of how lethal Lucy was on the training and battleground even when she was the smallest wolf in the room. Margaret wasn't small, but she was still a wolf, and therefore was still potentially dangerous.

After a few quiet moments, Margaret murmured, "Sorry."

"Hey, don't worry about it. I'm glad we're talking." Tate's lips curled up into a soft smile as his hand closed in on hers on the armrest, leaving the smallest space.

Her wolf wanted to close the remaining distance but her human was still scared, despite not showing it, so all she did was offer Tate a small smile and confess, "I'm glad we're talking too. You're a good listener."

That statement made his wolf howl in happiness. They were finally get-ting somewhere. But what Margaret had just said was also devastating. Life as a rogue wasn't just hard; it was lonely. Fear equated with weakness. Inner frustra-tions and turmoils were fought alone. Margaret probably had no one to hear her out, so Tate and Lucy, even Stella, bore the brunt of all her bottled-up anger and frustration in the interrogation room on that first day and days after that.

Come to think of it, Stella didn't have anyone to talk to either. But the solitude affected her differently. Whenever Tate started a conversation with the teenager on their way to and from the police station, he never seemed to have to do or say anything after asking one question. Stella would babble about scen-eries, angles, and lighting, and sometimes even share stories about her childhood, how she was allowed to skip firewood duty if it was her birthday or how she killed her first snail with salt when she was seven before feeling bad after the animal died and praying to the Goddess to send the dead snail to heaven.

"Thank you . . . for taking care of her," Margaret said gratefully.

"You don't have to thank me. I did it for purely selfish reasons," Tate admitted. Her confused orbs met his affectionate ones when Tate explained, "I want to take care of her, look out for her, and so does my wolf."

Margaret mm-ed as she returned his smile, diving into her own thoughts again. It was so strange to her that her daughter's birth father didn't care if Stella existed and was more than willing to cast Margaret out even with the possibility of her bearing his child. Now, Tate—who hardly knew her or Stella—was protecting her daughter like she was his own. She saw the willingness in his eyes and heard the sincerity in his husky voice. It wasn't done as an act of duty or a way to make her fall in love with him. He looked after Stella because he wanted to. Period. The thought thawed her cold heart and soothed her damaged soul, making her question everything she knew—or thought she knew—about love and mates.

Her past mate was nothing like Tate. Alpha Draxon was a textbook playboy, alcoholic, and self-entitled brat who got everything he wanted thanks to his status. The only good thing about Draxon was that he was brought up to be respectful to the elderly of Fleet Wood. He helped old men and ladies carry things, got a cat down from a tree, those kinds of things. It wasn't a lot to some, but it was a lot to many. Despite these occasional gestures, every parent who had a pup around Draxon's age couldn't ignore the fact that their future alpha was not the kind of creature they wanted their own pups to be around.

Draxon and Margaret found out that they were bonded mates on her twentieth birthday, which was three months before Draxon was bound to accept the alpha title from his widowed mother, who ruled Fleet Wood alone as luna for three years after her husband's death.

Being the naive girl that she was, Margaret dreamt of taming the untamable Alpha Draxon. She was over the moon to be bonded to the attractive bad boy whom she had a huge crush on since they were children. She'd steal glimpses of him at school and even found it "cool" that he skipped classes and talked back to teachers, especially the younger ones. Basically, she liked him for doing things that no one else could do without suffering severe repercussions. Where the elders saw impertinence, she saw bravery.

And she wasn't alone.

Every girl knew Draxon was trouble, but it was that very element that made them want him, crave him, submit to him. It was the thrill of the unknown and his indifference to just about everything that made many girls seek his attention, despite their parents' repeated warnings and advice. There wasn't a girl who didn't flash a coy smile or blush in innocent bashfulness if Draxon threw them a microsecond of a glance. Margaret was, unfortunately, no exception. Her cheeks used to heat up on their own whenever she walked past Draxon, even if he didn't see her.

"Hey, what's on your mind?" Tate's voice of concern brought Margaret out of the flashbacks.

She blinked, met his worried brown orbs, and shook her head slightly, muttering, "You're just . . . not what I expected."

Tate's wolf whimpered, thinking that she meant they weren't enough, that Margaret expected more for a second-chance mate. His voice turned a little hoarse when he asked, "What are your expectations?"

"Hm?" Margaret's eyebrows raised in surprise. She was sure she had heard him wrong.

Tate cleared his throat and tried again, "What do you . . . want in a mate? What do you expect him to be?"

His sorrowful face bothered her and her animal. What had she said? Why did Tate's demeanor take a 180-degree turn in a matter of seconds? She essentially had thrown out a compliment, which didn't happen often. After groping for the right words, she settled with, "Well, I didn't expect to get a second-chance mate, especially after thirteen years. So I never really thought about what I wanted in him. But you're definitely not what I . . . pictured as a mate, especially when you're . . . an alpha."

What? Tate was lost. Did Xandar and Lucy find it this hard to communicate when they first met? What about Juan and Hale? Did they have the same problem? Did Zeke and Zelena have to deal with this?

After swallowing a lump in his throat, Tate uttered sheepishly, "I'm not following, Margaret. What do you mean?"

Margaret then realized she couldn't make Tate understand without telling him about her past, but she wasn't ready to share that part of her life with him. What if he judged her naivety? What if he lectured her on how stupid she was to give into the mate bond by falling for someone who reeked of trouble from the start? What if Alpha Tate and Alpha Draxon were *friends*? That wouldn't just be the icing on the cake; it'd be the cherry on top of the sprinkles on top of the icing on the cake!

But she couldn't deny she was caving in. Her wolf wanted this. Her human part now saw Tate as a second chance at the type of love that left her broken and damaged the last time. But was he really all that he was showing? Was this really not an act? Alpha Draxon was nice to her because he wanted to sleep with her, and as soon as he got what he wanted, he tossed her out like she was just another she-wolf he'd fucked, not someone special he'd made love to.

After mentally deciding to only tell Tate as much as was necessary for him to understand, she began, "My first mate . . . was an alpha."

Tate knew that, of course.

"He . . . wasn't like you."

That was definitely good to hear, seeing how that bastard had left Margaret and Stella.

"You're not what I expected because you don't fit into the stereotype most of us have of an alpha. Apart from the handful of good ones, most young, mateless alphas are more focused on womanizing than they are on pack business."

"I used to be like that," Tate admitted in a shameful whisper.

Margaret's ears perked up. "Used to be? When did you stop?"

"Uh. . ." Tate did a mental count and said, "Six or seven years now, more or less."

"Well, you're definitely in the club of good ones now, and that's what I mean. The alphas I knew or heard about were controlling. Abusive, even. You don't seem to be like them." One shoulder lifted and fell. "You're not what I expected."

Tate pressed his lips together before updating Margaret on the alpha stereotype, "I'm flattered that you think of me that way, but I have to break it to you that those controlling and abusive alphas are facing extinction." Giving that some thought, he corrected, "In fact, I think they're already extinct today."

Margaret's head cocked to one side as her bright eyes urged Tate to continue, which he did. "For years, a few of us have been challenging these ruthless alphas, even some lunas, before taking their packs, all with the intention of giving those packs better protection and welfare. The initiative started with one of our closest allies, Alpha Juan of Blue Crescent, and the rest of us followed his lead."

"The rest of you?"

"Alpha Zeke and Luna Zelena from Blood Eclipse, Luna Lovelace from Midnight, and me from White Blood. Alpha Juan did most of it though. We just picked up what he was too busy to do."

Margaret blinked and leaned back into her seat. Rumination pulsed the veins on her temple. Her rosewood eyes of disbelief flickered back to Tate when she asked, "Alpha Ken retired?"

Of all the questions. And it came out like she was asking if the old man had died. Tate laughed. "Yes, he made way for Juan almost a decade ago. You've met Ken?"

"No, but I've heard of him. He was one of the good ones. I remember my parents talking about him quite often when I was young. My father admired him a lot. He said something about Ken being kind enough to adopt a child?"

Tate smiled as he nodded. "And that child grew up to be our queen today."

Margaret froze, and her reply came out in a conspiratorial whisper, "That's her?" She was so absorbed in the conversation that she wasn't even controlling her facial expressions anymore. "That's strange." Slumping back into her seat, her blabbering continued, "The news my followers and I got was that the king visited Blue Crescent one day and some unranked maid caught his attention with her innocent, helpless demeanor when she was serving him food at a dinner party. The king, overcome by lust, forced himself on her, before her submission to his dominance and repeated mistreatment made him fall in love with her, and he eventually crowned her as his queen."

Tate's wolf pulled its ears, wanting to tear them out and throw them away like doing so would rid them of whatever they'd just heard. His human cringed and pressed his fingers on his forehead at that preposterous suggestion when he whispered, "Better not say that ever again after today because that whole thing is . . . a tale that's very badly spun. The king and queen are bonded mates. They met in the annual collaboration hosted by the monarchy. Lucy herself was the fiercest gamma of our generation long before being bonded to the king. Sex was not forced, and it came *much* later in their relationship—when she learned to trust him. And Lucy is anything but helpless. She trained so many wolves, and then lycans, even the warriors around us right now. She's also nowhere near being submissive or forgiving to mistreatment. The king adores her and protects her with his life. The whole kingdom knows he'd do anything to please her, even before she knew it herself, before she fell for him. I mean, he is the only lycan king to ever consider mingling with werewolves *and* the first to kneel and bow to his mate. Seriously, Margaret, where do you and your people get your news? Everything you've just said is insane. If the king heard that, he'd throw those creatures in solitary confinement and they'd face an endless cycle of torture. I feel like I'm committing treason right now for not reporting this."

Margaret responded matter-of-factly, "Well, seeing that we didn't have access to the Internet, we rely on word of mouth. I really do apologize for this." She rubbed the back of one of her hands as she muttered, "Goddess, I feel bad for speaking to her that way now. I thought she was a cowardly, hypocritical, spineless whor—"

"You don't have to finish that sentence, Margaret, really. We're good." Tate stopped her when he noticed a few warriors around them, all of whom were fiercely loyal to and protective of their queen, seemed to be speaking less as their ears perked up in attention.

Margaret got the hint and continued pondering on her newfound knowledge, "You said she was a gamma?"

"Yeah, of Blue Crescent. Alpha Juan gives her full discretion in training and battles."

"The gamma of Blue Crescent . . . as in, Gamma Paw?"

"How did you know?"

Margaret scoffed. "Rogues fear that name. If we hear that Gamma Paw has been to a specific pack, we avoid it at all costs. Odds are, we won't survive the warriors he . . . well, she trained. I always thought it was a man."

Tate chuckled. "Yeah, me too, until I met her. Her brother called her Gamma Paw in her early years, not wanting packs to belittle his sister just because she's a woman."

"That's sweet," Margaret said with a smile, wishing she had someone like that in her life.

"Yeah, it is." A thought came to Tate, and his smile diminished before he held his breath when he cleared his throat. "Did we . . . happen to kill any of you?"

Her response came casually, "Blue Crescent slaughtered ten of our elders about nine years ago. A year after that, Blood Eclipse killed about fifteen. We ran into Midnight completely by accident and lost another eight. White Blood killed seven out of eight. The last one came back severely traumatized. And the last run-in we had with a pack was with the wolves from Forest Gloom three years ago. We lost two."

Wow. Every alliance member made it to the list. Tate scratched the back of his head and was thinking hard about the best way to respond.

"There's really no hard feelings," Margaret noted when she noticed Tate's uneasiness. "The ones you guys killed were stupid, to say the least. They did no research because their ego forbade them to ask around or send a wolf or two to check out the level of danger before striking. They were, by no means, careful when they snuck through packs, running through them like it was their territory. And the most infuriating thing about them was that they didn't know when to retreat. They'd just stubbornly hold their ground and threaten their followers with punishment if they had the brains to know that retreating was the best way forward. Idiots, really. So you and your friends have actually helped my pack get rid of a lot of unwanted creatures with unneeded opinions. The downside is that some good ones were also killed in the process because they couldn't escape fast enough. But they were stupid for following in the first place, so . . . there really are no hard feelings."

Tate let out the breath he had been holding onto. That was a relief to know. But the question was, "Why did you guys attack? What did you want?"

Margaret shifted in her seat, and one hand clutched the hem of her shirt. "For our pack, most of the time, it's just food and supplies. It kind of sucks to just eat sick animals all the time. And we can't touch the healthy ones anymore, of course, becau—"

"The hunters would kill you."

She nodded. "Yeah. That new law never stopped the elders, but it sure stopped me. The right that the kingdom gave hunters to hunt down any wolf who feeds on healthy herbivores without contractual agreement?" Margaret shook her head. "It's like it was put there to sniff us out and get rid of us."

"It was," Tate confessed, recalling the meeting he attended with other alphas, lunas, and gammas several years back in a mediation with the hunters.

"Well, it worked for some time. Lots of rogue packs we knew were lost," Margaret said.

Tate knew. Everyone knew. It was considered a small victory for non-rogues everywhere. Lucy and Toby even joked about how they might befriend hunters one day for helping them get rid of a notable part of the rogue population.

"I'm really sorry," Tate muttered.

Margaret continued pinching the hem of her shirt as she forced a small smile. "I doubt any of you knew. Before I became a rogue, I was also hardwired to hate every wolf who didn't belong to a pack, to look at them in disdain, to have no sympathy or empathy. I was brought up to believe that if no one wanted them, there had to be something wrong with them. I was taught that all rogues attacked for the pleasure of destroying our pack and murdering innocents." She scoffed. "But nothing could be further from the truth. I've met a few good ones leading rogue packs throughout the years. They never wanted any trouble. They just wanted to be safe and to . . . survive. The more optimistic ones even find ways to be content with whatever they have. It's not that no pack wanted them; they just . . . don't see the need to . . . bend and beg to be taken care of, to be accepted, to pledge allegiance to a pack leader who might one day turn against them if an alliance is formed with their former pack leaders." Margaret paused, reminiscing about the ones she met throughout the years. "I suppose what I'm saying is, if I hadn't left my pack, I would've done whatever you and your allies have been doing, killing rogues on sight. Because we've never been taught the other side of the coin. How would anyone expect us to see it?"

Tate got lost in her rosewood eyes for a moment before he uttered in a pained whisper, "I just wish it didn't take you becoming a rogue for one of us to see it."

Margaret's lips curled up at his sincerity. "But it did. There's no way to change that. Besides, only a rogue would know that side of the coin. I . . . do mind being tossed out, but I don't mind what it has taught me. I used to be so . . . reliant on the people around me. I used to think that I wouldn't survive a day without my family and friends, especially friends I trusted with every secret and fear. Only after I was forced to leave did I realize . . . I'm stronger than I gave myself credit for. And I get stronger each day, driven by nothing more than a sheer will to survive. I thought I wouldn't last a day after the rejection. But I did, and that gave me a little hope. Then I lasted another day, and I began to wonder whether I could last a week. When I did, I saw that I could last a month, then a year, even with a child. I don't like what happened to me. I really don't. I hate it. I hate that it had to be me. But I can't deny that . . . it has taught me something, something that, I feel, no other experience could have taught me. I never thought I could lead a pack, that's a given, and I planned to just stand by my first mate's side and look pretty as his luna." She chuckled briefly with derision. "I never saw myself as a leader. Being a rogue changed that."

After trying but failing to swallow a sniffle and wiping away her tears, mourning her lost innocence, the simplicity of her life, she chuckled depressedly and said, "I used to be a sweet, bubbly creature-pleaser. After I got tossed out, let me tell you, I became a grade-A bitch, especially after I had Stella. I wasn't just defensive; I became selfish, even cruel at one point. It wasn't until I met those few good rogues that I changed my perception. They showed me that— just because I was a rogue—it didn't mean I had to behave like the bad batch. Like the good ones, I could choose to be a little different." Shaking her head slightly as she reminisced about her childhood and teenage years, she muttered, "If you met me fourteen years ago, you wouldn't recognize me. I'm just . . . not a nice creature anymore."

A calloused hand, large and firm, wrapped around her slender one. Her fingers were lifted, brought to Tate's side, where his lips pecked a kiss before he spoke with a wide smile, "I'm glad."

Margaret was too stunned to react, to merely move. When Tate started stroking her fingers, she was brought out of her daze and slowly retracted her hand, trying not to show how much she enjoyed the feeling when his skin brushed against hers, already regretting pulling away from his touch. She averted her eyes again and hung her head low. Tate admired her slightly pink cheeks as he thought about what a great luna Margaret would make. A single mother who had to raise her pup all on her own while rising through the ranks as the leader of a rogue pack that was still surviving when other rogues were eliminated throughout the years. Undeniably phenomenal.

The jet landed, and the whole party escorted Margaret out with Tate by her side. Once everyone had stopped on the field, Chief Dalloway repeated a warning as he held a key before her cuffs, reminding her that if at any point in time she turned against the agreement, they had full authorization to kill her and her followers on behalf of the government and monarchy.

Tate's wolf tried to push forward to defend her, despite knowing that Dalloway was a trusted figure. But his human held back, understanding and appreciating systems and procedures better than his animal.

Margaret nodded with an emotionless face, and the cuffs were taken off.

Right before Margaret howled to summon her people, Tate interjected, "Wait, Margaret. I need to tell you something."

Everyone's gaze pivoted to Tate in confusion and disapproval, including Margaret's. Phelton was ready to shift and attack if Tate decided to help his mate escape.

Tate ignored everyone and uttered, "I appreciate you opening up to me, truly. But I haven't been completely honest with you. The truth is . . ." Margaret's eyes turned wide as she waited. Tate swallowed a lump in his throat, confessing, "The truth is that I knew you were rejected by an alpha, not because Stella told me, but because I've been listening to every one of your conversations in the station since the first day."

Margaret blinked, brows coming to a slow arch. "And you're choosing to tell me this *now*? You have a serious timing issue, Alpha. I'll deal with you later. If you'll excuse me." She turned to face a dense forest and howled her lungs out.

Tate would worry about how Margaret was going to deal with him later, but the trace of humor in her eyes wasn't just encouraging; it also made his heart flutter in happiness. She was warming up to him. He watched her in pride as her howls blared across the field. At the third howl, the rogues came into view in their wolf forms, snarling and growling—an unambiguous declaration that they were ready to attack.

The lycan warriors and policemen took their positions. Only Tate seemed confident that everything was going to be fine, crossing his arms as he studied the pack of wolves with curiosity.

Margaret's eyes glazed over, linking her right-hand woman, *'Azalea, we received an offer from the government: there's a new threat against them. If we help them uncover the culprit and get rid of the threat for good, they're pardoning us of all crimes committed in the past. I'm going to get everyone to stand down and shift back.'*

Azalea, the gray wolf leading the rest, snarled, *'Like hell you are! We didn't know where you went for days! These creatures took you and the others, and now they're forcing us to work for them? And WHERE IS STELLA?'*

'Stella is fine. She's with the king and queen. And they—'

'SHE'S WHAT? AND YOU LEFT HER THERE?'

Margaret lost her patience. Her foot stepped forward when she growled to remind her who was in charge. Some of the warriors were beginning to surround her, suspecting that she may be trying to escape.

In the pack-link, Margaret instructed, *'We are boarding this jet and helping the government. In exchange, we're freed from death or any other sort of punishment they can impose on us for everything we had to do to survive. No more running and hiding. We help them and they help us. If any of you chooses to walk away from this, these creatures around me will kill you. We can't outrun lycans.'*

Azalea argued, *'That doesn't mean we shouldn't try!'* She received support from a few others around her, but the rest were already hesitating. Azalea continued, *'They've tried to exterminate us in every possible way for YEARS! And now they're offering us this? It's stupid to think they want to help us! How do we know this isn't just some plan to coop us up in some cell before killing us all at one go?'*

Margaret yelled back, *'Azalea, shut up! If they wanted to kill us, they would've attacked by now. Do you see any of them attacking?'* A moment of silence passed, and Margaret ordered, *'Stand down and shift back. We can't win this. Trying is stupid. Any attempt to run will be futile, not just because these are lycans, but because these lycans have been trained by Gamma Paw.'*

A few rogues instinctively took steps back. Azalea stood her ground, but her voice got softer and unsure. *'That's not . . . possible. It doesn't matter how skilled he is. No lycan would ever be trained by a wolf. Their ego forbids it. It always has.'*

Margaret scoffed. "Yeah, funny story. It turns out Gamma Paw is a woman and is bonded to the king, which makes her our queen today."

Another rogue, Zane exclaimed, *'Holy shit, that's a major plot twist! Can't believe we've been running from a girl all these years!'*

Margaret and Azalea growled, *'What's that supposed to mean?'*

'Nothing. Nothing. I take that back. It was absolutely nothing.'

Azalea's heart raced. Her mind went through all the people they lost when some of their pack members ran through any wolf pack Paw had touched. When her eyes returned to Margaret, she noticed Tate. Registering how his soft gaze kept finding its way back to Margaret when everyone else's fixed glower was on her and the people with her, Azalea connected the dots and linked, *'That's your second-chance mate, isn't it, Margo?'*

Her teasing question changed the atmosphere in their link completely. Margaret tried to mask her embarrassment by responding, *'That's not relevant, Az. Wha—'*

'So that's why you're so sure this isn't a trap. This one must be different.'

'Az, that's a topic for another time. —Tate is jus'

'Tate, eh?' Azalea chuckled through the link when she noticed how the usually callous leader said that name with a degree of gentleness. Azalea was the first to go behind a tree to shift back. *'C'mon, people. Let's shift back. Don't want to embarrass our leader in front of her new boyfriend.'*

'A bonded mate is not necessarily a boyfriend, Az,' Margaret retorted as Azalea and the rest shifted back and dressed up.

Zane, for some reason, saw the need to add, *'This day just gets more and more interesting. I wonder if there'll be more plot twists today. Good plot twists, that is. Can't believe Gamma Paw is a girl. Did you meet her?'* he asked while pulling up his pants.

'Yes,' Margaret entertained one of the earlier friends she had made.

'Cool. Is she like how we imagine? Big, scary, kill-on-sight kind of creature?'

'No.' Margaret wiped a hand down her face before she pestered, *'Would you guys hurry up?'*

'Is she pretty at least?' Zane continued to ask.

Azalea scoffed and stepped out from behind the tree as she said aloud, "Zane, you do know you're talking about the queen—a married woman?"

"It's not like I want to hit on her or anything. And in the midst of all this bad, we've got to talk about some lighter things every once in a while. It keeps any creature sane."

Azalea, Zane, and a few more senior rogues were more confident in approaching the authorities because they trusted Margaret and she didn't sound anything less than firm and sure. The new ones were still considering running away, but the fact that these were Gamma Paw–trained lycans made them abort their plan to escape.

Once they were all before Margaret, Azalea gave her a hug before she registered Tate's aura. Her eyes went back to her leader, and she noted, "Looks like you were destined to be a luna after all. Good luck, sis. We'll be right here with you." Her gray eyes shifted to the jet as she said, "Ooo . . . nice ride."

Before she took another step, a straight-faced Dalloway stood in her way and ordered the twenty rogues to put their hands in front of them for his men to fasten the silver cuffs around their wrists. On the plane, most of the rogues were still constantly looking over their shoulders, internally terrified. Azalea and Zane, on the other hand, called dibs on window seats and chatted about the view like they weren't just arrested by the creatures they had been running away from for most of their lives.

Despite already being told that Margaret and Stella had no other family members, what Azalea said earlier made Tate ask, "Is she your sister?"

Margaret followed his sights to Azalea. "No. Azalea is an old friend. So is Zane, the one with her. Azalea and I were lone rogues before we ran into each other. We found Zane about a year later. Inseparable ever since."

"That's nice."

"Hm. They are the more trustworthy ones. They've even helped look after Stella when I was sick or out hunting." Margaret stopped herself from saying anything more. She trusted Azalea and Zane more than anyone in the pack, but she never learned to trust them fully. She never trusted anyone fully after her rejection.

Tate studied the ponytailed blonde woman and the brown-skinned man pointing out the window with large smiles, and he found himself matching their smiles when he muttered, "I'd love to meet them later."

Margaret's surprise was quickly replaced with a small smile. "You've already won over Az. I doubt Zane would have a problem with you either."

Tate's sights returned to his mate, and he placed his hand over hers before he said, "That's good to know."

This time, Margaret didn't retract her hand, and she bit her bottom lip to press back a smile before choosing to look out of the window when she knew she'd failed to hide her blushes.

Tate gazed at his mate and couldn't stop smiling. He had already found her stunning from the first moment they met, but after learning about her past, he didn't just find her stunning. Margaret was remarkable! How did he get so lucky? He thanked Goddess for bonding them, and then thanked karma for not being too hard on him after his years of messing around. Sitting next to her, Tate had never felt happier.

The police and warriors, on the other hand, kept their guard up. Phelton was eavesdropping on as many conversations as he could to see if any rogue would pose a threat to their safety. As his predatory eyes scanned each rogue, he found his heart softening at the sight of a larger-than-average wolf. She was looking at him from her seat and averted his gaze as soon as Phelton's eyes found hers. His lycan became curious and started studying her. Her brown skin appeared smooth from where he stood, and her bobbed hair allowed that beautiful neck of hers to be exposed.

No mark. Mateless. Her black orbs shone despite the trace of fatigue in them. Phelton had never seen a creature this attractive. Who was she?

CHAPTER 20

In the police station, Deputy Chief Lauren uncuffed Greg Claw before the king and queen. As Greg rubbed his wrists and inhaled deeply, embracing the return of his lycan senses, Xandar subconsciously held Lucy closer as his eyes fixed on the cousin he thought was locked up for a longer period of time than this.

Greg noticed his cousin's glare. His brows raised before he decided to have some fun. "Nice to see you too, cousin. And looking at me like that is not going to burn me to ash or put me back behind bars. Be grateful I'm helping the queen clean this shit up. After that, I'll r—"

Xandar's voice sent a shiver down the ordinary creature's spine when he interjected, "*One* misstep and don't think I won't throw you back in there after breaking *every* single bone in your body. Your request had better not mean trouble, Greg, because I can promise you, you won't survive the consequences."

Greg scoffed darkly, stepping toward Xandar and looking him dead in the eye as he boldly declared, "Brain is still as slow as it always was."

Xandar was about to land a punch when Lucy pushed Greg out of the way, and the duke steadied himself when his back hit the wall.

Lucy swiftly caught her husband's clenched fist that almost flew at her face, pecking a sweet kiss on his knuckles. His eyes softened, regret filling them fast. His fist loosened and opened up, and his warm palm cupped her cheek, thumb grazing her skin like he was looking for traces of injury, the apologies already at the tip of his tongue.

With her hand over his, tracing his knuckles, her voice came out stern, "Darling, I love you. But for the next few months, I need you to rein in your anger when it comes to him. Not only are our people counting on us to cooperate, but diplomatic relations are also at stake. Living, breathing creatures are relying on us to get along in the next few weeks. We are their best chance. Every time you feel like beating up your cousin or anyone we're working with, remember to breathe first. Alright?"

Gently raking his fingers through her hair, he promised, "Okay." His doting response was rewarded with his wife's small, adorable smile.

The queen then turned to face the duke. "For the record, Your Grace, your cousin helped in arguing *for* the granting of the conditional pardon. And when I told you to play nice, I meant play nice with everyone—your cousins, the ministers, the police, the warriors, the rogue wolves, me. Everyone. Do I make myself clear?"

Greg didn't mind playing nice with her, but the long list of people she'd mentioned before herself made his animal groan. That was one long list. With an arm stretched across his chest and an obedient bow her way, he uttered, "As you wish, my queen. I apologize for my earlier misbehavior . . . and every other misbehavior prior to that."

"Head up, Your Grace. It's time to discuss business." Greg's eyes met Lucy's when she continued, "Knowing you, you already have a plan in mind. Care to enlighten us?"

Enlighten her? With pleasure.

Enlighten his dim cousin? Ugh. Did he really have to? Wait, where was the other dim cousin? Never mind. The fewer fused bulbs, the better.

Shoving those thoughts aside, Greg said, "With your permission, Your Highness, I'd like to mind-link four from the ninety-eight lycans first, to meet you."

She shrugged and responded with a smile. "Alright, sure."

Greg instinctively matched her smile, which made Xandar glue her to the side again before Greg's eyes glazed over. *'Get in here. Four of you.'*

When his eyes cleared, Lucy asked, "So where are they? Where do we meet them?"

Greg watched his people walk in through four separate doors as he answered, "Here."

"Here?"

"As queen," Greg began matter-of-factly, "there's no need for you to travel to any part of the world to meet creatures, especially not rogues. They come to meet you." Goddess, why didn't she know that? Why didn't his cousin tell her that? Why give him the best mate if he didn't even know how to spoil the hell out of her?

Greg's thoughts were broken by Officer Katie suddenly yelling, "THAT'S IVORY HOFFMANN! ARREST HIM!"

"Oh no," Lucy muttered.

"Damn it," Greg cursed. Sprinting to Ivory, the duke shielded the man as he uttered to the police in a cold voice, "He's with me."

Officer Katie snarled, "Step aside, Your Grace. This man has b—"

"Katie, everyone, let them through. He's one of the ninety-eight." Lucy's firm voice cut through the space, and every policeman lowered their pistol or baton in compliance with their queen's order. But their fierce eyes stayed on the rogue and the duke.

As Greg and Ivory approached Lucy, Greg hissed, "What did I say about using contact lenses whenever you aren't in the Den?"

Ivory adjusted his eyepatch. "Well, we are meeting the queen, Your Grace. It didn't seem good to disguise my true face."

"Save those smart answers for the collaboration with less smart creatures, Ivory," Greg muttered after he couldn't think of a counterargument.

The duke looked ahead, a dominating, authoritative glint in his eyes as he snapped his fingers once. Lucy and Xandar followed his gaze and noticed that three lycans in caps with their heads hung low, leaning against the wall three feet from them, now looked up.

Lucy flinched at their presence. She didn't see them there.

Greg gestured the four of them to stand before the rulers as he stood next to Lucy, and everyone felt the awkwardness seep into the space. Lucy was about to thrust out her hand to start the introduction. But before she could, Greg exhaled hard and said, "I thought you four would have at least practiced."

Realization hit them, and they got down on one knee and bowed low before they greeted, "My queen."

Lucy's eyes widened, and she frantically said, "You really don't have to do that. Please, stand. All of you."

They stood and managed polite smiles before the upward curl of their lips flattened when they glanced at Xandar and then back at Greg. Greg said, "Yes, him too. I promised I'd play nice."

Their sights returned to Xandar. And with a synchronized curt nod, they reluctantly uttered, "Your Highness."

Anyone could feel the coldness in that greeting, maybe a little hate. Lucy tried her best to mask her discomfort as she suggested they continue the introduction in one of the empty interrogation rooms. Officer Katie and Deputy Chief Lauren requested to join them out of concern, and the rulers graciously thanked them for volunteering to sit in, allowing them to enter.

In the interrogation room, Lucy smiled and thrust her hand Ivory's way first "Ivory, was it?"

Ivory looked at her hand for two whole seconds before Greg sighed. "It's a handshake, Ivory. Seriously, what is wrong with the four of you today?"

Lucy turned to the duke. "Your Grace, playing nice includes your own people as well. I didn't think I had to tell you that."

Greg's eyes softened, visible enough for anyone to notice. "I'm sorry about this, my queen. These four are normally not this . . . slow."

Xandar snorted at that last word, which garnered everyone's attention and earned a glare from Greg.

Ivory got to it, giving Lucy a firm handshake with the same polite smile. "Ivory Hoffmann, ma'am. Arrested and indicted for involuntary manslaughter after a mining accident, and—"

He stopped at Greg's slight shake of the head. Lucy ignored the duke and urged, "Go on, Ivory."

"Well, um . . ." Ivory seemed uncertain, and his three teammates by his side thanked Goddess he went first.

Lucy uttered, "Ivory, it's okay. Just say what you were going to say."

Greg closed his eyes and pinched his nose before giving a wave of his hand, the green light for Ivory to answer. Ivory swallowed a lump in his throat and continued, "And um . . . after serving the sentence, I've worked under His Grace ever since."

"How long has it been?"

Ivory did a mental count before he said, "Forty-six years, ma'am."

"I see," Lucy muttered, then asked, "Is it because you've developed an interest in this line of work?"

Ivory scoffed at first but quickly turned it into an innocuous cough when he inadvertently met Greg's glare. Clearing his throat, he said, "Well, not at first, my queen. It's just . . ." he glanced at Xandar, who was also waiting for him to finish, so he did, "Convicted creatures don't get second chances in this kingdom. Not in this reign, not in the reigns before. Unless one could fabricate his professional history *and* change his face after being found guilty of a crime that grave, there really is no industry that would hire."

"I see," Lucy muttered again, sadness evident in her eyes and uneasiness obvious from her frown.

Greg noticed Xandar's thumb began stroking her waist, and the duke coped with the discomfort before his hand gesture signaled Ivory to wrap things up. "Anyway, that's in the past, ma'am. Money was an issue at first when I couldn't find a job, but after I began working with His Grace, the problem was solved. My ex-fiancé and daughter are doing quite well now, so all is w—"

"I'm sorry. Your ex-fiancé *and* daughter?" Lucy interrupted in disbelief.

Greg's animal wanted to tear its fur out. What were they thinking? They probably should have made his people rehearse with him before allowing them to meet the queen. Greg was considering making the introduction session stop at Ivory, but he knew that he wouldn't be able to stop Lucy if she was adamant about continuing this process with the next three. He prayed to the Goddess they wouldn't say too much. Whatever happened to the creatures before they were under his supervision was not her fault. The blame lay with his cousin, his uncle, and the kings before them, all of whom made no effort to change the system to offer second chances.

Watching Lucy's subtle look of guilt and despair now was pure torture. She shouldn't be blaming herself. She didn't know about any of this. When she was a wolf, she was subjected to equal—if not worse—discrimination from the entire lycan community.

Ivory gave up trying to guess what to say and what not to say. He was getting more and more confused by the minute. Besides, what was the worst that could happen if he told the queen everything? He was already going to be pardoned as long as he helped. With that in mind, he smiled and spoke to his heart's content, "Yes, ma'am. She was my chosen mate, and we were scheduled to be married a month after the mining accident. Intercourse was performed, but we saved marking for our wedding night, which is rather a relief in hindsight. Her job opportunities would've been narrowed as well if the employer knew she was marked by a felon."

Xandar then asked, "So what does she tell her employers?"

Ivory's lilac eyes had faint traces of onyx when he said, "That she slept with an untraceable creature after meeting him at a bar and became a single mother."

"And your daughter?" Lucy prompted, bringing his attention back to her.

Ivory smiled again. "Well provided for as soon as the duke offered me a job, ma'am. I visit my family once a week, and Iridessa, uh . . . my daughter, has been very good at keeping my anonymity."

"I see," Lucy repeated almost inaudibly, not knowing if any other response existed as her mind swirled around and around the information.

Ivory began to understand what the duke didn't want him to say when her voice weakened, so he added as cheerfully as he could, "Dessa graduated many years ago and is now an associate professor at Shlem University, my queen. So everything really *is* going well."

Lucy managed a forced smile. "That's good. What does she teach, if I may ask?"

Ivory grinned like a proud father. "Criminal justice, ma'am. Her approved thesis was on criminal psychology." Only when the words were out did he and Greg realize that there was one word that shouldn't have been in that sentence, and they both prayed that Lucy wouldn't catch it.

Fat chance.

Lucy's smile had faltered, brows drawn tight. "What do you mean *approved* thesis, Ivory?"

Ivory chuckled apologetically, knowing all too well that the duke was going to give him a full-hour lecture later. Alissa gave him an encouraging pat on the back while she held back a teasing smirk as Ivory responded, "Dessa wrote another two prior to that, but they were rejected by the faculty."

Please, no more questions. Please, no more questions. Please, no more questions, he prayed.

Prayers denied.

"And what topic were the rejected theses on, Ivory? Prisoner re-entry into society?"

Eyes bulged wide and brows raised from everyone around her, except Greg. The duke wasn't surprised she guessed that. Her ability to connect dots was one of the many reasons he fell for her in the first place.

Desmond, one of the four, turned to Hailey and muttered excitedly, "She's good, ain't she?" Hailey pressed back a smile and nodded subtly.

Ivory really wanted to wrap things up now so that Greg's lecture wouldn't be longer than it was already going to be. With a firm nod, he murmured, "W-Well, the full title was longer, but in essence, yes, it was prisoner re-entry, ma'am."

"I see," Lucy muttered yet again. "If it's not too much trouble, I hope I can get a copy of those theses. I don't know much about prisoner re-entry either. It'll be great to hear from someone who has gone through the trouble of researching."

Everyone froze, even Greg this time. As seconds passed, a smile replaced his shocked and frustrated features. He was touched, as was Ivory. Registering the silence, she asked doubtfully, "Unless the theses are no longer available?"

"No, Your Highness! They still exist. My wif—I mean, my ex-fiancé and I still have the hard copies. I'll fetch them on my next visit." A glimmer of hope appeared in Ivory's eyes. After so long, it felt like there was finally an authoritative figure who just . . . cared.

"That would be great. Thank you, Ivory."

When Lucy's sights moved to Hailey, Ivory sighed in relief, stepping to the side. Hailey smiled graciously as she shook the queen's outstretched hand and started speaking like a bullet train, "Hailey Hutchinson, ma'am. Former kindergarten teacher. Sued and found liable for civil negligence after one of the pups ingested six crayons during my supervision of a class of forty."

Lucy blinked a couple of times before she asked in disbelief, "*Six* crayons? Did those have a particularly flavorful taste?"

Greg found himself snorting and chuckling at her question. Amusement filled Xandar, too, until he heard his cousin's irritating chuckles, making his grip around his wife's waist tighten.

Hailey had to control her own laughter when she replied, "Well, um . . . I don't know about that, ma'am. But he did look like he was enjoying himself before I started panicking."

Lucy pondered. "So surgery was needed."

"Oh no, my queen. They gave him a laxative and got the feces out before sending it to the lab. I'm told that the substances in crayons are harmful to our digestive systems, but not fatal if they're removed within thirty-six hours. But my teaching career was over after that incident." Learning from Ivory's mistake, Hailey quickly added, "On the bright side, my queen, my negligence made kindergartens in many regions revise their operating procedure. One teacher for every ten children, to prevent these kinds of incidents from happening again. They didn't care about the extra costs of hiring more teachers anymore. The safety of the children finally came first, not second to their own pockets."

Lucy's steady eye contact held a degree of comfort when she said, "But your own employment opportunities were hindered nonetheless, weren't they, Hailey? Even though there are numerous other sectors that didn't pose a risk of pups ingesting crayons."

Like Ivory before, Hailey gave a firm nod before she muttered, "Yes. Negligence is . . . well, it's not wanted anywhere. Mistakes are . . . neither celebrated nor commended in any sector. If anything, it's a flaw that—when serious enough—can scar one for life. Errors might be tolerated in our younger years, but not in the workforce, unfortunately . . . or fortunately, depending on whether you're the person offering or receiving the service."

"Would you still have been teaching kindergartners had it not happened?" Lucy asked in curiosity.

No one had ever asked her that question. Hailey stared at the ceiling, then answered, "I think so. It seemed like the dream job. I was never one to go after those big, glamorous careers like being a doctor or lawyer. I just wanted a simple life. I do like baking. I guess I would've been a part-time baker and a kindergarten teacher, but I don't think I would do anything beyond that. I don't need a lot to be happy. Doing what I love keeps me happy, and teaching pups and baking muffins seemed more than enough."

Lucy cleared her throat to stop her voice from cracking when she said, "Teaching pups *is* a big dream, Hailey. It may not be big and glamorous to some, but choosing to dedicate your whole life to building the lives of future generations is not only huge but also noble. Don't let anyone tell you differently."

Hailey's lips parted, but no words came out as her eyes glistened. When she still had her dream job, it was never validated, valued, or praised to be "huge" or "noble" by even her closest friends and family. Never in her wildest dreams did Hailey imagine that an authority figure would be the one to make her feel like she had dreamt big.

Lucy touched her arm and whispered gently, "Are you alright, Hailey?"

Hailey was brought out of her daze. Blinking away the tears and turning to wipe away the excess, she chuckled and said, "Y-Yes, my queen. Thank you."

"No, Hailey. Thank *you*, for telling me all of this."

After Hailey offered her a gracious smile, Desmond pushed Alissa forward, his way of saying, "You go first." Alissa's eyes narrowed at Desmond before she turned to face the queen, shook her ready hand, and spoke with a wide smile and zero filter, "Alissa Arden, ma'am. Arrested, tried, and convicted for manslaughter after castrating my bonded mate and setting him on fire."

Lucy's eyes got an instant enlargement, and her brain sped up to keep up. That short sentence felt longer than it was. Taking it in, her black-and-lilac orbs narrowed in suspicion when she ultimately asked, "What did he do?"

Greg snorted again as one hand covered his mouth to hide his wide smile. This was actually getting quite entertaining. Xandar's hand went from Lucy's waist to her shoulder, where he pecked a kiss on her hair and hid his own smile while taking a whiff of her scent. This wasn't so bad for the king as long as he mentally blocked out his cousin.

Alissa seemed encouraged when even the duke was trying to mask his own amusement, so she continued speaking animatedly, "Oh, that's *quite* the story, ma'am. Let me tell you. So we met and found out we were bonded at a local grocery store. We both had someone at that time, but as soon as we met, he dumped his girlfriend on the spot, like right in front of me, which was *very* romantic at first blush. My then-boyfriend and I had a couple of years of history, so I was rather reluctant to just break up with him, you know? Anyway, I caved after a week, which is, by far, *the* biggest mistake of my life. My mate followed my boyfriend and me home without us knowing. After that, he just kept sending flowers and these cute messages that made me and my animal melt. When my boyfriend got mad and started threatening to end what we had if I didn't reject my mate soon, I uh . . ."

Alissa chuckled depressedly before saying, "I got really stupid. I thought that . . . him threatening to end our relationship meant that he was going to use that against me every time we had a fight. For some reason, my brain didn't remind me of all the other times we fought, when he never said that he would leave me if I didn't give in. We always found a middle ground. Everything worked. Not immediately, but it eventually worked. We even ended up strengthening what we had with each argument. But not this last time."

She paused to take a breath. "Being . . . blinded, I dumped him, and even had the audacity to move in with my mate the very same day I moved out from my boyfriend's place, utterly convinced that he was the one. For an entire year, things with my mate were . . ." her eyes zoned out as she reminisced about the past ". . . great, really. The romance made my heart flutter like butterflies; the sex was addicting. We even had a set of triplets together. The only problem was that he never seemed to want to let me mark him, nor did he want to mark me. The reason . . . no, that's not the correct word. *Excuse* is better. The excuse he gave was that he wanted us to be deeply in love first, then mark each other. I was confused, but I didn't say anything, thinking that everything would eventually work itself out. Goddess, was I wrong."

Despite her smile, they saw the pain and anger in her eyes when she continued, "After that magical year, his job suddenly required him to work late, sometimes a little too late. And it was weird when he smelled . . . clean when he got back, like he took a shower before he returned. Strawberry body wash. When I got suspicious and started asking questions, he just said I was being paranoid and that his heart was mine before throwing in a sex session to stave off my doubts. Then one day, we ran into his ex at a park. It was the day I realized he was still seeing her behind my back."

Alissa started staring at the floor with a sad smile. "They were both shocked to see each other there, but it wasn't an awkward shock. He just looked like he was trying to avoid getting caught when he turned away and dragged me along. She wasn't embarrassed or anything and just . . . smirked at me. My brain finally started working right. I stormed to her just to smell her. And there it was— strawberry." A film of moisture began forming in her eyes, tears of rage. "The most *monstrous* thing was that she didn't even budge, like she wanted me to smell her, to rub it in my face that my mate was seeing her, fucking her. I pushed her into the fountain, and my mate . . . went to help her out. It was as clear as day after that. He slept with her and showered at her place before coming back to me and our children."

Shaking her head with a self-critical curl of her lips, one shoulder shrugged when she deduced, "Everything made sense. His sudden need to work overtime, his unexplainable clean scent, the fact that he never wanted us to mark each other. He wouldn't be able to sleep with another woman behind my back without me knowing if we were marked, so he delayed it and used it to his advantage. The butterflies I felt turned into a traumatized experience of betrayal. I was so angry that I couldn't speak, couldn't scream. Everything just began to bottle up inside, and my mind went . . . oddly calm and quiet. He brought us home and apologized, saying that he wouldn't see her anymore, that I was his 'one and only,' though he still insisted that we hold off the marking. I didn't speak for the entire hour after that. I just stared at him blankly. I was hurt, but I don't understand why I didn't cry. I just sat there, feeling the fire burning in me. My animal was unusually quiet too.

"I tucked the kids in, as usual, and it was the first time my mate helped. We went to bed, and he dozed off quite quickly. Naked—this is an important detail. You'll see why. Anyway, after two hours of staring into space, it was like something overtook me. I got out of bed, went to the kitchen, got a knife, a lighter, and a bottle of wine, and made my way back to the bedroom. And uh . . ." she caught Hailey and Ivory's slight shake of their heads, so Alissa decided to end her story with ". . . well, I'm sure you know what happened from there, my queen. I'll spare you the details."

"I want the details, Alissa. Do go on," Lucy insisted with large eyes like she was watching a movie and was secretly rooting for the female lead—Alissa herself.

Alissa's eyes widened for a moment before she chuckled lightly. "I pulled over his covers when he lay flat on his back, poured half a bottle of wine around the frame of his body, chopped off his balls, heard him scream when I poured the remaining wine all over his body, and then used the lighter to . . . light him up?"

The men around her cringed as subtly as they could, but their discomfort was still visible from their faces. Greg, Ivory, and Desmond had heard the story before, but it didn't make it any less mortifying.

Xandar, in his silence, was finding her story more and more familiar by the second. When it hit him, he murmured in realization, "You're Arson Arden." She looked so different from the time she was tried. Her hair used to be longer, and her face was haggard even from the pictures. Now, Arson Arden looked fresher and healthier, and her hair only reached her chin.

Greg was glaring daggers at his cousin, not that Xandar cared.

Alissa forced herself to face Xandar as she suppressed the hate as much as possible, "Yes, Your Highness. That was what they called me in every news report."

Lucy remembered this case too. "But the news didn't mention the events leading up to that incident. They just reported that you started the fire because of a so-called common relationship issue, making it seem like you overreacted. And what was worse was that your then-mate said that you were mentally unstable."

Alissa nodded in confirmation. "Which was all fiction, I must add, my queen. He came up with events that never even happened. His rich family practically fabricated evidence that the court accepted without question because I couldn't produce evidence to contradict whatever the prosecutor submitted. And I was seen as the crazy one in court when I screamed my lungs out to deny the assertions."

This was getting more wrong by the minute. The queen recalled the last bit of facts. "Even when your lawyer tried to use the mental instability argument to your advantage, pleading diminished responsibility to absolve you from as much blame as possible, it didn't really work. Your sentence was lightened so little that it was almost negligible. And your children were taken away because no relatives were willing to take them in, while the court found you unfit to be a mother."

"Yeah, that was . . . definitely what happened." Alissa forced a brief smile before wiping away her own tears. "But uh . . ." she looked at Greg, her way of asking for permission, which he granted with a nod. Alissa said, "I've seen them grow up. All three were adopted by different families, and I make time to see each one."

With a hopeful twinkle in her eyes, Lucy asked, "Have you met them?"

Alissa shook her head. "It's too risky, my queen. My case took six years to complete. And in the years I've been in police custody and court, my triplets were raised by creatures who told them that their mother was a psychiatric patient who incapacitated their father, who then subsequently died from his injuries. I've thought about meeting them, telling them, but with the law and history against me, I came to terms with the fact that they might report me to the police, who would then take me away. I didn't see them for six years because of what I did to my bonded mate. I can't risk not seeing them for Goddess knows how long more if I'm caught and put behind bars again."

"That's understandable," Lucy mused.

Gently detaching herself from Xandar's grip, she stepped forward and wrapped Alissa in a hug. The mother who lost her triplets was shocked. But her animalistic instinct made her squeeze the queen in return as tears flowed down her cheeks when Lucy whispered, "I am so sorry, Alissa."

The sight even made Xandar sad. Arson Arden. How could the media label someone who was treated so badly by combining their name with a crime like it was funny or catchy? It was so insensitive and inhumane. The system back then even confirmed a creature to be clinically insane just because her mate had the means to fabricate such evidence? And the fact that she denied it in court by screaming just magically cemented the fiction that she was insane? What bullshit! How was it that the need to authenticate evidence never crossed the judge's or lawyers' minds?

Greg watched the two women in each other's arms and was moved. Lucy had no responsibility over what happened to Alissa, yet it was so obvious that she cared. Greg didn't recall a single instance where his late aunt, Queen Vera, would take the mildest interest in a subject. Heck! The late queen didn't even take an interest in him, and he was her nephew!

Lucy was now listening to her people's plight like she was a friend or a sister, even when she didn't have to. Everything about her was just so . . . different.

After Alissa felt a little better, she loosened her grip, and the queen got the cue to let the woman go. Alissa offered her a firm nod and a smile as a sign of gratitude, and Lucy returned her gesture before turning toward Desmond.

Desmond approached her with a wide grin and extended his hand. "Sup, queen? The name's Desmond Derulos."

Xandar's brows raised for two reasons. One, for the informal way Desmond was speaking to Lucy, who—in Xandar's eyes—was the most powerful creature in the kingdom. Two, for the very reason that Desmond Derulos was the infamous con artist who posed as CEO of a ghost company that sucked trillions out of investors. The king's sights moved to his wife, who showed no animosity toward Desmond, so Xandar continued to watch in silence.

Desmond continued, "Professional pickpocket and former con. Arrested and convicted for con work."

Lucy smiled in recognition. Her eyes shone with interest as she acknowledged in realization, "The Money Retriever."

Desmond chuckled. "Yeah. Wasn't good at covering my tracks at that time. Only got better when the boss hired me." His head motioned toward Greg, who was pressing his fingers against his lips to hide his smile, which was very hard to hold back.

The general public called Desmond the Money Retriever, but Desmond had been pinned as one of the most wanted criminals by law enforcement. What was fascinating about this crime was that he only conned wealthy business people who were exploiting their employees by paying them abusively less while taking most of the profits and dividends for themselves.

Desmond's heist began with researching the creatures he'd go after first, then attending events that his targets would attend. At the event, he would single them out and make an impression with sophisticated mannerisms and language while displaying just the right amount of confidence and charm when talking about the likely success of his fictitious business ventures to lure his victims in. Those who met him without knowing he was a fake later testified that Desmond appeared well-mannered, poised, and posh and was the epitome of a successful businessman.

If someone who wasn't his target expressed an interest in investing, Desmond would act pompous and wave them off like they weren't worthy of being his investor. But the truth was that Desmond didn't want to con the non-targets for money because those were good people who treated their staff right. After bagging the targets, Desmond would disappear.

On every Nouvelan, Desmond took all the money he collected and dispensed the sums in equal amounts to the abused employees with the message, "Happy Nouvelan. M.R." The thing that warmed Desmond's heart was when these employees posted pictures or videos of themselves expressing their thanks on the Internet, saying that the money helped in paying rent, buying daily necessities, getting insurance, or even getting new clothes and toys for their children.

Sadly, the heist only lasted four years before he was caught around two decades ago, before Xandar ascended the throne. The investors were elated, of course, and demanded the justice system make Desmond repay every last dime they were cheated out of, even asking for compensation for the "traumatizing experience."

But Desmond didn't have the amount of money he'd stolen since he had already given it away. The victimized investors knew about their employees' windfalls, which came merely months after they were conned of their money, and sought a court order to make their employees return the amounts.

The only problem? There was no hard evidence showing that the investment money given to Desmond was the "same money" that was later channeled to the employees. Desmond conned a few companies at once and pooled everything into one account. Essentially, the money was "mixed" before being used to make legitimate investments in legal, reputable businesses, and Desmond took the sum back out along with the small amounts of dividends made a few months later.

Now, this "new" money was considered to be Desmond's earnings from smart investing. Since the money was his in legal terms, it was *his* money that went to the abused employees. It was no longer the employers' money. Therefore, the court couldn't grant a court order and the recipients of Desmond's heist were legally allowed to keep the money.

Desmond was convicted of money laundering and theft, which carried a measly fine compared to the hefty amounts he took and gave away over the years. The biggest blow for the investors was that their stolen funds couldn't be recovered when Desmond filed for bankruptcy when he couldn't pay the fine. And since he had almost no assets that could be seized and sold, none of the investors were ever paid back. To say that they were furious would be putting it too lightly. Most of them resorted to taking matters into their own hands. Assassins were sought out and hired, which was where Greg came in.

Lucy uttered, "So you weren't abducted and taken hostage like what the media presumed after your disappearance from police custody. You disappeared because the duke offered shelter and protection."

"*And* tutorials to up my skills," Desmond added like an excited friend. "Ain't like those college classes but like real practice in the field, ya know? And that ain't even the best part. 'Cause the boss is this big guy in the rogue world, I became 110 percent bulletproof. The boss told those killers that if they touched me, he'd burn their family and friends. Ain't that great?"

Xandar's brows raised at what Desmond termed "great." He looked at his cousin leaning against the wall and had to ask, "You weren't really going to do that, were you?"

Greg's eyes reluctantly met Xandar's disapproving scowl as he declared in a low voice, "I don't make empty threats, Cousin. It's not good for my reputation. And the plan was never to burn them to death, just to incapacitate them so creatures would think more than twice before crossing me."

Sensing the rising tension, Lucy quickly moved the conversation along with the rogue. "I've been itching to know something for years, Desmond: did you have everyone in your net before you were caught?"

Desmond's smile froze for a second before he glanced at the duke with an excited grin. "I like her, boss. She cool."

Greg rolled his eyes but was also finding it hard to suppress his smile. "Get on with it, Desmond. The queen asked you a question."

Desmond continued, "Damn, ya're a cool queen. And if ya askin' 'bout that game I pulled off twenty-two years ago, then, no. There were three more on the loose. Din get to bag them on time, ya know?"

Greg wasn't sure how to feel about his people over-talking anymore. He found it amusing when they spoke about their pasts because Lucy's follow-up questions were more hilarious than awkward, and the fact that she displayed no disapproval was not only surprising but also encouraging.

Even so, Greg felt that she shouldn't have to carry the emotional baggage of people she hardly knew. She was a queen, not a therapist. Then again, wouldn't the best queen be one who at least took the trouble to get to know her people, no matter what their pasts were and what society labeled them as?

As Greg's mind trapped itself in this conflicted loop, he eagerly awaited another one of her brilliant follow-up questions that was nowhere near predictable. The suspense had his animal wagging its tail in excitement and his heart pounding in anticipation.

Upon hearing that Desmond didn't get everyone he was out to con, Lucy frowned. "Well, that's a bummer."

Greg snorted, and Desmond chuckled. "Yeah. Tough playin' superhero when ya play alone, ya know what I'm sayin'?"

"I do," Lucy nodded with a smile, easily relating when Toby and so many others came to mind. She glanced at Ivory, Hailey, and Alissa, commenting, "Good that you have a team now, then."

"Oh, this ain't the team, Queen. We all just the top four. Boss's team is huge!" Desmond said with pride.

Lucy turned to Greg. "I guess I shouldn't expect anything less."

Xandar then whispered into her ear, "But if it's so huge, how have they been moving about? We have policemen and warriors on constant duty in all corners of lycan territory."

She whispered back, "They probably used clever disguises and scent sprays, darling."

Desmond clapped once like he had just won a game of bingo and pointed at Lucy. "Ya're good, ya know that? Man, if ya ain't queen, boss will definitely take ya in."

Xandar's hand went from her waist to her abdomen as he held her even closer. Possessiveness surged through him. Lucy then spoke to him in a gentle, assuring voice, "Darling, relax. That was purely hypothetical."

Greg begged to differ. He would have *definitely* taken her in . . . No, that wasn't an accurate way of putting things. If Lucy weren't the queen, she'd be the first creature Greg would *beg* to let him take under his wing . . . but she might have to humiliate him before a crowd first, like she did in the dining hall when they first met. It was her creative comeback and killer retort at that time that sparked the interest Greg had in her, and the interest turned into admiration before it deepened into something far greater than anything he could ever imagine feeling.

"Shh . . . Xandar, we're okay. We're okay. Shh . . ." Lucy's hushed cooing brought Greg out of his thoughts, and the duke finally noticed that his cousin's glare was on him while Lucy was stroking her husband's cheeks. Realization dawned on the duke that he'd been staring at the queen for too long. With extreme difficulty, he rolled his eyes before looking the other way to avoid having to see Xandar place a statement kiss on Lucy's head.

When that was settled, Greg asked whether Lucy would prefer to meet the rest of his people at the station to discuss the plan. At this point, Lucy expressed her wish to go to the rest instead of having them come to her. Greg seemed reluctant to allow her to make the trip to the Den, purely because she had the power and status to *demand* anyone's presence, but when Alissa and Ivory mind-linked him about how it was better to bring her there and to come clean of everything they had in their arsenal from the very start, the duke gave in.

Ivory tossed Greg the car keys, which the duke swiftly caught like he'd done it a hundred times before, and the two of them, along with Alissa, got into Greg's car. Xandar and Lucy tailed them; Hailey and Desmond followed behind; and Lauren, Katie, and Dave came behind them in two separate police cars.

CHAPTER 21

Lucy was looking out the window, eyes large and bright—a sight that Xandar never got over admiring. He reached for her hand, wanting to talk to her, hear her voice. "How did you know to trust them?"

"Hm. What was that, darling?" She blinked herself out of her daze.

The shine in her eyes never ceased to make his heart skip a beat. With one hand on the steering wheel, he placed a kiss on her knuckles, explaining, "Greg's team, baby. How did you know to trust them?"

She shrugged. "They had more to lose than to gain by backstabbing us. Besides, it didn't feel like they were up to no good."

That got him thinking. "How did you . . . *feel* it though?"

"Like how anyone feels it, Xandar. That instinct built in our subconscious that tells us whether someone is good or . . . not so good. Humans have it too. Ours is better, of course, thanks to our animals' heightened awareness and all of that."

"So you just . . . felt that they were okay?"

"Yeah. You did too."

Xandar cackled in laughter. He thought she was joking, until she didn't laugh along. Brows arched, smile still intact—one of incredulity—he said, "Babe, c'mon. We both know that's not true."

Her brows rose. "You're doubting the instinct of the most powerful animal in the kingdom, my king?"

"For the record, the most powerful creature in this kingdom is *you*, my love. And I never doubted yours or your animal's instinct."

Under her breath, she muttered, "You've got to be kidding me." Adjusting herself in her seat so she faced him, she persisted arguing, "Xandar, your animal didn't feel any danger from them. If it did, it wouldn't have let me stand anywhere close to Ivory and the others. You would have pushed me to the back, using yourself as a shield, like when we thought the vampires were going to attack the other night in Polje."

Xandar felt his animal concede, but something still didn't sit right with him. "I wasn't completely comfortable back there, though."

"Yeah, but was that because of them or because of your cousin?" Xandar's grip instantly tightened before he sighed and loosened his hold. Unrelenting, she said, "Let's try this, Xandar: when you heard about their pasts, what did you feel?"

"What do you mean?" Xandar doubted he felt anything.

"Did you feel the threat of danger, sadness, happiness—"

"Goddess, definitely not happiness. What happened to them is wrong in so many ways."

"Exactly," she mused. "If they weren't good people, you wouldn't feel like they had been wronged after what they did. Think about it. You've met many creatures in your years as crown prince and king. How often have your preliminary instincts about creatures you just met been wrong, especially as you aged?" She gave him a moment before continuing, "Creatures with the right moral compass have the ability to feel anyone with accuracy, Xandar. Those of us with a firm set of principles and values have an innate ability to detect both good and bad intentions, from one's choice of words and actions, if not from one's presence. When we allow our animals to guide us in meeting new people or gauging a new situation in an unknown environment, some part of us just . . . knows how to differentiate between good and bad."

Xandar's smile broadened by the second. Pulling his car to a stop at a red light, his gaze fell upon hers when he said, "You're amazing, Lucy."

The usual warmth crept up her cheeks as she pressed her lips in a thin line only to fail at suppressing her smile. Her hand reached for his chest, resting right over his beating heart. Her touch was so gentle that it blurred out his surroundings, so assuring that he'd never felt more at peace, and so warm that he had never felt more loved.

With a soft gaze, she whispered, "Try to . . . be consciously aware of how your animal really feels in new situations with new creatures, Xandar. Trust what you feel. It'll hardly ever be wrong. I doubt it was wrong very often in your past."

Xandar leaned in and brushed a kiss on her temple before Lucy pushed him back to his seat when she noticed the lights turned green. Xandar chuckled and began driving again. "Now that I think about it, I did always have the urge to scratch the Kyltons' faces whenever either of them spoke, especially when my late parents forced me to sit through hours of nonsensical chit-chat with them."

"There you go." Lucy leaned back into her seat, a satisfied smile plastered across her face like she'd completed a task.

A mischievous glint entered Xandar's eyes. "So that means I should've scratched their faces all those years ago. It would've saved us a whole lot of trouble."

He felt his wife's glare aimed at him, her sudden urgency to retort surged through their bond, but when she opened her mouth with the intention to protest, no words came out. She ended up pausing, then pondering. Her urge to fight him diminished, gradually replaced by concurrence, although reluctant concurrence. Smirking, she said, "Well played, my king. Well played."

"So you agree?" Xandar asked, excited that this was one of the rare occasions that he could persuade her that spontaneous violence was the right way forward.

"I'm not supposed to." She was finding it harder to press back her smile. "But you do."

"Let's just say, as queen, I don't agree."

Another roar of laughter escaped him. "Oh, c'mon, babe. You can't deny your animal's instinct."

"You're right, just as my animal can't deny my logic and rationality. We coexist to balance out each other."

Xandar shook his head slowly at her rebuttal before he sighed. "Lucy, you are amazingly frightening and incredibly sexy when you're inhumane. You really don't have to restrain yourself from being merciless sometimes."

"I don't, Xandar. I just . . . want violence to be the last resort, that's all."

"Because you're the queen?" Xandar teased.

"Because I believe in second chances," she answered simply. "Some creatures do change for the better. I'm not just talking about Greg. I've seen so many before him making that change. Tate, Lovelace, Raden, and numerous others from so many packs." She paused when a thought came to her. "Our animal's intuition is great to gauge how careful we ought to be in the present. But the downside of it is that it can't sense if a creature is capable of changing. It can only detect the energies and intentions at a given time. If we act on it without letting time show us that someone is capable of being . . . better, we might be prematurely eliminating a possible ally and destroying a possible relationship that could blossom into a lifelong friendship. As much as I trust my animal's instinct, I also trust my own logic and intuition, which is more inclined to consider future possibilities."

In all seriousness, Xandar asked, "You're saying you considered that Greg . . . could change?"

"Honestly, no. Greg's case was very unexpected. If I were being honest, I thought I'd kill him myself before the end of the collaboration last year."

"What changed?"

"He did. He committed a long list of heinous acts in the past, Xandar, but despite the difficulties he'd face in coming forward, despite the losses he'd suffer by giving himself up, he still chose to do it. That not only takes courage, it also takes an insane amount of humility. You heard what he said about him never making empty threats to keep his reputation intact. His reputation was compromised in the rogue world the moment he chose to side with the government. But he did it anyway."

"And we both know why he did," Xandar muttered in dissatisfaction before he stopped at another traffic light and leaned in to kiss her lips. Staring intensely into her eyes, his deep voice reverberated through her ears, "I do trust you, baby. And I know you'll be with me despite how Greg feels, but it's just really . . . agitating when he looks at you like that."

Lucy's eyes narrowed. "I hope you see the irony here, dearest. You're not the one who has to resist scratching someone's eyes out every time we go shopping."

"What do you mean?" Xandar started driving again.

Turning to him in disbelief, she questioned, "You didn't feel my annoyance on those trips?" A small part of her felt overlooked, and feelings of abandonment began crawling in. Those instances got intense. He must have felt *something*. Why didn't he?

Their conversation paused when the convoy came to a steady halt at the far end of town with no soul in sight, only ruins from abandoned construction projects. It was so quiet and dusty that eeriness exuded.

Greg pressed open a tiny compartment on his steering wheel and tapped on the small red button there twice. Paused. Tapped another three times. Pause. And twice again. His phone screen lit up, the device echoing in a robotic voice, "Requesting voice recognition."

In a commanding tone, he said, "Make sure everyone is in the lounge. Be ready to greet the queen." His systems were programmed to recognize his voice, but the added feature sent out instructions if he urgently required any of his people's presence and assistance.

The same robotic voice responded, "Identity confirmed. Welcome home, Your Grace."

Greg continued driving forward as Xandar, Lauren, and the others began wondering whether they were driving right into a trap. Just when Xandar was about to say something, large metal floor panels covered by sand and rusty construction materials folded upward to reveal a route that seemed to lead to an underground tunnel. They followed Greg's car and came to a well-lit parking space. As soon as Lauren and his followers were in, Greg shut the panels.

Xandar parked in a random lot, then turned to his wife and asked, "Weren't you only annoyed on those shopping trips because the books, clothes, or shoes weren't to your taste?"

Lucy frowned and exclaimed with elaborated hand gestures, "Are you kidding me, Xandar? You want to talk about shopping when your cousin just opened a freaki—"

Waving his hand, he interrupted, "Yeah, yeah, that was all very impressive, but really, baby, those weren't the things that bothered you on those trips?"

She decided to just go with what her husband wanted to talk about for now. "No! Xandar, seriously? How could you not see the sales staff, cashiers, waitresses, and female customers look at you like they would gladly submit to you as and when you please?"

He pecked a kiss on her nose to calm her increasing agitation before explaining in defense, "Forgive me, my little freesia. I was preoccupied with trying to subtly scare off any man looking at my wife like I wasn't right next to her. Why do you think I've always kissed your hand that holds your ring? It's to show those fucking bastards that you're *taken*. By *me*." Lucy paused, registering that she was neither overlooked nor emotionally abandoned, then blinked to retrieve the memories of which hand he kissed on those occasions, not knowing that Xandar was far from done complaining when he added, "And can I just say that I have it way worse? Even the little boys seem to be so mesmerized by you that the toys in their hands don't seem to be able to hold their attention."

Lucy calmed down a little after Xandar's kiss, and her mood improved further now because she still found it amusing that he had the tendency to be jealous of little boys. With a smile playing at her lips, her hand reached out to stroke his shoulder. "Don't worry, my indecent beast." A low, appreciative growl filled the space between them before Lucy added in a conspiratorial whisper, "I'll only reciprocate Russell's attention."

His dreamy gaze widened in shock as his smile fell. Lucy dashed out of the car with a chuckle and a grin, closing the door behind her, effectively cutting her mate off when he was exclaiming, "WHA—"

When Xandar got out, he heard her saying, "Lead the way, Your Grace."

Greg nodded with a small tug of his lips and approached a white wall.

Xandar was at Lucy's side in an instant, his arm on her lower back. "You didn't play fair, sweetheart."

"How do you think I almost always win, darling?" Her smile pulled at Xandar's heartstrings, making him give in to his urge to squeeze the flesh at her waist before kissing her temple.

From afar, the white wall in the underground parking space looked innocuous enough to match any normal wall. Up close, there was a row of very subtle, minute, vertical lines, like they were carved there for decorative purposes. Greg didn't even need to count from the far left to know which line was the fifty-second one, and he inserted his car key into the slit before giving it a twist. When he pulled the key back out, the wall raised.

So it wasn't a wall. But a concrete roller shutter.

Lucy's eyes grew in wonder and awe at the sight, which was when Desmond exclaimed, "Ain't that cool, Queen?"

Greg cringed at the informality and threw a disapproving glare at Desmond, making a mental note to talk to this one about basic—incredibly basic—formalities. Desmond's attention was still on Lucy when she said, "Very cool." The awe in her tone soothed Greg's irritation. He could almost picture the shine in her eyes. And it took a lot of restraint not to turn around and start staring at her.

Lauren and the other policemen remained wary.

But Alissa, Hailey, and Ivory smiled at the queen's words. They could see how their boss had fallen for her. The queen was so . . . real, expressive, and open-minded for a royal. And they could tell that when they spoke to her about their pasts, she wasn't just listening out of duty, sympathy, or with the intention to judge. They felt her sincerity ooze. She listened to understand and feel their plight, making them feel heard and less alone.

Behind the cement roller shutter were motion-detecting glass doors that opened to each side as they stepped into another space with beige-tiled floors. A small, black-colored cubical device was right in the middle of another white wall with a mahogany door at the far right. After Greg punched in a twelve-digit code on the cube, the device scanned his retina before the door opened with a click.

In a hushed, excited tone, Lucy exclaimed, "So cool!"

Xandar loved seeing her being a curious cat, but maybe not when it came to this cousin's stuff. He placed a kiss on her temple to remind her that he loved her so much he would give her anything, and if this extensive security system was what she wanted, he would make it happen.

Greg finally allowed himself to look at her before gesturing at the door his people just went through. "After you, my queen."

As she approached the entrance, Xandar mind-linked her, asking if this was what she wanted for them. She looked at her husband with narrowed eyes. *'Darling, we don't need this system. We're not being shunned from society or hunted down by the authorities. I like it, but it doesn't mean I want it.'*

He smiled and whispered, "Okay," by her ear.

The moment they stepped through the door, Lucy froze at the sight. Ninety-four lycans in the large-spaced lounge were down on one knee with their heads hung low as they echoed in firm synchronicity, "My queen."

Greg's voice echoed through the lounge, "And her mate too."

Some of them raised their heads to glance at Xandar before they all muttered with blatant reluctance, "Your Highness."

Lucy slid an arm around her husband's biceps. Any ordinary creature could feel the chill in that greeting. They didn't even want to acknowledge Xandar as their king, only greeting him by royal address. Not wanting to let the room go quiet for too long, she smiled and said, "Rise. All of you."

When they did, most were already smiling her way, getting the gist of what she was like from the top four. In the crisp silence, Lucy added, "Don't take this the wrong way, but please don't do that again. I'm quite fine with a smile and a wave, or a simple handshake, really."

Surprisingly to the authorities but unsurprisingly to the top four, all eyes moved to Greg, which was a clear indication of who was in charge here in the Den. It didn't matter that Lucy was queen. The duke was still number one here. These were *his* people.

Hearing her words made Greg smile. So humble. So perfect. With a firm nod, he obliged, "As you wish, my queen."

"Thank you, Your Grace."

A familiar ringtone blared through the quiet space. Lucy's eyes widened, and embarrassment took over as she rummaged through her bag.

The lit screen read: "Pelly."

CHAPTER 22

Shoving aside thoughts of how good the reception was underground, she turned and picked up the call.

"Pelly?"

The response came out ominously, "Aunt Lucy, there's been another abduction. Twenty adults and two children have been taken from another village, Saber Vagary."

Lucy's neck stiffened, and her facial expression squinted in despair. "How far was this from the Falling Vines?"

"Twenty-three miles north."

"Without bloodshed?"

"Without bloodshed," Pelly confirmed. "We're still here and everything seems the same. Lycan and werewolf scents, which—we're positive—would fade to reveal the proditors that were here. The prints are like the last time as well—some real, some fake."

"Have your trackers managed to follow the trail from the last abduction?"

"Maddock sent sixteen vigils after your visit, but the trail was lost before they recovered any further clues. They've been suspended since, and Maddock has been stripped of his title."

Lucy blinked repeatedly before she found her voice again. "I'm sorry, what?" Pelly suspended sixteen vigils and a viscount? Well, now a former viscount. The vigil suspension came as a great shock because vigils were not just policemen but high-ranking investigative officers who were talented, skilled, and trustworthy figures, loyal only to the imperial family. A vampire had to have served for at least a century *and* done some form of noble work to be *considered* for this exclusive role.

Pelly couldn't fathom how what she said was hard to understand, but she responded nonetheless, "Octavia and I suspended Maddock for a week, along with those he sent who came back with nothing but an apology."

"Don't you only have thirty-two vigils in your empire, Pelly?" Lucy had been reading up on everything about vampires since the empress's first email. She remembered this particular fact easily since being a vigil would be her dream job if she were a vampire.

"That's right. The suspension ought to keep the remaining half on their toes."

Lucy reminded herself that Pelly had been ruling for centuries, so she would know what she was doing, and chose to ask, "Did the suspended ones find anything? Anything at all?"

"They followed the trail from Falling Vines toward the south, where the weather wasn't as sunny. Crossed over three rivers. Ran through a forest and an abandoned castle."

"So they went inside the castle?"

"Yes, they followed the trail through a broken front window and went to the second floor, and the scent was strongest at another window on that floor, which faces the second forest, the Forest of Oderem. Once they took two steps in, the trail was, understandably, lost."

Lucy knew about the Forest of Oderem too. Many did. It was an ancient, scent-confusing place. The forest itself produced its own odors that could be anything, from as wonderful as a field of flowers or as delicious as freshly baked pastries, to as foul as decomposed bodies.

It was grown by Count Dracula, who paid a witch for enchanted seeds that eventually grew into this forest. Dracula either brought the man he owned in there for private moments or lured his enemies into the forest before using the confusing scents to lure them deeper in and ultimately killing them and feeding on their blood. It was a nightmare for the authorities but a dream come true for proditors seeking refuge.

A snarl came when Pelly added, "That forest should have been burned a long time ago."

"Pelly, we both know why no one can do that."

Many emperors had tried to get rid of the Forest of Oderem, but their attempts were not only futile, but also it was a guaranteed way to suffer from some kind of misfortune. Some emperors who tried had their closest confidantes fall ill from unknown illnesses and die a painfully slow death; some lost their spouses; others even lost their only child—their heir—effectively ending their ruling bloodline.

"How about this, Pelly? Let Xandar and I meet the suspended ones. They might have seen more than they know."

There was a pause, and then Pelly's voice came out with visible relief. "That would be wonderful, Aunt Lucy. When?"

"I'm a little occupied right now, so . . . tomorrow evening?"

"Sounds good. We'll get them ready."

"Thanks, Pelly."

Her voice came out less exhausted, more hopeful. "Thanks for helping us with this. Send mine and Octavia's love to Uncle Xandar."

Lucy chuckled. "Will do. See you soon."

After hanging up and heaving a sigh, she returned to her husband's side and told him and Greg everything. Xandar's thumb on her shoulder started drawing comforting circles as he combated the frustration with her.

When the facts came to an end, Greg questioned in disbelief, "Isn't the Forest of Oderem like any normal forest, my queen? The thing about fake scents is merely a fairy tale spun by some author to teach children to avoid wandering into unknown places exuding pleasant scents, isn't it?"

Fairy tale? Where did that come from? Xandar's brows knotted in confusion for a brief second before he realized that Greg remembered the enchanted forest from a children's bedtime storybook, making him snort before burying the bottom half of his face in Lucy's hair to hide the teasing smirk and chuckles.

Lucy's hand fell gently on her husband's arm. "Darling, be nice. It really did exist in a fairy-tale book before we all learned the real thing in school."

When the king managed to compose himself, an amusing smile was still stretched wide when he commented not too loudly, "Greg, I knew you were bad at history, but I didn't think you were this bad. Goddess, a fairy tale."

Although only Greg's top four heard the king, Greg was still embarrassed that his weakest subject back in school was disclosed in front of the queen, so he argued in defense, "To be fair, Cousin, that class was nothing but a *nuisance*. What's with the mandatory requirement about needing to take history, forcing us to know every little thing about the past? It's in the fucking past! Leave the damn thing there and move the hell on!"

"Darling, seriously, stop," Lucy pleaded as Xandar continued trying to hold back his chuckles. She was neither smiling nor laughing at that moment, but Xandar's burst of humor through their bond was making it harder for her to fight against the urge to laugh with him.

Facing the slightly red-faced Greg, Lucy spoke with as much composure as she could manage, "I'd like to meet everyone, Your Grace. Shall we start with the introductions?"

"Of course. Right this way, my queen," Greg responded instantly as he gestured her to the first lycan on his left.

The fact that she was speaking to Greg replaced Xandar's humor with possessiveness, making him hold his wife close as they approached the first lycan. They spent the next few hours shaking hands and getting a brief background on the ninety-four lycans, who were pleased to meet her but still showed some resistance toward Xandar despite Lucy's repeated attempts to let them know that he had helped her argue for pardon to be granted.

Like Greg, they knew where the true power lay, and they felt it was with her because their lives had been stuck in a rut until she came along. Pardon was in the law for aesthetic purposes. It was almost never granted. If any police, warrior, or king heard about them living in the shadows, they would never be in a position to bargain once they were found.

Some of them were skeptical when they heard that Greg was surrendering their presence at first, but now that they'd met the queen, they couldn't help but concur that they would have done the same thing if they were him. The queen might not admit to having vetoed anything in the meeting when pardon was discussed, but her presence brought a change, not just in their boss but also in the kingdom. She was giving them a chance they had never gotten from anyone else but Greg.

When the introductions were done, the authority figures followed Greg through a cream-colored corridor that had so many turns that it felt like they were in a maze. There were doors the entire way in, but some were actually red herrings—opening up to walls, not rooms. It was a precaution taken to buy time to escape if they were ever found.

They finally entered a room with the same cream walls with a rectangular glass table placed in the middle. What was odd was that there were no chairs. Not one.

When the last policeperson entered, Hailey closed the door. Greg placed his palm flat on the table. A faint blue glow scanned his handprint horizontally, vertically, and around the shape of his palm before the blue words "ACCESS GRANTED" appeared in the middle of the table.

Lucy's eyes widened in awe again as Greg tapped on a button that was so subtle that one couldn't see it because it looked like it was part of the glass. A clear hologram appeared right in the middle, floating right above the table. The duke opened up a map of all territories, zooming in just enough to identify the inhabitants around Falling Vines and Saber Vagary.

Deputy Chief Lauren spoke, "As impressive as this is, Your Grace, why are we looking at a map that can be found in any stationery store?"

Greg's tapping paused before he continued tapping as he asked rhetorically, "Do all maps in stationery stores show this?"

Red and green dots appeared everywhere on the hologram in different densities. Lucy's legs developed a mind of their own. She gently detached herself from Xandar's hold, taking slow steps to get a better view of the dots, studying the color pattern with wide, analytical eyes, not aware that she was only two steps behind Greg's left shoulder, a little too close for her husband's comfort.

Xandar stood two feet away from his cousin before pulling her in front of him. He gently wrapped her shoulders and abdomen from behind just to make sure she stayed where she belonged—in his arms.

After a minute, she muttered, "Green ones are the wolves. That's the Lone Light Pack. Moving south, Misty Dawn and Cold River. The red ones—" Her head cocked to one side at the two measly red dots in wolf territory on the hologram. Greg waited for her to figure it out as he stole a glimpse of her beautiful thinking face. She eventually guessed, "Probably rogues."

Desmond's excited voice boomed from the corner, "Damn, the queen's good!"

Greg smirked. "It's funny how you're still surprised, Desmond."

"I ain't surprised, boss. Just celebratin' that, for once, a royal is smart *and* ain't judgy."

Greg's sharp eyes zoned in on Desmond. His fingers on the hologram hung in midair. In a low voice that sounded somewhat offended, he challenged, "And what the hell does *that* mean?"

Hailey patted Desmond on his shoulder as she pressed back a smile. Ivory looked at him and shook his head with a "you're doomed" expression. Desmond released a brief and ominous chuckle, then explained as cheerfully as he could, "Boss, I love ya. But ya gotta admit. Ya're judgy. Ya're smart, but reeaally judgy."

Xandar swallowed his enthusiastic agreement, but Lucy chuckled lightly at the remark. And because of that, any venomous words Greg was going to spit at Desmond couldn't come out through his parted lips. That melodious sound just softened . . . all of him.

Desmond glanced at Lucy and then back at Greg, suspecting that the queen might have just saved him from his own boss.

Greg smirked at the former Money Retriever. "You got lucky today, Desmond."

When Xandar's grip around Lucy's abdomen tightened, she began stroking his strong arm when she asked, "Is it safe to say that the red dots come and go, Your Grace?"

Greg's eyes stayed on the screen when he replied, "Yes, my queen. We came up with this three months ago. But this is not recorded in real time. My followers scout sites like these once a week or once in two to three weeks depending on the popularity of a particular location for rogue inhabitation and activity. This was updated two days ago, so perhaps w—"

Xandar's eyebrows furrowed when he cut Greg off with a question, "Does this mean you knew where Kylton's third supplier was this whole time?"

The cousins locked eyes as the duke admitted in a dead tone, "Yes."

Xandar's voice turned homicidal. "And you didn't mention this because?"

"Because they're also my supplier. Without them and their products, my followers would have no jobs, no money, and no life. I have legitimate businesses, but it isn't enough to sustain ninety-eight creatures and the security measures required to keep them safe. There's also the fact that most of my people don't like being dormant. Selling, transporting, and trafficking the supplied goods were the only ways to make an income and not die of hunger and boredom. You already had the suppliers you needed to do what you wanted to do with the Kyltons and former ministers. You *didn't* need this last one, Cousin." Greg spat the last word with intense hate that he didn't bother to mask.

Lucy's voice cut through the tense atmosphere, "Just out of curiosity, Your Grace, is that supplier also made up of previously convicted felons by some . . . error on the justice system's part?"

The duke's eyes softened, but he felt guilty for keeping this information from her, so he avoided her gaze and answered, "You could say that, my queen. The reason they're there as suppliers and not here with us is because it's safer for them to be there."

"What do you mean by that?"

After taking a breath to steady himself, he explained, "It's riskier to be on the field, be it as transporters or traffickers. Moving about without raising suspicions is not a skill that's easily mastered by all. Those in the supply department either lack the talent or have a family, so they themselves cannot risk getting caught."

"So . . . unlike Ivory's situation where his mate is *not* associated with him in formal documents, the suppliers *are* rogues, as spouses?"

Greg nodded before adding, "And some have rogue children. No parent wants their pups to end up in an orphanage, brought up by creatures who'd tell them that their parents are traitors who never cared what happened to them."

Lucy instinctively glanced at Alissa, whose eyes fixed on the ground as she stared into space, no doubt thinking about her triplets.

Xandar spun his mate around to face him. His hard gaze penetrated into her eyes when he linked, *'Baby, there comes a point where we need to draw a line in this. He knew where the third supplier was but didn't tell us.'*

'Can you blame him?' Lucy retorted.

A pause followed, then Xandar linked in disbelief, *'You're taking his side?'*

'No, Xandar.' That simmered down some of his rage as she continued, *'I'm taking the side of whoever's been scarred for life because of* one *legally punishable act that the law says they committed, which might not even be wholly their fault to begin with. If they're wrong, sure, punish them. But there's an endpoint in making them carry the blame that is, sadly, not practiced in this kingdom. We have to change that.'*

'And we will. But Greg can't be exempted from further punishment. He kept this information to himself despite knowing we were hunting down the suppliers. It's like he was laughing at us behind bars while we were on a wild goose chase!'

'He kept that to himself for the sake of his people, Xandar. And he could've lied when you asked him that, you know? Why do you think he didn't?' When her husband stayed silent, she continued, *'He's learning to trust us, Xandar, to trust* you. *He's helping us. He could've left us to fend for ourselves. Look at him. Look at his followers. Do you think they have anything to gain from helping the government? Do you think they wouldn't have been fine and safe on their own? From the way I see it, they didn't need the pardon to continue staying alive. This current situation is a gamble for them. They're putting their lives at risk to help us with this new threat. They could have gone on minding their own business and let the concoction happen, watching from the sidelines while the rest of us struggled to fight off those trying to challenge my Authority. They stepped up* without *being asked,* before *we knew about the threat. We don't have the bargaining power to draw any lines with them.'*

'So you're just going to let him get away with everything? It doesn't matter to you that Dalloway, Christian, and I, even you on some occasions, have been popping around random parts of the kingdom because we were hunting down the very creatures he *was hiding from us?'* Xandar's eyes darkened, and his breathing got heavy. His animal was nowhere calm either, snarling in protest.

Lucy's breathing got heavy too. *'Why is it so hard for you to understand that they are only hidden because the systems we defend are oppressive to them? How would you feel if I were a rogue?'*

'You're nothing *like them, Lucy.'*

'That much is clear. After learning about their pasts, I dare say I got really *lucky with life. But if I didn't get so lucky, if I somehow attempted to murder one of my past mates and the law convicted me for that, putting me behind bars, and upon my release after serving the sentence, my only form of survival* was *to go rogue, and I somehow found the resources and made the connections to help build a place like this, would you draw the line with me when I decided to help you with what I'd learned and helped build?'*

Xandar's grip was already tightening with each word. It was painful to picture her being punished and put behind bars like that, having to find a way back up all on her own when the rest of society was against her. Despite his watered eyes, his stare was still hard when he declared aloud in a deep, firm voice, "I would *never* do that to you, Lucy. And I will never let anything *close* to that happen to you. Ever."

In an adamant, angered whisper, she challenged, "Then why is our situation now any different?"

Xandar was racking his brain for something as his thumbs stroked her cheeks just to assure himself that she was right there in front of him, and not behind bars or wandering about as a rogue somewhere, struggling to survive.

A moment of silence passed before she sighed and shook off the rage, then suggested, *'How about we get to the bottom of things first, then decide if certain ... past actions have to be ... reviewed, balancing them with the right actions they're taking now? What I'm saying is ..."* she inhaled *'... if your cousin's present commitment and attitude cannot offset the horrors of the past, we'll ... compel him in a ... reasonable manner. But we should only decide after we've put the abduction threat behind us. If we keep scrutinizing every past wrong, we'll be wasting time that we clearly don't have.'*

Xandar considered it, threading his fingers through her hair, reaching the ends before he muttered, "Fine." Getting on her toes, she conveyed her thanks with a kiss on his cheek.

Turning back to Greg, Lucy was about to say something before she noticed the duke's eyes were glazed over.

'Boss, we've pinpointed J.J. and Bundy,' Quinn reported.

'Where?'

'*They came out of Halo's place at 1:00 a.m., got into a car, drove for six hours, and checked in at Vent's twenty-four-hour inn. I hacked into the inn's system. It's for a two-day, one-night stay. Should we continue watching them?*'

'*No. That's enough information to go on for now. Halo's and Vent's underground passageways lead to very specific territories.*' After some thinking, Greg instructed, '*Get Nani to monitor the end of Halo's. Ask Taron to do the same for Vent's. Any word on Dormant Little Red?*'

'*Lepak is watching him, but he said Red looks more like he's trying to . . . act dormant.*'

'*Same bar, same drink, same solitude?*'

'*Yes, boss. Proceed or drop watch on this one?*'

'*Proceed, but get Lepak to swap with someone else. We don't want Red suspecting anything before we know what his game is.*'

'*As you wish, Your Grace.*'

Greg ended the link, turned, and found Lucy skillfully pinching and enlarging the hologram like a pro, not knowing that when she first touched it without knowing how it worked, the hologram disappeared, setting a panic in her before Ivory and Alissa helped her set it up again, then teaching her how to use it.

Xandar was already smiling because he found her panicky state absolutely adorable and irresistible, and it was amazing that she knew how to work the hologram with just a few basic tips.

Greg allowed himself a brief look at the queen before his eyes went to the hologram. She was looking into vampire territory, the Forest of Oderem, to be precise.

Without thinking, Greg muttered, "Why didn't they just station guards around the perimeter at all times?"

Xandar explained as cordially as possible, "Because if the forest senses creatures around it for an extended period of time, it'll produce an odor that can adversely affect a vampire's immune system."

That got Greg thinking. "It'll *only* affect a vampire's system?"

Lucy and Xandar blinked in realization.

With firm eyes directed to the duke, Lucy said, "Don't even think about it, Your Grace. We're not putting anyone there. We don't know if it'll affect *our* species."

"Well, I'm not suggesting putting the warriors or police, but maybe a few prisoners to experiment?" Greg urged.

Her brows furrowed deeper. "No."

Xandar then said, "I wonder if Kelissa Kylton's screaming would scare or annoy the forest into telling us where the abductors went."

Greg was on the same page with Xandar for once. "Maybe her nauseating scent could rival the scents of the forest and magically tear it down."

Lucy butted in, "Your Grace, we're talking about a forest that can produce and replicate *all* scents. And I highly doubt Kelissa Kylton's odor would scare anything." Her sights shifted to Xandar. "Darling, your history mind knows that screaming at an enchanted forest is *not* a solution!"

Fingers on his chin, he disagreed. "I'm not sure, babe. It's enchanted. Anything can happen, don't you think? If the books are right about the trees being—in a way—more alive than normal trees, then they'd experience some form of emotions: anger, annoyance."

Greg was staring at the table, uttering, "That actually doesn't sound stupid. Maybe one could throw in a few rogue wolves and—for lycans—throw in the Kyltons, Tanners, and Aphaels, maybe even those arrested in Wu Bi Corp. That ought to make a large-enough sample size for more accurate findings. The prisons holding those idiots might be getting a little too crowded anyway."

Xandar added, "Besides, some of them have been sentenced to life imprisonment. This really wouldn't make a difference. If the forest does kill them, then they'd be given a shorter way to death."

Lucy countered, "And if the forest *doesn't* kill them and gets annoyed, don't you think the curse of tampering with it would affect one of us or the people we love? Don't you think it'll affect Reida?" The mention of their daughter pulled Xandar's mind to a halt.

Greg's thought process slowed down but picked up again. "Well, it's not tampering with the forest per se, my queen. There's no deceit. We're just curious about how it works. It's just a simple experiment to . . . understand it. Perhaps the forest might even feel flattered."

Lucy's rage at the absurdity hit its boiling point. And just when she was about to explode, Tate's link came in to tell her that they had just picked up the rogues, effectively saving the two cousins from her wrath.

When her eyes cleared, she found herself wrapped into something hard and strong, comforting circles being drawn on her shoulder, the scent of acacia and forest trees soothing her earlier inferno. Hands on his chest, she parted their bodies and looked him dead in the eye. "We are *not* putting *anyone* in the kingdom around the Forest of Oderem."

Xandar blinked, then with a suggestive smile, said, "Well, we could put them *in* the forest instead, it'll b—"

"XANDAR!"

He chuckled, kissed her forehead as his hands ran up and down her arms, and then assured her with a smile. "Okay, okay. Until we know more about the forest, we'll keep the experiments in our mental archive." Another kiss on her cheek before he muttered, "Over-merciful queen."

Lucy sighed with relief and turned, only to have a still-thinking Greg say, "Instead of lycans and werewolves, I suppose I could get a few willing humans to exper—"

"NO!" Lucy growled.

Greg and his animal raised their hands in surrender. "Alright, alright. Point taken, my queen. I'll stop here."

Desmond and the others were biting back laughter. Greg had never shown fear in any situation. He would be worried sometimes, but fear was not a word they'd associate their boss with. He actually looked comical being daunted right now.

Lucy inhaled deeply and composed herself before her tone returned to normal when she turned back to the hologram, adjusting the scope to show wolf territory. "So the red dots are our next points of attack, Your Grace?"

The duke's hands lowered. "Well, I wouldn't say that. Not all rogues are lethal. These . . ." he tapped on one of the red dots, and the screen enlarged to show a detailed assessment of the population before he continued, "are definitely harmless."

"How can you tell, Your Grace?" Lauren asked.

The assessment listed the population as follows:

Brown (light): 1 male
Brown (dark): 1 female
Gray: 2 males; 1 female
Black: 0
White: 0
Others: 0
Total: 5

Greg tried not to sound too exasperated as he answered, "One, the 'others' category is nil, meaning that they're normal wolves without any of those legendary special abilities. And if you remember basic science, Deputy, you'd know that black-furred animals are known to be more rebellious or ambitious, or both, thus dangerous, so their absence is something to be happy about. Three, no white wolves, which are generally known to either be harmless or only look harmless but are quite lethal. No offense intended, my queen."

"None taken," Lucy muttered with a slight shake of her head, and actually felt flattered by that generalization.

Xandar noted, "Basic science also taught us that creatures with light brown fur are known to be scheming or secretive, or both. What makes you think that one won't be a problem, Greg?"

Greg's brows raised, taking umbrage because his own animal was light brown. Xandar's question could advance into whether Greg himself would be a problem. The duke wondered whether his cousin was pushing his buttons or genuinely asking a question.

Lucy touched her husband's chest and prompted, "No offense intended, right, my king?"

Xandar tore his eyes away from Greg and whispered obediently, "Of course not, my queen."

Despite still being suspicious, Greg began, "It's not a problem, because the light brown one is the leader, so there wouldn't be a point in scheming or being secretive to his own followers. It'd only disrupt the peace and efficiency within his own pack."

Dark brown wolves were—to Greg—mindless followers until, if they got lucky—or unlucky—a life experience woke them up and shook them so hard that they started developing a spine and a mind of their own.

Gray wolves—in general—were emotional codependents and had trouble monitoring and controlling their own emotions, hence were easily triggered and would go berserk and attack for physical and emotional self-defense. Due to their emotional instability and poor judgment thereof, gray wolves rarely ran with other gray wolves, unless one of them had already learned to control their emotions and led the still-unstable one; or these two were attracted to one another due to their mutual emotional instability, because they felt that no one else but this companion understood what they were going through or how they felt. But one wrong word or the slightest hint of indifference shown by their traveling partner, and they'd attack each other from feeling betrayed and abandoned, even if it was just a misunderstanding.

Greg said, "Our first step should be to make sure that the abductors and abductees aren't in wolf and lycan territories, so that we can confidently blame the bloodsuckers' inefficiency and poor handling of the issue if it ever comes down to it. We'll be able to assert that it was beyond any of our jurisdictions to do anything from our end."

Lucy had to press her lips shut to avoid spending the next few minutes protesting against blame-shifting.

The duke took her silence as the green light to proceed, "To search our territories, the best point to start would be here." He pointed at the hologram and continued, "What I suspect is that *if* the vampires and three lycans from the first village did bring the abductees into wolf territory, these would be the rogues to ask. If they didn't see anything, then the abductees never entered wolf territory."

One of the policemen questioned, "Why not just ask those packs there, then?"

"Because," Lucy thought out loud, "The rogues are nearer to the border than the wolf packs are. And if the wolf packs had seen any rogue lycans, we, as the authorities, would have been alerted by now."

"Precisely," Greg chimed. "And if they saw no rogue lycans, then it's definitely good news."

Lucy blinked. Xandar's brows furrowed when Lucy asked, "Is it? Why?"

"It just means that the rogues used hidden passageways instead of the direct routes."

"And how would that be good news, Your Grace?" Deputy Chief Lauren prompted, failing to understand how *hidden* passageways were any better.

Greg didn't answer. His sights fixed on Lucy, giving her time to figure it out because he knew, without a doubt, that she could. Lucy's eyes went back to the hologram. She pinched the screen to reveal the whole werewolf and lycan territory. Her eyes squinted slightly to see if there was anything underneath the familiar geographical area everyone was familiar with.

Greg came over to tap on the "routes" icon, and hundreds of red lines appeared on the hologram. Lucy took a shocked breath as she stared blankly at what she was seeing, taking a step back to get a fuller view.

Greg murmured, "It's good news because the underground territories connected by those hidden passageways are limited. If no one saw them aboveground, then the search should expand underground. If they're not there, they're not in lycan or wolf territories."

Lauren suggested, "We could deploy forces to—"

Lucy immediately said, "No, Lauren. Once they know that we know where they are and who we're looking for, they'll either heighten security measures, throw in false trails, or resort to blackmail. Even if they're not down there, we don't know if our presence will alert the culprits who may be in the vampire's territory. It's too risky. We need to get the vampires back, but risking more lives and alerting the rest of the . . . rogue population is not the best move to make."

Alissa uttered, "Exactly why His Grace didn't let us do it."

Hailey continued, "Not that our numbers are enough to accomplish such a feat anyway."

"Yo! Our numbers 're enough! It's the too-many-of-us goin'-'round-at-the-same-time-and-raisin'-suspicions thing that's the problem," Desmond argued.

Greg said, "Partially correct, Desmond. Because Hailey was right about our numbers. We're a lot but not enough to look through every underground passageway without getting caught. There are highly sensitive territories here that I won't consider sending less than twelve of you in phases of two, three or four just to get everyone back here alive. And there's also the issue that the rogues beyond our circle who've been paying attention would recognize some of your faces, so subtlety and anonymity isn't a luxury you're entitled to any-more if you enter their turf."

That got Lucy thinking. "So . . . what you're saying is that it's better for us—non-rogues—to enter these turfs, using scent sprays to mask our scents?"

The two cousins' eyes bulged in wide-eyed horror.

Xandar spun her around and lifted her chin gently before he spoke in a dangerously low voice, "No. Fucking. Way. Don't even think about it, Lucy."

"It was just a suggestion, darling." She shrugged, looking at him with wide doe eyes.

Greg also spoke with some anger. "My queen, the whole point of sharing this with you is so that you're kept *out* of danger. There's no way any of us in this room will let you anywhere near uncharted waters. It's too dangerous. Plus, your cover would be blown sooner than you think. Everyone in our world knows your approximate size and recognizes your face."

Xandar sighed with relief and pressed his wife into his chest, muttering, "Thank Goddess."

In protest, Lucy loosened herself from her protective husband's embrace and questioned Greg, "So the whole point of sharing this with me is for me to sit back and do nothing?"

Greg scoffed. "I highly doubt you'd be doing nothing, my queen. Perhaps you could scare the law-abiding vampires a little so that they're more alert as to who goes in and out of their own territory."

Lucy was quizzically silent for a moment before she stated the obvious, "That's not within my jurisdiction, Your Grace. And their empress already suspended half of the vigils in existence. What else do you expect her to do?"

"Use the Empress's Authority definitely tops my list," Greg muttered as he opened up a list of names to pick the most suitable followers to get information from the two rogue packs.

"She doesn't have it."

Greg's finger on the hologram halted. His head turned. "She told you that?"

"Yes, and I doubt she'd lie about it. Xandar and I met her in a different life. We were close then. When she mentioned that she didn't have that power, she looked disappointed, even ashamed."

Xandar added, "Vampire history also supports that only emperors wielded the Authority in the past, never the empress."

Greg sights went to his cousin. "Lycan history also supports that only kings wielded that power until our queen came along to prove that damn subject wrong."

"Not true, Greg," Xandar retorted. "The first to wield the Queen's Authority was Queen Bellea."

"I suck at history, but I remember that this was the one who married a commoner, and this commoner became the only king without an Authority. Their own guards assassinated them in their sleep because no one in that time was ready to kneel before a supreme female ruler."

Xandar nodded. "That's the one. And that's our point. The Queen's Authority existed for lycans, but there's no equivalent of that in vampire history."

Shutting his eyes in exasperation for a moment, Greg exhaled then shot back, "No, Cousin. This is the point: like it or not, this is the first time in lycan history that we have someone you'd never expect wielding that power—a woman; a commoner; a former wolf."

The last description got Xandar thinking. "Lucy started wielding it when she was still a wolf, actually."

Greg's eyebrows raised. This was news to him.

"That means . . ." Lucy began.

Greg managed to get a hold of himself on time to finish for her, "That means the Empress's Authority can exist and start with your bloodsucking-ruler friend. But she might need a trigger to get it out."

"Trigger," Lucy repeated in a whisper as she recalled her first time being told that she was emitting her Authority. She was protecting the people she loved. That was the trigger. "But she'd have to believe that she might have the power first though. Before Xandar told me I had an Authority, I never channeled it, not to its maximum potential, at least."

"Great. That's done," Greg said.

"Done?" Xandar questioned, lifting a brow.

Greg tapped on four of his followers' names on the hologram, the ones he decided on sending to question the two rogue packs near the border, as he responded, "The queen is good with creatures, Cousin. She'll be fine. Let her put that thought into the empress's thick, bloodless skull. If I do it, I might start a war. And I'm sure none of you goody-two-shoes want that."

Lucy's eyes glazed over again, and Tate informed her that they were scheduled to land in twenty minutes. Once her eyes cleared, she said, "They're landing soon. We should go meet them."

They left the Den and headed for the jet hangar. Xandar linked Christian to bring Stella and Reida along to join them there.

CHAPTER 23

At the hangar, Greg and his top four minded their own business. Ivory and Desmond admired the interior while Alissa and Hailey chatted as the former chewed on gum. The officers who followed them continued keeping their guard up, just in case the rogues decided to strike.

Christian arrived, carrying Reida in one arm as he shot Greg a disgusted glare while he and Stella made their way to the king and queen. Stella scanned Greg and his people with curious eyes, the distance between them too wide for her to smell that they were rogues like her. But there was just something oddly familiar about the woman chewing gum.

Lucy thanked a smiling Christian when she took her daughter from him and started speaking animatedly to her little girl. Taking a quick glance at Greg, Lucy mind-linked her husband with her large orbs. Xandar gave Greg a precautionary look before giving into his little freesia. Lucy smiled and pecked a grateful kiss on his cheek before approaching Greg with Reida in her arms.

Ivory and Desmond stopped looking around. Hailey stopped talking. Alissa's gum-chewing came to an awkward pause, but no one was as shocked as Greg.

When Lucy was right in front of Greg, she positioned Reida to face him. In a hushed voice, the queen spoke with starry eyes, "Reida, this is Uncle Greg. Want to say hi?"

Reida looked at Greg with wide lilac eyes and—like she was trained—gave Greg a little wave before her mother cooed, "Good girl." Greg had long accepted that it was going to be difficult to see Lucy with her pup because it was not made with him, but the fact that she told her daughter he was her uncle made him feel . . . he belonged in his own family, something he'd hadn't felt since his late uncle passed away.

A film of moisture glossed over his eyes, and franticness overcame Lucy when she automatically assumed that she was being insensitive by introducing her daughter to him, so she hastily apologized, "I am so sorry, Your Grace. This was probably not such a good idea. I had no intention of making you uncomfortable. I am so sorry. I'll just go over there and wait." She hid her daughter's face in her bosoms and turned.

But before she took a step, Greg exclaimed, "No, wait!" His voice echoed through the entire hangar. Xandar had had enough and sprinted to his wife and daughter.

Embarrassment washed over the duke as Xandar held the two most important people in his life close.

Clearing his throat, Greg said, "Apologies for my outburst, my queen. And you didn't make me feel uncomfortable . . . well, you did at first, but not when I was introduced to the princess. I just . . ." In a very low volume so that his people couldn't hear, he said, "It's been a long time since anyone with royal blood saw me as family."

An uneasy feeling crept into Xandar. Before it was blanketed by conflict. Greg pretty much had asked for the hostile treatment he was given. Xandar and Christian weren't bullies. They both hit a boiling point before deciding to cut him off from government affairs entirely. Greg was lucky they still allowed him to attend social events and training practice before he was sent to prison!

"Oh, uh . . ." Lucy looked at her wide-eyed daughter, considering her next move. Looking to Xandar, she linked, *'Would you mind if Greg . . . held Reida for a little while?'*

His grip on her shoulder tightened instantly, and she got her answer. Dropping the subject and the link, Lucy then brought her pup to Alissa and the others. "Reida, want to meet some new friends?"

She took slow steps toward the top four, introducing them one by one, and Reida waved to each of them. Desmond was the most excited when he said, "Damn, ya're a cutie."

His compliment made Reida's small lips lift into a smile before she chuckled in the most adorable manner and yelled, "Fuck!"

"Oh dear Goddess," Lucy muttered in embarrassment.

Greg's brows furrowed in disbelief. "What did she just say, my queen?"

It was like Reida understood the question, so she chuckled before yelling again, "Fuck!"

Lucy's eyes turned stern, setting on her daughter. "Reida," the mother then shook her head slowly and spoke in a drawn-out manner, "No more using that word, okay? No." A sliver of fear entered the pup's eyes, and the princess cleverly leaned into her mother's chest to avoid having to look at that pair of fierce eyes.

Greg's top four were holding back smiles and chuckles, but Greg was still in shock.

With downturned lips, Lucy explained in discontent, "This is your cousin's fault, Your Grace. He used that word around Reida, and now my pup's first word is a curse word."

"Babe, to be fair, it was *his* letter that made me say that word." Xandar's head motioned at Greg.

Greg's furious sights went to Alissa. "What the f—what did you write in the message?"

Alissa's eyes widened the moment blame was directed to the letter. "Nothing in there was a curse word, Your Grace. I can assure you of that."

Lucy interjected, "It wasn't the contents, really. We just knew what a note from you meant."

"Bad news," Christian said the moment he came over and joined the rest with Stella.

Lucy reframed, "I wouldn't say that. It was more like . . . information that we don't expect to get from anywhere else."

No one could argue against that because it was true. Every note from Greg to Lucy was not mere clues, but clear answers that no one else could have given them. Greg and his people were touched that they were defended, and they started to love the queen more than they already did. Hailey was particularly interested in Reida, so when Lucy asked if she wanted to hold her, Hailey's eyes watered as she held her first child in years. The former kindergarten teacher was still great with pups, evident from the way she held Reida in her arms like it was second nature to her. Hailey didn't struggle to find the right way like those who had never held a baby would.

The sight of a rogue holding the princess was only glaring at first, but as the seconds passed, no one saw the labels anymore. It was just a woman holding an infant. That was all there was. Reida started playing with Hailey's hair, which made Hailey chuckle lightly, before wiping away her own tears.

Even Christian, who was the most skeptical about this whole idea of working with the rogues, had to admit they were more humane than he'd imagined.

Xandar strode to his wife, left a kiss on her hair, and linked, *'Sweetheart, if you still want to let Greg hold Reida, I'm okay with it.'*

Her glazed-over eyes shot to his own when she asked, *'Are you sure, Xandar?'*

Another kiss on her temple, and he uttered with a smile, "I'm sure."

She scrutinized his expression, then his emotions through their bond. When she was sure that *he* was sure, she looked to Greg. "Would you like to hold her, Your Grace?"

Greg blinked in surprise and instinctively glanced at his cousin before asking, "Are you sure, my queen?"

With a small smile, she replied, "Only if you want to, Greg."

Hailey brought Reida to the duke, and it was like Reida knew she was going to be handed to the next nearest creature, so her arms spread open, ready to cling onto the next adult like a sloth would a tree. With Hailey's guidance, Greg held Reida properly in his arms and was too afraid to move a single inch for fear of making Reida uncomfortable.

Since Greg's hair wasn't long enough for Reida to play with, her small hands reached for his chin, lips, and nose, and Greg didn't realize he was actually moving his face downward so that Reida could reach whatever she wanted to touch. That became a mistake. Before he knew it, Reida's fingers gently poked at his right eye, making Greg mouth "ow" before he turned away to blink off the sensation.

Lucy dashed to his side and uttered in guilt, "I'm so sorry, Your Grace." She looked at her daughter, held her tiny hand, and reprimanded, "Reida, no poking your uncle." She wanted to take Reida back, but the baby was so scared of her increasingly furious mother that she leaned into Greg, refusing to let go.

Xandar came over when Greg was still blinking and took his daughter's hand from his wife, kissing the small, soft chubbiness, and whispered with a proud smile, "That's my girl."

"Xandar!" Lucy protested.

Christian joined the conversation, "I think this might just be my favorite niece."

With narrowed eyes, Lucy said, "She's your *only* niece, Christian."

When Greg was alright again, he looked at Reida and muttered, "You're really not as harmless as you look, are you, Princess?"

Reida chuckled and yelled, "Fuck!" Her mother sighed in defeat. There was no way to unteach that now.

Greg scoffed lightly, smiling broadly when he said, "Fuck indeed, Princess."

"Your Grace!" Lucy exclaimed with seething eyes.

A loud rumble came from a distance and closed in fast. Everyone in the hangar witnessed Tate's jet landing. When it came to a stop, the door opened, and each rogue onboard descended the airstair with at least one lycan escort.

Tate and Margaret stood close, hands clasped, fingers interlaced. Lucy instinctively touched Xandar's arm. Her eyes sparkled when they met his own smiling ones. "Looks like it went well," he murmured.

Margaret's surprised eyes shot to her daughter, and Lucy motioned Stella to go to her. Although hesitant, Stella obeyed and strolled toward the group. Margaret let go of Tate's hand when she wrapped Stella in a relieved hug. Tate gave Stella's shoulder a hello squeeze before coming forward to embrace Lucy and greet the king and the duke.

As Tate filled them in on the extraction, his eyes darted to Greg some distance away holding . . . wait, was that *Reida*? His speech hung mid-sentence, his eyes squinted for another three seconds before he asked, "That's the other duke?"

They matched his gaze before Lucy confirmed, "Yeah, why?"

"And that's Reida?"

"Yeah."

"The other duke is holding Reida."

"Yes."

"Reida, as in your daughter, Reida?"

Lucy's eyes narrowed. "Congratulations, Tate. You have eyes and your mind is working just fine."

Tate chuckled. "I just never pictured that duke to have it in him to be anywhere near a pup."

"Well, none of us did," Xandar admitted as they glanced at Greg.

The other duke was now being more careful with Reida's prying fingers as he mumbled, "You're not as boring as the Blackfurs, are you, Princess? On the outside, you have a dull, Blackfur-resembling face. On the inside, you're just like your mother—seemingly harmless but *dangerous*. And it's a good thing. You know why? Because we don't want you ending up dim and slow, now, do we? That's right—we don't." And Greg went on talking to Reida despite knowing that she couldn't understand a single word.

After Tate managed to tear his eyes away from that weird sight, Lucy's eyes shone with hope when she asked, "So how was your first date?"

That wasn't an official first date with Margaret, but it sure felt like a good-enough private moment with her. Tate couldn't hide his widening smile. He glanced at his mate busying herself with watching Azalea interrogate Stella about how she was treated in the past few days before Tate whispered, "It went better than I expected. She's really opening up to me."

"Aww . . . that's great!" She offered him a congratulatory hug as Xandar patted him on the shoulder.

Christian teased, "So when's the wedding, Alpha?"

Tate's cheeks developed an unusual shade of pink as he chuckled, "That might not happen so soon, Your Grace. I don't want to rush her."

Christian's eyes snapped to his cousin and cousin-in-law. "Welllllll, that sounds *very* familiar, Cuz. Remind me, where have I heard it before?" It was Lucy's turn to blush. Xandar forgot about his cousin's question as he held her closer and planted a kiss on her hair.

Margaret came forward with the rest of her pack members. She glanced over Christian and Xandar before her eyes met Lucy's. Anyone could see the guilt swimming in her rosewood orbs. She offered a quick curtsy and uttered, "My queen."

Her people behind her followed suit, addressing Lucy in a non-synchronized way. They then greeted Xandar and the duke in the same manner. The three royals bowed back in return, shocking all the rogues present.

Azalea and Zane shot Margaret a "What do we do now?" look. Their leader had no clue.

To their surprise, Lucy stepped forward and wrapped Margaret in a hug. "It's good that everyone got here safely, Margaret. Thank you."

Margaret was so stunned by the hospitality despite her crudity with Lucy on the first day that her mouth opened but she didn't know what to say. Her body went on lockdown, stiffening as her brain scrambled. She thought of apologizing for her earlier behavior, or was thanking the queen for taking care of Stella a better way forward first, or maybe she should convey her gratitude for giving her and her people a chance?

"YOU?" Greg's roar drew everyone's attention to him as his look of disbelief fixed on Margaret. Even Reida was looking at Margaret with large, clueless orbs, blinking innocently.

Margaret went from being vulnerably speechless to frustratingly shocked. Her eyes turned wide and fierce when she whisper-yelled at Tate, "You said we were working with rogues!"

Tate glanced at Greg. "Those are rogues, Mar."

The affectionate way he spoke her name had some effect on calming Margaret down, but it clearly wasn't enough. "No, that's a royal! His followers are royal rogues. It's different!"

Lucy's eyes pivoted to Greg and the top four, and a smirk that carried awed realization tugged at her lips. "Royal rogues, I see."

Desmond proudly declared, "Best of the best, Queen."

Margaret scoffed darkly and exclaimed, "More like pushiest of the pushiest! Most disrespectful of the most disrespectful!" It wasn't a whisper anymore. Her voice blared and echoed clearly through the hangar.

Alissa argued, more calmly, "We asked one damn question, maggot. If you just gave us the answer, we would have moved on without a fuss."

Lucy's humor from the earlier revelation died down, and she was too afraid to ask but had to, "What fuss?"

Alissa's defensiveness diminished when she cleared her throat and explained, "Well, my queen, we crossed paths with this pack a few years back when we were tracking down a mole that infiltrated and escaped our circle. We asked around, and this pack was particularly . . . reluctant to offer direct answers, so—"

Azalea yelled, "You surrounded us at 3:42 in the morning! Did you expect us to be anything less than defensive? And you set our supplies on fire!"

Desmond yelled back, "After y'all refuse to give answers! If y'all knew nothin' 'bout what we asked, then say it! Why were y'all tryin' to delay us like y'all hidin' somethin'?"

"WAHHHHHH!" Reida's sudden cry stopped every adult's bickering.

Greg's eyes widened in shock and—he didn't think it was possible—but his heart cracked. He held the little girl closer, burrowing her face in his chest, drawing her sights away from everyone as he threw Desmond a glare so sharp that Desmond covered his mouth immediately while his animal shuddered, probably already turning to ash from the glare.

Lucy sprinted over and took a red-faced Reida from the duke. "There there, Reida. Shh . . . shh . . . It's okay. It's okay. Mama's here. Everything's okay. Shh . . ." Xandar was by her side with pained eyes, stroking his daughter's arm as Lucy cooed and planted soft kisses on their pup's head. Reida's cries gradually subsided with her mother's assuring voice and scent and her father's comforting touch. The cries eventually turned into softer sobs and sniffles before her tiny hands reached for her father's thumb, holding it close to her chest just to feel safe.

The royal couple sighed in relief when that was over, as did everyone else, especially those who hollered. Since Reida clung onto her father's thumb, Xandar took her, coddling her. The indecisive baby then let go of her father's thumb and took her mother's fingers, gluing them to her chest before leaning into her father for his scent.

With a soft smile, Xandar muttered, "Looks like we're both stuck with her again." He met his wife's eyes, unable to contain how happy and thankful he was for her and for their pup. As Lucy's fingers stroked their baby girl, her free hand reached out to stroke Xandar's arm, and elation overflowed from her being to his.

Their smiles fell when sounds of shuffling intruded their moment. As they tore their eyes from Reida, protectiveness made Xandar pull Lucy closer without a second thought. The royal couple's eyes turned defensive by instinct, their Authorities ready to be invoked.

Greg and every rogue in the room got down on one knee and started conveying their apologies at the same time, most of which was caught by the king's and queen's sharp hearing.

Greg was saying, "I'm deeply sorry for the distress my followers and I have caused the princess and you, my queen."

Desmond followed, "Really sorry 'bout that, Queen. Ain't gonna happen again."

Margaret was saying, "I should've controlled my temper. I'm so, so sorry, Your Highnesses."

Azalea spoke very fast. "I didn't mean to shout. I just got mad. We lost weeks of food that day and—"

Reida started getting restless again, attempting to toss and turn with a frown on her face. Xandar covered her exposed ear as his animal emitted a low, warning growl to silence everyone. As Lucy stroked his biceps to smother the raging flames, she spoke to the rogues, "Everyone simply acted on instinct. I'm partly at fault for choosing to ask about the time your groups crossed paths. Please, stand. All of you. Let's just head for the meeting room at the station now."

"As you wish, my queen," they uttered in unison in a synchronicity that surprised Xandar, Christian, and Lucy herself.

As they trotted to the ready cars, Margaret felt a sharp pain that surged from her nape to the top of her head, bringing her to her knees. Her eyes were shut tight, her body was fidgeting, and cold sweat beaded on her forehead as Tate—panicky and helpless—cautiously lowered her onto the floor.

He asked Azalea in dismay, "What's happening to her? Is this normal?"

Azalea looked worried too. "No, I've never seen her like this."

"Mom!" Stella screamed, hoping her mother could hear her.

Lucy gently tugged her fingers away from Reida's grip and rushed over. When Margaret's eyes forced themselves open, they weren't their normal rosewood color. They were bright red, and Margaret muttered, "Blood. There's a lot of blood."

"Blood?" Tate repeated as his worried eyes locked with Lucy's own. Before either of them could say anything, Lucy's eyes glazed over.

CHAPTER 24

'*A*unt Lucy?' It was Lucy's favorite nephew; his voice was soft, unsure.

'*Liam, sweetheart. You can mind-link!*'

Liam had just turned four. Wolves could only mind-link when they were six or seven, with a few exceptions like Liam. '*I t-tried so many times. Um . . . Aunt Lucy, a-are you coming home soon?*'

That was a very unusual question. The fact that Liam forced himself to mind-link her was another thing to be worried about. She tried to mask her anxiety, speaking to him in a soft, assuring voice, '*Well, I'll have to ask Uncle Xandar. We'll discuss it and make the trip there with Reida soon, okay?*'

'*NO! AUNT LUCY, DON'T BRING REIDA!*'

'*What? Why not?*'

Liam sounded devastated and afraid, like he was close to tears, '*Aunt Lucy, Daddy told Mommy there was a f-fight at the border. Big Guy Albus and Big Sis K-Kiera are in the p-pack clinic.*'

Lucy's heart sank. Kiera was the newly appointed gamma. Her skills were second only to Lucy in Blue Crescent. Albus was normally very swift too. What happened?

Liam's scared voice continued ringing through the link, '*Daddy and Mommy said stay in our rooms. I s-snuck out. Daddy's office door was open. I heard him tell Mommy someone wants something from you, Aunt Lucy . . . and— and if they don't get it . . . they might come after Daddy, and then Mommy.*' Liam was sobbing now as he pleaded, '*Aunt Lucy, please come home and fight for us. Please.*'

Lucy's protective instinct over her birth pack took over, and any fear and anxiety she felt was buried when she linked in assurance, *I'll be home soon, Liam. Stay in your room until I get there, okay?'*

'Okay. Thank you, Aunt Lucy. I love you.'

'I love you too, Liam.'

When the link ended, Lucy found herself in Xandar's arms. Christian was holding Reida, looking at her in concern. It was when Xandar clasped the sides of her face and started gently wiping away her tears that she realized she was tearing during the link. Without hesitation, she said, "We have to get to Blue Crescent. Now."

"What happened?" Tate asked, equally worried.

After wiping away the last of her tears, more roughly than the way her husband did, she announced, "There was an attack at the border. Kiera and Albus are in the clinic, injured. Juan suspects that whoever ordered the attack is after me. I have to get there before any of my friends lose their lives."

Staring into space, Xandar muttered, "It's a little strange for Juan to tell you this, actually." He knew his brother-in-law well enough to know that Juan wouldn't ask his own sister to come home when there was a threat against her.

Lucy's eyes turned fierce, and a scorching flame burned from her center when she said, "That wasn't Juan. *Liam* told me. When we get to Blue Crescent, I'm going to kill my brother for keeping this to himself."

Christian nodded like things made sense again. "Now that sounds more like Alpha Juan. You two go ahead first. I'll put Reida at my place with Mrs. Clifford and Annie, then round up more lycan warriors. We should be able to catch up with you guys within an hour."

Margaret asked Stella to stay behind, too, much to the teenager's dismay. Margaret had a vision when she felt that sharp pain. In it, as she told Tate and everyone else, she saw wolves, lycans, and vampires fighting each other. Bodies were thrown and blood was splattered everywhere as the howls of anguish filled the air. Margaret got half of her followers to stay behind because they weren't trained enough to fight yet, while the trained ones were following her to Blue Crescent.

Greg linked thirty more creatures from the Den, ordering them to meet him at Blue Crescent.

They boarded Tate's jet. Lucy stared out of the window, her thoughts far away as she sat on her mate's lap. Xandar rubbed her shoulders and forearms and pecked kisses in her hair, but nothing was working. Her worry was still surging strong.

Tate came over with Margaret, harrumphing to get their attention.

Lucy blinked herself out of her daze and managed a smiled. "Yeah, what is it?"

The two sat facing the king and queen before Tate casually began, "So . . . I linked Zeke and Zelena about this, and then Lovelace too."

"Okay," Lucy noted, and waited for him to continue. Those were their strongest allies. There was no issue in telling them about the threat. Everyone had to be alert.

"As it turns out, they already knew and are on their way there," Tate uttered, almost like he regretted the words as he said them. Lucy's brows furrowed as Tate concluded, "Meaning to say only White Blood and you weren't invited to Blue Crescent's pack-defense party this evening."

The lilac part of Lucy's orbs turned a deep onyx, and the rise and fall of her chest emanated an intimidating vigor that made her enemies think, "RUN!" Despite that, her voice came out steadily calm when she said, "I see."

"Juan probably just wants you safe, Lucy," Tate suggested meekly.

In a deathly, hushed tone, she admonished, "Keeping something like this from me while putting my friends' lives and his own at risk . . . does *not* keep me safe. Whoever it is will get to me eventually. I doubt they care how many creatures they'd have to kill to get my attention." A moment of silence passed before she asked, "You told Toby, too, right?"

"Yeah, he was pissed until he heard you didn't know either. Now, he's just waiting for a show when we reach Blue Crescent."

"He'll definitely be getting a show," Lucy muttered.

CHAPTER 25

In the early evening at Blue Crescent, Alpha Juan got Luna Hale to promise she would stay in the pack house with their pups while he came out to greet Alpha Zeke, Luna Zelena, and Gamma Raden from Blood Eclipse, Gamma Sylvia from Crimson, and also Luna Lovelace from Midnight, along with the pack warriors they brought with them. Juan stationed six of his own warriors around the pack house just to keep his family safe.

Juan embraced his allies and uttered gratefully, "Thank you for coming on such short notice."

Zeke swallowed a lump in his throat and exchanged uneasy glances with Zelena and the rest before he began, "There's something you should know, Juan. See, when we were on the road, Tat—"

"AHEM!" A familiar voice pulled the pack leaders' attention away from each other, and they witnessed Toby stalking toward them in large strides, his car parked right next to Zeke's.

Surprise entered Juan's eyes, but when he saw that his allies didn't share his shock, he knew he was alone in this. Toby patted Juan on the back and spoke without a smile, "Hope you don't mind, Juan. I invited myself."

The gears in Juan's head turned as he muttered, "If you're here, that means…"

"AUNT LUCY!" Juan's youngest son screamed in excitement, drawing everyone's attention to the little boy dashing out of the pack house, stealthily bypassing the warriors while his mother followed closely behind as six cars entered the compound. As soon as the first one pulled to a stop, Lucy alighted from the passenger's seat before Liam jumped into her open arms.

Turning to Zeke and the others, Juan issued his complaint. "You know, the whole point of not telling her was so that she *wouldn't* be here if and when they attacked again."

In defense, Zeke exclaimed, "None of us told her!"

"Then how did she find out? How did *he* find out?" Juan gestured at Toby like he wasn't right next to him.

Toby sniggered. "Ooooo . . . looks like someone snitched, Juan. Who could it be?"

Juan's eyes narrowed, and exasperation coursed through him. "It really does kill to get White Blood to side with me instead of my sister, doesn't it, Toby?"

"Considering White Blood didn't get an invitation when the rest of the alliance members did? Yes."

"It's my pack. I make the decisions here. I send the invitations. And the only reason White Blood wasn't on my list was because Tate was where Lucy was. Lucy would've suspected something was up. If she didn't, Xandar would. Tate is not hard to read." Juan spoke while praying that Lucy would speak to Liam and Hale a little longer so that he could come up with a good excuse.

The truth was, if their positions were reversed, Juan would have wanted Lucy to tell him about this threat too. He would have wanted to know. And he would be enraged if Lucy kept this from him. His eyes would be on fire, much like how her own orbs were at that moment she began barging toward him.

Juan wondered why his brother-in-law still had almost no control over his sister. He was the king, Goddess damn it! Then again, it wasn't as if Juan himself could control Hale either.

"Any advice?" Juan muttered ominously as he watched Hale and Liam disappear into the pack house. His sister's hair was up in a tight bun like she was ready for a fight. This was not good.

Zeke bit his upper lip, empathizing with Juan that the walking apocalypse was drawing nearer when he suggested, "Ask about Reida, maybe? It might cool her off a little. Good luck." After a good luck pat on Juan's back, every ally took three steps back as Lucy entered their circle with Xandar, Tate, and Margaret.

Lucy looked at her brother with an "I'm going to kill you" smile and began, "Hey, Juan. I had the sudden urge to visit. Looks like I picked the right time. All our closest allies seem to be here as well."

Juan cleared his throat and asked, "So how's Reida?"

"She's alright, now in Christian and Annie's place. We didn't bring her along. You know why?" She took one step closer and growled, "Because I heard there was a threat that put two of my friends in the clinic this morning—an intel that *didn't* come from *you*."

Juan shot Zeke an unappreciative glare, "Ask about Reida to cool her down? Does she seem cooled down to you?"

Zeke shrugged. "I tried."

Lovelace unhelpfully added, "Juan, honestly. She's your sister. Shouldn't you know best?"

Lucy's fist was about to land on Juan's jaw when Xandar restrained her arms and held her back by her abdomen, taking a few steps back himself to create a safe distance between the siblings. "Breathe, baby. Breathe," he cooed into her ear, which was also heated with fury.

And she *was* breathing. Breathing in pure *rage* where every breath was like steam in a sauna.

Juan decided to use this little time to explain to the struggling, onyx-eyed monster he'd grown up with. "Lucy, I was going to tell you."

Toby interrupted in disbelief, "*Were* you?" Tate nudged Toby, prompting him to be quiet.

As Lucy continued struggling to break away, Juan continued racking his brain for a plausible explanation. "We just wanted to be sure about our suspicions before we told you."

Xandar was now familiar with Lucy's forms of attack, so he knew that he had to restrain her by her arms and one leg to hold her in place. But he threw Juan a worried look, his way of saying, "I don't know how much longer I can hold her."

"Baby, please. Just breathe. Save your strength for battle. How about that? If you fight Juan now, you'll have less strength to fight later if we have to fight."

She took a few heavy breaths and stopped trying to escape. Xandar started loosening his grip before he realized that she was misleading him to do just that to break free. He pulled her back immediately, and her growl echoed through the pack, miles beyond their circle. Some of the Blue Crescent folks who were minding their own business even flinched at the sound. Several warriors on their way to border duty almost tripped.

"Aunt Lucy?" Liam's sudden voice put her struggling and murderous thoughts to a halt. Every adult's eyes zoned in on the little boy who dared approach the monstrous creature when everyone else was kept at a safe distance from her.

Xandar felt her mood go soft and set her free, knowing that she wouldn't be violent around pups, especially not this one. Lucy went from a ready-to-kill lycan to the sweet-and-attentive aunt, smiling brightly when she squatted to give her nephew her full attention, stroking his brown locks when she asked, "Yes, Liam?"

"I made this for Reida. Can you give it to her?"

She looked at the rocket ship Liam had drawn and colored, with two kids inside—one with the label Liam, and the other labeled Reida. Her animal cooed as her heart melted, their earlier intention to kill evaporated and forgotten. Liam even glued a small piece of folded cardboard on the back for the drawing to stand. Moisture gathered behind her eyes as she wrapped the little boy in a hug, whispering, "Thank you, Liam. Reida would love it."

Leaving a kiss on his forehead, Liam then asked with guilty eyes, "Aunt Lucy, are you angry at me for asking you to come back?"

"*YOU* ASKED HER TO COME BACK?" Juan exclaimed. Of all the snitchers! Juan thought he'd made his pups stay in their rooms before he spoke to Hale. How did Liam even tell his aunt? He had no phone!

Liam was visibly frightened and instinctively took a step closer to his favorite person. Lucy cupped one of his cheeks and gently made him look at her as she said, "No, Liam. Aunt Lucy isn't angry. I'm very proud of you. Thank you for telling me." She made him promise that he was going to stay with his mother and siblings in the pack house now while the adults dealt with things. At the pack house entrance, Liam gave Lucy a little wave before disappearing behind the door. Juan signaled the warriors he'd stationed there to lock it.

Lucy's sights returned to Juan when she showed him the drawing. "If secrets like this are kept from me again, it'll be you alone on this rocket ship on a one-way trip to space."

Toby scoffed. Greg and the others pressed back smiles.

Juan rolled his eyes, not knowing whether to reprimand his son later for doing something behind his back or buy the boy ice cream for saving his ass. Archiving those thoughts, he pointed at the path ahead and said, "Let's just talk about this at the crime scene."

Lucy safely tucked Liam's rocket ship in the glove compartment of the car. Then Juan led the entire party to the far side of the pack, near their river—where Lucy came on her 4:00 a.m. runs when she still lived in Blue Crescent. She'd sit right next to that boulder that had some blood stains now. Her predatory eyes started looking for a trail and found a few more drops here and there on the ground and dried leaves. "Seriously, Juan, why didn't you tell me?"

"Lucy," he sighed. "What did you expect me to do? This could have been you! The vampire scent is still lingering over there, across the river, meaning

Kiera and Albus were attacked there and thrown over here. And do you know what the doctors found in their blood? Vampire venom. And the biggest joke?" He let out a short, depressing chuckle, "No one who saw Kiera and Albus being tossed saw a single vampire during the attack!"

Fear came and left Lucy's eyes. She swallowed, then tried to put on a brave front. "See, was that so hard to say?"

From the side, Toby remarked, "Well, I don't know if it was hard to say, but it was definitely hard to hear." His hand subconsciously moved to his neck, because wolves learned in school that during the war, vampires went for their enemies' necks when it came to injecting venom with their fangs. It was the fastest way to kill them.

"Toby, you're supposed to be on my side."

"I am. But still, no one saw any vampires, which is kinda creepy. You haven't happened to develop some sort of super vision to see what the rest of us can't see, have you, Lucy?"

Juan continued, "And, Lucy, before you kill me or send me to space, I'd better show you what one of them left in Kiera's hand after she collapsed."

He rummaged through his left pocket and extracted a crumpled sheet, handing the ball to his sister. Lucy unfolded it and read the note aloud, "You know who we want. We're waiting for HER."

Xandar's hold on her shoulders tightened. Greg's forehead creased, as did Lovelace's. Toby's jaw clenched taut. Tate held Margaret closer. Zeke started rubbing Zelena's right shoulder to reduce her anxiety.

Christian and the warriors arrived and entered the discussion circle. Greg's followers got there at about the same time as well. As soon as Christian registered everyone's ominous faces, he sighed. "Okay, how fucked up is it this time?"

Lucy muttered, "I'm hoping less fucked up than it was 204 years ago. We don't need another war."

Christian's flat brows arched before Xandar filled him in. The lycan warriors matched everyone's ominous expressions. At the end of the tale, Christian heaved a heavier sigh and shook his head. "So long story short, it's *super* fucked up."

As Lucy continued staring at the blood on the boulder, she asked Juan, "Has anyone smelled any vampires since the attack, apart from those across the river?"

"No. I've put every warrior to work. Literally everyone is sniffing around the entire pack right now. I sniffed my own house ten times and I'm still worried."

Christian asked in dismay, "Alpha Juan, if your warriors are sniffing around . . . are you saying that the vampires could still be *in* the pack?"

Sharing a gloomy look with Lucy, Juan muttered, "It's possible."

Greg questioned, "For clarification's sake, you have warriors everywhere, correct? Streets, trees, homes, borders, trails?"

"Yes, everywhere."

"Then I doubt they're in the pack." Greg's tone relaxed in a way that was not reciprocated by anyone else. "Their scent wouldn't vanish that quickly. If no one has found anything, there's probably nothing . . . that, or they're hiding in the sewer."

An awkward silence followed before Lucy asked the question going through everyone's minds, "Your Grace, is that a joke or—"

"Oh, it is a joke, my queen. I saw a few sewer openings on the way here. No adult vampire could fit through them. And I doubt a child did this." He gestured at the blood trail.

Xandar then said, "A discretus can see other discreti. We should contact the empress for help. Maybe she can send a few of her people to guard Blue Crescent in case the intruders return."

Juan's sights went from his brother-in-law to his sister, whose black-and-lilac orbs were begging him to accept the assistance. The alpha nodded gratefully. "That'd be great, Xandar. Thank you."

As soon as the green light was given, Lucy got out her phone from her back pocket and began scrolling for Pelly's number, when a sudden gust of wind came from her side and snatched her device right out of her hand. Everyone watched her phone flying across the space like it was thrown before it stopped midair. The phone was held facing them, and they watched it being tossed up and down in thin air before the device was crushed against a tree trunk.

Greg cursed, "Damn it."

Everyone's nostrils picked up the striking smell of chrysanthemum and pine leaves surrounding them—the general scent of vampires. Foreign, individual scents wafted around them as well, putting their animals on guard. A stream of cackling laughter came from across the river. The warriors and rogues took their positions as a shirtless man leaped from one of the trees across the river and onto Blue Crescent's territory, landing perfectly on his feet and one fist on the ground.

At that sight, Lucy exhaled in frustration. "Seriously, why can't you rogue alphas just die?"

Xandar positioned an arm in front of her, blocking her as much as she allowed him to, which practically put him to her side anyway. He didn't know who the hell the bare-chested six-footer was, but this one had definitely pissed off his wife before.

Former-alpha of Fleet Wood, Draxon, smirked that same obnoxious way from over a decade ago. "That's not very nice, Lucy. And for the record, Jake really did like you, which was stu—"

Xandar growled at the mention of Jake and pounced on Draxon. Draxon didn't avoid the king's attack fast enough, so Xandar caught his leg, broke his limbs, and was cracking his neck slowly. Draxon howled in pain before he whimpered and scratched Xandar's hands to loosen his tightening grip, but to no avail. Then, a gust of the wind from behind Xandar nicked the left side of his arm. Another gust came from the front and nicked the right side.

Before he knew it, his arm lost strength and Draxon was dropped before something threw him across the river. Lucy dashed to Xandar and examined the injury. Gray lines began to form. He was losing the ability to hold his arm up and his senses were faltering. Lucy was about to rush him to the pack clinic before she felt his prickling numbness and weakening grip . . . subsiding. The gray lines disappeared even before reaching his elbow. His arm regained its strength and sensory volition.

Lucy didn't trust her eyes or their bond telling her that he was fine. With a suspicious look in her eye, she traced his forearm before stepping back to see if any other part of his body was affected. Before she was done scanning every inch, Xandar pulled her into him and kissed her hair. "I'm fine, baby. You healed me. Our bond healed me. I'm okay now. Thank you."

Sighing in relief, she thanked Goddess that her ability to heal from poisonous substances was shared with Xandar after they mated and marked each other. It was fortunate that the vampire venom was so little that his immune system fought it and won within seconds.

"YOU MORONS COULDN'T STOP HIM SOONER? I COULD HAVE DIED!"

At the reminder of the selfish, imbecile of an alpha, Lucy's angered eyes turned sapphire blue, but before she could do anything, Draxon lifted a finger. "Ah, ah, ah. Don't even think about it, Lucy. You have no idea how many amigos I brought with me. Wouldn't want everyone here to get vampire venom by accident, now, would you?"

She recalled the strong scents of chrysanthemum and pine leaves. As if through silent agreement, she and her allies began subtly sniffing out the individual scents on top of the general vampire odor, to count how many were surrounding them and where their exact positions were.

Lucy, Xandar, Christian, and Greg smelled six in front; Toby, Tate, and Margaret could detect another six on the right; the warriors counted only five on their left; and everyone else behind knew that there were about twenty behind them. The vampires were outnumbered. If the wolves and lycans acted fast, they could kill every single one in no time. But their aim had to be very, very precise. They only had one shot.

"Get on with it, Draxon. What do you want?" Lucy decided to engage in nonsensical chit-chat while buying her friends and family time to pinpoint through scent.

"It's really simple. Just stand where you are while we do a test run."

"Of what?" she continued as her allies took small steps toward their targeted opponents.

Draxon pushed his shoulder-long blonde hair behind his ear as he shrugged. "Controlling you, or killing you, depending on what works."

A rumble of ferocious growls channeled his way, and the ones who stood closest to Lucy were about to cross the river before her outstretched arms stopped them. Thankfully too. Those in front smelled vampires creating a barricade between them and the river. One more step forward and one of the lycans might have been attacked or nicked, maybe even both. There was a presence directly in front of Lucy. In fact, she felt the creature glowering down at her, so she threw a sharp glare and emitted a low growl into the air, then felt the creature take a step back.

Her sights returned to Draxon. "You know, if you still can't make up your mind on whether to control or kill me when you're just across a river in a territory I'm very familiar with, you're even dumber than I remembered."

Though offended, Draxon was controlled, scoffing darkly to shake off the humiliation. "Keep talking, Lucy. That mouth of yours might have gotten a lot of creatures to kneel at your feet, but not me. Trust me, when the dust settles, ALL OF YOU will be at MY feet."

Juan sniggered. "Us? At the feet of someone who doesn't even have the balls to be on the field ready to fight his opponents? One who had to use another species just to get an upper hand, and even then still chooses to stay eight feet away because he's too afraid to die?"

His allies chuckled condescendingly, but hisses and growls came from over the river when ten vampires appeared next to Draxon.

Juan linked every other warrior in Blue Crescent. Once his eyes cleared, Draxon noted with a sinister smirk, "Linking for help is a big mistake, Juan."

In her brother's defense, Lucy snarled, "How about you think about the way your beta kicked your ass and claimed your title *and* pack before you tell my brother what to do as alpha!"

Draxon tsked. "Lucy. Lucy. Lucy. Still so presumptuous. My former beta was *not* better than me. Not before he took my title, not after that either. He couldn't even keep his own mate and pups safe when my amigos paid a . . . friendly visit. Weak, like I always said he was. But no one listened. And look where it got them."

The realization shook them. They knew Fleet Wood was decimated by rogues, but they didn't know they were Draxon's rogues. Margaret gasped a little too loudly, drawing attention that she didn't want from her former mate.

Draxon threw Margaret a bored look. "Yeah, I saw you back there. Still not worth my time. But your parents died a quick death, I can tell you that."

"You killed them!" Margaret hissed, eyes glistening as her animal howled in pain at their loss. It had been thirteen years, but she still missed them every single day. Tate held her by her shoulders when he growled at Draxon.

Explaining casually like he didn't order a massacre of his own pack, Draxon corrected, "Well, no. The people I hired killed . . . everyone, really. Whoever said revenge wasn't the answer should really do a reality check." He chuckled darkly. "It felt really good. The smell of blood that day—" he whistled "—it smelled like accomplishment."

Lucy snarled, "Enough of this!" Her claws protruded and plunged through the vampire in front of her. The discretus shrieked and came into view before he fell onto the ground, and the rest got the cue to start attacking. One thing good about harming vampires—they won't heal.

Lucy's eyes turned sapphire again, compelling Draxon to kneel and stop breathing as he choked out, "Do . . . it."

The ten vampires by Draxon's side got to work. Their teal-green eyes turned pitch black, confirming that they were decipimus, who channeled their manipulation powers on Lucy.

Xandar was helping those at the back and had just killed another discretus who almost got one of the Blue Crescent warriors when he felt his wife's mind being compressed and her legs giving way. He began sprinting toward her before he was knocked away by two other discreti. The king pushed himself up, and his claws blindly scratched the air in front of him as he sprinted toward his mate, whose heart rate was increasing as she continued the mental battle with ten manipulators.

With a thunderous growl, he ordered, "Get those motherfuckers across the river away from my wife!"

Disregarding their own safety, every lycan and werewolf tried their best to charge forward, but many were blocked by the invisible freaks. Some lycans and werewolves even got nicked and fell to the ground.

The discreti were working in pairs now. One to distract and one to bite. Draxon was smiling broadly at how things were playing out. He especially enjoyed seeing Lucy on her knees. Before *him*. Her hands dug into the ground and pulled at the grass to cope with the mental torment, and her panting was visible as the droplets of sweat fell from her head. Draxon smirked wider, taking steps to cross the river, intending to lift her face and relish in looking into her anguished eyes while he pulled out her tongue and tossed it into the river to shut her up for good.

But within a few moments that felt like an eternity, Lucy's growl came out louder than anyone had ever heard before. The strength echoed through the forest as she pushed herself up like she had merely experienced a simple fall when—in reality—it was like she was crushed by ten boulders.

The queen radiated her Authority, which pushed back the manipulators' compression just enough for her to get to Draxon.

The manipulators were visibly stunned, and exchanged uncertain glances before trying to manipulate her mind again, trying to confuse her into thinking that they and Draxon were her allies and those on her side were enemies. Lucy exerted her full strength and blocked it all out, wasting no time in compelling Draxon to raise his hands.

Horror entered Draxon's eyes when his claws extended without his control and he began attacking the manipulators around him. Lucy managed to make him kill two and injure one before another twisted his neck. Draxon's lifeless body fell to the ground with a thud, and Lucy was the first to jump across the river with another ferocious growl and fiery eyes, shifting into her lycan form as she did.

The decipimus panicked and fled from the white-furred, striped-tailed beast. Lucy easily caught up to the slowest one and killed her first decipio, then a few moments later, her second. Xandar, Greg, Christian and the alliance members were catching up as well.

The decipimus mind-linked one another, hastily trying to hatch a plan as they kept running. One tripped, and she met her demise when Christian ripped her head off. Juan crushed her detached skull when he leaped over her corpse.

Xandar closed in and—after a quick estimation—leaped off the ground and landed flat on one, ripping off his arms and hearing him scream before snapping his neck.

Six down. Four to go.

The four remaining decipimus leaped on separate trees and climbed higher and higher. Lucy and the others were not backing down. They started climbing, albeit slower since they didn't practice climbing anything. The wolves had to shift back to do the same.

The vampires picked whatever they could find on the branches and threw it at them, mostly fruits and nests. Greg was still in his human form, and he got so frustrated at the mangoes smacking his face that he started catching the fruits just to throw them back.

When the vampires were at the highest branches, they exchanged a firm nod and targeted Xandar's mind. Xandar instantly fell onto the ground with a loud thump. Lucy leaped off the tree, hands on his chest and arm, frantically linking him if he was alright. She didn't feel that any part of his body was broken, but the fact that his animal seemed to feel trapped was worrying her. *Xandar. Xandar, darling. Can you hear me?'*

His animal pushed itself up as it wobbled around, shaking its head hard to get the caging sensation out. Lucy's lycan steadied him by his arms as her animal whimpered, trying to get her mate to open his eyes. She felt his annoyance, struggle, and frustration, and it was getting worse by the second.

As she cupped his face, her thumb stroked his cheek to calm him and her nose brushed against his. His breathing hastened instead of steadied. And when his eyes opened, they weren't the lilac or onyx ones she had fallen for. They were dark green.

'Xandar, listen to me. You can fight this. Trust your animal. It knows AHHHH—' Lucy's lycan howled in high-pitched anguish when Xandar's claws plunged right through her abdomen before his second set of claws scratched her face. As if that wasn't brutal enough, he then tossed her with full force against a tree. The smell of her blood filled the air, and those climbing the trees didn't think twice before aborting their plan to chase the remaining decipimus.

Xandar felt her injuries and pain through their bond, and he, too, held his abdomen as he steadied himself, anger and worry set in his eyes. Even so, he wasn't done with her, as she was still trying to recover as she endured.

Xandar towered over her, shifted back, and proclaimed in a cold baritone, "You *will* regret hurting *my mate.*"

As her lycan continued whimpering—an express plea for him to wake up—her human part tried to do the same. *'Xandar, snap out of it! I am your mate!'*

His face started twitching, like he was fighting off something before the manipulation engulfed him when he snarled, "Never! You will *never* be my mate!" He was about to pounce on her before Greg knocked him out of the way. Without wasting a second, the duke lifted the king and threw him as far away as he could from the queen.

With distressed eyes, Greg helped her sit up as gently as possible. When he heard a disgruntled growl and saw Xandar getting back up again, shifting as he did, the duke barked his order to his followers, "WE SWORE ALLEGIANCE TO THE QUEEN, NOT THE KING! PROTECT HER AT ALL COST!" A claque of howls echoed through the space as every royal rogue shifted and charged toward the largest lycan.

Christian approached the queen and Greg pushed aside his reluctance to speak to a Blackfur, instructing him, "Stay with her." He allowed himself another brief look at Lucy, fighting the constriction in his chest at the bloody sight of her, before joining his people, shifting with them to stop his idiotic cousin.

The sight of Xandar fighting against their friends and allies was so agonizing to watch that Lucy's eyes glassed with tears. Christian blocked her view and linked gently, *'Focus on your recovery, my queen. They can slow him down, but you might be the only one who'll be able to stop him.'*

She tried to look away to do just that, which was when she witnessed a sight that would forever be etched in her memory, that would now invade her dreams and wake her up as nightmares—her closest friends attacking one another.

Blood was already oozing out of the wound on the left side of Zeke's torso, and he was still dodging blows from his dark green-eyed mate. "Zel! Snap out of it! It's me!"

Toby was fighting off a manipulated Juan. "Juan! C'mon! I didn't invite myself for this! It's just vampire magic! Fight it, Goddess damn it!"

Margaret was facing the same dilemma with Azalea. "Az! Quit it! The real crooks are getting away!"

And that was how it was everywhere Lucy looked. Tate was trying to land blows on a dead-faced Lovelace without hurting her too much; Phelton was struggling to find his best forms of attack without over-hurting Raden; and even Lauren was blindly attacking her colleagues.

With the little strength she had, Lucy linked them, *'Knock them out cold!'*

They threw her an "Are you sure?" look before dodging another attack from their opponents, concluding that blacking them out was the only safe way for now.

Toby aimed at the back of Juan's head, and the alpha fell flat on the ground. "Sorry about this, brother. You can punch me in the gut later." He went on to help the next one.

Margaret saw what the others were doing and got the idea, so she knocked Azalea out with little difficulty but a lot of guilt.

Zeke dodged a few more attacks before saying, "Babe, I'm really sorry about this. I love you." Zelena growled before Zeke knocked her out, then sat on the ground and held her in his arms, burying his face in her hair as he whispered an endless stream of "I'm sorry."

The sound of bone cracking brought Lucy's attention back to Xandar. He was snapping limbs and throwing wolves and lycans. Their anguished howls and blood weren't making him any more merciful. Greg began wrestling with him, but it was clear that the duke wasn't going to win. The mate bond made the lycan king almost invincible.

Lucy turned to Christian with alarmed eyes. *'Help Greg!'*

Christian seemed hesitant before his queen's order came out fiercer in her weakened voice, *'Help Greg Claw, Your Grace. That's an order.'*

Nodding in compliance, he left to join the effort. Xandar punched Greg to the ground before landing two merciless blows on his face and abdomen. He then held Greg by his neck with one hand and lifted him off the ground. His fingers were slowly tightening, and Greg's dazed animal began losing air.

Christian thought to himself, *'I'm so sorry for this, Cuz.'* The second-in-command plunged his claws right through Xandar's arm, earning an angry growl as the other duke slipped right out of the king's grip.

Greg was visibly surprised, but not for long. After exchanging a knowing glance with his distant cousin, both dukes pinned the king to the ground on either side. Their combined forces seemed to hold him. Just when Greg was about to ask Ivory to knock Xandar out, the king growled again and flicked the dukes away like they were mere insects. Both his cousins flew and knocked against trees at a significant distance away. The impact hurt their spines and heads, and they were trying their best to heal as quickly as they could.

In that time, Xandar sped toward Lucy in strides so large and with a force so strong that it plowed through anyone standing in its way. When he reached Lucy, his hand pinned her neck to the tree. She knew mind-linking him wouldn't work, so she resorted to using her Authority instead, directing the power to his mind, focusing on connecting with his animal. Right there, in the center of his animal's control room, she helped him push away the manipulation effects just like how she pushed her own earlier.

Xandar's eyes flickered. His head shook violently, trying to fight it off with her, and eventually, he did. His grip around her neck loosened, and Lucy gently removed it. The lilac shades returned to his eyes, and the sight of his injured mate petrified him. *'BABY! WHAT HAPPENED TO YOU?'* A hand, with claws retracted, hovered over her face before his deep, homicidal voice dominated their link, *'Who did this?'*

A relieved smile crossed her lips. Her animal cooed and pressed its forehead against his. When she still heard snarls, howls, and shouting, realization dawned on her that the battle was still ongoing. She faced the battlefield and emitted her Authority once more, channeling it through them, removing the effects of the manipulation.

The manipulated ones came to an abrupt halt in their attack as they looked at their ally, colleague, or friend in utter confusion. Some weren't even embarrassed to ask, "Uh . . . what am I doing?"

'Baby, talk to me. Who attacked you?' Xandar questioned as patiently as he could, his animal already growling, ready for revenge.

'Get me to the river, please. I need to wash this off.' She motioned to the blood stains on her face. It was just so much more visible with her white fur.

Xandar's black-furred animal carried her ever so gently and dashed to the riverbank, nuzzling her face along the way. Her lycan was drained from the physical and mental battle, so she retreated from exhaustion. By the time Xandar reached the river, Lucy was in her human form, naked.

It was the first time Xandar and his animal were not aroused by her fully exposed body. Their worry and anger took precedence. After sitting by the riverbank, he shifted back as well for easier conversation. When Lucy was done cleaning her face and abdomen, she covered her breasts with her arms, and Xandar's broad arm shielded her lower region.

He sat butt naked on the ground when his onyx eyes pierced into hers. "*Who* did this to you, Lucy? Tell me." He felt her animal's exhaustion, and the insides of her abdomen were still healing as well.

One of her hands reached for his face. "It was the vampires, Xandar. Really."

"No." Xandar knew she was lying. "You wouldn't have sustained an injury this grave if it were a vampire. Their claws don't make a wound this deep. Tell me who did this, Lucy." His best guess was another wolf or lycan. Maybe Draxon brought friends that none of them saw at first?

"Darling, it really was the rogue vampires—the proditors. The decip—"

Xandar looked her dead in the eye and asked again in a low snarl, "That's *enough*, Lucy. No more trying to protect someone else over yourself. Who. Did. This?"

Greg's cold voice came from behind, "If you let the queen finish, Cousin, you'd know that the one who injured her was you."

Xandar turned and growled at his cousin, who didn't even flinch like many others around him did before the king declared in a low, firm voice that held nothing but ferocious certainty and undeniable devotion, "I would NEVER hurt MY MATE!"

"Cuz . . ." Christian's somber look and cautious interruption gave Xandar second thoughts.

Then everything started to come back. How he felt his mind being invaded when he was climbing the tree, chasing down a vampire; him falling to the ground; his mate's white lycan coming to him; him . . . plunging his claws right through her abdomen, the very area that was still in the midst of healing when he carried her to the riverbank; and him . . . scratching her face. One of the scratches was so close to her right eye that he could have blinded her had she not turned away in time. He then . . . tossed her against a tree, like she was nothing. He almost blinded and killed the very creature he'd sworn to protect, the one he'd vouched to love.

His sights moved back to his mate, his hand gently touching her now-healed abdomen, and his fingers gently ran across her now-flawless face. He could still see the scratches he made there in his mind even though they were no longer visible in reality. His breathing got heavy as the memories of the real events came back and his eyes glistened in hot tears as his heart squeezed until it got hard to breathe.

Lucy cupped his cheek and made him look at her. Despite her weakened physique, her voice still rang strong when she said, "It wasn't you, Xandar. You would NEVER do that to me. You love me. You and your beast would never hurt me. That wasn't either one of you. It was the decipio proditors. They manipulated you to do what you did. We'll deal with this. We'll talk to Pelly and Octavia, and we'll end this. Okay?"

Xandar's face was still hard and eyes were still filled with tears. His jaw was clenched taut, and he swallowed. His head slowly turned to the left, where Christian was, before his voice came in a low, shivering command, "Tell the empress we're meeting her in her castle within the next hour. I want her entire governing body and security forces ready to meet us. I want full access to every corner of their empire to hunt down the proditors who were here and those they work for. I want answers to every question we'll have when we land. One absentee, one rejected request, one vague or wrong answer, and I *will* declare war to annihilate *every* decipio in existence."

"On it," Christian noted, and ran back to get his phone in his trousers among some torn-up garment somewhere.

Lucy tried to calm Xandar a little by stroking his arm, but it was clear that it wasn't working. He planted a deep kiss on her forehead, knowing that a million apologies would never make up for what he did nor would a million kisses and declarations and promises of his love for her rectify the past hour.

Lucy felt his hot tears fall on her hair and she cooed, "Shh . . . I love you, Xandar. I love you. We'll get through this together. We always will. I love you."

Many wolves and lycans were sent to the pack clinic for blood transfusion. Some were so incapacitated by the venom that their friends and allies had to carry them. Eighteen wolves and ten lycans, two of whom were Greg's followers and one of whom was Phelton, were in a coma as the Blue Crescent's chief of medicine called two ally packs for supplies and asked for extra doctors and nurses. Xandar got Dr. Yeil from lycan territory to send over some of his staff and bring more blood as well.

Seeing how dangerous the proditors were capable of being even in small numbers, everyone refrained from sending trackers to follow the decipimus' scent trail. The royals and alliance members cleaned up, dressed, and headed for Tate's, Toby's, and Christian's jets with stoned faces.

Liam was regretting asking his aunt to come back when he saw how tired she was just through her eyes, which shone less than they normally would. Juan made sure Hale hid all their pups, especially Liam, before Xandar brought Lucy into the pack house to use the bathroom.

Before they left the pack, Lucy mustered as much strength and assurance as she could to tell Liam that he did the right thing, and made him promise that if anything like this happened again, he'd tell her. Liam nodded in obedience and waved goodbye as the convoy of cars left Blue Crescent.

On the jet, Xandar placed Lucy in a window seat before sinking into the seat next to hers as he held her hand. It felt weird, so Lucy got up and made her space on his lap, where she always sat when they traveled by air. Xandar hesitated. Nonetheless, his strong arms held her in place, careful to avoid touching her abdomen.

She leaned into his warm chest and listened to his heart that was beating at a slightly-higher-than-average rhythm. Her fingers ran across his torso, planting a deep kiss over his shirt, right over his heart. Xandar's anger subsided just the slightest. His animal was still furious that they had been made to harm the very creature they claimed to love most. The curse of being manipulated was that it didn't wipe out one's memories of reality. Hurting his mate—the mother of his daughter—would be an image that would be etched in his mind forever.

Kissing her head in return, he uttered, "I love you, baby."

Her tired eyes still sparkled a little when she whispered, "I know, Xandar. I love you too."

He managed a small smile. "Sleep, my little freesia. We're not reaching there anytime soon. I'll wake you when we land." Lucy mm-ed and snuggled into him as his fingers trailed down her hair while she drifted off.

On the same jet, Zelena's face was as hard as cold metal as Zeke continued stroking her hand and cooing her through their link. It was taking every bit of patience for Zelena to not start screaming profanities at the proditors who were no longer in sight. Lovelace had her fingers pressed against her forehead, staring out the window, unable to accept her actions on the battlefield. Juan apologized to Toby for the third time before the defense minister decided to take a nap after telling the alpha—again—that it wasn't his fault to begin with. Azalea replayed the memory over and over, somehow wishing that she was remembering things wrong.

CHAPTER 26

The jet roared through the castle courtyard when it touched ground in less than an hour. The lycan ministers who were not involved in the Blue Crescent battle received an urgent link from Christian and met them there. Sir Weaver spotted a very weak queen in the king's arms when he was descending the airstair and would have fallen had Lord Yarrington not held him by his arm.

The two vampire servants who were there to greet them looked hospitable at first, but the moment they saw the faces of the wolves and lycans—which were nothing short of murderous—they became visibly frightened, jittering as they waited. One servant nudged the other as he himself became invisible—courtesy of his defense mechanism. The other servant, who was a velox, fought the urge to sprint away and fidgeted when he forced a smile and said, "R-Right th-this way, Y-Your Highnesses."

Once they were inside, the servant stuttered again when he asked them— or pleaded with them— to wait while he and his still-invisible colleague informed the empress of their presence.

Lucy finally managed to convince Xandar to put her down, and she studied the surroundings. Black-and-white tiled floors and cedar-colored walls opened up to a gray ceiling that would have made the room a dark cave had there not been five chandeliers and wall lamps lighting up the hall. Huge portraits of past rulers crowded the space, all of which shared the same bronze frame of the same size. It was as if vampire rulers were forbidden from smiling when each emperor looked more menacing than the next.

"HOW MANY MORE FUCKING DAYS DO YOU NEED TO COME UP WITH A DAMN PLAN?" an ear-piercing roar came from upstairs, and those who'd met Pelly recognized that it was her voice. "YOU'VE MADE ZERO PROGRESS IN THE PAST WEEK! OUR PEOPLE ARE STILL MISSING! YOU REFUSED THE LYCANS' HELP TO FIND THEM! NOW, FOR ALL WE KNOW, THE ONES WHO TOOK OUR OWN ARE THE ONES WHO MADE THE LYCANS AND WEREWOLVES ATTACK ONE ANOTHER! THEY COULD HAVE LOST THEIR QUEEN TONIGHT!" The slamming of a table resounded before the empress's voice continued ringing angry and strong, "DO YOU IDIOTS HAVE *ANY* IDEA HOW DIRE OUR SITUATION IS? IF I HADN'T MET THEIR RULERS, IF OUR PRESENT RELATIONSHIP DIDN'T START OUT SMOOTHLY, WE'D BE AT WAR RIGHT NOW! YOU'D BEST BELIEVE IF THAT EVER HAPPENS, I'M SENDING YOU AND YOUR FAMILIES TO THE FRONTLINES *FIRST*! I DON'T CARE IF THEY CAN'T FIGHT!"

Like the rest, Greg's eyes rested on the door on the first floor. Pressing his lips in mild satisfaction, he remarked, "I'd say we're off to a good start."

Lucy's eyes narrowed at what he termed "a good start." The empress was screaming her lungs out now. Who knew if she wasn't going to break a few necks soon. Then again, knowing Greg, breaking necks might be termed "a better start."

By her side, Xandar uttered, "And we're here to make sure that the momentum stays that way." To signify her disapproval, the back of Lucy's hand hit his chest with the little strength she had left. But Xandar simply took her hand and left a quick kiss, caressing it and hoping it'd regain its hardiness soon.

By his side, an unsmiling Christian patted his shoulder. "We will, Cuz. We will."

These cousins. Lucy thought to herself. Her insides began to boil, which only simmered down after Xandar pressed a deep kiss on her hairline.

"WHAAAAT?" Pelly shouted when the servants—the discretus had to force himself to be visible from the waist up—popped their heads through the timid opening of the door. Their legs wobbled when they told her that the neighboring species had arrived.

For a brief moment, the unsynchronized chirps of crickets outside seeped through the cracked windows like the murmurs of an audience after a stage performance. But the sound of nature faded away when the brisk clicking of heels and shuffled footsteps grew louder.

Pelly and Octavia exited the room, leaving the door ajar. Both dashed to stand before Xandar and Lucy. The queen smiled instantly and wanted to offer

Pelly a hug, but Xandar's hand on her waist held her in place as the king waited for the vampires to extend the greeting first.

The empress and consort bowed with no hesitation and visible remorse. Lucy was about to return the gesture, but her cold-faced husband held her up, refusing to let her knees bend even by an inch. She started throwing him an annoyed glare before Pelly began apologizing in a tone that was so different from mere seconds ago that a normal creature would think that the one who screamed and the one speaking to them now were two different creatures. "I don't even know where to begin, Aunt Lucy, Uncle Xandar. I cannot tell you how . . . embarrassed and sorry I feel that this happened on my watch. Uh . . . Octavia and I have no issues with giving you and your people full access to look under every nook and cranny of this empire at any time of day. Our governing members, security forces, and even the vigils, remain at your disposal. You have full authorization to go wherever you want and speak to whoever you wish."

"Even the prisoners?" Greg asked, surprising everyone present.

Octavia's left brow rose in confusion when Pelly replied, "Well, if that's necessary, then, yes. We can make arrangements for anyone you'd like to see, um . . ."

Pelly threw Lucy a puzzled look, not knowing how to address Greg because she didn't know who he was. Lucy explained simply, "This is the duke from Xandar's paternal side."

Nodding in comprehension, she addressed him, "Your Grace." It was then that curiosity entered her emerald orbs. She took a longer look at Greg, feeling his familiar energy, then stepped toward him and stretched out her hand. "May I, Your Grace?"

"What?" Greg questioned with squinted eyes like she had just spoken in another language.

Lucy murmured, "Give her your hand, Your Grace. She'll listen to the rhythm of your blood flow. It'll tell her if you two met in another lifetime."

"*What?*" Greg asked again, his quizzical look given to Lucy this time.

Xandar's patience was running out. "Just give her your damn hand, Greg. Stop wasting time. We've got work to do."

As Greg put his hand into the empress's pale one, he fired back, "The fact that we're all still here and not in that chamber up there with those other blood-suckers *is* wasting time. I would've barged in through those doors without an invitation if I were you."

When Pelly had her answer, she let go of Greg's wrist, smiled wryly, and said, "Thank you, Your Grace." She then gestured the lycans and werewolves toward the stairs. "Right this way, please."

Greg paused, protesting, "Woah, woah, woah. I let you listen to my blood, and now you just want to get on with business without telling me whatever the queen said you were going to tell me."

Lucy's eyes widened in irritation when she suggested, "Maybe if you ask nicely, she'll tell you."

Pelly, who paused in her steps the moment Greg started speaking, smirked at him and gave him a "What's it going to be?" look. Octavia tried to mask her amusement by pressing her lips together but her smiling eyes gave her away.

Greg looked at Lucy in disbelief, like he was asking her to reconsider. In a hushed tone that only those with the sharpest hearing could catch, she said, "What happened wasn't the rulers' fault, not entirely, at least. No one wanted to screw up. We can, and we have, bargained for more help, more access, and more say in this matter. But we do not stoop to the level of bullying this species or any species. We negotiate, we argue, and we fight for our people's best interests. Unless there is clear evidence of willful ignorance and intentional lack of care, we won't resort to condescending any individual creature to get what we want. Is that clear, Your Grace?"

Greg knew he was supposed to be afraid of those partially onyx orbs piercing into his soul, but he wasn't. Her commanding energy simply reminded him of why she was the only creature worthy of being the queen in the first place.

Although Lucy was speaking specifically to Greg, Xandar absorbed every word like a sponge. His lips curled into a soft smile as he fell even more in love with her, and he muttered affectionately, "As you wish, my queen."

Greg was brought out of his daze and repeated the same line with a smile of loyalty. Now came the hard part: to actually be nice. Bullying was just so much easier. Greg cleared his throat, met the empress's gaze, and monotonously said, "Please."

"Really, Greg? Please? That's all you got?" Lucy questioned.

Pelly seemed satisfied when she continued trotting up the stairs, "Oh, that's a big improvement from his last life, Aunt Lucy. My late father and I failed to fathom how Aunt Rosie managed to hold a conversation with him without exploding. She'd always protect me from his disparaging remarks, and without her smothering the flames, father would've killed him just for the way he spoke."

Xandar asked, "So who was he?"

"Aunt Rosie's personal bodyguard, Sir Gerald Knightly. He came when Uncle Reagan couldn't. History records that before Uncle Reagan killed his own father, he killed Knightly for failing to uncover the plot to poison Aunt Rosie before she was poisoned."

That really was a surprise. Xandar hadn't mentioned anything about Rosalie having a bodyguard because he didn't find any material in lycan territory recording such a person himself.

The nemesis cousins exchanged glances before Greg whispered in frustration, "Who the fuck are Aunt Rosie and Uncle Reagan?"

Lucy pointed between her and Xandar, and everything started falling into place for Greg. If that bloodsucking empress was telling the truth, and that damn subject was right, Greg wondered if this constant need to protect Lucy was because he failed to do just that in the past. He wondered if he pissed her off in their last life like he did in this one. He wondered if he fell in love with her more than a millennium ago like he had fallen for her now.

When they reached the meeting chamber, Pelly pushed open the two doors and stormed in, gesturing the wolves and lycans to the empty seats at the long table on the left. The vampire officials were at the long table on the right. The moment Lucy sat in the chair that Xandar had pulled out for her, she noticed the vampires had bruises and cuts on their faces. Some even had black eyes.

Did Pelly slam the table with her hands or their heads? Lucy wondered.

Christian was next to Xandar, and Greg beside Lucy. The alliance and remaining ministers took their seats alongside them. Greg followed Lucy's worried gaze and noted the vampires' freshly beaten-up faces, then leaned toward her and muttered, "I have a very good feeling about this meeting, my queen." Lucy threw him a warning look, and the duke tried hard to press back an amused smirk. Toby sat next to Greg just in case Lucy needed a good comeback to silence this duke.

At the sight of Maddock, Xandar's bubbling anger neared eruption. Lucy reached for his clenched fist on the table, making it loosen as their fingers laced together. The sparks made a feeble attempt to soothe his raging inferno.

As soon as Pelly sat with Octavia, Rafael, and Amber at the four-seater table perpendicularly positioned between the long tables on the left and right, the empress gave Xandar a nod to begin.

Scowling at Maddock, Xandar's low voice came out in a manner that would've paralyzed the faint-hearted. "Walk us through every single step of the investigation since we last met, Maddock." Despite the innocuous request, the tone made it sound as if only good news and useful information would be allowed. Anything less would warrant the murder of the minister.

Maddock had a cut near his left eye, and he tried not to glower at Xandar as he gave the details. "I asked for thirteen vigils from Their Imperial Majesties and sent them to track the scents picked out from Falling Vines. They lost the trail at the Forest of Oderem, so I'd say following the scents wasn't a good way to start the investigation to begin with. We invested time there, and we lost more time when the venture yielded no results."

With immense restraint, Xandar swallowed a growl before questioning, "And what would you have done if it wasn't to follow the scents?"

"Order a search party, perhaps."

Christian pressed, "In which part of the empire?"

"The vicinity of Falling Vines and, later on, Saber Vagary." Maddock couldn't believe he was being interrogated by creatures less than half his age. What made it worse was that these were low-life lycans!

"Is that so?" Lucy taunted.

Everyone on her side either leaned back to enjoy the show ahead like Christian and Juan, or sat up in anticipation of what was to come next, like Xandar, Greg, and Toby. Once Lucy spoke in that tone with that look, one can be assured that whatever came out next would either be deathly humorous or mercilessly frightening.

Lucy could see why both Xandar and Toby didn't like Maddock now. "Well, your hindsight must be *extremely* insightful, Maddock. No one could have *possibly* thought to search within the vicinity of the villages upon hearing about the abduction." A few vampires didn't get the sarcasm and were smirking obnoxiously at the young queen's ignorance when the joke was actually on them.

Maddock, however, wasn't deaf to it. Forcing a smile, he uttered less confidently, "We have thought about it and executed it in a timely manner, Your Highness."

Lucy mocked a bewildered look, but powered just enough strength in her voice to make it clear that the lycans' inferiority in ruling status did not mean that they could be stepped on. "I'm confused, Maddock. Why would you want a solution that you've already executed in a timely manner which did not even reap *any* results? At least we gave a trail that led your deployed forces to the Forest of Oderem. Where did your own instructions lead to?"

Silence ensued before Octavia prompted, "Answer the queen's question, Maddock. Stop wasting everyone's time."

Maddock swallowed a lump in his throat. "Only around the village." Clearing his throat to muster a little more confidence, he spoke again, "I . . . apologize for what I said earlier, Your Highnesses."

Toby and Christian would have cheered if they were allowed to. Lucy wasn't celebrating just yet. Her voice demanded respect when it echoed in the chamber, "The best apology is a changed attitude, Maddock. We shall see if you're *capable* of that. With regards to the investigation, is it safe to say that you didn't personally join the vigils?"

Maddock tried to walk around answering the question, "That's . . . not how we handle things here, Your Highness. I'm an administrator. I don't go on these expeditions. Not anymore, that is. My job is simply to find the best creatures for the task. I've long retired from being on the field." Embarrassment seemed to have rained over the vampires at his response.

Xandar couldn't hold back the low snarl when he leaned forward. "So as the administrator who led the investigation, you have *no* insight as to what happened that you wouldn't have the slightest hint of how twenty-eight of my people are in a coma, thirty are hoping that they won't join the twenty-eight while they wait for blood from allies, and you have ZERO idea of who was behind forcing me to almost . . . kill . . . my wife?"

The chill from Xandar's voice made some of the younger vampires shudder, even though they themselves were older than the king. The atmosphere was never this tense since the war more than 204 years ago when the vampires used this chamber to discuss the stages of attack and strategize their troops. The vigils, who stood in a row behind the governing ministers, prayed to the Lord that the king wouldn't declare war. Their families really couldn't fight. There wasn't a need to learn since the truce. But from the way Xandar was speaking, many knew that the truce might just be coming to an end.

Lucy stroked Xandar's tightened grip. Her free hand reached out to touch his forearm as she whispered, "Xandar, I agree that none of this is okay. But please, there's still a way. They can still help us. We just haven't found the right creatures to ask yet. Let's find the ones who can give us answers. Let's find *the* way. What do you say?"

Xandar tore his onyx eyes away from Maddock, who was turning whiter than he already was with each passing second. Every fiber and bone in Xandar's body was ready to tell his wife that enough was enough, that these creatures were given enough time and came back with nothing, that there was no point in wasting more time.

But the moment Lucy's soft orbs held his hard ones captive, the king miraculously forgot what he was supposed to say. His features softened. Like his animal had been trained, he took a few slow, deep breaths to calm himself as he focused on her comforting touch, ultimately kissing her forehead, replaying her words from earlier and muttering, "Okay."

A few vigils sighed in relief at Xandar calming down, and this did not please Toby or the rest of the alliance members. Greg even muttered, "Lucky bastards."

Toby couldn't help but agree. The vampires should be groveling on the ground thanking the queen right now for saving their asses. This party was not over.

Lucy's face turned business-like serious when she proceeded to speak to the vampires, "Those who were personally involved in the investigation, please come forward." Thirteen suspended vigils took the requested step with still-terrified eyes. "Which one of you led the tracking?" the queen demanded.

A ginger-haired man took another step forward. "That would be me, Your Highness."

Lucy nodded. "Your name?"

He seemed surprised. Normally, officials merely asked for his code, which would be VIG 001. He couldn't remember the last time he was asked for a name by someone of higher authority. He blinked like he was processing the two-word question before answering, "Duica, Your Highness."

"Duica," Lucy noted. "Walk us through the investigation, but only specify every odd detail along the trail."

Every odd detail? He exchanged a puzzled look with his comrades before sheepishly admitting, "I'm sorry, Your Highness. I'm afraid I don't understand."

He was pleasantly surprised that Lucy didn't sigh in exasperation like the empress would. The queen simply explained, "What stood out when you and your team went down the trail or when you were in the old castle next to the forest? Did any of you see, hear, smell, or feel anything that was unusual for a vampire territory? Perhaps one of you sensed a presence or heard a sound when you didn't expect to? Did the forest emit any scents when you were within its proximity?"

A wave of comprehension washed over them. Duica mind-linked those who joined him that day, and they exchanged firm nods at the end of the discussion. VIG 001 glanced nervously at the empress, then back at the queen, cleared his throat, and spoke, "In the abandoned castle, when we were at the castle window next to the Forest of Oderem, we detected a scent that matched . . . the empress's."

CHAPTER 27

Octavia was the first to exclaim, "WHAT THE HELL ARE YOU SUGGESTING? THAT THE EMPRESS ABDUCTED HER OWN PEOPLE?"

Lucy's voice rang through the chamber a little more calmly, "Yes, Duica. What are you suggesting? Was this only detected at the window?"

Duica gulped. "No, in fact. It was . . ." he looked to his comrades for support, who all gave him an ominous nod for him to disclose the whole truth ". . . we realized that it was the empress's scent at the window, but when we investigated the rest of the castle, we found that the scent was . . . in every room and corridor, albeit less concentrated than by the window."

Before anyone could say anything, Lucy murmured, "Odd." Turning to a still-shocked Pelly, she asked, "You've never been there, have you, Pelly?"

Gratitude entered the empress's confused eyes. "No, I've never even seen it."

"Very odd," Lucy muttered.

Everyone heard the contemplation in her voice. Almost every wolf and lycan—even some of the vampires—were starting to suspect that the empress and consort were the real culprits all along. The only ones who were sure of their innocence were Lucy, Xandar, Rafael, and Amber. Greg was on the fence on this one. He didn't have enough information to decide.

Pivoting to the duke, Lucy asked, "Greg, can scent sprays be . . . custom-made to match a very specific creature, like the empress, for example?"

"Not to my knowledge, my queen. But . . ." Staring into space, he gave the feasibility some thought. "I must admit that it's not impossible, with an empress's close associate and with a very high fee due to the risks and dangers of getting caught using the scent of a ruler to cover their tracks."

Toby voiced out his view, "Lucy, it couldn't be scent sprays. By the time the vigils got to the castle, any of it would've vanished, wouldn't it?"

Greg pointed at Toby and added, "That would be right, unless the empress's scent was sprayed there a lot later, after they received word that a search party had been sent down that trail."

Xandar offered an alternative suggestion, "Perhaps it wasn't synthetic scent sprays to begin with, but the natural one?"

Pelly's eyes widened in disbelief when she thought Xandar was suggesting that she was there in person when she wasn't. Octavia was about to defend her wife again before Xandar continued, "Perhaps the scent was naturally produced by the Forest of Oderem, which then diffused into the castle through the window. The trail *is* the strongest there, after all."

Upon hearing this, Greg thought aloud, "So what you're saying is that the empress has never been to the abandoned castle, but she's been to the forest for it to replicate her scent?"

The vampires glowered at Greg like he had just said something offensive. Lucy quickly explained, "Greg, I doubt Her Imperial Majesty has been there. No ruler has. The only member of the imperial family who has—in the whole of history—is Count Dracula, who is . . . not the most celebrated figure, so following in his footsteps to enter the Forest of Oderem is considered . . . a sin in most regions of the empire. Plus, due to the . . . incomprehensible mystery of the forest, there's an unspoken rule that no emperor, empress, consort, or heir to the throne is ever to visit that place."

"Oh," Greg noted simply, and shifted his sights to Pelly before casually saying, "Pardon me. I'm not well-versed in forest voodoos."

"Greg!" Lucy reprimanded.

Octavia interjected, "It's alright, Lucy. Off the record, we give it unflattering names here too."

Greg looked at his queen with feigned innocence, and his hand motioned Octavia's way, his way of saying that he didn't say anything wrong.

Several vampires were impressed with Lucy's knowledge and were touched by the respect she had for their culture and taboos, even the indecipherable ones. Some were even beginning to grow fond of her despite what she had done to Maddock. But they were unanimously getting very annoyed with Greg's insensitivity.

Lucy only calmed down with Xandar stroking her hand as he continued speaking, "The prime mystery of the forest is that its curses can reach to the far corners of the empire, even those who've never stepped foot there, and it's still a complete enigma of how it can replicate *every* scent. But *why* it would do so is the question."

Amber's brows furrowed, sharing his frustration. "If only we knew, Your Highness. Our guess is as good as yours, that it's doing it to confuse us—the authorities."

Toby countered, "If that's true, why did it specifically copy the empress's scent? Why didn't it spray something that matched—excuse me for suggesting—yours, Duica's, or even Maddock's?"

Amber exchanged a nervous look with Rafael. She and everyone else were made fully aware of Xandar's threat to declare war if they gave vague or incomplete answers. Flustered and fearful, she admitted, "I want to give you the answers, Minister. I really do. But the forest is not something that any of us can understand."

"Except for those who used it to escape," Greg suddenly mentioned.

Amber agreed, "That's true, Your Grace. But those who used it to escape *have* escaped. We don't have anyone to ask."

"I wouldn't be too sure about that. Someone in prison might know something."

"I doubt it. Those were put there for petty crimes that were nowhere near the forest."

Greg scoffed. "This is where those of us in the rogue world have an upper hand. For some reason, you authority figures often believe that we operate solo when the fact is many of us don't. But, of course, I speak for lycans. I don't know if proditors are accustomed to doing things as a team, but the events in Blue Crescent today show us that—accustomed or not—rogue vampires who can work in a team *do* exist. And rogue teams that can work together are dangerous at best and lethal at worst."

Rafael said, "We do catch burglars working in teams of three from time to time, and crimes similar to those. But there are still some who work alone. In essence, whether proditors are indeed . . . communicating with one another and cooperating seems . . . varied from the records."

"Records show you nothing." Greg gave up trying to explain the obvious. Turning to Lucy, he declared, "We need someone on the inside who knows something, if not everything, my queen."

Lucy looked at Xandar like she was asking for permission, which he gave with a small smile and a subtle nod before she turned back to the duke. "I don't disagree, Greg. But, knowing how rogues operate, I have a feeling we aren't going to play fair. So I must ask: how are we going to get them to tell the whole truth?"

Greg spoke casually, "Well, if the Empress's Authority is out of the question, then torture should work. It has been effective on lycans."

Lucy's eyes widened, but not for the noble reason of not wanting to torture another being. Swinging her head, she said, "We are *not* doing that. The books say that the forest offers its followers some sort of protection. Whoever tortures its followers receives the same form of torture in return. They have this protection mark on their nape that only becomes visible when it's too late. It's not a legend. It's hist—"

"History. Damn that subject. Stupid forest." Greg slumped back into his seat.

Xandar used to be fascinated with the forest, but now, even he shared Greg's frustration.

Lucy continued cracking her head, and when an idea came, she asked Xandar, "Just to clarify, the books said nothing about *non*-vampires getting cursed, dearest?"

"Not from our archives."

His sights then went to Pelly, who confirmed, "Not from our archives either."

The queen nodded and looked back and forth between Xandar and Greg when she speedily muttered, "For the record, I'm only changing my mind now because I can't see another way."

Before Xandar or Greg could decipher her intention between the lines, she faced the vampire rulers and said, "Let *us* enter the Forest of Oderem."

"NO!"

Lucy didn't know how many creatures growled that word her way, but their combined volume was enough to make her animal cover its ears.

Xandar turned her to face him, squeezing her arms a little tighter than usual. "Babe, when we talked about this, we said we were putting our prisoners there, *not you.*"

"The prisoners won't necessarily do things our way or ask what we want, darling."

Juan exclaimed, "Lucy, are you out of your mind? No one knows how that thing works, and you just want to trespass like it is your own territory?"

His sister meekly countered, "Well, we're not trespassing if we have the forest's permission."

Greg was close to exploding as well. "How the *fuck* do we even get that? And you didn't think of bringing this up earlier, my queen?"

Xandar wasn't done either. "What about our daughter? Didn't you say it might affect her?"

"I don't think it will affect her or anyone else adversely in our case. It's like Greg said before: we're just trying to understand the forest. I get where he was coming from now. The forest might really feel flattered and give us what we're looking for—answers through scents or something like that."

Xandar threw Greg a piercing glare.

Greg was equally pissed. "My queen, putting what I said that way isn't fair. Like this cousin of mine, I suggested putting prisoners there. Or humans. Disposable creatures who are better off disposed. You—as I'm sure everyone will agree—*do not qualify*."

Adamant, Lucy persisted persuading her husband, "Think about it, Xandar. Every historical curse took effect *after* a ruler sought to destroy the forest. There's nothing in history that says one died of an unknown disease or had someone they loved taken from them by simply passing through."

Greg argued, "Didn't you mention that no guards are stationed there because it'll emit some sort of lethal odor, my queen?"

"Yes, because the guards weren't just passing through. They were there 24/7. How would you feel if someone watched you 24/7, Greg, someone who controls who comes to see you and invades your space as and when they please?"

Greg refused to answer that question. Glowering at his cousin, he uttered, "Even the most insignificant speck of dust in the kingdom knows you're powerless when it comes to the queen, but for the love of Goddess, don't pick this time to be powerless, Cousin. She *cannot* be allowed to go there."

"I don't need you to tell me that," Xandar replied in a low rumble before speaking to his stubborn mate much more gently, "Alright, babe. How about this? We'll send someone else in there for a test run. If what you're saying is true—that it's safe—we'll go in. Deal?"

With askance, she questioned, "Who are you suggesting?"

Pelly immediately offered, "I have twenty-six vigils at my disposal."

Lucy's eyes widened in shock, then stated the problem with that suggestion, "Pelly, the idea is to send non-vampires."

Octavia argued, "We heard that, Lucy. But if all that is needed to keep harm at bay is to enter the forest without intending to destroy it, then it won't matter what species we send in there, don't you think?"

None of the werewolves and lycans were on board with letting Lucy go either, so the queen was on her own when she tried to persuade the vampire rulers to reconsider. "We're talking about sending your most trusted investigators, Octavia."

Pelly and Octavia nodded like they were on the same page. Pelly replied, "Exactly. Who better to send than the very creatures with commendable track records of bravery, dedication, and undying loyalty? And you've said yourself, Aunt Lucy: the forest never cursed anyone who didn't want to demolish it. They'll be fine."

The lycans and wolves were conspicuously grateful that the empress was on their side. Pelly had just gotten back the person she thought was lost forever. She wasn't going to let Lucy put herself in unnecessary danger now that she had the power to protect her in a way that she couldn't do with Rosalie.

The chamber fell into dead silence as they waited for the queen's answer. Her eyes studied the vigils. Some of them might have families, spouses, even children. But what assured her was that they showed a readiness to serve, reminding her of herself and her friends. There was a willingness to fight and die trying. Sighing in defeat, she concurred, "Fine. Okay."

Those holding their breaths exhaled a relieved sigh. Greg slowly leaned back into his chair and muttered under his breath, "Goddess, this creature takes stubbornness to a whole new level."

Toby found himself responding, "Well, now you know what it's like to be us, Your Grace." Even he was surprised by what came out of his mouth. The minister had expected to speak against this duke in support of his best friend, not the other way around.

But everyone jolted when Lucy said, "But don't send them all at once, Pelly. Maybe two at a time? And don't wander too deep in at one go. Take it slow. Maybe the first pair could go as far as six feet in, the second pair could go ten feet, something like that?"

Pelly turned to her vigils and sternly prompted, "Noted?"

"Duly noted, Your Majesty." They bowed and uttered in unison.

Pelly's voice softened when her sights returned to the king and queen. "We'll start executing the plan tomorrow."

"And two days after that," Xandar insisted.

Before Lucy could argue, Octavia uttered with a firm nod, "And two days after that."

When that was settled, Toby raised his hand. "Can we borrow a few decipimus and discreti to guard Blue Crescent?"

"Of course, Minister," Pelly obliged with a smile, and signaled a team of six custodes—police persons—who complied with her silent command with a bow.

Octavia added, "Perhaps it's best if we send a few to all packs, Minister, just to be safe."

Shock made the heads of wolves and lycans turn to the consort. But Pelly merely gave her mate's hand a gentle squeeze, signifying her appreciation.

In genuine concern, Toby questioned, "Do you have enough to spare, Your Majesty? Your territory isn't exactly . . . proditor-proof yet."

Octavia grinned and reassured, "Well, Minister, I must admit that our species will be spread very thin across your packs, perhaps only two of each in each pack other than Blue Crescent. They will only act as a pair of eyes to see what wolves and lycans cannot. Some of them might not have sufficient skills for battle, so the burden of fighting must still be borne by your people, I'm afraid. With the abduction threat still present and our limited population, that's the most we can offer t—"

Before he could finish, Zelena exclaimed gratefully, "It's more than enough!"

Juan agreed, "Yes, that really is all we need—a pair of eyes that can see something that we can't. Thank you, Your Majesties."

Every pack leader's scowl was replaced with grateful smiles. The cold and distant atmosphere lifted, a connection that they never imagined being established with vampires formed.

Just when Pelly thought that was all, Rafael whispered something into her ear, then waited for her answer. Her brows furrowed when she reminded Rafael with concerned eyes, "Just be . . . very mindful about how you're going to phrase things."

Rafael nodded with a nervous smile, faced the king and queen, and said, "What I'm about to say is going to be potentially triggering for some . . . or for everyone, uh. . ." He chose his next words even more carefully. "When the decipimus . . . manipulated, what did it feel like, Your Highnesses?"

With that, the lightened atmosphere that took a lot of time and effort to reach was instantly and effectively tossed out the window. Tension rose intangibly and with speed in the pin-drop silence chamber, the weight pushing the other decipimus further into their seats despite not having anything to do with the attack.

Xandar's grip on Lucy's hand tightened when he explained, "Linguists haven't come up with a word to describe how I felt. The ordeal was a nightmare at best, a shattering experience at worst—the kind that puts you at its mercy. In the beginning, I felt caged before I was released into a world that's supposed to be real but really isn't. When the manipulation took effect, what I saw around me were only enemies—creatures we put behind bars less than a year ago. My friends and family who were fighting alongside me miraculously disappeared. My wife . . . was missing." He paused for a moment to be conscious of Lucy's thumb stroking his hand, and continued, "Some part of me felt that she was in danger, that she was hurt, and I had to find her. But the so-called enemies were standing in my way. The worst part? When Lucy was right in front of me, I didn't see her. I saw Kelissa Kylton—the very creature that did everything within her reach to hurt my mate with the goal of being crowned. When the manipulation effects wore off, I started remembering. Every detail of what I did to my allies are now more vivid than I'd prefer. As for every way I attacked my mate? Evocative: the way I looked dead into the eyes of the creature I love most and plunged my claws into her, the way she screamed through our link and howled into the sky, the way her blue eyes pierced into mine—with so much fear and obscurity, like she didn't even recognize me."

Juan, Lovelace, Azalea, and every other creature who had been manipulated easily related to his words. But no one dared suggest or could deny that Xandar and Zelena had it worst. They were both manipulated to hurt their mates with the intention of killing them.

Xandar looked away from Rafael, pressing away the hot tears from the corners of his eyes, and focused on Lucy cooing him through their link, *'It wasn't you, Xandar. It was the proditors. It really wasn't you, darling, please. You and your animal wouldn't have done that had you both known what was going on.'*

His head snapped to hers when he whisper-yelled, "But we should have known, Lucy!"

Her soft and assuring orbs peered into his when she whispered, "It's a power that none of us of this generation is familiar with yet. It really isn't your fault. Now that we know a little more about it, we might just be able to find a way around it. There might be a weak spot somewhere or a defense mechanism that no book has taught us yet. We'll find a way, okay?"

"It's an archaic power that's as old as the King's Authority. No one has ever found a way around it. What if we can't find a way?" Xandar questioned in worry and dismay. What he really was asking was: what if he was made to kill her? The thought of her dying by his hands shot an excruciating pain right to his heart. It constricted his chest, tightened his veins, and strangulated his soul, making it so suffocating that his animal curled up into a tight ball just to cope with the torment.

With determined eyes, she declared, "If we can't find a way, we'll *create* one. Another first, right?"

The power in her voice drew a smile along his hard features. The tormenting thoughts stopped. Determination built within him and he could breathe again. As the fear and agony subsided, he leaned in and pecked a kiss on her nose. "Right. Another first." A quick kiss on her lips before he muttered, "You're amazing."

After trying and failing to suppress her pink cheeks and shy smile, she gently pushed her husband back into his seat. Her eyes went to Rafael, but when she opened her mouth, Rafael immediately said, "If you'd prefer not to describe it, Your High-ness—" his voice cracked at the acknowledgment, and he harrumphed while one of his legs shook under the table "—I completely understand. Perhaps that was a very inappropriate question to ask."

So much for wanting to help. If the king's answer could turn the faces of warm-blooded creatures stone-cold when he was only manipulated by four proditors, imagine what the queen's answer was going to do when her mind was invaded by ten! Rafael prayed to Lord he didn't just ask a question that could further jeopardize diplomatic relations or, Lord forbid, start a war. His best friend would probably kill him before he even made it to the frontlines.

With as much diplomacy as he could muster, Christian queried, "I don't mean to be rude, Rafael, but if you knew it was inappropriate, why pose the question in the first place?"

Rafael was thankful that Christian didn't make him feel even more intimidated and explained apologetically, "In all honesty, Your Grace, I was trying to assess the level of skill of those who were there, to see what we're all up against."

Greg had the most brilliant retort to assert that whatever Rafael had just said was complete bullshit, but before the words came out, Lucy said, "Then let's assess that together."

Greg, in effect, had to deliberately shut his opening mouth. Being nice was getting painful.

Rafael wasn't even subtle in taking a breath and holding it as she began, "When the manipulation started, it felt like my mind walked into a wall, and when I turned, I just knocked into another wall, then another, and another. It was like they were trying to close my mind to all possibilities but one—the one they wanted me to see. My animal and I kept pushing back, because we could . . . sense that the route they were pushing us toward wasn't the right one."

Rafael's eyebrows pulled together. "You could *sense* the manipulation, Your Highness?"

"I think so." Contemplating on how to explain things, she said, "You see, my animal's sense of smell could tell that what I was made to see wasn't real.

They were trying to get me to see that Draxon was Xandar and the vampires were my family and allies. The only problem was that Draxon smelled nothing like my mate, nor did the vampires smell like my allies, even though they looked like them in my head. And the other problem with the illusion was that the creatures I was being persuaded to side with didn't exude the warmth that I'd normally feel with my loved ones. It just felt cold and suspicious. My animal could sense that my eyes weren't seeing what was real, and I just . . . trusted her."

There was a moment of stunned silence before Rafael turned to Pelly and said out loud, "So it's true then! They really can sense the manipulation. We haven't heard of a creature who could do that since Bernard IV and his fifty espions. And that was . . ." he slumped back into his seat to do a mental count and exclaimed, "more than two millennia ago!"

Leaning toward her husband, Lucy asked, "Bernard IV?"

Xandar's gaze fell on hers sparkling with curiosity. His fingers ran down her soft hair as he explained, "Bernard IV was the director-general of the Secret Service that used to exist, sweetheart. The Service started with him, who took in creatures of any species as long as they possessed enough aptitude, attitude, mental stamina, emotional stability, and psychological mastery. They operated independent of governments and monarchies, loyal only to civilians, but . . ." his gaze took an uneasy turn when he continued, "his successor didn't possess the same vision or nobility, and soon it became apparent that politics played a role in how the Secret Service operated."

Lucy looked around, seeing a few judgmental faces from across the table, then turned back to her slightly guilty husband. "Let me guess, his successor was a lycan?"

Xandar gave a slow nod, staring at her fingers. "And the lycan was his daughter." Her mouth fell open while the rest of the wolves and lycans tried their best to keep their shock to themselves.

Rafael quickly added, "It wouldn't be fair to blame the lycans as a whole for the successor's . . . incompetence, Your Highnesses. Bernard IV was a lycan as well, and things were phenomenal! He became a legend!"

Xandar forced a smile. "That's very kind of you to say, Rafael. But the fact is as quickly as something legendary was built by a lycan, it was also quickly demolished by another." Giving his mate his attention once more, he completed the story, "The rulers of every species reached a unanimous decision to dissolve the Service. And that was the end of it."

In the quiet, devastating atmosphere of loss, Greg's voice permeated with a gleaming smile, "Finally. Something about the damn subject worth learning about." Even his animal had paid attention to a historical tale for once.

Ignoring him, Xandar said, "About *sensing* a decipio's manipulation . . . I've never read about such a thing."

Rafael chuckled. "We're not taught that over here either, Your Highness. But in the unpublished royal archives, it says that Bernard IV and his espions were the only ones who had abilities that others did not, and not because they were born that way, but were trained that way. So, Your Highness—" his enthusiastic eyes shifted to Lucy "—I would very much like to know how you trained your senses to smell things like that."

Already sad that she'd have to disappoint them, she replied, "Well, my sense of smell has always been a little better than most, Rafael. You see, I can smell things like silver, oleander, and mercury, substances that are scientifically proven to have no distinct odor. I'm . . . like this. So I guess I don't qualify as an espionne in the Secret Service if it still existed today."

Rafael continued questioning, "Does that also mean that for usual scents, you are innately born to smell them better?

"Uh . . . I . . . don't know?" *How does one even measure that?* she wondered.

Rafael pondered, and when his eyes went to Pelly's cup of red liquid, a smile spread across his serious face. He took her cup away, earning an annoyed, "Raf, that's mine!" from the empress, which he ignored when he asked Lucy, "Can you smell this, Your Highness?"

Greg had his arms crossed when he grimaced. "Don't patronize her. It has to be blood."

"It's not," Lucy remarked.

Her friends and family stared at her when Greg blinked. His eyes focused like he was scrutinizing a written plan as he studied the queen's face, which was nothing less than sure. "It's not?" Greg prompted, more in disbelief of her smelling abilities than of the drink not being blood.

"It's not," Lucy repeated. "Blood scent would have circulated in any room. We've been here for more than an hour. No one smelled anything yet. There's no way that's blood. What it smells like is more of . . ." she turned to the cup, scrunched her nose, and said, "raspberry, strawberry, and a whiff of . . . something fizzy. What is it, Pelly?"

"Phosphoric acid, Aunt Lucy."

"Ah. New one." Lucy made a mental note.

Greg internalized her unusual ability and muttered, "A very new one."

Turning back to Rafael, she asked, "Anyway, do you mean to say we just might be able to defend ourselves with our noses . . . and other senses?"

"I do believe that it's possible, Your Highness. And the good news is that the decipimus who attacked weren't even *that* skillful, so—"

"*Weren't* even that skillful?" Xandar questioned.

Christian went on, "And those decipimus are considered *good* news?"

Rafael's mouth promptly shut.

Lucy stroked Xandar's hand as she explained, "Perhaps what Rafael was trying to say is that with the most basic practice, we'd be able to go around their . . . mind-attack, darling. That's good news. We don't have to train very long to protect ourselves."

Without peeling his eyes off Rafael, he placed a kiss on his wife's hand before asking, "And what is a skillful decipio like, Rafael?"

Xandar, Christian, and Toby recalled their conversation with him and Amber at Falling Vines, about Rafael being the most powerful decipio in the empire. If anyone could provide insight into manipulation powers, it'd be him.

"Well," he began, "a skilled one would be able to enter your minds slowly and subtly to avoid detection for as long as possible. From whatever you've both just told us, Your Highnesses, it seems like these never . . . bothered to enhance their abilities. They barged right into your minds. Only below-average players do that. And instead of building walls and caging you, a very good decipio would be able to slither his way in. Less effort, better results."

"That's amazing," Lucy praised in awe.

If it was anyone else who'd said that, Xandar would've torn off that creature's head and thrown it out the window, or—if he was feeling civilized—he'd use his royal prerogative to subject the creature to solitary confinement for the rest of its living days. Since this was his little freesia, all he could do was sigh in despair at her amazement of the very power that had almost killed her, and mutter, "No, baby. It's not. It's deadly."

"Well, I'm not saying that it's not dangerous, Xandar. But to have the ability to manipulate someone without them knowing just opens up a whole new level."

"One that I hope we won't have to unlock, my love."

"Better to unlock it now than later, don't you think?"

Toby muttered, "I knew this was coming."

Christian questioned, "What is?"

Greg rolled his eyes because—unlike his distant cousin—he knew what Toby meant. Those infected with the Blackfur gene were just so slow.

The minister exchanged a knowing glance with the queen and said, "Lucy is going to get Xandar to agree that we should practice with skillful decipimus over the next few days or weeks to be ready for the next attack. Can't believe she's already getting my vote on this even before she said the words."

Rafael was the most excited. "I have no problem with volunteering for these practice sessions, Your Highnesses!" His enthusiasm was not shared by many of his own, but he didn't care. If neither Pelly nor Octavia stopped him, he was going to go with it. He'd always wanted to see the way an espion's abilities would play out, and perhaps now he could train one to see one.

Juan murmured, "Well, better now than later." Similar murmurs spread amongst them, especially the pack leaders.

Looking at Xandar with doe eyes, Lucy awaited his decision, and the king sighed in defeat before leaving a kiss on her glabella as he conceded, "Better now than later, then."

CHAPTER 28

T oby and Tate would discuss practice schedules and make arrangements with Rafael. The meeting was dismissed, and everyone went home.

Xandar and Lucy picked Reida from the Blackfur residence and put their pup into bed before hitting the hay themselves. As soon as Lucy made her space in Xandar's arms and was going to drift off, he kissed her head and muttered in a voice full of sorrow, remorse, and vulnerability, "I am so sorry, Lucy."

Looking at him with droopy eyes, she murmured, "Darling, again, it's not your fault. It's not his fault either." Her hand traced his cheekbone, making his animal coo as their foreheads met. "Stop blaming yourselves and each other. Neither of you would have done such a thing. We found a way to solve this. Let's just focus on being better, being more than what we are now, okay?"

He dropped a kiss on her lips. "Mm-kay." Just when she was going to fall asleep again, Xandar murmured, "At least I saw your tail glow when you used your Authority today, and it was beautiful." A final peck on her nose, and he muttered, "Night, sweetheart."

His eyelids fell when her eyes shot wide open. "My tail what?"

Without waiting for Xandar to answer, she detached herself from his loose embrace and jumped out of bed, eliciting an annoyed groan from her mate, who was about to surrender to fatigue with her in his arms. She undressed and shifted in the middle of their bedroom. Xandar thanked Goddess she wasn't very large, and the empty space in their bedroom was enough to accommodate her size.

He watched her observe her own tail as she channeled her Authority. The thickest stripe of the tail emitted a faint blue glow, and when she strengthened her power, it emitted a brighter blue. What was odd was that none of the other stripes were glowing, not even a little.

"Beautiful," Xandar muttered.

Lucy was still staring, unable to believe her own eyes. When her husband got impatient, he demanded, "C'mon, babe." Patting on the empty side, he said, "Neither of us needs a night light to sleep. Just turn that thing off, shift back, and come back to bed."

Her animal smirked before Lucy came back into view, putting on her shirt and panties. She then rooted in her spot, muttering to herself, "I wonder if I've missed anything on species peculiarities in that book."

Right when she was about to leave the bedroom and head for her Reading Wonderland, Xandar leaped out of bed and stopped her at the door, scooping her up and putting her back into bed, caging her between his arms, where he said, "It's late, baby. Sleep."

"I just need to check on something, Xandar. It won't take very long." Try as she might, she couldn't escape his grip.

Xandar bluntly responded, "Lucy, we both know that's a lie. Once you step foot into your wonderland, you'll be gone for hours! Besides, don't we have a private rendezvous with Pelly and Octavia tomorrow morning?"

"But I need answers! How can you sleep after seeing that?"

His eyes peered into hers when he firmly declared, "I can sleep because I know that you and our daughter are safe. We can start searching for answers tomorrow. Besides, I doubt you overlooked anything in the books. You flagged every page and highlighted every fact that stood out. The books aren't going anywhere, Lucy. Just sleep."

After coming to terms with the fact that her exhausted physique was not going to enable her to escape, she gave in with a reluctant grunt. Xandar smiled with eyes closed, then positioned his nose right above her hair, taking in her scent as he drifted off. Lucy let herself relax by concentrating on the rhythm of Xandar's beating heart, and she, too, surrendered to the darkness.

They were both awakened by the device connected to the detector in Reida's cot at 3:54 a.m. Reida was crying, demanding a diaper change, so the sleepy couple sped to the nursery next door and spent the next few minutes cleaning her up, changing her sheets and blankets, and putting her back to sleep.

As soon as Reida's breathing rhythm slowed and steadied, Lucy whispered, "I think I'm just going to take a short nap."

"Thank Goddess," Xandar murmured.

They went back to bed and were woken up the second time by the doorbell.

Lucy gasped when she saw the time. It was close to 7:00 a.m. Their meet-up with Pelly and Octavia was less than an hour away! Xandar let Mrs. Parker in while Lucy took a quick shower and got ready. She then handed Reida to Mrs. Parker and dashed through making breakfast while Xandar got ready. They kissed Reida goodbye and had their breakfast on the jet.

The king and queen were ten minutes late when they landed on the castle grounds in better spirits than the night before. They embraced the vampire rulers and headed for the castle garden. Octavia and Xandar were fully aware that Lucy and Pelly wanted to speak privately, so they wandered down a different route.

As they strolled down the stone pathway, Octavia began, "I must say, Alexandar, you and Lucy impressed everyone with your combined knowledge on our species last night. No one could remember the last lycan king and queen who managed half of what you both did. But that paternal cousin of yours was . . . a little more difficult to like."

Xandar chuckled. "Yeah, Greg is a very hateable creature. I can genuinely see us going to war solely from the way he behaves."

Octavia laughed, appreciating that Xandar took no umbrage. "I feel quite certain that wouldn't happen while Lucy remains queen, Alexandar."

Xandar's smile faded. "Tell me something, Octavia. Did Sir Gerald Knightly fall in love with Rosalie?"

Uneasiness clawed at the consort's skin when she eventually muttered, "He did, but from Pelly's and her late father's observations, it was never reciprocated. Rosalie's heart was only given to the very persuasive Prince Reagan, a malicious-looking creature who only turned harmless in the presence of his bonded mate."

"Didn't Reagan know about Knightly's affection for Rosalie?"

Octavia's head gave a brief shake. "Not at first. From what I've read and heard, Reagan didn't simply appoint Knightly because he was the kingdom's best professional in keeping anything and anyone safe; it was also because Knightly and Rosalie didn't start off on the best of terms, so the prince felt assured that nothing could possibly happen between them. But that proved to be wrong later on, of course. Knightly was good at masking how he felt, but Reagan eventually found out, mostly through the way the knight behaved around Rosalie."

"How *did* he behave around Rosalie?"

"It is said that Knightly was chattier around her, even smiley at times, which was rumored to be very unusual for the famously brooding knight. When Reagan found out, Knightly was promptly dismissed. A female bodyguard replaced him, but Knightly was still leading a team of five that watched over Rosalie. He just wasn't allowed to be anywhere near her anymore."

After a few quiet moments, Xandar remarked, "I wonder why I never came across his name when I went through the research material. I mean, I know he was probably removed from lycan history because explaining his death would open a can of worms about Rosalie's existence, but why hadn't I come across his name in papers written by vampires?"

Octavia's lips twitched. "Let's just say not a lot of vampires liked him, and since he wasn't one of us, most historians didn't see it as their duty to include him. But most of them loved Rosalie. Every historian kept Rosalie in, but only the most objective and professional ones extended the same courtesy to Knightly. Believe it or not, one of those who kept Knightly in the archives was Pelly's late distant uncle, who disliked Knightly to the core but wrote about him anyway, with a balance of good and bad. His work stopped circulating widely because, after his death, the later emperor restricted circulation. It's even rare to have heard about Knightly in our empire, let alone in your kingdom."

Xandar remembered the distant uncle, the one Rosalie had successfully operated on. After another pause, he muttered, "This is probably not a good thing to say, Octavia, but I feel better knowing that the insufferable disease of abusing one's power to bury the truth is not confined to our kingdom."

Octavia chuckled and patted his back like he was a brother. "That's a universal hereditary disease that infects generations of rulers, so you're not alone, Alexandar. I simply hope that . . . when the time comes for us to tell the truth, we won't do what our predecessors did. I hope that no matter how badly something would affect our legacies and tarnish our reputations, Pelly and I would still find the strength to own up to what we did, rather than hide it."

"Lucy and I definitely want that for ourselves too."

"I'd like to know more about your father, Pelly. What was the late Emperor Kosh like?"

Lucy and Pelly sat on a wooden bench facing a large pond with a few papilionibus—singular: papilio—small, green-colored animals that each had the body of a bee and the wings of emerald swallowtails.

"Father was . . . strict and protective, like most fathers, I suppose. We lost Mom when I was three, and my governess brought me up after that. Father was often busy with royal duties." Her emerald eyes met Lucy's orbs when she continued, "He really liked you—Rosalie, I mean. She was—in his words—a trusted ally. He used to say that Rosalie was someone one could turn to for the cold, hard truth. She was the one who made him realize that he should be spending more time with me, because I'm his daughter. Rosalie was probably the only creature who dared spelled out how irresponsible he was being as a parent to intentionally bring me into the world and then leave my upbringing in the hands of servants when he could block out time to be with me the way he blocked out time for work. Our family dynamic changed a lot after that."

Pelly smiled as she watched the papilionibus fly from one water lily to the next. One inevitably met its demise when a yellow tongue coiled around its body and pulled the insect underwater with a plop.

Pelly continued, "I was the first heir to enter a meeting chamber at the age of six and a half. He never forced me to go in and made it clear that if I ever got bored, I could always find something else to do with that time rather than listen. I never knew what went on in that room in the first few months. I was just glad that my father finally . . . saw me and I got to sit beside him for more than twenty minutes a day. When I started picking up on the meeting agenda, I brought colored pencils and paper to take notes, but the adults always spoke too fast for me to get everything . . . or I was too slow in jotting down everything."

Lucy chuckled.

"The thing about Father is that he never fails to put on a brave face, a confident front. When he put me into bed every night, he always reminded me to fight the nightmares if I ever got any. 'Start by putting on a brave face,' he'd say. 'Then whoever or whatever the nightmare is will get confused. That confusion will make you braver, and that's when you'll win.' I still practice that to this day. But I learned that it doesn't work on nightmares when it comes to the loss of loved ones. Still, it was the most useful thing he taught me. The royal duties always came second to that. After Aunt Rosie . . . left, he was probably the only adult who truly believed I could lead the empire."

Lucy's thoughts drifted to the times Pelly had been brutal to her own governing members, like how she stripped Maddock's title after a failed tracking expedition and suspended the vigils for a dead end that was beyond their control. She carefully asked, "Is that why you're . . . strict with your ministers and vigils?"

"Partly," she murmured. Her brows furrowed like she was recalling something painful. Her voice came out in a despaired whisper, "You have no idea what it was like to step into the meeting chamber the first time as empress, how invisible and incompetent I felt when the room didn't acknowledge my presence even when I cleared my throat to get their attention. Father never needed his presence announced. For some reason, I've always had to prove myself worthy to sit where he sat. I tried being respectful, approachable, but that made things worse. Many were beginning to step on me, cutting me off as I spoke. Rafael, Amber, and Octavia weren't in the governing body at that time, so there wasn't anyone I could turn to for help. I felt so ignored, so . . . lost." Her face hardened with determination when she continued, "As I thought about the situation I was in, I began asking what Aunt Rosie would do if she were me. I didn't know. Then, I started taking out anything that she gifted me during her visits, just trying to find . . . something. And I found what I was looking for—a notebook."

She took a breath like freedom was finally within her reach. "Her words on the back cover were something I've read over and over again just to draw an ounce of strength to make it through the next day or even the next hour. She wrote—and I quote—'When you've grown into a woman, you'll most likely find that everyone around you expects you to listen and obey without question. Few people expect you to have the brains to analyze and the bravery to speak up. Do the unexpected and leave your mark. Every woman has the innate ability to inspire hope, instill fear, and demand respect with nothing more than a few irrefutable words and the right amount of ferocity in her eyes. Harness that power, Pelly, but wield it wisely. With love, Aunt Rosie.'"

A soft smile brightened Pelly's features. "I never understood the depth of those words at a young age, but after ascending the throne, every word made so much sense. I tried to be a beacon of hope, but the ministers looked like they were trying not to laugh at me. I tried being respectful, and they started getting comfortable with telling me what to do without even listening to what I wanted to say. So I used fear. And things went upward after that. For me, at least. I dismissed anyone who countered my arguments with no hard evidence or plausible facts, and their immediate and unexpected dismissal jolted *a lot* of the other ministers. They began being more careful about what they said to me, how they behaved around me."

Her brows furrowed as she rubbed the back of her hand. "I never wanted to do this, to be . . . cold, brutal, unnecessarily demanding as a ruler, but when I'm not these things, the old-timers just never give me the respect and commitment that they'd give my father. I would've long let them go had they not been so careful that I have no valid reason to dismiss them. Being obnoxious is, unfortunately, a highly subjective trait that is not a valid reason for dismissal."

"There aren't many old-timers left though," Lucy mentioned, her mind breezing through the ones she'd seen.

"True. There are only six left. Thank the Lord. The new ones . . . most of them are alright. But being a little too friendly with them would make the old ones relax and slip back into their obnoxious mode. I tried. So now, I'm like this."

The helplessness in Pelly's voice spoke for her dissatisfaction with who she was. The doubt in her eyes was unmasked now that she was with one of the creatures she trusted most. Pelly didn't want to be a monster, but she couldn't gain respect or get things done any other way. She wasn't happy with who she was, but she'd sacrifice that in order for the empire to thrive.

Something clicked in the queen's mind. It made sense now. What if the sole reason that Pelly couldn't channel her Authority was that she didn't like who she had to be as a ruler, because she didn't believe that her true self could rule efficiently and intimidate those who needed to be intimidated? What if Pelly felt that—to be on par with past emperors—she'd have to be like them and not herself? Each emperor left a legacy that was—in some way—a reflection of their own personality. Pelly could and should do the same, Lucy thought. And come to think of it, maybe she already has.

Recalling her own awakening of the Queen's Authority, Lucy realized that the gift didn't fully unleash until Xandar made her aware that she was bestowed it. In essence, one needed to allow oneself to shine with every flower and thorn in her soul *and* to have an awareness of that gift before being able to fully radiate it. That decided, Lucy began, "Pelly, when you're on the throne . . . how do you feel?"

After letting out a depressing scoff, she replied, "Terrified. Every single day. The last thing I want is for this empire to crumble on my watch."

Her self-doubt was laced heavily in her voice and emanated from her eyes. Lucy wouldn't have guessed Pelly had any problems ruling had the empress not shown this side of herself. Where she thought Pelly was strict and fierce, the empress was actually . . . scared. The fear she instilled in her governing members was a defense mechanism to shield her from her own fear of being stepped on, being overlooked, being a puppet to more than willing puppeteers.

The fear was also probably another reason Pelly channeled the Empress's Authority. She probably couldn't draw out her power because confidence and emotional security weren't something that she'd properly developed yet. She doubted her own ability to properly lead an empire. It was a given that she'd doubt her ability to wield the archaic gift.

"Pelly," Lucy began. "In your years as empress, what is the moment you're most proud of?"

Pelly's lips tugged upward. "Closing the gender pay gap by the end of my fourth year on the throne. That was . . ." she sighed, proud ". . . phenomenal. No one thought I could do it when I brought it up, especially not the men who still saw me as a little girl, but I proved them all wrong. I was ecstatic. I still am." She chuckled.

"Do you happen to have a second proudest moment?"

"I do. Choosing to be with Octavia despite the backlash. The elders claimed that homosexuality was going to ruin the sanctity of the imperial family since I'm the ruler. Some of them even started talking about overthrowing me. I asked for evidence of how my preference would inhibit the growth of my reign, and since there was none that was solid, I dismissed those who wanted to kick me out." She laughed again, a hearty cackle. "Rafael said that that was the most impactful thing that I'd ever done, but removing the gender pay gap is still my first love."

Pelly's pride was contagious and even made Lucy smile. "Pelly, I hope you can see that you've proven to be more capable than many of your predecessors."

Her smile faltered slightly when she admitted, "I do try to live up to the giants who once sat on the throne, but sometimes, I just feel like I still . . . lack something."

Lucy's hand reached for hers. "You don't lack anything, Pelly. You are more than enough. You have everything you need to defy all odds. The will that drove you to fight for all those successes speaks for itself. And if you feel up to it . . . we believe you're able to awaken the Empress's Authority in you."

Pelly's eyes widened in shock before her head swung side to side. "It's not in me, Aunt Lucy. There's no such thing. There never has been."

"That's only true if you want it to be, Pelly."

She blinked in confusion. "Pardon?"

"Your ability to break boundaries and shatter glass ceilings show that you have the ability to wield a power that others before you have not. It's in you, Pelly. But you have to believe that you have the power and the capacity to use it. I understand that the last empress didn't have it, but what if you were destined to be the first empress to wield it?"

A moment of silence followed as Pelly gave that some thought, after which she asked, "You really think I could?"

Seeing the hope in her eyes, though a mere flicker, Lucy nodded. "I do." She refrained from telling Pelly about the glowing streak on her tail, not wanting her to force the Authority out because anything that was emotionally forced was unstable.

"If I had that power, you don't think . . . do you think I could somehow . . . control the more magical parts of the empire, Aunt Lucy?"

Lucy had read about those too. The first emperors were so powerful that everything that was imbued with magic in their empire was at their command because it was in their territory. The Forest of Oderem came after these emperors, so no one knew whether it could be controlled.

Lucy wasn't going that far, if she were being honest, but that suggestion had definitely gotten the queen even more enthusiastic. "That's actually a wonderful thought, Pelly. I was more focused on unlocking the highest potential that's hidden deep within you, but controlling the magical aspects of your empire does sound like a great bonus."

Those words hugged Pelly the way Rosalie once did. The warmth and love were so clear, so irrevocable. It wasn't about what she could do for Lucy if and when she emitted that power. It was about helping her develop herself.

At 10:00 a.m., the rulers bid each other goodbye for the nocturnal ones to go to bed.

Xandar and Lucy went home and spent time playing with Reida. When the villa seemed a little too quiet, Xandar asked, "Babe, where are Tate and Stella?"

Her eyes snapped to him. "The Labyrinthe Vert with Margaret. Tate told us after we landed last night."

"Oh," Xandar muttered as his hand stopped the red rubber ball in his daughter's hands from entering her mouth. "Right, that's today."

CHAPTER 29

Despite having already met and spoken to her, Tate's heart still thumped in trepidation about seeing Margaret, who remained in her holding unit, just like her followers.

Tate thought about asking for more leniency in terms of freedom and accommodation for her and her people, seeing that Greg and his followers were free to come and go wherever they pleased and do whatever they wanted. But the stark difference was that Greg had proven trustworthy when he gave himself up after exposing the Kyltons, pledging loyalty to Lucy. The duke and his followers even kept her safe during the Blue Crescent attack. Margaret and her people had not done anything close, so there wasn't a strong enough reason to satisfy granting more leniency than they were already offered.

Tate was in a light green shirt and black jeans. Stella was in a white shirt and yellow shorts. They left the villa for the police station, and after Tate signed the papers, Officer Katie escorted Margaret out, reminding her and Tate that they were only allowed two hours.

Although Margaret embraced Stella, the daughter's returned gesture seemed frigid and appeared . . . forced. Margaret tried to mask her sorrow and acknowledged Tate, who saw through the front that wasn't properly put up to begin with.

The drive to Labyrinthe Vert was nearly soundless, save for the quiet roar of the engine, gentle blast of the air-conditioner, and faint music playing in the background. Tate found it strange that Margaret and Stella didn't say a word to each other throughout the twenty-minute journey. He thought he'd be able to get a glimpse of the mother-daughter's usual subject of conversation, but—

clearly—he was wrong. He wondered if it was because he was there, if *he* made it uncomfortable for them to speak freely.

The rearview mirror offered him a peek of an unusually quiet Stella seated obediently at the back. It was strange to see her so tight-lipped. She'd normally be chatting non-stop about anything.

They reached their destination, and seatbelts unbuckled with clicks. Tate parked in front of a gated property with concrete walls covered with lush, green moss—a sight that drew a shine from Margaret's eyes as she gasped in awe. Hopping out of the car, she dashed forward to feel the moss under her palm, savoring the soft, spongy, uneven surface.

Tate thanked Goddess there was an all-green place that was suitable for a date in lycan territory. As he pulled out the key from the ignition lock cylinder, Stella finally spoke, "See, what did I tell ya, Dad?"

Tate's head snapped to the teenager in the back seat. "What did you just call me?"

With a straight face, Stella gestured to her mother. "Look at her. She'll cave in in no time."

As his sights returned to his mate, who was still distracted by the moss, Tate muttered, "I hope so. This is my first time bringing a woman out on a date, so I really don't know what I'm doing here." Stella scoffed, which was when Tate said, "And go easy on your mother, Stella. She's been through a lot. She might be tough on you sometimes, but she loves you."

"I know that. I just . . ." Stella sighed in frustration. "Her love is just a little . . . closed off sometimes, like you'd hit a wall if you got too deep or too close. Does that make any sense?"

A smile graced the alpha's features. "I thought it was just me." Seeing Stella slumped back into the seat in disappointment and deciding to cheer her up, he added, "Who knows? Maybe she'll love me more than you."

The teenager protested without a second thought, "In your dreams! I'm the daughter!"

"Yup, and pups wait in the car with the doors safely locked while their parents—"

In an instant, Stella clicked open the door, getting out while declaring, "No way! You promised I could take pictures." Once Tate shut the last door and locked the vehicle, Stella asked, "Can I go in first?"

"Sure. Tell the lady the tickets are booked under Tate Brownan."

Seemingly on purpose, a cheeky grin appeared on Stella's face as she glanced at her mother and exclaimed, "Okay! Thanks, Dad!"

That word jerked Margaret and pulled her back to her surroundings. Her palm was still glued to the moss, but her shocked eyes went to her daughter, who was smirking at Tate as the alpha dragged out an exhale, then muttered, "Really?"

Stella chuckled before dashing toward the ticket booth.

Tate approached Margaret in careful steps. Why did that teenager have to be so insensitive about him taking small steps with her mother?

When he reached Margaret, she instinctively gazed into his eyes and was once again reminded of how tall and well-built he was. When she didn't say anything, he asked in a soft whisper, "You okay?"

It was only then that Margaret realized that she had been staring at him longer than expected. The thought painted her cheeks crimson. Her eyes darted to the ground as she nodded and said, "Yeah. Yeah. Um . . ." She registered her hand was still on the wall. And she was the only one doing it. Several passersby were giving her weird looks, like she was an uncivilized creature, so her hand immediately left the wall alone.

Tate saw it too. He managed to glare daggers at three of them, all of whom recognized him as the deputy defense minister and offered a polite bow as an implied apology.

His eyes went back to his mate, reaching for her hand. "Forget about them, okay? It's just you and me. Just be yourself."

A warmth spread from the center of her chest as the sparks from his touch ignited her senses. "Thank you."

Tate's smile broadened when he asked, "You ready to go in?"

Margaret nodded again with a brighter smile, and excitement exuded from the way she paced to the ticket booth with him. This was the first time he'd seen her like this—walking toward something she wasn't dreading. She dawdled in the rocky beginning of their meeting and trotted like a full-fledged luna in Blue Crescent as they approached danger, but never did she walk like this—toward something she looked forward to. Her eyebrows didn't arch, and the alert and violent glint in her eyes was absent, replaced by eagerness and hope, her defensive energy now inviting and exuberant.

Beautiful, Tate thought.

Upon entering through the gates, they saw Stella on the far left in a squatting position with a phone in hand as she gauged the best angle for the bed of orange flowers swarming with ladybugs. The teenager zoomed in on one of the insects, muttering, "Don't move. Don't move. Just one second, and . . ." In the microsecond before she tapped on the button, the ladybird flew away and the teenager groaned before falling on her bum and sulking while she silently cursed the uncooperative insect. That was when the same ladybird landed on her knee. Stella swallowed a grateful shriek and very carefully positioned her phone at the angle she was going for. Her phone clicked with a perfect snap. Her lips curled into a successful grin as she squealed to herself.

Tate couldn't help but smile at the sight, as did Margaret. She hadn't seen her pup being this animated about anything since her fifth or sixth birthday.

Seeing that Stella had no problems keeping herself entertained, Tate prompted Margaret, "Shall we?"

He gestured toward the right, where the entrance of a maze stood. She nodded, and they entered together. When Margaret noticed they were alone, her free hand ran over the plants and leaves that made up the maze. The alternating red and pink flowers beautified the leafy background, and the rays of light only made the flowers stand out more than they already did.

"This place is stunning," Margaret said.

"It pales in comparison to you," Tate rasped.

Her eyes snapped to his soft brown orbs, and she felt the familiar feelings of affection. But her smile faltered when memories came flooding back in of how that same emotion left her the last time. Even so, she couldn't deny that she found it easier—much easier—to trust Tate. The way he looked at her and spoke to her amplified his desire to know and understand her. Her wolf fell for him instantly. Her human started falling for him on his jet when they collected the rest of her pack members. A large part of her wanted this to be real, to be her forever.

As these thoughts went through her mind, she cleared her throat and asked as confidently as she could, "You truly know how to get into a woman's heart, don't you, Alpha?"

Tate's lips twitched awkwardly. "I wish that was true. I suppose the ability to charm creatures is supposed to be an alpha's in-born talent?"

"It most certainly is."

Coming to a pause, he took her hands and looked into her rosewood eyes, whispering, "I only ask for the ability to charm a certain red wolf. I wonder if that's too much to ask."

Despite her widening smile and pink cheeks, Margaret feigned ignorance. "Well, you've already charmed Stella, so I'd say you got your wish. That little red wolf sticks to you like a magnet."

He closed their distance, prompting with a smile that made him irresistible, "And what about the not-so-little red wolf?"

As Margaret's lips tugged higher, she confessed in a murmur, "You're getting there."

Tate's wolf howled in happiness as he placed a soft kiss on her knuckles before leading them deeper into the maze where the flowers were white and blue. Her hand in his made him feel light. The three words she said in bashfulness made him feel powerful. He wondered if she was ready to go deeper.

"What were your parents like?" Tate asked carefully, testing the waters.

Eyes on the flowers, she casually replied, "Hm. Mom and Dad were conventional creatures. The no-sex-before-marriage kind of parents. Dad was a nurse in the pack clinic, and Mom was a botanist. I take after my mother, loving greenery and all."

Tate wondered if he would be pushing it too far if he asked his next question, and decided to just give it a go. "Any brothers or sisters?"

"No." She then added, "Fortunately." Her eyes dimmed, the shine from before shadowed.

"Goddess, I'm sorry I asked, Mar. I didn't mean to hurt . . ."

"You didn't," Margaret insisted, and their gaze locked. "You don't have to apologize for trying . . . Tate."

That was the most beautiful thing he'd ever heard. He could listen to his name in her voice on repeat all day. He wanted to keep talking to her, hoping that he'd get to hear her say his name again. He was convinced he was blessed when—without him asking—Margaret went on, "I miss my parents every day, and sometimes, I just wish I was at least given a chance to say goodbye." Taking a few quiet steps to mentally decide how much to share and where to start, she eventually continued, "I ventured back to Fleet Wood a few times after I was cast out, but every time I went near the border, I just . . ." She trailed off, eyes dampening.

"Got stuck," Tate finished for her. "Because the Alpha's Authority was used to keep you out."

In dismay, she uttered, "I'd never imagined the power could be that effective. I thought I would at least be able to howl from afar and my parents would hear me. But I couldn't even howl or scream when I tried to do it near my pack. I could never reach out to them to tell them where I was, to let them know that I was alive. I have no idea what Alpha Draxon did to my parents' phone numbers, because when I tried calling them from random phone booths, the line was suddenly non-existent. After twenty-three times of trying to enter Fleet Wood in two years, I just stopped trying." There was a pause; a breeze that could've been invigorating now felt cold. She ultimately muttered, "I've never felt more alone."

The sharp pain from reliving the memory of that helpless moment in her life cut through her heart, and Tate's arms wrapped her in a tight embrace as he let his shirt soak up hot tears. "You're not alone, Mar. Not anymore. You have me, and I'm not going anywhere."

Her tear-stained face looked up at the most handsome man she'd ever seen. The way he held her made her feel sheltered and protected. His scent was as soothing as it was assuring, calming the anxiety and fear that she had hidden under lock and key for more than a decade. Tate's very presence assured her that she could be at her most vulnerable with him and not be taken advantage of. She may have had a mate before Tate, but Tate made her feel like she was falling in love for the very first time.

Tate carefully clasped the side of her face to wipe off the tears, whispering, "You don't have to go through these things by yourself anymore. I wasn't there for you then, but I am here for you now. I need you to know that you'll never be alone ever again, that we'll get through the rough patches together, okay?"

Margaret looked deeply into those brown orbs that held nothing but a promise—a promise that she didn't have to run anymore, that she was safe, that she was somewhere she could belong. "Thank you, Tate."

Tate smiled wider from her saying his name and opening up to him. "Mar, you have to know you don't have to thank me for things like this. You really deserve nothing less."

They came to the center of the maze where there was a fountain. Gushing water dominated the orchestra of nature, of which Margaret was its faithful audience. When they stood before the stone structure, she leaned forward. Her hand dipped into the cool water before she noticed—through their reflection—that Tate was staring at her side profile with a beatific smile.

Margaret's wolf pushed her human to take a leap of faith, closing the distance with their mate when Margaret asked, "What about you, Tate? What's your family like?"

Tate sat by the fountain and gently pulled Margaret by her hand to sit next to him as he began, "Mom was a math teacher, and she'd throw a fit if I scored anything less than the highest in my class. When I was nine—the first time I was the second-highest on a math test—when I got my test back and saw my grade, I erased the answer I got wrong and wrote the correct one before going up to the teacher to ask her to review it again. She realized what I had done, and it was the beginning of a very horrifying experience." Margaret's eyes sparkled with interest as he went on, "As it turns out, my math teacher and Mom were friends, so when I got home, I was given an hour's lecture, grounded on the night of a concert I'd been waiting to go to for six months, and—to my dismay—given more math homework. There was so much that I started seeing numbers in my dreams." Margaret chuckled lightly, warming Tate's heart. "Mom was strict as a mother and a luna . . . and she was a stationery addict. She particularly loved weird-shaped paper clips."

"Those are cute, actually," Margaret remarked.

"Not if you have like a thousand of them at home," Tate retorted.

Margaret weighed up that fact, then shook her head. "Sorry, Tate. I'm with your mother on this. Weird-shaped paper clips are cute even if there are a thousand of them." Tate chuckled before Margaret prompted, "And your father?"

"Pop was a typical businessman, focusing on buying land and properties in strategic locations and turning them into commercial estates."

"Which of his businesses was your favorite growing up? Was there one?" Margaret asked in curiosity.

That question took Tate by surprise. Normally, people would ask about the businesses that his father owned and passed down to him, or they'd venture into making small talk—saying how lucky he was that White Blood had a consistent, lucrative income that had been established before he took the helm.

Margaret's question was more personal, about what he personally thought of his father's work.

While he stroked the back of her hand, he said, "That would have to be the nature park that was about to be torn down had he not bought the land. The trees and plants there are exotic and gorgeous. And there's this lake right in the middle of the park, so Pop, Mom, and I would go there every fortnight for a canoe ride. I'd put my hand into the water and feel the fish. There was even once when I fell into the pond." He laughed, but registering his mate's eyes that widened in fear, he quickly added, "Nothing bad happened, really. Pop scooped me up before I went too deep."

Margaret sighed with relief, then reprimanded, "What were you thinking?"

Tate shrugged. "The fish were just clearer underwater."

Margaret narrowed her eyes and smirked. "I'm sure they were."

Her candid reply made him laugh. "I'd love to take you there one day . . . if you'd like to see it."

A soft smile buried Margaret's smirk. "I'd like that."

Their eyes met long enough for Margaret to start blushing again, and she looked away.

Very carefully, Tate's free hand reached for her face, gingerly cupping her warm cheek, gently lifting for their eyes to meet once more. The backdrop of flowers, leaves, and water faded into oblivion as Tate's attention was sucked into two rosewood whirlpools. "You are so beautiful," he muttered in stupor. Margaret tried to look away to hide the widening smile that she was getting very embarrassed about, but Tate muttered, "Don't hide from me, please? I want to see you."

That soft gaze seemed to be knocking on her rosewood windows, and time spent with him beseeched her enough to crack her windows open, allowing him to penetrate into her soul. His touch was comforting yet stimulating, like a soft pillow and a live wire—two completely opposite things that have nothing in common suddenly did.

Tate's heart rate raced when he inched his face closer to hers. The tip of their noses touched, tingles teased their skin, and their lips were barely an inch away before Margaret subconsciously held back.

"Oh, c'mon, Mom! That was so close to perfection!" Stella's sudden presence and outburst made Tate and Margaret flinch.

Margaret shot up in an instant, and Tate threw the teenager an annoyed look, complaining, "Really?"

"Dad, that was her fault. Why are you looking at me like that?"

"What did I say about going easy on your mother, Stella?"

Stella's head cocked to one side. "I think it was something about her loving me more than you."

"Terrible memory," Tate commented with a shake of his head.

Stella chuckled before stating the obvious, "Anyway, I only came because I thought you two lovebirds needed a reminder that we only have twenty minutes left before Officer Katie calls."

Tate's eyes widened as he checked the time on his phone. How in the world did time pass so fast? They were just here for . . . five minutes?

He took Margaret's hand without hesitation and spoke in a hushed voice that only a lover would use, "We should head back."

"Yes, we should." Margaret nodded, replying in the same hushed tone.

###

In the car, it got uncomfortably quiet again. Clearing his throat, Tate casually asked, "So, Stella, what's your favorite part of Labyrinthe Vert?"

"Mm. . ." Her index finger on her chin, she feigned contemplation. "Definitely the fountain. I saw a couple almost making out there."

Margaret flushed and mouthed, "Oh Goddess."

Tate couldn't wipe the smile off his face. "And your second most favorite, Stella?"

The teenager's smirk was on full display in the rearview mirror. "Trying to change the subject so soon, Dad?"

Tate's heart stopped every time Stella called him Dad around Margaret. The pessimistic part of him thought that Margaret would be angered and tell her daughter to stop acknowledging him in that manner. But when Margaret said nothing the first time, he felt relieved; the second time, he felt hopeful; the third time, which was now, he felt like the most blessed creature in the world. Matching Stella's smirk, he said, "Says the one who's trying to converge every conversation to only one topic."

"Which topic is that?" Stella questioned.

"You're doing it again."

"I know," Stella chuckled, and as flustered as Margaret was, she couldn't help but smile at her daughter's happy face. There was no worry or fear. For once, Margaret saw a cheerful teenager. It was amazing how Tate could give her that. Stella finally decided to cooperate and started talking about some bushes with small flowers that had white-and-gold petals being her second favorite part of that place. "What are they called?"

Tate smiled. "Coincidentally, those are estellas."

There was a brief silence before Stella accused, "You're lying."

"Why would you say that?" Tate asked with zero humor.

Stella waited for the ball to drop, but when it didn't, her brows drew together when she turned to her mother, addressing her for the first time since they got into the car, "Mom! You told me estellas were blue and black!"

"They are, Stella," Margaret responded in her strict voice. "They were blue-and-black estellas all around Fleet Wood. Now watch how you're talking to me."

Tate decided to butt in, "That flower has many colors. The soil, temperature, and overall humidity of this part of lycan territory must be different from that in Fleet Wood. I'm not sure if they have blue-and-black estellas here, but white-and-gold ones seem to grow pretty well in this region."

Stella relaxed. "Oh, that's not so bad. For a minute there, I thought mom had lied."

Tate sighed in frustration and threw her disapproving look. "Stella, seriously."

"Fine." Her eyes went to her mother through the rearview mirror for a brief moment to mutter, "Sorry."

Tate nodded in satisfaction. "Much better."

It bothered Margaret but impressed her wolf that Tate had better control over her daughter than she did. How did he do it? He didn't have any siblings he had to look after, nor did he mention having any experience with dealing with children or teenagers. How did he know what to say and do to get Stella to behave?

They reached the police station with two minutes to spare. Stella opted to wait in the car. As soon as they both entered the station where Officer Katie had been waiting, Margaret began, "Tate?"

His feet pulled him into an automatic stop. His beguiling eyes peered into her hesitant ones when his voice came in an affectionate whisper, "Yeah, Mar?"

"Um . . ." She glanced at the car outside and then back at him. "How . . . How do you get Stella to listen to you?"

Tate's eyes widened in surprise before he scoffed in amusement. "Mar, that teenager doesn't listen to me. She's a teenager. I asked her to go to bed at 9:30, and she kept telling me it was too early."

"9:30 *is* too early."

"Hey, hey, hey. Are you on my side or hers?"

"Sorry. It's just . . ." She sighed. "She might not listen to everything you say, but I can see that . . . she listens to you more than she does me. Most of the time, I just . . . don't know how to reach out to her."

Her helplessness constricted his chest. He began thinking about what had worked so far with Stella before suggesting, "Maybe talk to her about what she loves and ask her why she loves it? She loves taking photos, especially at night. Maybe try to ask to see a few of those next time you're with her?"

After a moment, she muttered, "I'll try that."

They saw Officer Katie, who was nice enough to give them a grace period of another minute for Margaret to add, "How did you find out about that hobby of hers though? How did you make her talk?"

"I didn't," Tate admitted sheepishly. "Lucy did."

"The queen?"

"Yep. She loves children and is naturally good with pups. She has a way of making them feel heard and important, even if whatever comes out of their mouths has little significance. For Stella, Lucy just asked her what she liked to do at the dinner table the other night, and your pup started showing us photos from her phone. I took a leaf out of Lucy's book and started talking to Stella about what she liked and hated when it was just the two of us. Before I knew it, I was learning that she could skip firewood duty on her birthdays and doesn't like rooms with windows because she's terrified of what she may see if she looks out, like a possible intruder or a fight."

Margaret didn't blink, learning about her daughter of over thirteen years through her mate she'd just met days ago. Officer Katie gave Tate a signal, and Tate reluctantly nodded her way before assuring Margaret, "Stella knows that you love her, Mar. She knows that you'd do anything to protect her. Getting to know her at a deeper level might be . . . awkward at first, but once the gears are warmed up, you'll get her talking in no time. She might even grow the guts to ask about you, and when she does . . . try not to shut her out. Life hasn't been easy on you, Mar, but Stella shouldn't have to go through the aftermath of what you had to become to survive and bring her up. You've come a long way. Your pup deserves to know the strength you cultivated throughout your journey. She might even draw inspiration from you one day, you never know."

Margaret's eyes glistened when she responded in a whisper, "I just wanted to protect her from all that I couldn't avoid. I didn't think I was shutting her out."

Tate held her and tried not to make eye contact with Officer Katie. "It doesn't have to stay that way, Mar. We can fix it together, okay?"

After another squeeze, she reluctantly parted their bodies, giving him a gentle nod. "I'd like that. Thank you, Tate."

"I'll see you tonight."

Margaret remembered. "Practice with the decipimus."

"Yup. Let's hope for the best."

CHAPTER 30

At 8:00 p.m. in Polje, a hundred decipimus led by a flamboyant Rafael joined the werewolf and lycan monarch, ministers, warriors, and rogues. Both sides closed their distance, which was when Toby uttered to Lucy, "You gotta admit, if they weren't on our side, what we're seeing now is shit scary."

"Not if you think about what's at stake, how many creatures we have to protect."

After exchanging bows and acknowledgments, Rafael and Toby got their species to partner up, one decipio for every two lycans or werewolves. Rafael then threw out a stern reminder, "As I've mentioned before, we're here to *train* them to battle with us in their minds while they physically battle with another creature in front of them. It's a practice session. *Don't* let them get hurt."

Pelly was there, and this was the longest she'd gone without handing out orders, giving her friend full discretion to lead. When the species started pairing up—some reluctantly—Rafael's strict demeanor turned polite and more cordial when he faced Lucy and Xandar. "I'm afraid Your Highnesses don't have the privilege of choosing a partner. As the creatures with the sharpest senses in the kingdom, our recommendation is for you both to train with Pelly and I."

"That'd be great," Lucy responded.

"Also," Rafael added in concern. "We plan to push Your Highnesses to your limits, probably to the point where you might have to summon your Authorities. There is a . . . danger that you might hurt your opponent, so I strongly suggest *against* practicing with one another."

Lucy blinked. "Wait, wouldn't you be able to stop us before we did anything? You just told the rest to not let our people hurt each other."

"And that is very possible for them but not for us, Your Highness. My instructions to the other decipimus here are to start from the lowest level—manipulate your people slowly and conspicuously enough to facilitate familiarity in sensing the walls that a decipio builds and then fight against being caged in. That basic level of manipulation can be torn down in less than a second, before any harm is caused. You both have a different level of . . . aptitude and sensory functions. According to the books, lycan kings require a collaborative manipulation by a minimum of twenty decipimus. Anything less would require them to be of very high caliber or—in the case of Blue Crescent's attack—use a chemical to enhance their power in order to control their target. Only an emperor can manipulate the lycan king alone. I haven't read anything similar on lycan queens, but I doubt it's very much different, Your Highnesses."

Xandar clarified, "So in essence, because the level of manipulation you're going to use with us isn't . . . basic, it'll take more time to tear down even if you wanted to?"

Rafael nodded. "The effects take time to fade. Pelly and I can speed it up, but we haven't found or developed a technique to tear it down in an instant as of yet."

"I see," Xandar registered.

Pelly elaborated, "So to keep Aunt Lucy safe, you need someone who you don't mind . . . hurting during practice, Uncle Xandar. But try to pick someone who'll also benefit from the practice and not just end up running away and getting hurt all the time, someone who can rival your strength and senses, at least in the very beginning."

Lucy's eyes widened when she realized the only creature who ticked all of those boxes. "No. No, no, no, no, no. Those two together are already dangerous without manipulation, Pelly. I really don't think it's a good idea. Besides, wouldn't using me as Xandar's opponent better train him to fight off the manipulation since he'd never want to hurt me?"

Pelly begged to differ. "As logical as that sounds, we mustn't forget that neither of you has any skills to fight off manipulation effects yet. You *will* hurt each other in the initial stages of practice. And the psychological effects of those who have been touched by a decipio can also be detrimental. If Uncle Xandar continues to hurt you, or if you hurt him to a degree that you both never intended and regret when the effects wear off, it will scar your minds. You both might start holding back during practice, and it will neither serve you nor the kingdom. We strongly recommend *against* practicing with one another."

Already on board even before the empress's caution, Xandar took his mate's hands and pecked a sweet kiss. "Lucy, what happened in Blue Crescent is a nightmare that I wish I could forget. I don't want to keep hurting you. It's better if I practice with Greg."

After going through her mental library on whatever little she knew about decipimus, she looked at Xandar in dismay and admitted, "I really hate that I cannot come up with anything to argue against the three of you right now."

Xandar placed an assuring kiss on her forehead and muttered, "We'll play nice, baby. I promise."

Despite the affection in his voice, Lucy frankly said, "No you won't. You both won't. But what choice do we have?"

Funnily enough, Xandar couldn't deny that he and Greg were now given the perfect opportunity to tear each other apart. They got Greg to join them. Rafael briefed him. Greg's animal was secretly pleased that they could now use being manipulated as an excuse to harm the cousin they hated, maybe get even for what Xandar had done to him at Blue Crescent. But they also had to weigh in the fact that hurting him would end up hurting Lucy, so they had to be very selective in how they wanted to get even.

When Rafael came to the end of his briefing, Lucy declared, "If practicing with one another does more harm than good, I'm pairing with Xandar, okay?"

That contingency plan made the cousins' ears perk up. So much for finally having an excuse to harm each other or even out any score. The cousins exchanged a worried look as they aborted their mental plan before Xandar assured her, "You won't have to pair with me, baby. We'll be fine."

Greg affirmed, "We'll behave professionally, my queen, for the sake of the kingdom." He was going to add "and for you" but stopped himself.

"I really hope so," Lucy murmured, more to herself than anyone else.

Rafael ushered Lucy toward a large tree, and as they walked away, Xandar asked Pelly, "Wait, you're training us? I thought we were getting Rafael."

Pelly smirked in amusement. "Trust me, Uncle Xandar. You don't want to get Rafael yet. Besides, I'm softer on Aunt Lucy. I'll go easy on her. Alright, let's get started. Maybe create a distance? Yes, that's good. Alright, whenever you both are ready."

They took their positions facing each other, and Pelly warned, "What's going to happen is similar to the events at Blue Crescent. I'll be building walls, and you both have one of two options, go down the only path I'll be pushing you toward where you'll have to rely on your animal's senses to detect what's real and what's not, and move from there; or push the walls back while trying to find me, the source."

"Simple enough," Greg muttered.

Pelly noted. "In theory, yes. In practice, no. I'll start at the lowest level and we'll work our way up."

###

When they were far away enough, Rafael said, "May I just say that was a game well played back there, Your High—"

"It's just Lucy, Rafael, really. And I wasn't playing anything. Those two cousins hate each other more than anything and anyone. If they don't improve when everyone else does, I *will* be practicing with my husband despite the risks."

Rafael took a peek at his best friend now manipulating the king and duke and said, "I doubt the king and duke would let that happen, Lucy."

When they reached the tree, Lucy asked, "So who am I fighting, Rafael?"

With a smile, Rafael said, "Me."

Her shoulders fell. "You can't heal like us if I hurt you. Are you sure I shouldn't just get one of my warriors?"

"I'm quite certain, Your H—Lucy. And this may sound arrogant, but I doubt you'll be able to hurt me tonight. Unlike the rest, we're not starting with wall-building. It'll be far too easy for you. I'm going to slither my way in and we'll start by seeing if you can sense it. Once you do, see if you can differentiate the authentic from the inauthentic. And if you do manage to attack me tonight..." he patted on the tree trunk next to them and continued, "this is my escape route. My family owned an orchard, and I've climbed trees since I was a boy, so I'll be able to climb fast enough for the manipulation effects to wear off from your mind."

Her relieved eyes went to the tree, then back to Rafael. "That actually makes me feel a lot better."

"One more thing, Lucy. If practicing with me alone proves to be . . . too doable, I'll have to involve Pelly. The two of us will combine our powers to make it a more . . . productive session for you. Being the lycan queen, you should have the ability to fight off the manipulation of a non-vampire ruler, maybe not in the beginning, but you will be able to eventually. It's a muscle that's probably dormant for now, but it will be activated when we start practicing."

"Alright, let's do it."

With a firm nod, Rafael's smile faltered and he began his work.

Lucy didn't realize that her mind had already been invaded, because she didn't see Rafael's smile falter. What she saw was Rafael taking his position before she heard the snarl of two proditors from the tree. One landed right on top of Rafael, and Lucy heard his bones break as he groaned in pain and was kicked to the side.

The other proditor landed perfectly on the ground next to his friend, and both glowered at Lucy. She took a quick look around and realized that the proditors were invading Polje. Her people and the decipimus on their side were already trying to fight them off.

Lucy reflexively charged at the ones in front of her after sizing them up. When she saw the one on the right throwing his body forward, intending to make her fall, she abruptly stepped back and let him fall to the ground before the proditor on the left charged and tried to land a few blows at her face, which she easily dodged before her claws plunged through his arm, earning a deafening shriek. Her claws then went through his body, and she gave a forceful kick, throwing him to the side like how his friend kicked Rafael.

The first one charged at her again. As Lucy dodged his attacks, she tried to guess what their abilities were. Neither of them would be a discretus, or they would've been invisible to ease their attacks. Not a velox because their attacking speed was too slow. Definitely not a fortis with how easy it was to destabilize them just by a simple kick in their chest. Plus, it was odd that when her claws went through, it felt . . . light, like she was attacking thin air. Decipimus? But if they were decipimus, why weren't they attacking her mind?

And then the truth hit her, maybe they were already in her mind.

As she dodged attacks, she realized that she didn't detect any strong smell of chrysanthemum and pine leaves. In fact, those scents were faint, meaning that they were a distance away. After her claws went through the proditor's chest and she watched him fall to the ground, she began focusing on her other senses apart from sight.

Her nose told her that there was only one vampire within her vicinity, and her ears could hear the two on the ground groaning and struggling with their wounds. Her animal prompted her human to close off anything they were seeing and hearing, concentrating fully on their noses. When she was trying to trace the only vampire she could smell, she heard more snarls and found herself being surrounded by more than ten proditors, who were pacing toward her in slow, taunting steps. Most had blood on their faces, which made Lucy automatically conclude that some of her people were already dead. That very thought threw her off course from her scent-tracing effort as regret and blame engulfed her.

Her animal thought differently. She was still focusing on scents. When she still smelled only one vampire, it made its human aware of that. Lucy wiped away her raging tears and lowered herself to pick up the rock by her foot, letting her animal pinpoint the one they were really after.

What was worrying was that Lucy's nose started picking up more than one vampire, which was beginning to confuse her animal. But the other vampires smelled like they were further away than where they now stood. And she was even beginning to smell wolves and lycans even though she was seeing none.

Cascading confusion threatened to drown her like a tsunami now. Still, her lycan continued to sniff, and when she pinpointed her target, at their seven o'clock, Lucy swiftly turned and threw the rock with great force. The rock flew through the air and fell on the ground.

Lucy thought her animal had made a mistake, until she realized that the proditors around her had vanished. But she still smelled vampires. Confusion eased away like a low tide as the winds of frustration pricked her senses. But right before she growled into the emptiness out of pure vexation, reality entered her field of vision.

Rafael was at the very spot where she threw the rock, tossing it, letting it fall back into his left palm and tossing it again as he waited for the manipulation effects to wear off, a broad smile filled with awe etched across his face.

Lucy stubbornly tried to hasten the process by shaking her head. Then she started remembering. Rafael was never harmed. There were no proditors, so she was actually avoiding and attacking the night air. Her animal covered its face in embarrassment at how it now looked.

When she started smelling more vampires, lycans and werewolves, it was her friends and allies, along with their vampire partners she detected. They were taking a break and had decided to see how Lucy was faring since their decipio partners told them that their queen's training was different. Rafael made sure they stood a considerable distance away for tonight, not wanting to add that type of confusion at this stage yet.

When she threw the rock, Rafael caught it with an awestruck expression. The rock never landed on the ground. And finally, she remembered how everyone around her gasped and wowed when the rock made a direct hit at Rafael.

Her bright, relieved eyes met Rafael's still-amazed ones when he said, "That was bloody well done, Lucy."

When Xandar knew she was back, he took steps toward her, pride exuding from his being.

Toby's voice of mock discontentment cut through the silence, "Okay, that wasn't really fair. Lucy had a rock nearby. I didn't."

His vampire partner, Joseph, turned to him. "You did, Tobias. You tripped over it."

When laughter ensued from the rest, Toby accused, "That was only because you manipulated me into thinking that there wasn't anything there, Joe."

"No I didn't. I was only trying to manipulate you to see Lovelace as your enemy. The absence of a rock was the result of your self-manipulation, Minister."

When Toby ran out of arguments while everyone around him cackled, his narrowed eyes found his best friend—who was now wrapped from behind by her mate—when the defense minister declared, "I've grown a sudden hate for walls, Lucy."

As her indecent beast inhaled from her hair, Lucy argued, "At least you could feel the walls, Toby. I didn't even know the manipulation started until after I killed two imaginary proditors. I was fighting literally nothing."

All contemplative eyes turned to Rafael, who looked at his own best friend and scratched his nape. "Perhaps I entered a little too quickly for the first practice."

Christian then said, "No, Rafael. That's not the point . . . well, not my point at least. The question is: you can create a creature out of . . . nothing?"

"Every decipio here can, Your Grace."

Some of the werewolves and lycans cursed under their breaths, then quickly apologized to their decipio partner.

Zelena asked, "Why would you want your victims to fight nothing? I thought the whole purpose of manipulation was to make your enemies fight each other."

Rafael explained, "That is the endgame, yes. But we can't deny that, sometimes, when our enemy is charging toward us, there may be no one between us and them. So creating an illusionary creature between the two sides buys us time to escape, maybe even attack."

Toby nodded in understanding. "That's actually pretty clever." The objective compliment made the decipimus so proud of themselves and their abilities that most—if not all of them—smiled without effort.

Xandar then asked, "For comparison's sake, Rafael, is it easier to create something out of nothing or change how a creature sees another creature?"

"Creation takes more effort and skill, Your Highness. We'd have to quickly pull out information from your mental archives to understand what you're prone to find true. Then, we'd have to conjure up what the imaginary creatures would look like and how they'd react to threats and attacks. If we're merely changing the physical aspects of another creature in our victims' minds, we wouldn't have to think about how our creation would react to our victims' attacks since the reaction comes from the actual creature that our victim is made to fight in real life. Swapping really is much simpler than creating."

As everyone processed this, Rafael added, "But creation takes decades of practice to perfect, and even then, it requires a certain level of concentration during execution . . . and proximity to the victim, of course. So decipimus can't have someone attacking us while we're creating something out of thin air. Any level of distraction tampers with its authenticity. Personally, when I'm distracted, the . . . thin-air manipulation I create is . . . unrealistic, such as the sounds that should be louder come out illogically softer. Take this for example: you won't have a ready-to-attack creature standing right in front of you snarl so softly that you start suspecting he's having a sore throat."

Toby shrugged like he didn't mind. "I'd probably laugh at him before fighting him."

Replaying the Blue Crescent attack, Greg said, "I suppose we should count ourselves lucky the decipimus from the other day didn't forge something out of thin air."

Rafael ventured, "And that could be for two reasons, Your Grace. One, they can't do it for lack of skill, which would be good news for us; two, the fact that they were being chased and attacked didn't offer them the luxury to focus on doing something like that."

Greg uttered the thought running through everyone's minds, "Let's hope it's the former." He was usually open to new challenges and "worthy opponents," but this was not something that he'd want a challenge in. He knew close to nothing about keeping himself and the people he cared about safe from the power.

When no one else had questions, everyone got back to practice. Rafael slithered his way into Lucy's mind exaggeratedly slowly this time. Even then, Lucy still couldn't feel him in the first three intrusions.

Greg and Xandar didn't hold back. In the manipulation, Greg saw Tanner, sometimes Livia. Xandar either saw rogues, the Kyltons, or Sasha Cummings. They both acted on instinct and attacked each other as soon as the manipulation took effect in their first two rounds, never bothering to fight back the mental walls that pushed them toward an illusion. After that, however, the cousins started noticing illogicalities.

When they attacked, their opponent appeared more ferocious than the actual person would be, so Greg was seeing a ready-to-kill Livia or Tanner when in reality, they'd cower when he was about to attack. Xandar noticed the same thing with the Kyltons and Sasha Cummings. The rogues were a little trickier for him since those had always appeared fierce in reality.

What was different, Xandar realized when he circled a hand around Greg's neck and lifted him off the ground, was that he smelled his cousin. Sure, he hated the guy, but his animal somehow knew that killing and hurting Greg was not on its to-do list. As they practiced one round after another, they'd even throw in reluctant apologies if they ended up hurting one another, so it was mostly Xandar apologizing to Greg after the manipulation effects wore off.

In their sixth round, they started trying to push back the mental walls. Greg got so frustrated at one point that he cursed, "Fuck this shit," and summoned his animal's strength to punch through the mental wall with his fist. And the thin wall Pelly created shattered like glass.

The effects wore off, and the empress looked at the duke with a congratulatory smile. "That was very creative, Your Grace. But know that strength will only work with thin walls and very untrained decipimus. In the end, awareness of a decipio's intrusion will still triumph, so reliance on your animal's senses remains a must-master skill."

"Yeah, I just got sick of it," Greg muttered frankly.

Pelly smirked. "I can tell. We should take a break."

The empress went to watch another pair while Xandar and Greg lay flat on the ground, mentally drained. Looking at the night sky, Xandar murmured, "Why is it that—even with our human and animal instincts combined—we still trust what we see more than what we smell or know?"

Greg pinched the bridge of his nose. "Basic science, Cousin. Light travels faster than anything. Sight is our quickest sense in detecting stimulus, so to speak. The rest of our senses take a little more time to catch up." He then closed his eyes to find some peace from his cousin.

Xandar looked past Greg's condescending tone and thought out loud, "That means . . . when we're in the presence of decipimus, it's better to start off with our eyes closed."

Greg's shut eyes snapped wide open. That was actually not a stupid idea. But the question was, how long should their eyes stay closed?

Xandar elaborated, "If we memorize the scents of our followers and allies, which our animals have already been doing, any foreign scent is the enemy. Then no matter what or who we see, we'll know it's safe to kill."

The duke sat up in silence as he tried to find loopholes in Xandar's reasoning. When silence ensued, Xandar pushed himself off the ground as well, which was when Greg said, "It's good to know that a glimmer of light is appearing from your dimness, Cousin. I credit the queen for that improvement. Let's get the empress. We should start putting our theory to the test."

Xandar protested, "Our theory? I thought of that whole thing, Greg."

"After I told you about how quickly our eyes detect stimuli. I get points too."

They shared "their" theory with Pelly, who was more than ready to see it in action. Practice began. When they felt the mental walls beginning to build up, both cousins closed their darkening eyes, letting the manipulation guide them toward the illusion they were being made to see. Pelly moved from her original spot, traipsing around them but being careful to manipulate the cousins' hearing so they couldn't hear her footsteps.

Without sight, Xandar and his animal could only rely on their senses of smell, sound, and touch. Their ears picked up growls from at least ten creatures, but their noses only detected two creatures within his vicinity. One was moving. One wasn't.

Greg only heard one snarling creature, but it didn't sound like a wolf or lycan, more like a vampire. Scents guided him to a different conclusion—there were two creatures, one who smelled like a vampire who was moving in slow paces somewhere behind him, and one who smelled like a lycan not far in front of him.

Xandar opened his eyes and was made to think he was in a random wolf pack. The imaginary wolves snarling at him were vivid, and the manipulation influenced him to believe that they had killed Lucy and a few alliance members. Anger and remorse flooded his being. His tampered thoughts pinned the one in front of him as the leader, who looked unusually large for a wolf.

His claws extended, but right before he attacked, his lycan concluded that the scent of the so-called leader matched Greg. They stood in their spot and contemplated, finally coming to the revelation that Lucy couldn't be dead. Their mate bond was still intact. He could feel that she was alive. He didn't even feel her enduring any form of pain, nor was she scared. She just felt . . . curious, and maybe a little frustrated. But she was safe. He just didn't know where she was.

Greg's tampered thoughts told him that he had entered a bad bargain with an anonymous business associate who turned out to be a vampire, who was now threatening to kill all his followers after finishing him off. This was a duel, and whoever won would kill the other's followers. He emitted a low growl and shifted into his brown-furred animal, ready for the fight.

Greg charged at Xandar, and Xandar dodged his attack, letting his cousin fall onto the ground as he yelled, "Greg! Snap out of it!"

But what the duke heard was, "That's the best you got?"

Greg growled louder and fiercer. His claws extended, and he started trying to plunge them into his opponent. Xandar continued trying to yell some sense into the duke but to no avail. Greg tripped him, and the king fell on his back. Before the duke's claws went through the king's chest, Pelly wiped off the manipulation. At the same time, Xandar kicked Greg with force, and the duke flew toward Pelly, who reflexively took quick steps back as she exclaimed, "GAH!"

Some of her people dashed to her, but she shooed them back to practice after ensuring them that she was okay. Octavia felt her shock and immediately linked her from the castle study, asking her what was going on.

Once reality welcomed the king and duke, Xandar took quick, relieved breaths as he got up. Greg tried to process and accept how misguided he had been when he didn't trust his sense of smell. He had to admit the manipulation was top-notch. The empress somehow knew his weakness . . . well, one of the main ones anyway. His number one weakness was Lucy and his people, who were equally important and irreplaceable to him. His second weakness was his ego. In the rogue world, he didn't like being fooled or challenged. If he were challenged, he'd like to win. The Kyltons fooled and challenged him, and look where that got them.

His ego to win the fictional duel and preserve his status made him blindsighted to the fact that the scent of his opponent was familiar. If he had given himself a little more time, he would've easily connected the scent to his cousin. So the lesson was to prioritize scents over ego and pride, at least in such battles.

Xandar reached Greg and Pelly. The king's voice held a hint of concern when he asked, "Are you alright?"

"Fine, Cousin," Greg muttered.

Xandar's brows rose, and his eyes flickered to his cousin still seated on the grass. "I was talking to the empress, but . . . I'm glad you're okay, too, Greg."

Patting his cousin on the shoulder, Xandar tried to press back a smile. Greg sensed his amusement, and it made the animal in his head growl.

Pelly's eyes sparkled when she said, "That was amazing, Uncle Xandar! How did you do it?"

Xandar shrugged with a smile. "I trusted the scent more than sight. It really is better to start off with closed eyes, but I'm not sure if we'll have the luxury of time during battle."

Greg stood from his spot and questioned, "Were you even trying to defend yourself, Cousin?"

"Why else would I be backing away from you when you attacked?"

"And *you* didn't attack! I could have killed you."

"No. I wouldn't have let that happen, which is why I kicked you away. Didn't you smell me?"

Greg swallowed his pride and admitted, "With hindsight, I did. I just..."

After an awkward and embarrassed pause, Xandar finished for him, "Didn't focus on the scent long enough to match it to me?"

"You could say that," Greg murmured. There was something about the decipimus' power that was really beginning to bother him, so he turned to Pelly and asked, "Do you see what we see? Do decipimus like you see the manipulation?"

"To a certain extent, we do."

"What the hell does that mean?"

"Greg," Xandar admonished, exasperated.

Pelly's brows raised, waiting for him to rephrase. Greg took this as a cue to start practicing lowering his ego and swallowing his pride. "May I know what that means?"

"It means that we see the number of figures and objects around you, but we don't see who or what they are."

"Really?" Xandar asked, surprised.

Pelly nodded. "Take our latest practice, for example. I knew the number of creatures I set around you both, but I didn't know who they were or what they looked like."

Greg asked, "How do you know who to use if you can't see who you are using?"

Taking a moment to consider the best way to explain the concept to non-decipimus, Pelly finally said, "Think of your minds as compartments. Each compartment is an aspect of you or your lives—love, fear, resentment, pride, and so on. When we invade the general archives of your minds, we normally pull out only one specific piece of material to deceive what you see. Stronger decipimus can pull out more than one piece at a time. My personal record is eight. Rafael's is ten. As great as that sounds, it's actually not that mind-blowing if you explore the intricacies of our ability. How do I put this . . . uh . . . when we pull out a specific material, we know it'll affect you, but we don't see the creature affecting you. We can guess what or who it is, but it will just be that—a guess. If the point of the manipulation is to scare you, I'll pick out your fear archive and take the most extreme one to bring to life. If—hypothetically speaking—it's a spider, then I can see the outline of the spider myself, but I won't see the finer details like the color or the look in its eyes, those kinds of fine features."

"What about sounds?" Xandar asked.

"That's also from your own archives, Uncle Xandar. You see, for it to feel real to you, it has to be something that you've heard before or have imagined hearing, so that it's easier to convince you. Even when we create thin-air manipulation, I can increase or decrease the volume and pitch based on logic, but I really don't hear what you hear."

Greg muttered, "That's a relief to know."

She replied, "I agree. Invasion of privacy can be disturbing, not to mention wrong if our power is abused."

After giving some thought to how little the lycans and werewolves knew about vampires, Xandar found himself mumbling, "I've got to get Yarrington to stock up on vampire material in our territory."

"Uncle Lucas should have done that centuries ago," Greg uttered in dissatisfaction despite talking about his favorite royal family member.

Pelly watched Lucy and Rafael, commenting, "I'm surprised Aunt Lucy hasn't read anything about this. I wonder what's in the libraries and stores of lycan territory these days."

Xandar sheepishly admitted, "Mostly about our history and feuds, written and edited to villainize vampires. We took back textbooks from schools to be rewritten a couple of months ago, so those will show differently by the end of this year or the next, at the latest. There are a few books on your species' biology but not a lot. Lucy has only three of them, and she said it was pretty much the same thing, nothing as in-depth as everything you've just told us."

"Looks like your education minister and ours have to discuss business once this ends, Uncle Xandar."

As Xandar nodded with a smile, Greg murmured, "That's long overdue."

After Xandar, Greg, and Pelly shared the theory with everyone else, the cousins attracted lots of shocked and surprised looks, apart from a few gaping mouths. Christian, Lucy, Toby, and Greg's top four couldn't believe their ears when they heard those two actually worked together and came up with something constructive. They wondered if they were in the midst of a manipulation as the explanation of theory went on.

With disbelief lingering at the back of their minds, they got back to practice to try out the technique.

Close to the edge of Polje, Phelton requested a break when Zeke started asking the decipio, Brienna, about him seeing mental walls as mirrors. Phelton made his way toward the rogue wolf he found attractive the other day on the jet. She was scrolling through her phone and sat a notable distance away from her wolf and decipio partner, who were taking a break.

He plopped next to her, which made her instinctively hold her phone closer to her chest as she leaned away, even shifting more to the side to create a larger distance between them.

"Kate, right?" Phelton began.

"Yeah?" she responded suspiciously.

"I'm Phelton."

"I know. What did I do?"

"Nothing. I just . . . wanted to talk to you."

"About what?"

Phelton didn't think of that. "Anything, really." Registering Kate's blank, annoyed look, he chose to add, "Well, we could start with how you became a rogue?"

Kate's eyes turned defensive as she snapped, "That's personal. It's not part of the deal, so I don't have to say anything."

"I'm not speaking on behalf of the government, Kate. I just want to know you."

Frustrated now, Kate asked, "Why?"

Phelton didn't even need to think before uttering, "You seem special."

Kate blinked when realization dawned on her. She stood, making Phelton panic internally as he followed suit. "I'm flattered, Minister, but not interested."

"Kate, this isn't some manipulative scheme to get you t—"

"I'm not saying that it is. I'm just not interested."

"Why?" Phelton asked with furrowed brows.

"You're not my type and I already have someone."

His voice took an angered and possessive twist when he asked, "Who?"

"That's none of your business, Minister. All you need to do is respect my choice and never bring this up again." Kate trotted away, internally relieved that Phelton didn't demand she show him her phone.

Phelton imagined a ton of scenarios of how that would play out before he spoke to Kate, but it had never crossed his mind that she'd say she was with someone else. He'd been stealing glances at her since the day on the jet, then at

Blue Crescent before the proditors attacked. He couldn't deny that she was careful not to return his gaze, but that didn't stop him from protecting her when he noticed that her arm was being pulled by something none of them could see.

During that attack, Phelton charged at the emptiness next to Kate and successfully tore the discretus away from her before he was nicked twice in the back by another two discreti that no one saw coming. He passed out and woke up in Blue Crescent's pack clinic hours later, and the first thing he asked the doctor about was Kate. The warrior was relieved to learn that she wasn't in the clinic with them, but was sad that he couldn't see her until he returned to lycan territory.

Tonight, Phelton genuinely thought he'd have a shot at getting her to open up. He'd even expected a simple thank-you for saving her from the venom that could've put her in a coma.

How was it possible that she was with someone else? In the numerous times he'd stolen a glance, Phelton had never seen another male or female look at her with interest or affection, nor did she look at anyone that way. Perhaps her lover was from a different rogue pack? If that were the case, Phelton thanked Goddess that she and her lover were separated for the time being. He doubted whoever Kate was seeing was her bonded mate. If it were, she would have said so because it would have been a sure way to keep Phelton away.

Perhaps Kate was lying. Maybe, just maybe, she wasn't actually seeing anyone, and she said what she did to keep him away. Did she declare she was not interested because he was a loyal deputy minister, or because she really wasn't interested?

Phelton replayed their exchange and had to come to the upsetting conclusion that it was the latter. There wasn't the slightest shred of desire in her eyes. He'd seen two people in love before, either due to the mate bond or by choice. The way they'd look at each other was different. One could easily see a connection that amplified when they were together. Kate showed nothing close to that with him.

"Phelton! Ready for another round?" Zeke's voice pulled him out of his thoughts, and he jogged toward them to resume practice, but not after stealing another glance at Kate.

Neither Kate nor Phelton knew that Hailey witnessed their exchange. She and the other royal rogues didn't need reminders about having to remain alert at all times. From her extensive experience of watch duty under Greg Claw, she could easily tell that Kate was hiding something.

CHAPTER 31

Mental practice with the decipimus drained the lycans and wolves, so most of them slept in the next day.

Lucy and Xandar only woke up when Reida demanded diaper changes and feeding, and the parents were utterly—and guiltily—relieved that Mrs. Parker was coming at noon to babysit. They'd get a few more hours of rest then.

After a nap, Lucy entered her reading wonderland and started studying one of Iridessa's two theses on prisoner re-entry, which Ivory handed to her before they parted ways the previous night. She only left the bedroom for ten minutes before her husband came looking for her.

It took Xandar zero brain power to figure out where she'd gone. He groaned at the emptiness of the bed and dragged his groggy self from their room to the library before dropping chest-down on the couch where she sat, hugging her thighs to prevent further escape, and continued his nap. Lucy's hand instinctively went to his hair, and her thumb ran through his thick locks. His animal purred into deeper slumber.

Page after page, a large part of Lucy found it more and more unfair that the thesis was turned down. There was so much in here that a layperson didn't know about. It held viable solutions, substantiating evidence taken from the past and from other species, precautions, and backup plans. She went through only a quarter of the document before being forced to take a mental break. As Lucy sipped Earl Gray from the white mug that Xandar bought for her on their honeymoon, which had the words, "Shh . . . I'm reading," in big, black font, she pondered on the thesis and wondered how there was more.

As Lucy stroked Xandar's locks and listened to his breathing, she couldn't help but feel guilty that former convicts had never crossed her mind when they were discussing the kingdom's affairs. It almost felt like the governing body didn't know they existed, or didn't want to acknowledge their existence. It also made her feel that Greg was better than any of them in government. He protected and looked after the people who were shunned by the kingdom, giving them a second chance that was never offered because of one mistake.

Objectively speaking, not all of those crimes could be labeled as mistakes. Negligence qualified, but crimes like defrauding abusive employers or setting a mate on fire did not, because none of those were done by accident. Of course, there were also those who harmed and stole without good intentions. It was complicated.

Was that why it was easier to just put all of them in the same jar, a jar that was sealed so tightly that redemption was never opened to any creature that was put in there? She started wondering whether any rogue lycans from Wu Bi Corp suffered the same misfortune, and prayed that those who went there failed the vetting session—if there was one—with her cousin-in-law before joining the corporation.

Setting down her steaming mug and getting back to reading, she was admittedly terrified of turning to the next page to learn more about how second chances could've been given but weren't.

Xandar woke up an hour later when Lucy was halfway through the bundle. The yellow highlighter in her hand brushed over another line before she placed the cap back on, and her hand returned to her beast's hair. Despite knowing he was already awake, the movement of her thumb didn't stop, and Xandar's eyelids closed once more to indulge in her touch while his animal cooed in tenderness.

When the mental fatigue returned, Lucy heaved a soft sigh and placed the thesis on the table. As soon as she did, Xandar pulled her downward and made her lie on her side. His hands gently lifted her shirt to reveal her bare tummy. He could still see his claws going through the now perfect-looking skin. Guilt and anger returned as he pressed a deep kiss there.

Lucy whispered a stream of soft "I love you" as he hugged her abdomen, pressing his mate close to himself, channeling the depth of his love for her through their bond, which she reciprocated in equal strength. After a few minutes, he pulled her shirt back down and moved up to bury his face in her bosoms, listening to her steady heartbeat, inhaling her scent.

When Xandar felt better, Lucy said, "I wonder if the vigils are okay. We haven't heard anything from Pelly yet."

"Mm . . . sure they're fine," Xandar muttered, snuggling deeper into her breasts.

Another quiet moment later, Lucy tried to push herself up. "I'm just going to check on Reida."

Xandar groaned and tightened his grip. "Our daughter is with Mrs. Parker, babe. She's fine. Just . . . stop moving."

"I haven't moved in the past hour, Xandar."

"So what's a few minutes more?"

After trying but failing to escape his grip, she remarked, "You're a little clingy, darling. You know that?"

She felt his lips at her breasts tugged upward when he muttered, "Can you blame me? I waited 178 years to meet you. You made me wait this long. It's your fault that I'm clingy."

"No, my love. Being clingy is one's own choice. If you're like this when I simply want to see our daughter, imagine how you'll be if and when we have a son."

Xandar chuckled lightly, pulling himself up to plant a kiss on her neck, lips, and forehead. "I like the daycare center idea you had. I wonder if there's also a . . . night care center."

With fierce eyes that turned up his amusement, she said, "It was sarcasm, Xandar."

He chuckled and left a kiss between her brows before surrendering, "I know, babe. I was just joking. Relax." Her remaining rage evaporated. His lilac eyes peered into her black-and-lilac orbs as he whispered, "How about we spend a few hours together this weekend, just the two of us? We haven't gone on a date since our honeymoon."

Despite her flushing cheeks, her eyes narrowed in suspicion. "Christian gave you the idea, didn't he?"

Xandar smiled wider, and his fingers traced her blushes. "Something like that. In the eighteen years he and Annie were married, he'd make time at least once a week to just spend some time being with her, talking to her. He said it makes him fall even more in love with Annie. It's once a fortnight now that they have Lewis and Ianne, but they still do it." The tip of his nose gently nudged hers. "I don't know how it'll be possible to be more in love with you than I am now, but I do want to spend more time with you."

Her smile continued to broaden with each word. Her thumb stroked his lower lip when she whispered, "If I don't say yes, would you still try to seduce me?"

Xandar's soft features turned coy when he turned their bodies, making her lie flat on her back while he hovered over her. His lips attacked her neck without warning, and she angled her head to give him full access as she moaned in ecstasy. Their skin heated up, and when she whispered his name, he licked and sucked on her mark, which made her body arch toward his, electricity coursing through her. His hardened shaft was pressed against her slightly wet area, and the only boundary left was their shorts.

Xandar glued their bodies together as his lips moved up to her ear, where he sucked on her earlobe, muttering in a seductive whisper, "Say yes, baby." He planted a soft kiss on her earlobe before he repeated, "Say yes."

Her dazed eyes were fixed on the most amazing, handsome, loving, romantic, patient, supportive, and understanding creature in existence, and it was moments like this that she couldn't thank the Moon Goddess enough for giving her the jackpot of a mate after all the heartbreaks and disappointments.

Registering her silence, Xandar smirked and spoke in a deep voice that turned her on, "You're making me up my game, aren't you, my little freesia?" Planting more kisses on her cheek and jawline, he finally pressed his lips against hers, licking the inner walls of her mouth and her tongue as he linked, *'Still not a yes, baby?'*

Lucy moaned unintelligibly as Xandar squeezed her bum. When she broke away for air, his face hid in her neck. His lips left a trail of butterfly kisses until he reached her collarbone.

After Lucy caught her breath, Xandar's nose nudged hers again, and she cupped his cheeks. Her blissful eyes peered into his when she whispered, "I love you."

His radiant smile spoke for his happiness. "I love you, too, Lucy. But that is still not a yes."

A familiar ringtone chimed, and Lucy reflexively pushed Xandar off, but he pinned her back down and urged, "C'mon, baby. Just say yes."

She bit her bottom lip, then gave up hiding and letting her smile light up her face when she pointed out the obvious, "I was already going to say yes when you first asked. Now get off, my king. That could be important."

He chuckled and reached for her phone, handing it to her. His face returned to her chest when Lucy answered the incoming call from Tate. He and Stella were out visiting Margaret, so Lucy assumed he was passing on a message from the police force before taking Stella to another park to take pictures.

The moment she tapped on the answer button, Tate's grim voice came through, "Lucy, Margaret predicted a possible attack in Polje tonight."

Tate couldn't get her through the mind-link when she and Xandar were having their private moment, so Tate resorted to calling her instead.

Xandar heard Tate's ominous message, and his defensive eyes snapped up to meet his mate's hardened features when she said, "Tell Toby, Phelton, Langford, and Dalloway about this. Xandar and I will let their Imperial Majesties know, and we'll request for backup. See you tonight."

CHAPTER 32

It wasn't really "tonight" for anyone. Everyone was at Polje by late evening. The sunset dripping off the horizon would've been a breathtaking sight if it weren't for the fact that everyone was there because of Margaret's vision. She saw fire and heard growls, but thankfully, no blood or anguished howls like the last time.

Octavia and Amber came tonight, along with a few other discreti and fortes. The eyes of the consort and the other ten discreti they brought along roamed the surroundings, scanning for proditors. When they did this for a good fifteen minutes but saw nothing, the discreti asked their wolf and lycan counterparts whether they were hearing or smelling anything. None of them did, not even Xandar, with the sharpest hearing, or Lucy, with the sharpest sense of smell.

Most of them didn't doubt Margaret's vision at first since it proved to be terrifyingly accurate about the Blue Crescent attack. But after an hour in which half the time was nightfall, some began looking at the clairvoyant with suspicion, wondering if she was pulling their leg. Tate was beginning to glare at anyone who was looking at her in disdain, which was mostly the royal rogues.

Lucy saw it, too, so she suggested, "How about half of us resume practice while the other half stand guard? We'll take turns. An hour of practice for the first group, and then an hour with the second."

Desmond was the first to shrug like it was no big deal. "Better than w'all standin' 'round doin' nothin'. Yo, Zane! What d'ya wanna do first?"

Greg's animal was scratching its face at Desmond's casualness before the duke's hand went for the Money Retriever's nape as he delivered a stern, shivering reminder, "After the queen finishes speaking, we place an arm across our chest as a sign of loyalty and say the standard words of, 'As you wish, my queen,' as a demonstration of obedience. Is that understood, Desmond?"

Desmond nodded without needing to think. He might have been afraid of the way Greg looked at him with that partially onyx glare, but the follower was more afraid of disappointing the very creature who had helped him stand on his feet again than he was of the warning.

Lucy's voice then rang through the space, "Greg, let him go. Desmond did nothing wrong." Turning back to everyone else, she said, "The ministers and royal family will stand guard with the discreti first. Warriors and . . ." It was on the tip of Lucy's tongue to say "rogues," but the word didn't feel right after reading the thesis, so she thought fast and chose to say, "mavericks." Her own animal was covering its face in embarrassment for its human, but Lucy pushed through. "Train first. We'll swap after an hour."

The queen quickly turned and jogged toward a random spot to guard, not wanting to see any weird looks that may be shot at her for her lame choice of word. She really should have thought that through before opening her mouth.

But Lucy didn't know the word "maverick" made the rogues who understood it feel better about themselves.

When Desmond saw that the queen had left the circle and he didn't need to be all nice and polite around the king, he faced his boss and said, "That's a cool word, boss. Ain't know what it means though."

Greg's smile was getting broader by the second. He allowed himself another two-second look at Lucy's retreating figure before answering, "Mavericks are unorthodox creatures who don't follow a prescribed set of rules, customs, or beliefs. Independent thinkers and believers."

The duke then turned in the other direction for his own guard duty when Desmond asked, "That's a good thing, ain't it, boss?"

Greg smiled radiantly when he yelled out, "Beats being called a rogue like you don't belong anywhere."

The rogues turned to their queen again, who was speaking animatedly to Octavia and another discretus, and the rogues couldn't deny the warmth she gave them just through a simple swap of one word. For once, they didn't feel like they were being ostracized by society. She made them feel . . . special, maybe even above those who blindly followed rules.

Even the non-rogues felt they'd learned something. If they were being honest with themselves, they'd admit that they'd been keeping their distance from the rogues, who "earned" that label after causing some form of trouble.

But now that Lucy had addressed them as mavericks, it somehow felt like they may attempt to . . . forgive, and possibly accept these creatures who were now helping them with the present threat.

When Lucy looked around and realized that she was the only one standing guard, with the exception of Greg, who was moseying like he was on a stroll, her confused eyes darted back to everyone who was still staring at her in awe and appreciation. With nothing but annoyance since she didn't know what went on after leaving the circle, her arms raised into a "What?" sign as she shouted across the field, "WHAT ARE YOU GUYS DOING STANDING THERE? THE FIRST HOUR OF PRACTICE STARTED TWO MINUTES AGO!"

Upon hearing that, Greg's animal prompted him to ditch walking and sprint to stand guard, which they reached in three seconds flat. Everyone else's eyes bulged wide open as they cursed under their breath before frantically searching for their decipio partner and pulling their wolf or lycan partner to start practice.

Xandar, Christian, and the ministers sprinted to cover the edges of the field. Toby and Juan even knocked into each other by accident when they were in the midst of rushing. It didn't matter how long they had known Lucy; it was still very possible to be scared of her when she barked out orders like that.

Xandar approached his wife and left a kiss on her temple to calm her agitation, muttering, "Sorry for delaying their practice, babe. And you're amazing, by the way. You have no idea how many eyes lit up when you called them mavericks instead of rogues."

Before he could sprint away, Lucy protested, "That can't be right, Xandar. That word is so ancient that it's lame to use it today. Calling them rebels would've been cooler, but there may be some . . . negative connotation to it that would create further friction between them and the rest of our people. I'll definitely be thinking of a better word for their group."

Xandar chuckled. "Lucy, that word is perfect. *You* are perfect. You gave them what you've already given the rest of us—hope. There's nothing lame about it at all. It baffles me how you still can't see the effect you have on creatures. If you stuck around after saying what you did, you'd feel the tension between our kinds eased a little with the change of one word."

Her eyes went to the mavericks, who'd begun practicing. She let her sympathy show when whispering, "Not all of them are what we thought they were, Xandar. We have to fix this. We have to fix what history and our predecessors have done to them and what we've been taught to keep doing to them."

Wrapping her in an embrace, he promised, "We will, baby. We will."

Margaret was practicing with Azalea with their decipio partner, Dylan. They shut their eyes like they had been taught. After five seconds were up, their lids lifted. Since they reminded themselves and their wolves to trust smell over sight, the first session wasn't very difficult to ace since Dylan only made them both see each other as enemies, removing himself from the picture. The real challenge came when the three of them agreed that it was time for Dylan to help them level up. That was when things got a little bit out of hand.

Before the five-second cue was up for round two, Margaret's ears caught fierce snarls, the type that normally hit her eardrums when her rogue pack was surrounded by other rogues ready to attack to either steal their supplies or kill her to assimilate her followers into their own pack.

Her survival instincts took over. She opened her eyes to find that she was surrounded by more than ten rogue wolves. A part of their shelter was already on fire. It was exactly like her vision.

She didn't realize the choking smell of billowing smoke was not present despite the fire, and it didn't occur to her that their pack had never and would never take shelter in an open space like Polje with no trees to hide them. These logical conclusions were not at the forefront of Margaret's mind because it was dominated by the sight before her.

Then, she heard a scream—Stella's scream, coming from the room close to the fire. Her animal pushed through, and the red wolf came forward. Three of the imaginary rogues pounced at her. One unshifted rogue was patronizing her, taunting her for being an incapable mother who was going to lose her pup.

Margaret's claws sunk through one of the three attacking as her canines scratched one of its eyes. She then kicked the second one toward the third, getting them both out of the way at once before making a run toward the burning shelter. Another rogue pounced on her, but she flipped him away with one swift movement, somehow failing to register that the rogue was too light for its size.

The leader came and stood in her way with one of his followers right behind him, when Stella's screams got louder.

Margaret tried mind-linking Azalea, and her friend kept yelling, *'Margo! I'm right in front of you! I can smell you! Whatever you're doing, stop it!'*

'Stella's in danger! Get to her quick!'

'No, she's not! We're being manip—'

'SAVE MY DAUGHTER, AZALEA! THAT'S AN ORDER!'

'IT'S NOT STELLA! USE YOUR NOSE!'

Dylan watched Azalea trying to get to Margaret without hurting her as he wondered whether he'd be attacked himself anytime soon. Taking a deep breath and hoping that he wasn't going to regret his next move, he made Azalea seem like the next rogue who was about to attack Margaret. The red wolf growled thunderously and leaped off the ground, at which time Dylan immediately removed the manipulation effects before pushing Azalea away, retaining a slight scratch along his forearm when he narrowly avoided Margaret's claws. As soon as Margaret landed, she began looking around, astonished that the sight before her took a complete turn within seconds.

Tate asked Yarrington to help guard his spot for a few minutes as he dashed to his confused-looking mate. Getting down on one knee when he reached the red wolf, he steadied her by clasping her face. "Mar, you okay?"

The red wolf's racing heart steadied, and its disheveled mind calmed as the sparks from his touch coursed through her being. Reality returned, and Margaret turned to Azalea and Dylan. Azalea threw a towel over Margaret, allowing her to shift back. As soon as she did, Tate helped her up.

With nothing but guilt in her eyes, Margaret asked Dylan, "How bad is the wound?"

Dylan showed her the scratch and said, "Not at all bad, Margaret. It was my fault. I probably should have stopped you sooner."

"I am so sorry."

Dylan waved his hand with a sincere smile. "It really is nothing. I wouldn't call it a wound to begin with. Perhaps we should take a short break here."

When nods of agreement went around, Azalea and Dylan went to watch different pairs, seeing them struggle and trying to learn something themselves.

Once they were alone, Margaret muttered, "Gosh, that was a disaster."

Tate's hands stroked her shoulders in soothing motions. "It's only the second day of practice, Mar. You'll get there."

"No, what I mean is . . ." she looked around, then whispered, "The vision I had . . . wasn't of reality. It was of my own manipulation practice. I just wasted everyone's time and messed up every creature's peace of mind by telling them that there was going to be an attack tonight. The attack already happened . . . in my mind."

"Hey," Tate clasped both sides of her face and uttered. "It wasn't wrong to warn us about it. Any one of us would've done the same thing. It's no secret that psychic abilities take time to develop. Mistakes are bound to be made. It wasn't wrong to tell us what you saw. It's better to be safe than sorry, Mar. No one can blame you for this."

After heaving a heavy sigh, her eyes went to the queen, who had gotten bored and started weaving leaves, looking into the forest ahead every few seconds. Octavia and the other discretus she was with were now at a distance from her to cover a larger perimeter of the field.

Margaret murmured, "I have to tell her."

Tate followed her sights to his old friend and chuckled lightly. "You really don't have to worry about Lucy. She isn't the type to make us feel bad for a mistake."

His lightness was contagious, and it made her less anxious, to the point where she managed to say, "So you're saying that I'm supposed to worry about the rest of them who may make me feel bad for my mistake, Tate?"

"Those loyal to the king and queen understand that mistakes happen. As for your own followers . . . I doubt they'll make you feel bad for this, Mar. And I don't think you give a damn about what the royal rogues think of you."

It was amazing how—with just a few words—Tate made her feel that much better. Tate reached for her hand, and his fingers cautiously laced with hers. His wolf stood so still in his mind, wondering if that was the right move to make at the moment. When Margaret's fingers tightened around his grip, Tate let out an audible sigh of relief, at which time Margaret teased, "Am I really that scary, Alpha?"

Going along with her humor, he replied, "Considering that, one, you have a wolf that can try to push through silver cuffs; two, you climbed to the very top of the rogue ladder while raising a daughter by yourself for more than a decade; and three, the fact that your followers just trusted you when you asked them to follow a plane full of lycans that we're taught to stay away from, I'd definitely say you are terrifying."

Margaret chuckled, and the sound made Tate's wolf wag its tail in happiness.

Lucy's ears perked up when she heard footsteps approaching her, and Octavia offered to keep watch while the queen paused her weaving as her attention went to Tate and Margaret. To Margaret's surprise, the only thing that came out of Lucy's mouth was a relieved "Thank Goddess."

There wasn't the slightest hint of anger, annoyance, or judgment. In Margaret's rogue pack, there was no room for mistakes. It was worse when misogynistic wolves still led the pack. Those late elders *never* let her or any other female forget their mistakes. When Tate and Lucy didn't make her feel sorry to begin with, it reminded Margaret about her birth family, who'd never judged her for blunders.

Lucy informed Octavia, and the consort glanced at Margaret before linking Pelly. Lucy herself linked Xandar before she linked the others, strictly emphasizing, *'If we had her power, we would've warned each other just how she warned us. We're not blaming her for this.'*

Toby linked back in amusement, *'Lucy, if there's anyone who's going to blame the future luna, it's going to be the other duke and his followers.'*

Zelena retorted, *'That's nonsense. Once Lucy gets that duke to drop the matter, he'll obey like a good pup, and his followers will fall in line.'*

Yarrington somehow saw the need to add, *'I personally think that the royal mavericks would not criticize the error because they themselves are pledging loyalty to the queen, not because the duke chooses to obey per se. Yes, they obey Greg Claw, but surely none of us can deny that most of them are growing fond of the queen.'*

Lucy had no intention of making the royal mavericks loyal to her. All she wanted was smooth cooperation, but she had actually grown fond of many of them herself. Their strength and resilience were attributes she admired, and their plight was something she was determined to help alleviate.

Xandar's deep, commanding voice rang through the link, *'Yarrington's right. They already love her; they'll comply. Since there isn't a threat, half of us here should resume practice. The other half of us stay with the discreti, just in case.'*

Utterances of agreement were sent through the link before they decided who should go first. Xandar began, *'Babe, you go first. I'll take the first round.'*

Left abashed at the affectionate way Xandar spoke to her in their group-link, her cheeks heated up. She could've sworn she heard Toby's not-so-subtle chuckles when he saw the way his best friend responded to the king's gentle tone.

After Lucy briefed Octavia about the new arrangement, the queen threw away the partially woven leaves and left her spot, which Xandar immediately went to retrieve before returning to his spot, studying the half-done craft with interest.

His features softened when he watched his queen jog across the field to his hated cousin. His smile fell as his predatory eyes watched their exchange. Lucy made sure she stood in a way that Xandar could see hers and Greg's side profiles when they spoke. The duke's features hardened before his eyes instinctively roamed the space in search of the unreliable fortune-teller. But his search was brought to an abrupt halt when Lucy's stern eyes brought his attention back to her, and he nodded in compliance before Lucy thanked him and left his side. Greg's eyes glazed over to link his followers.

Xandar only felt at ease when she was far enough from Greg, but when she reached a smiling Rafael, he tried to control his jealousy again, hoping Lucy wouldn't feel it through their bond. As he reminded himself that he and his mate were mated, marked, married, and still deeply in love, his sights returned to the forest.

Christian found this the appropriate time to link, *'Next time Annie brings up my jealousy, I'm going to use you as my buffer and say that you're worse, Cuz. At least I'm not worried about a vampire stealing my wife.'*

'How would you know? Annie's not even here. Have her come tomorrow night, and we'll see if you really won't fume like me.'

Christian considered it. With a quick glance at Lucy, imagining that it was Annie with Rafael instead, the duke harrumphed and linked, *'I'll bring Annie when Rafael is less good-looking and more assholish.'*

'You're not really helping, Christian.'

'My primary job as your favorite cousin is to annoy you. Helping you comes second.'

'You are so lucky you have no competition.'

'I know, Cuz. Your love for me is eternal, as is mine for you.'

Greg's eyes glazed over to link the royal mavericks, *'The fortune-telling was a false alarm, and the queen has emphasized the need to refrain from exerting blame on the maggot, so refrain. But keep an eye on them, all of you. The queen's safety is our top priority. Investigate at the first sign of danger.'*

'Yes, Your Grace,' they uttered in unison through their link like they'd done a hundred times before.

When Greg ended that link, Hailey's private link came through, and she told him about Kate. He asked, *'Anything of use tonight?'*

'She seems to have some aversion to the empress. When the queen was speaking to us and everyone's eyes were on her, this rogue kept glancing at the empress with . . . hatred. It's just a preliminary suspicion, Your Grace. I'm still trying to see if it happens again.'

'Physical profile?'

'Brown, six feet, bob hair, in a faded green top tonight.'

Greg's eyes scanned the field for Hailey before finding Kate not far away. *'Get another two of our own to help you keep watch, those nearer to her practice spot. Good work, Hailey.'*

After the break from their third round, Rafael prompted, "Ready?"

Upon Lucy's nod, Rafael began. She felt her awareness diminishing, like she was being induced into a daydream, which decipimus have found to be the perfect place to start at manipulating their victims. As hard as Lucy tried to fight to stay alert, she couldn't completely clear the seemingly innocuous fog invading her mind. Instead of trying to focus on making her mind clear of the fog, she channeled her concentration to her nose and skin, smelling any creatures near her in reality and trying to feel their energies.

There was only one vampire—as far as she could tell—taking slow, cautious steps at a safe distance around her, but she was being manipulated to forget that it was Rafael. When she began approaching Rafael, he painted a fictional scene that pulled her to a halt.

She was hiding behind a tree. About five feet away, her late parents were in their wolf forms, both white, lingering behind high bushes as their eyes glazed over, mind-linking one another.

Right when Lucy was about to run to them, she heard disgruntled murmurs and heavy footsteps. Her parents heard them, too, and they lay even lower. Lucy instinctively dropped herself into a squat behind the tree as she watched two men—one beer-bellied and one lanky—and one large-sized woman, in chaps carrying rifles that were slung across their backs.

Hunters.

The insides of Lucy's stomach churned, until she remembered they weren't at war with the hunters anymore. Diplomatic relationships had been established years ago. Rafael noticed her certainty, and his fog of manipulation slithered deeper into her mind.

Her lycan stubbornly held onto their knowledge about the hunters and even recalled that her parents were dead. Besides, in reality, she should have been able to smell her parents from where she was, but she wasn't detecting any of their scents at present.

These logical revelations made Rafael certain she was ready for the next level, so he turned it up a notch. The hunters noticed her parents and aimed their loaded rifles at them.

Rafael began assessing whether Lucy would give in to her emotional urges instead of trusting what she knew to be true.

Before the hunters pulled the trigger, Lucy turned the other way and ran in the opposite direction, not wanting to witness her parents being fictionally killed. She ignored the sounds of gunshots and her parents' anguished howling, repeating to herself and her animal, "Not true. Not true. Not true. Silver blade. Silver blade. Silver blade." Her parents had died after succumbing to the silver-laced blades used by hunters, not through rifle bullets, so this was probably a nightmare. She must have been dreaming.

Rafael smiled in awe, and he put her through one last test for the session, dead certain that she was going to ace it. The enthusiastic decipio was already mentally planning on what to do in the following practice session.

Lucy ran until she knocked into something hard. It was someone's back, someone in a black suit. The frame was so familiar that it didn't take her long to recognize it as Xandar's back. He turned, towering over her like he always did in reality. The difference was that his eyes held no love or affection, only disgust and annoyance.

"What are you doing here?" Xandar's voice came out low and callous.

"Xandar, it's me. What happened? Where are we?" she asked, looking around. They were in the dining hall where the annual collaboration was held many months back. There wasn't another soul in sight.

Xandar's cold voice drew her attention back to him. "What did you just call me?"

His question sent a wave of confusion through her. Her animal was backing away, sensing no warmth from their mate. Her human was too shocked to move. "I called you by your name?"

He took one step closer, looking her dead in the eye when he snarled, "And who gave you the right to call me by my name? I am your king."

"You gave me that right, Xandar. You made me your queen."

Xandar scoffed darkly. "It really is that hard to accept a rejection, isn't it? I thought it'd be a piece of cake for something like you, having already gone through five. I guess I was wrong. You're more incapable than I thought."

The stabs from the words *rejection, something,* and *incapable* made her animal howl as her chest constricted; her heart bled. Her emotions were spiraling out of control, and her focus subtly left what she knew to be true and was fully given to this blatant lie. She took a step back, already believing what she was seeing.

Rafael's attempt to block her awareness was getting more successful, and she forgot that she and Xandar were marked, married, and had a daughter together.

She was made to believe that they were bonded mates, but when they met, Xandar looked at her with nothing but disdain and rejected her in front of everyone on the first night of the annual meet-and-greet for a chosen mate, who was . . .

"Hello, Xandar." Kelissa Kylton appeared from behind Xandar's large frame. The beautiful lycan wore a stunning dark purple dress that accentuated her slim figure, and her slender fingers hung comfortably on Xandar's left shoulder.

Xandar's features softened, and his hand snaked around her waist in the most natural manner. A smile replaced his hardened face as he pecked Kelissa on her lips. "What took you so long, my love?"

Lucy's heart raced and stomach churned. It was getting harder to breathe and harder to see because of the moisture forming over her eyes. How had she fallen in love with him despite the rejection? She told herself that she was never going to fall in love again after Sebastian Cummings. She was so sure that she didn't want a mate anymore, so why was she upset? Why did she feel like she was being betrayed when he had never misled her to think that he wanted her, that he had made her and the rest of the kingdom aware that only Kelissa was his rightful queen, that Lucy herself was everything that a queen shouldn't be—a wolf, physically violent, overly opinionated, unwanted, too small to be noticed let alone be given any attention and respect to.

Adamant, she refused to wipe away her tears in case she accidentally saw Xandar and Kelissa again. Her feet only carried her two steps before Xandar's cold voice made her stop. "Where's your respect for your queen?" She looked up, and even through her blurred vision, she could see Kelissa smirking, her body glued to Xandar's side. Xandar continued to spit, "Are all wolves this disrespectful, or is it just you? Kneel before your queen."

Kneeling may not be a problem at all, not because she'd give that brat any form of respect but because her legs were weakening. Everything in her felt heavy. But despite her heartbreak and tears, her face hardened when she mustered the little strength she had left and looked Xandar dead in the eye as she uttered a clear and defiant *no*.

Xandar's lilac eyes turned onyx, a rage that Kelissa easily matched. Lucy shambled toward the door again, hanging her head low. Then a large hand caught her arm and spun her around. She was pulled into something hard and instantly recognized Xandar's scent. His arms wrapped around her and held her tight. Her tears sprung free as she tried to push him away, but he was refusing to let her go.

Back in reality, Xandar's voice came out in a panicked, desperate plea, "Baby. Baby, please. It's me."

In the manipulated illusion, she heard him snarl, "You're not going anywhere yet, you uncivilized wolf!"

The manipulation effects were fading very slowly despite Rafael's effort to speed things up, and the Xandar of reality coped with the pain when his little freesia punched him in the chest, gut, and jaw to attempt escape as he tightened his grip around her. The blows were nothing compared to what they were doing to his heart. His animal couldn't understand what was happening and combined his strength with his human to hold her close, cooing into the link, trying to reach her lycan, wondering why she, too, was shutting him out.

"What did you do to her?" Xandar hissed at Rafael.

When Lucy's latest practice session began, Xandar felt her doubt through their mate bond at first, and assumed it was normal because of the manipulation. But when that doubt grew into disbelief, then painful acceptance and distance, he tried to decipher what she was distancing herself from. That was when he realized that his worst nightmare had come true—she was distancing herself from their bond, from him. The way her heart was squeezed made his animal howl in torment. He didn't think twice before dashing to her, not caring that she was in the midst of practice. He pulled her into him only to have her try to push him away.

When everyone saw their king sprinting across the field, those taking a break started watching and were shocked to see the way their queen was trying to break free. Xandar caged her in his arms and dodged punches, holding her in his embrace as Lucy sobbed and whimpered in a futile attempt to run away.

The others blinked countless times. Some even shook their heads to make sure they weren't in a daze and squinted their eyes to verify that they weren't seeing things. Many began considering they were undergoing their own manipulation practice and thought this was an easy test to pass. The king and queen of reality would never behave like that. But they didn't understand what they were supposed to do with this information. Was this a build-up before an attack that they'd eventually have to defend?

Christian asked Toby if they were both looking at the same thing. Pelly came over, as did Octavia, and all eyes then shifted to a very guilty Rafael. The most powerful decipio watched the lycan couple helplessly as he swallowed a lump in his throat before admitting sheepishly, "Perhaps it's still too early to tamper with the mate bond."

Finally giving Rafael his undivided, murderous attention, Xandar questioned, "You. Did. WHAT?" His growl echoed across Polje.

But Lucy heard him say, "She's. Your. QUEEN!"

Knowing he meant Kelissa, Lucy tried to wriggle out of his slightly loosened grip, but Xandar repositioned his arms and held her in place again, gently muttering, "Babe, hold still. Just give me a minute, please."

She didn't give him another second when she heard, "When I'm done teaching you about respect, you'll wish you'd knelt." It only made her struggle harder.

"Let me go. P-Please, just let me go, Your Highness," she pleaded, deciding to deal with the humiliating aftermath later.

Xandar's heart shattered at her feet, and the worst part of it was she didn't even know. Anger and hurt coursed through his veins as his animal growled with full force through their link, trying to wake their mate from the manipulation. His human glued her to him and restricted all movement, uttering in her ear, "No. Not now. Not ever. You're *mine*."

Those words made her shudder as her grappling continued, bringing tears to Xandar's eyes despite knowing she wasn't seeing or hearing what was real yet. Not knowing what else to say, he planted a long, deep kiss on her forehead, sending a shower of sparks right down to her toes. Her struggling paused and confusion came, and she stood very still, trying but failing to comprehend the gesture.

Taking advantage of her motionlessness, Xandar's eyes went back to Rafael as he snarled, "What the *hell* were you thinking? Do you have *any* idea how *fucking* hard it was to get her to open up to the idea of having me as her mate, to persuade her to accept the crown, TO MAKE HER BELIEVE I LOVE HER? Do you know how many blows she took from the mate bond before we met? HOW DARE Y—"

"Xandar, please stop," Lucy's weakened voice came in a shaky whisper.

His onyx eyes darted to her, relief cascading through him at the sight of her pressing herself into his embrace. Even her animal opened up to his now. Gently lifting her chin, he looked into her teary orbs and firmly declared, "I love you, Lucy."

The urgent anticipation in his eyes obliged her to whisper back, "I love you too."

That wasn't a good answer. He heard the hesitation in her voice and felt the doubt lingering through their bond, so he planted another deep kiss on her forehead before demanding in a softened voice and a hard but pleading gaze, "Tell me you know that I love you, baby."

That familiar line sent the usual warmth into her heart. The doubt she was struggling to flush out on her own melted away. Her small hand reached for his cheek, and Xandar leaned into her touch as he waited in dismay.

She managed a small smile and finally said, "I know. I love you too."

He pressed another kiss in her hair. Their foreheads touched when he muttered, "We'll talk about this later, okay?"

"Okay."

Ear on his chest, she indulged in the beautiful rhythm of his heartbeat, feeling the depth of his love for her for a few more moments before deciding that she was ready for round five, not yet realizing that neither her decipio partner nor her husband was ready for that.

Lucy gently broke loose and turned to a still-remorseful and much paler Rafael, but as soon as her mouth opened, Xandar spun her around once more and said, "Perhaps that's enough practice for one night, my love."

"I'm fine now, Xandar. I can go again." She actually sounded normal, which perplexed Toby and many others.

Rafael immediately added, "Your Highness, I have to agree with the king. We should stop for the night."

"But I'm fine," Lucy protested, and started using her doe eyes on Xandar.

But before they possessed the lycan king like they always did, he said, "We know you are, sweetheart. But it's my turn to practice and your turn to stand guard. Here—" he put the half-woven leaves into her hands "—you can finish this up. I'll come check on you later, okay?"

Lucy gaped when she realized her husband had picked up something she had casually thrown away. It wasn't even good work. Her sister-in-law was way better at this than she was.

Xandar took advantage of her surprise, pecking a kiss on her temple and gently ushering her toward Weaver and Phelton, who were both in the second round of guard duty too.

The ministers understood the king's silent command and led their queen away, toward the edge of Polje. Xandar's lilac orbs followed them, and his heart softened when Lucy's hands began working on the leaves again. She looked absolutely adorable doing that.

His animal reminded him about Rafael, and Xandar reluctantly tore his eyes away from his wife before looking at the decipio, mustering as much diplomacy as he could when he questioned, "Was that really necessary?"

Rafael counted himself lucky that Xandar spoke with less ferocity. "I am very, very, very sorry about that, Your Highness. I sincerely believed that she was going to pass that final test with nothing more than mental exhaustion. My decision to . . . touch that part of her mind was, for all intents and purposes, an effort to motivate the rest of the lycans and werewolves that they too can start . . . slithering practice. Mental walls are very basic. I'm only worried that the proditors have more skillful decipimus with them, who may well be able to tap into the mate bond and use it to their advantage since it has proven to be the most effective way to fully distract and derail its victims. I am terribly sorry for the . . . overexertion. With hindsight, it really wasn't smart of me to tap into it when she'd already gone through three rounds."

Greg couldn't stop himself, firing, "If you want *us* to start slithering practice, rush *us*, *not* her."

Xandar threw his cousin a glare. "She's my mate, Greg. I can handle this. We're starting slithering practice tonight with the empress."

Pelly immediately said, "That's not possible. I won't do it. Your foundations on recognizing and maneuvering around mental walls aren't even stable yet. Slithering won't only crush your minds; it'll demolish your confidence, both yours and your animals'. The last thing we need is having a lowly motivated set of creatures to help us fight the present threat."

Greg groaned in dissatisfaction. "Fine. We'll do walls first."

Xandar took another look at Lucy before he spoke in a commanding voice, "We should all speed up trying to improve. Push ourselves beyond the limit. We don't want to have to rely on the empire's decipimus to carry our weight, nor should we let Lucy expend unnecessary energy to help us fight off the manipulation with the Queen's Authority when we can train ourselves to do it."

They listened to every word. Their fatigue and reluctance dissolved when they saw and felt the urgent need to step up. Their sights instinctively followed Xandar's to Lucy, whose fingers on the leaves paused when she looked left and right. She then turned with the same confused and annoyed look from earlier, but before she could say anything, everyone scrambled and either took their positions around Polje or started practicing.

Lucy shut her opening mouth, and her eyes went to her brooding husband taking his position with Greg and Pelly. She admired his muscular figure and determined eyes that were highlighted by the moonlight. A shy smile graced her features as she returned to the leaves in her hands.

Xandar came to check up on her whenever he and Greg were taking a break, and was happy to see that she was back to normal.

They reached home at around 11:00 p.m., checked on Reida, and then got into the shower. After that, Xandar carried Lucy—who was in her underwear and his shirt—to the couch of their bedroom. He placed her on his lap and held her close, listening attentively as she told him about the manipulation. She didn't smell him or Kelissa, but the image of them consumed her mind so much that even her lycan had completely ignored that the scents weren't present.

His grip tightened when Lucy mentioned that she didn't even remember being marked or married to him, nor did she recall having their daughter. A storm brewed in him as the tale went on.

Lucy tried to lighten the mood by finishing with, ". . . and the whole time, I was actually talking to a tree, so I was technically being heartbroken that the tree rejected me."

With another kiss on her temple, he said, "That's not funny, Lucy. That power is just so . . ." he sighed and rubbed a hand down his face before choosing the word ". . . dangerous."

"Explains how the vampires could've won the war if our ancestors didn't surrender." She snuggled deeper into him and stroked his chest, jaw, and chin—the parts she punched earlier. "I'm sorry for hurting you."

"Goddess, Lucy. Don't apologize for that. After what you were manipulated to see, I'd be worried if you didn't do what you did." They sat in silence for the next few moments, feeling each other's presence inside and out. After taking a greedy whiff of her hair, he cupped her cheek and lifted her face. Their eyes locked when he said, "Whatever happens, wherever we are, know that I love you, okay?"

"Okay." She left a kiss on his chin, adding, "Know that I love you too."

A soft smile replaced the hardness in his face. His nose grazed hers when he whispered, "Thank you, baby. We should get some sleep now." He carried her to bed, and they fell into a deep slumber in each other's arms.

CHAPTER 33

In her holding unit, Kate crawled under the sheets and deleted the messages of the day out of habit. She then extracted the SIM card and hid it in her bra. The practice tonight was horrible for her. She'd just received news from the person she'd been communicating with, and it did nothing to ease her anxiety.

###

On another end, Hailey had just gotten Jade to hack into Kate's phone before the signal was lost. Frustration took over when she asked, "Really? Now?"

"What a time to be taking out the SIM card," Jade mused.

"Well, she's not supposed to have a SIM card to begin with," Hailey noted. "We should ask the duke to report her to the queen. She's hiding something."

Jade, who watched Kate when Hailey couldn't during manipulation practice, said, "I dunno. That'd be the direct thing to do, but personally, I'd ask the boss to just sit back for now. This rogue might know something we could use."

"We snatch her phone, use it as evidence of betrayal, the queen uses the Authority to make her vomit whatever shit out, and boom! We get everything."

"Really? What if there's something in there that none of us has thought of?"

"That's kind of the point of the Queen's Authority, Jade."

"No, Hay. This is the point: the Authorities only work with very specific commands. They tell us to sit, we sit. They tell us to kneel, we kneel. They tell us to go to battle and not die, we go to battle and . . . try not to die. But if they say something generic, like, 'Tell me the truth,' or 'Tell me everything you know—'" Jade threw his hands in the air "—it's basically the same as not asking."

"Give the queen more credit, Jade. She'll know how to phrase those questions. Even we can, like, 'Tell me the truth about this text,' 'Tell me everything you know about this creature you've been contacting.'"

Jade's hands raised at chest level. "In no way am I saying that the queen is stupid, Hay. But if we converge the truth to the text, information will be limited to the text. If we narrow it to individual creatures, information will be limited to them. We may be looking at a network here, one that Kate herself might not even know yet."

"Kate?"

"The rogue's name, Hay." Looking at her with judgment creases on his forehead, he said, "You've gotten better at eavesdropping, but it still needs work. Anyway, the point now is even the smartest creature cannot know or predict everything. Take our boss, he didn't know the Kyltons had brains to do shit and look what they'd been doing for almost two decades. He's one of the smartest creatures we know, and even he didn't know he was being used."

Hailey recalled the debacle, murmuring, "That was a very careless mistake on his part, to work with someone without knowing who was at the top of the chain."

"And it's a mistake that he won't repeat, but the point stands. So we should extract whatever we can from Kate's phone the next time the SIM card enters, before making a move."

Hailey sighed in impatience. "Fine. I'm going to bed. Tell the boss."

"Wait, me?"

"Yep," she replied nonchalantly.

"I'm not one of his favorites though."

Hailey proudly declared, "I am, but I'm sleepy, and I might not be as convincing as you are in putting this point forward. If you impress him enough, you might become one of his favorites."

"I highly doubt there's room for me up there, but, yeah, I'll link him."

"Tonight," Hailey insisted.

Jade shut down the computer and shot her a smile when he confirmed, "Tonight."

After Hailey left, Jade linked Greg, who got on the same boat as him even before Jade finished explaining. Jade couldn't help himself from asking, *'Will you be . . . telling the queen about this, Your Grace?'* Maybe that was why he wasn't one of the duke's favorites. He tended to ask questions that were—perhaps—better off left unasked.

Greg was asking himself the same question. After a moment of flicking the pen in his hand, he said, *'I have to. This is a cooperation, not a solo project amongst ourselves.'*

'She wouldn't . . . stop us, would she?'

'I hope not,' he muttered, then added, *'I can't speak for the queen, Jade. She's smart enough to know that what we want to do is the most strategic way forward, but she's forgiving enough to offer this rogue a chance to explain herself.'*

'The latter way is too soft and may be ineffective. How do we know Kate won't lie?'

'Exactly.' Greg sat up. *'I'm sure the queen will weigh in all these factors before deciding.'*

Jade sure hoped so. *'Alright, then. You know her better than we do anyway. Night, boss.'*

'Thank you, Jade. Goodnight.'

Greg's eyes cleared, and he continued flicking his pen in his office as he returned his attention to the penned-down information he'd received from the deployed teams. Those sent to wolf territory reported back that the rogue wolves saw no vampires. Good. That meant the bloodsuckers' abduction problem was within their own territory.

As for his watchers, however, it wasn't all good news. In fact, there was no news at all! After the team he sent to examine the passageways accessible from Halo's and Vent's businesses led to nothing, they took the initiative to begin watching J.J. and Bundy again. The two loud talkers were still not loud-talking. Greg still couldn't understand why J.J. and Bundy had not done anything besides visit bars with a low profile and then check in to random inns for the usual two-day, one-night stay. Dormant Little Red hadn't progressed or regressed either. This wasn't just getting odd; it was getting infuriating.

He linked Lepak, who began watching Red again, *'Tomorrow, whisper some nonsense into the bartender's ear and tip him ten bucks. Then leave. See if you can feel Red staring at you.'*

'As you wish, Your Grace.'

He then linked Nani, who swapped with Quinn in watching J.J. and Bundy with the same instructions.

All there was left to do was wait.

CHAPTER 34

The next morning, Lucy packed the baby essentials before she and Xandar left for the Den. Xandar was hesitant to allow their daughter to come with them at first, but seeing that both he and Lucy could use their Authorities on those creatures if they had to be used, he gave in.

Lucy didn't want to spend too much time away from Reida, so she brought her daughter anywhere that didn't pose a risk of danger. She had already met the royal mavericks, and they were all loyal to Greg. Since Greg was on their side, she wasn't worried about bringing Reida along.

They reached the Den, and many were fascinated by the princess, who was looking around with those curious lilac orbs in her mother's arms. Hailey came over and was elated that they had brought the pup. She dashed to her room, got the small teddy bear she bought after meeting Reida the first time, and handed it to the princess.

The king and queen thanked Hailey for the kind gesture. The softness of the plush toy clearly pleased the baby girl, but the scent didn't. She hugged the bear for only a brief second before holding it away. After a moment of contemplation, Reida rubbed the toy mercilessly against her mother's bosoms. The pup's head then turned to Xandar, and her arms stretched out. Her father got the cue to carry her, but she dropped the toy into her mother's arms on the way, so she exclaimed, "Ah!" demanding the bear before rubbing it against her father's chest next. When she was satisfied with the scent of her new gift, she held it close to her chest and cooed aloud in happiness.

Hailey and Desmond led them to the discussion room, and they noticed chairs had been added around the table. When Xandar walked past Greg, Reida caught her uncle's familiar scent, so she turned and yelled, "FUCK!" with a big smile.

"REIDA!" Lucy exclaimed with eyes and a tone that made Reida's smile falter as she snuggled deeper into her father, seeking protection.

Xandar pecked a kiss on her daughter's forehead, whispering, "Well done, cupcake."

Greg simply chuckled lightly and said, "Good morning to you, too, princess."

Lucy began apologizing when Greg interjected, "I doubt she knows what that word means, my queen. It really isn't an issue. It's probably her way of saying hi."

To Reida, Xandar muttered, "Daddy will explain what it means, cupcake. But you'll have to promise to keep saying it when you see Uncle Greg, okay?"

Lucy warned, "Don't. You. Dare. Xandar. She's too young. She shouldn't be saying that to *anyone* yet."

Of course Xandar didn't mean it. He was simply eliciting a response from his mate. The proud father doubted Reida possessed the vocabulary required to understand that word anyway. After stroking his fuming wife's hand to calm her, they started the discussion.

Greg brought them up to speed about Dr. Tanish and Madame Psych. The good news was that this was a false alarm. The scientists behaved normally, speaking only to each other while closing off their field of vision, hearing, and opinion to everyone else. They were—in Greg's words—still dabbling in random nonsense without any prospect of a breakthrough. When they moved on to J.J., Bundy, and Dormant Little Red, Lucy's brows knitted when she questioned, "Are these three from the same . . . clique, Greg?"

"Never was. And I doubt they'll ever be. They aren't in any clique, clan, or group per se. No one wants them. Apart from being able to keep themselves alive, they're practically useless."

Lucy's arms crossed as she leaned back into her seat. "Useless," she muttered in contemplation. "How are the two females affording the stay at the inns?"

"They're pickpockets."

"Pickpocket who? The other rogues?"

Greg nodded. "Sometimes. There are also a number of dim creatures in our territory who wouldn't know what these two were up to until it was too late, even if it had happened several times before. Other times, they use scent sprays and disguises to steal from those in crowded places of the kingdom. Malls, markets, airports, and the like."

"So . . . you're saying they're useless despite being able to pickpocket because their skill isn't up to your standards?" Lucy asked.

"I suppose you could say that, my queen. Beyond knocking someone's wallet or cash stack out of a bag, they can't do anything without alerting their prey. They can't even steal from someone's wrists or pockets where most valuables are found."

Lucy got to thinking again. "Have they been staying in the same inns this whole time?"

Greg looked at Nani, who nodded in confirmation.

Same inns. Same routine. Same frequented locations. Nothing had changed except the fact that they both had quieted down. The usually drunk Red sobered up. Why would creatures need silence *and* sobriety?

When Lucy figured it out, she looked straight at Greg and said, "You think they're watching your people."

Greg admitted in a low voice, "It's a preliminary suspicion for now, my queen, but, yes."

Xandar asked, "Why would someone want to watch your followers?"

Greg replied, "Like you, not everyone likes me, Cousin."

"I thought you had everyone under your power."

"I had everyone under the impression that no one can or should mess with me and my followers. That's my power. Not every rogue lycan is my follower."

Xandar then uttered in revelation, "There's someone who wants to challenge your position. That's the present threat."

Greg muttered in dissatisfaction, "Suspected threat."

The king turned to his queen and uttered, "The other day at Blue Crescent . . . you were the only one who wasn't physically attacked by the proditors. They want to control you with the concoction and use you to control the rest of us. Whoever is behind this is playing the big game, to control not just those loyal to the kingdom but also those who aren't. The proditors and whoever they're working with are looking to overthrow me *and* the king of rogues here. They think they can do it, but they need time. Those watching his followers right now are just buying time by . . . being red herrings."

No one could mask their surprise at Xandar acknowledging that the duke was a king of something. Xandar had long acknowledged that the royal mavericks exuded the willingness to serve Greg, the same type of energy that Xandar himself got from his own ministers, police, and warriors. Sure, Xandar had the King's Authority to compel any rogue he pleased, but Greg had power over them without any Authority.

Lucy was the first to blink and said, "That does seem to be the case, darling. Uh . . ." her sights returned to Greg ". . . will there be anything you need, Greg? Something within our system or . . ."

"What we need from you, Your Highnesses, is permission for another matter." Greg then explained the situation with Kate, and Lucy held her breath. A mole? Already? Well, a potential mole at the moment.

Mind-linking Xandar to discuss the matter, her eyes cleared as she instructed, "Do whatever is necessary to keep our people safe. Every single one of them, including the mavericks."

In the Forest of Oderem, the vigils were *not* having fun.

CHAPTER 35

Duica and VIG 002, Bernadette, went in as the last pair on their third day of forest testing. They were relieved that no unexplained misfortune was reported by the palace or their families and friends and were immensely grateful that the forest exuded only fresh and pleasant scents when they entered each time. Despite the positive signs, they were still anxious and daunted because of their knowledge about past curses.

Duica and Bernadette went half a mile in, and Bernadette took out her notepad to record the scents of buns and waffles she was smelling before Duica suggested, "Perhaps we can go a little further today. Maybe see what's another half a mile away."

They were both veloces. Running wasn't a problem. Bernadette agreed, "Her Imperial Majesty didn't draw any limits on how deep we can go, after all."

They sped another half a mile and reached a river with the clearest water they'd ever seen. The rocks at the riverbed and the odd-looking fish swimming in the water looked a lot like the illustrations in books that were about this place.

Duica muttered, "The River of Heres. It exists."

"I wonder if the source exists," Bernadette responded, eyes trailing upstream.

Without further discussion or contemplation, they marched up north, admiring the turquoise seaweed and pink-colored rocks in the clear water. As they continued on their path, the smell of buns and waffles got stronger. It was as if the forest was leading them somewhere. Duica was wary, as was Bernadette. They hoped if they were being lured into a trap, they'd have enough time to link the other vigils before they passed out or were killed. Not long later, they found themselves before a coursing waterfall.

Bernadette murmured in awe, "The Misty Waterfall of Heres. It's real."

"It's just like in the books," Duica said. "With the water and food source, there's absolutely no reason to leave this place. I wonder if those who hide here eat the fish."

As soon as he said that, a random yellow flower nearby opened and sprayed a scent of animal dung at Duica, taking offense. Duica choked on the horrible odor and said aloud, "I suppose not. Sor—" cough, cough, cough "—Sorry about that."

The foul odor disappeared, replaced with fresh buns and waffles once again. The observation fascinated the two vigils. As they neared the waterfall, they heard something—rustling leaves.

Their feet stopped as their investigative eyes roamed the place, trying to pinpoint the source. They spotted a large leaf on the ground that was swaying to a stop when their eyes were fixed there, and Bernadette was about to skip across the river before Duica held her back. "There are only two of us. We shouldn't try to follow it yet. It isn't wise. We should head back and get the others."

"What if they escaped by then?" Bernadette hissed.

"I doubt they would, Bern. They have nowhere else to hide. If they run from the forest and enter where we are, the custodes will have a field day arresting them."

Bernadette's hard gaze stayed on the now-still leaf as she hissed, "We should link the others and ask them to meet us here!"

"Sure, while we stand here and wait for any creature in there to surround and attack us when we're clearly outnumbered."

Shooting him a glare, she concurred through clenched teeth, "Fine. Let's head back."

A woman with the abilities of a discretus stood still behind the leaves until the vigils were out of sight. She conveyed a silent thanks to whatever sent them away before heading back herself.

Ella exited the hideout for a daily stroll and breather before she heard two un-familiar voices. As soon as she registered their faces along with their clean-and-tidy appearance, concluding that they were non-proditors, her defensive instincts took over, and her invisibility ability hid her in plain sight as she froze, being careful to not move an inch or make a sound.

An unhelpful insect found it appropriate to land on her leg and bit her through her pants, causing her leg to jerk reflexively and hit the large leaf next to her. Internally, she cursed while resisting the urge to manually stop the swaying leaf. Ella prayed neither of the vigils were discreti, and was relieved when they couldn't see her even though they were looking straight at her.

When she saw the woman ready to cross the river, Ella's heart stopped, and she was about to turn and run, which would have effectively blown her cover. But when the man stopped his companion, she thanked the Goddess and Lord.

Once they left, Ella dashed back, hoping that she wasn't seen or followed, taking the longer route just to make sure she wasn't leading the intruders to their community hideout. Relief washed over her when she concluded that they were still safe. But it was as if she was relieved too soon. The forest's protection mark on her nape started to sting, and when her fingers instinctively flew to that area, there was a slight electrocution that she had never felt before. What was going on?

'Ella! Where are you?' Their leader, Saxum, linked, worried and angered.

'I'm only half a mile away from our place. I'm getting there as fast as I can. Saxum, the protection mark . . . it . . . '

'I know. Get back here quickly. We're leaving. I'm calling for an emergency meeting after we've reached the safe house. We're hastening the Callows.'

'But the sting and the burn . . . what does it mean?'

'The forest might be . . . switching allegiance. It's contemplating for now, so we still have its protection. But we don't have much time. Just get back here and pack up whatever's important so we can leave!'

Ella figured this wasn't the best time to tell him about the non-proditors. He already sounded frantic as it was. And why wouldn't he be? Who knew what the authorities would do if they found out hybrids like them existed and had been living right under their noses for centuries.

CHAPTER 36

According to Saxum, Emperor Kosh had slaughtered many of them because they didn't obey the laws of nature. This horrific tale was passed down to generations of hybrids, justifying the need to stay hidden. To be killed for what she was wasn't a fate Ella wanted for herself or for her friends and family.

The Forest of Oderem was switching allegiance? Could that really happen? She never took the forest for being fickle-minded. They'd been protected for centuries. The authorities and imperial family were so afraid of getting cursed that no one who wasn't protected would enter or even come near.

She finally reached the place she called home. After kicking away the dried leaves that covered the metal opening, she knocked on the metal surface three times, once, and then five times before pulling the cover and climbing down the wooden ladder, closing the cover behind her. As usual, the forest produced a gust of wind that blew the dried leaves back to hide the metal cover.

Ella found everyone running about and didn't even offer her a glance as they stuffed valuables into suitcases. Some who'd already packed were trotting through the newly dug tunnel leading to lycan territory.

Saxum extracted a large box that arrived not long ago, which had the word Fragile written in red. He then instructed the veloces and hybrids who possessed the same ability to place the item all around their hideout. Without question, each of them took as many as their hands could carry and sped around the place, putting it in every place that held it.

"What are you waiting for? Hurry up and pack!" Saxum exclaimed in irritation when Ella didn't move from her spot.

"Right." Sprinting to her room, she opened up her suitcase to pack a few clothes, the only notebook she owned, and her mother's scarf.

On her way to the tunnel, a three-year-old toddler came forward and took her hand. Ella hid her anxiety and smiled. "Your mama and dada ready, Isla?"

Little Isla smiled and nodded. Ella noticed her parents weren't far behind; both frowned in worry. Isla asked, "Ella, where're we going?"

In a hushed tone, Ella said, "We're going on a trip together, someplace nice and cozy."

"Will that place have big, green paa-pee-lionibus?" Isla had been fascinated by papilionibus ever since she noticed the protection mark on everyone's necks that bore the symbol, even her own. Ella once told Isla that papilionibus were green, showing the girl a picture of the insect from a book that had been handed down for generations.

In a conspiratorial whisper, Ella uttered, "Who knows? We might just see them."

Isla giggled and excitedly marched forward with Ella's hand in hers. Ella turned and locked eyes with Saxum, whose brows pulled together before he and three other hybrids pushed a boulder to cover the opening of the tunnel. A short distance forward, Saxum pulled a rope to let down a grill with sharp points that dug into the soil below. About a mile forward, Saxum linked Ella, *'As soon as the kids are at the safe house, link me. I don't want them to hear the explosion.'*

It took them twenty minutes to reach the safe house. That was the quickest they could manage even with those with super speed carrying those who didn't have that gift. The accommodation was their accomplice's hotel, which was thought to be out of business long ago. Klementine, the lycan owner, ushered them upstairs. Ella counted the twenty-five children twice before she clapped her hands in excitement to get their attention. "Now, let's play a game."

The children's eyes sparkled as they formed a circle on the floor. Ella sat among them, explaining, "Here's what we'll do. When I say *go*, we cover our ears and scream. The one who screams the loudest and longest wins. Ready?"

Some of the over-enthusiastic children even started screaming before the game started. Ella chuckled before asking them to save their vocal cords for the game. Their parents were trying to look as normal as possible, but they, too, covered their ears.

"Ready? One, two, three, GO!"

When Gerella saw every child covering their ears and screaming their lungs out, she linked Saxum, *'NOW!'*

Back at the forest hideout, Saxum's ready thumb pressed the red button on the control to detonate the explosives that completely covered the ten-mile gap with rocks of all sizes. That should keep them safe, he thought, then made his way to join the others, who felt the vibration but chose to say nothing to the kids, while Ella lied to the children by saying that the strength of their voices had shaken the earth.

Saxum didn't even sit when he reached Klementine's place. Every administrative creature of their community was at a worn-out wooden table. Ella went to Saxum's side, whispered about the non-proditors' presence into his ear, and waited. Saxum's blue eyes darkened, and he gave a firm nod before Ella left his side to take her seat at the only empty chair left next to him. The hard-faced leader born with the ability of a fortis began, "Callows. Get to it. How much longer?"

The Callows were lycan triplets—Matthew, Nessa, and Ourelia. Gifted and ambitious didn't even begin to describe these three scientists, who shared a home lab since they were kids. Science fairs and competitions were for losers who favored wasting time and potential on small-scaled successes that would be forgotten once the heat of the competition was over or extracted by the government, who'd restrict the heights that science could reach. Being delible or controlled did not suit these triplets, who'd never aimed for anything less than world domination.

Matthew Callow, with a bushy white beard that covered his jawline and chin, peered at Saxum in annoyance as he repeated the same thing he'd been saying since the failed attack in Blue Crescent, "I can't give a definite timeline, Saxum. Tests and experiments can run for years before we see the slightest hint of success, especially one as ambitious as this."

His sister, Nessa, with wild, short brown hair that had prominent white strands here and there, affirmed, "If it were that easy and quick to come up with the formula for the chemical, someone would've done it by now. Sustainable success takes time. For the hundredth time, Saxum, this *will* take time!"

Saxum's fist fell on the table, and all the creatures but the triplets jerked upon the impact. "Time . . . is not something we have a lot of left. The Blue Crescent attack triggered them. Now they're out for blood. Seeking refuge in the Forest of Oderem isn't an option anymore."

Matthew countered, "I thought you claimed that no authorities ever dared enter the Forest of Oderem."

Saxum glanced at Ella, then responded, "Not until today." Now the triplets were worried. Saxum continued, "You have to speed things up. I don't care how you do it. Just do it. Stop trying to be so careful with the vampires."

Ourelia, the youngest triplet, taunted, "You really know nothing, do you, Saxum? We're not being careful with them because we don't want to hurt them. They're just raw material at the end of the day." She leaned forward and continued speaking slowly like she was explaining to a child, "Extracting segments of their brain is a very delicate process. We're being careful about taking out what we want. It's not. About. Their lives."

Saxum pressed, "Then speed up being careful. When I agreed to work with you three, efficiency was promised."

Ourelia smirked arrogantly. "When *you* sought help from the world's three geniuses, *you* promised bulletproof protection and anonymity. Weren't we supposed to hide in the forest should something go sideways?" she chuckled condescendingly. "Looks like we both fucked up."

Saxum's fist slammed the table once more, demanding the respect that Ourelia was more than happy not to give. Nessa placed her hand over her sister's wrist to stop the words at the tip of Ourelia's tongue from spilling out. Ourelia flicked her long brown hair to the back and crossed her arms, pressing her lips shut.

Matthew took over. "Slamming the table repeatedly is not going to get us anywhere, Saxum. I told you to refuse that wolf's request to attack the pack. It was bad enough that he wanted to outright show our species are now working together. It's even worse that—of all the packs in existence—he chose the birth pack of the queen!"

Another vampire, Regina, spoke in Saxum's defense, "It was Draxon's idea. We weren't familiar with wolf and lycan territories. We trusted his judgment because he was a wolf."

Ourelia simpered and muttered, "One of the most stupid ones I've ever seen."

Saxum brought everyone back to the problem at hand. "Draxon was an idiot and is dead. We'll be joining him, too, if you three don't speed things up. You have the formula to make the shell. Why is it so difficult to replicate and modify it to shield us against the queen's power? If you can't create something to manipulate her into controlling another, at least create a shield!"

Nessa spat, "Do you think we haven't been trying to do that? The problem with that former wolf's power is that no one knows how it's different from the King's Authority, nor does anyone know how much more powerful it is."

"How is that possible?" Chong, a wolf and Regina's mate, questioned in disbelief. "She's a wolf. She's not supposed to be more powerful than a lycan, and we're talking about the lycan king!"

Nessa uttered, "That's an enigma that we can only hope to uncover *before* they find us. The duke is already spreading his forces at every corner, showing the faintest trace of abnormality."

"Are the distractions still working?" Saxum asked.

"For now, they are," Nessa uttered. "His people are still watching our puppets. That ought to keep the royal rogues busy for a little while longer."

Ourelia mumbled, "But not much longer. They'll figure things out soon enough."

Regina simpered, "If they were that smart, they'd know you three were still alive, wouldn't they?"

The triplets glared at the woman who—to them—was nothing short of an imbecile, when Matthew said, "It wasn't easy to make the duke *and* his followers believe that our end came with an experiment that went wrong. He already had people tracking us before they lost our trail. Knowing the duke, he'll still suspect that we're alive since our bodies were never found."

Ourelia hissed at her brother, "I *told* you we should've left fake corpses behind!"

"And then what?" Matthew yelled back. "When the duke gets the lab reports, he'll know they're fake anyway! And then he'll be certain that we *are* alive! At least now, it's just a suspicion."

"Shut up. Both of you," Nessa said sternly.

Chong sniggered. "At least one of you has some sense."

Nessa threw him a sharp glare, speaking in her siblings' defense, "Their reactions are justified. We argued a lot on the best possible solution to get off the duke's radar. In the rogue world, Greg Claw either likes you enough to recruit you, respects you enough to leave you alone, finds you displeasing enough to keep you out of his turf, or finds you dangerous enough to kill you. You don't need to be as intelligent as we are to know where the three of us fit in."

Saxum let out a short, dark chuckle. "You three aren't the geniuses you proclaim to be, are you? From what I've heard, the duke only takes the best of the best."

Matthew refuted, "He takes whoever works *for* him, and we don't work for anyone. Our aptitude far surpasses everyone's in the rogue community, even Greg Claw's. He saw us as threats when we questioned his position. And he was plotting to get rid of us."

Regina commented, "For creatures who claim to possess superior intelligence, it's odd that you've made close to zero progress."

Matthew simmered in anger. "Your memory must have eluded you through those jumbled-up curls. Let's see if I can help you remember—in Blue Crescent, we couldn't control the queen, but what we gave the decipimus controlled the king. Acario and Maurine said the last glimpse they caught on the battleground was that the king attacked the queen. Isn't that true?"

Saxum muttered, "It is."

Matthew seemed calmer. "Well, then. That's progress. Instead of wasting time that we don't have trying to control the queen or shield ourselves from a power that could take years to understand, I say we control the king."

Ella spoke for the first time, "Isn't his Authority inferior to hers?"

Ourelia smirked. "It doesn't matter. The queen didn't even try to attack, which means she won't do anything to hurt him while he is under our control. And that will be her demise."

Nessa confessed, "But the one we gave the proditors the last time wasn't . . . strong enough, I'd say. Those who manipulated the king reported back saying it was a close call. Their combined power might not have been enough to overpower him, even with the help of our chemical. The king was close to shaking off its effects."

Ourelia muttered thoughtfully, "We'll just increase the concentration."

Matthew added, "Which would then require us to make further adjustments so it doesn't harm the proditors' systems in any way. For the rest of us, it's wise to ingest the shell. It won't shield us from the queen, but if the king can't be kept under our command after he manages to kill the queen, we'll need the shell to make our escape."

"Agreed," Nessa uttered.

Saxum then asked a pressing question, "Are the vampires in your storage enough to manufacture a higher concentration of the chemical you gave the proditor-decipimus last time?"

Matthew did a mental count. "It's enough for half of them, maybe a few more, but not enough for the rest."

Chong immediately asked Saxum, "Should we send them to get more from the villages?"

Saxum didn't hesitate when he gave a slight shake of his head. "No. It's no longer safe. We used to be able to rely on the forest to keep authorities out. Now, they can go in and leave without getting cursed. We don't have a proper escape route anymore."

Regina's brows pulled together as she tried to console her leader and friend, "Saxum, we don't know that yet. It's too early to tell. Perhaps the forest's enchantment will work within the next few days."

Saxum's hard look stayed on the table as he declared, "Merely hoping that someone in the imperial family will be cursed is not a good option. Hope is not a strategy, Regina. We are not waiting around to see if they manage to find us. The Callows will manufacture the . . . king-controlling chemical with whatever they have, and we'll have to move out of here by tonight."

His decision sent a shockwave among the creatures who had just moved hours ago. Ella's voice came out in a way that was beseeching him to reconsider, "Tonight?"

His worried gaze met hers. "We're only safe for now. When they dig their way through that tunnel, we will be found. It's better to leave now when we still have time." Mentally running through his plan again, he added, "Send an urgent message to Neptune, Ella. Tell him we need that spare hideout tonight."

Everyone dispersed. Ella got a sheet of paper from Klementine and wrote out a message in proditor code before handing it to Klementine's assistant, Feva, who sped to Neptune's residence.

CHAPTER 37

Eighteen vigils entered the Forest of Oderem with Duica and Bernadette, and the forest graced their nostrils with the same scent of freshly baked pastries once more. When they reached the River of Heres, they felt the ground tremor for a brief moment, which made them pause, as the fish in the water swam away out of fear. When nothing happened for the next few moments, the vigils followed the trail up to the waterfall. Two vigils stayed at that spot while the remaining eighteen crossed the river and started sniffing.

Bernadette caught a faint mixed scent of vampires and lycans, so they headed in that particular direction. After dashing for only a mile, the trail just stopped.

"Scent sprays. Damn these proditors," VIG 009, Dominic cursed.

Duica murmured, "This is the Forest of Oderem. This whole place is practically a scent-producing factory. Do synthetic sprays even work here? Wouldn't the forest just wipe them out?" His eyes scanned the place, unconvinced this was the end of the trail. He and a few others traipsed around, and that was when they stepped on the metal cover. Pausing in surprise, Duica swept away the dry leaves, when the breezy fingers of the forest helped blow over the rest.

The cover contained a symbol of what appeared to be the front view of a papilio, the very type of insect that was only found in the palace pond and nowhere else in the empire.

Dominic hesitantly asked, "Do we still think their Imperial Majesties have nothing to do with this?"

Duica squatted and studied the cover. The metal held a thick layer of rust. Certain parts were beginning to chip off. "If they had something to do with it, why send us here to find the purported closet hiding their skeletons?"

Dominic looked around and suggested in a whisper like he was about to say something forbidden, "To lure us in there and kill us, perhaps?"

Bernadette's brows furrowed. "Why would the empress want to kill us? We've only ever been loyal to her and her consort."

Dominic sighed before asking, "Alright, then. Who's going in there?"

"I am," Bernadette was the first to volunteer. Another nine vigils did, too, including Duica.

Apart from two vigils who bent over the cover, getting ready to pull it open, the others got ready for a possible attack at the opening. Upon Duica's firm nod, the two pulled it open, and to everyone's relief, nothing came out.

Now, on to the next step: entering.

Duica hopped in first, followed by Bernadette and the rest. They instantly noticed the rope attached to the opening that appeared freshly cut. There wasn't another soul in sight. Their visions adjusted to the darkness, and one of them switched on the lamps on the floor, walls, and tables. There was a lot of furniture around containing no dust.

Bernadette concluded, "They either left before we got here, or they'll be coming back."

Duica said, "I doubt they'll be coming back. There are no valuables here. These are just things that no one takes with them when they run."

"But if they ran . . ."

Duica finished for her, "Someone saw us. They knew we were coming. Search the place, everyone."

They scoured the hallways lit by more wall lamps, going through room after room. The mixed vampire-lycan scents were everywhere.

Like the vigils were taught to do with the case from Falling Vines and Saber Vagary, they sniffed any clothes and belongings left behind before recording the scents.

Duica noticed a fresh trail in the soil and traced it to the boulder. He got three fortes to move it to the side, and they were astonished to find a tunnel that led to a grill, which was being pushed back by a wall of rocks. Everyone awaited instructions, and Duica calmly said, "If the Forest of Oderem has led us here, unharmed, we can assume that it's safe for their Majesties and Highnesses to enter. We should return to the castle and report our findings."

After the quick sniff-and-search, the lights were turned off and the vigils came out from the opening. Duica was halfway through suggesting they scour the rest of the forest before the smell of rotten eggs was sprayed by a staghorn fern in his face.

How is a fern even capable of producing any scent? Duica wondered.

Dominic bit his bottom lip to stop himself from laughing. "I don't think the forest wants us to do that."

Duica coughed and distanced himself from the harmless-looking plant before he uttered louder than usual, "Fine, fine. We'll just return and report." The fresh scent of pastries replaced the foul odor once more.

Pelly and Octavia granted them an immediate audience, and they didn't even need to consult one another before Pelly called Lucy right after. Lucy and Xandar rounded the defense ministers, alliance members, Greg and his top four, Margaret and two of her followers—Azalea and Zane—Chief Dalloway, and fifteen lycan warriors before making their way to the Forest of Oderem.

The abandoned castle next to the forest looked oddly familiar to Lucy and Pelly, though neither of them knew why. They hadn't even been here before. Perhaps it was just a memory from seeing a picture somewhere?

The familiar scent of pastries graced everyone's nostrils, and Pelly couldn't help but smile and chuckle lightly with glistening eyes.

"What is it, my dear?" Octavia asked in confusion

Her emerald eyes were soft when she said, "That scent reminds me of mom. The whole castle would smell like a bakery when she baked and sent pastries to everyone, even the servants. When I smelled that as a child, I'd drop whatever I was doing and go look for her just by following this scent. It was like a mother-daughter game of smell-and-seek."

The vigils didn't connect the pastry scents to the late empress, and no one could blame them. The woman passed away more than a millennium ago.

Xandar smiled and said, "The forest is welcoming you."

Greg rebutted, "Or luring you into a trap."

Xandar argued, "If that were true, Greg, those who escaped that underground hideout wouldn't have had to escape."

"How do we know the hideout isn't just left empty to mislead us to think that they escaped? What if there was another hideout that the forest didn't want us to find. It did spray foul smells at Vigil 001 over there when he wanted to look."

In the midst of their argument, Lucy was looking straight at the forest and feeling its energy. It felt safe, warm, and . . . welcoming, like an old friend. She had a habit of feeling a creature's energy, but never a forest's. This was very odd. Intrigued, she approached it.

That was when Greg came right in front of her and stopped her in her tracks. "My queen, the king and I are still arguing about this."

Lucy's curious eyes narrowed in annoyance. "Then you two can stay here and finish the argument. I'm going in."

The duke stopped her again and heaved a heavy sigh at her stubbornness, suggesting, "Let some of us go in first to make sure that it's saf—"

"No," she cut him off in firm defiance. "We all had a deal the other night, Greg. The vigils test the forest for three days, and if nothing happens, I'm allowed to go in. Nothing happened. I'm going in."

Greg faced Xandar and asked in despair, "Is there a reason you're not doing anything to stop her?"

"Greg, look at it. Feel it. Do you feel any danger?" Xandar's hand gestured to the forest.

No, he didn't. In fact, his lycan was curious about the forest too. The duke couldn't believe his own animal was on board with this. This beast was trained to be more logical and rational than most. How could it not be the least bit suspicious now? Greg hissed at his cousin in hopes of making his own animal listen as well, "You're basing whether it's safe on *a feeling*?"

Xandar responded, "Any victim in history who was lured in and suffered an unfaithful death or injury felt a degree of danger and uncertainty when they entered, despite the pleasant scents. I don't know about you and your animal, but my lycan isn't picking up any danger from that place."

"Despite the tremor the vigils reported *feeling*?" Greg spat at his cousin and his own animal.

Greg's lycan was nodding its head in certainty when Xandar replied in irritation, "Yes! They all got out unharmed, didn't they? If the forest really wanted to go for the kill, it would've caused a second tremor to drop rocks on the vigils when they were in the hideout, don't you think?"

The hypothetical suggestion made the vigils jerk internally. Dominic muttered something about thanking the Lord nothing like that happened.

Without waiting for Greg's response, Lucy groaned and walked around him, heading toward the forest. The cousins dropped their argument to follow her. Pelly was as sure about the forest as Lucy was and strolled by her side.

The moment they entered, Lucy felt a warmth wrap around her body. She looked at her hands and legs but found nothing beyond the ordinary. It was then everyone started gasping. She looked around, and her eyes widened in shock at two of the five copper streaks in Pelly's hair glowing—one in blue, the other in green.

Greg muttered sarcastically, "Great. Now that we have a live glow stick, we can stay here until nightfall and nothing will happen."

A yellow flower near Greg bloomed instantaneously and sprayed scents of animal dung at him. The duke choked on the pungent smell and moved far away to another plant, only to be sprayed by the same foul odor by another yellow flower.

Seeing how Greg was suffering, Christian turned to Xandar, grinning as he declared, "I like it here, Cuz."

Xandar himself had to look away from Greg to make sure he didn't chuckle out loud. At that point, Christian felt something at the sole of his left foot before two green tendrils wrapped his shoe from each side and entwined with one another. Then, two red roses bloomed to exude that all-too-familiar rosy scent.

Amber, Rafael, and Octavia were pressing back smiles when the duke turned to his cousin and asked in bewilderment, "Am I supposed to know what this means, Cuz?"

Xandar's eyes amplified playfulness when he patted his cousin on the shoulder. "Looks like the forest likes you, too, Christian. It's flirting with you."

Rafael burst into laughter, as did many others when the duke's eyes widened in shock.

"Please tell me you're joking, Cuz."

Christian's right shoe was wrapped by tendrils the same way before another two red roses bloomed there. Lucy started chuckling as the king said, "Well, now that I think of it, flirting is too shallow. I'd say the forest has already fallen in love with you."

"Uh . . ." Christian would have thought Xandar was pulling his leg, but the looks on everyone else's faces—especially the vampires—confirmed that his best friend may be serious.

Christian had no idea how to reject a forest's advances—a forest that had the ability to curse anyone in the empire if it was angered. His lycan was of no help when it told him to just pull his leg out and break the tendrils because only Annie could be tender with him like that. His human knew that doing what he truly wanted would be reckless. He didn't want random creatures cursed because of him. And he sure didn't want the forest to go after Annie or their pups.

Christian bent down and looked at the fully bloomed roses, swallowed a lump in his throat, awkwardly patted the two flowers on his right foot, and muttered, "I'm flattered, really, but uh . . . I have someone." The petals started wilting, the red turning brown. Christian didn't want to upset the forest, so he added, "You're definitely something special. I'm not saying that we aren't good enough for one another, but it's just . . . we might not be . . . the best fit in the long run. I hope you understand."

Lucy had to bury her face in Xandar's chest to muffle the laughter, and Xandar did the same by hiding his mouth in her hair. The burst of humor in their bond was out of control, and neither of them was capable of stopping the other.

Toby had already pulled up his turtleneck to cover his mouth, and the other wolves and lycans were using various ways to hold back the humor. They envied their animals, who were chuckling and laughing uncontrollably in their minds when their humans had to put on a straight face. Some of the vigils who wore jackets used those to cover the bottom half of their faces, but anyone who saw their smiling eyes would have known how they were really taking in the situation before them.

The roses and tendrils at Christian's foot withered. When nothing happened in the next five seconds, he turned to the vampires and asked, "I didn't do anything wrong, did I?"

Rafael reluctantly removed his hand from over his mouth and spoke as seriously as he could, which was not seriously at all with that broad, teasing smile. "Your Grace, you just broke the forest's heart. How *dare* you presume that you've done nothing wrong!"

Lucy snorted, and then she and Xandar burst out laughing again, their voices echoing through the forest. Some river water splashed on the royal couple, making Lucy protest, "Hey!"

It was finally Christian's turn to laugh. A beige flower with small red polka dots in the inner regions of the petals appeared an inch away from his left foot. The duke looked at it in confusion. Annie had shown him most types of flowers and plants and taught him what each one meant, but he had never seen such a flower in lycan territory.

Rafael teased, "If the flower of friendship doesn't appease you, Your Grace, I'm sure the forest would be more than happy to replace it with the romantic ones from before."

Upon hearing that, Christian leaned down to snatch the flower off the ground and put it into his coat pocket as he spoke to the grass, "Thank you. I really appreciate this. I'm glad there are no hard feelings."

His sights turned to his still-smiling cousin and cousin-in-law when he linked them both in seriousness, *'No one tells Annie about this.'*

Lucy linked back with an excited grin, *'EXCEPT FOR ME!'*

Xandar responded, *'Christian, what are you worried about? It's not like you cheated on her with the forest. You ended the relationship before it could even start. And I thought your heartbreaking and friend-zoning days were over.'*

Octavia's hand landed on Christian's shoulder when she spoke with more humor than any vigil or minister had seen, "I won't be surprised if our empire is suddenly blessed by your visit, Your Grace. On behalf of our people, Pelly and I send our . . . most sincere thanks in advance."

The duke's eyes narrowed.

The mention of Pelly drew Lucy's sights to the empress's still-glowing streaks. "I wonder . . ." Lucy murmured, swinging her head to look behind her, where her tail would be if she were in her animal form.

Xandar pecked a kiss in her hair to get her attention, whispering affectionately, "Only one way to find out."

Her eyes shone in excitement as she went behind a tree to strip and shift, and lo and behold, two of the five stripes glowed—the thickest one in blue, the stripe next to it in emerald green. Xandar's eyes never left her when he picked up her clothes, leaving a kiss on her furry forehead as he muttered into her ear, "Beautiful."

Her lycan cooed under his loving stare. His animal made him nuzzle her nose to elicit her human's soft chuckles through their link. He then took her hand and led her out of her changing spot. When everyone saw her tail glowing, mouths gaped and eyes snapped wide open for the second time that day.

The forest found this an appropriate time to exude a scent that certain insects were attracted to. Within seconds, a swarm of minuscule bugs flew along the scent trail that led into the opened mouths. The alert ones closed their mouths quickly enough to avoid them. Toby and a few others weren't so lucky and had to spit out the insects when they realized their mouths had been invaded.

Pelly was looking at herself in the reflection of the River of Heres. Her eyes snapped to Lucy when she emerged. They stood side by side, and the surface of the water rippled to remove Octavia and Xandar from the reflection, leaving the two women before it added three silhouettes next to Pelly and a human-form Lucy—one next to the empress and two next to the queen.

"What does this mean?" Pelly muttered, brows drawn in.

Lucy shifted back to make talking easier.

The silhouette next to Pelly appeared to be someone with a high ponytail and toned arms; the one next to Lucy looked like a figure who was wearing a cloak; and the last one on the far right had her arms folded, probably crossed in front of her chest, and there was something frilly at her left ear that was visible because her hair was pushed over her right shoulder.

Pelly uttered, "I don't recognize any of these."

"Neither do I," Lucy mused as everyone crowded around them.

Xandar's arms snaked around Lucy's shoulders and abdomen from behind as he looked at the one with a cloak and thought aloud, "That one has to be a witch. Cloaks are most common among their species. And that one . . ." he pointed at the one with the frilly ear, and declared, "is probably a merfolk. This last one on this side looks like . . ."

Before he could finish, Greg said, "A huntress."

Juan questioned, "Could this be one of the huntresses we met in the mediations, Lucy?"

Lucy studied the silhouette more carefully. "I don't know. The silhouette is a little too generic if you ask me. Most huntresses have lean bodies and their hair up like that. Without the hair color and approximate height, I won't be able to tell if we've seen her before."

Toby questioned, "Has anyone met any witches or merfolks, by any chance?"

When murmurs of "no" and headshakes came from everyone present, Lucy said, "It's impossible to have such an opportunity, Toby. Those species closed themselves off centuries ago."

Toby shrugged. "So did the vampires. Look where we are now. I wouldn't say that integration is impossible after the events from recent weeks."

None could deny the truth in Toby's words. The thought of being able to live in harmony with every species in existence still seemed far-fetched to some like Greg, Margaret, and the vigils, who knew that species couldn't even live in harmony amongst their own kind, let alone with another; it seemed possible for some like Juan, Toby, and Lovelace, who used the current interaction with the vampires as a basis for how integration could work; and it became an ambitious goal that Lucy, Xandar, Pelly, and Octavia were determined to reach.

Seeing the river was not going to project anything else, they left and followed the scent trail of baked goods to the Misty Waterfall of Heres. Duica explained that the hideout he and the others found was up ahead, so they crossed the river.

When Margaret was stepping on one stone after another that formed a path leading to the other side, she couldn't help but look at the riverbed with the abnormal seaweed, rocks, and fish. Her red wolf was wagging its tail as she admired the sight through her human's eyes. Margaret didn't realize the last stone was more slippery than the rest. Her foot glided, and she gasped, bracing herself for a fall that never came because Tate turned and caught her just in time.

In his arms, her rosewood eyes locked with his brown ones, and he whispered, "You okay?"

She heard him but couldn't respond. The last time their faces were this close was at the fountain of Labyrinth Vert, when they were close to kissing. Despite her instability, the atmosphere felt the same. It was like their surroundings muted and blurred out.

After making sure Margaret's feet were planted firmly on the ground, Tate's hand reached for her face. The way his thumb traced her cheek made her feel precious, special.

Toby nudged Lucy's arm, putting a finger to his smiling lips as his eyes gestured her to follow his—to Tate and Margaret. There was no distance between the two, and when their noses touched, Tate instinctively closed his eyes before he leaned in. Margaret was leaning in, too, until a flashback from her past came back to haunt her for a microsecond, making her pull away.

Lucy's bubble of excited anticipation burst, and she linked Toby, *'Dang! That was so close!'*

Toby chuckled. *'Relax, Lucy. It'll happen.'*

'What if we don't see it when it happens? The first one's always the best.'

Toby glanced at Xandar before he teased, *'Better not let your mate hear that, Lucy. He might think the ones that followed weren't as good. And he'll start smooching you in front of everyone here. Besides, who are you to demand to see Tate's first kiss with the luna? I don't recall seeing yours.'*

Lucy pressed back a guilty smile. Xandar looked at the two best friends who were giving him funny looks before he asked, "What?"

Lucy shook her head and uttered, "Nothing. Let's go."

She barged ahead. Xandar's furrowed brows landed on Toby, who patted his shoulder and said, "Nothing serious, Xandar. It was just about how much you love her."

Xandar blinked. "You did tell her it's more than anything and anyone, didn't you?"

"Y-Yeah. Yeah. Definitely." Toby made a mental note to think before he lied next time. He was a good liar with strangers and enemies, but not with friends and family.

Xandar saw right through the minister's terrible attempt. He dashed to Lucy's side within the next second. *'Everything alright, babe?'*

She gave a firm nod. *'Of course.'*

'What were you and Toby talking about?'

It was frustrating how the mere mention of that conversation could warm up her cheeks and make her lips curl up without effort. She looked ahead and replied, *'Just . . . you and me . . . about the earlier stages of our relationship.'*

Xandar's fingers laced with hers when his voice softened, *'What about it?'*

Her thumb stroked the back of his rough hand. *'Toby said . . . I didn't have the right to demand to see Tate's first kiss with Margaret since our first kiss happened in private.'*

'Hm . . .' his voice took a coquettish turn when his large hands stopped her at her waist as his face closed in on hers while he whispered, "We could try to replic—"

Her fingers pressed his lips to stop him as she uttered sternly, "No. Not here, my king. This is not the time."

She left a kiss on his cheek before breaking free and striding forward. Xandar and his animal were happy enough with the kiss and caught up to their mate again.

Not far behind them, Toby wriggled his eyebrows at Tate when Margaret wasn't looking, and Tate linked, *'Knock it off, Toby. I don't want to make her uncomfortable.'* Toby chuckled to himself and turned away.

Margaret witnessed Lucy's interaction with Xandar and began to wonder how Lucy managed to open herself up to a bonded mate's love again after all her rejections. Margaret learned from Zane, who had partnered with the very talkative Desmond in manipulation practice, that Lucy had been rejected five times. That was more than anyone had ever heard of. The chatty lycan also reminded Zane at least ten times to avoid raising the subject because both the king and duke didn't like the queen's rejections to be brought up, even though the queen herself didn't see anything wrong with it.

Margaret had only been through one rejection, and she'd been cursing the mate bond ever since. That was the reason she was finding it so hard to open up to Tate. She no longer had as much faith in the Moon Goddess's choice as she once did. She wanted to believe that the connection she felt with him now was true, but there seemed to be an emotional block that was stopping her from getting closer in a way that he wanted her to, that she wanted to too.

As these thoughts occupied her mind, a sharp pain shot up her nape and went to the top of her head as her rosewood eyes turned bright red.

CHAPTER 38

L ike the previous time, Margaret fell to her knees and grunted in anguish. Tate knelt before her and pulled her into him, increasing the intensity of the sparks and hoping that it would soothe some of the pain. It did.

The discomfort easing away enabled Margaret to focus on her vision: she and everyone else around her were in a dimly lit space, and there was something . . . suspicious about the surroundings.

Before Margaret could delve deeper, the vision ended.

That was it? Her rosewood eyes blinked in disbelief. Her awareness brought her back to the present. Everyone circled her and Tate, giving Margaret enough room to breathe but also allowing them a good look at her.

Tate's thumb was stroking her shoulder. His scent comforted her wolf and melted her anxiety.

When Toby had had enough of the silence, he prompted, "Luna?"

Margaret jerked at the title, and Tate shot Toby an "Are you kidding me?" look, which made Toby respond in hushed defense, "What?"

Margaret pushed herself up with Tate's help, then explained what she saw.

Greg pinched his nose bridge, commenting, "It'd be a lot nicer if your visions contained more details and elaboration, Maggo—Margaret." He promptly replaced the nickname after noticing the sharp glare coming from the queen that could slice through armies. The alpha was scowling at him, too, but the duke didn't feel anything from that one.

They weren't in a dim place yet, so nothing could be done at that moment. Their attention returned to the task at hand. Lucy turned, facing the metal cover with the symbol of a papilio, her brows pulled together in contemplation.

Octavia muttered, "We were meant to come here."

"What do you mean?" Lucy asked.

Octavia nodded at the cover. "The papilio is only found in the castle pond. And those animals only reappeared after Pelly's birth."

Xandar's eyes pivoted to Pelly. "When did they last appear before your birth?"

"When Count Dracula was still alive," she confessed. "The fact that his birth and mine were the only times in history that brought about the papilionibus' existence in the castle pond was more of a taboo than a celebrated coincidence. Father forbade it from ever being raised or spoken about, so not many people know about this. He didn't want our people to start a rebellion to dethrone me for the coincidental similarity I shared with Dracula."

Lucy's sights went back to the papilio. "It doesn't feel like a coincidence anymore."

Xandar agreed, "You've probably the heiress to this forest. The papilionibus were a sign of inheritance."

Pelly begged to differ. "It's strange though. I know my family's history, and I'm not related to Dracula in the faintest way. Out of all the rulers that led the empire after his death, why am I the destined one?"

"That's the billion-espèces question," Greg muttered.

Pelly gave Duica and Bernadette a firm nod to open the cover, and they did. Like the last time the vigils came on their own, nothing came out, much to everyone's relief. The two vigils entered first, and when they turned on the lights and announced that it was safe, the royals dropped themselves down the hole.

The vast space surprised them. It was large enough to house villages of vampires. The moment Margaret entered after Tate, she recognized the surroundings as the one in her recent vision, and she immediately informed Tate, who then linked Lucy.

Lucy paused, turned, and reminded everyone to exercise caution, to be careful of where they stepped and what they touched. There might have been a trap that the vigils were lucky enough to avoid the last time.

The walls were the first structures Greg checked as soon as his feet hit the ground, but he felt nothing but dry dirt. He then checked the ceiling, and it was odd to him that there was no technology there either. He kicked some dirt off the ground, trying to see if there was anything underneath the surface, but after about half a foot into the dirt, which effectively created a hole, he found nothing. He wasn't satisfied, so he and his top four dug another few holes of equal depth around the area.

Blackfur even asked him why he and his people were "playing" with dirt. Greg would have retorted with sarcasm had the queen not explained to the dim duke first that Greg may be looking for detectors and traps.

As the royals stood in the middle of the main room, looking for any clues that might lead them to the culprits, some dirt on the ceiling fragmented off, falling onto Pelly's hair. She moved aside and looked up, when Octavia pulled her further away. A small object fell to the ground, and the dirt stopped disintegrating.

Even Greg didn't have the technological knowledge to understand how that worked, so he asked, "Okay, what was that?"

With a shrug, Christian answered, "Magic."

Greg's frustrated eyes pinned him as he drew a long exhale. Christian didn't even bother pressing back his smile when he exchanged a look with Xandar. It was nice to annoy Greg for a change.

Lucy, who Xandar firmly held by her abdomen during the dirt disintegration, tried to lean as close as possible to the pile to see the last thing that fell. The king was not letting her go any nearer as he scrutinized the ceiling, which didn't seem to be chipping anymore.

Octavia made Pelly stay where she was and went forward to retrieve the object, handing it to the empress. It was a scroll. The foreign linguistic characters scrawled through the length—with curlicues twisting in various directions—were presented before them, ones that no lycan could read.

"Succoglyphs," Xandar murmured.

"Translation?" Greg reluctantly asked, once again reliving his hatred for history.

Lucy murmured, "Ancient vampire writings."

Once the scroll was pulled to the end, Pelly read with pinched brows, "Only the creatures willing to go to any lengths to protect those who need protection most shall inherit the Forest of Oderem."

At the end of it was a signature that vampires had only ever seen in museums—the one of Count Dracula.

Greg's eyes went back to the ceiling when the pessimistic part of him spoke, "I wonder how the inhabitants planted it there."

The intrigue in Pelly's eyes tore away, intruded by wariness. "You suspect those who hid here put this there, Your Grace?"

His eyes were still glued to the ceiling. "I don't know. I'm not well-versed in . . . forest magic."

Christian questioned, "Wouldn't they have to forge Dracula's signature before even putting it up there? And have you seen the count's signature? The strokes are illegible *and* complicated."

"Doesn't mean it can't be done. For all we know, that whole thing is forged." As Greg continued scrutinizing the ceiling for signs that it had been manually tampered with, a small chunk of dirt fell straight into his eyes. He cursed aloud, and Christian tried very, very hard not to laugh.

Before Lucy could follow her instinct to help Greg, Xandar held her back and got Ivory to lead the duke to the river to rinse away the dirt. Ivory got his boss out.

Xandar faced his wife and came up with the best excuse he could think of, "You're needed here, babe. Let Ivory do it."

Lucy exhaled a long, sharp breath to stop herself from starting a petty argument with her husband, and Christian swallowed the chuckles as he said, "Well, I guess that confirms the scroll is authentic. It's nice to have a place that does this sort of true-or-false thing, especially when it does it on Greg. We should have something like this back in the kingdom, Cuz."

Instead of agreeing, Xandar chose to say, "I'm beginning to see why the forest fell for you, Christian. You're quite the flirt."

Xandar was elated with the growing humor in Lucy. Christian, on the other hand, didn't find it funny anymore when he narrowed his eyes at his cousin and heard the light chuckles from his cousin-in-law.

When Greg returned, he was still murmuring profanities under his breath. Upon reaching the discussion circle, he grudgingly asked, "Since that thing is . . . not forged, does this mean you're the heir, Your Majesty? Do you have control over this ceiling dirt?"

Pelly was also trying not to laugh for courtesy's sake and attempted to respond as neutrally as she could, "The scroll doesn't say whether I am the heir, Your Grace, but I currently have no control over any dirt in this place."

Greg bit the inner walls of his mouth to stop a stream of sardonic comments before he eventually gestured to the grill partition pushed back by a wall of rocks, suggesting, "Let's check that, shall we?"

Octavia then asked, "Should I get a few fortes to break it?"

Lucy replied, "We should have the whole partition checked to see if it's connected to any traps first, Octavia. I'm linking Toby, Tate, and Phelton."

###

When everyone was granted the green light to commence investigation after they entered through the opening, Toby, like everyone else, picked a random corridor to investigate as they left the royals to study the main area. As he trooped down that corridor with the rest, his wolf had a sudden fixation on a particular scent, something that smelled like gardenias and apples. At the end of the corridor with ten rooms, he didn't even pause, entering the second room from the left.

There were dry leaves at the corner piled up to shape a bed, which seemed to be only large enough to accommodate one adult creature. This was strange to Toby because the general species scents confirmed that there was at least one vampire and one wolf who frequently occupied the room. He wondered if vampires preferred sleeping on the dirt floor. He knew for a fact that he didn't like that option as a wolf.

At the opposite corner stood a wooden table and chair made from poor carpentry. The general scent confirmed that the inhabitant was female. Picking up a strand of long dark hair and taking a whiff, Toby became more perplexed when it carried both vampire *and* wolf scents. Even mates, whose scents were mixed, wouldn't be able to attain such a balance in their odor. Their own individual scent would always dominate over their mate's even after marking and being marked.

Why was this scent different?

Toby shifted his attention to the table, where he found rocks of various shapes, no doubt for various uses. The long-shaped rocks with sharp tips could be a carving tool and the oval-shaped ones could be used as . . . Goddess knew what. Paperweights?

There was only one book, and he flipped through the pages without thought. A dried-up, slender leaf fell out. Picking it from the floor, he noticed there was writing on it and held it against the little light in the dim place. Squinting his eyes, it took him a while before making out the word—Ella.

The name made his wolf howl in excitement. His human was so shocked that he froze, staring at the leaf in disbelief. It wasn't until Lucy mind-linked him, Tate, and Phelton that Toby blinked. He left the book on the table but placed the leaf gently in the inner pocket of his jacket, careful not to damage it.

When he met Lucy and the others at the grill partition, Lucy took one look at him and asked in concern, "You okay, Toby?"

Toby tried to act natural, figuring this wasn't the best time to say something like, "I think I smelled my mate in the room I was looking through."

Instead, he said, "Yeah, yeah. So uh . . ." he noticed the grill ". . . we have to dig through that, right?"

Lucy wasn't convinced and made a mental note to speak to him later. "Well, we have to see if it's safe to break the grill first."

"Right. Okay. Let's have a look." He came forward, joining Xandar, Christian, Phelton, and Tate.

Lucy's sights lingered on Toby, worry etched across her forehead, which Greg noticed. The duke had also picked up the sudden change in the minister, so he turned away to link Alissa, *'Keep an eye on the defense minister. He's hiding something.'*

'As you wish, Your Grace.'

Greg then joined the others at the partition, feeling the grill with his hand, and said, "It feels . . . new."

Tate added, "Even where we're standing feels new compared to the ground inside. Wherever this leads to, this tunnel was a recent plan."

Lucy went to the far left and stepped on boulders on the side, supporting herself with the grill as she stepped higher up to look for any strings, ropes, or anything that may be triggered if the grill gate was tampered with.

Her husband sprinted over with wide eyes and held her lower back as he whisper-yelled, "Lucy, you could've asked me to do that!"

"I'm fine, Xandar. I'm just climbing. You guys don't happen to see any strings or ropes connecting to booby traps, do you?"

Everyone checked. Xandar left one hand on his mate just to assure himself that she was stable before looking around as well. Greg pondered on what he would do if he lived here. He'd kill whoever tried to track him down after his escape. It was a given that he preferred torture, but the scale of this infiltration made torture a little too tedious for his taste.

Kill. That was what he'd do. But *how* would he do it?

He turned away from the grill, observing the space they'd entered. It would have been nice to have installed some kind of motion-and-weight detector into the ground, programming it to detach and release those large roots protruding from the ceiling, killing whoever was unfortunate enough to stand below them. As for the creatures who weren't below those structures, Greg probably would've had a device installed in the walls to fire something at them, something that killed them slowly, like lethal scents of sorts.

Desmond and Ivory came up to Greg in the midst of his thinking process, and the two said nothing until their boss was satisfied with where his train of thoughts paused before he asked, "What?"

Desmond went first, "Boss, I dunno if whoever lived here dumb or we dumb."

"I don't take dumb rogues, Desmond."

Ivory elaborated, "It's as if there are no security measures around this place at all, Your Grace. No detectors, no traps, no cameras. Nothing out of the ordinary. Picture a ceiling of a house with tiled or hardwood floors, and this is actually like any other house we've broken into. Even those houses had cameras!"

When Lucy and the others found nothing, Octavia got a fortis to break the grill and linked a few more to start moving the rocks before the royal members turned their attention to Greg's conversation with Desmond and Ivory.

Though his frown was deep, Greg insisted, "I agree that it's odd, but there *will* be something here. We just don't know what it is yet. If this tunnel is new, then the creatures who lived here didn't see the need to escape until very recently. If there was never a need to escape, there wouldn't have been a need to take any security measures. Whatever they've just installed, it'll be as new as the tunnel, and it'll be something that takes the least amount of time to put in place yet can still create very significant damage."

Tate uttered in Lucy's direction, "Please tell me he doesn't mean a bomb."

Greg threw Tate a berating look as Lucy replied, "I doubt it, Tate. Something that can detonate wouldn't have been hidden this well. The royal mavericks would've found it even if it were. I guess what we're looking for is something that looks ordinary but really isn't. It may contain some kind of . . . dangerous substance."

"Like oleander?" Christian asked in worry, making Xandar's grip on Lucy's waist tighten.

Lucy contemplated, then said, "No, it'll probably be a substance that's harmful to vampires. No wolf or lycan has ever stepped foot into this forest before today, so I doubt precautions are being taken against us."

Smart, Greg thought. He was beginning to worry at the mention of oleander as well.

Octavia's pondering eyes met Pelly's. "Substance harmful to vampires. It's just beta-keratin at a very high concentration and . . . allicin."

Ivory asked, "Where are those found? Tablets, sprays, laced on weapons?"

Xandar muttered, "Beta-keratin makes up our claws and canines. Allicin is a precautionary chemical that was injected into the wolves and lycans before battling in the war. It made the vampires in their proximity hallucinate. Some lycans carried allicin around to jab it into the vampires, but speed was crucial because allicin degrades fast when it's exposed to air, making it lose its effectiveness with prolonged exposure. So if allicin is here, then . . ."

The two-second silence was killing everyone, so Lucy gently shook his arm and prompted, "Then what, darling?"

Xandar got lost in her eyes. A soft smile graced his features when he reached out to stroke her fingers on his arm. "Then it's possible that some of us have already found it, but we didn't recognize it because it's inert."

Christian built up on that, "Inert, meaning that it needs a trigger to be activated. Heat, water, chemicals."

Greg started eliminating possibilities from there. "It won't be chemicals. That'd be way too complicated. The trigger would be something simple, something that any vampire would touch or use by reflex, something . . ."

POP!

The bulbs on all the lamps exploded, and the chemicals within took up the space like haze. Agonizing shrieks of vampires pierced through everyone's ears. Lucy didn't think twice before she carried Pelly and dashed out, and Xandar did the same for Octavia.

As Lucy placed the quivering empress under a tree about ten feet away from the opening, the queen linked everyone, *'Get the vampires out of there! Whatever it is, it might kill them!'*

The wolves and lycans who were confused at first now sped around looking for every vigil and minister, and got them out. While everyone was worrying about the bloodsuckers, Greg yanked out one of the lamps before leaving, and got his followers to help evacuate the hideout. After that, he leaned against a tree at a considerable distance away from the weakened bloodsuckers and took the exploded bulb out of the lamp.

Tossing the exterior of the lamp to the side, his full attention was given to the bulb that lost two-thirds of the glass that was originally there. When he figured out the workings of the ingenious invention, a menacing smile spread across his face as he muttered, "Clever, but not clever enough."

Two vigils and one minister were rendered unconscious because they stood too close to one of the lightbulbs in a room during the explosion, thus inhaling too much of the scent. Another twenty of them were nearing that stage as well.

Pelly and Octavia were weakened but were the least affected since they were the first to be brought out. Just then, the forest exuded a lemony scent, which soothed the stinging sensation, reducing into a prickling one before the discomfort disappeared completely.

One by one, the vampires tried to get up on their own with the wolves and lycans by their side ready to catch them should they fall halfway. It was astounding that none of them needed that support when they couldn't even move less than two minutes ago. Still, most of them sat back down because they were still weak and their insides still felt unusually heavy, though they were regaining their strength with each minute.

Even though everyone appeared fine, Lucy persuaded the rulers to at least agree to link the royal medical team for a standard checkup. It didn't take a lot of pestering to persuade Octavia, but it took a little more to get Pelly to agree.

The empress pushed herself off the ground, intending to approach the hideout again. Lucy stood in her way and looked sternly into her eyes. "No, Pelly. We'll take it from here. We got lucky this time. Whatever else could be in there might be instantly lethal. You stay here with the others and wait for the doctors. We'll continue the investigation and update you and everyone else."

Octavia bolted upright when Pelly stood, about to tell her wife that it was too dangerous to continue today but Lucy beat her to it. Upon hearing the queen's words, the consort grinned broadly and let her mate's hand go, leaning back against the tree, and closed her eyes in bliss, uttering "After 193 years, it's nice to have someone else stop my wife's adamance for a change."

Rafael, who wasn't far away with Toby, knew that he shouldn't be laughing after everything that just happened, but he couldn't hold back an amused snort, and Pelly shot him a "You're supposed to be on my side" look. Octavia took Pelly's hand and pecked a sweet kiss on the back, uttering, "Let them do it, Pelly. It's not worth the risk. The poison doesn't affect their species. They'll be fine."

When the lemony scent dissipated, the vampires felt a tingling sensation on their napes. Some of them thought pesky insects were biting them at first, until their hands went to the back and felt something was being etched on their skin.

Octavia slowly stood, and her wife moved her blonde hair to the side for the consort to see the faintest green glow appearing in the shape of a papilio. When the tingling sensation ended, the mark disappeared from view.

Lucy spoke with more relief than awe, "Well, it's nice of the forest to finally offer protection."

Octavia glanced at Christian before responding, "I was certain that a blessing would come soon, but I didn't think it would be this soon. It must have taken a special someone to woo the forest to offer us its mark."

A beige flower with red polka dots promptly grew by Christian's side, and the duke restrained his animalistic urge to tear up the flower. Instead, he bent down, ignored the chuckles and giggles, gently plucked the flower off the ground, and thanked the forest like he previously did, before he said, "We should get back to investigating."

When Pelly and Octavia followed behind, thinking that they'd be fine now that they were marked by the forest, a fern by a tree sprayed a foul odor in the space between the vampire rulers and the rest of the lycans and werewolves, who all stared at the leafy flora in disbelief. Duica, still slumped against a tree on the other side, shook his head at the fern.

Xandar deduced, "It's probably still not safe down there even with the protection mark. You and your people should stay here. We'll handle this."

The wolves and lycans returned to the hideout entrance, wondering what triggered the bulbs to explode. Lucy's eyes found the lamp exterior Greg had flung aside, and Greg approached her with eyes and smile still glued to the bulb, completely fascinated by the invention.

The duke handed her the bulb, and Lucy held it close to her face. His own face softened as he watched her think, enamored with the way her eyes converged on the broken thing, the way her brows arched in that particular way when she mulled over a thought. When her furrowed brows were replaced with wide-eyed realization, he had to look away to press back a smile. *Beautiful.*

Toby tapped on the thin broken glass and got the ball rolling, "So instead of putting the tungsten wire in the bulb like a normal lightbulb, they lined it along the internal wall of the glass. With the heat accumulated from an extended period of the bulb being lit, it cracked the glass."

Phelton continued, "When the glass broke, the light went out and the substance inside got out."

Lucy took a whiff and finished off, "The substance is allicin, which would have decomposed and lost its effectiveness if it was overheated by the wire. That's why the wire was lined with the intention to break the glass, to make sure that the allicin remained effective when it got out."

Tate glanced at the vampires, some of whom were carefully testing their limbs, before he turned back to the discussion group and whispered, "I know this may not be an appropriate thing to say right now, but this is smart."

Greg said, "I agree. But, fortunately for us, they weren't smart enough."

Lucy handed Toby the bulb, and the defense minister studied the object when his best friend asked the duke, "Who even makes these things?"

Greg pointed at her like she'd just asked the right question. "Exactly. I am still not familiar with the proditors, but I do know that there is only one rogue lycan in our territory who prides himself on having every accessible poison stocked up. In my last . . ." he glanced at Christian ". . . business enquiry, which was quite a while ago, I do recall seeing allicin in his catalog. But he only had one bottle because no one thought to trespass in vampire territory until very recently. So our answers will start with him—Nash Beaufort."

Phelton asked, "Is one bottle even enough to make hundreds of light-bulbs, Your Grace?"

Greg narrowed his eyes at the deputy. "I doubt he was the supplier of the allicin for these bulbs, Minister. The one we'll be looking for is *his* supplier."

Lucy asked, "So where is this Nash Beaufort?"

Greg exchanged a quick glance with Xandar before saying, "You don't need to know, my queen. It's better if we take this one."

Xandar got the message and pinned Lucy to his side as he spoke to her gently, "He's right, baby. It's safer if they did it."

Her eyes darted to her husband. "No it isn't. Rogues aren't stupid. And I doubt they'll refrain from gossip. Many—if not most of them—know that Greg and the mavericks are working with us now. If the mavericks ask for information, it'll take someone living under a rock to not know that it's being asked on our behalf."

Well, Xandar couldn't argue with that.

Greg tried to walk around the problem. "Our people are more familiar with the routes and . . . culture down there, my queen. It really is better if we executed this task."

Greg couldn't believe he was siding with his cousin, but if this was what it took to keep Lucy out of that territory, he'd do it. The duke acknowledged she had the Queen's Authority, but what if she didn't use it before she got hurt? What if she used it to save someone else before herself? Or—in the worst case scenario—what if there were decipio proditors down there now which would practically render her power useless?

Lucy firmly said, "I'm not agreeing to this until you give me the location, Greg. I don't want anything to happen, but if the plan does go sideways, I want to know where to start looking."

All the more reason not *to let it go sideways*, he thought. He would never want her to find her way there. Seeing that she wasn't going to negotiate any more than she already had, he nodded and gave her the coordinates and route they'd take to get there, then informed everyone that he and Ivory would be the ones paying Nash Beaufort a visit later that day.

Lucy bit her inner bottom lip, attempting to mask her shock at the route they'd take from the kingdom to rogue territory.

Xandar and Christian weren't as composed when they shot each other looks of disbelief, and the second-in-command whisper-yelled, "The rogue gateway has been there this whole time?"

CHAPTER 39

Contact lenses cloaked Ivory's blinded eye, and concealer hid his scar. Greg wore a pair of shades and a hoodie before the two took a subway to Primordial Station, which was only a thirty-minute drive from Xandar's and Lucy's place.

After stepping onto the platform and using the loo to kill time while waiting for the crowd to disperse, they entered the elevator that was designed to only go up. The moment Greg slid a plain white card into the slit between the closed doors, the built-in scanner granted access. Pale yellow lights in the elevator turned pale blue, and they descended.

Once the doors opened, Greg removed the hoodie and adjusted his formal wear underneath. Ivory rubbed off some of the concealer and proudly put on his eyepatch. The row of cabs was there. Greg and Ivory hopped into their regular one and gave him the location, and the driver stepped on it.

They arrived at their destination within ten minutes. Disregarding the long queue outside the nightclub with neon lights that read Nash's Escape, they headed directly for the entrance, approaching the two bouncers, who'd stepped aside to let them through even when Greg and Ivory was still several steps away, muttering, "Your Grace," with an arm across their chest as they passed.

Greg immediately spotted Nash boasting about his business at a table surrounded by six female lycans, all of whom he himself had slept with at least once before. As soon as the duke got the nightclub owner to spot him, Greg made his way toward Nash's office. Nash emptied his beer mug, then excused himself and signaled his bouncer outside the office to open the door for Greg and Ivory.

The door closed, leaving the three men alone. Nash's finger flew to his lips—a sign to talk about anything *but* business. This was what Greg was worried about. In his absence, someone had asserted dominance—or was trying to at least—and they'd even gotten to independent proprietors like Nash, whom Greg had left alone out of mutual respect. The duke offered Nash an empathizing gaze when he spoke in a business-like manner, feigning normalcy, "I'm looking for something, Nash, something strong."

"The same as the last?"

"No. This is to end a very powerful creature. Instantly."

"This doesn't fit into your usual modus operandi, Your Grace. May an old friend ask why?"

"That depends on whether you have what I want or not."

Nash chuckled and gave a firm nod to acknowledge the duke's empathy given by a brief left nod. Nash then strolled across the room to a small, round table where a miniature lycan in a fighting position stood. He bent the tail, and the bookshelf moved to the side, revealing his storage space.

Every type of poison in existence had its own special place on the shelves that covered the four walls. Greg and Ivory immediately spotted bugs placed on the inner shelves. There were ten that they could see, but none were positioned to face the table where business was normally discussed, so it was safe to conclude that these were just listening devices.

The round, glass table in the middle had only two chairs. Greg plopped into one with Ivory behind him. Nash extracted a round-bottom flask with brown liquid and set it on a stand on the table.

Nash sat, smiled, and began, "This is called Neplus Vivre, Your Grace. It's effective as it is quick. This . . ." he wrote something on the notepad and slid it toward Greg. ". . . is my quote for one milliliter."

Greg read the "quote" on the notepad: "You took too long, Your Grace."

He noticed there was a folded paper underneath the first page, and after exchanging a look with Nash, he took it out to unfold it quietly as he kept the conversation going. "The last time I was here, it was a long time ago. Has the traceability of poisons improved or deteriorated?"

It was a stupid question to buy time. He and Nash knew that poisons would always be traceable.

"Well, you got away the last time, didn't you, Your Grace?" Nash played along.

"Barely. If this leads back to me, I don't want it."

"Perhaps something with a more common scent then." Nash rose and continued pretending to be looking for some other poison.

Greg sped read the note:

I wrote this in advance waiting for your arrival, Your Grace. Six months after your imprisonment, we were all paid a visit. Klementine's assistant, Feva, turned against her and has a new employer, who is now forcing us into submission. We have been instructed that—should you ever return—we are to treat you as we normally would, not to raise suspicion while they monitor your and your followers' movements. I can't tell you how grateful I am that they can't plant bugs in mind-links. Emily, Jordan, and I agreed that we remain at your service, Your Grace, as always. But we fear that your own safety may be compromised. The main reason this new, anonymous employer is gaining influence is because we are told that you will give us up to the kingdom's authorities—to the queen herself—once you're given the chance.

Greg scribbled his reply, and when his pen returned to the table, Nash grabbed another glass bottle and returned to his seat, where the notepad already was as his quick eyes scanned through the duke's response:

Klementine would die before allowing one of her goons to continue living after betraying her. This new story claiming her as the victim does not sit with logic. She has to be involved in challenging me. As for the kingdom's authorities, I give you my word that I won't let you or the others be found unless I can guarantee everyone's safety. The queen is different when it comes to accepting us. That was the only reason I disclosed my followers to her. If we help her, she'll help us. There's a threat against her, involving vampires, which I'm sure you've heard about. I need to know where your supply of allicin comes from.

Nash lifted the purple liquid's bottle and began promoting its benefits, "This one is special because it carries the general lycan scent. The inventors were very clever to neutralize the original odor that it would seem as if any lycan could've committed the murder."

"You're guaranteeing me that this one has no loopholes? Not even if an autopsy is performed?"

Nash replied in mock impatience, "Your Grace, an autopsy would only reveal the cause of death. And it so happens that this has such common elements that those bird-brained police would take decades to track it, if they're able to track it at all!"

Greg asked monotonously, "And the quote for this is?"

Nash scribbled the purported quote on the notepad and pushed it back to the duke. Greg smiled, then said, "I'll take this one then."

"Of course you will."

While waiting for Nash to fill up a small vial using a dropper, Greg reread the name and address, committing it to memory, before he smiled softly at the question Nash added at the end. The duke scribbled on the notepad again to answer why he was helping the authorities when he could've just stayed out of the whole thing, adding his own last question to the message.

When the vial was ready, Greg stood, handed over a stack of cash, shook Nash's hand, and uttered the usual, "It's been a pleasure doing business with you."

At the entrance of the room, Greg turned back, awaiting his answer to his last question, to which Nash chuckled silently, shaking his head, mouthing, "No."

Greg nodded with a smile in acknowledgment and composed himself before he and Ivory left the office.

Nash turned off the lights and let the bookshelf hide the secret room once more. He stood by the fireplace and threw the whole notepad into the flames but for one sheet, Greg's last response, which intrigued Nash so much that he had to read it again: "If you ever fall in love with a creature that stands apart the way she does, Nash, you'd understand why. By the way, is this thing really untraceable?"

Nash chuckled to himself at the question but couldn't help but feel sad when he reread the sentence preceding that. *So it's true. The duke has fallen for the queen.* Nash sighed and threw the sheet into the fire. The fire crackled as the sheet turned from white to black and then disappeared into the amber flames. He leaned against the fireplace and—for the first time since he was a young boy—his eyes went to the ceiling while he conveyed a silent prayer, "Goddess, spare him the torment. He may not be the best man, but he is a good man."

###

Greg and Ivory got back into the cab and went straight to the address Nash gave him, reaching the factory within forty-five minutes. When they barged to the entrance, two guards glowered at them. Unperturbed, Greg announced, "I'm here to see Ruby Lyworth."

"Ms. Lyworth did not mention any visits or appointments being scheduled today."

"Tell her Greg Claw demands an immediate appointment."

Greg's name got the guards on full alert. The duke—on the other hand—was insulted. How could there still be creatures who didn't know his face? The rogue world wasn't even that big . . . alright, in all fairness, it did expand over the years, but shouldn't these newcomers at least know the face of the person who was in-charge here? He hadn't even been gone for a year!

Sensing their hesitation, Greg murmured in a low, homicidal tone, "You have thirty seconds to let me in, or I kill you both. If you have families, pray that I'll never find them."

Knowing that Greg had a good track record in hunting down creatures and torturing them, one of the guards linked Ruby while the other politely said, "Give us a moment, Your Grace."

Greg crossed his arms, and his left foot tapped on the ground, as if intending to increase their anxiety on purpose. His mental count reached twenty-nine when the guard who was mind-linking swiped his access card on the monitor plastered at the gate and invited them into the compound, offering a slight bow and uttering, "Apologies, Your Grace."

As Greg and Ivory walked into the compound, they caught the look the two guards exchanged. There wasn't the usual unwavering submission to the highest power, but a knowing glance that Greg might not be the one they'd be obeying in the near future. Maybe Nash was right—he *had* been gone for too long.

Within the factory of machines pumping in chemicals of various colors into bottles and vials of numerous shapes and sizes carried by conveyor belts, heads of employees carrying shipment boxes turned to glance at the unexpected visitors.

Greg and Ivory ascended a flight of cement stairs and came to a metal door, which was left ajar. Before the guard could knock on it, the door opened and a short, plump woman with bronze-colored curls offered a slight bow and a forced smile. "Your Grace. Please, come in."

The guard saw himself off and the two men entered, closing the door behind them and taking the two seats in front of the office desk piled with a high stack of paper on the left side and with about ten figurines of mice standing, some on all fours and some on their hind limbs.

"Interesting decor," Greg mentioned in passing.

Ruby's eyes followed his sights, and then she smiled and uttered, "Ah, the rodents. Well, they've proven to be quite useful in my line of work, so I'm sure you can imagine how they can have a special place in my heart."

Yeah, the part of her heart for experimenting and killing the animals.

"Anyway, to what do I owe the pleasure, Your Grace?"

Greg got to the point, "I understand you produce allicin?"

"I do."

"I want the list of all your purchasers of that particular product."

"That . . . wouldn't be possible, Your Grace. Client confidentiality is something we adhere to in this business. Being in your own line of businesses, I'm sure you can understand."

Greg smirked darkly, and with his legs crossed, he declared, "I respect confidentiality when it's *not* used to piss me off, Lyworth. If they guarantee you a higher status or protection, you can be assured that is sales talk for you to keep your mouth shut. Have they done anything to alleviate your status so far?" Silence followed, and Greg proceeded fanning the flames, "Not even some form of partial payment?"

Ruby tried her best to control her expression when she cautiously challenged, "Using your line of reasoning to assume that such a client exists, how can I be assured that you can top their offer?"

"I've never touched you in the years you were here, have I?"

He knew of the existence of this factory, but it was just labeled as Poison Production in his system's archive. When the business started decades ago, it didn't have a large catalog. Although Greg got his people to keep tabs on all rogue businesses—skimming through how each one grew or deteriorated— Greg didn't have information that was kept on paper, since he couldn't hack into those. For whatever he could hack into, he'd learned that time did help Ruby Lyworth scale her business.

Lyworth couldn't argue with Greg. She was the handful of lucky ones who were neither touched nor visited by the king of the rogue world. Pushing the same simulated smile, she concurred, "Well, I can't argue with that. But I do have a question, Your Grace—how am I to be guaranteed safety seeing that your style of work has . . . altered recently?"

Greg knew this was coming. Lucy was right: it was no secret where his loyalty lay as soon as he chose to give himself up.

Smirking and deciding to hurt this woman's confidence and pride enough to make her think twice before asking any questions about his decisions next time, Greg uttered, "For a long-established entrepreneur, I would've expected you to at least have the due diligence to conduct basic research. Looks like I've overestimated you. Have any of my followers been caught since I decided to take a short vacation in police custody?"

"The fact that you didn't try to get out was troubling, Your Grace."

"Why would I get out of a place that has such promising individuals? Looking for new recruits is part of the job," he fibbed.

Silence. Ruby didn't expect that answer.

Greg caught the hint of uneasiness in her lilac eyes, and continued, "A certain customer of yours somehow managed to piss me off while I was taking a break. So before I forcibly take what I want, your best move would be giving me what I asked for."

Ruby considered her options while Greg looked her dead in the eye. She mentally went through whatever she knew about this duke, and whatever little she was told about the people who were trying to challenge him. Although she was promised a better status—one of power and monopolization in the poisons industry—she couldn't be sure if that was grade A-sales talk or a contractual agreement. There was definitely nothing written on paper, and even if there was, it wasn't as if she could go to court and make her case. The case would be struck out for illegality, and she'd be thrown into prison. Her business and legacy she had worked so hard to build would perish with one simple mistake.

But what if she played it safe? What if she gave Greg what he was asking for, then—in order to remain in this anonymous player's good books—gave Feva a heads-up? If Feva's new employer won, Ruby could make her claim for what was promised to her. If Greg won, Ruby would be as safe and prosperous as she always had been. It was a win-win!

Her lips tugged into another smile when she took a white ring folder out of her desk drawer that was kept under lock and key. Opening it from the back and extracting the last invoice, she handed it over and said, "I believe this is the only document you need, Your Grace."

Ivory stood and took it on Greg's behalf, then remained standing as he waited. Greg didn't even glance at the sheet in his hand when he prompted, "When I say I want all the purchasers of allicin, Lyworth, I mean *all* purchasers."

"One can never be too careful, I see," she muttered with a fake smile, taking the thin stack between the red-and-blue dividers before handing it to Ivory.

Only then did Greg stand, Lyworth following suit. The duke gave a firm nod and said, "Thank you for your cooperation." He headed for the door, but right before he touched the knob, his head turned and he delivered a warning, "I hope we have an understanding that *this* is confidential. Should word be sent to the new player, you can rest assured that I will find out, and when I do, our next encounter will be on less civilized terms."

"I wouldn't dream of doing such a thing, Your Grace!"

"You'd better not. Good day, Lyworth."

Once the door closed, Lyworth reconsidered her plan and still decided to send a message by old-fashioned paper to the anonymous new player.

CHAPTER 40

Lucy's lycan was practically scratching its face when they knew that Greg and Ivory had begun executing the plan. Her eyes would go to the wall clock every few seconds, despite the stack of files she deliberately placed in the middle of her office desk when she thought they would keep her mind properly occupied while waiting for the time to pass. She envied how well Reida was sleeping in the baby cot by the left corner.

Saying that the queen was worried would be an understatement. She started regretting not forcing Greg to take Desmond, Hailey, and Alissa as backup, though she doubted he would. Too many creatures would make him look desperate, and that vulnerable trait couldn't be shown in any business negotiations in the kingdom, let alone in the rogue world.

Xandar made her a cup of tea and took a chocolate bar out of the fridge before making his way to her office that was now next to his, separated only by a glass wall because he loved watching her work when he took short breaks from his own work. The moment he stepped in with the snack and drink, Lucy covered her face in guilt, realizing that her emotions were not under control. After Xandar moved the files to the side and placed the steaming cup in front of her, his strong hands found their way to her tensed shoulders as he kissed her cheek.

"Sorry," Lucy muttered and heaved a sigh, then took deep breaths to calm herself for the sake of her mate.

"Don't apologize, baby."

He lifted her off her seat and sank into her chair, placing her on his lap, guiding her head to lean into him as he handed her the chocolate bar. She looked at the bar in amusement and tore the wrapper from the top before biting into it. Xandar stroked her arm, letting their skin contact and proximity ease the stress. Lucy found comfort in his touch and scent. His beating heart felt like it was assuring her that everything was going to be okay.

After some quiet moments, Xandar said, "They'll be fine, Lucy. They've probably done things like this a million times before."

"That was before Greg was on our side."

"If anything happened to him or Ivory, his followers would have alerted us by now . . . well, alerted you. As long as we don't hear anything, they're fine."

"I hope so."

After she snuggled deeper into his embrace, Xandar casually asked, "How's Toby?"

"I spoke to him. He said he's fine but his head is a little in the clouds if you ask me."

"Like he's keeping a secret?"

"Yeah. Maybe he's not ready to tell anyone yet."

"I wonder what it is."

A strain of possessiveness entered her. "Whatever it is, he'd better tell me first. I'm his best friend."

Xandar chuckled at her territorial nature when it came to this particular friendship, which Toby easily matched. "I'm sure you'll be the first to know, sweetheart."

As soon as everyone left the Forest of Oderem, Toby breezed through the good-byes and took his jet to a place he once went to with some friends in his teenage years. On his way, Lucy linked him, and it felt very uncomfortable not to tell her the truth. He was sure she suspected something was up and wondered how he was going to break it to her.

He had gotten excited over a name on a leaf.

There weren't any living creatures there to confirm that he was getting excited over a bonded mate. The most unsettling thing was that his wolf was so sure it was his mate. He'd never heard of a creature finding their mate through their things. The mate itself normally came first, not the objects they owned.

His jet landed in a green space, and he sprinted for half a mile to get the frustration and confusion off. The wind grazed his skin as the scent of leaves and grass invaded his nostrils. Not long later, Toby was welcomed by the sound of waves crashing on the shore and the squawking of seagulls.

He paused to catch his breath and took off his shoes to feel the grains of sand beneath his feet. His sights went to the boulders where he and his friends sat to take a group photo when they came here more than a decade ago as teenagers. It was a group of six guys, five of whom were now dead from fighting off rogues over the years. He lost the last one two weeks before he met Lucy.

He still missed them, and never had the strength to come back to this beach since then. Somehow, on this day, he felt that he had to come here, that he was being pulled here, though he couldn't fathom why.

At the six boulders, his hand went to the names engraved on each one. When he reached his own name, he sat on the boulder, the same place he sat when they took the group photo. He found himself tearing up and muttering, "I do have new friends now, but I still miss you guys."

He watched the sun that would be setting in less than an hour. A part of him wanted to leave to avoid having to watch the sunset like he once did with his friends, but a larger part of him asked him to stay, not to remember what he lost but to honor the memories he shared with those he loved.

When the sunset began, he took a deep, steady breath, recalling his friends' laughter and the stupid things they'd say and do together, and he felt lighter, happier. He knew for a fact they were in a good place, and smiled at the boulders before talking like his late friends were right there listening to him, telling them about the progress White Blood had made over the years, how the wolves were faring now, how much he had personally grown.

He saved the best topic for last. "I have a best friend now. Her name's Lucy. Now I know the six of us swore that we'd never pick one over the other for exclusive friendships, but . . . I'm sorry, guys. She's really cool . . . and really scary. You guys should have met her. She definitely would have kicked your asses in ten seconds flat, bruised your egos if you hit on her, and probably even broken your spines if she was in the mood. She broke Tate's spine in their first spar, by the way. Also, Tate's not an asshole anymore. He just met our lu—"

He paused when his wolf caught a scent of gardenias and apples. Getting up, he followed the trail that led him to a few palm trees not far behind, where he saw a female in a gray sweater and black pants looking straight at him, her wide blue eyes amplifying shock and even a little fear. Toby had never been struck by anything more gorgeous. While his wolf declared *mate*, he uttered, "Ella."

CHAPTER 41

In the new hideout, Ella had just explained to the kids—again—that they couldn't go out to play yet because the weather wasn't good. The truth was they were never going out to play now that they were hatching yet another escape route. After reporting to Saxum about the food supply, Ella went for a stroll in the forest.

She was enjoying the coolness and peace in her invisible form. Then, she heard something. A rhythm. Lup-di-duh-di-dup. Over and over again. It was the most beautiful sound she'd ever heard. But where was it coming from? There wasn't a soul in sight, unless this was another discretus? Was she hearing the bodily fluid of the mate their Lord had bonded her to?

Excited but nervous, she followed the sound and found herself walking toward the beach—the very location Saxum had told everyone to steer clear of because there was no cover. The blazing gold of the sunset spilling over everything within reach was blinding. She was nearing the edge of the sand when she noticed someone on one of the boulders. He appeared to be talking to himself. Her eyes moved away from him until she realized the beautiful rhythm was coming from this creature.

Who was he? Why was he sitting out in the open like that? Wasn't he afraid of getting caught or killed by the proditors and rogues nearby? Was he a local?

Her shoes hit the sand, and she started noticing his features: his tanned skin and onyx eyes, which were more striking with his dark hair. Her footsteps paused, and her excitement was put to an abrupt halt. He wasn't a hybrid like her. He was a pure wolf. She doubted he was a rogue. He'd be with Klementine if he were. This was her turf.

Ella racked her brain for what to do next.

But before she could decide, Toby's talking stopped and he started sniffing the air. Her heart raced, and while her invisibility power would normally hide her when she felt scared, it revealed her this time even though she was terrified. She stood paralyzed even when Toby was right in front of her.

The way he said her name when he towered over her melted her entire being. It was so soft, so gentle, so full of wanting. They stared into each other's eyes for the next few moments, and Ella couldn't believe the Lord and Goddess would bond someone this handsome to her. She craved to trace his bushy eyebrows and Greek nose, to run her fingers through his dark hair.

Toby, on the other hand, wanted to take her hands and feel her fingers, to feel what it was like to have her bury herself in his chest. His animal, like the uncivilized animal that it was, encouraged him to go for it, but Toby knew better than to do something that spontaneous. They hadn't even heard her voice yet.

Very carefully, he took out the leaf from his jacket and handed it to her, whispering, "I think this is yours, Ella."

She stared at the leaf she used as a bookmark, harrumphed, and managed to utter, "T-Thank you."

Her voice was warm and alluring—like hot chocolate on a cold winter's day. It made him forget about the present threats, troubles, and problems of the kingdom for a while. At that moment, he just felt at peace.

"Um . . ." Ella hesitated.

"Yeah?" Toby closed their distance and prompted in a gentle whisper.

"Wh-What do I call you?"

Oh. He had gotten so caught up in her that he'd forgotten that he hadn't introduced himself. His smile turned into a short, soft chuckle, and then a grin when he said, "It's Toby, Ella."

"Toby," she repeated, sending a spark that shot through his bloodstream. "S-So you . . . don't mind?"

"Mind what?" He took her hand, and found that it was a little colder than the average creature's.

Ella could see him slowly coming to realize she wasn't like him, and filled in the blanks for him. "That I'm a hybrid, born from the union of a wolf and a vampire."

Toby's eyes widened as his mind shut down. All that came out of his mouth was, "Oh. I definitely didn't expect you to say that."

Ella would've been discouraged, but the fact that he didn't look disappointed or upset made her hopeful. He just looked shocked and confused, and he explained why, "Not that I don't like the idea of . . . that, but I just . . . didn't know hybrids existed. Like how do you operate? When do you sleep? Do you drink blood seeing that you're technically . . . half a vampire?"

She felt his warmth, his curiosity, his genuine effort of wanting to know her kind, and that touched her soul. She couldn't help but find his way of asking questions amusing, endearing. Life as a proditor under Saxum's command had very little laughter, if any. Ella herself was only smiley around the kids to cheer them up, but it would've been nice to have someone make her smile and laugh for a change.

She chuckled, then replied, "Those things are different for each hybrid. It all depends on which genes our bodies are inclined to adopt. Personally, I sleep at night. I find more beauty and life in the morning, so it's sad to just be sleeping throughout the day."

"That's good to know," he whispered affectionately as his thumb stroked the back of her hand.

Ella felt an unfamiliar warmth creep up her cheeks. No one ever had this effect on her. Then again, she lived underground. There weren't really any opportunities to meet creatures who weren't in hiding. She tried to stay focused despite how hard it was with Toby looking at her like he'd just gotten a new pair of eyes and was seeing for the first time. Still, she cleared her throat and continued, "I do drink blood, but it's not my staple. I mean, I don't vomit when I drink it, but I wouldn't say that I crave it every single meal. It's just another food option for me."

Toby weighed this fact and mumbled, "That does make sense, actually. So . . . when you guys hunt, do you drink its blood first or eat it first?"

Pressing her lips together to rein in her laughter from his random question, she then answered, "Blood first, then eat. It's less messy. And we don't hunt. The Forest of Oderem spoils us: exuding scents to lure in animals. We're practically killing what's being brought to us."

Toby scoffed in amusement. "And here I was feeling sorry for you guys that you'd have to eat nothing but those fruits in the trees and fish in the water."

"Oh, those fish can't be caught or eaten," she clarified. "They're like the forest's pets and have been there for centuries. Someone tried to catch them once. He got a fever for a week."

Toby's brows shot to his hair. "Huh. Pets."

He wondered if his next question was going to be offensive, and Ella made their eyes lock when she asked, "What is it?"

Toby ran through how he was going to ask his next question three times in his head before putting it out there, "Do hybrids . . . age?"

A crook of a smile curled the corner of her lips. "If you're asking how old I am, Toby, I'm forty-five. Hybrids do age, and it differs from one hybrid to the next. Though for some reason, our appearance always adopts the slow-aging one of vampires. It's not an accurate indicator of how long we'll live though. Some live up to three hundred years old like wolves; some up to five hundred like lycans; and a handful live up to around two thousand like vampires. Our leader, Saxum, fits into that final category."

Only when the words were out did she realized she'd just steered their light conversation toward a serious, melancholic one. There was something about Toby that just made her feel safe to say anything that came to mind. Recalling the leaf he gave her, it was safe to say their hideout had been found.

Toby returned to reality at the mention of a leader. He was the kingdom's defense minister, the queen's best friend, one of the strongest and most trusted allies. Now, the Moon Goddess had seen it fit to bond him to a proditor. The worst part was he didn't even mind. He would take her on a date right now if she let him. But circumstances and responsibilities had to get in the way.

"Ella," Toby began uneasily, his hands held hers so that she wouldn't run away. "I think you know who I am. I'm sure you know how and where I found that leaf. Please, I don't want to hurt you or anyone. But I need to know about the creatures trying to challenge the Queen's Authority."

Ella wished she could just disappear, but her ability seemed to have malfunctioned all of a sudden. She glanced back into the forest and whispered, "Part of those involved are basically my family, Toby. We may not be related by blood, but they're family nonetheless. You can't just ask me to give them up."

"Why does your family want to challenge the Queen's Authority? If you wanted a place in the kingdom, all any of you had to do was ask. I doubt Xandar and Lucy would mind."

"Xandar and Lucy?"

"The king and queen. She's the same queen whose power your family is trying to challenge." He tried not to sound too harsh but it did come out somewhat accusatory.

Ella knew she wasn't an innocent party here, so she calmly explained, "Asking isn't an option for us. Some of those who've lived long enough to try saw the repercussions of that."

"Like Saxum?"

"Yes."

"What happened when he tried?"

She peeped into the forest again, making sure no one was watching them. "It was during Emperor Kosh's reign. Saxum's mother was a vampire, father a lycan. They had a set of twins together. The late ruler felt hybrids like us defied the laws of nature and had to be eliminated, so they killed Saxum's twin brother and the creatures who made them, sending a warning that no such union would be tolerated. Saxum only survived because he was with his governess when the attack started, and she brought him to nearby families. He went through a few trusted hands. One after another they kept him safe for at least a few days, until a witch advised that Saxum be brought to the Forest of Oderem, where she was sure he'd be safe, so that was what they did. The forest had long hated rulers preceding Emperor Kosh, but the moment Saxum was brought in there, it was as if the shield strengthened. Authorities used to just fall ill from intrusion to search for non-hybrid proditors who used the forest to get away. After Saxum entered, the forest would choose the lethal methods to deal with authorities. It was like Saxum's presence made the forest hate those running the empire even more than it did before."

She gave Toby a moment to take this in before proceeding to say, "In the decades that followed, vampires would run into werewolves or lycans at the border between the two territories and find out they were bonded by fate. It's reckless to remain in the empire because of what Emperor Kosh did to Saxum's family, and it wasn't wise to live in wolf or lycan territories seeing there was still tension between the species. A wolf mate might not have killed the vampire counterpart, but they didn't feel safe knowing that another wolf might do it."

Toby challenged, "So now the solution is to come up with some chemical to attack a creature who'd *never* attacked any of you, who had not invoked any violence unless it was to protect those she loved?"

Ella didn't think that there was such a ruler. She was trained to think that all rulers were the same—cold, reckless, devoid of empathy. Swallowing a lump in her throat, she muttered, "We just want to be safe, Toby."

"Tell that to those your family abducted, Ella. Can you tell me that they feel safe now?"

She bit her bottom lip and checked the forest again. "I didn't agree with taking the children. But everyone felt that leaving them behind left a loose end, and they didn't want that."

Toby was too afraid to ask but had to, "Are they dead?"

She hesitated before answering, "The first death was yesterday. The rest of them are still in an induced coma for now."

"Even the kids?" His brows furrowed to the maximum.

She nodded, lips pressed together, downcast eyes filled with guilt. "We didn't want them to see anything by accident."

Toby pressed the bridge of his nose and sighed before asking in a low voice, "Where are they, Ella?"

She murmured, "I don't know. They've been sent to the three scientists working on . . . the chemical. Only Saxum knows where their lab is."

"Ella, you've got to admit this has gone too far. Sure, Emperor Kosh didn't do right by Saxum and his family, but that's no excuse to attack the present rulers of both the lycans and vampires. You have no idea how close we were to war after the Blue Crescent attack. Wait, was that you guys, or was that another player?"

She bit her lip, then admitted, "It was one of the creatures we were . . . collaborating with, but we knew about the attack."

His eyes drilled into hers. "Knew about it or helped plan it, Ella?"

Her dimmed eyes, pressed lips, and overall uneasiness gave Toby his answer. He sighed again. A moment of silence passed between them before Ella said, "It was meant to be a simple test."

Toby scoffed darkly as he replayed the events from the other day. "A simple test that could have sacrificed so many of my closest friends . . . my best friend—our queen, leaving the king who had just found her heartbroken and alone, leaving *me* alone. Do you people know they just had a daughter together? Your plan was so close to leaving a child motherless. And not by accident. By the way, that little lightbulb trick in the forest hideout? Really? You guys had to install a genocidal weapon to kill a kind that you share half of your genes with? Those vampires would've been dead if we weren't there to get them out!"

Confusion flowed through her. Lightbulb trick? Was that why Saxum got the veloces to change the lightbulbs in every lamp during their departure? It was a weapon meant to kill whoever found their hideout?

Toby used the silence to assert, "This doesn't feel like you guys are fighting for a chance anymore, Ella. It feels like revenge. Your family—especially Saxum—wants blood."

Ella argued in defense, "I didn't know about the lightbulbs. But I can tell you whatever we're doing *isn't* for revenge. As long as hybrids are safe, we won't hurt any more than we have to."

"Have to? You have to control and potentially kill my best friend or have someone kill her to feel safe. Do you hear yourself right now, Ella?" Toby didn't feel the blossoming love anymore. What was engulfing him instead was disbelief and disappointment.

"That's not the plan anymore," she muttered, not even knowing why she was blurting everything she knew. "The scientists found that . . . they don't have time to come up with something to control her power, so that isn't the plan anymore."

"So what is the plan now? Controlling the king and then getting him to kill her?"

Ideally, Toby would have wanted Ella to deny his suggestion—preferably while looking at him like he was crazy, but her silence was worrying. There was nothing to control the Queen's Authority yet, but he and the others knew for a fact that the shell worked well to shield the rogues against Xandar. Tweaking the shell to be offensive rather than defensive might take less effort and time than having to come up with something from scratch to control Lucy. It already worked so well in Blue Crescent. With some improvements on the shell they gave the decipio proditors, there was no doubt the hybrids would succeed.

This was getting more messed up by the second.

Ella cautiously uttered, "The queen has garnered many enemies over the years, being one of the main players who had them kicked out of their packs . . ."

"BECAUSE THEY WERE HARMING THEIR PACKS, ELLA!" Even Toby was shocked he'd started yelling at his mate, his voice echoing through the forest.

Ella panicked and looked around to make sure it was still empty, but she knew she had to head back before Saxum suspected anything. She didn't plan to tell anyone about finding Toby yet.

"Ella," Toby's voice brought her attention back to him. "Please really think about what you, your family, and whoever else you're working with are all doing. Saxum's enemy is dead. None of the ones you're targeting now have done anything to any of you. We're not the villains here."

Ella hated that he was right. Abduction was a very difficult thing to see being executed. She hid in the room with the hybrid children when the abductees were brought into the hideout and through the tunnel. She didn't want to get nightmares at that sight, knowing she had a hand in it.

When she said nothing, Toby continued, "Knowing how rogues operate, I'd say you guys are going to escape soon. I don't know how you're going to hasten them without raising suspicions, but if you don't want us to find you in the next twenty-four hours, you'd better think of something while you wrap your conscience around this whole plan, Ella."

Ella blinked. "You're letting us . . . go?"

Toby scoffed depressedly. "Not really. I just know I'm outnumbered this time." He reluctantly let go of her hands, and Ella felt cold all of a sudden. The defense minister fought through hot tears as he uttered, "I'd love to get to know you and be with you, but the fact that I'd have to get involved in your . . . family business and protect those on your side, which essentially hurts and kills my own family and everything I stand for, is making me doubt this bond."

Ella was battling tears. Her voice went up a notch when she hissed, "Not everyone in your family is innocent either, Toby. Only two decipimus returned from the test run the other day, and you're saying that none of you have blood on your hands?"

With a numb gaze that couldn't hide his sorrow, he said, "Tell me, Ella. Whose land were they on and what were they doing before they were killed?" Her lips pressed in a tight line as she looked away when he continued, "We only kill to protect. We always have. We're not innocent in that we still kill, but we don't invoke a war and then play the victim."

Her eyes glazed over when Regina asked where she was. She sounded worried and panicky, asking her to return immediately. When her eyes cleared, Toby asked, "Are you even thinking about trying to call this off? Or if your safety is at risk, are you even considering coming with me?"

Her hushed reply came out almost helpless, "I can't go with you. I can't just abandon them. And we're not calling this off. We have . . . business partners counting on this venture to succeed. We had a deal. We have to hold up our end of the bargain."

Toby bit the inner walls of his mouth so hard that they were starting to bleed, the metallic stench falling on his taste buds. He had been hoping she wouldn't say that. He was hoping that she would—at the very least—let him bring her to safety or—at the very best—say that she'd try to stop the plan.

His memories of meeting Lucy and spending years growing, laughing, arguing, and fighting with her came to mind, then he recalled how she was almost killed in Blue Crescent the other day. He had already lost so many friends to ruthless creatures, he couldn't afford to lose another one, especially not the only one he'd cliqued with like a perfect puzzle piece, especially not for a creature he'd just met, who seemed comfortable maneuvering through life with a moral compass that starkly contradicted his own.

"What's your full name?" Toby asked as steadily as he could.

"Why?" she asked suspiciously.

"I'm not going to kill you or anyone today, Ella. Just tell me your full name."

"Gerella Graymont. Why?"

Toby heaved a heavy sigh, cleared his throat, and recited, "I, Tobias Tristan, reject you, Gerella Graymont, as my mate."

Ella's eyes widened before a sharp pain shot straight to hers and Toby's hearts as his wolf howled in anguish at their loss, a love that could have been, now cut short.

Ella used the tree to steady herself while Toby had the boulder next to him for the same purpose.

When she didn't say anything, Toby prompted, "This is the part where you accept it, Ella."

With her energy drained from escaping, looking after the children, and now the rejection, she could only mouth in disbelief, "What?"

Toby's phone beeped, and he saw the reminder to head for decipio practice. Looking at his still-confused mate and with heaviness in his chest, he murmured, "Ella, I know I'm being a dick by pushing you to do this quickly, but you know we both need to hurry back."

Ella had heard about rejections and bond snaps, but she never imagined it would be this painful, and she never thought it would happen to her when she had done nothing but follow orders and help out her whole life. She didn't deserve to feel this pain, did she? Despite her weakened state, she muttered, "No."

Toby's brows raised in surprise. No? His wolf was already wagging its tail, as if it was celebrating getting back their mate. Even his human couldn't deny his hopefulness. Maybe not all is lost? "Ella, come with me," he urged.

"I can't. I'm needed here. I can't turn my back on everyone I know."

"Not even if you can see their plans are more destructive than beneficial? Do *you* find them more beneficial than harmful?"

She didn't have an answer. She was so sure the hybrids were the victims before Toby spelled out how creatures—innocent creatures—had almost died from their plans. She thought she was okay with experimenting, but now, she wasn't so sure anymore.

Toby allowed himself another two-second look at her, who remained tongue-tied, before he said, "Something to think about, I suppose. Take care, Ella."

He waited for another two seconds before sprinting to his jet.

Alissa beat Toby by two minutes after spying on them from a distance, so she had time to discreetly cover her tracks with scent spray. And it was too easy to get past the not-so-alert pilot anyway. As she hid under a seat in the back row, she linked Greg to report.

CHAPTER 42

Greg had just exited the elevator and stepped onto the subway platform, waiting to catch the next ride when his watchers' report came in, telling him that his suspicions were right—that they were being watched all along. He instructed them to bring in Dormant Little Red, J.J., and Bundy, then called off watch duty immediately.

The new assignment was to start looking for Klementine and her assistant, Feva.

Alissa's link came through next. Greg said nothing throughout the report, even when he stepped onto the train. When the report came to an end, he ordered, *'Get to Polje for the bloodsucker practice as usual. We'll fill in the queen if the defense minister stays silent about this affair.'*

That night, Lucy wasn't even subtle in sighing with relief when she saw Greg and Ivory emerge at Polje. Alissa approached the duke, handing him a white envelope containing the pictures she had taken from a distance with her camera contact lenses. "Good work, Alissa."

Greg spotted Toby, so he got Ivory to greet the queen first as he himself went for the defense minister, who was approaching the king and queen's circle. The duke didn't even bother checking the pictures before he slammed the envelope at Toby's chest, delivering a warning, "You tell her, or I will."

Toby looked at the envelope, then back at the duke, recalling his skills and network before the defense minister eventually guessed what the envelope contained.

He took it and was not surprised to see pictures of him and Ella. He was so ashamed of missing her already.

Greg's stern voice brought him out of his thoughts, "The last thing the queen needs is a mole in her circle, Minister. My people and I swore to protect her, and we'll keep her safe even if it's from her own allies, even if it's from y—"

"If you didn't hear the conversation between us on the beach, Your Grace, don't act like you know everything. It's making you look stupid. I have watched Lucy's back *long* before you showed up, *long* before you became her ally, and I have no intention of stopping anytime soon. You're more than welcome to protect her, but don't attack me while you're at it. She may be your queen, but she has been my sister for almost a decade. Just as she'd kill to protect us, we'd kill to protect her. I am no exception."

"Even if it means killing your own mate?" Greg pressed mercilessly.

Toby scoffed sadly. "Somehow I'm questioning whether I should still call her that."

Greg was going to tell Toby that didn't answer his question, but they were stopped by Lucy, who yelled, "Toby! Greg! Everything alright?"

Toby looked at his best friend and muttered at a volume that only Greg could hear, "No, it most certainly is not, Lucy."

He dashed to her, as did Greg. Lucy wrapped Toby in a bear hug like she always did. He squeezed her in return, but Lucy felt the unusual tightness in the embrace and some sadness in his energy. She looked between him and Greg and declared, "Okay, things are definitely *not* okay with you, Toby. What happened? What's wrong?"

He took note that the alliance members were present, as were the ministers, warriors, top mavericks from both sides, and vampire rulers, and thought to himself, "Fucking fantastic."

Lucy shot a look around and was going to drag him away by his arm. "How about we take this—"

"No, it's fine, Lucy. They should know too." After clearing his throat, Toby told them everything, down to the smallest detail of Ella's eye color. "Not like dark blue or sky blue but like pale blue, like sky blue mixed with a little gray."

Lucy was holding onto her breath throughout the tale, with Xandar stroking her waist, before being the first to eventually speak, "She sounds really pretty."

Toby appreciated she didn't just completely flush away his attempt to keep things lighter than they actually were. "I guess hybrids have the best genes from both species."

Christian found himself saying the very words going through everyone's minds, "Why you though?"

"Christian!" Lucy hissed, knowing fully well where the duke was headed.

Tate chose his words carefully. "It just looks like a mistake now, Toby. It might not be one."

Toby looked at Margaret, then back to Tate. "I'm not sure if I'll get that lucky, Alpha. My mate, her family, and the creatures cooperating with them are basically the ones we're hunting down."

Greg was, by far, the least empathetic one when he said, "Funny you didn't link for backup when you realized who she was."

Lucy's eyes took a fierce, protective turn. "That's enough, Greg. Retreating was the only way to guarantee his own safety. She might not have killed him, but I don't think we can say the same about her family."

Seeing that he had angered her, Greg lowered his head and uttered, "Of course, my queen."

Sighing to herself, she then declared, "Let's just focus on finding solutions now. Ella gave us . . . a lot to go on, assuming whatever she said was true."

Juan cautiously asked Toby, "Did she look like she was lying?"

Toby bit the inner walls of his mouth when he replayed their exchange. "Not to me. But it's hard to say. I've only met her once, and I don't know if hybrids feel the mate bond as strongly as we do to actually feel uncomfortable lying. And I already began questioning her conscience anyway, so . . . I don't know."

With a hand on his shoulder, Lucy assured him gently, "We'll figure it out together, Toby." He forced a smile and was immensely grateful that she was giving him the support he so desperately needed at the moment.

Lucy did a recap of facts, "So her family are hybrids and anyone who produced hybrids who hid in the Forest of Oderem because the late Emperor Kosh killed their leaders' family. They don't trust wolves or lycans either because of the conflict with the vampires. They're working with three scientists . . . whose names we don't have yet. The abductees are in their lab . . . which only the leader knows where. And the current plan is to . . . manipulate Xandar to . . . gain control."

No one dared say the ultimate plan was to make Xandar kill Lucy, even though everyone knew it. Xandar's lycan had been growling in anger, and its human's breathing got heavy as Lucy's thumb stroked the back of his hand, letting the sparks calm him as her animal cooed to his through their link.

Pelly tried desperately to meet Lucy's gaze, and when their eyes locked, Lucy knew exactly what she wanted to ask, so she gave a firm nod. The empress glanced at Toby before she linked all twenty-six vigils, giving them the hybrids' location, and instructed, *'Take the custodes with you and arrest every one you find. Kill only for self-defense.'*

'Yes, Your Majesty.'

When Pelly ended her link and registered that it was still silent, she decided to get the ball rolling. "What this woman said about my late father killing a hybrid isn't true. He killed a vampire who married and marked a lycan because the lycan was part of the conspiracy to end Rosalie's life and put Reagan in solitary confinement. The reason was never that they defied the laws of nature or anything of the sort. He was merely avenging an ally."

Tate asked, "Then why kill one of the children?"

Pelly replied, "That's where it gets more erroneous. There were no children."

A long moment of silence passed before Toby whispered to Lucy, "I'll believe whatever you believe, Lucy. I don't know what's real anymore."

Lucy was not doing any better, equally confused. "Pelly, how was Emperor Kosh . . . certain that there weren't any children? How did he get the information?"

"Like any ruler before him, he sent the vigils to investigate." Something came to her mind, and she added in a low murmur, "Maddock was in-charge."

Lucy nodded, murmuring, "That's our next point of investigation for the child issue, then."

Since verifying the presence of children didn't concern Greg, he moved on to what really interested him, asking Toby, "Minister, did she give any descriptions of the three scientists?"

"No. With hindsight, I wish I'd asked."

Lucy gently consoled, "You had a lot on your mind."

Tate added, "And she might not even know, Toby."

Toby begged to differ. "It's really nice of you to want to help defend my mate, Alpha, but let's face it, if she's privy to planning the Blue Crescent attack and the abductions at Falling Vines and Saber Vagary, I doubt she won't know who the scientists are."

Greg muttered, "The number *three* is quite peculiar."

In exhaustion, Toby asked, "What does that mean, Your Grace?"

Greg explained, "Most scientists in our world don't play well with others, so most work alone, and come up with close to nothing in their lifetimes. This is with the exception of Dr. Tanish and Madam Psych, but they never worked with anyone beyond themselves."

Xandar questioned, "Is it possible that those working solo have altered their working style?"

"Maybe. Maybe not. It depends on what they're being guaranteed."

Lucy asked, "What would swing the odds in our rival's favor?"

Greg thought about that. "Power. That would be my best guess, my queen."

Toby wasn't even trying to think anymore. "What? Everyone wants to vacuum the Authority out of Lucy?"

The duke's mouth opened, intending to deliver the usual harsh retort, but the sight of the tired and saddened minister made Greg feel a little bad, so he chose to answer cordially, "Power in status was what I meant, Minister. Everyone wants to be in the highest position, to be untouchable, to overthrow the one who sits on top so that they'll be the one to make the rules."

"Oh. Of course," Toby noted casually, like he heard about a revolution every single day, to the point where he was jaded.

Lucy asked, "What do they even want with that power? Why are they so pinned on being untouchable? They're rogues. They already have more leeway than anyone in the kingdom . . . as long as they don't do anything to go against your rules, that is."

This made Xandar ask, "What *are* your rules, Greg?" Maybe they weren't as flexible as he thought.

Greg shrugged. "Nothing complicated. Just don't do anything to piss me off, which can range from something as simple as becoming intolerably loud in a bar I'm in, to something more complicated like planting a mole in my circle."

While everyone processed this in silence, Xandar commented, "That's a very wide range of subjective circumstances, Greg."

Greg countered, "Says the one who came up with the complicated tax system to suck money out of individuals based not just on earnings, but property, business, shareholding, foreign income, investments. And let's not forget the exemption only for people who can claim family support, child support, and a whole list of other things that would take me days to recite! And what's with that tax-exemption incentive about some history shit?"

In defense, Xandar argued calmly, "Research and publication of historical events that have been buried or burnt by our predecessors are useful because we can gauge the best approach to take when we're with the other species. It helps the kingdom as a whole in the sense that it preserves peace without being taken advantage of. Of course, there'll be a tax exemption for the time and money that goes into anything like that."

Christian added, "And that whole list of things you're complaining about isn't placed there to target anyone in particular, Greg. It isn't personal, so it's not subjective. It's just economics, unlike your rules, which are strongly based on emotions—your emotions."

Greg responded without effort, "I'm level-headed most of the time, so I doubt involving my emotions is a problem, distant cousin. It really isn't that hard to avoid pissing me off. Just do as I say, stay out of my way, answer questions when I ask them, and don't conspire against me. It's that simple."

Christian heaved a heavy sigh and threw his hands in the air before deciding to give up explaining how that whole *simple* thing was a problem.

Xandar was not surprised. Apart from Greg's lack of birthright, the whole dictatorial line his cousin had just recited was the reason Xandar was determined to never let Greg take the throne.

Seeing that the cousin-bonding time was over, Lucy got the subject back on track. "Greg, do you happen to have a list of creatures who aren't happy to do as you say, stay out of your way, answer your questions, and not conspire against you?"

The way she recited the list in the same sequence earned a few soft chuckles and made some of the judgmental faces turn into ones of amusement. Desmond snorted and abruptly stopped when Greg's fierce eyes shot to him.

Lucy prompted, "So there *is* a list, Desmond?"

"Queen, ain't no list needed. Almost anybody with an ego and who ain't workin' for boss don't like doin' those things. And it ain't personal. These folks just don't like being bossed around, ya know?"

"That's . . . understandable, I suppose." Her sights returned to Greg. "So which scientists are the most . . . rebellious ones, Greg? Surely, they can't all be certain they can overthrow you."

Flattered by her confidence in his ability to keep the rogues in line, he couldn't help but smile when he proudly answered, "I haven't had a problem with self-proclaimed geniuses for more than two decades, my queen. The last ones were . . ."

That was when it hit him.

His smile withered as his eyes went to his top four, who were lost for a brief moment before they, too, realized who they were looking for. It made sense! The Callow triplets were the only ones who worked in three—the only scientists who defied Greg by spreading tales about how he was not fit to stay on the top of the rogue chain, the only ones who died without leaving corpses.

Lucy squeezed Xandar's hand to cope with the painful silence and gnawing anticipation. She didn't want to interrupt their thinking, but the wait was an ordeal! Christian and the alliance members weren't doing any better.

It was like the royal mavericks were discussing amongst themselves, but that couldn't be possible, seeing that their eyes were clear. They weren't mind-linking. It really looked like they were having an internal discussion just using their eyes. Lucy began wondering whether she and the alliance members could do that after fighting alongside each other for so many years.

After the royal mavericks recalled the last time any one of them mentioned the name Callow in their own investigation, Greg scoffed darkly and uttered with a sinister smile, "Those bastards are going to die for real this time."

CHAPTER 43

After Toby left the beach, Ella ran as fast as her legs could carry her back to Neptune's hideout. She was still amazed by how close the two rogues were that Neptune was allowed to set up his own hiding place on Klementine's land.

Ella cracked her head for a plausible excuse to evacuate as soon as possible. Arriving at an abandoned hut, she went to the back, where there was a worn-out truck. She slipped underneath the vehicle and slid open the metal casing covered by dirt and dried leaves before sliding into the hideout.

Her eyes scanned the significantly smaller space, looking for Saxum.

Neptune saw her franticness. His head gestured to a room behind a tattered curtain. "There. One of your friends has fallen ill."

Fallen ill? Now?

She barged into the room without an invitation, and she saw Delancy, who Saxum had dated on and off, lying flat on the rubber mattress on the floor with her eyes closed. Her face was pale, as were her lips. Regina and Chong were there, along with the only hybrid with medical knowledge—Zepine.

Before Ella could ask what had happened, everyone felt their napes sting before it turned into a burn. The anguish spread from their napes to the rest of their bodies. It felt like their organs and vessels were coerced into constriction before the pain found its way to their hearts, and that was excruciating enough to bring them to their knees.

Ella could hear the hybrid children screaming, but she couldn't even get up to go comfort them, battling with the same ordeal herself, now drenched in a cold sweat.

Only when the papilio marks had vanished entirely from their napes did the torment come to an end. The kids were still crying and screaming while the adults took heavy breaths. Normally, Gerella placed the children first, but since she was still struggling to stand from the burn and internal constriction, her eyes locked with Regina and Chong when she asked between lungsful of air, "What . . . happened?"

Chong recovered first and explained, "Delancy was creating an inventory of food supplies with me, and she just fainted. I brought her here and linked Zepine and Saxum before we realized that . . . the mark on her nape was already gone."

Ella's eyes bulged wide. "She didn't scream, sweat, or shiver? Nothing?"

With a shake of his head, Chong muttered, "Nothing."

Ella's panicked sights went to Saxum, who was holding onto Delancy's lifeless hand as he held back tears. No one had ever seen Saxum cry, and only Delancy had ever made him smile.

Although Ella knew Saxum wanted space and silence, the fact that the authorities would be coming for them soon made her forget about empathy. If they didn't leave soon, they'd all wished they ended up like Delancy. After the ten times she practiced in her head, she now fibbed effortlessly through her teeth, "Saxum, we need to evacuate. I smelled something when I was in the forest and tracked it to the beach. There wasn't anyone, but there were fresh footprints on the sand."

Saxum was still staring at the only woman he'd ever loved, but he heard every word. Regina and Chong were scowling at Ella at first, but at the mention of a fresh scent and footprints, they too knew that this was not the time to mourn the death of a dear friend.

Regina asked Chong in a worried whisper, "Where do we go next? Even Neptune has been a risky creature to contact."

Chong muttered, "Klementine probably has another friend or something. Or maybe we can seek refuge in the triplets' lab."

Regina was practically panicking by now when she whisper-yelled, "That place isn't big enough! They made that clear! We can't just leave half of our own behind."

Saxum's voice came out in a low murmur, "We won't. Neptune has another place that's kept off the radar. We'll go there and stay about a week."

Ella didn't like the ambiguity of what came after, so she pressed, "And then what?"

Saxum reluctantly tore his eyes away from Delancy and sighed in impatience. "The tentative plan B is to hide in lycan territory, but we'll have to reach out to Klementine for a few associates before deciding on the exact location. If that doesn't work, Rudolpho has someone in wolf territory, so we have that option as well. Any more questions?"

Out of the hundreds she had since Toby planted the seed of doubt in her head, she decided to pick the top one. "Is this even right, Saxum? Should we be doing this?"

Saxum's impatience turned into shock before it was replaced with anger. He slowly stood, and Ella followed suit. The leader growled, "Is it right to protect ourselves? What do you think, Ella?"

Swallowing the lump in her throat, she softly stated, "Kosh is dead, Saxum."

"The people he worked with are still alive, Ella! His daughter is alive! She's ruling the empire with the same iron fist she inherited from that bastard who killed my family! Do you want to end up like them?"

At that moment, Ella didn't know how to tell Saxum that he might be wrong without telling him about Toby. Then, doubt entered her mind—how was she so sure that Toby was telling the truth, that even if the vampire rulers didn't want hybrids in their territory the lycan rulers would gladly take them in? He wasn't even a member of the royal family. He mentioned the queen was his best friend but was there even a friendship strong enough for one to make a guarantee on the other's behalf?

Ella felt like a complete monster for pressing Saxum one more time, but she just needed the answer to one last question for the time being. "Apart from them, did the administrators of the empire slaughter another hybrid or the couple who produced them?"

Saxum took a heavy breath to avoid losing his temper. "Another six infants that he came across when he was hunting me down were sacrificed, and I hope the numbers stay there. Go help the mothers and children pack. And send Neptune in on your way to their rooms."

They packed up and left within the next hour, using scent sprays that matched the forest trees—custom-made by Klementine in case of emergency—to cover their tracks. No one dared mention anything based on suspicion, but it was worrying the parents that their children seemed to be coughing a little too much for normal children. Regina and Chong were worried about their own toddler, too, and hoped that it was just the result of fatigue.

###

The vigils and custodes only reached the beach and abandoned hut two hours after the hybrids left. In the darkness around 11:30 p.m., it took them another thirty minutes to find the entry of the hideout under the wrecked car. In the hideout itself, they could smell that the scents matched those found in the Forest of Oderem. The only difference was that no belongings were left this time.

They searched the forest before Duica had the idea to start looking through the wooden hut again. The fact that the floorboards had uneven gaps in between and the plank walls weren't evenly constructed depicted that this shelter was not built by a professional. Perhaps it was a family project of sorts.

If there weren't any clues here that would lead them to the hybrids, maybe there was something that could tell them who this shelter belonged to. To his disappointment, there didn't seem to be any scent. This place had been abandoned for a very long time. He could smell the thick dust, and the rooms with closed windows and doors only smelled musty, nothing more.

He and five others ran their hands over the layers of dust on the furniture and walls, hoping to find something hidden. When Bernadette decided that she wanted more ventilation, she plodded to the slightly opened window. Stepping on the floorboards hard like she was punishing the hut for their dead end, Bernadette shrieked when one of the boards broke and her leg went right through the hole she'd created, alarming her colleagues, who sprinted from all corners of the hut as she cursed at the pain.

Dominic and Duica had to break the board around her leg before carefully pulling her out as she tried not to make a big deal out of the wood splinters that went through her flesh. Dominic and Portia started helping her take those out while Duica took out the broken floorboard and ran his fingers through the cobwebs and dust that filled the space underneath. When his fingers felt something solid, he froze for a second and his heart raced when he took out the small, slender object. Flicking away the dust, Duica found that it was a pen.

"That's it?" Duica thought to himself. He opened and closed the cap, finding nothing out of the ordinary. After opening the cap the second time, his fingertips ran over every inch once more. He felt an unevenness near the tip of the fountain pen, so he went to the window to get a clearer view of the engraving using the moonlight.

"Are you even going to share, Duica? You wouldn't have found that without me, you know?" Bernadette protested as Portia and Dominic continued trying to get all the splinters out.

Duica turned to his friend with one raised brow. "Well, it's good to know your arguing abilities remain unaffected by the splinters."

He threw her the pen, which she caught with ease. When Bernadette felt the engraving, she asked, "What does this circular thing mean in lycan territory? Is it a company logo or something?"

"That's a question for the lycans. We should check in with the others, and if there's nothing, we'll head back and report . . . and get you to a doctor, of course."

Half of the vigils stayed behind to wait for the synthetic scents to fade while the other half made their way back. The half who stayed discovered a few hours later that the scent sprays used weren't premium ones. It was nowhere near the forty-hour mark but they could tell the natural scents were becoming detectable. They began tracking for only five minutes before a downpour ruined everything. It rained for two hours, and after it finally turned into a drizzle, both the natural and synthetic scents were no longer present. They explored the trail with the faint natural scent from earlier, but found nothing so they decided to return to the empire.

CHAPTER 44

reg got back from decipio practice and went straight to the Den. His followers were as tired and cranky as he was, but they had to get this done tonight. The invoices Ruby Lyworth gave him led them nowhere because they were filled with company names that were unfamiliar to him, which made sense. Only vampires would see the need to buy allicin, and Greg didn't keep tabs on proditors and their businesses because there was never a need to. Besides, it would have been difficult to check up on their progress since proditors weren't on his turf.

Greg entered the first room, where J.J. and Bundy were each tied to a chair. After the duke plopped into another chair—positioned backward—his legs on each side like he was riding a horse, he began, "I'm tired. I'm pissed. I'm impatient. So let's make this quick and we all go home happy. Delay me and someone will get hurt. Concise answers only—who's promising you two scatterbrains and Red power after trying to overthrow me?"

Bundy's neck stiffened. J.J. subconsciously shifted in her seat and pretended to be clearing her throat when she noticed how Alissa's fiery eyes were pinned on her. The two besties had agreed that if they were ever caught, they'd just lie. Since Alissa looked like she was choking J.J. with that glare, the rogue decided she should say something to not look like she was hiding. "We don't know what you're talking about, Your Grace. We have been minding our own business, whe—"

Greg was so tired from practice, and now he was further drained from this bullshit. He merely waved his fingers and leaned his head against the headrest of the chair for some quick shuteye as Alissa took over. Alissa's hand circled

J.J.'s neck, tightening her grip and choking the woman before her fingernails went through the rogue's skin.

It was one thing to be desperate for air but another to be enduring the blades of long fingernails slowly impaling into one's skin. Sweat beaded along J.J.'s forehead and drenched her armpits, blood oozed from the incisions made by Alissa's nails, and J.J.'s screaming was as annoying as it was piercing.

Greg groaned in irritation. Well, a fifteen-second rest was better than nothing. He watched the pathetic woman struggling in her chair as a dead-faced, exhausted Alissa continued her work. When J.J. finally gave the asking-for-mercy look that Alissa was waiting for, her hand detached only slightly from her victim's neck as she waited.

J.J. took the breaths she needed, and her skin healed the wounds, stuttering, "S-Some say that . . . o-once you served the k-kingdom, y-your right t-to govern rogues is f-forfeited, Your G-Grace."

"Forfeited?" Greg asked in a low, shivering tone.

The chair grazed the floor. He stood, plodding toward J.J., towering over her, making her feel like an insect squirming in fear. He held her chin and gave her cheekbones a painful squeeze as his onyx eyes bore into her fearful ones when he declared, "*I* make the rules in the rogue world. The mere question of my right is a conspiracy that I will not have. Who. Started. This?"

"I don't know the leader, Your Grace, I swear. W-We were told t-that . . . if successful . . . we wouldn't have to work another day in our lives."

It was almost hilarious how they considered pickpocketing "work." It was so simple that it might as well have been considered a leisure activity. If Greg were ever to meet a rogue child he favored, this would be the first skill he'd teach the kid, who he was certain could beat these women by the end of a six-month intensive practice.

Greg moved on to Bundy, and Hailey came to position her hand right in front of Bundy's throat, a silent threat of strangulation before Greg asked, "What else has your friend not told me?"

Bundy didn't even need to think before blurting the facts like she was pouring out hot gossip, "We were paid. In cash. We used it for drinks . . . the hotel. And in exchange, we only had to lay low, stay in inns they asked us to stay in, and k-ke-keep an eye of your f-followers."

"Keep an eye on my followers," Greg repeated in a coldness that left one shuddering, with a rage that made one quiver. He prompted, "For what?"

"They didn't say. But from what we understood, Your Grace, you might not be the only one they want to kill."

What a laughable venture. These creatures actually thought they could kill Greg Claw and his followers. They must have been underestimating the size and aptitude of his network. But the whole plan made sense. Watch his followers to know which ones to kill after trying to kill the leader. His followers were loyal to him, so killing only Greg himself was not enough to guarantee unconditional and sustainable loyalty to a new rogue ruler.

Greg scoffed and pressed the corner of his eyes for more quick shuteye when he murmured, "If I weren't so tired, I'd be laughing right now. Name of the creature who came to you?"

It couldn't be the triplets. They wouldn't risk being seen. Was it Klementine? Her assistant, Feva? Or was it Ruby Lyworth this whole time?

J.J. gulped and muttered, "El-Elvis and Sivle."

Alissa groaned. Another set of names. Another routine tracking. Another search. Something this simple used to be nothing to her, but with the decipio practice and vampire helping, this whole conspiracy issue was getting agitating with lack of sleep.

Greg questioned J.J., "Was that the truth or a lie?"

"Truth," she answered immediately.

Greg's homicidal eyes bore into both of theirs for another few more moments. "Talk to me about the Callows."

Bundy mouthed the word "Callow" like it was something foreign. Her perplexed eyes locked with her friend's own before J.J. whispered from where she sat like Greg and the others couldn't hear them, "Is it Gallow? As in, Ben Gallow?"

Alissa heaved an angry sigh before exclaiming in a way that made the two hostages jump, "IT'S CALLOW, YOU IDIOTS! MATTHEW, NESSA, AND OURELIA CALLOW!"

J.J. looked at Alissa in further confusion for another moment before realization dawned on her, and she questioned, "Didn't they explode with their lab more than twenty-five years ago?"

Bundy added in a gossipy whisper, "Aren't they dead? We heard the royal rogues made sure they were dead."

There were no traces of humor in their eyes. There was only curiosity and a zest for the truth, or at the very least, something worthy to gossip about.

Greg knew he couldn't get anything else from them, so he got up and said, "I'm going to ask Little Red the same thing about the Elvis and Sivle thing. If he says something different, you both won't live through the night."

In the next room, Dormant Little Red registered the bloodstains on Alissa's fingernails the moment she stepped foot into the room, and Greg didn't even finish his question before the little man spat everything he knew. He was paid. In cash. But he had to sober up to be aware of who was watching him because he was told that those were Greg's followers, who were going to be eliminated as soon as their leader was removed.

When asked about the Callows, Red seemed as deaf to the name as if he was drunk, having no recollection of the triplets until he heard the three names and vaguely remembered a destroyed lab. Other than that, he, too, was clueless.

Greg was satisfied with the smooth heart-to-heart session. He stood, patted Little Red on his head, and thanked him before leaving the room. The top four left with him, and Desmond turned off the lights and shut the door, leaving the sober lycan in the darkness.

CHAPTER 45

At 4:15 a.m., Lucy dashed to the front door when she heard a light tap. She and Xandar had asked Mrs. Parker to babysit much earlier this morning so they both could spend a few hours together.

Lucy got the picnic basket while the food that she and Xandar prepared the night before was being heated up. After Xandar stuffed the picnic blanket into the basket, they left through the backdoor, shifted, and made their way to the freesia field. Xandar still carried her across the river, and when they reached their destination, they made their way across the field of flowers and placed the basket under the largest acacia tree—their usual spot. Shifting back, they set up the food and drinks.

When Lucy was satisfied with the arrangement on the picnic blanket, she lowered herself next to Xandar before his hands went to the sides of her bum to pull her into in his lap, making her gasp.

Her eyes snapped to his, and he was gazing at her with the most beatific smile. As his arms tightened around her shoulders and abdomen, his lips trapped hers in a slow, loving kiss. Her cute moan came out in a way that made his heart swell and his animal coo. He would never get tired of hearing that sound and loved the fact that it was because of him.

What made the experience of kissing the most beautiful creature in the kingdom more amazing was that—ever since they marked each other—he could feel her *while* kissing her. He could feel how she let herself forget everything and be completely vulnerable with him when he touched her, how she was pouring her love into his being through her lips and touch, and how at peace she felt just by letting their lips collide until she was out of breath.

When she broke away for air, Xandar's mouth moved to her jawline, neck, and shoulders. He was ecstatic that she had chosen to wear a strapless tank top and short skirt that gave him full access to her neck, shoulders, and thighs. Her fingers pulled at his locks each time he sucked on her skin and squeezed her flesh.

A stream of sexy moans followed as Xandar's hand at her inner thigh felt the heat radiating in the small space, and this made him emit a dangerous yet alluring growl before his hand went up to her butt, giving it a rough squeeze. She gasped and whispered his name, and when Xandar's mouth gave her mark extra attention while his fingers found their way into her wet folds, her legs parted slightly to offer him more room to continue his work there as she moaned in ecstasy.

Xandar's fingers gained speed when she was close, and her fingernails dug into his skin when she came with a scream. As she took rapid breaths, her indecent beast carefully pulled out his hand and licked the nectar he collected from the morning's harvest. His eyes closed as he and his animal savored in the taste— the most delicious thing to ever meet their taste buds.

Lucy's hand touched the hardened part of him in his shorts. Their eyes met, and the temptation to give into each other's desires right then and there was evident. But they both remembered that—once upon a time—someone was watching them when they thought they were alone in the field. Their eyes roamed the surroundings out of defensive instinct, and when they saw, heard, and smelled nothing, Lucy's hand snuck into his pants to bring his erection into full view. Xandar growled and speedily placed her on the grass as he pushed down his pants and boxers before helping Lucy remove her underwear.

He entered her in one go and began pumping, pulling down her top to reveal her ample breasts moving to the rhythm of his entry and exit. His rough hands touched the softness of her breasts as his fingers and thumb played with the swollen nipples.

"Mm . . . faster, Xandar."

The lycan king smirked and sped up as they moaned in pleasure. Xandar knew he wasn't going to last much longer and went all out to make sure Lucy got there first. When her body arched, she screamed and locked him in, and he, too, came with a satisfied smile as he lay on her beautiful body.

The moment they caught their breaths, their animals pushed forward and did two rounds of their own before allowing their human parts to regain control.

Xandar adjusted Lucy's top after pecking kisses on each boob, and slid her underwear through her legs just to have an excuse to kiss her thighs and butt. She helped him with his boxers and shorts after giving his shaft one last loving stroke.

He leaned back against the acacia tree and guided her to his chest. With a euphoric smile, her free hand that rested on his shoulder moved to his abdomen before sliding up his well-defined muscles, and his animal lay on its back, savoring her touch. Her palm stopped over his beating heart, and her thumb stroked the area affectionately.

He gazed at her as she smiled dreamily at his chest, where his heart was. With his hand over hers, he pressed a kiss on her forehead and declared, "It's yours, Lucy. Every part of me is yours."

Her eyes glistened before her lips smashed against his, pulling him close for a deep kiss, which Xandar was more than happy to return. Grips tightening, emotions intensifying, sparks from their bond hitting a new high, their hearts beat in a complementary rhythm and souls entwined in reciprocated devotion.

When Lucy freed him, she whispered, "I love you . . . so much."

His forehead touched hers, and he whispered back, "I love you, too, baby. So much."

They stared into each other's eyes for another few more moments before Xandar's growling stomach decided it was time to eat. Despite already being married to her, his animal still felt embarrassed at that barbaric sound that had ruined the romantic atmosphere.

Lucy chuckled before reaching for the blueberry muffins. Carefully tearing off bite-sized bits, she then fed her indecent beast who had no intention of freeing her from his embrace. He tried to suck her finger and thumb with every feeding, and his animal released a pleading whimper every time his human missed, which in turn made Lucy's lycan prompt its human to leave a kiss on Xandar's jaw.

After the muffins were done, Xandar started feeding her croissant sandwiches, carefully tearing enough so that a bite would have a bit of everything but not so much that she would struggle to fit it into her mouth. When the fruits, mini tarts, and pudding were done and they felt stuffed, Xandar put tea bags into two mugs as Lucy opened the flask and poured the hot water. They let the drinks sit and relaxed against the tree, into each other.

Lucy began, "How's the practice with Pelly and Greg? She's not going easy on you, is she?"

Xandar scoffed. "With the things she's making me see, I sometimes wonder if she resents me for not getting her the doll I promised her as Reagan."

Lucy giggled and stroked his shoulder before she asked, "What did she make you see?"

His smile faltered when his fingers combed through her soft hair. "In the beginning, nothing terrifyingly overwhelming. It was normally the rogues, you being in danger, or our friends and allies either slaughtered or taken hostage."

Lucy's spine straightened in attention. If those were not *terrifyingly overwhelming*, what was?

It was as if Xandar could see the confusion that arched her eyebrows, the curiosity and worry that swam in those gorgeous black-and-lilac orbs. He pecked a kiss on the back of her hand before he answered her silent question, "In the uh . . . latest practice session, we started with the slithering manipulation. I was made to think that . . ." he swallowed a lump in his throat before proceeding to hold onto her hand tighter ". . . that my parents' plan to make me mate and mark Kylton succeeded, and I saw you . . ." he harrumphed before choking out, "marked . . . by Greg."

That was not just *terrifyingly overwhelming*. It was monstrously torturous, heartbreaking and soul-crushing. It was basically the strongest cocktail of all his fears combined into a single scene.

Lucy's hands reached to stroke his cheek and shoulder, ensuring him that she was right there in front of him, that she was his and only his, that they weren't apart and never would be so. He leaned into her hand and kissed her palm before she asked in a small, encouraging voice, "How did you fight it?"

He managed a smile. "For a while, I didn't think I could. My instinct was to pounce on Greg, who was holding you a little too close for my comfort . . . actually, I prefer if he didn't hold or touch you at all." His grip around her instinctively tightened. Lucy made no move to loosen it, leaning closer into him, letting the sparks travel through his being as she waited for him to continue. "I think what made that so convincing was that I *did* smell Greg, but when I didn't smell you, my animal started to suspect something was up." He let out a short, dark scoff when he continued, "The setting was a royal ball, and you should have seen the shock and anger on Greg's face when I pulled you right out of his arms and onto the dance floor. When I held your hand and waist, you felt . . . light, too light for any living being, and your skin felt like the cold night air— lifeless. It was odd. With hindsight, I should have just focused on your lack of warmth and the absence of your scent, but whatever I was seeing just . . . consumed my mind." A pause, and he uttered, "You . . . didn't approve of the way I 'stole' you from my cousin, but you just went with the flow—my purported theft—to avoid starting a scene. I asked why you chose him over me, and the fact that you *reminded* me our Goddess chose him for you made the manipulation practice top my nightmare list. I then asked if you . . . had a say in the Moon Goddess's choice, would you have chosen me over him. You said no without needing to think, like you'd never consider me good enough to be that—to be someone you'd have by your side. You even looked . . . disgusted and uncomfortable. And unsafe. Around me."

Xandar's heart squeezed at the thought of his little freesia disgusted by him, and his strength was drained when he recalled how she'd distanced herself from him, like he would break her heart if she ever gave it to him, like he wasn't good enough to take care of her, like he could never be the one to make her happy.

Lucy started leaving kisses on his chin, jaw, and cheek, reminding him about what was real. He took a deep inhale from her hair before continuing, "When Greg came over, wanting to take you out of my hands, I lost it. I issued the mate challenge and used the Authority to compel him to accept. In the midst of all the creatures around us—including you—telling me that I couldn't issue such a challenge when I myself was marked by and married to . . . another, my vision cleared and the manipulation effects wore off, no doubt with the help of the Authority. It was like . . . when I refused to believe that was my fate, our fate . . . the Authority pushed away the lies and nonsense."

Lucy wondered why she didn't feel any of this during practice. Then, she realized that she did, and she got out using her Authority too. She recalled Rafael was manipulating her with her relationship with Xandar the previous night as well, warning her beforehand this time.

The two vampire best friends must have timed their practice to synchronize hers and Xandar's heartbreak to make it convincing. She didn't blame them for using this method. It was a given that proditors would stoop to any level to win, so it was better to practice and be ready now than to be taken by surprise later.

In her own practice, before Lucy came to realize that the person in the manipulation wasn't really Xandar, her heart squeezed to the point that it became hard to breathe. After coming out of the manipulation, she still felt the residual anguish, which her dazed self thought was her own pain when it was actually her mate's. It was also no wonder Xandar felt so relieved when they held each other in a long embrace during their break after that round. It wasn't just her who was seeing these nightmares now; it was him too.

After Xandar pressed a kiss on her forehead, he finished the tale with a merciless complaint, "It's unfair that all Greg saw was his mother being snatched away from his side by a strange-looking lycan, when what I saw was my mate being taken away from me."

Lucy carefully uttered, "His mother must have meant a lot to him too. The fear and pain would've been an equal challenge to cope with." She left an assuring kiss at the corner of his lips before asking softly, "Did Pelly at least warn you before doing that?"

"She did. Three times, in fact. But I still didn't see it coming. Probably because it was my first time, so it still hurt. And do you know what the most infuriating thing about that whole session was, sweetheart? When my eyes cleared, that little vampire girl-turned-empress was actually sitting on the grass, looking at me with those green eyes and wide smile like she was watching a movie. Instead of giving me pointers of improvement, the first thing she said after that whole nightmare she just gave me was romantic. Last I checked, we were supposed to be practicing for battle. I didn't sign up to be an actor in her movie. Was she even supposed to sit there like that? What if I lost my temper and started randomly throwing and kicking things in the manipulation, including her?"

Lucy tried not to chuckle at how he described Pelly as being *little*, and when he complained about being in a movie that he didn't sign up for, she had to try very hard to press back a broadening smile. After a sweet peck on his lips, she looked into his eyes and said, "Well, my king, you'd make a very good-looking actor."

His mood improved with that compliment, and he gazed coquettishly into his favorite pair of eyes and noted the beautiful blushes before asking in a deep voice, "Does that mean you would've let me drag you onto the dance floor?"

She traced his eyebrows as her cheeks continued heating up. "I think so. I've always accepted and refused dance requests based on the vibes I get from each person, and I've never gotten any bad vibes from you. To me, you've always exuded confidence and assurance."

"Well then," he pulled her impossibly closer and muttered, "guess I shouldn't have done away with royal balls after my parents' passing. Maybe a formal dance on the first day of the annual collaboration would've kept Cummings's hands off you and bound us a little sooner."

Lucy chuckled at his line of reasoning. "Yes, an annual ball would've been a good idea. Imagine the number of beautiful women you'd get to dance with year after year before we met. I wonder how many times you'd have to spin Sasha Cummings around."

"Well, if I spun her once straight into a fireplace, I doubt there'd be a second." Lucy laughed at the image he'd painted, and the melody calmed any storm left in him. With his forehead on hers, he uttered firmly, "Without my parents nagging at me about the duty to mingle, I doubt I'd dance with any woman. None of them were my type, and there was almost no common ground beyond our privileged status, so it was hard to hold a conversation with them about anything other than their businesses and inheritance." He inched closer to feel the warmth on her cheeks with his lips, making her heat up even more before he whispered, "You coming into my life just made me understand why I was never drawn to anyone else. I was waiting for you, my little freesia."

Although Lucy was deeply touched, eyes already welling up, she continued teasing in a whisper, "I have to admit, it feels nice to be complimented by a good-looking actor, my king."

Scoffing in amusement, he noted, "If I ever go into that line of work, my queen, I'm dragging you there with me. And there is no way Greg will be on the same set."

She felt the flash of insecurity come and leave his being. Her thumb traced his lower lip. Looking deeply into his eyes, she said, "Whatever happens, wherever we are, know that I'm in love with you. Only you, okay?"

A film of moisture formed over his eyes when he felt the strength of her love in those words, the depth of her devotion through their bond. After pressing a slow, deep kiss on her lips, he murmured into the small space between their parted lips, "Thank you, baby. Know that I'm only in love with you too."

He waited for the usual answer, and Lucy responded, "I know. Thank you, my love."

They stayed and watched the sunrise—the golden spilling over the horizon and the field, pushing back the darker tones as the vibrant palette took charge of the sky, bringing out the colors of nature wherever its light touched. Beads of dew dotted leaves and grass as the flowers bloomed slowly, shyly.

When it was time to leave, they decided to take a slow walk back. Hand in hand, they strolled across the freesia field, walked through the forest, and crossed the river before coming back to the forest behind their backyard, reaching home just in time for Lucy to get ready to visit Margaret, who came up to her the night before and asked if the queen had time to spare because she wanted to talk to someone who could relate to rejections and its effects.

Mrs. Parker went home, and Xandar took over looking after Reida.

When Lucy was dressed and came to see if Xandar needed anything else before she left, Reida pooped. But the moment Lucy rushed to the cupboard to get a fresh set of baby clothes, Xandar snatched them out of her hands and insisted he could do it, asking her to leave so she wouldn't be late.

Kissing his cheek and their daughter's forehead, she left and drove to the station.

CHAPTER 46

One of the perks of being the queen was that Lucy was fully trusted to take suspects and criminals out for however long she wanted. It wasn't advisable or customary because of issues of safety, but Margaret's case was different since she was working to get pardoned. Even if she attempted to harm the queen, Lucy's Authority would stop her.

In the car, they talked about Stella until Lucy pulled up at an outdoor café. Inside, potted plants filled every corner and hung from the ceiling. A water feature for a wall that had the most invigorating sound drew Margaret closer—an unconscious action that told Lucy where to sit.

After placing their order for slices of cake and cups of coffee, they thanked the waitress and got down to business.

Margaret pressed her fingers at intervals when she started with her rehearsed question, "Lucy, after the rejections, how did you . . . sort of . . . paper over the pain?"

Lucy immediately said, "I didn't paper over the pain, Margaret, and I highly recommend against doing that. It doesn't work. The pain still lingers and grows, staying longer than it's welcome. And the debilitating effects of it shows. Not everyone will see it, but we definitely see it when we're by ourselves."

"So what then? You just let the pain show?"

She offered a small nod. "Yes. I'm most comfortable letting it show when I'm alone. The thing about pain is that we have to feel it to get through it. Let the pain come. Let it flow through your entire being. Cry. Scream if you have to. Being strong doesn't take away one's right to be vulnerable, not even yours, Margaret. I'm not saying you should cry in front of your pup, but you are allowed to cry. You're allowed to be you, to express yourself in ways that feel right for you."

An unfamiliar shimmer appeared over her rosewood eyes, and the edge of her mouth wobbled as she looked away. Emotions within her—ones of loss, anger, grief, deep sorrow—awoke, surging to her chest and turning the shimmer into a puddle. In the silence, the puddle overflowed. When her hand came to wipe the tears away, it felt like she was sinking, her being getting heavier and heavier, nearing the bottom of life. But the moment Margaret told herself she'd continue this some other time and stopped the tears, drawing her first breath, listening to the water feature, a certain lightness gave her a moment of peace. The sensation was brief, but she had to admit it was liberating.

After that moment with herself, she questioned, "Why do I do this? I know I've buried the pain deep down because of the need to survive as a rogue and all, but . . . I feel like since I came here, since I . . . met Tate, I'm trying to move past the pain . . . but every time I do, every time I think I'm moving forward . . . I'm just slapped with the truth that everything I don't want to feel anymore is still very much alive within me. I . . ." She sighed. ". . . I don't even know what I'm asking, Lucy. Goddess, I'm so sorry."

Lucy reached for her hands and gave them a gentle, encouraging squeeze, making their gaze lock. "Don't be sorry, Margaret. You *are* moving forward. You *are* progressing. You wouldn't have awakened your psychic abilities had you not chosen to make peace with your past. The process is just . . . slow. It takes time, but you are getting there. We can see it. Stella and Tate can see it."

In a dismayed whisper, Margaret pressed, "Then why does it feel like I'm stuck? Why do I keep reverting to this loop of pain when I know it isn't good for me, when I know I don't deserve to feel this? Is it because my heart wants to feel this?"

"No, Margaret. It's not what your heart wants. It's just what your heart is . . . used to feeling. It takes a reasonable degree of awareness and discipline to fight through it, to refuse to believe that you're trapped in that loop forever and choose to believe that you deserve all the gifts that life can offer you, the gifts that you can offer yourself."

"The gifts that I can offer myself?"

"Yeah, you know, things like self-respect, self-love, taking chances. Essentially, things that make you love yourself more than you already do, things that make you happy."

Self-respect was something Margaret understood. It was how she rose through the ranks. Taking chances was not unfamiliar, seeing that rogues have to move around, never staying too long in one place, taking a chance that a new venue with no known wolf-patrolling was safe. Self-love was a bit more foreign to Margaret. As for the things that made her happy . . . it was a lot of things before she became a rogue, when life was much simpler.

Leaning in, she asked, "Lucy, after the rejections, how did you find happiness again? Family and friends' support aside, how did *you* find it again?"

"Well, this may sound . . . self-entitled, but um . . ." She was sure it was going to sound entitled. "I told myself that I deserve to be happy."

"Because you have the love of the king?" Margaret asked in curiosity.

She shook her head. "No, not exactly. I actually started telling myself that long before I met Xandar. On my worst days, to calm the storm in me, I tried as hard as I could to convince myself that I deserve to be happy because I'm . . . not a bad person. And I'm taking action to be better every day. I know I'm no saint, and I admit that I pissed off and killed a lot of creatures over the years, but I would never hurt someone for the sake of it. Xandar does make me happy, and his love is something I didn't think I'd be lucky enough to get. But before him, I found happiness in the little things in my life—training, memories made with friends and family, a quiet run, a cool breeze, a good book, betting against Dad . . ." Lucy laughed just thinking about it, adding, "To be loved by a creature who you love just as much is wonderful, but, as individuals, we are still something without it, and we still deserve happiness as long as we wake up every day and just . . . keep going."

The coffee and cakes arrived. Margaret took a sip and processed everything before asking, "How do you tell yourself that you deserve to be happy? I've just tried saying it in my mind, and I already feel guilty doing it. It's as if I . . . don't believe I deserve that. I mean, I did a lot of wrong things before I ran into you and Tate."

"You did what you had to do, Margaret. I'm not saying the things you did were right, but I do acknowledge that you did what you knew to be the best way forward for you and your pup, and later on, for your pack. What's important right now is that you . . . refuse to go back to how you were. As for the guilt, it might have stemmed from the stereotypical image you have of a deserving, happy person. See, most of us are programmed to believe that wanting to claim happiness is wishful thinking instead of an achievable goal. Our subconscious is trained to think that only the purest creatures deserve happiness, but . . .

personally, I really do think that . . . unless one finds pleasure in harming others or is harming someone to fulfill their own selfish desires, no one deserves to be unhappy."

Margaret took a bite of her cake and couldn't help but find Lucy's response . . . logical, rational and fair. She definitely had no plans to return to rogue life, especially now that they were earning a chance at safety, and Stella looked a lot healthier and happier ever since they came to lycan territory.

Margaret then asked, "When you mentioned that we are still something even without the love of a mate, that we still deserve happiness, does it mean that it's . . . wrong to find happiness in someone else? For the past thirteen years, I've only found happiness—pure and lasting happiness—in Stella."

"And that isn't wrong, Margaret. It isn't wrong at all. It's natural for a mother to find happiness in her pup. But in the midst of finding your happiness in your daughter, it's also healthy to find happiness in yourself."

"Isn't my daughter . . . part of me, in a way?"

"Stella is a unique masterpiece that you created and raised. She holds a large part of your heart, but she's her own person. You are your own person, too, Margaret. While loving Stella and finding happiness from her existence, it's also . . . good to find happiness with your own existence. Be happy with what you gave life to, but also be happy with what you can continue giving life to, and I'm not just talking about children. You can give life in so many ways, be it researching the best spots to find food to feed a pack, or merely showing up to add your dash of magic in the lives of those who matter to you. Your worth doesn't deteriorate or end after Stella was conceived. Your individuality as a fellow pack member, a loyal friend, a trusted ally are still there. Stella just added an extra category that you're proud to carry with you."

"I like that," Margaret murmured with a smile. "I love my daughter, and I'm proud to be able to call myself her mother, but it's also great to know that . . . I'm also someone valuable in the other aspects of my life. It's like I . . . appreciate what and who I've grown to be."

"Exactly," Lucy's lips tugged upward at Margaret opening up, her smile increasing in hope and radiance.

When Margaret's brows furrowed, she got to her next question. "Are you always . . . happy with who you are?"

Lucy chuckled and shook her head without hesitation. "I can think of more than a hundred things wrong with myself, and I'd love to tell you all about it, but we'd probably be here for days!"

Margaret was encouraged to laugh in response, feeling less alone. "Don't take this the wrong way, but I'm glad you said that, Lucy." After more chuckles, Margaret looked from the napkin on the table to Lucy, then asked with a sad smile, "It's never going to be easy to be happy with who we are, is it?"

"It's never going to be easy to be unhappy with who we are either, don't you think?" Lucy turned the question around with a smile.

That got Margaret thinking, and when she realized what Lucy was trying to tell her, she smiled wider and said, "I've never thought of it that way. I actually . . . like it."

Lucy could tell. It was as if a flicker of light shone from Margaret's eyes, a rejoicing smile dancing on her lips, so Lucy continued building the momentum, "As difficult as it is to be happy with who we are, it's also difficult to be unhappy with who we are. You and I both know how self-blame and self-hate can be draining—mentally, emotionally, and psychologically. We should be accountable for our actions, but we shouldn't have to punish ourselves forever for our faults and flaws. If we don't like something, we can always find ways to improve rather than complain and hate on ourselves all day long. If it's difficult either way, I'd rather be happily working on myself than unhappily sulking and ranting for the rest of my life."

Margaret confessed, "I guess the concept never crossed my mind. Self-love isn't something I'm very familiar with. Growing up, it was even portrayed to be selfish."

"It isn't though. Many of us are taught that, but it really isn't. Loving ourselves is as essential as breathing." Lucy took a sip from her mug and reminisced about her past when she admitted, "Self-love is . . . work. Like with any kind of love, it's a constant practice of kindness, patience, tolerance, and forgiveness, and the desire to do better by ourselves, for ourselves. It'll always be a work in progress, especially if we make a mistake. If we can find it within ourselves to forgive the people we love, we sure as hell should be more than okay to forgive ourselves."

Margaret took a few more sips and uttered, "What I like about that is we can be happy on our own. I love the power in that. It emanates control, and we hold the remote. It just shows that we're . . . not reliant on someone else's love or happiness to actually . . . be happy."

Lucy agreed. "If we rely on something outside to make us happy, it's neither stable nor reliable because once that thing disappears, our happiness goes with it. It's better to choose to be happy with what you are or what you strive to be. It's more sustainable, and frankly, more doable."

Margaret decided to go deeper. "I hope you don't mind me asking this, but when you're alone, do you sometimes feel . . . empty?"

"I used to."

"What did you do when you felt that way? How do you fill up the emptiness, the cold, barren wasteland that you gave no permission to build up?"

Lucy looked back into her past, then responded, "I fill it up with the things I love and appreciate. I'm quite sure we both can always love and appreciate our strength, our independence, our ability to get things done—all those things that we're proud of. The beautiful thing about this process is that, once we recall what we're made of, it gives us a sense of fulfillment, even happiness."

Margaret crossed her legs and leaned back. "I do feel a sense of pride when I think of those things, like I'm an absolute badass."

"You should, because you are," Lucy encouraged, then whispered behind her teacup with a knowing smile, "Not everyone survived rogue annihilation."

Margaret chuckled, and then Tate came to her mind. The times they almost kissed but didn't because she pulled away, which brought her to her next question, "When you met the king, how did you know the bond was . . . going to last? I haven't told anyone this, but . . ." she sighed ". . . as right as Tate feels now, there's a part of me that just wonders whether this would abruptly end."

This was the first time Lucy admitted, "I felt exactly the same way with Xandar. His status and the fact that he's a lycan made me certain that the mate bond wasn't going to last. Even when we gave our bond a chance in the beginning, I was just . . . waiting for him to get tired of me and eventually come to terms with the fact that rejecting each other was the way to go. But instead of drifting apart, we only got closer. Everything he was and still is, everything he said and did just . . . pulled me closer every day. Even after I fell for him, I was still so scared to commit fully that I kept him at a distance for a while. In hindsight, distancing him was ridiculous. But at that time, I was just being careful. I was scared, scared of having to go through another heartbreak that I didn't ask for."

Margaret resonated incredibly well with that. It wasn't that she didn't want to be with Tate. She was just scared. She just wanted to be careful.

Lucy continued, "But my brother and friends made me realize that . . . Xandar could be different, and I shouldn't use my past to justify running away from something that could very well be . . . it."

Margaret started pressing her fingers at intervals again. "Tate does make me feel special, seen. He does seem like a good person, and I love that he's already bonded so well with Stella."

"Does he bond well with you though?" Lucy asked. The cup in her hand stopped in midair as she waited for her answer with large, curious orbs that didn't hide her anxiety.

Margaret nodded like it was obvious. "Of course."

Lucy sighed in relief. "Tate is my friend, and I'd love for him to get the woman he's fallen for, but not if the woman doesn't want it, so I had to ask. It's great to hear you want this because you personally do, and not just because it's what Stella wants."

A blissful smile curled up Margaret's lips. "When I speak to him, I forget to keep a straight face. I feel comfortable saying whatever comes to mind. And he's been incredibly patient with me. I still feel bad for the way I treated him in the beginning, but he doesn't seem to be holding a grudge. I can't remember anyone else who has been that patient with me. After that rough start, he still looks at me like I'm some precious treasure."

"You are a precious treasure, Margaret. He's hoping that you'll be *his* precious treasure someday."

Margaret chuckled lightly as faint blushes crept up her cheeks. She'd never thought she'd be gifted a second-chance mate, and she sure as hell didn't think he'd be as perfect as Tate was to her, especially when he was an alpha.

Lucy noticed the way Margaret lit up and her features softened just by talking about Tate, and it took a lot of restraint not to lift up her phone and snap a photo to send it to her alpha friend, who could very well use it as a screen wallpaper.

When Margaret came out of her thoughts, she said, "Maybe it's time to take a leap of faith." Downing the rest of her coffee, she confessed, "I wonder what I'll do after this whole vampire thing is resolved. The easy thing about being a rogue was that the day-to-day planning required little creativity. Basically, find supplies or run. I'm sure I'll be helping Tate, but I wonder if there's anything beyond that."

"Something to do with plants maybe?" Lucy suggested, making her judgmental animal smack herself on the forehead as it basically conveyed *lame*, a response that had her human pointing out that the beast living in her didn't even have any ideas to begin with.

Margaret didn't seem to find it lame when she said, "Yes, but what? I don't want it to just be something aesthetic. I want it to be something that helps creatures find peace, to feel like they're heard and supported, like a safe place for people to open up."

"Like a therapist?"

"I wish I had the qualifications to be that . . . maybe I will pursue that field once all this is over. But how can I help with what I have now, I wonder."

"Huh," Lucy muttered when she recognized that energy, the zest and enthusiasm for wanting to make a change.

"What?" Margaret prompted with wide eyes.

"You remind me of someone. You two have quite a bit in common now that I think about it. We should go meet her. C'mon." Lucy immediately got up.

Margaret followed suit when she asked, "Her?"

After settling the bill, Lucy drove them to the Blackfur residence. The guards let her in and told her that the duchess was at the other end of the villa with her guests.

"Perfect. Thank you, Frederick," Lucy uttered with a smile, and the guard tipped his cap in response.

Across the estate, Lucy parked right in front of a single-story building that was detached from the villa. She and Margaret got out. When Lucy's hand was inches away from the doorknob, her ears perked up. She left the door alone and began walking around the building. "They're over here, actually."

The moment they reached the back, Margaret gasped at the gorgeous greenhouse. It was the largest structure she'd ever seen, and she had seen a lot of greenhouses back in her childhood. The moment they stepped inside the glass structure, her rosewood eyes were immediately glued to the lush, green moss covering the entire left wall. The flowerbeds that lined the right wall were filled with small flowers of red, orange, and yellow. Above those hung an entire row of potted ferns of various kinds. Purple and yellow morning glories climbed the wooden pillars. This place was nothing short of a paradise for the red wolf.

What Margaret loved about it most was that part of the ground was covered with soil and not just cement, and she could tell that the plant arrangement partitioned the space in a very subtle way. There was a corner with two pots of roses; another corner with jasmine; another with cacti; and the last with a small lime plant, which was where the duchess and her three guests were at that moment.

"Lucy!" Annie called out when she saw the queen, and she strode over to her, wrapping her in a warm hug.

"Thank you for letting me come on such short notice, Annie."

"My queen, what are you talking about?" Christian walked through the entrance, carrying one child in each of his arms as he continued, "You know you can drop in anytime, even without notice."

"Oh, they're up!" Annie exclaimed with a grin, taking Ianne from Christian as he handed Lewis to Lucy when his son's body began tilting toward her so much that he was close to falling off.

"Hello, Lewis. You didn't poop on your daddy again, did you?" Lucy asked in a hushed tone that made the little boy chuckle in the most adorable way.

Margaret scoffed at her question, and the duke uttered, "It really happened. It's not a joke. He hates me."

Annie retorted, "Christian, infants defecate whenever they please. Ianne did the same thing to you last week and you're not complaining about it."

The duke argued softly and sheepishly, "She didn't look like she did it on purpose."

Annie rolled her eyes, and everyone knew that the little girl that resembled Annie already had her father wrapped around her little finger. Lewis had gotten his father's eyes, nose, and mouth, but his hair color was leaning toward his mother's.

Margaret admired the twins, commenting, "They are just adorable."

"Thank you," Annie uttered, elated and grateful.

The duke circled his arm around the duchess's waist and placed a sweet kiss on her cheek before he said, "You know, it would have been nice for you to tell me the queen was coming. I feel left out, and my cousin was gloating through our link about him knowing what you ladies were up to before I did for once. I'm lucky my favorite niece wet her diaper, or would have been boasting for more than two minutes."

Annie argued, "You said you were going through a few files while the twins slept, so I sent you a text about Lucy coming to avoid disturbing your work."

He gazed at her in affectionate disbelief, whispering, "How many times do I have to tell you that your links will never be bothersome no matter what I'm doing, my duchess?"

"Well, this is only the thirty-second time since our marriage, so we can still work our way up," Annie replied, despite her reddening cheeks.

Lucy whispered in Margaret's way, "Aren't they just the cutest thing you've ever seen?"

Margaret couldn't deny that the duke and duchess looked beautiful together, much like Lucy and Xandar. Their relationships exuded not just love and affection, but amplified deep assurance and wonderful communication.

She wanted that.

Christian then spoke to Margaret with a warm smile, "It's great to see you getting close to having something like this, too, Luna."

Margaret flinched at the title, which was when Lucy said, "Oh, that. Yeah, Christian has an obsession with titles, save in very exceptional circumstances. I mean, he even calls his wife by her title."

Christian pressed back a guilty smile as the duchess chuckled.

Margaret found it amusing as well, but she managed to respond to Christian's earlier remark, "Well, I've been in a good, supportive circle that exemplifies what a relationship should look like, Your Grace. And may I just say that you both have the most gorgeous greenhouse I've ever seen."

Christian replied, "Oh, this greenhouse is Annie's masterpiece. It was a plain piece of nothing here, and my duchess worked her magic. Fun fact, she didn't let me pay for anything."

Annie protested, "That's not true! You got those stools!"

"Ah, yes." His sights returned to Margaret, speaking like he was resting his case, "I made the very significant contribution of purchasing those twenty mushroom-looking stools you see in the corner over there."

Lucy chuckled when Annie elbowed her husband before the duchess explained, "He already paid for most of the plants I wanted around this estate and even in the house, never letting me take out a dime, and would pay me back if he found out I bought a plant in secret, even if it was just a small cactus. This greenhouse was something I wanted to create and pay for on my own."

Margaret uttered, "I get that. It's not that you don't want his money or help, but you want something that came entirely out of you."

Annie smiled broader before looking at her husband. "See, she gets it."

Christian sighed in mock frustration. "Luna, you're not supposed to side with someone you just met. It's dangerous. You don't know what she has up her sleeves."

Margaret was getting more comfortable with the hospitable atmosphere. "I've seen danger, Your Grace. Your duchess is nowhere near that trait or even on that spectrum."

Annie threw Christian a triumphant smile, and he took the opportunity to kiss her lips, making her cocky features soften in tenderness. After clearing her throat, Annie decided to start introducing her guests. "Margaret, these are Wanessa, Xelda, and Yelena, my fellow co-founders. We had just completed our discussion on future projects when Lucy linked me."

"Oh, pleasure to meet you." Margaret shook each of the ladies' hands before asking, "Cofounders of what?"

"A non-profit organization called L'Auditeur. It's aimed at helping those who've been emotionally and psychologically scarred by something that happened in the past. We just started a few months ago, but the response has been positively overwhelming, so we're looking at plans for recruitment. We use this greenhouse for most sessions for now because it's soothing enough to feel welcoming, but we're thinking of getting a bigger place due to the increasing demand." Margaret's eyes sparkled as Annie went on, "Wanessa and Xelda are certified therapists, and Yelena works and volunteers in programs involving abused women and children in human territory. None of us have a perfect past, and we wished we had something like this, someone who could understand and relate to what we were going through, so we started this initiative to be just that for creatures who may need this form of support but might not be able to afford it."

"That's . . ." Margaret was so awestruck that she was groping for the right word, and finally managed not to embarrass herself and say, "amazing! Wow! Can I join?"

"About that," Annie shot the smiling Lucy a knowing look, inadvertently making her husband feel left out again before the duchess continued, "when Lucy told me you were coming, the four of us here were hoping you could help us expand our work to werewolf territory."

"Me?" Margaret asked in shock.

"Yes, but you don't have to start right away, of course. We all need time to heal ourselves first. You, like everybody else, are more than welcome to join the activities and healing sessions, but we were hoping that, one day, you'll take a chance to help lead this initiative with us—if you want to, that is. This isn't an obligation or . . ."

"I'd love to!" Margaret exclaimed, then wrapped Lucy in a spontaneous hug when she uttered, "Thank you, Lucy."

After their brutal exchange from the first day, Margaret would have never thought she could find a friend in the queen, nor did she think Lucy would connect her to people who could help her get what she had begun to want since she realized that she didn't have to be a rogue forever—a purpose, a chance to make an impact in someone's life, leaving them in a better place than the one they were in before.

Lucy squeezed her in return until her ringing phone made them let go of each other. Everyone saw the word Greg on the lit screen before she swiped to answer.

Greg spoke so speedily that Lucy could easily tell it was an emergency. When Greg was halfway through, Lucy's eyes turned onyx as the rise and fall of her chest grew more visible.

Xandar felt her anger and tried mind-linking her, but she didn't answer, so he linked Christian instead.

Christian explained, *'Well, the bad news is that it's Greg. The good news is that she's pissed.'* When Christian noticed Lucy's clenched fist and Lewis's small hand reaching to gently pat his aunt's heated cheeks, trying to cool them down, the duke added, *'Really pissed. I'm genuinely hoping she won't combust, Cuz. You might get burned trying to put out her flames.'*

Xandar hoisted Reida and linked, *'I should come to her.'*

'No, no. Wait, she's going to speak.'

Lucy muttered in a voice so calm and monotonous that a creature who didn't know her wouldn't be able to guess what was really going through her mind, "I'll send word to Dalloway. We'll meet you in the Den soon. Thank you, Greg."

The only thing Greg said after that was, "Please don't bring the princess this time, my queen." He knew for a fact she was enraged, because that was the only time her voice would go that low and flat.

"We're on the same page there. I don't plan to. See you soon."

Hanging up, her eyes locked with Christian's glazed-over ones before the duke murmured to Xandar, *'Looks like we're working through the weekend again, Cuz.'*

CHAPTER 47

The defense ministers; Margaret and her mavericks; and Lucy, Xandar, and Christian reached the Den. Chief Dalloway, who was escorting Kate, looked at the duke as if asking him an unspoken question.

Greg pointed at the only chair to his left. "Over there, Chief."

Despite being surprised that this duke actually addressed him politely, he complied.

Kate was confused. What was happening? And why did she have to go first? None of her friends knew what this was about, not even Margaret. But Tate knew, and it was killing him and his wolf to not say a thing to their mate.

Lucy had to discuss with Xandar for two whole minutes before deciding whether they should tell Tate. Even now, she wasn't sure if they had made the right decision. She hated to be the reason Tate had to keep something from his mate, who he'd been trying so hard to get close to.

The present test was to see how many in Margaret's pack knew about Kate's movements and communication. The royal family members and defense ministers stood at parts of the room that gave them a good view of the clueless faces, which they hoped would remain clueless. Greg's top four dawdled around the room like it was just another workday for them.

Lucy envied how casually Alissa could chew gum. Although the queen kept her composure, she was boiling like a kettle on the inside. She gave her word that, should there be betrayal or treachery, she'd torture the traitor until she was satisfied. She hadn't seen the evidence Greg and his mavericks found against Kate yet and hoped—for Kate's sake—that there was a plausible explanation to the evidence, but that seemed unlikely.

Xandar's hand was on her shoulder, his thumbs drawing comforting circles. Lucy offered him a small smile and touched him lightly on his chest before Greg got the ball rolling, "Kate, how long have you been in contact with this creature named Rudolpho?"

Kate's body stiffened.

Lucy and the others were relieved to see that Margaret and her followers had squinting eyes, arching brows, and creasing foreheads, looking confused and muttering, "Who?" to each other.

Kate cleared her throat and uttered, "I don't know who that is."

Greg had expected that answer because not everyone knew that deleted messages could be retrieved. The duke continued reading from the screen and questioning monotonously, "You don't know who you've been sending, 'I love you. Please be safe,' text messages to? Really?"

Margaret's confused eyes widened in wrath, scowling at Kate, waiting for her answer. They weren't supposed to be sending messages to anyone! They were allowed to have phones for any function *except* communication.

Kate gulped and insisted, "If that's in there, it's fake. You must have put it in."

Lucy saw the way her foot subtly moved and her eyes averted. Kate's steady voice made her a good liar, but her less-than-perfect body language showed that she wasn't good enough. The queen walked up to Kate in slow steps, and the click of her shoes echoed against the walls. In a voice that sent a shiver down everyone's spines, she questioned, "You're certain that the duke is lying, Kate? Think *very* carefully before you answer me."

Kate ignored the warning and exclaimed, "It's fake! We're not allowed to contact anyone! I didn't do it! This high-tech guy and his goons must have gotten it into the system to frame me somehow."

Azalea asked in genuine confusion, "There are forty of us. Why frame you?"

"I don't know, Az, okay?"

Lucy saw the body signals of a liar again, and it pissed her off that she was being lied to in her face more than once. Her eyes turned blue, emitting her Authority as she pinned Kate to her chair and asked, "Is the duke lying?"

Kate fidgeted in her seat, trying to fight off the compulsion, but she couldn't and ended up answering, "No."

That made some of her pack members gasp. Half of them growled without thought, shooting Kate a glare that could've burned through her skin.

Lucy continued asking, "Who is Rudolpho?"

Tears rippled in her eyes at the way she was made to go against her will. "My . . . boyfriend."

Azalea hissed in a whisper, "What the fuck! Since when?"

Kate was glaring at Lucy now. She had never hated anyone more at that point. The queen remained unperturbed when she parroted, "Since. When?"

"Two years ago."

"So he's a chosen boyfriend, not a bonded one?"

"Yes."

Margaret let out a low growl and was about to pounce forward out of pure rage had Tate not held her back. The alpha was beyond relieved with her reaction. At least his mate was clear from this.

Lucy proceeded to ask, "Does he know about the conditional pardon?"

"Yes."

"What did he say?"

"That it wouldn't mean anything soon because they have a plan to re-move you."

Xandar was at his wife's side within the next second as he glowered at the woman in the chair. Greg came over too. Both were trying to rein in their animals, who demanded to be released.

Lucy scoffed darkly. "So your boyfriend and his pack are the ones we're after?"

"Partly."

"Meaning?"

"They're collaborating with a few other groups. I wasn't told how many. He said the less I know, the better."

"Well, he got that right. Too bad he already told you so much. Anyway, did you know about the Blue Crescent attack?"

Kate tried with all her might to press her lips together, but eventually she answered, "Yes."

"So the attack wasn't just an attack, was it? It was also supposed to be your escape route."

"Yes."

"Who was supposed to take you away?"

Kate breathed heavily in anger and said, "A discretus. I don't know his name."

"Where were they supposed to take you?"

Kate smirked. "I don't know."

Greg's hand was about to go to Kate's neck, but Lucy stopped him with a gentler tone, "Not yet, Greg."

Her attention returned to Kate. "So it's safe to assume that you've met up with him before?"

"Yes."

"Where?"

Hailey and Ivory turned more alert and immediately brought up the hologram of the map as their index fingers got ready to pinpoint every location they were about to hear.

"Grotte, Ravin, Forêt, Bordure, Talus."

Margaret lost it when she yelled, "So basically, EVERYWHERE we've been in the past two years!"

Kate bit her lip and refused to meet her leader's eyes.

Greg then confirmed Kate's account, "Those locations are also where her texts were sent from, my queen."

Lucy proceeded to ask Greg, "And the texts from Rudolpho? Where were they sent from?"

In a flat, discontented voice, Greg exhaled and replied, "The almighty, *magical* Forest of Oderem, my queen."

More gasps followed. Zane and Azalea exclaimed "What the fuck?" in a frustrated whisper.

Lucy gritted her teeth when she asked Kate, "Earlier, you told me that you didn't know where those who invaded Blue Crescent were supposed to take you. Now, the trace is showing that your boyfriend is from the Forest of Oderem. Are you saying that you didn't know where he was from?"

"No."

"Then how are these two contradictions both the truth?"

"My boyfriend wasn't going to bring me to the forest first. He said he needed permission to do that, not just the leaders' but also the forest's permission. I was supposed to go to a transit location. And he said that if permission was ever refused, we'd just live somewhere else."

Margaret spat, "Oh, how ROMANTIC! Risk having the whole pack found and elope with a lover you don't even know!"

Kate shot Margaret a glare. "I've known him for two years. He loves me. I know him better than you know *your* mate you met less than a month ago!"

"That. Is. Enough." Lucy started to make Kate slowly stop breathing, then made her slap herself on both sides of her face with force, leaving her own handprints on her cheeks before the queen asked everyone around her in a low voice, "Does anyone have any further questions?"

Too shocked to speak any louder, Zane asked innocently and softly, "Did anyone else know about you and your boyfriend?"

Lucy reluctantly let Kate breathe. Her lungs began replenishing themselves with the sudden air supply, but Lucy didn't allow her to fully recover before compelling her to give a response. Since Kate couldn't speak yet, her eyes went to a fair-skinned man.

Zane and everyone else followed her gaze to him before Zane murmured, "Oh, you've gotta be fucking kidding me."

Azalea managed to land a punch on the guy's jaw before Phelton held him by his arm and brought him before the king and queen, kicking his knees to make him kneel.

With her sapphire eyes, Lucy began, "Howard, right?"

"Yes, Your Highness."

"How long have you known?"

"A year and a half."

"Why didn't you tell anyone?"

He was beginning to look ashamed. But the Authority eventually made him utter, "I was promised that I could go with them if they ever succeeded—be in a polyamorous relationship with Kate and Rudolpho."

"Have you met Rudolpho?"

"No."

"But you are sure he is okay with the plan you have in mind?"

"Yes."

"Why is that?"

"Because Kate told me that it was okay."

"When did she tell you that?"

"About a year and a half ago after I caught her seeing Rudolpho. He ran away before I could meet him. Kate told me to keep it a secret and said I could go with her when the time was right, that three in a relationship wasn't a problem for them."

"So you also knew about the plan to *remove* me?"

Xandar's grip around her abdomen tightened as they waited.

"No. I thought it was a simple escape when no one was noticing, like wandering off to find supplies and just never returning to the pack."

"And the escape during the Blue Crescent attack?"

"I didn't know I was supposed to escape then."

"When did you think you were going to escape?"

"I don't know. I was waiting for Kate to give the signal."

"Which never came, I presume?"

He nodded.

"Where did you catch them on their rendezvous?"

"Bordure."

Lucy turned back to Kate. "Do you have a picture of Rudolpho?"

Her pressed lips were no match for the lycan queen's power. "Yes."

Greg swiped through his tablet and murmured, "There are hundreds of photos of men here." He turned the device to Kate, asking, "Which one?"

It was baffling that Kate was still trying to be defiant. There was already no way out. Cooperating would give her better chances of getting a more merciful outcome, yet she still chose to remain adamant.

Lucy snarled, "Which. One?"

The many random pictures were a precaution Kate took in case someone went through her phone, a precaution she didn't expect would backfire. Kate reluctantly studied the screen and muttered, "Seventh row, second one from the left."

Greg tapped into that image and showed it to her again. Once Kate nodded, Greg murmured to Lucy, "I'll deploy a few mavericks to ask around in the rogue world, my queen."

The duke then handed the device to Toby, who came forward and muttered like he was talking to the screen, "I'll get our warriors to search the kingdom."

Xandar instructed, "If there are others with Rudolpho, retreat. They might be decipimus. We're not risking lives for a few bees. Let's see if we can use him to find the nest."

"Goes without saying," Greg muttered as he swiped through his phone.

"Yeah, will do," Toby murmured casually as he took the picture of Rudolpho using his own phone.

"You'll never get to him." Everyone's eyes darted to Kate, who added, "It'll be a mistake to go after him and the others. You will lose. It wouldn't matter if you brought the empress and her vampires. You will all lose. Look what happened in Blue Crescent."

Xandar's thunderous growl made every other growl in the room inaudible. He lifted Kate by her neck and started strangulating her slowly. When everyone heard the first few crackling sounds of breaking bones, Lucy stood on her toes and pecked a kiss on Xandar's cheek before she whispered affectionately into his ear, "Thank you, darling. I'll take it from here."

"No," his immediate response came in a low rumble.

"Please?" Her softened voice and the way her hands circled his biceps made their eyes lock. His animal was trying its best to fight against her doe eyes and tender touch, but it knew it was losing.

"Baby, no," Xandar said again, much gentler and with more desperation, already bending.

Every single creature in the room already knew the ultimate winner. Toby was just waiting for his best friend to win again while he sent out Rudolpho's photo to every gamma and lycan warrior with attached instructions. Christian was counting the seconds before his cousin gave in, wondering if the queen was going to break her record again, making a mental note to tell Annie if that happened. Funnily enough, Chief Dalloway was secretly counting the seconds too. He couldn't be more thankful that the queen always calmed the king whenever he or his colleagues had to deliver bad news, and when it wasn't him that she was saving, he found it entertaining to just know how long the queen needed to cool their king.

"Please? For me?" Lucy asked in a small voice, innocently blinking her large eyes.

After Xandar pinched his nose bridge and sighed, he threw Kate back into the chair. Greg's ready foot tilted the chair back so that Kate didn't fall off.

While Kate took her time to heal and catch her breath, Xandar was rewarded with his wife's smile and a quick kiss at the corner of his lips before she whispered, "Thank you, my love."

His frown eventually turned into a smirk when he linked, *'You didn't play fair, sweetheart.'*

With a bashful smile, she replied, *'I know. Thank you for letting me win again, darling.'*

Leaving a kiss on her forehead, he whispered, "Anything for my little freesia."

Despite still being slightly breathless, Kate choked out, "What? You stopped your mate from choking me to death just to make yourself feel better by doing it yourself?"

Even Toby paused from replying to a long line of incoming messages, looked at Kate, and said, "You and the cult you want to join take ruthlessness to another level."

"Says the ones who support an empress whose father set out to slaughter hybrids!"

Lucy argued, "That isn't confirmed. There are no records or evidence showing such a thing. If Rudolpho told you that . . ."

Kate cut her off, "If the fucking empress told *you* that, you're dead stupid!"

Another round of growls followed as Lucy used her Authority to mute Kate and pin her to her seat. The queen's finger and thumb lifted Kate's chin, and she began squeezing it so tightly that Kate felt her fingernails digging into her flesh as the queen conveyed a chilling promise, "I'm not going to kill you today, Kate. Unfortunately for you, I'm not that nice. As promised to the government and to you when the offer was spelled out, I'm going to break you. Slowly. Until I'm satisfied. I'm going to find Rudolpho, and the three of us are going to have a rendezvous to get to know each other. On that day, you're going to wish I'd killed you."

Kate's eyes bulged wide. She wanted to scream, but nothing came out. Lucy's force on Kate's chin increased to the point where the bones there cracked and broke. Kate's fingers dug into the flesh on her thighs on her own accord to cope with the pain. Tears and cold sweat beaded on her face, but no one cared, not even Howard or Phelton. Lucy's fingers then rested on Kate's right cheekbones, and the torture continued there. Even when the smell blood filled the room, the queen didn't stop.

Lucy uttered, "You think *this* hurts? How do you think the creatures who trusted you feel? How do you think the creatures who gave you a chance feel? You didn't just make us look foolish, Kate. You turned against everyone who's been protecting you. You turned against all of us over someone who can't even guarantee your safety. You'd best pray your boyfriend's theory on hybrid slaughter isn't fiction, or you'll spend a long time behind bars in a never-ending cycle of torture and recovery." After her cheekbones broke, Lucy broke Kate's nose and right ear, which made her continue screaming voicelessly.

The queen instructed Dalloway, "Take her into custody and start running through the archives for any crimes that left a scent trail that matches hers, Chief. The prosecution can start building their case against her."

"Duly noted, my queen. And the . . . other one?"

Lucy's eyes went to Howard, which was when Xandar instructed, "Same procedure."

"As you wish, my king."

As Dalloway and his forces took Kate and Howard away, something beeped, and Greg went to extract the thumb drive from his laptop before handing it to Toby as he muttered, "Your copy."

"Uh . . . thank you, Your Grace." Toby blinked in shock before accepting it, then locked eyes with Lucy when he linked, *I haven't lived very long, but that was—by far—the weirdest shit that's ever happened to me—Greg Claw handing me information without coercion.'*

Lucy shrugged. *'It just shows he can be nice if he wants to.'*

'If he's doing this because he's in love with me, I'm going to kill myself.'

Lucy's eyes narrowed as her head gave a slow shake while Toby chuckled at his own joke.

Xandar decided to ask what that was about later. Lucy had been making more time to speak to Toby lately just to make sure he was okay, that she was there if he needed anything, so Xandar knew better than to interrupt them, especially now when Toby needed her more than ever.

CHAPTER 48

s soon as the vigils returned to vampire territory after the investigation of the hut and hideout in midafternoon, they made their way to the castle once again. Outside Pelly's study, Duica took a deep breath, knocked twice, and waited.

"Who is it?" Pelly's familiar voice came from inside.

"It's VIG 001, Your Majesty."

"Come in, Duica," came the reply.

Duica was surprised. That was the first time the empress had acknowledged him by name. Dominic nudged him and teased through their link, *'She might have a favorite after all!'*

After Duica rolled his eyes, he opened the door, and Pelly, who was seated, looked up from the map spread across her desk. Octavia was perched on the armrest of the empress's chair with one leg on the floor as her furrowed brows flattened just slightly to acknowledge the vigils' presence. They were trying to guess where the tunnel of the hideout from the Forest of Oderem could lead to, before Duica's knock came. The lycans had moved the rocks and boulders, but it just led to a dead end because Klementine demolished her accommodation after everyone left her place, thus covering her end of the tunnel.

"Your Majesties," the vigils addressed in unison.

Pelly did a mental headcount twice, then asked, "What did you find, and why are there only twenty-four of you? Where are the other two?"

Duica responded, "One of our own was injured, Your Majesty, and the other brought her to the hospital. Her leg went right through the floorboard of a dilapidated hut in the forest behind the beach, and the accident was actually how we found this."

He came forward, placed the pen on her desk, and stepped back to wait. Pelly glanced at the pen before her eyes scanned the vigils again. "Who's injured? Portia or Bernadette?"

"B-Bernadette, Your Majesty. My apologies, I should've been clearer."

"It's no issue," Pelly uttered monotonously.

When did the empress even learn their names?

The truth was that Pelly and Octavia had always known their names. All twenty-six of them. But because of the constant need to make their authoritative position clear to the vigils and the ministers watching Pelly instructing them, the empress had chosen to address them by their code ever since she ascended the throne.

Recently though, Pelly had watched how Lucy and Xandar addressed everyone by name, regardless of their position, and the empress liked the fact that everyone, even her own people, tended to speak more freely when they were addressed that way, so she decided to give this change a chance.

The empress lifted the pen, then opened the cap and scribbled on the square notepad, which was when Duica said, "I tried that, Your Majesty. The ink dried up long ago. But what is peculiar is the carving."

"Yes, a . . . patterned circle," Pelly murmured as she studied the carving with her consort.

"Anything else?" Octavia prompted them to continue.

They gave information about the smell, covered trails, and hideout underneath the abandoned car. Pelly groaned aloud when they said whoever was there had escaped. Again. And how the downpour only made things worse.

"How long do we have to keep doing this?" Pelly murmured to herself.

As Octavia stroked her tense shoulders, Duica said, "We're doing everything we can, Your Majesties. Finding the abductees has never been anything but our top priority, I can assure you." The vigils thought they were being blamed when Pelly was just complaining out of fatigue and frustration.

Brows raised, Pelly said, "We've never doubted that, Duica." Her sights returned to the pen that meant absolutely nothing to her. "I'll ask their Highnesses about this, and we'll see if there are any leads from there. For now . . ." her eyes went to the grandfather's clock ". . . I only need two of you to stay behind to help with the talk I'm going to have with Maddock in fifteen minutes. The rest of you can go home after checking on Bernadette. Send us a status on her condition once you do."

"As you wish, Your Majesties."

Duica and Dominic stayed behind and were asked to remain in the study, when custom dictated they waited outside. They stood around awkwardly until Octavia gestured them to the chairs in front of Pelly's desk. Their immediate, conventional response would be to refuse since they weren't going to be the one who was to be questioned soon, but seeing that the consort insisted and the empress didn't object as her eyes returned to the map, they sat in the very comfortable sapphire-colored furniture. Dominic was even beginning to get very comfortable, feeling the velvet of the seat with his finger pads.

Octavia handed the vigils a file that concerned Maddock's matter, and the vigils combed through the papyrus pages together, realizing very quickly that it wasn't as thick as it was made to seem—a third of the thin document had been redacted.

At two minutes to 5:00 p.m., there was a knock on the door. Upon Pelly's permission, the servants allowed the former viscount to enter. He bowed, then took the only empty seat. Maddock didn't mask his surprise and disdain when he saw the vigils seated. Had their Majesties forgotten yet another royal custom that they were allowing such disrespect from commoners?

Pelly went straight to the point, "Maddock, what do you know about hybrids?"

Maddock made a wild guess, "It sounds like what the word suggests, Your Majesty. The product of two different species."

"Like a vampire and a lycan, yes?"

"I suppose."

"Do you remember any vampire being with a lycan by any chance?"

The vigils were watching his reaction as well. Maddock checked his cards and said, "Once."

"And what happened in that case?"

"If memory serves me, the late Emperor Kosh ordered the execution of Lady Luisa Lybarth and her mate—a lycan official named Heros Pas."

"And?"

"That's . . . all I know, Your Majesty. I suggest studying the file containing this particular c—"

Exhaling in exasperation, she said, "I have studied the file, Maddock, and do you want to know what I found?" Pelly lifted the folder, flipped to the pages that troubled her, and then turned it for the document to face him. "Most of what I want to know has been redacted, so here's my question: why?"

"I wouldn't know, Your Majesty. The execution was a closed case long before the late emperor's death."

"You don't know who redacted a case in the royal archives, despite being the only one who would be given access to do such a thing because you led it?"

"I didn't do it, if that is what Your Imperial Majesty is suggesting."

"What I'm suggesting is that you know more than you're saying."

A pocket of silence filled the space. Maddock looked between the increasingly angry rulers before eventually saying, "When the plan was executed, I was sworn to secrecy." He cleared his throat, then continued, "Lady Luisa and Heros Pas were assassinated for what your late father deemed to be treason, which many couldn't imagine how. Rosalie was never a royal aid or anything of the sort in the first place. That decision did not help with the tension with the lycans at all. The untimely death of Heros Pas—one of the most prominent lycan officials— was one of the strongest bits of propaganda used by their kind to instigate hatred and disharmony, encouraging the wolves and lycans to kill us."

Pelly refuted, "Rosalie was closer than a royal aid. She was practically family. My father did something any ally would have done—avenge her death. As for Lady Luisa, wasn't she a close family friend of yours, Maddock?"

"She was, though I don't see how that's relevant."

"You both went to the same schools, took very similar courses, and attended the same events. Before she met Heros, you'd be her companion at those events."

Maddock kept a straight face. "You're suggesting that I was in love with her, Your Majesty?"

"Were you?" Pelly looked him dead in the eye, daring him to blink.

Maddock simpered before he murmured, "That was a long time ago."

"Are you saying you both were no longer friends at the time of executing the plan to get rid of her and her mate?"

The last part made Maddock subtly stiffen. "We weren't as close as we once were. That's all I can say about it."

Pelly glanced at the folder again. "When my father asked for someone to take lead for this particular task, I understand you volunteered?"

"I did."

Her brows arched. "And you expect me to believe that your initiative had nothing to do with wanting to help Luisa escape?"

Maddock considered his options, and since Pelly didn't have the Empress's Authority to choke the truth out of him, and anyone else who was involved in the task had passed on, Maddock chose to say, "I delivered what was asked of me. The task . . . amplified when we discovered the presence of two children. Never mentioning the infants . . . was a precaution taken to make sure the late emperor didn't have to abdicate the throne for cold-blooded murder."

Despite the uneasiness in her chest, Pelly's voice continued ringing steadily, "So the twins were killed after their parents?"

"That is my understanding, Your Majesty."

"You didn't *see* the children being killed?"

"No. My assignment was the parents. The twins were a separate task on their own because their governess took them away as soon as Luisa and Heros heard rumors about our plan. The search team took months before they were able to track down the governess and end her along with the children she took."

Octavia questioned, "Luisa sent her children away *without* going with them herself?"

"Yes," Maddock asserted. "And it's quite clever if you think about it. It would've been easier to find her children if she were with them, since we were already hunting her down. To keep her children safe, to give them the best chance of survival, she had the governess take them away."

Pelly questioned in disbelief, "How was Heros okay with that? He didn't do anything to keep Luisa safe, even if it meant temporarily separating her from their children?"

"I am not privy to what went on in the lycan's head, Your Majesty. All I know is that they were going to leave together on the night we found them in one of the Lybarth holiday estates, almost done packing when we knocked on the door." The way he said the word *lycan* didn't go unnoticed. There was judgment, distaste, perhaps even jealousy.

Pelly continued, "What were their reactions when they saw you and the two vigils you brought along that night?"

Maddock remained unperturbed. "They begged and pleaded. Luisa was in tears, asking me to let them go for old time's sake. But I gave the signal for the vigils to fire the beta-keratin arrows. We retrieved their bodies and returned."

Duica then asked, "How did you know that there was a child if there weren't any there to begin with?"

Maddock was surprised that a vigil spoke without being asked, and shot him a disapproving glare, as if waiting for an apology for what Maddock saw as discourtesy.

His wait backfired when Pelly prompted, "Did you not hear the question, or are you buying time to come up with something to cover a lie, Maddock?"

Maddock's shocked eyes returned to the empress. "I'm simply surprised that he spoke without permission, Your Majesty."

"If Duica and Dominic are in this room joining the discussion, they have been given permission to speak whenever they deem fit. Now, answer the question."

Masking his discontentment, Maddock said, "There were pacifiers and some of the infant's clothes scattered around the home."

Dominic pressed, "And how did you know there were twins? Those could belong to one child."

"Not if there were two sets of items that had each child's name on it." Maddock's sights returned to Pelly when he continued with the names, "Audax and Saxum."

The name Saxum was a dreaded thing to hear. Pelly then questioned, "Where were the children found?"

"The team reported it was in a nursing home where the governess later sought shelter and employment."

Octavia's voice rose in more suspicion, "Why is it that you speak as if you're not sure about what truly happened to the children, that what you know is merely from a report? What was the evidence showing that the twins ended in that gruesome manner?"

"Unfortunately, technology wasn't with us at that time, Your Majesty, so I can't provide any pictures to prove what I'm saying. If necessary, I'll happily provide a deposition to replace those redacted pages."

After a long moment of silence, Pelly spoke, "That would be helpful. We'll ask our lawyer to contact you for the session within the next three days."

The empress stood, signaling Maddock's cue to leave. He stood with a smile. "I look forward to it, Your Majesties. I shall take my leave now. Thank you for your time."

He stepped out, and the moment the door shut behind him, Duica felt the duty to say, "Your Majesties, I'm not saying that whatever Maddock said was a lie, but not everything may be the truth."

Pelly murmured, "I agree. We're taking his words with a grain of salt."

Octavia complained, "Or a pot of it. The downside of digging up the past is that there is no one else to verify or debunk his facts."

Dominic, being encouraged to speak when Duica did it, said, "The facts about the late lady seem rather unbelievable if you ask me. Did anyone see the way he spoke when he described the assassination?"

Deep in thought, Duica uttered, "He showed no sadness. Or remorse. It's odd."

Dominic continued, "Even if he had moved on from the lady, which I doubt, seeing how his voice softened when she was mentioned, there should have been some kind of emotion, especially when he was talking about killing an old friend or past lover. There has to be some anger, at the very least. Or jealousy. Or loss. Guilt, even. The fact that his face remained straight is very concerning."

Rage and helplessness pulsed through Pelly. If only she had the Authority like past rulers, she'd be able to simply extract the truth from Maddock. She wondered if the Forest of Oderem would be so kind as to curse whoever lied to those it gifted its protection marks to. She doubted it. Nothing in history recorded such a thing had ever happened.

Octavia suggested, "With time, I'm sure the truth will reveal itself. For now, let's just wait for his deposition while we send word to the lycans about this pen you retrieved. We'll notify you once we get an update."

The vigils got the cue to leave, so they bowed and left, leaving the rulers alone.

That was when Pelly went straight to the point with her wife, "Sometimes, I wonder if what Aunt Lucy said is true—that I have the Authority but it's not . . . awakened."

Octavia felt her disappointment. Hands caressing Pelly's shoulders, the consort tried to assure her as best as she could, "Well, she's never been wrong, has she?"

The rhetorical question made Pelly chuckle. "I keep wondering how she manages that. Never being wrong. Not about Dad. Not about me."

Octavia's hand went to Pelly's cheek, gently lifting her face for their eyes to lock. Her emerald eyes were a sight that would make Octavia melt in happiness every single time, even after being together for so long. She muttered, "Lucy saw something in you when she was Rosalie. She still sees something in you now. Perhaps it's time to see yourself through her lenses, Pelly. Remember what she said the other day? About you not being any less extraordinary without that power?"

A soft smile brightened Pelly's features. She reached out to stroke Octavia's hand as she whispered gratefully, "Thank you, my love."

Octavia pressed a kiss in her hair before pulling her out of her seat because it was time for their nap, but not before sending a photo of the pen to Lucy first.

###

At her end, Lucy forwarded the message to the ministers, alliance members, and Greg.

Greg studied the pen in a laid-back position of his office chair after reading about the vigils' report on . . . nothing. That was what the report was on—absolutely nothing. As he mumbled to himself on how the bad weather had cursed the already less-than-competent bloodsuckers, he found his ranting come to a stop when his eyes fell on the familiar carving of a planet near the tip of the fountain pen.

His back shot up, leaning forward, staring at the carving for another few more moments before murmuring, "You traitor." He didn't even run things through with Lucy before linking his top four in an anger-suppressed growl, *'Locate Neptune. Now.'*

CHAPTER 49

In the part of the kingdom bordering the empire, Ella and the others were in Neptune's warehouse, where Neptune claimed no one ever came unless he authorized them to come. He had an older warehouse, too, but using it wasn't smart since the authorities would've already found the abandoned hut. If the duke somehow managed to figure out the hut belonged to Neptune, he might send his followers to other old, vacated properties to look.

This was simply a precaution because Neptune doubted Greg Claw would know the hut belonged to him when he deliberately left it out of the duke's annual check on rogue assets. Greg did this check to ensure that rogue assets either remained off the authorities' radar or were registered to be legitimate in the authorities' systems.

The hut was in a well-hidden location, and Neptune liked it to be kept from the duke because it made him feel superior to Greg in a way—that he knew something Greg didn't, even if it were about something as petty as an abandoned shelter.

In the warehouse, Isla and five other children were falling ill. The coughs were making their throats sore and voices hoarse. At first, it became a game among the kids to see who had the greatest change in voice, but the playful mood ended when their bodies weakened. Two of them were struggling to keep their eyes open as their bodies gradually heated up. Their parents—including Isla's—urged Ella to bring it up with Saxum, to tell him that whatever the Callows were doing might be causing their children's illnesses.

The administrative hybrids stood at the corner for a discussion on their next move, with Neptune and Klementine in their circle.

Saxum began, "Rudolpho knows a few good spots in wolf territory. He explored it with a friend of his. We can go there next. I particularly like Bordure's location. It's the safest out of all our options."

Klementine questioned skeptically, "Is that even wise, Saxum? The Blue Crescent attack would've placed every other wolf pack on high alert."

"We won't have to hide there long. The Callows have the modified chemical ready. We're waiting for the delivery of capsules. The decipimus will ingest it and control the king from there. The rest of us hybrids will ingest the shell, just in case. We should discuss our plan of attack, so . . ."

Ella backtracked the discussion when she questioned, "Saxum, what do you mean we're leaving for wolf territory? Have you seen the kids? They can't travel."

Saxum glanced at the sick children coddled in their mothers' arms and back at an almost-fuming Ella as he calmly explained, "We have to hide."

"We are hiding! Running to wolf territory is not a good move, especially after angering one of the strongest packs. And you're certain about the safety of this new location because Rudolpho's friend says that it's safe? Have you ever met this friend of his?" Ella gestured at Rudolpho, who took umbrage and was about to say something.

But before he could, Saxum responded instead, "No, but I've met Rudolpho and so have you. He's standing right here among us. The authorities may be closing in, Ella. We have to move. We don't have a choice."

"We do have a choice, Saxum. The choice is *not* to go there and open ourselves to getting caught."

"We have the decipimus to help if wolves do eventually find us."

Ella challenged, "You're certain the decipimus amongst us are enough to hold off a wolf attack, bearing in mind that the children can't run fast enough, some adults are tired and weakening?"

Saxum knew Ella. He knew her to be obedient her whole life, and if she was speaking against this, there must be a reason. Reluctantly, he asked, "What do you suggest we do?"

Without hesitation, she hissed, "Pull the plug, Saxum. Tell the Callows to stop."

Chong exclaimed, "Are you mad?"

Regina added, "Out of the question! We've already come this far."

Ella gestured to the sick ones, her voice now an angered whisper, "And look what it has cost us!" Her sights went back to a contemplating Saxum. "You have to admit that this can't be a coincidence. Delancy only died a day after the

Callows killed their first vampire. They're tampering with the vampire children's anatomy to modify the chemical right now, aren't they, Saxum?"

A dead silence lasted two long seconds before Saxum admitted, "It was the most malleable component they needed, children being less susceptible to heeding to any Authority."

That did it. That snapped her thread of patience and obedience. She took a step closer, uttering with angry tears, "The deal was that the children remained *off*-limits, Saxum. This is crossing the line. We didn't agree to this."

"Look, Ella. I understand you care for the little ones, but we've come this far . . ."

"You're still going through with this?" she asked, infuriated. "So it doesn't matter that more of us are going to die?"

"Any death would be in vain if we don't finish this. Stopping now won't bring the dead back to life, Ella." His orbs held deep melancholy as his voice weakened toward the end.

"This isn't just about Delancy, Saxum. It's all of us. Look at those parents. Do you want them to end up feeling what you're feeling?"

Saxum could see that the inferno in her eyes was nowhere near the cooling edge, and to him, she wasn't in a good state of mind to listen to reason, so all he said was, "Why don't you go for a walk and calm down. When you come back, we'll talk."

That got her even more enraged, fire upon fire. He actually thought *she* was being the unreasonable one? "I am not overreacting, Saxum. I'm the one trying to keep them safe. You can't possibly disagree that the more we push this, the more likely we'll lose lives. Is it even worth it?"

Without hesitation, Saxum replied, "It is. If you've lived in the shadows for as long as some of us have—for as long as I have—you'd know that harmonious reconciliation is naive, wishful thinking. The only way to guarantee safety for everyone is to fight for control."

Ella couldn't believe her ears. Their original plan of having something to shield them from danger had now turned into a plan to control the highest power at all cost, even if it meant sacrificing their own. How was he okay with this? How was it that none of the administrators but her had an emotional attachment to the other hybrids, especially to the kids?

Registering her silence, Saxum prompted, "Go for a walk, Ella. You'll feel better."

She expelled heated breaths, then trotted out of the warehouse, barging into the forest, and stepped on every twig in her path, savoring the sound in each snap. After the silence and thickness of the forest cooled her a little, she thought about Isla. Ella felt so helpless when she held the girl in her arms earlier that morning. How was she an administrator when she couldn't even fight against sacrificing more lives?

Then, it hit her.

Maybe she wasn't as helpless as she thought.

With each step she took, she began forming a plan—a plan that might save Isla and the rest of the weakening children. She had seen an old map of wolf, lycan, and vampire territories in one of the old books, so she roughly knew where she was and where the routes around her led.

When Ella mentally ran through her plan for possible loopholes, her walk turned into a run. As her feet hit the ground in gradual succession, it was clear there was only one thing she needed to make sure everything went smoothly—speed.

CHAPTER 50

It was early evening when the royal family, alliance members, ministers, warriors, mavericks, and ten vigils were at Bordure—the part of wolf territory that was most susceptible to rogue attacks when attacks used to be frequent because of its significant distance from larger and stronger packs.

They were also here because these packs were the closest to vampire territory and—according to Greg—rogue lycan territory. No pack leader reported seeing any rogues or proditors, but the fact that this was the most vulnerable part of wolf territory *and* a rendezvous point for Kate and Rudolpho made them pick this particular location to stand guard.

They stood between the wolf packs and the neighboring territory ahead, hoping for an uneventful evening. The instructions were simple: stand guard, and if nothing happens, half will return to Polje for decipio practice that night.

Everyone formed temporary mind-links, just in case. Juan was pleasantly surprised that all Xandar did when Lucy was forming a link with Greg was stand and watch. Even after the link was formed, Xandar didn't grab her hand and lick it like Juan thought he would. As soon as Greg moved on to the next creature, as did Lucy, Xandar shifted his attention and locked gaze with his brother-in-law.

Juan linked, *'Surprising improvement, Xandar.'* His chin gestured at Lucy as he half raised his own hand.

Xandar smiled sheepishly. *'I'm trying. It still bothers me sometimes.'*

Greg hadn't been inappropriate thus far, just annoying. Plus, it wasn't as if Lucy had shown the mildest interest in his cousin, so Xandar and his animal came to terms that there wasn't a need to show who Lucy belonged to. Everyone knew, and everyone respected that.

When the links were formed, Xandar went to Lucy, pulling her into him, looking into her eyes, and muttering, "If and when he links you, tell me, okay?"

He didn't even need to be specific for her to know he meant Greg. "Of course, just as you'd tell me if any woman happens to link you, I presume?"

The teasing tone lightened Xandar's mood before he pointed out the obvious, "Babe, you know I tell you everything."

"So do I . . . except for that time when Margaret almost attacked us. Then again, I *was* going to tell you . . . just not right away." Her eyes darted to his shoulder, recalling the events from the other day.

Xandar's nose gently nudged hers to get her attention again, and with furrowed brows, he insisted, "Right away this time, promise?"

Lucy was pulled into the only pair of lilac orbs that generated all kinds of emotions—light, deep, safe, strong. With her doe eyes, she whispered, "I promise."

Xandar smile, then closed his eyes for his nose to press against her hair. Only after that did he give into his little freesia's pestering about needing to take their places.

A team of ten was sent to the exact location Margaret and her followers used to reside at, to check the vicinity for a probable rendezvous point. Jade had been keeping tabs on Kate's phone, waiting for incoming calls or messages, but there was nothing. He even impersonated Kate by sending a few messages to Rudolpho, but there were no replies.

Jade would have suspected that Rudolpho was alerted about the forceful change of ownership of the device, but the last message was days before Kate was caught, so the only logical conclusion was that Rudolpho had ghosted her.

Temporarily or permanently? No one knew. Not even Kate knew this when Lucy made the trip to the police station to ask the additional questions the mavericks needed answers to. Kate did say the rendezvous point with Rudolpho was somewhere in the forest where the trees grew so high that their branches and leaves formed a canopy, dimming the forest.

The team of lycans and vigils, along with Margaret and Tate, marched through forest trees. As serious as things were, Tate couldn't stop himself from lacing his fingers with Margaret's, whose insides fired up in excitement when she felt his rough skin against hers. She wondered if it was even possible that her heart felt like it was pulled closer to his simply by holding his hand. The sensation was as soothing as it was magical.

When Margaret's thumb began nervously stroking the back of Tate's hand, the alpha was so surprised that he paused in his steps and looked straight at his beautifully flushed mate. He didn't expect her to make a move, especially not now when they weren't even on a date.

His lips twisted into a smile before he leaned in to kiss Margaret's left cheek, which was when she pulled his lips into a deep kiss. Tate's eyes shot wide open at first, but his impatient wolf got him to snap out of it, and his lips began responding to hers in equal enthusiasm. His tongue danced with hers, then delved deeper to explore her inner walls, tasting her as the sparks coursing through their beings brought every part of them to life.

When their lips parted, slowly coming back to reality, they came to terms that those with them were either looking away out of courtesy or looking straight at them with teasing smiles.

This was not the place Tate imagined when he thought about their first kiss. It was more than perfect to him, but it was also unexpected. Peering into her shining rosewood eyes, he muttered, "Looks like I'm not the only one with a serious timing issue, Mar."

Margaret broke free and barged forward, struggling to suppress a smile. "You started it with the unnecessary hand-holding."

Tate chuckled before matching her pace, sliding his hand back into hers. "Well, if unnecessary hand-holding ends up with us making out, I really don't see the point in not doing it."

Just when Margaret's mouth opened to deliver a retort, her eyes turned bright red, and Tate's smile fell, his humor instantly replaced with frantic worry when he held her close to ease the ordeal that was on the verge of hitting his mate.

What Tate didn't realize was that—unlike the previous times—Margaret felt very little anguish even without their skin contact. It was as if when Margaret chose to take a leap of faith, to start welcoming a new life while making peace with her past, she was liberated. She was liberated from feeling like an outcast, from letting her upbringing in the majority conventional society of Fleet Wood dictate how she—as a rogue—was supposed to feel, how she should react, how she should live. Freeing herself from her past gave her strength and psychological stability, allowing her red wolf to amplify its power.

Now in her vision, Margaret saw wolves and lycans battling with eyes darkened from decipio manipulation. They were maneuvering around as their noses sniffed the space. And many new faces were present, snarling at them as they attacked. Margaret tried to concentrate on the surroundings to find that precise location. The moment she recognized it, her vision ended.

After the team of ten left, everyone else took their places along the border separating the two territories. After a while, Lucy picked three leaves from a plant nearby and started weaving as she stood guard. When she felt the prickling of her skin—telling her someone was staring at her—she traced it to the source and found herself looking at her husband, who had his arms crossed as his smiling eyes met hers.

'Focus, my king. You're supposed to be looking up ahead, not at your side.'

'Mm . . . but I prefer the view at my side, my queen,' his coquettish response came, and his animal saw the need to emit the dangerous and alluring growl through their link.

She noticed the six smiling creatures standing between Xandar and herself had taken a step or two back to give the king and queen an unobstructed view of one another, one of the six being her brother. She then linked Xandar, *'Maybe I should stand a little further away to make things easier for you, darling.'*

Xandar's eyes widened and his smile faltered. *'You wouldn't.'*

'Then eyes up ahead, Xandar.'

Xandar shifted his body so that it faced her before he replied, *'I am looking up ahead.'*

Lucy was more frustrated by her inability to press back her smile and control her blushes than she was of Xandar twisting her words. She was now trying very hard to cool down her burning cheeks with the back of her hands, and her reaction tickled Xandar's heart so much that his animal began cooing and wagging its tail while his human part smiled even wider at the gorgeous sight.

But that blissful moment came to an end when he and his animal felt Lucy's humor and irritation die down—when her eyes glazed over. Her confusion was evident from her face and their bond.

Juan wondered if his youngest son was linking the favorite aunt again. He quickly checked in with Hale to make sure everything was fine in Blue Crescent. Luna Hale assured him that nothing was happening out of the ordinary and Liam was right next to her, reading a book. Eyes clear.

When Juan came out of his link, his eyes locked with Xandar's still-perplexed ones, and the alpha shrugged. "Not a message from my pack, Xandar. It's probably from Tate or someone else from the team of ten."

In the midst of the link, Lucy tried to wrap her head around how this person had managed to link her without them ever forming a mind-link in the first place.

CHAPTER 51

Ella stepped into the empire's civilization, wondering if she was in the right place. She pulled up her gray hoodie, trying to draw as little attention to herself as possible, not knowing if it was smart to go invisible. She decided against it, not wanting other discreti to think that she had something to hide. She was glad to see that whoever else was on the street hid their heads as well, but they did it because they hated the early evening sun and wanted as little of it as possible.

On her way here, Ella already knew she'd have to hide her eyes since their blue color didn't match the green ones of the population. Trying to find something that would do the trick, something outside the subway station suddenly caught her attention. It was an advertisement for contact lenses in five distinct colors, and the model's eyes were blue, like hers.

Ella's face morphed into confusion as her head cocked, trying to fathom the concept of contact lenses.

Two ladies with shopping bags and blood-flavored slushies in their hands noticed her discombobulation. Their nosiness forbade them from taking another step, making them join Ella at the advertisement board when one of them said, "Don't bother with this brand. It's a safety hazard."

Blinking in surprise, Ella asked, "W-What?" She wasn't even sure if talking to someone was part of her plan.

The same lady pointed at the board and explained, "They should've taken this down two days ago. Someone bought contacts from this company, but the color from it peeled and entered her eyes. After the surgery to remove the color fragments, she filed a suit, asking for hundreds of thousands to cover the medical costs. I think she bought the purple ones."

"Oh," Ella responded, not knowing what else to say.

The other one was sucking on her slushy before she said, "If you're looking for good contacts, try Optimum. That one's been around here forever. No lawsuits whatsoever. Where do you get yours, by the way?"

"Uh . . . Optimum, actually." Even Ella was surprised by how smoothly that lie came out. She wasn't even sure she heard the lady right.

The lady turned to her friend and said, "See, I said it remains the most popular brand, and I was right. That other gal we saw earlier uses Optimum, she uses Optimum . . ."

They were walking away before Ella called out, "Hey, um . . . could you tell me where the rulers live?"

They turned and blinked, and the second one questioned, "The empress and consort?"

"Yes."

They found her question rather odd, and began scrutinizing her attire to decipher which region she might have been from. Everyone in their town knew where the castle was. But Ella's clothes were too generic for them to pinpoint her origin, even with the knowledge they had on the stereotypical dressing of foreigners. They didn't want to be late for their ride, so the first lady pointed to her right and said, "Go around the corner, walk until you see the custodes station, then make a right, and keep going until you see the castle."

"Thank you!" Ella exclaimed out of pure relief, and dashed away.

The two friends exchanged odd looks before waving their transit cards and waiting on the platform. "What do you think? Is she from Occidens or Orientem? Her accent *is* different but I can't tell how. Like, from which region?"

Ella followed the directions, but after a minute, she wondered if she was being too trusting to only ask one set of individuals. Her doubts were put to rest when she walked past the custodes station, where she saw creatures in uniforms. She made right like she was told, and blocked out Saxum's link for the third time since she left, before striding as quickly as her legs could manage.

The sight of the castle sent a stream of pure relief through her. The upward curl of her lips radiated elation, until she saw the guards.

How was she going to get in?

Pelly heard the knocks on her bedroom door. She was waiting for Octavia to get ready when she went to answer it. At the sight of one of the castle's guards, she asked, "Yes, Dolly?"

Dolly appeared apologetic. "Forgive my intrusion, Your Majesty, but there's a young woman requesting an immediate audience with you and the consort. She claims to be a hybrid." Pelly took a long blink, failing to hide her surprise. Dolly continued, "She said her name is Ella. The guards at the gates tried to get rid of her, but she said something about needing to warn you that the lycan queen will be in danger, and something about hybrid children dying because of some experiment? And she said she was a bonded mate of Tobias Tristan, claiming to have met him on a beach. Isn't Tristan one of the kingdom's ministers, Your Majesty?"

Octavia was next to her by now. Pelly took a moment before stepping out of the room, pacing down the corridor while asking, "Eye color?"

"Blue, Your Majesty."

"What did she smell like?"

"Apples and gardenias."

"Send her in."

The guards brought Ella into Pelly's study, where she blurted everything she knew and begged the rulers to find a way to stop the whole thing before any more hybrids were sacrificed.

Dolly and her colleague kept looking at their Majesties throughout the confession, waiting for the signal to arrest this woman for treason, abduction, false imprisonment, and a whole line of other things that could make a very lengthy case in court. But Pelly's and Octavia's eyes never left the frantic hybrid.

At the end of it, Ella was already taking quickened breaths when Pelly asked, "Do you know whether they've moved on to the next location without you by now?"

"No. I've been blocking out Saxum's links. Regina's as well."

Octavia clarified, "If they chose to move, you said that they'd be going to wolf territory?"

Ella nodded.

"*Which* part of wolf territory?" Pelly asked, eyes wide, breath held.

The moment Ella said, "It might be Bordure," Octavia linked Rafael and the rest of the vigils and custodes.

Pelly rummaged through the papers on her table for her phone as she muttered, "C'mon, where is it? Where is it?"

Pelly's urgency and the persistent way she was picturing Lucy in her head made something miraculous happen—her eyes glazed over and her rummaging was brought to a brusque halt when she heard Lucy's confused voice ringing through her mind, *'Pelly, I don't recall forming a mind-link with you.'*

Pelly stayed silent for a second before skipping over the formalities, practically yelling through the link, *'Aunt Lucy, Ella is here. In the castle. She said the next location the hybrids are planning to run to is most likely Bordure.'* Lucy held her breath as Pelly continued, *'The hybrid children are falling ill. Ella kept emphasizing the need to end this before any little ones die. Octavia and I are leaving for Bordure now. We're bringing everyone at our disposal. Aunt Lucy, should you see the hybrids first . . . please don't engage in battle until we get there.'*

At Lucy's end, a sudden howl pierced through the air—the kind of howl that wolves and lycans used to warn each other about an incoming attack. Her head turned in the direction of the sound, where the team of ten was sent, and she saw the vigils, shifted wolves, and lycans retreating.

At the sight of a few foreign faces that were gradually increasing in number, Lucy ran toward them as she linked Pelly as calmly as she could, *'Pelly, get here as soon as you can. We might be able to slow this down, but there's no doubt the battle is starting soon.'*

Pelly cursed before Lucy ended the link.

CHAPTER 52

Sprinting across the space, Lucy growled in a way that made the new faces halt. Some even took a few steps back. She positioned herself between them and her people, as did Xandar, Greg, Christian, Phelton and the alliance members, who stood by her side, claws already out.

Xandar's hand at Lucy's abdomen made sure she didn't take another step further as they assessed the situation.

Lucy linked the vigils by her side, *'Anyone familiar besides Rudolpho?'*

'Not at the moment, Your Highness.'

No one could help but take a slightly longer look at Rudolpho, who was scanning faces, undoubtedly looking for the only one that mattered.

Lucy put his search to a stop when she said, "Kate isn't here."

Rudolpho's eyes snapped to hers in shock before quickly looking away. And those around him began muttering questions like, "Who's Kate?" It was surprising to everyone on Lucy's side to see Rudolpho mouth, "My contact."

Your contact? That was it? A few hybrids even asked whether someone called Hilda knew about Kate, and what she thought about him having contact with another female. They all knew he had a contact in wolf territory, but they assumed it was a man.

Alissa shook her head when she recognized the traits of a cheater who had been caught red-handed. Lucy and Greg exchanged a brief gaze when they, too, understood the game that had been played against Kate.

Sympathy for Kate channeled through the queen, but this wasn't a sentiment shared by everyone. Greg's animal was scoffing at how Kate had just gotten double-crossed after double-crossing Howard and betraying everyone. "Karma at its finest," the duke thought.

Saxum linked his people, prohibiting further interrogation of Rudolpho, and claimed that he was given full authorization to do what he did. Although the hybrids obeyed their leader's command, their mental gears were still turning. Several linked Hilda in secret, only to be told that Rudolpho's partner of three decades had never heard of Kate.

The moment Saxum's eyes cleared, he was pulled into the penetrating gaze of a pair of black-and-lilac orbs. Lucy asked, "I'm assuming you're Saxum?"

Saxum registered Xandar's aura and then Lucy's own before he noted, "You must be the queen."

He would've guessed who she was even without her aura announcing so. She truly was as beautiful as the rumors went. Even Saxum, who had seen so many females in his lifetime, had to admit her beauty was only second to Delancy's. It was a pity they were on opposite sides.

Lucy got to the point, "We are not out to kill hybrids, nor are the rulers of the empire. End this. We can give you a place. You don't have to kill to secure your or your people's safety."

Many were shocked. How did she know so much? Saxum connected the dots and linked it to the still-missing and unreachable Ella. Everyone behind him started calling bullshit on Lucy's promise, thinking she was simply luring them into a trap.

Those on her side knew their opponents were going to strike soon, and Lucy wondered if her Authority would work on hybrids. They were technically half of the species she could control. She was thankful that there weren't any children present . . . unless they were all already dead? The possibility that they were too late sent a surge of sadness into her heart.

Xandar retracted his claws and stroked her hand as he issued a low warning to the hybrid leader, "Whatever you've been told about a hybrid massacre, Saxum, there has to be a flip side of the coin you don't know about. The empress was given a different set of facts. Ask your people to stand down and let's discuss this."

"Discuss?" One of Saxum's brows rose like the word was a strange concept. He scoffed darkly and said, "You think you can discuss a slaughter that happened before you existed?"

Xandar countered, "If you are right about what happened, you should consider the fact that we are not our ancestors. Just because our predecessors didn't treat your kind right, it doesn't mean we won't. We have nothing against hybrids. There is no need to challenge us to feel safe. The rogues you're collaborating with aren't worth the . . ."

Saxum's chuckles intending to humiliate Xandar cut him off midway, which made Lucy's eyes flare as she attempted to step forward, only to be pushed back by her overprotective husband. Those by the king's side took their positions, ready to charge.

Saxum spoke, "For a king, I expected a little more . . . ferocity, if I were being honest."

Lucy took over, "For a leader, we expected you to possess more common sense, if we were being honest." The leader's taunting sights turned into ones of fury when he glared at the petite queen. Before he could get a word in, she proceeded to say, "If you do this, what makes you better than the ones you say killed your family?"

Saxum noted with a cocky smirk, "I will win."

"No you won't. At least not without a price." Although Lucy looked confident on the outside, she was struggling to remain calm within, wondering how much longer she could delay the hybrids. "You already know how we know so much. She came to us because she didn't want another hybrid to die from your expedition of trying to kill me. How many of your own people are you willing to sacrifice before calling it quits, Saxum? Is losing the creatures closest to you really worth all of this?"

Saxum swallowed a lump in his throat and bit his teeth to hold back tears before he spat, "The one closest to me is already dead. I will fight this because I will not let her sacrifice be in vain."

"Did she sacrifice *for* the quest, or was she sacrificed *because* of it?" she questioned.

This didn't just get Saxum thinking. It made his own followers grow contemplative. Saxum's train of thought was pulled to a stop when his eyes returned to Lucy. "You're playing me. You're tricking me into surrendering."

Lucy simply responded, "I do want you to surrender, Saxum. But none of what I said is trickery. Your own logic will tell you that this is going to cost lives. It's going to sacrifice not just my people but yours as well. Don't do this."

Fast-growing seeds of doubt grew into full-grown trees in Chong. Regina and their toddler were still at Neptune's warehouse because their child was too sick to travel. All the children were. Those who came to Bordure were just here to scout the site after Ella expressed her skepticism, so not everyone came. They didn't expect to run into anyone.

Chong had been with Regina for almost a century before they were blessed with a child. He didn't want to leave without watching his little boy grow. He was confident about their plan at first, but now, he wondered if the queen was right, that some of them really might end up dead. And it was odd to him that neither the queen nor king had used their Authorities on him—a pure-bred wolf—yet.

With much hesitance, he linked Saxum, *'What if they're right?'*

Saxum glared at Chong, who was right next to him. *'We have the chemical to overpower the King's Authority. They have nothing to challenge that. That's why they're asking us to give in, Chong!'*

'What if the Queen's Authority overp—'

'Look at them!'

Chong did. The king and queen looked like a very close couple, a very devoted couple, one that would put each other's lives before their own.

Saxum linked him again, *'She. Won't. Kill. Him.'*

'But should he kill her?' Chong questioned in dismay. He wouldn't mind if Regina killed him from a decipio's manipulation, but he could never forgive himself if he was manipulated into killing the love of his life. He might just take his own life out of remorse and heartbreak.

'Listen here, Chong. We have deals to uphold, promises to keep. Delancy has already given her life for this. There's no . . .'

'Delancy didn't give her life for this, Saxum. Her life was taken because of this. There's a huge difference. She was killed from an illness not even Zepine knew of and—coincidentally—after the first abducted vampire was sacrificed in the triplets' experiment. That's how the Forest of Oderem works: a life for a life. The forest took away the creature you loved most because the one who died must have been someone with a significant other. We can manipulate the king to kill the queen, but it's not going to end well for us in the long run. The forest's curses overpower everything.'

Saxum turned to fully face the creature he thought was his loyal friend and follower, who would support him no matter how high the stakes were. First the obedient Ella went rogue, and now Chong was chickening out?

'Chong, think very carefully about the stand you're taking. Ella's rebelliousness will not go unpunished.'

Chong's eyes drilled into Saxum's when he declared, *'Ella went against all of us because the sick children were the last straw for her. She asked us to pull the plug, but we paid no heed. If she can stand for our people without having any blood ties with any of them, it doesn't take much to comprehend that I will stand with making sure my son won't end up dead.'*

'Your son is going to join Delancy if we don't follow through with what we've started. Rudolpho already said the king and queen share close ties with the empress and consort. Should the latter pair ask for our decimation, what do you think the former would do?'

Chong didn't know how to answer that, so he walked around the question. *'Saxum, all I know is that neither of them is using their Authorities on me or on any other pure-bred wolf or lycan here. They don't want this fight.'*

Saxum took one step closer. *'Do you want this fight?'*

In a firm, defiant tone, Chong said aloud, "No."

Chong howled in anguish when Saxum's claws went right through his guts, ripping them out before snapping his neck. At the warehouse, Regina drew everyone's attention when she shrieked at the sudden abdominal penetration that no one could see. When Chong's neck was snapped, Regina's screams and wails filled the entire warehouse as those who had no children came to see what the commotion was about. The physical excruciation ended only to be replaced by an emotional loss when the other end of the mate bond became cold and barren. Lifeless. Non-existent.

On the battleground, Lucy's eyes bulged wide as her breathing got heavy. When Chong's lifeless body fell to the ground, Saxum's eyes locked with hers, and her look of dismay was replaced by one of disappointment and anger.

There was nothing that could stop Saxum. He was determined to finish this.

Greg knew it, too, so he linked his followers, *'Everyone knows the drill: protect her at all costs.'*

'Yes, Your Grace.'

Saxum scoffed at Lucy's expression. "Your mind tricks work on some people, probably because he was your kind, but not on me." They exchanged hard stares for the next few moments before Saxum taunted, "Still don't have the urge to commence attack even after what you've seen?"

Lucy simpered. "I know how this will go down in history. Until you attack, don't expect us to make a move."

Saxum found himself matching her smirk as he stated the obvious, "When one is in power, history . . . is something that can be rewritten. If you've talked this long to buy yourselves time, then your luck just ran out. It's time to play."

The moment Lucy felt the mental walls building up, she allowed her animal to push forward. The thickest stripe on her tail glowed in bright blue as she not only broke the mental walls but also tried to compel every opponent that she could compel to stand down. Xandar used his Authority as a shield, helping his people push back the manipulation the same way Lucy did for everyone back in Blue Crescent, and they charged forward.

It was on the tip of Greg's tongue to say it was going to be too easy, seeing they'd been familiarizing themselves with a decipio's power and both the Authorities were obviously giving them the upper hand, but the duke chose to save that cocky declaration for later, when they actually won.

Some hybrids found it harder to move, but Lucy soon realized she couldn't completely compel them since the vampire part of their genes wasn't tailored to heed to a lycan's Authority. Those with a dominant wolf or lycan genotype were easier to compel, whereas those with a dominant vampire genotype—like Saxum—were much more difficult to coerce.

Many vampires were trying to distract her by appearing behind her or getting in her way, which made holding the hybrids with her power slightly more difficult. It was especially hard to target the discretus hybrids since she couldn't see them to compel them. Her allies came to help, but this in no way made it easier to pinpoint her targeted creatures.

As Xandar held the shield for his people, he targeted the proditors who were in his way of getting to Saxum. The king landed punches and broke his victims' limbs before throwing them at trees to render them unconscious or kill them if the proditors were still stubborn about attacking despite being injured. He found beating them to be surprisingly easier than he had anticipated.

Then again, he had been training with his wife for months, beating her almost half the time now, so his speed and agility had improved tremendously. The veloces couldn't rival the king's speed. The fortes were the easiest to defeat. And after the manipulation practices with Pelly, the mental attacks by the decipimus on the ground weren't as insurmountable. The most annoying, thus far, were the invisible discreti.

The king even had a second here and there to briefly glance around the battleground to see how the others were faring, especially his wife and family. Lucy had help, and as soon as she was done tripping her opponent with her tail and kicking them in the head to knock them out cold, she and the one or two creatures with her moved on to the next one.

Christian was doing well, too, swiftly dodging attacks before delivering his own blows with techniques that Xandar himself had never seen him use, deducing it to be the result of Christian's weekly private training sessions with Lucy, which the duke always groaned and complained about yet continue taking.

Greg seemed to be enjoying himself a little too much for the king's taste, smirking right before he injured or killed his opponents.

Juan and the alliance members were doing better than fine too.

The only advantage Saxum had was in numbers, which was dwindling when more hybrids, proditors, and rogues either fell unconscious or dead. Even the discreti were decreasing when the vigils took them down one at a time.

After more attacks and kills, Xandar managed to reach Saxum. The king growled in rage as he pounced on the leader, which was when Saxum yelled, "NOW!"

Xandar broke Saxum's left elbow and tore off his right arm, neither indulging nor caring about the sharp shrieks coming out of Saxum's lungs even as he broke the leader's knees. But the moment the king reached for Saxum's neck, he paused. His eyes alternated between dark green and onyx, and the intrusion made Lucy kill her opponent just so she could see what was going on with her husband.

The decipio proditors who were given the capsules created by the triplets stood safely in high branches as they manipulated the lycan king. The shield that the King's Authority created for the lycans and werewolves was torn down, with the king losing focus and control over his own power and autonomy.

"Fuck," Greg muttered when he and the others felt the protection from his cousin vanish.

"Got that right," Juan, who was right behind him, agreed.

Saxum managed to crawl out of the king's hold when his elbow was healed, and he watched how the toughest animal in the kingdom was struggling to fight off the manipulation effects, internally cursing the triplets for not improving the chemical enough to take control of the king from the first second of manipulation.

Of course, the leader didn't know Xandar's mental strength was now superior to past lycan kings' since he was the only king in history to practice with the second most powerful decipio in the empire, so the lack of effectiveness of the chemical was technically not the triplets' fault. There was simply a variable that they didn't know had to be taken into consideration.

When the vigils were close to reaching Saxum, the proditors made Xandar shift and fling the vigils away. Instead of trying to reach Saxum again, the vigils went for the proditors, only to discover that there were more than thirty of them. Yes, thirty were manipulating the king. But there seemed to be a team B with another forty decipimus making sure the thirty were undisturbed as they intruded the minds of anyone who attempted to reach for team A.

Lucy tried to reach Xandar with her Authority, but three discreti caught her by surprise, tripping her before attempting to plunge their claws through her gut. Lucy caught their scents and tripped them with her tail. She pounced on the seemingly empty space and found herself standing right on top of one before her canines dug into the discretus's being, making the creature shriek and come into view.

One of the other remaining two was the female discretus's mate, and he, too, shrieked and appeared as he pushed Lucy off. Ivory arrived and broke the discretus's limbs before ultimately snapping his neck, then throwing his lifeless body at Hailey's opponent.

A third discretus was sneaking up on Lucy. Her claws were inches away from Lucy's chest when the queen identified her scent, narrowly dodging her attack by backing away before attempting to land a punch. That was when the discretus's claws went through her arm, and she groaned while pulling the discretus's arm right off with that attack.

As the discretus came into view with nothing short of anguish, anger, and hatred, she used her last ounce of strength to pounce on Lucy, making her fall to the ground. Before Lucy could push her away or kill her, the discretus bit into her shoulder, collarbone, and chin, letting the venom enter the queen's bloodstream.

Lucy only managed to scratch her opponent's face once before she started losing strength. Toby came to kick off the discretus, and his claws went straight into her chest. The minister turned the body over to hide the creepy, sinister smile of accomplishment on the now-dead discretus's face, then leaned forward to check on his best friend.

Lucy quivered as her immune system tried to fight off the high concentration of venom. Her own Authority that held their opponents wore off, giving them a surge of energy and unencumbered liberty to attack and defend. Those on her side were still holding up fine, but many were glancing at their queen, whose state offered the explanation of their opponents' sudden vigor.

Hailey, Ivory, Toby, and Dominic formed a circle around her, fighting off incoming attacks.

Lucy was trying to reach Xandar with her Authority again when she heard him groan in pain, which was most likely because he was feeling her pain.

Juan linked her, telling her to stop trying in the midst of recovery because it would only slow down the process. Whilst breaking necks and kneecaps, the big brother sternly told his sister to focus on herself for now if her ultimate aim was to help everyone else.

Lucy gave in because she couldn't find a plausible retort. But she began desperately trying to reach Xandar through their mind-link. Her animal cooed and whimpered, and they could tell that his animal felt her, but he was struggling to connect with her.

Toby shook her and exclaimed, "Lucy, quit it! If you want to stop him, you need your full strength, and you know that! Stop trying to use up whatever you have left. Your gamma mind knows you can stop him, but only if you just fucking let yourself recover!"

She continued quivering as she linked, *'O-kay. Je-ez.'*

To take her mind off Xandar's ordeal, she chanted the word *recover* in her head. Nothing she'd been through could beat the difficulty of blocking out Xandar's struggle, but she reminded herself and her animal that they were playing the long game. The proditors wouldn't kill Xandar—at least not before making him kill her—so Xandar was going to be fine.

The vigils and lycan warriors headed for the trees as soon as they could, but the decipimus were annoyingly skilled at jumping from branch to branch as they continued collectively taking control of the king's mind.

Team B was making their victims see things that weren't there, so many chose to close their eyes and use their noses to find their way around. Sure, they knocked into a few bushes and trees and each other, but that didn't stop a few of them from finding their way to those in the branches, which petrified those up there when they were being shown that their mental tricks weren't as effective as expected.

Xandar felt Lucy's agony, but he couldn't see her. He felt her, but he didn't know where she was. His awareness of reality slowly diminished along with his mental strength. With the final shred of awareness, he and his animal reminded each other to trust the scents and warmth of creatures or lack thereof before killing. His eyes turned dark green, and he snarled before charging toward his wife.

At that sight, Greg muttered, "Goddess damn it." The duke then linked the creature he had hoped he wouldn't have to link, *'Blackfur! We have to slow our dick cousin. Let's go!'*

Christian ignored Greg's insolence for once and focused on sprinting toward Xandar. Greg tripped Xandar just in time, and Christian pinned his knees to the ground. A fortis vigil helped pin Xandar by his left arm while Greg placed his full weight on Xandar's right.

Greg was beginning to question the Moon Goddess's intelligence and rationality when she decided to strengthen a creature with the mate bond. Did she consider such circumstances? Even with three of them holding the lycan king, they could feel Xandar would eventually break free.

When Greg saw Christian's eyes going to Lucy before glazing over, he immediately linked him first, *'Don't even think about hastening her, Blackfur. She's already trying as hard as she can.'*

Christian gave in to his burning urge to argue, *'What is it with you and always thinking you know everything?'*

'Well, am I wrong?'

'Yeah, you are. I was just going to ask the vigils when the empress and other decipimus were arriving. I wasn't going to link the queen.'

'It doesn't really matter when the other bloodsuckers will arrive, does it? Unless they can teleport here, we're on our own until they actually arrive.'

In the midst of their bickering, Xandar registered his cousins' scents and was made to think that his late father was still alive and was compelling Christian with his Authority, which was why his best friend was stopping him. It was easy to believe that Greg would take his favorite uncle's side without question.

Xandar growled in a way that shook the battleground as he spun his body to fling the vigil away before throwing Greg at a tree and flinging Christian to another tree. Both dukes grunted upon the impact, but only Greg had the strength to mutter, "Goddess, I hate you, Cousin."

When Greg saw how close he was to some of the decipio proditors, a light-bulb moment came. He picked up a few rocks and pebbles and started throwing them at the decipimus. His aim wasn't perfect, but he managed to make two fall from the trees when they lost their balance. The ones who fell met their demise when the wolves on the ground went straight for the kill. A few of the team B decipimus started trying to control Greg, and the duke managed to make one more proditor fall before his own animal made him close his eyes to avoid acting on reflex based on sight.

Once his nose confirmed the scents of those on the ground, his eyes opened and he killed every single creature whose scent he didn't find familiar, even though they were portrayed as his loyal followers and, in one case, the queen. That last one was—by far—the most difficult one to see his claws plunging through. He had to pause and breathe heavily for a moment as he and his animal assured one another that the creature stank too much to be Lucy.

Xandar was made to think that the ones around him were warriors and guards who were loyal to his father, and they were trying to stop him from attacking the parent he was after. In the manipulation, the late King Lucas and Queen Vera influenced Lucy to sever the mate bond with Xandar. Xandar "remembered" how painful it was to hear the words of rejection leaving her lips, how he sunk to his knees and begged her to take it back and give him a chance, to which she further refused, albeit with tears.

The manipulation went on to convince Xandar that Lucy was held in some underground dungeon that only the late king and queen knew the location of, and they were doing everything they could to keep Xandar from finding it while waiting for the next full moon so the mate bond between their son and the worthless wolf would be severed by default. Xandar seemed to think that his current plan was to choke the location out of his father. If that failed, the plan was to kill his father, then use the King's Authority, which he would subsequently inherit, to force the truth out of his mother.

His animal smelled warriors all around but felt that it didn't have the time to kill. He needed to find his mate! Xandar sprinted toward Lucy, who could finally feel her limbs again as she slowly stood.

Seeing her mate charging at her, she frantically linked those around her, *'Get out of here, all of you!'*

Toby was the first to respond, "Not a chance, Lucy."

Ivory insisted, *'We have strict instructions to . . .'*

'Damn it!' She either pushed or kicked away those stationed to protect her when Xandar pounced at her way with stuck-out claws. Her timing was—fortunately—impeccable. One second later and Ivory would've been dead, and Dominic could've broken more than a few bones. Lucy only retained a light scratch along her arm, which healed in seconds.

She dodged Xandar's attacks and tried to use her Authority to reach his animal. The decipimus in the trees saw the lycans and werewolves heading for the queen, and they got Xandar to emit his Authority to keep them at a distance.

It was as if Xandar's power had created an invisible wall, forming a circle that stopped any wolf or lycan from entering the perimeter. The manipulation told Xandar that it was his own father who kept those around them at a distance, wiping out the memory of channeling the power himself.

The warriors and alliance members looked at each other in dismay, as did the mavericks. How were they going to protect the queen when they couldn't even reach her?

CHAPTER 53

L ucy kept a safe distance from Xandar, trying to come up with a plan as he growled at her and took a wider stance to assert his dominance. In a low, threatening tone, Xandar linked his father, *'Tell me where she is, or I'll kill you* and *Mom.'*

That was when he realized something was off. There was nothing at the other end of the link. And it was even odder that he wasn't detecting his father's scent. He was smelling something unusual, beautiful—butterfly pea and jasmine. Despite being manipulated, he knew of only one creature who carried that scent, and his mood instantly softened.

'Xandar, darling,' Lucy linked gently as she took a hesitant step toward him.

When Xandar saw his father approaching, he snarled in defense to keep him at a distance. Lucy backed away, which was when he replied in the softest and gentlest tone, *'Lucianne, h-how are you mind-linking me? Wait, that's not important right now. Where are you, sweetheart? What do you see around you? I can smell you, but I can't see you. Tell me where you are, my love. Please. Let me come get you.'*

'I'm right here, Xandar. I'm right in front of you. If you're seeing someone else, know that it's not real. It's me. I'm standing right in front of you. Trust your nose. Feel me. I'm not whoever you're being made to see.'

His snarling came to a stop. His animal became more aware of the energy radiating from the creature standing before him. It exuded a warmth that touched his soul, wrapped his heart, and carried an inviting presence that gravitated him.

He knew his father. He was anything but inviting, especially when they didn't see eye to eye.

It was difficult to accept that he was staring at his mate when he could only see his father down to the finest details of the faint wrinkles on the old man's face. By instinct, he closed his eyes and took a few more moments to confirm that it was highly possible that it really was Lucy before taking slow, cautious steps toward her.

Juan, Toby, and Christian went the most berserk at the sight, thinking that Xandar was about to attack. Lucy raised a hand to get them to stop growling, shouting, or banging at the invisible wall.

The vigils came to help, but the moment they stepped into the space that no wolf or lycan could, Lucy's stop sign made them halt. They watched from a small distance, getting ready to push her away if Xandar lost control.

Very carefully, Lucy channeled her Authority. That was when Xandar—with eyes still closed—linked her again in awe, *'Lucianne, is that coming from you? That power. It feels like . . . like. . .'*

'Like an Authority?' she chuckled, melting his heart when she continued, *'I didn't know that it was, not until you told me.'*

'I told you?' he questioned in doubt as he went closer. Lucy stayed put, giving him time and letting him come to her.

'Yes, Xandar. About two weeks after we first met, you told me I had this power, that I was bestowed the Queen's Authority. You made me realize that I have it, that you felt it.'

'Two weeks . . .' Xandar was made to think that he never spoke to her again after the second day of finding each other—after she rejected him. The decipimus were trying to tamper with their mind-link, but there seemed to be a block, and that block was the Queen's Authority.

'Yes, Xandar. Two weeks. We were in my room when you told me about this. You explained how you channeled your own Authority, teaching me to channel mine.'

'Your room,' he repeated in an inaudible murmur. The mention of his own Authority completely bypassed his thoughts when full concentration was given to trying to recall being in her room, in a place so close, so intimate—one that he just couldn't remember. Then, something of higher priority hit him, and he blurted, *'Does this mean you're taking back your rejection?'*

He could feel amused disbelief, but it didn't feel like that emotion was his. He couldn't understand where it was coming from.

Lucy's firm link dominated his mind when she declared, *'Dearest, I never rejected you. I could never. I love you.'*

His animal cooed aloud, and the last three words made him so happy that he pounced on her before any vigil could stop him, which sent a second round of heart attacks amongst those watching.

After realizing that Lucy was still safe, the vigils sighed in relief, thanking the Lord. Toby used the invisible wall for support as he recovered from the shock. "Goddess, I'm going to die young with this amount of stress," he thought to himself.

Xandar's eyes were still closed as his tail wagged, which further infuriated the decipio proditors. Lucy could feel—from the reduced compression in Xandar's mind—that the thirty decipimus were down to twenty-three, and they were giving it their all, trying inexplicably hard to make Xandar see what they wanted him to see, trying to pull him away from her.

Some knew their plan was failing. The most strategic ones were already coming up with a plan B as they continued hoping that plan A would still pull through.

'You love me?' Xandar asked again, hovering over her, his nose close to her forehead. Oddly enough, this closeness felt familiar, though he couldn't recall a time they were in this position.

Lucy leaned closer to his nose as she linked affectionately, *'Of course I love you, Xandar. I'm your mate.'* In a possessive whisper, she added, *'And you're* mine.*'*

Without remembering he had the King's Authority, Xandar channeled the archaic power because that seemed to be the only way his animal knew to connect to the Queen's Authority, to connect with his mate.

The manipulation effects wore off in waves as their combined power cleared his mind. When his darkened green eyes returned to lilac, relief and elation cascaded through Lucy as she nuzzled his nose and the rest of his face.

His animal cooed and buried his face in her neck, greedily taking in her scent before he asked, *'Babe, I don't remember what exactly happened yet, but I'm going to think I was being manipulated. Can you tell me why I'm on top of you when we aren't in our bedroom?'*

She chuckled. *'Because you're my* indecent *beast, my king.'*

He pulled away and smirked, nudging her nose when he argued, *'I'm not* that *indecent.'* Getting off, he offered her his hand like a gentleman. *'Come, my queen. Let's finish this.'*

The decipio proditors put the impromptu plan B into action, manipulating the king and queen's allies and friends to attack them instead.

It didn't take as much force to mentally invade those without the king's strength and power, but the situation still annoyed the proditors because most of their victims were shutting their eyes and refusing to follow through with what they wanted them to do. Fake sounds were added just to get their victims to move in a particular direction. Everyone ended up running into trees and each other rather than letting the fabricated knowledge make them give into their urge to attack and kill.

Those who were manipulated by more skillful decipimus did end up attacking Lucy and Xandar, who had to watch each other's backs as they tried to channel their Authorities again.

Right before one sneaky discretus hybrid could plunge its claws right through Lucy's nape, a dash of breeze whizzed past Lucy, pushing the hybrid away and making him fall to the ground. The hybrid quivered in fear at the sight of a murderous pair of emerald eyes boring into his blue orbs.

Pelly plunged her claws right through the hybrid's being, relishing in his shrieks before Lucy's casual link calmed her down when the queen said, *'Oh. Hi, Pelly. You're here!'*

The empress got up, hurriedly dusted the dirt off her pants, and turned her attention to them when she said, "I am so sorry we're late, Aunt Lucy, Uncle Xandar."

Lucy replied, *'Don't worry about it. You're here now. Let's finish this. Saxum is somewhere over there, I think.'*

"On it." Pelly sprinted and went looking for the leader with Octavia and Amber right behind her, albeit catching up slower since neither of them had the abilities of a velox.

Saxum and a few alert and quicker decipimus had begun retreating the moment they saw Pelly and her forces entering the battlefield. Their instinct was to return to Neptune's warehouse, but logic told them that they might not be able to outrun whoever was chasing them down, so the current plan was to find a place to hide.

On the battleground, Ella scanned the place, feeling relieved that none of the children had come, but guilty when she witnessed friends either struggling, unconscious, or dead. Her blue eyes didn't stop searching until she found Toby.

She gazed at his wolf in gaping awe as the rhythm of his blood sang to her. But her smile faltered when she noticed his eyes were darkened green from the manipulation, and he was walking right into Rudolpho's claws that no one could see, seeing that he was a fellow discretus. Ella sprinted and pushed Toby away, causing Rudolpho's claws to plunge through her arm as she shrieked in anguish.

His knitted brows drew close like he was asking, "What are you doing?"

Heaving from the pain, Ella simply said, "Rudolpho, get your fucking claws OUT OF ME!"

Although still confused, Rudolpho retracted his claws as she groaned. It was the first time she felt blessed to have the healing abilities of a wolf.

Before Rudolpho could start lecturing her about her loyalty, Alissa kicked him in the head, and he fell to the ground unconscious as she muttered, "Asshole." She was very tempted to use the lighter in her back pocket but felt that she wasn't the right person to finish him off the way she wanted to, so Rudolpho was left there with the others.

Toby came out of the manipulation when Joseph—his decipio partner—sped up bringing him back to reality. Ella dropped to her knees by his side as she frantically asked, "Toby. Toby, are you okay? Can you hear me?"

Toby was blinking, trying to recall the events from the last minutes when he lost mental autonomy. When he remembered being pushed away and falling, then looking up at the creature who made him fall, his heart ached and vessels constricted when the memory of Rudolpho attacking Ella entered his mind.

"Toby! Can you hear me?" Gerella continued yelling before turning to Joseph. "What's wrong with him? Why can't he hear me?"

She was pulled into a sudden embrace, shock evident from her widened eyes. Toby shifted back and leaned his forehead against hers, uttering, "Please don't do that again, Ella. That was fucking terrifying."

Joseph left the two alone as Ella sighed in relief when Toby finally spoke. Her arms circled his neck, hugging him back as she whispered an endless stream of, "I was wrong. I'm sorry."

Toby pressed her deeper into his embrace, hooking his chin on the crown of her head as he cooed, "Shh, it's alright."

An energy sprung from the very depths of their hearts, which was left bare and in pain after Toby recited his part of the rejection. The moment Toby pulled her into his arms and Ella embraced him in return, a small flame rekindled, a gentle warmth filled the emptiness. That flame was a sign that the rejection had been retracted, its effects lifted.

Although one could verbally retract a rejection to keep the mate bond alive, a simple act of love and affection would also have the effect of rekindling the bond, so long as that act was reciprocated, just as Ella was reciprocating now.

The wolves and lycans were having a much easier time seeing that Rafael and many decipimus of the empire were on the field. Rafael's fiery eyes exhibited an intensity of anger that no vampire, wolf, or lycan had ever seen. Upon identifying the remaining decipio proditors, he entered their minds all at once, making them leap to the ground and walk toward him like trained pets before shutting them down, putting them to slumber.

Toby—while still holding Ella—couldn't stop himself from saying, "That's pretty neat."

Rafael turned to Toby with a humble smile and nodded in acknowledgement. "Thank you, Toby."

Seeing that the situation around them was under better control, Lucy took a quick glance at her best friend's mate and couldn't help herself from smiling before she sprinted deeper into the forest, hoping to catch up with Pelly.

Xandar, Greg, and Christian ran after the white lycan, wondering how she always managed to move on to the next prey without much of a break in between.

CHAPTER 54

Pelly only had to speed for a bit before Saxum and the runaway proditors came into her field of vision. She entered their minds and made them think that they were running into a wall, bringing them to an abrupt halt. The empress put the decipimus to sleep, and only Saxum was left standing.

At a safe distance from the leader, Pelly got straight to the point, "How sure are you that my father killed your family? Who told you that was what happened?"

Saxum saw only the two of them in a white space. He scoffed when he came to the realization that she'd entered his mind, and fired a remark, "You're going to manipulate me into thinking that what I know is a lie."

"No. I'm making you think you have nowhere to go so that I get answers."

"What right do you have to demand answers? You're just a spoiled little princess, born into a luxury of choices and freedom, never needing to care how the odd ones have to fare because Daddy provided everything. I don't answer to any ruler, especially not one who doesn't even have the basic skill of wielding an Authority."

That wasn't the first time Pelly was being ridiculed for not having that archaic power. She merely simpered and retorted, "Funny how this spoiled little princess didn't even need the basic skill of wielding an Authority to trap you and your runaway friends, Saxum."

She found strength in her own words, confidence in her self-recognition of her worth even without the archaic power. She couldn't see it, but a streak in her hair glowed in bright green. Fibrous roots came out of nowhere and crept up Saxum's body, holding him in place.

Lucy and the others arrived, instantly feeling an energy radiating from Pelly's being. Her wide, sapphire eyes met Octavia's proud ones as they exchanged smiles, both internally happy that Pelly finally had unlocked the Empress's Authority, wielding it like it was second nature to her.

Everyone's sights then went to the roots around Saxum, and Xandar wondered if those were what he thought they were.

His question was answered when some roots appeared next to Christian, making the duke flinch as his animal readied itself to attack. But when a familiar beige flower with red polka dots grew instead of the strangulating structure they saw on Saxum, Christian reined in his animal's urges and made his beast pluck the flower diplomatically, then awkwardly conveyed his thanks with a hand gesture before linking his cousins and cousin-in-law, *'The Forest of Oderem is miles away. How the hell did this get here?'*

Greg found this the perfect moment to retort by simply saying, *'Magic.'*

When Christian's eyes narrowed, Xandar explained, *'Pelly's Authority must be one of the most powerful—if not the most powerful—in history. Not only can she control the magical parts of her empire now, but also summon them to help her if she is in foreign territory. No emperor has ever managed such a feat.'*

Pelly wanted the truth. Nothing but the truth. The forest heard her silent command, and small flowers with transparent petals grew and bloomed in the roots closest to Saxum's face. The odor exuded made Saxum more susceptible to heeding to the empress's demands.

Pelly didn't know just yet what the flowers were for, so she emitted her Authority with full force when she asked, "Who. Told. You?"

"The witch and vampire who raised me."

"Do this witch and vampire have names?"

"They never gave them to me, saying that it was for my own safety."

She didn't see the point in pressing for the witch's identity any further. Witches only lived to five hundred years old, so there was no doubt that she was already dead.

"Is the vampire still alive?"

"Died four centuries ago."

"Did either of them ever leave the forest?"

"Not that I recall."

"Anyone come to visit them to bring them supplies?"

"Our supplies are found all around the forest. There was no need for external sources."

Reducing the intensity of her power, she continued, "They said my father killed your family?"

"He ordered their assassinations. Kosh might have gotten someone else to do the dirty work for all I know," he spat.

Pelly contemplated, then asked, "Does the name *Maddock* ring a bell?"

"No," Saxum mumbled, then added on his own, "Who's he?"

Looking into his angered but tired blue eyes, she simply murmured, "Someone who I hope didn't lie to me."

Unbeknownst to him, a complex web of possibilities was expanding in Pelly's mind. She couldn't help but feel that Saxum might just be acting based on false information he was brought up to think was the truth.

"The three scientists you're working with—where are they?"

"In their lab."

"And where is that?"

"It's accessible by an inn, owned by a lycan named Vent."

Greg immediately refuted, "That's a lie. My people searched that place. There's no such room."

The flowers made Saxum clarify, "It's an underground lab that's only accessible through their freezer. The keypad is on one of the shelves, hidden by blocks of cheese. Perhaps that's how your people missed it."

"Bastards," Greg muttered.

When the questioning was done, Pelly put Saxum to sleep. The vigils and custodes who arrived began carrying Saxum and the proditors back to the empire as the rulers discussed their next move.

Greg was given the green light to go after the scientists, and he only had one question, "Am I allowed to end them as I please?"

The rulers mind-linked amongst themselves. Pelly voted *yes* without much thought, as did Xandar. After the whole mess those three had caused, they were lucky the decision was to end them. However, the duke decided that torturing them first was simply a punishment before death. Octavia and Lucy couldn't find a reason not to agree as well.

Subjecting the triplets to a cycle of eternal torture wasn't wise because the rulers didn't want to risk them breaking out and then disappearing. If Greg couldn't locate them for so long with his reach and network, the rulers knew they stood less of a chance if it happened to them.

Lucy gave Greg a firm nod and uttered, "Do as you please."

Xandar added, "As long as they end up dead."

Greg rolled his eyes. "That goes without saying. I'll take my leave now. Have fun collecting the other hybrids from Neptune's warehouse."

A thought occurred to Octavia, so as Greg was walking away, she asked, "Your Grace, do you need a few of us to help carry . . ."

Without looking back, Greg waved a hand and replied, "No, we'll be fine. I doubt your kind is that heavy."

He left with twenty of his followers and linked the rest scattered across the rogue world to make sure Vent didn't leave his inn.

CHAPTER 55

Ella led everyone to the warehouse. The kids were so happy to see her that they ran into her open arms without giving much thought to the new faces, thinking she simply brought new friends from the trip their parents told them she spontaneously had taken.

Ella's eyes glistened in happiness when she saw they were all okay. She thought a few of them would have died by now, but the death on the battlefield compensated for any deaths of children that were sustained during the triplets' experiment.

Neptune wasn't with them. He'd already fled on his own without telling anyone the moment he received the link about trouble from Saxum. The adults left in the warehouse weren't fighters, so they cooperated when the vigils, custodes, and warriors escorted them out. The kids were the least affected, since the adults told them that they were simply going on another trip.

A few little boys' eyes sparkled in awe when they were walking past Lucy. One of them even stopped in front of her as his babysitter went ahead with her own daughters. His mother had passed out during the Bordure attack and was now being carried by one of the lycans, so his babysitter took over watching over him as they waited for his mother to regain consciousness.

The way his eyes glued to Lucy made Xandar mutter, "Goddess, hasn't this day been long enough?"

Lucy levelled herself with the boy, a welcoming smile stretched across her face. He looked a little intimidated, so she carefully opened her palm like she was asking for his hand. After blinking his eyes, considering for a moment, his little hand went to hers. He liked how warm it felt.

"What's your name, sweetheart?" Lucy asked gently.

"M-Michael," he answered shyly. "What's *your* name?"

"It's Lucy," she replied, gently touching his hair.

He gazed at his babysitter nervously. Most of the adults had stopped traipsing as they watched Lucy's interaction with Michael. The boy turned back to her and asked, "A-Are you our new friend, Lucy? Are we going to share the same room at bedtime?"

Oh, hell no.

Xandar's hand went to Lucy's shoulder as he curtly noted, "Actually, Lucy and I share a room at bedtime, Michael."

Michael's neck craned to the tallest creature he'd ever seen when he innocently said, "We only have one more bed in our room at home. Can you pick another room?"

Little piece of shit.

Before Xandar said another word, the back of Lucy's hand hit his leg when she spoke to the boy again, "Michael, we are going to find you and your family a new home, one that is as comfortable as your bedroom in your old home, okay?"

"Will you be living with us?"

"No, sweetheart. But I'll come visit."

"Promise?" His pleading blue eyes gazed into her black-and-lilac orbs.

She smiled wider and pecked a kiss on his forehead, making Michael blush as she whispered, "I promise. Come now. Let's get you to a . . . temporary place while we find you a suitable home."

As she held his hand and started walking, Michael asked, "What's *temporary?*"

Lucy entertained his questions, keeping him distracted as they left the warehouse together. She didn't know yet that Michael was Chong and Regina's son. The boy inherited most of his maternal family's features, so no one matched him to his now-dead father.

Most of the captured adults didn't know what to make of the situation. They liked that the queen was not scaring the children, but knew that the consequences of their administrators' actions left them with a very bleak future.

There was a group of angry widows and widowers whose mates had just died on the battlefield, but they knew better than to start a row under these circumstances, so they simply barged out as some sobbed and others put on brave faces.

CHAPTER 56

At Vent's inn, Greg barged in without batting an eye, as if he owned the place. Two of his followers took Vent, and the rest followed him into the kitchen. Even the chefs with choppers and knives didn't dare attack the duke. They merely watched—stunned—kitchen weapons hung midair.

When Greg's arm wiped the cheese off the shelf with the force of his anger, the chefs sprinted out of the kitchen, not knowing that his followers stationed outside were ready to lead them into a truck for a torture session.

In the freezer, Jade did his thing with the keypad that was recessed into the shelf layer and got the hidden wall to open.

The moment the triplets heard the freezer door open, Ourelia, whose eyes gleamed into the chemical reaction taking place in the test tube in her hand, shouted, "We didn't ask for you, Vent!"

The scoff they heard in response jolted their senses and sent a shiver down their spines. Only one creature possessed a deep, dark scoff like that. Before any of them took another step or said another word, the duke's followers dashed forward, slamming the triplets to the walls and pinning them in place.

Greg caught Ourelia mouthing, "Fuck," when their eyes locked, so he decided to start with her. His rough hand held her by her face when he asked, "Where the fuck are the bloodsuckers?"

Matthew questioned in return, "Does that even matter?" Desmond and Ivory kicked his kneecaps, a warning to never speak unless being spoken to as Matthew groaned and cursed under his breath.

Ourelia kept her lips sealed, but when Greg began squeezing her face and fracturing her facial bones, she choked out, "If you want . . . answers, why didn't you just . . . bring your new girlfriend to question us . . . instead?"

Greg had *never* had a girlfriend. The term was used to push his buttons, but had he prepared himself for this. Every living being with ears in the rogue world would have known about this weak spot of his by now. After what he had done to the Kyltons and to himself, any future enemies he may have would use Lucy to throw him off, to make him feel that he wasn't as great as he presented himself to be, to bruise his ego since he couldn't get the woman he wanted. From the cousin he claimed to be a weakling, no less. Many would go so far as to say that Greg didn't even have the balls to challenge his cousin.

It wasn't about balls. It never was.

Lucy's happiness was the determining factor in his decision to just let her be, and if the shallow-headed imbeciles in the rogue world couldn't understand that, then fuck them.

Instead of retorting with anger to give his opponent the mildest satisfaction, Greg smirked darkly at Ourelia, responding, "The queen . . . had more pressing matters to attend to, and she *knew* I wanted this assignment. I didn't even have to put in a request. Great chemistry we share, don't you think? Besides, having her use the Authority on you three would have been *way* too easy. She extracts answers with minimal torture. And you know me, I don't do minimal torture. Life is made to be much more interesting than that. Now, let's stay on subject. My subject. Where are the bloodsuckers you three put in a coma?"

Ourelia wasn't going to budge. The cracking of her bones echoed through the walls of the laboratory when Nessa exclaimed, "Stop it, you idiot! Stop it!"

Greg's lilac eyes went to the other sister as his hand continued pressing Ourelia's cheekbones when he said, "Tell me what I want to know, and then I'll stop. For a moment, that is."

Nessa breathed heavily as she sealed her lips. Alissa would have punched her in the gut had her eyes not given her away. She was looking at a tall, metal rack in the corner.

Greg snapped his fingers twice to ask for two followers as he, too, approached the rack. After moving the rack aside, he ordered, "Find the keypad. It must be the same as the one in the freezer."

The two pushed everything off the shelves, searching. Greg stared at the wall as his hand ran along a line he could find traveling from the floor to the ceiling. One of the two followers found the keypad and punched in the same six-digit code as before, and the wall opened as Greg stepped aside.

He took two steps in and glanced at the place with furrowed brows, plodding to the section where the children were kept. Then he heaved a heavy sigh and shook his head, utterly disgusted by this sort of experimentation.

The two followers stood at the entrance awaiting instructions, which Greg ultimately gave, "Get every bloodsucker out of here. We're sending them back to the empire. I only need three of you outside Vent's place. The rest of you, load them into the cars and get them back."

"Yes, Your Grace."

When his people got to work, he got back to the main reason he'd made the trip. His anger seethed through his onyx orbs and sinister smile when he began, "As nauseating as you three are, I can't deny we still have something in common—a love for science. I'm more of a physics guy myself, but I remember you three love playing with chemicals. Now, where's that thing you siblings used to be so obnoxiously proud of?"

He moseyed through the lab like it was a shopping trip, searching for syringes of oleander he once saw lying around their old lab when he first visited. The triplets once mentioned that they mixed oleander with other chemicals, seeing if a stronger substance would ever come out of it just in case some goody-two-shoes scientist came up with an antidote for the lethal poison in the future.

Greg found what he was looking for at Matthew's side of the table. He lifted one of the syringes and held it inches away from his nose as he took a whiff before setting it back on the table. "Concentration of whatever the fuck you three added with oleander is too high in this one. How about this one?"

He sniffed the second syringe. "Concentration's lower, but not sure if it's what I'm looking for. Hm." His shoe tapped against the floor as he thought for a moment. "You three like to do test runs, I recall. The one in Blue Crescent was really an experiment to remember, and perhaps it helped confirm or debunk whatever theories you three had. I have a theory now. Let's run a test, shall we?"

To the triplets' surprise, Greg walked over to Matthew and instructed, "Stick out your tongue."

Matthew's eyes widened and pressed his lips tight. He knew exactly what would happen if any of that chemical in the syringe made contact with his body.

Greg began complaining, "For Goddess sake, Callow. Can't you cooperate the same way we cooperated with your white mice in Blue Crescent? It wasn't as if we killed all of them."

Desmond hit the back of Matthew's head as Ivory reached in to pull his tongue out. Desmond held his head back, letting the pink, moist structure stretch.

Greg murmured, "Careful, Ivory. Fingers at the tip. We don't want this on your skin. Hold him very, very still, Desmond."

Matthew's indecipherable protests were ignored.

Greg carefully pushed the plunger. A single drop of liquid formed at the tip of the needle before falling onto Matthew's tongue. The three men observed the effects with interest.

Matthew screamed at the stinging sensation. His eyes teared up at the anguish as the chemical burned through his tongue to form a distinct hole. But the ordeal didn't end there. The oleander was slowly travelling throughout his mouth and spreading to his respiratory system. If the triplets' data was accurate, Matthew was expected to die in less than six hours.

Greg merely nodded at the sight. "My bad. This one's still too strong."

As he returned to the table to pick another syringe to play with, Nessa hissed, "You're despicable!"

Alissa's claw went through Nessa's ear, giving her a too-large piercing she didn't ask for, making Nessa scream before the claw was retracted as blood oozed from the area.

Greg's signature dark scoff reverberated through her ears. "Do you even know what that word means?" He picked another syringe, looking at it through the ceiling lights before setting it down and moving on to the next syringe. "It means morally reprehensible. I doubt any of us in this room have the right to use that word against each other, seeing that none of us are saints. Being who we are, the Goddess already has our places reserved in hell, where we belong."

He picked another syringe and approached Nessa, towering over her when he declared in a low voice, "I'm not despicable, Callow. I'm deathly. You fuck with me or the people I care about, and this is what happens to you and those you care about."

He stuck the syringe into her collarbone and left it there for a moment because Nessa began struggling. Alissa and Hailey held her against the wall before Greg pressed the plunger all the way through. It took Nessa a whole twenty minutes of shaking, sweating, paling, and croaking before she finally died on the floor.

Greg looked at the corpse and uttered, "Nope. Still not it. It has to be longer. I wonder how long it will take before I find the one I want."

He came back to the table of the neatly arranged row of syringes and—in mock amusement—said, "Ah, silly me. It's arranged by concentration. Highest to lowest from left to right. How could I have not known?"

No one believed he didn't know. The concentration on every damn syringe was labeled. In bold.

"Any last words, you two?" Greg asked, eyes still stuck to the table. "Matthew, you first."

Ivory let go of his tongue, but Matthew clearly still couldn't frame coherent sentences or utter any clear words. Between the incomprehensible muffles, everyone caught a curse word or two . . . or more, but that was all anyone could decipher.

Matthew panted when he was done, which was when Greg said, "Thank you, Matthew. Ourelia, you're n—"

"YOU WILL NEVER BEAT US! YOU WILL NEVER BE BETTER THAN US! EVEN ON OUR DEATHBEDS, EVEN IN HELL, NO ONE WILL FORGET THAT WE, THE CALLOWS, WERE THE ONLY ONES TO FOOL GREG CLAW!"

Greg's followers growled thunderously in their boss's defense, but Greg merely smirked as he offered Ourelia a slow, sarcastic applause. "That was a very well thought-out speech. Too bad I can't say the same for your plan."

"Your intelligence is becoming more questionable as this drags on, Claw! You get *nothing* out of this! Not the status. Not the respect. Not the woman. NOTHING!"

"I'm starting to question *your* intelligence now. I'd explain, but I'm a little short on time, so I'll just let you figure out how you're mistaken. It'll give you something to do while you await my arrival in hell."

He stuck the syringe with the lowest concentration of oleander into Ourelia. Jade and Nani held her to the wall as her body weakened painfully slowly. Greg then did the same to Matthew.

Greg didn't expect anything in return when he offered Lucy his help. He didn't want anything from her. Not the status, respect, or even her. But as time went on, he realized that he was given those things in a way.

His status during the cooperation as one of the most trusted figures couldn't be denied. Lucy never made him or his people feel left out. If anything, she made them heard and more accepted than they'd ever been in the kingdom. On a personal level, he was given the status of an uncle when he thought he'd been permanently cut off from interacting with any future royal family members.

Respect from the creatures beyond Lucy was more difficult to establish in the beginning, but with time, it became doable. Even the non-rogues became more open to accepting and respecting him and his people as the decipio practice sessions went on. It was unbelievable, but it had happened.

As for getting the woman . . . Greg admitted he couldn't have her the way he wanted, but he did get to work with her—something he never thought he'd have the privilege of doing after their rough start when they first met. He "got her" in the sense that he earned her trust, to the point that she trusted her daughter with him, that he had her confidence in retrieving every bloodsucker from the lab, and that he was given full discretion in ending the Callows.

Greg wasn't planning to demolish what they'd built. He knew how deep a betrayal would cut, and it wasn't as if he didn't look forward to interacting with his niece. He might even teach her a swear word or two then put the blame on his cousin just for a few laughs. The queen would no doubt find out eventually, but until that happened, it would be fun.

The ministers and warriors weren't so bad either. They weren't as slow as those during his late uncle's reign. He even grew to enjoy working with them, as did his people.

Seeing that he had time to kill as everyone waited for Ourelia and Matthew to die, Greg had a look around their lab to see what other toys they had. When he was done browsing through the shelves and books, his eyes darted around random things—the clock, switches, etc. Then, his eyes stopped at the bin, where he saw crumpled waste papers.

Since he had nothing better to do, he dug into their trash and emptied the bin onto the table. Carefully avoiding the broken glass pieces, his fingers extracted the papers, which he assumed would contain random equations and symbols written in illegible handwriting that he might not even understand.

He smoothened the first sheet and found a sketch of the lightbulb they found in the hideout of the Forest of Oderem. He then spread out the next sheet, and when he saw a beautifully written paragraph of words and sentences that any non-scientist could understand, his relaxed mental gears jostled and got to work again.

His eyes burned at the initials at the end of the note, and he thanked Goddess the siblings died at the two-hour mark. He couldn't wait any longer to get on to the next phase.

The mavericks carried the triplets' bodies out of the lab. On his way out with them, Greg said, "Finish up, Alissa. We'll wait for you outside. Make it quick."

"As you wish, Your Grace." Arson Arden embraced the name given to her, took out the lighter from her back pocket, and set the whole lab on fire, leaving no book or poison unscathed.

They left ten of their own to put out the fire and to make sure that everything was thoroughly burned through as the remaining twenty royal mavericks headed to Ruby Lyworth's factory. Greg gave the guards at the gate two choices: stand in his way and die a slow death, or let him in and spend maybe a few years in prison and have a chance at freedom. It didn't take a lot of thinking for them to choose the latter option.

Greg made a beeline for Lyworth's office.

The entrepreneur was about to run out the door after being alerted by one of the guards, who pushed the emergency button installed at the side of his earpiece. Greg grabbed her arm and pushed her back inside as he shut the door.

"Sit." He pointed at her office chair.

She complied, not seeing an alternative.

Greg took the crumpled paper out of his pocket and placed it on her desk. When the duke saw her face pale and lips quiver, he got his answer.

He scoffed. "Ruby. Ruby. Ruby. What did I say about confidentiality and not pissing me off?"

She tried to lie. "Y-Your Grace, I . . . I didn't write this, I swear. The initials are pr-probably a coincidence."

"Really?" Greg asked as he walked to one of the cabinets, pulled out a file, and flipped through it until he found handwritten notes before slamming it on the table, putting the note right below the document in the file when he pressed, "So it's also a coincidence that the handwriting is so similar?"

Ruby continued to shake as her brain scrambled for a plausible lie, but the duke's intimidating presence was making it very difficult. She wasn't hitting mental dead ends. She practically couldn't think. It was as if her brain had packed up and left her remaining faculties to deal with the consequences on their own.

Greg glowered, and a snarl escaped his lips. "Think *very* carefully before deciding to tell me anything but the truth, Lyworth. I found this note, so it's safe to say your new anonymous ally is as good as dead. Misleading me again is not going to end well for you. I'm already going to take you back to the kingdom, and we know how the queen's power works, don't we? If what you're about to say now isn't going to match what you're going to tell her when she compels you, we're going to have a problem. And I will submit a special request to end you personally. We all know that I've been in the queen's good books. And my cousin won't tell her no. So I have no doubt my request will be approved. Now that I've laid everything on the table, it's your turn. Answer my very simple question: did you warn the new players after my departure?"

In an almost inaudible murmur, she said, "Yes."

"See, that wasn't so hard, was it?" Greg replied somewhat innocuously.

Ruby was about to relax before Greg's hand reached for her forearm, bending it backwards and breaking her elbow. Her screams from the torture were nothing compared to what came after, when Greg's claws plunged right through her arm, staying in her flesh as he dragged her out of the office. Her blood made a trail on the floor.

Greg even dragged her down the stairs since she was in too much pain to get up or move on her own. Unaffected by her cries for mercy, Greg merely said, "On the bright side, Lyworth, it would have been worse if you lied."

Her employees complied with Greg's command to surrender themselves to the kingdom's authorities as soon as they witnessed their employer being hauled out like a sack of potatoes. After dumping Lyworth and her goons at the police station, Greg made his way to the mortuary to meet up with his cousins and cousin-in-law.

CHAPTER 57

"Was this really necessary, Greg?" Xandar muttered at the sight of Greg's fresh victims. The duke shot him a glare. "You were one of the four who told me to end them. And I was granted full discretion on *how* to end them."

"I know that. What I meant was . . ." Xandar sighed ". . . did you have to bring back the bodies?"

Lucy was studying the triplets with interest.

Christian didn't think there was much to see, seeing that they were just . . . gray.

Greg continued arguing with Xandar, "This. Is. Evidence. Evidence that our assignment was completed to perfection. I'll have you know, Cousin, that in the rogue world, this is first-class delivery."

That was when Lucy managed a small, grateful smile, finally looking up when she said, "Thank you, Greg." Her eyes then returned to the corpses.

Greg's sights returned to his cousin. "At least the queen appreciates good work."

"I'm not saying I don't appreciate it, but," his fingers pressed his forehead before he asked, "what are you expecting us to do with these? Build a memorial?"

His wife suggested, "We could just cremate them then use the ashes as fertilizer for prison plants or something, darling."

Greg gestured at her when he told Xandar, "That's one way. Though if it were me, I'd hang their bodies in town for a week for everyone to see. It'll scare a few creatures into obedience, *and* it might attract some new insects that can be used for research, you never know."

Christian's and Xandar's faces scrunched in disgust, which was when the light in Greg's eyes dimmed and he muttered, "You two are boring."

Xandar immediately decided, "We'll go with the cremation and fertilizing option." He turned and was about to drag Lucy out with him before pausing and turning to Greg again. "Oh, I almost forgot. The empress and consort sent their thanks. The abducted ones are in the hospital. Most of them are safe and will recover."

"What do you mean *most*?" Greg questioned. He liked his work to be perfect.

Lucy's features hardened when she explained, "Five adults and all eight children had most of their brains . . . removed. The children even had strings of nerves connecting to all four limbs removed."

"That's sick," Greg commented, his face squinted in revulsion.

Lucy nodded, agreeing. "The surgeons are trying to see if they can find a way around the problem, but . . . a solution seems unlikely. The most probable thing that would happen—we've been told—is that life support would be cut off by the end of the week after friends, relatives and family members have come forward to see the abducted ones one last time."

"Well, that's unfortunate. Looks like we weren't fast enough," Greg noted ominously. "What about the hybrid leader? What's going to happen to him?"

Lucy said, "Pelly is going to choke the truth out of Maddock in an hour's time. Would you like to come along?"

"Yes, I would. Thank you, my queen."

CHAPTER 58

In one of the many rooms in Pelly's castle, Saxum was tied to a chair positioned at the edge, away from the table with three chairs, two of which were placed facing the third one. He would mind-link someone, but the oleander and allicin cuffs got in the way.

Servants came to ask if he wanted water, which he declined every single time. He didn't want to drink something that might have contained poison.

The doors finally opened again, and Pelly and Octavia strode in, bringing a man that Saxum didn't see on the battlefield. Lucy, Xandar, Christian, and Greg took their seats at the opposite side of the room, facing Saxum.

Pelly and Octavia took the seats placed side by side, after which Pelly gestured to the chair and said to the new face, "Have a seat, Maddock."

The name caught Saxum's attention. He began observing the former viscount but found no familiarity. A servant came with a potted plant and placed it on the table, pushing it very near Maddock.

Maddock didn't dare move the flora away, but he shifted in his seat, then glanced at Saxum. "And who may that be, Your Majesties?"

"That's Saxum."

Maddock's eyes bulged wide in horror. He took another look at the leader, who began feeling suspicious with his reaction. Saxum couldn't stop himself from asking, "Have we met?"

Maddock chose not to answer and turned away, recognizing the way the hybrid's nose and lips matched Lady Luisa's. A crack split his heart, though he remained externally composed.

Pelly began, "I want the truth, Maddock. What happened during the assassination of Lady Luisa from our empire and Heros Pas from the lycan kingdom?"

Saxum sat up, back straightened, fatigue forgotten, hatred of the injustice taking a back seat and curiosity drawing his eyes to the old man.

Maddock insisted, "But I've told you what happened, Your Majesties. Your lawyers have also taken my deposition, and . . ." before he went on, the transparent flowers exuded their fragrance, and Maddock suddenly found himself more willing to get straight to the point and tell the whole truth.

Pelly didn't want to use her Authority to extract answers. She wanted Saxum to know that whatever Maddock was saying was the truth, and no information that followed was the result of compulsion by the Authority.

Maddock coughed at the strong odor and waved his hand in front of his nose in hopes of removing some of its effects before he started, "Well, after Rosalie's death, Emperor Kosh discovered that Heros Pas was instrumental in poisoning her. When Kosh demanded Lady Luisa cooperate in surrendering Heros, she refused."

Maddock was surprised by how frankly that whole thing came out, which was when he realized what the plant was for. Where on earth did they get this from?

"Go on, Maddock," Octavia prompted as Saxum's eyes grew wide in eagerness.

Maddock was forced to inhale the fragrance again. "After Luisa's refusal, she . . . wrote to me, asking me to convince Kosh to look past Rosalie's death and Reagan's subsequent insanity as an unfortunate consequence of a bond that was created between the right souls but at the wrong time."

"Did you respond?" Pelly asked.

"I did. I . . . have never stopped loving her." He pressed his lips together, knowing fully well that his confession contradicted his deposition and story told the other day.

The flowers got him to talk again, so he went on, "I didn't like the idea of her choosing to be with Heros with that sort of background, but I also didn't like that Kosh wanted to kill the man when it was not within his jurisdiction to do so. Muddling jurisdictional lines was one thing. What made it more complicated was the fact that, by exerting his decisions upon a lycan without the lycan king's permission . . ." he sighed in dismay ". . . it was a recipe for diplomatic destruction. The newly crowned king still saw Heros as a trusted figure, so you can imagine how messy things would get if we touched him."

"So you asked my father to reconsider his decision and he said no?"

"That is the . . . abridged version, Your Majesty. You see, Luisa then wrote to me saying that she was bearing twins. I saw this as good news because I thought the late emperor would never want to leave a set of children fatherless. I was later proven to be wrong. Kosh agreed that the children, despite having Heros's genes, shouldn't be touched. But he still wanted Heros's head. He didn't want a co-conspirator to a murder living a happy and lavish lifestyle in his empire, saying that letting him live here meant that he tolerated what the lycan did, which Kosh didn't."

After clearing his throat, he proceeded, "It was clear that Luisa was not going to give up her husband, nor did he want to give himself up since he felt that he was simply aiding the monarchy. He claimed that whatever he did . . . was an act of duty and loyalty to the late king and queen. I wrote to Heros—privately—telling him that Kosh was never going to negotiate more than he already did, and that if he wanted to live, he'd have to return to lycan territory."

Maddock continued, "What was shocking was that Heros couldn't return because the medical professionals' demonstrations and protests were also calling for his death. He wasn't safe there. The other conspirators who were involved already had their homes burned and their families dismissed from jobs, and most had been assaulted and battered one way or another. The new king was still trying to smother the flames, and the authorities were searching for the culprits, but the fact remained that Heros could also be in danger if he ever went back. He was scared for his family and himself. He pleaded with me to change Kosh's mind again, but we both know your father, Your Majesty. Almost no one could change his mind. Your father . . . began to question my loyalty, seeing that I was pleading Luisa and Heros's case when the whole world was against them."

Pelly murmured, "That's why you volunteered for the task—to prove your loyalty to the empire."

"That was one of the reasons. Another was to make sure that the task was done right. The issue was by the time the plan had to be executed, Luisa herself had garnered a lot of backlash for sleeping with a conspirative murderer, bearing his children. The public wanted Heros dead, and they didn't care if she survived. The children? Most people felt that it was better for them to be brought up by a normal creature who neither murdered nor supported murdering. I volunteered because I wanted to make sure that *only* Heros was killed, as Kosh ordered. Luisa was supposed to be left unharmed."

"She sacrificed herself," Octavia mumbled.

Maddock confirmed with a sad, firm nod. "She was a discretus. On the night we entered their private residence, my mistake was to have every discretus on the team search the property when I myself faced Heros with only a velox and decipio. We didn't see Luisa behind the curtain, covering the child she was holding with her garment. Heros refused to tell me where she was. I assumed she wasn't on the property. The moment I gave the signal to fire the arrow, I heard her scream and what I saw next . . . was . . . her appearing . . . in between . . . me and her mate . . . with an arrow going right through her and the child. My men fired the second arrow to kill Heros, and the oleander killed him slowly. Luisa could heal like a lycan after being marked, but the fact that the poison was oleander made the healing ability practically useless, and she . . . didn't survive."

Tears welled up in his eyes. Flicking a guilty glance at Saxum and the lycans, Maddock's attention returned to his rulers when he added, "The names on the infant garments were true, Your Majesties. We saw two names, but we couldn't find the second child. We started tracking the governess, whose things we found in the smallest room, and we found her eventually, but . . . upon Kosh's compulsion, she admitted giving the child away. We went down that trail and lost it when it was collected by a witch. We attempted to enter the Forest of Oderem fifty-two times, but it kept us out with its mist and odors."

"The mission was considered a failure. That's why everything was redacted," Pelly muttered.

Maddock nodded sadly. "That task was an embarrassing debacle on our part, on my part. When we went looking for Saxum out of genuine concern, word got out about our search. And those in the empire who hated Heros and Luisa started going on a hunt. They were hunting down hybrids. Hybrids were mere children, and those who gave birth to them were already a very discriminated against minority, but they kept to themselves, so they were safe, until the urge to kill a murderer's descendant gave them an excuse to justify killing the innocent creatures' babies, saying that they may be hiding a future killer, claiming that the child they were holding was actually Saxum, when, in reality, it was their own flesh and blood."

Pelly questioned, "Weren't they tried? Weren't these people punished for their own murders?"

"Of course they were. That's how it stopped."

Octavia asked, "Why hasn't anyone of our generation read or heard about this?"

Maddock explained, "You have, but you may not have known when you did. The courts didn't call the victims *hybrids*. Because they were merely infants, almost no description was given about them to protect their identities and families. Cases like Re V, Re Q . . ."

Pelly exclaimed in disbelief, "Those were hybrid cases? From the way the judgments were written, it sounded as if the victims were older, killed because their parents were involved in some . . . heinous act, something actually illegal."

Maddock nodded. "That was the whole intention—to mislead future generations."

"My father ordered this?" Pelly clarified.

"Not . . . exactly. But speaking objectively, he did . . . influence it. You see, Your Majesty, anyone loyal to the emperor knew better than to do anything that may minutely villainize their ruler, so everyone involved found ways to . . . walk around the problem."

Pelly scoffed depressedly. "A cover-up is a cover-up. My father knew about this and did nothing to stop it."

Maddock glanced at Saxum once more before murmuring to her, "He never wanted them dead. We really tried to find him. But we couldn't. Kosh felt . . . if the matter didn't die down . . . it might even cost him his throne, and consequently, your throne. As much as he was thinking about himself, he was thinking about you, too, Pellethia."

Pelly's eyes raged in tears when she spat, "Burying history to secure the throne . . . is NOT the best example to set."

Maddock then spoke to her more gently than he'd ever done during her reign, "And what would you have done if you were in our shoes, when the Forest of Oderem kept you out, when the hybrid massacre started before you even knew about it? I gather that you may have decapitated me for my own mistake, but apart from that . . . would you have tried anything else that your father hadn't to rectify the situation?"

After a long moment of contemplation, Pelly replied in an angered whisper, "I know I wouldn't have been able to sleep another night if I hid the truth."

Maddock smiled sadly. "None of us slept well after that failure. None. Not me, not the late vigils, and especially not your father."

Pelly knew her father had suffered from severe insomnia but she always thought it was due to work and missing her mother. She could never imagine that it was because of this.

Maddock then spoke on his own accord, "Kosh . . . really did regret the order. He admitted to being blinded by the thirst for revenge, that if he could've just let one bad person live, many innocent creatures would have survived."

The former viscount turned to Saxum again, who was staring at the ground as he took this all in. Maddock cleared his throat to get the leader's attention, and with nothing but guilt and sincerity, he said, "I'm sorry. On behalf of every-one involved, I must tell you . . . not a day went by that we didn't think about what happened, how we could have done better, how we could have done right. The error still haunts me to this day. I am terribly sorry."

Saxum swallowed a lump in his throat before asking in a low voice, "You loved my mother?"

"Y-Yes, but it wasn't meant to be, as it turns out."

"Can you tell me more about her?"

That question took everyone by surprise. Shouldn't Saxum have wanted to kill Maddock? Maddock instinctively shot Pelly a nervous look.

Pelly faced the hybrid. "Saxum, I'm going to use my Authority to know what's really inside your head. This is not an attack. It's a precaution, alright?"

Saxum nodded in understanding.

Her emerald eyes shone when she began, "Do you want to kill Maddock?"

"Yes and no."

"Elaborate on that."

"Yes, because it was his mistake that killed my family. No, because it was a mistake. My mother couldn't be seen, and my birth father was . . . sadly, not a good person. And neither am I." His head lowered, tilting toward the floor. "I can relate to the thirst for revenge and being . . . blinded to its rippling effect. I am . . . not optimistic about my future after what I've done, so with whatever time I have left, I want to know something about my mother. Anything."

Pelly wanted to help him, but after what he had done, it was impossible. Her own people had been calling for justice ever since the first abduction took place. When word got out that the lost ones were found, there was relief only for a few hours. Now, the public wanted justice for those whose anatomies were tampered with, whose lives ended before they even began.

Saxum was right. His future was bleak. The law didn't take misunder-standings as a defense. No legal system did.

"We'll have that arranged." That was all Pelly felt sure of saying.

After Saxum was escorted out by three vigils to have him sent to the dun-geon, with Maddock tagging along to tell him everything about his mother out-side the cell, the royal family members were left alone.

Pelly turned to Lucy, asking in a pained voice, "How would you have done what Father did differently?"

Lucy admitted, "I don't know if I could. After Maddock's unfortunate error, every other route available to Kosh seemed to have only led to either a dead end or another disaster." She wrapped Pelly in a hug. "Your father did everything he could, Pelly. He tried his best. None of us is perfect."

Pelly then asked everyone, "If we tried Saxum, and if he is sentenced to death . . . would we just be following father's footsteps?"

Xandar asserted, "Not the way I see it. Kosh had no jurisdiction to order Heros's death because Rosalie's death was within the lycans' jurisdiction, so only the lycans could and should have dealt with him. In our case today, Saxum's army harmed both our species, not just at Bordure but also in the hideout of the Forest of Oderem. We are in a position to try him."

Octavia added ominously, "Not just a position, but a duty. We owe it to the lives that were lost. He can never be freed, not after what happened. Whatever he did, no matter how sympathetic his past is . . . amounts to attempted massacre, treason, amongst other things. Even if we do let him go, there's no telling if he'll survive whoever's out there ready to kill him if they know who he is."

Greg murmured, "He's too deep in, crossed too many lines. He and the dead triplets practically led this whole thing that took this many of us to crack down. There's no way to help him."

In the uncomfortable pocket of silence, Pelly could only say, "Let's hand this over to the justice department then."

CHAPTER 59

Those from Neptune's warehouse were now placed in a guarded apartment building near the castle. They were given food, clothing, medical checkups, and therapy if they wanted it. Toys had also been donated by civilians from across the empire for the hybrid children.

Lucy, Xandar, Christian, and Annie made regular trips to visit the families with Pelly, Octavia, Rafael, and Amber, to see if the families needed anything that they could provide. Even Maddock and the other ministers visited a few times.

Several families began asking whether they could return to the lycan kingdom to visit families and show their parents their pups. Xandar and Lucy instantly granted such requests and even gave the families a few dates when a jet would be sent to pick them up.

They began trusting the royal family and close aides as the visits frequented. But the widows and widowers were still closed off. Most weren't even ready to begin therapy. But the therapists assured Pelly that, with time, those who lost their spouses would be ready to open up.

By far, the most difficult part of this whole thing was for the single parents to tell their children that one of their parents was never coming back because they had been sacrificed in battle. Most cried, some screamed, and many became closed off.

Michael—for instance—could sense that his mother zoned out every now and then, and he sometimes wondered if it was something he'd done. Regina tried her best to be there for Michael, but seeing Chong's face in her mind just made her miss him so much that she wanted to cry all the time.

Ever since Michael was told about his father's demise, he had only interacted with his mother, his mother's closest friend, Aisyah, and Lucy. He was finding it difficult to behave like he used to, even smiling a lot less. When he did smile, it was forced.

Lucy and Xandar were playing with him one day because he refused to join the other kids, and his eyes watered when he asked, "Did Papa die because he was bad?"

Gingerly placing him on her lap, Lucy explained, "No, Michael. Your papa was very brave. He stood for what was right."

"Then why did he die?"

"Because . . . doing what is right . . . isn't always safe. Your papa was not safe when he did the right thing."

Michael started sniffling and choked out, "Why . . . di-didn't . . . anybody . . . save . . . him?"

The memory of Saxum's claws going through Chong's gut came to Lucy's mind. The two were mind-linking before the sudden homicide. Lucy could hack mind-links. She should have hacked theirs. If she knew where things were going, she could've emitted her Authority to make Chong step back, or restrain Saxum, even if it were just a little. She had the power but didn't use it. She should've done more.

Gently wiping away the boy's tears, Lucy tried not to choke when she admitted, "We weren't fast enough, sweetheart. I'm sorry."

After some more sobs and sniffles, he looked up at her and asked, "Is Mommy going to die?"

She frantically asked, "What? Why would you say that? Is she okay?"

"She's not . . . talking much . . . like before."

Lucy stroked his hair and explained, "Your mommy is grieving, Michael. She needs time. You need time too."

"What's grieving?"

"It means . . . allowing yourself to be sad after someone close to you died."

"Do you grieve, Lucy?" Michael asked innocently.

Lucy nodded with a sad smile. "I do." Her own parents were killed when she was just a little older than Michael. She'd lost so many friends to rogues over the years. Grief was not unfamiliar, but it remained a difficult phase to soldier through.

"So Mommy and I will be sad forever?"

"No, sweetheart. It won't be forever. You and Mommy love your papa, and you will be sad that he's no longer here, but he's in here." She placed her hand on his chest and continued, "A part of your heart will always be connected to him. You will still miss him, as will Mommy. Both of you still have each other. There'll still be sad days, but there'll also be happy ones."

Michael sniffled some more and leaned into Lucy's chest as she stroked his arm. After a moment, Michael looked at Xandar and asked, "Do you have a papa?"

Xandar smiled and answered gently, "I did, but he died a long time ago."

"Oh . . . did you grieve?"

As Xandar ruffled the boy's hair, he replied, "I did."

Michael murmured, "Okay."

Lucy held Michael for an hour before he let Aisyah pull him away for lunch. Families like Michael's were left alone to grief, and when they requested to visit the graves the rulers claimed to have buried their loved ones in, their request was approved with the provision of transportation.

At the cemetery, they wanted to hate the creatures who'd gone against their loved ones in battle. But after learning about what Saxum and the other administrators had planned and executed, it was difficult to see their enemies as the true criminals.

Pelly granted permission for grave visitations no matter how frequent they were, sending regular reminders that she was willing to provide flowers for them to bring along, if required.

After the latest visit, Lucy stayed silent in the car and on the jet. On air, Xandar held her close and planted a deep kiss on her head when he began, "Chong's death isn't your fault, Lucy." He felt the guilt engulfing her when Michael asked why didn't anyone save Chong, and even he didn't have an answer.

Lucy argued in a whisper, "I'm gifted with a power that I didn't even use. I could've hacked their link and then pulled them apart. But I didn't."

He clasped both sides of her face and looked intensely into her eyes. "You did everything you could, Lucy. You always have and you always will. It's who you are. Bordure was no different. Hacking their link wouldn't have guaranteed Chong's safety. If you did something before Saxum attacked Chong, it would look as if you were trying to start a fight between them. Even if you did manage to get Chong to step back . . . Saxum's claws would've still gone through him, sweetheart. They were standing very close, and Saxum was swift in that kill. He might not have managed to tear out his gut right away, but Chong's death was certain. Saxum wasn't letting anyone get in his way." After wiping away her stray tear, he firmly noted, "The losses on their side are not your fault, Lucy. Alright?"

She sniffled once and buried her face in his chest, making him hold her close. His grip tightened, chin hooked on the crown of her head. She let his warmth wrap her, his heartbeat soothe her, drowning herself in his scent. Only after a few minutes did she manage a small smile, kissing his cheek before uttering, "Thank you, Xandar. I love you."

He pecked her lips before uttering with a soft smile, "I love you, too, my little freesia."

CHAPTER 60

The administrative hybrids and those who had fought at Bordure weren't given as much freedom or luxury as those who weren't involved in executing the plan. The remaining administrators were Saxum, Regina, Ella, Rudolpho, and Zepine.

Regina was under house arrest since she had Michael to care for.

Ella was confined to her apartment as well, escaping dungeons because she'd warned the empress and consort about the attack.

The other three were kept in the dungeons until trial. Unlike the other prisoners, they weren't allowed to leave their cells for meals or walks. It was a safety precaution taken to avoid prison riots.

On a trip that Lucy dreaded, Deputy Chief Lauren and Officer Laila escorted Kate when they boarded Xandar's jet for the empire. Once they landed, Duica and Bernadette were there to take them to the dungeon where Rudolpho was being held.

In the car, Bernadette politely informed Lucy, "We've already placed the one there according to your wishes, Your Highness. The other cell is ready as well. May I confirm that your prisoner has no dietary restrictions?"

Lucy turned to Kate and unmuted her, asking flatly, "Do you have dietary restrictions, Kate? Any allergies after consuming a particular food group?"

Kate was fuming all the way, not the least scared when she spat, "I'm allergic to your first-class hypocrisy, you AH—" Lucy muted her again when Lauren's claws went through Kate's hands bound by silver cuffs.

Lucy then responded, "No, she doesn't have any dietary restrictions, Bernadette. Thank you."

"My pleasure, Your Highness. Um . . . may I . . . humbly suggest extending the seventy-two hours to . . . a week?" Bernadette asked, taking umbrage in the way Kate spoke, even though Lucy was not her queen.

Only Kate had no idea what the duration was about. The original plan to break Kate was to put her in a cell right in front of Rudolpho's and send in Hilda to see what Rudolpho would do when he had to face both women at the same time. Hilda had already been warned about Rudolpho's betrayal, and she said yes to cooperating when her rage peaked. Hilda was free to leave if she wanted to, but Kate would remain where she was, forced to stay with the one she thought loved her and only her.

When the matter was discussed in the kingdom, Greg and Christian were visibly annoyed when Lucy said that she'd just keep Kate there for twenty-four hours. Xandar was as dissatisfied as his cousins were, so he talked his wife into extending the period, so it became seventy-two hours, which still wasn't enough for Greg.

That's the best you can do, Cousin?' Greg linked Xandar in secret.

Not needing to ask what it was about, Xandar refuted, *'Could you have done any better?'*

Ignoring the rhetoric, he said, *'No. But seventy-two hours? That's it?'*

'Think of it this way, Greg. She'll also be charged for her crimes in the kingdom after she's kept with Rudolpho for seventy-two hours in the empire, so this isn't the end of her punishment.'

'The sentence here better be heavy.'

'You know it will be. What she did was practically treason, and who knows what other petty crimes Dalloway and the others found? She'll most likely be behind bars for almost as long as Cummings and the others.'

'Fine,' Greg muttered, ending their link.

When Pelly received Lucy's link about the seventy-two hours, she immediately asked whether that duration was even enough.

Now in the car with the vigils, even Bernadette was suggesting extending it.

Lucy didn't give in at first, feeling somewhat sorry for Kate for being lied to by the one she had given her heart and loyalty to. On the flip side, Kate was really pissing her off with her attitude, and she had betrayed her pack along with everyone else who offered her a better life. With that in mind, the queen told Bernadette, "I'll be submitting my request to the empress to have it extended to a month, plus two whips per day." She doubted her husband and cousins-in-law would have a problem with the change, but she texted them just in case.

Their replies were instant: Christian sent a row of emojis containing thumbs-up and yellow faces, each wearing a party hat and blowing party horns; Greg replied that he'd be okay even if it were a year; and Xandar said he'd just fallen even more in love with her.

Bernadette and Duica exchanged surprised glances. A month! They'd hit the fucking jackpot! Not even their empress had managed to change the queen's mind! With a gracious smile, Bernadette replied, "That's . . . wonderful, Your Highness. I'm sure the empress would be happy to hear from you about the matter."

After driving through the gates and walking through doors, exchanging smiles and greetings with the custodes on duty, they were led down a flight of cement stairs as the custode on duty, Anthony, turned on the lights. The moment Kate saw Rudolpho in a prison cell, she tried to free herself from Lauren and Laila, but the lycan officers restrained her with ease.

Lucy began, "Remember that little rendezvous I promised you, Kate?"

Kate's eyes widened in horror, and after glancing at Rudolpho, who made no move to stand even when he saw Kate enter, Kate shook her head violently and looked like she was finally pleading for mercy.

The vigils threw her in the cell facing Rudolpho's, and Lucy continued, "It looks like I don't have to exert as much force as I thought. You see, Rudolpho already had someone when you two met, and their thirty-year partnership was never severed upon your arrival. So I'm going to leave you here, and do you see that projector up there?"

She pointed above her head, which even made Rudolpho look.

The queen continued, "That is going to project every photo in Rudolpho's phone of him and his partner on that white wall over there. So you're going to be here for a whole month to see every photo and watch every video of them celebrating birthdays, going on dates, those kinds of things. And they will be played over and over and over again. There's *a lot* of kissing and hugging, I should tell you. And when you're not enjoying the . . . documentary, you'll be escorted out for two strokes of the whip daily. I'll come fetch you at the end of this honeymoon period with your beloved for the kingdom's justice system to deal with you next, okay?"

Like she had a choice. Still, Kate's eyes amplified doubt.

Lucy asked, "You don't believe me, do you? Ask him yourself then."

After Kate was unmuted, she didn't speak right away. She looked at Rudolpho and was hoping he'd deny everything, but he didn't even bother meeting her gaze. The lights near the white wall were turned off, and intimate photos were projected. One by one, they entered Kate's vision and lingered in her mind, etching her memories. Kate was convinced these were photoshopped, that the fair-faced, ginger-haired woman was just some random model chosen from the millions of stock images on the Internet.

Rudolpho watched it as well, missing the woman in the pictures and wondering where she was now.

Suddenly, a small, tired voice came behind Lucy. "Is that her, Your Highness?"

Before Lucy responded, Rudolpho shot up from his bed and sprinted to the steel bars of the cell as he exclaimed, "Hilda! You came. You're alright."

Kate's worst nightmare had been presented before her. She saw the desperation in her lover's eyes, the affection and relief in his voice that was shown to another woman—the woman in the photos. Kate and her wolf started piecing things together, replaying every moment they shared with Rudolpho, and her breathing labored.

Lucy gave Hilda a light nod. "Yes. That's Kate. Would you like us to leave, Hilda?"

Although tired, Hilda managed to force a smile. "No, Your Highness. I . . . won't be here long either."

Rudolpho exclaimed, "Hilda, please! I can explain. I had to do what I did. Saxum said we needed a backup plan. We needed an insider. We . . ."

Hilda lost it, forgetting the queen was right in front of her when she blasted, "YOU NEEDED AN INSIDER FROM TWO YEARS AGO WHEN SAXUM'S PLAN ONLY STARTED MONTHS AGO? YOU HAD TO BE SEXTING AN INSIDER?"

In a hushed tone, he pleaded, "Hilda, that was nothing. Please, at the end of the day, I'm only yours. I only truly love you."

Hilda's eyes brimmed with hot tears, scoffing as she replied, "At the end of the day, you only truly love yourself. No one does this to the people they love! You can rot in hell for all I care!"

Hilda turned and—in a chopped voice—muttered to Lucy, "Ex-cuse me, Your H-Highness." She dashed out with the custode escort, not wanting to be seen crying in front of so many people, especially not the one who'd broken her. Rudolpho called out her name again and again, but Hilda never looked back.

Once the entrance door closed, Lucy looked between Rudolpho and Kate and casually said, "Well, that's that. Since everyone is fully briefed about the existence of any past and present relationships . . . or lack thereof, both sides can now start afresh on honest grounds. I'll leave you two here to . . . pursue your courtship. From a distance."

Everyone could hear the sarcasm in the queen's voice that was devoid of empathy. Rudolpho was glaring daggers at the queen without knowing that Kate was scowling at him. When Lucy turned to leave, she heard Kate scream in rage before taking the lamp on her nightstand and throwing it at the steel bars of her cell. The lamp broke into pieces, and Kate started throwing the shards at Rudolpho, screaming like a maniac. "YOU LIAR! YOU LIAR!"

Her aim wasn't good, and Rudolpho managed to dodge most of her attacks as he sat on his bed thinking about Hilda, ignoring the crazy bitch that was probably going to render him deaf by the time she left. How long was she staying again?

Outside, Lucy followed the sound of sobs to Hilda, who was seated with a custode offering her a cup of water. When Hilda felt her presence, she looked up to see Lucy dropping into the space next to her. "Would you like someone to talk to, Hilda? Or would you prefer to be alone for now?"

Hilda muttered, "Alone, please."

"Okay. If you need anything, let us know."

Hilda nodded again, and Lucy got up to leave. She linked Pelly on the jet, and the empress was more than happy to see through with the revised plan. Pelly got an update from the custodes, who said that Kate had thrown the prison lunch bowl at the projector but missed. She then started throwing her cutlery and food at Rudolpho as she screamed.

'They're telling me she's crying now, but the rage might return again soon.'

Lucy agreed, *'Yes, it will. It lingers for quite a while. Thank you for your help, Pelly.'*

'You're more than welcome, Aunt Lucy. Kiss Reida for me. And send mine and Octavia's love to Uncle Xandar.'

CHAPTER 61

Toby visited Ella twice a day, getting to know her and making sure she had everything she needed to make the experience less tormenting. She constantly assured him that she was fine, and always looked forward to his visits.

He learned that her mother had died giving birth to her and her father subsequently passed on from the grief and heartbreak. He learned that she liked children and had a favorite—Isla. He met the kid with Lucy. Isla really was an angel.

He also learned that Ella was fluent in proditor code, which helped those who left the empire transmit messages to their families or close friends. The main translator was a proditor who stayed in the Forest of Oderem for a few years before sneaking back into the empire, living in one of the most remote parts under a new alias. His years as a proditor enabled him to read the code, and he made a good fortune out of the translating business when families and friends sought him out.

Evidently, not everyone who entered the forest was escaping the authorities. Some entered as messengers whose napes bore the protection mark, which only became visible when they were in the forest. This convenience of communication was only available to vampires, seeing that the forest was in their territory. No one thought to dig a tunnel leading to lycan or wolf territory solely for sending messages.

Ella explained that many of the empire's criminals didn't actually stay in the forest. If their napes weren't marked within six hours, they'd have to leave. If they didn't, the forest would either spray foul scents to shoo them away, or curse them or their families. They left from a different part of the forest from where they entered and would disappear.

As Toby's thumb stroked her hand that was on his lap, he asked, "What if the same crook enters?"

She shrugged. "So long as they don't stay the night, the forest doesn't care if they are inside for a few hours."

"Huh. So it just hates law enforcement."

"It did. But you mentioned that that's not the case anymore, right?"

"Right," Toby murmured, gazing into her blue eyes before her head leaned against his shoulder.

Their mate bond strengthened with each visit, the scintilla of sparks now a strong stream coursing through them, intensifying with every touch and interaction. Toby never truly had understood how even the fiercest creatures could completely crumble upon their mate's touch. But being with Ella now, taking in her scent, knowing that he was the only one who had the privilege of holding, smelling, and touching her so intimately, he understood completely.

Pressing a kiss on her hair, he said, "Thank you for what you did, Ella, for standing on our side."

"Toby, this is the third time you're thanking me." Her thumb traced his brow when she said, "Which you really don't have to. I shouldn't have agreed with the plan in the first place. I'm glad I met you halfway through. I needed to know the other side of the story. Everything became easier to see after that."

He held her closer. "I'm glad I met you at that time too. Things would have been much more complicated if we ended up meeting in Bordure first."

She chuckled, a sound that never failed to jostle his heart. "Well, I wouldn't have killed you," she said.

"I wouldn't have killed you either, Ella. But come on. That may have been the worst setting to find out we're mates. We deserve something peaceful."

"Good thing we met at the beach then. Peaceful. Private. Romantic. Why were you there alone?"

A gentle wave of melancholy washed over Toby as he shared about his younger days and the friends he had and lost. It was then Ella understood why he was so protective of his existing friends. He had already lost so many that her heart ached for him.

She wrapped her arms around him, and the heaviness in his chest miraculously lightened. He gave into his urge to hold her tightly in return, and when she kissed his jaw, Toby felt like he owned the world.

When it was time for Toby to leave, Ella walked him to the door, as usual. Reluctance emanated from them. Toby sighed, leaned in, and pecked the usual kiss on her forehead, lingering for a moment before pulling away, which was when Ella pulled his face back and smashed her lips on his. Briefly stunned, Toby emitted an unceremonious growl and responded in hunger, tasting her and breathing her in, hand on the back of her head tangled in her locks as her own hands pulled at his hair. Their lips parted, but their noses remained glued as they shared the air supply in the small space between their mouths, locking dazed eyes, euphoria consuming them.

The visitor pass in Toby's pocket beeped non-stop. If he didn't return the card within thirty seconds, he'd be barred from seeing Ella. Leaving a hasty kiss on her nose, he said a quick goodbye and dashed out, handing the pass over at the twenty-eight-second mark.

On his jet, Toby replayed his time with her. His fingers traced his swollen lips and he smiled to himself like an idiot. Without thinking, he linked Lucy, telling her about it.

His best friend shrieked at the most deafening pitch through their link and demanded every last detail. He blushed so hard and grinned so wide as he went over how spontaneous and perfect the moment was, how Ella fit so well in his embrace. Lucy ended up sobbing, her jubilance for them exuded through their link.

But the moment Lucy asked if he'd be okay with her asking for the living room cameras to see his first kiss with Ella, his smile fell and brain froze. He forgot there were cameras in every part of Ella's holding apartment except the washroom.

Shit.

It was no wonder the lady he'd handed the visitor pass back to was suppressing a smile.

'Toby?'

Snapping out of the freeze, his mind thawed quickly. '*Where's your recording of the first kiss with your mate, Lucy? I don't remember getting a copy.*'

'*Oh, c'mon! You've seen us like that tons of times. I haven't seen any of yours yet!*' She chuckled, then added, '*I'm kidding, Toby. It's your special moment with her. I feel more than privileged that you're telling me about it.*'

'*You should.*' His voice took a playful, accusatory turn, '*Unlike you, I didn't make you ask before spilling.*'

'*You can't blame me for that. I couldn't even speak properly for days whenever I thought about it.*'

'*Yeah, I noticed. It was like he tamed a beast.*'

'Just like your mate tamed you, I presume.'

He chuckled. *'Without a doubt.'*

After saying their goodbyes and ending the link, Toby's mind went to the proditor code, and he immediately connected it to one creature he knew would be interested in the subject.

CHAPTER 62

Toby spoke to Greg about it, and the duke expressed his interest in learning more about the code, telling the minister that he might just reach out to Ella after the vampire's legal system was done with her and when the rogue world in lycan and wolf territories had been "properly cleansed."

Greg's followers hunted down Neptune, Klementine, and Feva. Elvis and Sivle were just Klementine's less-known helpers, so finding them wasn't as difficult as the top four thought. These traitors didn't suffer the same fate as the triplets, but the punishment they were subjected to was an eternity in solitary confinement . . . after being tortured by Greg Claw first, of course.

Chief Dalloway asked Greg if the black eyes, limping, and deep wounds that still hadn't healed were already on his victims when he found them, to which the duke replied with a curt "no" without offering further explanation. Dalloway nodded in understanding, thanked him, and got his people to run the rogues through the usual procedure.

Law enforcement on the vampires' side was busy running through their own procedures as well. After several weeks, a hearing was scheduled. There wasn't much of a fuss since all the administrative hybrids pleaded guilty.

The lightest sentencing was Ella's, who was to be imprisoned for a mere twelve months, with the guarantee of early release for good behavior. Toby's wolf growled in protest, but his human knew that was the lowest sentence that the judge could give. She wasn't just an accomplice for the most part. Ella was one of those who'd approved suggestions and made decisions, so she was on equal standing as any other administrator.

The second lightest sentencing went to Regina, who was asked to pay a hefty fine of two hundred thousand monetæ—vampire currency—over the course of fifty years, along with serving one thousand hours of community service. Regina didn't have any money yet, but once she was mentally and emotionally stable enough to work, the monthly deductions would be made from her salary. Should she default, Michael would be taken by an adoption agency in the name of providing the best form of care that a child is entitled to receive. This sounded like a threat to some, but a precaution to others.

Rudolpho, Zepine and the others who didn't back down from the plan down to the final battle were sentenced to three hundred years behind bars. Visitations would only be allowed after the one-century mark, provided that they had been on good behavior for those one hundred years.

Saxum's sentencing was ten whips a day for eighteen months before he would be decapitated. He was also not granted visitation rights, so Maddock wouldn't be allowed to see him anymore.

As for the lycans and werewolves who lived in the Forest of Oderem without the empire's approval, they were fined five thousand monetæ each, to be paid over the course of five years. Although deportation would normally follow, the court decided against it, seeing that there were many children to single lycan or werewolf parents. Deporting their parents would cause the children further distress on top of the deaths at Bordure. The court offered the parents a three-month grace period, and in these three months, the families had to decide whether to register as a citizen of the empire, or renew their registrations in the kingdom and register their children there as well. If they failed to comply, separation and deportation would follow.

Most chose to stay in the empire while a handful chose to leave. Luna Hale, as the minister of welfare, readied an accommodation in the kingdom to house these newcomers on a temporary basis. The newcomers were expected to seek employment and learn to sustain themselves and their children after a month of grieving. Otherwise, their children would be taken by the authorities to provide better care than a parent could offer.

CHAPTER 63

When Toby visited Ella in prison for the first time, his leg fidgeted as he prayed that she wasn't bullied or battered. The empress and consort assured him several times that Ella was safe, and that the prison guards always had things under control, so violence and bullying seldom happened behind those walls.

His animal had really been an animal lately. After the judge sentenced Ella and the others, his wolf kept asking his human to find ways to break into prison, pestering him to ask Ella which cell she was in so that it could save time sniffing her out. The wolf even encouraged Toby to ask for Greg's help to avoid getting caught.

As tempting as that was, Toby decided against it. There was no telling what would happen if he did get caught, especially if the prison guards found his scent in corridors or parts of the prison where he shouldn't have been.

He was in the private visitation room for two painful minutes before Ella entered with the policewoman, who took off the allicin and silver cuffs that bound her wrists while reciting the usual procedure and the two hours she was allowed. Ella was dressed in the teal-green uniform that everyone else wore, her hair up in a ponytail, and Toby sighed in relief that she still looked perfect.

Ella's brows arched in confusion when she took her seat facing him and skipped over the usual *hi*. "Did you think I was going to refuse to meet you?"

He saw the humor swimming in those gorgeous eyes, and his hands reflexively reached out to hold hers, his thumb stroking the back of her hand when he confessed in a distressed whisper, "I was just worried. I wasn't sure if you were safe in here."

Ella slid her fingers between his when she uttered with a smile, "I am. We all are. They're really strict about not touching another inmate here, especially if voices start to raise."

"Oh no," Toby muttered in dismay at the last part.

"It's a good thing, Toby."

"Were they raised at you?"

With a gentle shake of her head, she replied, "No."

"Okay." He sighed in relief. "It's just twelve months. Six months if we get lucky." As hard as Toby was trying to be here for his mate, he was really assuring himself more than her. Despite being the one in custody, Ella seemed as calm as clear skies.

She gave his hands a gentle squeeze. "Hey." The worry in his eyes melted away with the tranquil blue orbs that held him captive. Ella continued, "We're going to be okay. Thank you for coming to see me."

Toby scoffed as his mood improved by the sound of her voice. With a wide smile, he confessed, "Ella, don't thank me for this. I never want to *not* see you. If possible, I want to stay with you in there until they let you out."

Her heart swelled at his declaration, yet she still chose to state the obvious, "Inmates are separated by gender, Toby. We wouldn't see each other or be together even if you were in there. You'd be in the other block."

Toby groaned and complained, "Can't you let a guy dream for once, Ella?"

Ella chuckled. "This might be the first time I'm hearing about a dream that curtails liberty."

"When my mate is in prison, I feel as trapped as she is. It might feel a little more liberating if I could see her more than twice a day or hold her longer than a few seconds each time." His wolf nodded in agreement.

A tinge of pink colored Ella's cheeks from the way he looked at her when he said those words. There was no hesitation, no need to think. It was like he just knew this was what he truly wanted. Being an administrator, Ella had always been seen and heard, and knew what it was like to feel important.

But Toby seemed to have taken it to a whole new level, or a different spectrum altogether. He didn't just see and hear her. When they spent time together, she could tell he wanted to see parts of her that didn't show, hear words that weren't said. He didn't just make her feel important, he made her feel like a special puzzle that he was more than happy to solve.

"What have you been up to lately?" he asked gently, bringing her out of her thoughts.

"Uh . . . making friends, mostly." A thought came to her, and her eyes sparkled when she shared enthusiastically, "I reconnected with a few forest messengers. Most of them are here for petty theft. They recognized me and welcomed me into their circle. We're getting along very well. What was interesting to me, though, was that they said they've been in prison before, like it wasn't a big deal. Some have been in and out more than ten times. Can you believe it, Toby? They know these walls and hallways like it is their other home or something."

Toby was definitely not expecting to hear that. "As unexpected as that was, it's definitely good news. At least you have company, but these messengers . . . they can't read the codes, right?"

"That's right," she added with a smile. "They've been complaining a lot lately, saying that one of their income sources has been depleted now that none of us live there anymore. They like me, but . . . they hate you."

"Wait, what?" Toby's eyes bulged wide.

Ella's smile grew when she explained, "They think it's the authorities' fault we left the hideout. Since you're an authority figure, they hate you."

Toby argued in a whisper, "Ella, that's not fair. The vigils went in first. I'm *not* a vigil. Hate on them. And besides, you guys left *before* any of us saw any of you."

She replied with a playful smile, "I know."

"Didn't you tell them?" Toby asked in dismay.

"Not at first. I do like to listen before saying anything. It gives me a good picture of what they know and where they stand in things."

"Baby, you didn't defend me?"

Her focus broke. Her cells halted in shock. He'd never called her *baby* before this day. That word felt like Toby was wrapping her in his arms even though they were seated across from each other. The way they were both leaning across the small table reflected their desperation to do just that, but they always saved this part for when Toby had to leave.

"Ella, hey, you okay?" Toby gave her hands a gentle squeeze when she said nothing.

She blinked several times before saying, "Yes, I'm . . . alright. For the record, I did defend you. I told them how we were the ones who were wrong, and that you're a really good person."

"And?" Toby's eyes widened in hopeful anticipation.

"They hate you less than Saxum now, but I think they have a propensity to hate law enforcement in general."

"Great," Toby murmured in dissatisfaction.

One brow rose in playful suspicion as Ella said, "I didn't know you cared about inmates' thoughts of you, Toby."

He simply replied, "I didn't, until some of them turned out to be your friends."

"I'm sure they'll warm up to you once they get to meet you. They have a soft spot for good-looking men."

The ears of his animal perked up, and Toby's own eyes shone when he tightened his grip on her hands as he asked in a whisper, "You think I'm good-looking?"

Ella didn't mask her surprise and annoyance. "Did you seriously just ask that, Toby? You know, when you told me your last attempt at intimate love was in your late teens, I didn't believe you. When you brought me to meet the queen and I saw what she looked like, it was *very* hard to believe that you two had only ever been best friends. You two look so close. And you're both very attractive."

Frantically, Toby insisted, "I wasn't lying, Ella. I've never lied to you about anything. Lucy really is just my best friend. We have no such history. We never saw each other like that. Ever."

Ella smiled warmly. "I know. The way you two interact and speak to each other made me sure of that. She seems nice."

Toby had the urge to specify, "Only when she's not fighting or training."

Ella shrugged and said, "That's fair. We hear things about her here in prison too. Even the forest messengers are a little scared of her, despite never meeting her. When they asked if I met her, and I said yes, they asked if the queen tortured me before I was thrown in here. Many of them didn't believe me when I said she never hurt me. No one believed me when I said she was nice. They think I was given some drug or potion to make me forget what was done to me, or that I have a threat hanging over my head if I speak against her."

Toby weighed that up, and a mischievous smile stretched across his face. "I think I have a way to befriend your messenger friends, Ella. We all love you and we're all scared of Lucy! We have those things in common. Isn't it great?"

Her brows furrowed. "Should you even be doing that to your best friend?"

Toby waved his hand like it was no big deal. "We've teased Lucy about her ferocity many times over the years. She's cool with it, even getting back at us sometimes. Her brother does it, too, but . . . I think I'm the worst one."

Ella chuckled again, stroking his hand when she prompted, "So what have you been up to?"

"Besides thinking about you? Mostly the usual: checking on the gammas and warriors, training, communicating with the vampires about decipio practice sessions for the wolf packs, reading stuff for the next meeting, those kinds of things."

The government was expanding training to include decipio practice, but there were several skeptical packs that weren't yet onboard with the idea.

Ella carefully asked, "How are they taking it? The decipio practice?"

"Some . . . still aren't very open to the idea yet, but the upside of this is that the strongest packs have signed up, and the majority of the other packs are saying yes to it. The problem is just those who . . . have a preconception that the vampires are cooking up some evil plan for wanting to help."

"That's a little sad."

"Or stupid."

"Maybe they just need time."

Nodding in agreement, he said, "I am one hundred percent with you on that, Ella. With time, these birdbrains will eventually die off, and we'll be safe from their stupidity."

Her eyes fumed in irritation, "That wasn't what I meant, Toby."

Toby chuckled and stroked her hands to soothe her. "I know, Ella. I know. And you're right. They just need time to warm up to the idea. Once they see other packs doing it with no issues, they'll get on board."

When the timer went off, a thread of melancholy weaved itself into the happy atmosphere. They looked at the annoying timer sadly like they always did when the visit had to come to an end. Chairs scraped the floor as they got out of their seats. Toby pulled her into his chest, taking in her scent, breathing her into his lungs, storing it there, and hoping to ration it until they saw each other again.

As they parted their bodies, his hand reached for the back of her head, pulling her into a kiss. Ella's eyes fluttered closed as she indulged in the feeling of his warm lips against hers. The sparks that coursed through her body with each brush made her feel protected, desired, and loved.

When the guard tapped on the metal door twice, Toby reluctantly pulled away. He pressed a kiss on her forehead and uttered, "I'll see you in the evening, okay?"

She nodded and managed a smile. After giving his hands another squeeze, she let them go and walked toward the guard at the door, who put the cuffs back on before opening the door to let her back out. She briefly turned back to see Toby one more time before disappearing from view.

Toby left the prison and boarded his jet, keeping Ella at the back of his mind while scrolling through the morning's news.

CHAPTER 64

Xandar was in bed scrolling through his phone when he read the news from the empire. Many were awed and touched by the level of commitment the kingdom offered to their Imperial Majesties, vigils, and governing body during the cooperation.

They were grateful to Greg because he had tracked down the triplets and brought back the abducted vampires before killing the scientists and destroying their lab. When he was reported to be "the only royal family member who is—at present—single," some women from the empire boldly expressed their interest in "meeting" the duke.

Xandar took a screenshot of that segment and sent it to Greg, whose reply came seconds later with only four words, "I hate you, Cousin," along with the middle-finger emoji. Xandar chuckled to himself and continued reading.

Journalists quoted civilians saying how much they were looking forward to collaborating with lycans and wolves, be it in business, education, or environmental issues.

In recent weeks, Lucy gained popularity within the empire for how skillful and powerful she was reported to be during the battle, and how Pelly credited her for helping unlock the Empress's Authority. They also liked the fact that the queen spent time with the hybrid children even though they weren't housed in her kingdom. It was not a short trip, but she and her husband visited frequently despite that.

Xandar, on the other hand, became popular when the vampires were told that he broke and tore off Saxum's limbs during the battle. They mentioned liking Xandar visiting the hybrids as well, but his ferocity was the more favored element. They loved that he was seen to torture the proditors before ultimately killing them.

The king himself wondered if torturing and killing another creature was even an appropriate way to gain favor with their species. The war with vampires over two centuries ago started with violence and willful lack of consideration, and no one was celebrating then.

A sleepy and fully bare Lucy felt his deep contemplation through their bond. Scooching into him, she murmured with closed eyes, "Darling, what is it?"

His lilac eyes snapped to her, and his conflicted thoughts melted into blissful happiness as he admired his beautiful flower when her arm slid across his chest. After leaving a sweet peck on her hair, his thumb drew circles on her smooth shoulder as he filled her in on the news, concluding with his own thoughts, "I never doubted they would love you. I knew that—being the one of lycan descent—I'd be the one that they'd have a hard time accepting. But when I dreamt of fixing our kingdom's relationship with the empire, impressing them through violence was not what I had in mind."

Lucy chuckled lightly, pushed herself up to kiss the corner of his lips, and whispered, "Darling, you are amazingly frightening and incredibly sexy when you're inhumane. It's okay to be violent sometimes."

"Hm, is that so, my love?" The way she repeated his words flipped on a switch in him, and the delicious view of her perfect body only made him more aroused than he already was. After placing his phone back on the nightstand, Xandar flipped her over, hovering above her. The previous night was amazing, and both were satiated after the session, but when they woke up this morning, they realized that they wanted more.

They needed more.

His hand spread over her thigh, sending a fiery rush of want through her. His mouth began at her neck before moving down to her breasts, where his tongue awakened her nipples. His hand traced her smooth skin from her breast to her waist, then her butt. Her small hands ran along his broad shoulders and neck and up to his thick hair. When Xandar headed back up north to suck on her neck, he linked, *'Oh, you are a Goddess-given masterpiece.'*

"Ohh . . ." she moaned softly as his fingers played with the moisture at her lower region.

His mouth went further up, stopping by her ear, where he whispered, "Louder, my queen."

His touch made her moist, but his deep, alluring voice made her wet. Xandar knew this, too, and he moved south before his tongue began toying with her wet folds, making her gasp and moan louder than before. He loved the way her body responded to his touch. The sounds that came along got his tool hardened and ready. His tongue and fingers sped up when she was close. When Lucy screamed and her body arched, Xandar drank and licked up every bit she gave him as her chest rose and fell.

He trailed to her neck again, teasing her mark by sucking all around it but never on it, and Lucy whimpered as his tool teased the part of her that ached for him to fill the emptiness. Xandar decided to put them out of their miseries, sliding into her in one swift motion, savoring the look on her face that morphed from relief of his entrance into unquenchable hunger signaling him to move. He went rougher with her this time, slamming at her flesh with each thrust and biting on her skin, holding her mark in his mouth as her moans and whimpers continued driving him and his animal insane.

When she screamed and her core tightened around him, his body tensed, and his own orgasm shot into her.

Flipping them over, Xandar lay on his back and held Lucy on top of him as their lungs replenished themselves. As their breaths steadied, he gave her butt a surprise squeeze to elicit her gasp and cute moan before whispering, "Does this mean you love me when I'm rough and violent, baby?"

Their eyes locked, and Lucy's starry eyes made him forget everything as she reached for his cheek. "Xandar, I love you when you're a lot of things, not just when you're rough and violent. I love you when you're soft and vulnerable too. Your violence seems more like protectiveness to me. I love that you're fiercely protective of our people. I also love that you only resort to violence if there is no other way to keep the ones under your care safe." Her finger traced his left brow when she continued more softly, "Apart from your protectiveness, I love that no matter how busy you are, you always make time for the ones who matter most to you, like Christian and Annie, and now me and Reida. I love the way you light up when you talk about history or anything else you love. I love the contemplative look in your eyes when you're thinking through a problem. I love that—no matter how hard or tedious it is to do things the right way— you never resort to shortcuts if it isn't in the kingdom's best interest to do so. And those are just the main ones. Darling, there are so many things to love about you. It's not just your ability to be rough and violent."

Xandar's eyes gleamed, and the softest smile lifted his lips. He and his animal were touched beyond words, and his animal pushed forward for a full minute just to lean its nose and forehead against hers, cooing aloud to express his love for her. When his human regained control, he trapped her lips in a deep kiss, turning her over and pressing her into the pillow, feeling the smile in their kiss as her legs wrapped around his hips and pulled him in. At her neck, he chuckled before giving himself to her again, one with more love than lust.

Much to their animals' disappointment, there wasn't time for another round. They had a meeting scheduled and had to pull themselves out of bed to get ready.

CHAPTER 65

In the meeting room of government headquarters, notes and copies of Iridessa's theses were either clutched in one's hand or poured out from one's bag as ministers walked in and took their places around the table. Toby was pacing to his own seat, striding past Lucy when he muttered, "I've never seen that many words in a single document in my entire life."

Lucy merely scoffed in amusement, whereas Xandar saw the need to respond, "It's a thesis with research taken from all species, Toby."

"Wrong. It's TWO theses, Xandar," Toby argued, raising two fingers to substantiate his point.

Lucy covered her mouth, biting back chuckles when Xandar continued, "Exactly, so what did you expect?"

Unabashed, Toby declared, "I expected more graphs and charts, preferably with color."

Weaver exclaimed, "That was *exactly* what I said!"

When Weaver and Toby high-fived, Yarrington shook his head with an amused smile directed at the queen.

The moment the last minister had arrived, they began.

Toby came up with the simplest way to steer the discussion. "I work better with short words and notes, so from whatever I understand from these encyclopedias, it's essentially three parts of support that we can be expected to provide: personal, professional, and environmental."

Personal support, as the theses noted, was aimed at helping inmates understand and make peace with the whys. Why was the crime committed? Why did they do it? After this, it would be emphasized that they may not have known better then, but they did know better after the incident.

For Ivory, his colleague's death was an unfortunate mistake. The consequence of remembering that his negligence led him to kill his colleague, however involuntarily, would stay with him longer than his sentencing. He wasn't careful then, but he undoubtedly became more careful after that. Hailey's child-swallowing-crayons scenario, though didn't end up with a deceased victim, was another one which fitted under the Mistake section.

For Desmond, the crime was intentional fraud, but in one of their chats without Greg being present, Desmond confessed to Lucy that his own father had been cheated of 60 percent of his retirement fund that was supposed to help him and his sister go to college. The fund was monitored by a third-party company which was headed by the employer's brother, hence Desmond's anger and resentment toward abusive employers. Filing a lawsuit to claim the money took another thirty percent of the fund. Although Desmond's father and many others won on paper, the company filed for insolvency, and the sum stolen couldn't be restored.

The support that the government aimed to provide was ways to help inmates understand that what they had done was not entirely their fault, like Ivory and Hailey; and it sought to open the minds of those like Desmond, who would be given suggestions on how to further their cause in a legal manner.

Alissa's type of circumstance was very delicate because it involved the mate bond, betrayal, and loss, which would inevitably entail strong and justified emotions of infuriation, resentment, devastation, and the burning desire for revenge. Personal support would be more frequent for inmates like her, to encourage them to get better and ensure them that they wouldn't be alone when they assimilated themselves into society once again.

At the end of the discussion for the first segment, it was agreed that therapy should be provided to every inmate for at least thirty minutes a week. Annie and Hale were to see this through. They were to reach out to organizations and professionals to collaborate with the government and ensure that only when inmates were mentally, emotionally, and psychologically stable would they be released from prison. If they didn't reach this threshold even after completing their sentence, therapy would continue, which would be scheduled by parole officers at the convenience of ex-inmates.

As an incentive to encourage related professionals and organizations to help, the government decided to offer a 10 percent bonus for a therapist's time at every eleventh inmate if the first ten had successfully reached the threshold.

Vanessa said, "How many professionals would have to certify that an inmate has reached the clinical threshold is now the question. I'm voting on three."

Some voted five, others two. But the majority swung toward three, so three it was.

Xandar called for a short break, which was when Christian heaved an exhausted sigh and uttered, "One down."

Toby slumped into his seat to get some quick shuteye when he murmured, "Two to go."

Christian and Annie, along with some ministers, left the room to get some air. Xandar placed Lucy on his lap and guided her to lean into him. His eyes closed, and his nose buried in her hair as he inhaled his preferred type of fresh air. She, too, leaned into him to let the sparks replenish her energy.

Everyone came back a little fresher after the fifteen-minute break and got on to the next item: support to rebuild them as a professional.

Inmates should have been required to take up a class that would teach them some kind of skill, giving them a competitive advantage when they entered or re-entered the workforce. Yarrington and Benedict were assigned this segment since they were already working closely with teachers, mentors, lecturers, and professors at every level of education. The point was to make sure inmates could do something to feed themselves when their prison term was over.

Yarrington and Benedict pointed out that the issue of finding employers who wanted to take ex-inmates was of concern, and that was where Christian came in. Since he had inherited companies from various sectors, he'd be able to absorb a significant number of ex-inmates.

Xandar and Lucy disclosed that they were mandating removing the section of job application forms which asked whether the applicant was an ex-inmate and declaring a company discriminatory if it was found that this topic had been raised during an interview. Companies found to be discriminatory would be fined and their taxes increased.

The king and queen also pledged to meet housekeeping agencies, food and beverage owners, and the like for further employment opportunities. Zelena and Tate offered to do the same in wolf territory to speed up the process. The minister of justice, Pamela, even offered to propose recruiting them as clerks and runners in the next meeting with the judiciary.

"That should suffice for now," Yarrington said.

Everyone looked to their king, waiting for a signal for a break.

Xandar was already lifting Lucy off her seat while she was still running through her notes. Placing her on his lap, he then told the rest, "Yes, go ahead. Fifteen."

Lucy continued scrutinizing the points when most of them left for a breather. The moment Xandar felt a drumming throb in her head, he snatched away her notebook, placed it back on the table, and pressed her into his chest. Lucy was too drained to protest, so she simply closed her eyes and leaned into him, concentrating on his heartbeat.

Round three: environmental support

Weaver agreed with Iridessa's suggestion that public housing should to prioritize ex-inmates instead of excluding their eligibility just because of their record and that the government should subsidize the first two months of rent and provide a small congratulatory payment if the ex-inmates eventually managed to move out; the earlier they moved out, the higher the reward.

On the miscellaneous side of things, the theses emphasized the need to raise public awareness of the fact that many creatures were capable of changing for the better and how acceptance would only benefit society, the economy, and harmony in the long run. There should be media coverage, talks, and seminars to educate the general public. The government unanimously agreed that they wanted Iridessa to lead this initiative, and Lucy offered to speak to the woman herself.

When everything was concluded by lunch hour, Weaver was the first to get up and stretch out his limbs when he said casually, "How I love a meeting without Cummings, Whitlaw, and the other morons."

That was probably the fifteenth time Weaver said that after a meeting was concluded. Still, those who went through the years of ordeal working with those time-wasting, anti-change, and solution-repelling ex-ministers could never get tired of hearing that line.

Yarrington merely packed his things as he entertained his mate for the fifteenth time, "I'm sure you do, dear."

Lucy was looking at them like she was saying "Aw, you guys are so cute." The education minister met the queen's gaze with a smile and said, "We'll see you later, my queen, my king."

"See you." Lucy's significantly softer and weaker voice surprised even herself.

Her husband hoisted her out of her seat and speedily packed her notes as he said, "Let's get you something to eat before we meet Pelly and Octavia. You'll get some shuteye in the car and some sleep on the jet." He pecked a quick kiss on her forehead before he slid his hand into hers and uttered, "Come," before leading her out.

CHAPTER 66

A fter lunch, the rulers met to discuss bringing back the Secret Service. They had been observing Greg and his followers. Not only did they conclude that none of them went out of line, but they also agreed that none of them went anywhere near that line. The initiatives they took were highly commendable; their commitment in the cooperation was unwavering; and their loyalty outshone their pasts, no matter how dark they were.

Octavia even mentioned that it didn't feel like they were doing what they did to be pardoned. The royal mavericks helped because they wanted to help. Margaret's followers were more split—about two-thirds helped because, like the royal mavericks, they grew to like working with others beyond their own. But the remaining one-third were just there for the pardon, excluding the traitors, Kate and Howard, of course.

As a precaution for the sake of the kingdom and empire, Lucy suggested all rulers be given a regular update on the ins and outs of the Service for the first ten years. If all went well, less frequent updates would suffice. The mavericks would have discretion as to how they operated, but the rulers had the power to stop assignments or shut down the Service altogether if such a time ever came.

Xandar was relieved when she brought this up the previous day when they were discussing the matter between themselves. At present, Lucy didn't want to give Greg unrestrained power and authority, but she didn't do it for her husband. As much as she personally trusted Greg now, she couldn't deny that, as queen, she had a duty to make sure precautionary measures were taken for the sake of their people. If the mavericks ever went too far, the rulers would be able to terminate any task and hunt down the ones involved. She definitely hoped this would never happen, but if it did, they'd know what to do.

When the decision was finalized, Pelly noted the obvious, "So the question that remains is, *does* the duke want to lead something like this. They've been free for so many years of their lives. What we want as precautions for our people would stifle the mavericks' movement to quite an extent."

Xandar argued, "We're not stifling their movement. We just want to be kept in the loop. They'd be safe to move around the kingdom without needing to hide their faces or mask their scents. The need for updates isn't that bad, but it might involve . . . a level of tediousness that my cousin is allergic to."

Octavia disagreed. "His Grace may not like procedures the way we uphold them, Xandar, but he doesn't hate being tedious, I find. In the tasks that interest him, he strives for perfection as much as we do. Look at the way he brought back our people and dealt with the scientists."

Lucy stroked the back of Xandar's hand and reminded, "He also had to be tedious in his security measures for him and his followers to live right under our noses for so long."

"Under mine and Christian's noses," Xandar corrected before taking another sip from his mug.

When it was time to leave to visit the hybrids, they left the castle and headed for their destination. Weaver and Yarrington arrived shortly after meeting with the ministers of education and environment on the vampire's side, and they checked up on the families with the professionals looking after them before taking their leave.

###

Back in the kingdom, after getting Reida from Mrs. Parker, Lucy and Xandar made their way to the Den.

The moment they stepped into the lounge, Greg took a quick look at their exhausted postures and tired eyes, and asked, "Long day, you two?"

Lucy, with Reida in her arms, replied, "Two meetings. One hybrid visit. It gets busy like this sometimes. We're fine, really."

"Uh-huh," Greg replied, not at all convinced, eyes shifting to his cousin.

Xandar got to the point, "Yes, she's drained. This is our last stop for the day. Once we're done here, she'll be fine."

"That was more believable," Greg uttered before meeting the princess's large eyes looking straight at him. While Lucy was telling Xandar something about needing to give the hybrids more clothes, the baby holding her teddy bear gave her uncle a little wave as she mouthed "fuck."

Greg's smile had never been broader as he briefly waved back, utterly impressed at how she got around her mother at such a young age.

His sights were only torn off his niece when Lucy prompted, "Well, shall we, Greg?"

"Of course. Right this way, my queen."

In a small discussion room with a round table and three chairs, Lucy took a seat, placed her daughter on her lap, and began, "We spoke to Pelly and Octavia, and we've come to an agreement that we want to bring back the Secret Service, but only if you want to lead the initiative."

Greg's brows furrowed. His entire posture froze for two whole seconds before he blinked and asked, "Pardon me, my queen, but . . . could you repeat . . . that whole thing?" He had thought she was coming to ask for a favor and was cracking his head the whole day, wondering whether there were any loose ends that weren't properly tied up.

Registering his shock, Lucy clarified, "Would you like to lead a legally recognized body where you have full discretion of its operations and network, but would have to submit biweekly reports on any venture that you'll be sending your people on? The difference between what you've been doing all this time and what we're currently offering you is that your followers would no longer have to hide in the shadows or mask their scents. Those employed by your supplier and any other individual who want a second chance in the kingdom have the option of assimilating into society again as well. If they wish to continue in the . . . rogue line of work, it must be in the service of the kingdom, meaning it's to monitor suspects and sniff out threats. If they insist on pursuing intentions that harm the kingdom, we must hunt them down and run them through our legal system."

Greg muttered to himself, "Hm. Didn't think they'd get a pass too. They didn't even do anything."

"They got you your supplies, didn't they? Those that allowed your mavericks to earn some money before our cooperation?" Lucy asked, head cocked to one side.

"Yes," Greg uttered in defeat.

She continued, "And, Greg, there is also the . . . dreaded condition that we are to be kept informed about what's going on."

Looking at her like she just coughed up a furball, Greg replied, "That's not a dreaded condition, my queen. It's a rational requirement. I impose the same thing on every rogue and maverick living in the shadows of the kingdom."

Though surprised, she went on, "I should also mention that should we ever see the need to dissolve the Service, we retain the power to do so, in which case members would be expected to go their separate ways, and if any . . . questionable members are involved, we will hunt them down and run them through the law."

Xandar added, "Or, if the situation is severe, we'll use our royal prerogative to deal with them as we deem fit."

Greg scoffed and uttered, "It's funny how you never used that, Cousin. Uncle Lucas waved that thing like it was his own hand."

"I'm not him," Xandar noted.

Rolling his eyes, he murmured, "Clearly." Sitting up from his leaned-back position, he said, "Anyway, I'm interested in hearing the dissenting opinion of this venture." A smirk was shot at Xandar before Greg's attention returned to Lucy.

Her delicate brows pulled together. "There is *no* dissenting opinion, Greg. This is a unanimous agreement."

Greg's face morphed into disbelief, directed at his cousin, when he asked, "Really?"

Xandar managed a diplomatic smile. "Really. I'm not going to lie, Greg. I hated the idea of us working together . . ."

"The feeling's mutual," Greg interrupted.

Xandar let out a brief, amused scoff and continued, "Before we met your followers, I . . . expected some of them to stray and turn against us. Even when we started cooperating, I expected you to . . . do things that you weren't supposed to, both with regards to the cooperation and to me personally."

Greg didn't even bat an eye when he spoke crudely, "Cousin, as much as I hate you *less* than I did before, it doesn't erase the fact that whatever I did wasn't for you personally."

At that point, Lucy whispered affectionately to Reida, "Did you hear that, Reida? Uncle Greg hates Daddy less now, and Daddy is giving Uncle Greg a chance. Isn't that great? You're going to grow up with three uncles in our big, happy, and slightly scary family."

Reida chuckled even though she had no idea what her mother had just said. Their daughter's laughter softened Xandar's heart, and Lucy's words touched Greg's soul.

Tearing his eyes away from Reida, Greg turned to his cousin. "Anyway, it wasn't as bad working with you and Blackfur. As for the offer to lead the Secret Service, thank you for your support." Greg tried not to show how weird it felt to convey thanks to the very creature he'd spent so long hating.

Xandar took a moment snapping out of his own shock. "So you'll do it?"

"Yes, why wouldn't I?"

Xandar noted the obvious, "Because you hate law and the authorities?"

Greg retorted, "That was before I found out those under you two now have more brains and speed than those under Uncle Lucas and Aunt Vera. The present authorities are nowhere near perfect yet, but they're not a lost cause, unlike their predecessors. As for why I used to hate them . . . honestly, can you blame me? And I'm not just talking about speed and intelligence here, Cousin. Even with all those procedures and so-called precautions in place, they couldn't even do things right. I mean, just look what the ones from the past did to them." His hand gestured at the door leading outside, where his followers were.

Xandar understood. "I admit, we should have done more for them. We are doing more now. Prisoner re-entry was the only topic of discussion in government headquarters this morning."

Lucy added, "It's not right that they've been overlooked and neglected, Greg. We're doing everything we can to fix this now. We really do admire what you've done for them when no one else was there to help. It certainly explains your scent."

"My scent?" Greg asked, feeling somewhat small when he could tell that even Xandar understood where she was going with this.

Lucy explained, "Yes, Greg. Your scent. Ever since you disclosed housing ninety-eight rogues, none of us could fathom how you never smelled like a rogue. When you confessed to being the one leading the rogue world, the issue of why your natural scent was retained became even more perplexing. I thought you used scent sprays at first, but you didn't always have those on hand, even when you were in prison, so that couldn't be it. The only logical explanation is that you were never a rogue."

"O . . . kay?" Greg tried to keep up before he said, "That's probably because no matter what I do, I'm still of royal lineage, my queen."

Xandar countered, "That can't be it, Greg. In the past, any king or queen who had been dethroned and thrown to the rogues with their followers didn't retain their natural scent. And anyone who pledged loyalty to the rogue world through words or actions would inevitably smell like a rogue as well. You're *leading* the rogue world. You should smell like them, not us."

"I'm definitely feeling the love, Cousin," Greg murmured sardonically, but he couldn't help but agree that his situation was odd.

Lucy pushed her hair back to stop Reida from chewing on it before she said, "You've always served the kingdom, Greg. That's why you never smelled like a rogue. You were never one. You didn't . . . pledge loyalty to the rogue world over the kingdom. Your actions showed that you've always prioritized helping the creatures that this kingdom didn't help. You gave those who fell victim to the systems the second chance they needed to get back up again. You may have protected the rogues, but you were never a rogue yourself because you still cared about what happened to the ones no one bothered to empathize with. A rogue wouldn't have cared about what happened to a kingdom or anyone in a pack once they'd been cast out. But you . . . even when you disappeared for sixteen years, you never stopped caring for that portion of the population."

Greg couldn't deny any of that. He reminisced about the times he got creatures out of prison and trained them to be his followers. "Well, caring isn't very difficult when one is able to . . . relate to them." A quiet moment passed as Greg continued in a low murmur, "I wasn't the . . . most well-behaved student throughout school, which should come as no surprise, and it always got me into trouble. I did do those things on purpose sometimes, but other times, it was just a miscalculation that made a prank go too far. Teachers and administrators either tried to get me transferred or expelled. The only thing that kept me in was my family's status. I was viewed in a certain way, and suddenly everything that I was actually good at became . . . meaningless. I didn't want anyone else to feel that . . . just because they have a dark side . . ."

"It doesn't mean that they can't also be the light," Lucy finished for him when he was groping for the right words. He nodded in agreement, and she continued, "You harnessed their strengths the way you wished someone had helped harness yours."

"That sounds too noble to match what I became, my queen. Let's not forget, I do discriminate since I only take lycans. And I did certain—" he glanced at Xandar "—things that are not worthy of forgiveness."

Xandar muttered under his breath, "Good of you to know that."

Lucy's free hand reached for her husband's on his lap before she responded to Greg, "None of those *things* were right. But you don't need to be a pure, clean slate to be noble, Greg. You have a side that's darker than most and will go to great lengths to get what you want. But you've also been the light that your followers so desperately needed to climb out of the abyss, the beacon that kept them alive and going, and now thriving. You're not perfect, Greg. None of us is. But you are enough."

Greg's animal choked on tears, cooing at the acceptance, recognition, and appreciation that came from those words. His human was trying to get his beast to snap out of it, biting his bottom lip to hold back his own tears from surfacing. After a long moment with the only sound being Reida hitting the table with her teddy then checking to see if all parts were still intact, Greg replied in a small voice, "Thank you, my queen."

Xandar was very tempted to tease his cousin about those glistening eyes. Showing this much emotion was a big deal for someone like Greg, who had always presented a tough exterior. Lucy felt his humor, knowing exactly what he wanted to do, so she squeezed his hand and threw him a stern glare. Xandar ended up chuckling lightly and pecking a kiss on her hand before changing the subject.

"Greg, I have one question though: when you held office, funds went missing. Did you . . ."

"That. Was *not* me," Greg argued defensively, almost failing to suppress a growl, knowing both his cousins had been looking at him suspiciously ever since that issue surfaced all those years ago.

"Then who was it?" Lucy prompted.

Greg faced Xandar with furrowed brows. "Didn't you question how Uncle Lucas and his wife were suddenly able to afford a two-month trip halfway around the world, coming back with shopping bags of all kinds that took twenty servants three hours to get everything into the castle and in order? Also bear in mind that they weren't the money-saving type."

Xandar thought aloud, "They told me it was an education fund that was kept untouched for a second child that they never had. I checked the accounts. It confir—" Greg narrowed his eyes when their gaze met, and the king matched the duke's look when he deduced, "He tampered with the accounts."

With a broad smile, Greg said, "Don't you just love the old man, Cousin?"

"I *hate* you, Greg."

Greg snickered in amusement like it didn't bother him one bit. "Get those cops in the hacking department to check if you want. They should be able to crack this. It's not very complicated. And I do admit I wasn't very smart to buy that car at that time too. The timing was terrible. My businesses had a sudden boost, a legal one. With hindsight, I'd say I should have celebrated later."

Xandar clarified his last lingering doubt. "About that . . . when you prioritized profits over caring for the people, it was because . . ."

Greg's face was dead serious when he interjected, "Because the people in the kingdom weren't worthy of being cared for and protected the way the law said they were entitled to. They were the very creatures who shunned anyone who made mistakes, practically gave outcasts like Ivory, Alissa, and the others no choice but to turn rogue."

Xandar smiled in comprehension, "The profits were never for you. They were for them—your followers."

"That sounds a little too nice, Cousin. I would have taken some for my own hard work before giving them their cut. I'm not you or Blackfur. And up until I met the queen, I really didn't give a damn about wolves, so I didn't see a point in securing their safety or sharing anything with them, unlike the goody-two-shoes that you and Blackfur have been the whole time."

"That's . . . good to know, too, I guess."

Lucy whispered to Reida again, "See, Reida. They can get along. This was a good heart-to-heart, don't you think?"

Reida chuckled again.

Greg had the sudden urge to say, "My queen, why do I get the feeling the princess was brought here for a reason other than to be kept an eye on?"

Lucy mocked ignorance. "I have no idea what you're suggesting, Your Grace. My intentions have *always* been the very embodiment of directness and purity."

Xandar burst out cackling first. Greg tried but failed to press back his smile as he covered his mouth in an attempt to stifle his own laughter. It took a lot of effort to get a hold of himself before he managed to say, "If you say so, my queen."

When Greg walked them out, the sneaky princess mouthed the only word she knew at her uncle when her mother wasn't looking. After Reida was safely strapped in the baby car seat, Greg cleared his throat and said, "I've been meaning to thank you both." The couple's bewilderment snapped to him when he continued, "For what you gave Alissa."

The king and queen exchanged a nervous glance before Lucy said, "We really wanted to do more, Greg. We've consulted six legal advisers who've all told us that her case was properly tried in legal terms. The law applied and executed wasn't . . . wrong. Her excessive sentencing, as it turns out, was not excessive. It was legally permissible, so there was technically nothing wrong with how everything turned out."

Greg nodded with a small smile and confessed, "I know. I consulted my own set of lawyers when it happened too. But she is happy with what you gave her."

Xandar admitted, "We expected her to refuse, to be honest. It's just a journalistic story. It won't change what happened to her."

"Nothing will change what happened to her, Cousin. It's done. But the offer gives her a chance to emphasize parts of her story that were discarded by the media. If it goes well, she might be able to meet her pups without the risk of being arrested or shunned."

"Let's hope it goes that way," Lucy muttered.

CHAPTER 67

It took three months of countless interviews with Alissa and her acquaintances, friends, and colleagues before the assigned journalist pieced the story into a lengthy article entitled "Alissa 'Arson' Arden: An Ordinary Woman with a Scarred Past and a Thriving Present."

It was available in print and online, topping charts and pushing back any other headline for the day. The shares, likes, comments, and traffic garnered weren't even this high when the news of Xandar and Lucy's engagement went viral.

In her apartment that she bought for herself with the earnings made from working for Greg, Alissa let the article sit for two hours before she came to terms with the fact that it was time to read it. Her heart thumped like racing horses. She took a deep breath that did nothing to slow the franticness in her chest. Her thumb tapped on the link that led her to the website, and she started reading.

Love is what we all crave. Affection. Attention. Devotion. It is the very emotion that brings us together and blurs the lines between species. As lycans and werewolves, we are said to have an advantage. Said.

You and I have heard of the countless tales about how gracious the Moon Goddess was to do the heavy lifting, simply bonding two creatures together who then went on to live happily ever after. Tales like these have swept us off our feet and—for the most part—made us hope that we, too, would be so blessed to be bonded to that one very special creature who would be absolutely perfect for us.

On a usual day, after the usual cup of coffee, on the trip to the usual grocery store, you catch an unusual scent. You follow it. It follows you. At the end of the trail, you find it—your perfect mate.

But is this creature truly perfect?

Is the mate bond really a blessing of promised love and devotion, or is it sometimes a curse in disguise?

Twenty-eight years ago, a then twenty-three-year-old woman by the name of Alissa Arden had to find out the hard way that—in her case—it was unfortunately the latter. After meeting her bonded mate, Dickxon Ghouse, in a local grocery store, Dickxon did what we often see in movies—call it quits with the girl by his side in pursuit of the mate gifted to him by the deity.

Alissa herself left the man she was with for the same reason after a week of Dickxon's relentless persuasion through notes and flowers sent to the apartment she shared with her boyfriend.

The article went on to detail how they lived together and brought three pups into the world, how he began working late because he was seeing someone behind her back, how she found out, and—of course—how she set him on fire.

The day of the verdict came after six long years of arduous work. Her sentencing of twenty years imprisonment was seen as a failure of the legal system because, as *The Daily Piece* put it, "twenty years behind bars is not enough to balance the scales of justice. It does not compensate for the loss of a creature's life, and it is disrespectful to our Goddess, who bonded her sacred gift to this reckless monster."

The Central Headlines creatively curated public views for their article "Has Justice Been Served on Arson Arden?" which contained mostly views that Alissa "took things too far," as one anonymous respondent said, because if things really were that bad, "she should have just done the logical thing of taking the kids and leaving without a fuss. You can't change someone who doesn't want to change." When asked whether they would've let the same thing happen to them, most responded, "No," with only two respondents saying, "I hope not."

The Morning Message had a more varied set of responses, with some—like those who spoke to *Central Headlines*—saying that Alissa "brought that fire of hers from hell and should go back there," but others—who can be seen as being ahead of their time today—felt that there may be facts that weren't disclosed to the public. One respondent readily admitted to this by saying, "I don't know her, but I wouldn't want to mess with her. I've been a little more cautious with my own girlfriend after reading about it."

As much as there was to squeeze out of the tale, there will always come a time when the media will have to leave this dock and lower their sails in search of the next big scoop. Some argued that they have left the dock too early because as the vibrant flames of Alissa's case smothered with the execution of the prison sentence and everyone assumed that the ember was cooling into a cinder, turning it into something useless and unattractive, they were proven wrong when, two weeks into Alissa's sentencing, she was reported to have escaped.

Searches were conducted and news spread. The hunt for the "monster" who lost her home, job, dignity, and pups was on. Weeks turned into months, which turned into years.

Alissa Arden was never found.

We learn today that upon her escape, she was nursed back to health and commenced her training to work for the Duke of L'ouest, Greg Claw. When asked whether the duke assisted in her escape and kept her hidden for romantic intentions, Alissa laughed.

"His Grace isn't the type to ask you for one thing and then use you for another. If he gets you to work, you're his employee. If he gets one to serve his needs when she's offering herself or when she's in that particular line of work, then she is his companion for the night. Intentions and expectations have always been very clear when it comes to him, and it's something that I am very grateful for."

When asked whether she herself developed anything for the duke beyond their professional relationship over the years, she looked at me like I hadn't been paying attention before responding with a curt, "No."

Alissa claims that she works "mostly in the security side of things," which the duke has confirmed—via email—sufficiently describes her job scope.

Some may wonder whether she will be returning to prison to serve the remainder of her sentence now that she's no longer missing. The simple answer to that is no.

Alissa and many others who worked for His Grace have been granted pardon by their Highnesses after successfully helping the kingdom and our neighboring empire to track down and eliminate a set of rogues and proditors who were cooperating to challenge the crown. The conditional pardon covered all offenses except murder, so it covers Alissa's circumstance as well, seeing that hers was a case of manslaughter.

Today, she is a free woman who hasn't yet met the children she misses dearly, but she knows they're all doing well, having looked them up on the Internet many times over the years, expressing to me how grateful she is for having such "good, stable families" to raise them.

She remains unsure of whether she should reach out to them, expressing her fear of how she may be viewed, given what she did to their birth father.

Alissa doesn't plan to make any major shifts in her life at the moment, claiming to be paid well with a good professional and social circle. She intends to continue working for His Grace in the security department to see where her career takes her next.

When asked whether she would have done anything differently, her response was instant, "I would've rejected him. I should've never trusted him over my gut. I didn't know any better. If I went back and started over, I would've rejected him the day we met at the grocery store."

Alissa placed her phone back on the table and continued staring at the laptop screen displaying her sons' contact information. One became a physician, who'd undoubtedly be very busy; one was an assistant manager of a five-star hotel; and the last one became a firefighter.

Alissa couldn't help but chuckle to herself at the last one.

Perhaps she could just send them emails? If they allowed her to see them, she'd make the trip. If not, she'd just watch them from afar like she had been doing all along.

Once the emails were typed and perfected, she wondered if she was reaching out too soon. The article came out just hours ago. What if they needed the time and space to think things through? What if they hadn't even come across the article yet?

Then, there was a knock at the door.

CHAPTER 68

Alissa's furrowed brows and puzzled eyes shifted to the wooden structure. Her defensive instincts kicked in. She extracted the hard drive from her laptop and slid it into the custom-sewn compartment in her jeans.

Reaching for the loaded gun and heading for the door, she tried to guess who it could be. The property had been rented under an alias. Her landlady never came up in the last ten years she stayed here. Greg and the others usually gave her a heads-up before dropping by.

She looked through the keyhole. All she saw was a sand-colored shirt. She was also picking up a delightful yet somewhat familiar scent of oak and rain.

The knock came again.

She pressed her ear to the door, where she heard a heavy sigh before something ruffled at the foot of her door as footsteps retreated.

Alissa waited for the sound to fade further before she slowly opened the door. To her shock, a large bouquet of red roses that was placed leaning against the door fell on her feet. She picked it up and skimmed through the flowers for explosives, cameras, and bugs—none of which were present—and her head tilted out to get a glimpse of the creature who was there.

The frame at the end of the corridor looked very familiar, and when the man turned to his side, Alissa called out, "Gabriel?"

The man's face snapped up at her voice. Their eyes met as he mouthed, "Alissa."

He sprinted to her, brusquely stopping himself from touching her. His mouth opened, but he didn't know what to say. In the end, all he asked was, "Can I hold you?"

Alissa leapt into his arms, one hand still holding onto the bouquet and the other holding her gun. Familiar sparks coursed through her being like an electrical voltage as her lycan declared "mate."

Gabriel held her closely and inhaled deeply from her neck. His lycan already knew that his mate was behind the door the moment he stepped out of the elevator. He was relieved that the scent led to Alissa's apartment, but was also nervous and remorseful, somehow feeling responsible for what had happened to her. When he knocked and she didn't answer, he thought she didn't want to see him, and was leaving with a broken heart along with the intention to try again the next day.

He never imagined she'd jump into his arms. He'd missed her scent of chamomile and lemongrass, her frizzy locks that he'd comb through just to have an excuse to touch her hair. He'd missed *her*. In a chopped voice, he said, "I am so sorry. I should have never let you leave. I should have sent you flowers. I should have loved you more. I should have . . ."

Alissa smashed her mouth on his, and it didn't take long for Gabriel to respond with the same need of his own. When their lips parted, Alissa muttered, "*I'm* sorry . . . for doubting you, for doubting us. I was so stupid. I . . ."

"No, don't say that, Ali." His rough hand reached for her smooth cheek, and she leaned into his touch the same way she did so long ago.

The hinges of a door creaked as one of her neighbors came out, so they decided to continue their conversation inside. Sinking into the couch with Gabriel's arm caging her body from the side, not wanting her to sit too far away, he explained that he'd gotten her address from the journalist, who he bribed by offering her inside information on a rival company's scandal that she was investigating.

As Gabriel held her hand, he explained, "After you left, I thought about calling you, seeing you, but I always . . . chickened out. When I heard that you had kids with . . . him, I just . . . I thought my chance was blown. I left town. The next time I came back was when . . . the news about you and him exploded. I tried to visit you at the station, but they told me you were only allowed visits by your lawyer. I came to the trial a few times. I'm not sure if you saw me."

Alissa was visibly uneasy when she confessed, "I almost didn't see anyone during the trial. I just kept my head low to avoid the cameras."

"Yeah." There was a moment of silence before he said, "Your boys are doing quite well though. They have your eyes. The physician even has your smile." Alissa's brows furrowed in suspicion. How did he know? Gabriel scratched the back of his head and confessed, "I might have . . . stalked them online when I had the time. I didn't see anything before they had socials, I swear."

"How do you even know their names?"

"That wasn't the hard part. I just had to comb through the local authority's adoption list and find three kids with the dead guy's last name and make sure the kids' first names were from characters of your favorite movies."

Alissa blinked. "You went through an adoption list?"

Gabriel nodded. "It's a long list. Lots of weird names."

"So you found those families for my boys?"

Shaking his head, he sheepishly admitted, "No, Ali. I wished I had. I'm glad they've been in good hands, though. I uh . . . went through the list because I wanted to see if . . . if I could take them."

Alissa just stared at him like he had spoken gibberish. "You wanted to adopt my triplets?"

Gabriel pointed at her face and said, "The lady at the desk gave me that exact same look when I applied. My application was rejected, obviously. She very crudely told me that when it came to taking care of the kids, an ex-boyfriend is about as reliable as the imprisoned mother."

Alissa's eyes fumed when she snarled and cursed, "That mother f—"

"Hey, hey . . . calm down. The old lady was just doing her job." Gabriel began stroking her arms, both scared and elated that he was getting to see this side of her again. "Look, the point is: you lost them once. Now that you're free and your name is . . . less tainted after helping the royal family and all of that, maybe you should consider paying them a visit."

Gabriel recalled the part of the article where Alissa mentioned she was unsure about reaching out to her triplets. He gazed at her in concern, peering into her eyes as he tried to decipher what she really wanted.

Alissa confessed, "I drafted the emails but haven't sent them. I don't know if I should."

He whispered encouragingly, "Of course you should!"

"What if they don't want to see me?"

"What if they do? Ali, c'mon. What's the worst that could happen? We can still make the trip to stalk them if they refuse."

"I've already been stalking . . . watching them. From afar, that is," Alissa muttered.

Gabriel's franticness turned into realization. "So that's why you're delaying this. You've already seen them."

Head resting on his shoulder, she said, "Still, it'll be nice to meet them. I'm quite intrigued by my youngest—the firefighter."

Without warning, Gabriel carried her and put her into her chair at the desk, opened the laptop, and said, "Go on. Do it."

And she did. She took a deep breath and clicked the Send buttons. Now the pain was having to wait for a response.

Within an hour, one reply came—from the son who had become a hotel assistant manager, which said:

> Thank Goddess! We've been trying to find your location for hours, Mom. That journalist who interviewed you isn't very helpful, is she? Three of us called her asking for your address, and she entertained none of us, saying that everyone had been claiming to be your pups today.
>
> We were even willing to send our birth certificates to prove it, and she flicked us off. Said she already had seventeen poorly photoshopped copies and we shouldn't bother sending more. Fucking idiot.
>
> Anyway, the three of us already planned to meet tonight to figure out how to find you, but since you've reached out, we'd love to come see you. Looking forward to receiving your address. Let us know where you'd like to meet.
>
> Triplet #2
> Caleb
>
> P.S. The only reason this response came late is because triplet #1, Dr. Oliver, was too busy to check his phone. He's the worst amongst us, Mom. Busy. Busy. Busy.

Alissa cried so hard that Gabriel had to calm her long enough for her to send Caleb the address of a restaurant down the street. When that was done, he shut her laptop and continued letting her cry into his shirt.

After her sobs died down, Alissa got out of his embrace, washed her face, and went through her wardrobe to pick out her best dress. Checking herself in the mirror, Gabriel could tell that she was nervous by the way her chest rose and fell, so he asked in amusement, "Ali, were you this nervous when we went out?"

She forgot about her nerves for a moment, narrowing her eyes when she replied, "No. You're one guy. I'm meeting three tonight. There's a huge difference."

He chuckled, then reached out to hold her waist, telling her that she looked beautiful, making her smile wider and her eyes shine brighter. After sharing a kiss, they left the apartment and made their way to the restaurant.

They were twenty minutes early. Her crossed legs were fidgeting, and Gabriel did everything he could to distract her, from stroking her hand to speaking to her. When the twenty minutes were up and the triplets were still not in sight, Alissa started getting restless.

What if they changed their minds and stood her up? What if whoever sent the response was a prankster? The maverick part of her began mentally plotting how to make the prankster suffer if her triplets didn't show up, and she found out that it was someone pulling her leg.

Ten minutes later, three men with identical features stepped through the doors, and Alissa burst into tears again. They each took turns holding the woman who'd brought them into the world, with Caleb making sure that Oliver went last since he was the reason they were late.

The triplets sized up Gabriel when Alissa introduced them, Oliver being the most skeptical. Ryan and Caleb weren't worried. Their mother could always set this one on fire if he turned out to be a dick.

Much to Alissa's surprise and relief, none of her boys appeared to be carrying any resentment for what she'd done. The youngest, Ryan, even found it "cool." Caleb agreed it was cool as long as it didn't happen in the hotel he worked at. The rest of the night was mostly spent hearing about their childhood, schooling days, and university life.

It was the best date Alissa had been on. She didn't want it to end, but when it was time to say goodbye and goodnight, Alissa mentioned that she'd like to meet their adoptive parents. Only Caleb was horrified because he was nowhere near obedient when he was younger. This time, Oliver made sure that they all visited Caleb's parents first.

"Fuck," triplet #2 cursed.

Alissa linked Greg, Ivory, Desmond, and Hailey, telling them that she had reconnected with her sons and would be out of town for a few weeks, briefly mentioning Gabriel.

They were happy for her. When Greg was in the midst of asking her to "take care," he typed "Gabriel Bafford" on his phone and started his research. He and the other three of the top four only called it a day when they finished reading every single piece of information there was on the man, so they could go to sleep knowing that Alissa would be safe.

CHAPTER 69

3 months later

Alissa was leading Gabriel by his arm through the rows of white, yellow, and beige flowers in a nature park, where Tate and Margaret decided to have their wedding ceremony. In the sea of White Blood pack members, Alissa had finally found the creature she was looking for.

Pulling him to the smiling creature, Alissa began, "My queen, this is Gabriel, my second-chance mate and husband. Gabriel, this is our queen." Alissa beamed with the widest smile. Alissa and Gabriel had tied the knot two months before in the marriage registrar's office with the attendance of her triplets, Greg, Hailey, Desmond, Ivory, and Gabriel's brother.

Lucy observed the nervous-looking man in a tuxedo. "Well, it's a pleasure to finally meet you, Gabriel. We've heard a lot about you from Alissa. It's great to be able to finally put the name on a face."

"I-It's an honor to meet you, Your Highness. Uh . . . you look great. How far along are you, if I may ask?"

Xandar, whose hand was on his wife's shoulder, beamed while Lucy glanced at her baby bump and replied, "Fourteen weeks. This is our second and final pregnancy."

At that moment, a familiar voice from behind joined the conversation, "See, what did I tell you, Ella? There's a double dynamite in there."

Turning to lock gaze with her best friend, Lucy first offered Ella a welcome-back embrace. Ella was just released two days prior. The queen sensed a slight difference in the hybrid, but she didn't know what it was just yet.

Lucy then held her best friend. That was when she realized Toby felt leaner, his shoulders were broader, and he smelled a little different. She parted their bodies and looked him in the eye, which shone in unfiltered happiness as he tried but failed to press back a broadening smile because he knew he'd been caught.

Her eyes widened in realization before they went to his neck, where she saw a fresh mark. Her mouth hung open for a moment as she looked back and forth between Toby and an increasingly blushing Ella before wrapping Toby in a second hug while speaking intentionally loudly, "AWWW . . . I'M SO HAPPY FOR YOU TWO! IT MUST HAVE BEEN A GREAT NIGHT!"

Many paused their conversations and turned. The alliance members were already coming over, as were many White Blood members. Ella was flushed and stood closer to her mate. Toby knew exactly why Lucy did what she did. This was payback for exposing her and her mate's first time.

The minister's eyes narrowed when he complained, "Lucy, this isn't fair. I didn't wake you or anyone at 4:00 a.m. with my business."

In mocked innocence, Lucy asked, "So what time was yours then?" Ella looked horrified, which made Lucy add, "I'm kidding, Ella. Really. I'm just messing with Toby."

Ella sighed in relief, and the alliance members offered their appropriately phrased congratulations, as did the mavericks, easing Ella's anxiety.

In the midst of that, Toby locked eyes with Lucy again and linked, *'Around eight last night, so my point stands—you and your mate are still the insane ones.'*

Lucy chuckled as he ended their link to concentrate on Hale's conversation with Ella.

The moment Lucy's eyes cleared, Hailey came into her field of vision with a frown. "Reida isn't here, my queen?"

"She is. She's with her uncle." Her head craned and eyes started searching when she muttered, "Where is he?"

"Which uncle?"

"Greg."

Hailey's lips curled up. "I'll go find him."

"And this. Is. A. Spider," Greg said. He sat under a tree, securing Reida tightly with one arm, his free hand at a distance from her face for her to observe the spider on his palm which was lost on which way to go.

Greg was hoping to find animal manure that was used as fertilizer so that he could point to it and train Reida to say, "Dada," but there wasn't a single heap in sight, so he had to settle with entertaining her with the insects and spiders instead.

"Now, watch this, Princess." Greg turned his palm over, and the spider's legs reached for his finger before a sliver of white formed, and the arachnid hung by its self-made thread.

Reida's large eyes looked at the dangling eight-legged creature in wonder.

"My turn, Your Grace!" Hailey's voice made Greg flinch, and the spider fell and scurried away.

He turned and looked at her in annoyance. "What do you mean *your turn*? She's *my* niece."

"Exactly. You'll get invited to family events from now on. I don't. You'll have more opportunities to hold her than I do. Come on. Hand over the princess."

Greg groaned, turned to Reida, and said, "Auntie Hailey is going to take you now. If you don't like what she's doing, what should you say?"

"Fuck!" Reida could say "mama," "dada," "yay," and "no" now, so it was crucial to her uncle that she knew which word to use at any given time.

"Atta girl," Greg praised before planting a quick kiss on Reida's forehead, a gesture which shocked himself and Hailey. Reida chuckled like she did whenever her parents kissed her there, and her tiny hand reached out to touch Greg's nose before she let out a cute coo, melting her uncle's heart.

Gingerly placing Reida into Hailey's arms, Greg was careful not to look Hailey in the eye. Hailey knew her boss didn't want her to see the happy tears pooling there, so she walked the other way, plucking leaves, grass, and flowers for Reida to play with.

###

Lucy's feet weakened and wobbled despite wearing flats. Her hand instinctively went to Xandar's shoulder for support. He held her by her arm and waist, suggesting, "Babe, why don't we go sit down?"

"Yeah, okay."

Guiding her to the chairs, she plopped into one of those in the row reserved for the alliance members in the front row. Xandar kissed her temple before lowering himself to take off her shoes.

He began rubbing her right foot when she pulled it back and whispered, "I'm fine, Xandar. That's not necessary."

Xandar could feel that her feet were tired, but he also felt her embarrassment. When she glanced around, making him realize why she refused the foot rub, he sighed and leaned in to kiss her cheek, muttering, "I've already knelt to you before the entire kingdom and you're still embarrassed to have me rub your feet in public?"

Without hesitation, she replied like it should be a well-known fact, "Yes!"

He scoffed lightly. "Fine. I'll do this later on the jet." After washing his hands, he got her some water before returning to her side, arm across her shoulders as she leaned into him while his hand stroked her belly.

A kick—brief and strong—assaulted his palm, bringing mist to his eyes. Xandar chuckled and left a light kiss on the corner of Lucy's lips, muttering, "I love you."

Thumb stroking his thigh, she said, "I know. I love you too."

The wedding planner's voice boomed from the front, and everyone took their seats. Shortly after, the groom came into view, dressed in white with a blue-and-black estella pinned on the lapel of his tux.

Xandar helped Lucy slip her shoes back on before kissing her hands, then leaving her side to join Tate with Juan, Toby, Zeke, Raden, Christian, Phelton, and Beta Mannon. Juan, as Tate's best man, was the first to convey his congratulations to his old friend.

The alpha of White Blood got cheers and claps even before the bride emerged. He was pleased to see that his pack members were not giving the vampire guests odd looks, and he was proud that—when he raised this matter with everyone weeks before the wedding—they seemed more excited and welcoming than reluctant and disapproving.

What surprised him most was the vampires didn't sit at one place. They were scattered amongst the wolves and lycans. Tate wanted the integration, but he definitely didn't expect to get it this soon.

He took a good look around to commit the sight before him to memory—the memory of his closest friends and pack members here to celebrate his and Margaret's special day.

When his eyes fell on Lucy, she linked, *'Margaret's more than everything, Tate.'*

He instantly replied, *'Not more, Lucy. She's* my *everything, the same way that you are his.'*

Her sights reflexively went to Xandar, whose eyes were only on her. Those lilac orbs held so much devotion and affection even from a distance, promising her the world, promising her everything.

The music started, and everyone turned to the back to watch the bridesmaids walk down the aisle that was decorated with yellow and blue baby breath on each side. They were mostly women from Margaret's old pack and members of another rogue pack whose leader was friends with Margaret, all of whom had merged with White Blood. The last to appear was Margaret's maid of honor, Annie.

When the bride came into view in an elegant, sleeveless white dress with a low V-neckline, holding a bouquet of estellas, everyone stood, and many gasped at the picturesque sight of White Blood's luna.

Stella herself had opted to be a photographer instead of a bridesmaid. In the early weeks of planning the wedding, Tate specifically told Stella—in private—to mentally count to five before refusing to walk down the aisle with a bouquet in hand, then act sheepish when she told her mother that she wanted to take photos instead. However, Tate soon learned that things would not always go as planned when it came to his stepdaughter.

Before Margaret could finish asking Stella about becoming one of her bridesmaids, her daughter refused and said—very bluntly and shamelessly—that she wanted to take photos instead. Tate remembered Stella throwing him a cheeky grin right after. What was surprising was that Margaret didn't mind, and actually found Tate and Stella's exchange amusing, even endearing, much to his relief.

Stella practiced for weeks with the camera Tate had gotten her back in lycan territory, even looking online for any tips and tricks she needed to learn. So while everyone was watching her beautiful mother, she was recording the march with steady hands, finally including Tate in the video when Margaret joined him there.

Tate muttered something to Margaret while taking her hands into his, making her chuckle lightly and glow even brighter than she already was.

The marriage officiant began reciting from the Scriptures of Matrimony before it was time to exchange vows.

Tate began, "Mar, saying that I fell for you because of the mate bond or your beauty would be speaking like someone who didn't just spend the best months of his life with you. I fell for you when I saw the lengths you'd go to save your pup on the very first day we met, when you let me in on how you didn't let your past stop you from getting back up, when I saw the way you smile."

That drew a bigger smile from her. "And I still fall for you every day, regardless of whether you're just getting out of bed, helping someone, scrolling through your phone, or watering and fertilizing the plants in our home or within the pack. It's amazing how you can look so effortlessly perfect even when you're doing the simplest things, like walking across the room or just sitting on the couch. The way you collect leaves and put them in your scrapbook makes me smile, the way you smile makes my heart skip, and the way you touch me and put yourself in my arms makes me feel like the luckiest creature in the world."

A layer of moisture got increasingly thick behind Margaret's eyes as Tate continued, "I've never been acquainted with a leader of a rogue pack, and I sure didn't think I'd be blessed with a bond that gave me the strongest and most perfect one. I have no idea what I've done to deserve someone like you, Mar. You're so sure of who you are, so firm in what you want, so protective over the ones you love, and so determined and resilient that nothing from your past seems to be holding you back."

He paused, kissed her hands, and declared, "Running into our daughter has been the best thing that's ever happened to me, because it drew you out and led me right to you. You have no idea what it means to be able to call her mine, to call *you* mine. Thank you for letting me in despite your past, despite what I am. I promise to always have your back, to make sure you're never alone, to express how grateful I am that you'd have me, and to let my timing issues stay as timing issues. I love you, Mar."

Margaret was chuckling before she began crying. Annie came with tissues to dab away the tears.

Everyone else wasn't doing any better. Weaver blew his nose a little too loudly, which drew attention to him and his slightly apologetic-looking mate. Azalea was dabbing away her own tears. Lucy wondered why she even bothered with makeup when she had a front-row seat to such a touching scene, especially when she had been the lucky few to witness the progress of their relationship.

After a few moments, Margaret cleared her throat, looked into Tate's eyes that held so much love and assurance, and began reciting her own set of vows, "Tate, when we met, I thought our bond wasn't going to last. I thought a rejection would follow, from you or me, or even from the both of us. You haven't the faintest clue of how relieved and happy I am that I've been proven wrong. Very wrong. I was wrong to think that our bond is a mistake, I was wrong to judge you based on the title you inherited, and I was wrong to think that you could never love me the way I didn't know I needed to be loved. Never in my wildest dreams could I have imagined falling in love again, and never did I think it would be to someone as perfect as you are. I held so much hate from my past, carrying it throughout my life, yet you've never judged me for those scars."

Taking a breath, she continued, "There's this . . . thing that you do. I'm not sure if it's the way you look at me or touch me, the things you say, or the way you speak, it just . . . smothers the flames, and I know for a fact that it isn't solely because of the mate bond. You have a way of making me feel safe to be at my most vulnerable, to let out any sadness or vent off any frustrations. I love how you make time to sit with me whenever I need a listening ear, how you drop whatever's in your hands when I peek into your office and insist that you want to hear me out first. Your presence itself is a constant assurance that I'm never alone. In anything. I was convinced that I'd always have to fight and lead on my own. At that time, my only hope was that my daughter would have a better life than the one I was forced to live. It was fat hope seeing that she was born a rogue, but I never stopped hoping. It didn't occur to me that my prayers would be answered in the best possible way—through you."

Tate's Adam's apple bobbed, eyes turning misty. Margaret pushed through. "I love the way you interact with our daughter. It's amazing how you try so hard to bond with a child that isn't yours by birth, and I especially love that you can get her to do things that I *clearly* cannot."

Their eyes went to Stella, who rolled hers in response, making the attendees erupt in a round of laughter. Tate shook his head with a proud but slightly irritated smile, and Stella grinned and chuckled at his reaction.

When the bride's and groom's eyes returned to each other once more, Margaret vouched, "I promise to barge into your office or onto the training ground and pull you out of there whenever I can feel you need a break, I promise to hear you out whenever you need a listening ear, and I promise to be with you whenever you need me to be." She then added a line that wasn't in her original draft, "Thank you for welcoming me into your heart despite my past, despite what I am. I love you, too, Tate."

After exchanging the rings that were made from rose gold and brown diamonds, the officiant pronounced them husband and wife. They shared a kiss as the attendees burst into loud cheers and wild applause.

###

In the middle of the wedding banquet, the wedding planner announced that it was time for the bouquet toss. Single females who wished to be the next one to walk down the aisle gathered at the open space next to the banquet tables.

Ella had heard about this tradition and was excited to see her first one. A thought came to her: maybe she could even be in her first one! Her eyes shone when she gave Toby's hand a squeeze and asked, "Can I go?"

"Of course. Go ahead." Toby pecked a kiss on her temple before she sprinted to join the rest.

Lucy, next to Toby, had a knowing smile that couldn't be blocked by her sipping water from her glass.

Toby muttered, "Goddess, I hope this works." He downed the last of his wine before getting up, and Lucy hastily followed suit. She had already missed his first kiss. She wasn't going to miss this. Xandar took Reida out of the baby highchair and into his arms, following Lucy to make sure that she wasn't exerting herself with the excitement that was about to come.

The females got ready, and Margaret's back faced them. One, two . . .

Before the toss came, Margaret turned back around, walked straight to Ella, and placed the bouquet into her hands. Ella didn't know what was happening. This was not what she remembered from the tradition at all. She then felt someone taking her right hand. Her blue eyes darted to the source and found a smiling Toby getting down on one knee.

She was so shocked that she didn't hear the creatures around her gasp and squeal. Her mouth gaped when Toby took out a small jewelry box from his pocket, opened it to reveal a light blue diamond adorned by onyx diamonds along the band, and began, "Ella, from the first moment I saw you on the beach, I knew I had to get to know you. You are one of the bravest creatures I have met, the kindest I've ever known, and the most beautiful I've ever seen. I promise to give you only the best as my mate." His hand holding the jewelry box inched closer her way when he asked, "Ella, will you marry m—"

"YES!" Ella exclaimed and threw herself at him, making them both fall to the ground as she pressed her lips against his. A mixture of chuckles and cheers came from everyone who watched.

When their lips parted, Toby looked into her joyful eyes, muttering, "Ella, as much as I love what you're doing, I really do need to put the ring on your finger before I can feel at ease."

Ella chuckled lightly, seating herself on the grass next to him while he took her hand and slipped it onto her ring finger, after which he let out a relieved sigh and planted a sweet kiss on her lips, thanking her after he did it. A train of congratulations and well wishes followed as more tears and laughter spread.

CHAPTER 70

7 weeks later

"I've actually already had two. They taste pretty good," Toby said to Lucy as they stood by the table with trays of cupcakes. "I'm glad she decided to start a business out of this. Her baking skills are fantastic!"

Hailey made them. She was now a probationary kindergarten teacher on weekdays and baker on weekends. She and the other mavericks still worked for Greg, but they were free to indulge in their hobbies and passions when they didn't have maverick duties. Some even pursued career paths that earned a salary the "normal" way.

Jade opened a cybercafé which attracted lots of youngsters, and Hailey baked cupcakes or made pastries to sell to Jade's customers, offering him a small percentage of her earnings for his space. Some even came in just to buy the baked goods.

Lucy could see how tempting the cupcakes were, but she restrained herself from taking one to leave a visible hole on the perfectly arranged tray. She was so glad she'd already had Reida. Lucy had such severe cupcake cravings when carrying her firstborn that she had to have at least five cupcakes a day or her mood would spiral out of control. Xandar had to make sure there were bakeries or cake shops in their honeymoon locations for this exact reason.

"Is the tie okay?" Toby asked, adjusting the black necktie again.

Lucy's brow knitted as she gently slapped away his hands and hissed, "It was fine, Toby. Stop touching it!"

"Easy for you to say when you're not the one who has to think about looking perfect on your wedding day for your mate. I'm sure Xandar was just as paranoid when you were going to walk down the aisle."

Now that he mentioned it, Lucy did feel some of Xandar's nerves on their wedding day.

When she was satisfied with how it looked against his white shirt and light blue tuxedo, she looked Toby dead in the eye and warned, "If you touch it one more time, I'm going to tie your hands behind your back until Ella is right in front of you, do you understand me?"

Toby gave that threat some thought and murmured, "I wonder if we should do that right now, actually."

A sudden urge to punch Toby surged through her before a light kiss was pressed on the back of her head, putting those violent thoughts to rest. She turned to lock gaze with her husband, who was carrying one of their fraternal twins when he asked in concern, "You okay, babe?"

After taking little Enora from his arms, she declared, "If Toby touches his tie again, we have to break his hands."

Toby argued, "C'mon, Lucy. It's not like it isn't normal! Xandar, how many times did you mess up your tie when you two got married?"

With a sheepish smile, Xandar admitted, "I lost count. Christian was very patient with me, adjusting it over and over again."

Toby turned to Lucy. "Which is exactly what *you* should be right now, Lucy. You're my best woman. Well, now that I think of it, I can see why no one else I know has had a best woman."

Lucy smirked. "Regretting your decision?"

With a wave of a hand, he replied, "Nah. It'll be weird to have anyone else fill those shoes."

Toby's sights then went to the pup in her arms. "This is the one that hates everyone, right?"

Lucy rolled her eyes. "She doesn't hate everyone. She just . . . doesn't feel comfortable around anyone else yet." Lucy then spoke to her daughter in a hushed whisper, "But you will warm up to them someday, won't you, Enora?"

Enora merely leaned into her mother's chest without offering a response. This younger twin, for some reason, only let her parents hold her. If anyone else took her away, she'd scream and cry until she was safely back in her parents' arms. No one knew why she was the way she was, not even the doctors.

Ken was a little hurt when Enora cried in his arms until her face turned red, quickly handing his granddaughter back to his daughter to calm the child. What the old man loved about the baby girl was that her features seemed to be following those of her mother, from the hair to the shape of her eyes, nose, and lips. But neither Ken nor Janice knew whether Lucy was shy as a baby. As for Xandar, he didn't recall his parents saying anything about him being picky about who was carrying him as an infant. Not knowing where Enora's behavior came from, they let the mystery remain a mystery.

Toby smiled at little Enora when he asked the happy couple, "Where's the one you two cleverly named after former Alpha Ken?"

With a guilty smile, Xandar replied, "With Janice and the older Ken."

Lucy asked, "And Reida?"

"She was with Mrs. Parker before Hailey took her. Uh . . . there." Xandar pointed at the shoreline where Hailey was carefully dipping Reida's feet into the seawater as the little girl chuckled, and the happy father uttered, "Reida seems to be having fun."

Lucy smiled as she said, "The beach is a great idea for a wedding, Toby. The trees, breeze, sand, and sound of waves make this location really private and intimate. And *they* are probably here for you too."

Her chin gestured to the boulders. She knew about his teenage friends. It was the reason several seats in the front row would be left vacant.

Smiling at the stony structures, he murmured, "Yeah." Looking around, feeling the energy of the place, he admitted, "It didn't take much thinking to decide to have it here, to be honest. This is where Ella and I met *and* where I get to imagine *they*'re here." A moment of silence passed before he said, "I have to thank His Grace for making sure this place was rogue-free before using it. Also have to thank him for approving Ella's application to join the Service. She's having fun in their training sessions, by the way. Wakes up excited every day."

"Haven't you thanked Greg like . . . twice already?" Lucy questioned.

Toby shrugged. "You've just adjusted my tie four times. I doubt the duke has any right to complain." His hands were subconsciously reaching for his tie again before Lucy's hand came to gently slap them away.

When everyone was asked to take their positions, the guests took their seats in the rows of white chairs that each had a blue chiffon ribbon tied to the back. Toby marched down the aisle as he grinned and waved to friends and allies, even to the hybrid families who came.

Toby took his place next to his best woman and glanced at his row of groomsmen as he muttered, "I might have just broken the record for the number of groomsmen, Lucy."

"No kidding," she responded after taking a long look.

In that line stood Xandar, Christian, Tate, Juan, Mannon, Zeke, Raden, Rafael, Joseph, Weaver, Yarrington, Phelton, Desmond, Ivory, and Greg. Toby couldn't narrow it down any further than that, as he had told Ella and Lucy countless times, despite the fact that neither of them minded the number he had in mind.

When flower girls and page boys emerged with little baskets of petals, everyone watched the precious sight as some attendees whispered words of encouragement which got the more intimidated children to smile as they scattered pink petals all over the ground.

Michael was one of the last to emerge, and his eyes focused on Lucy's warm smile to block out the hundreds of other eyes staring at him, walking stiffly to the front with the others. While the children circled around and returned to the seats where their parents were, Michael went up to Lucy and reached for her hand.

Lucy's eyes searched for Regina and found the woman in one of the last rows. The vampire managed a smile, which Lucy gently returned. Xandar lightly patted Michael on the head before he took Enora from Lucy so she could focus on the boy. Michael stood closer to her because he didn't want Xandar to take him away the way he took the other pup. Lucy's thumb stroked the back of his small hand, and the sensation comforted him.

The bridesmaids emerged in a mix of vampires, hybrids, wolves, and lycans before Ella finally came into view. Toby's eyes shone, sighing in happiness at the sight of his gorgeous bride in the faded blue dress that hugged her figure with a bouquet of gardenias clasped in her hands.

While all eyes were on Ella, her sights stuck to her groom, who looked like he was close to tears as he beamed at her.

At the end of the aisle, he offered her his hand, helping her onto the platform. The music stopped, and the guests took their seats once more.

After the marriage officiant recited from the scriptures, Toby began, "Ella, from the moment we met, I knew that my life was never going to be the same again. Not only can I now boast about being the only one among my friends to get the most beautiful hybrid for a wife, but also your mark practically gave me the license to gloat about being able to see a discretus when they can't. You have no idea how much fun I'm going to have lying about a discretus's presence when we're training."

Laughter ensued from everyone, especially the alliance members, before Toby continued more seriously, "There's something about you, Ella, something magical about your presence, your scent, your voice, your touch . . . they all send the gentlest ray of light to soothe my darkest memories and ease my most painful losses."

Ella gave his hand a gentle squeeze as her smile and eyes grew softer. His thumb stroked her fingers when he said, "I am forever grateful to our Goddess for bonding us, and I promise to be the understanding, supportive, and loving mate that you deserve. Thank you so so much for giving me a chance after what I did on the first day we met. I've never taken you for granted, and I will never take you for granted. Never. You are a gift that I still can't believe said yes to marrying me. I want nothing more than to hold you close every night when we go to sleep and kiss you when we wake up. I promise to be your pillar of support when it comes to pursuing your dreams, to be your voice of reason whenever you need input, and to be your main source of comfort, protection, and laughter. Thank you for making me yours, baby. I love you."

As everyone sniffled, Ella quickly wiped away her own tears.

She took a moment to breathe and cleared her throat before reciting her vows, "Toby, I've never met anyone quite like you. You emanate a gentle warmth that feels welcoming, yet that warmth carries a protective presence that looks daunting but feels assuring. Your sense of humor always brightens up my day. The way you speak never fails to lighten any heavy atmosphere. I love that you have an impeccable balance of humor with seriousness, knowing immediately which to choose at any given time."

She took a deep breath and continued, "Thank you for rejecting me when you found out who I was and what I was up to. It was painful, but it was a much-needed wake-up call. Thank you for telling me how wrong I was to take the path I took, and for showing and offering me an alternative route that makes me happy, safe, and fulfilled. I only hope I'm able to match your bravery, nobility, and ferocity one day, but your humor is something that I have no intention of matching."

Light chuckles followed before Ella finished up, "I promise to be in your embrace whenever you need a hug, to hear you out whenever you have something to say, and to support you in your endeavors, however difficult they may be. Thank you for making me yours, Toby. I love you too."

Upon the marriage officiant's request, two hybrid children came with the wedding rings. Right after Toby and Ella slid the rings onto each other's fingers, Toby pulled her into a deep kiss even while the officiant was still making his final pronouncement.

The congregation erupted into loud applause as they celebrated the newly wedded couple.

During the banquet, Pelly sat between Lucy and Annie, sharing details about the ceremony to return the lycan's royal title that was to be held the following week, repeating at least three times that "it has to be perfect."

Octavia, who was next to Xandar, muttered, "Do you have any idea how many times Pelly says those words in a day ever since we decided to return the title, Xandar?"

Xandar let out a short chuckle, then made a wild guess, "More than twenty times, I'd say."

Rafael—next to Octavia—snorted, proclaiming, "More than a hundred times would have been a better guess, Your soon-to-be Majesty."

Octavia added, "Neither Rafael nor I recall Pelly being this paranoid when she and I were going through the details for our wedding. Our WEDDING."

Xandar felt a little bad, and uttered, "Lucy and I really don't mind something small and simple, and it really doesn't have to be perf—"

He was cut off by Octavia and Rafael shushing him, both nervously glancing at Pelly, and was relieved to see that she was too busy talking to notice them.

Octavia whispered, "Don't tell her that. It upsets her. She loves doing this and takes pride in the planning. If the empress wants grandeur and perfection, she will get exactly that, or the ceremony will be postponed. She wanted a type of flower that wasn't in season on the date we initially chose for our nuptials, and we ended up changing the date, not the flower."

Rafael clarified, "We're not telling you this to make you feel bad, Your Hig—Majesty. We're sharing this to let you know how seriously we're taking this in the empire, and the uh . . . detail-crazy empress that our Lord has blessed us with is making sure that everything goes right."

Xandar smiled. "Thank you. No one from our generation would have thought this would happen this soon . . . or even happen at all."

Octavia waved her hand and declared, "Don't thank us. After everything you, Lucy, and your people have done for us, the title is the least we can offer as a sign of gratitude. The business discussions our people are having with yours are going very well, we're told." She patted Xandar's shoulder and proceeded to say, "Yours and Lucy's reign has taken the kingdom to new heights thus far and will no doubt be breaking lots of glass ceilings in the years to come, both in terms of the inner workings of the kingdom and diplomatic relationships with the other species. Many congratulations to you both, Xandar."

Xandar's smile broadened by the second, and he stole a glance of his mate, who was holding Enora, before turning back to Octavia. "I don't know what to say, other than I'm lucky to be bonded to her."

Acknowledging he was doing better with his mate by his side, Octavia nonetheless insisted, "Give yourself some credit, Xandar. Your reign was already taking the unconventional route before Lucy showed up. Your Goddess wouldn't have bonded her to you had you been like past kings. Even if the deity did . . . I doubt such a bond would have lasted. Seeing the two of you are thriving, I'd say you've earned your right to be with her as much as she's earned her place with you. As individuals, you both may have been working on similar goals without ever realizing that you were working toward one another. As king, you're determined and sure of what you want from your people and yourself, and you implement changes regardless of what tradition dictates. Lucy is a gift that ensures you're going the right way, no doubt also using her own intelligence, skills, and character to help speed up that process and make the reign that much more revolutionary. Like Pelly and I, you and Lucy are lucky to have each other."

Touched beyond words, the king could merely utter, "Thank you, Octavia."

CHAPTER 71

The ceremony to return the title was held in the abandoned castle next to the Forest of Oderem. Pelly had an unexplainable feeling that it had to be there, as did Lucy.

When the servants went to have the place cleaned up, all praying that they weren't going to encounter anything out of the ordinary when they did their job, two among the sixty cleaners entered a room on the highest floor that was covered with a very thick layer of dirt and dust. They opened the windows to let in some air, and a dash of breeze came from the forest and blew at a part of the dirt on the floor, making the poor servants flinch before instinctively holding each other as they quivered in fear. When nothing happened for the next few moments, they slowly released their hold over each other.

Taking note of the carvings on the cement floor uncovered by the breeze, they braved through cleaning the room for the next two hours, looking over their shoulders from time to time. When they returned to the castle, they shared the spooky tale with their colleagues before reporting it to the empress and consort, who went to take a look but didn't know what to make of it. Even the experts who worked for the imperial family had to consult other experts on the matter, who all admitted they knew nothing at present, and that they would look into it, concurring that the carving meant something—they just didn't know what yet.

Pelly and Octavia now stood at the edge of the circular carving with Lucy, Xandar, Christian, Annie, and Greg in the room an hour before the ceremony was scheduled to begin. The circle was cut into five sectors—one sector had two vampire fangs, the second sector had a lycan's handprint, the third had the flipper of a merfolk's tail, the fourth had an old-fashioned bow, and the fifth one only had a line sitting right in the middle, which everyone guessed was a wand.

After a long while staring at the structure, Greg's voice cut through the silence, "Hurry up, Cousin. Just spit out whatever history shit this is so we can go."

Christian taunted, "You're not afraid of being in this room, are you?"

Greg's eyes narrowed when he declared, "I'm bored, distant cousin."

Enora was bored, too, but she remained quiet on Lucy's shoulder. The baby's eyes wandered to the view outside the window, where the Forest of Oderem was. What the adults didn't realize was that the forest started growing pink and amber-colored flowers that attracted butterflies, and the sight of the fluttering insects captivated the little princess, drawing out her smile.

The forest may not have known how rare it was to get Enora to smile, but Greg knew. Everyone who met Enora knew about her aversion to strangers and the difficulty of hearing her laugh or seeing her smile. Her uncle caught the lift of her lips and followed his niece's sights, noticing the way the forest was entertaining the pup. Approaching the child, he muttered, "That place is more than meets the eye, Princess. The yellow flowers are *especially* dangerous."

Lucy's confused eyes went to Greg before she turned to face the forest, and that was when Enora moved restlessly because she was denied her good view. Lucy positioned Enora's side to her chest, letting her daughter face the forest once more as she, too, looked in that direction. Instead of looking at the butterflies and trees like Lucy thought she would, Enora's huge orbs stuck on her uncle. She had never seen him up close before and blinked her large eyes a few times, studying him.

His animal prompted him to back away, the beast himself backing to the corner of his mind as well, not wanting to scare the pure, little creature when Greg asked Lucy nervously, "She's not going to cry, is she?"

This princess cried and screamed even when the Blackfurs attempted to hold her. As delightful as it was to witness the scene, he didn't want to be the cause of those tears.

Nonchalantly, Lucy explained, "No, this is her curious face. Her features will crinkle before she cries." Her tone lowered into a hush when she then whispered to her daughter, "This is Uncle Greg, Enora. You remember him, right?"

Enora blinked again before her little hand raised and she gave Greg a wave the way her sister always did. The sight made her mother gasp.

"Babe, what is it?" Xandar asked, coming over.

Lucy groped with words, "Enora. She just . . . she could . . . she waved . . . at Greg."

Xandar's brows raised in surprise, and he looked back and forth between his daughter and his cousin before Enora waved at Greg again, which was when her father uttered, "Well, this is a first."

Greg offered Enora a slight bow and a wide smile when he whispered, "I'm honored, Princess."

Enora chuckled as her arms reached out to him, something she only did to her parents and no one else.

Greg's smile fell when he asked in concern, "Are you sure?" Only when the question left his lips did he wonder why he bothered asking when he wasn't even sure if she could understand him yet.

Lucy was still trying to make sense of things when she offered, "Do you want to try holding her, Greg? I'll take her back if she gets upset."

Gets upset was the code word for "cries and screams her lungs out." No one didn't know. Even Pelly and Octavia knew. Enora was wriggling in her mother's hold, eyes looking up at Greg in anticipation.

Fear rattled through Greg like never before in his entire life. He had never attempted to hold Enora because he had seen how she pushed away practically everyone but her parents. All those times secretly laughing with his animal about how even the Blackfurs couldn't hold this princess without the child's objection suddenly wasn't funny anymore.

The shine in Enora's eyes dimmed, her lifted lips now downturned, and that put her uncle in an even worse predicament.

When he reached for his niece, his animal covered his eyes, ears folding inward. His human then murmured more to himself than to anyone else, "This is not going to end well."

As he gently took the baby girl, everyone braced themselves for the deafening screams that would usually follow. But what came next was just soft coos as Enora leaned on her uncle's shoulder, resting her head there with a soft smile.

After a few quiet moments, Greg glanced at the pup before looking back at her parents. "What did you two feed her this morning? What sorcery is this?"

Christian had a theory, which he shared as he approached Greg, "Maybe she's starting to warm up to us. Let me try."

As soon as Greg reluctantly detached Enora from his shoulder and the baby realized that she was going to a different adult that was neither one of her parents, her screams and cries echoed off the walls as she pressed herself to Greg.

"Holy shit. That was loud," Greg cursed as he placed Enora on his shoulder again, and the screams miraculously stopped.

Christian backed away, evidently hurt as Lucy apologized to him, embarrassed. Xandar gave his best friend an apologetic squeeze on his shoulder.

Enora's hand balled into a tight fist, punching her uncle's neck with all her little might, which was something she did to her parents every time they tried to let a friend or family member hold her. Greg had seen this reaction of hers before, and although no damage was done to his neck, the anguish in his heart was undeniable. His own animal began criticizing him for even considering handing the princess to a Blackfur. A Blackfur! Of all people!

As Greg gently stroked Enora's short, fine hair to calm her, he muttered, "I'm sorry, sweetheart. No more experiments on you, I promise. I'm sorry, okay?"

Enora, surprisingly, responded in a dissatisfied grunt as she began looking at the forest flowers and butterflies again.

Xandar shook his head and murmured, "This is weird," and then went back to study the carving again.

Lucy quickly added, "A good kind of weird, Greg."

Christian and Annie were still lost for words, and when the distant cousins' eyes met, Greg said, "What? You have your favorite niece. Now, I have mine."

Turning defensive, Christian retorted, "Let's face it. You don't have much to cho—oof." He paused when Annie elbowed him in the ribs.

The duchess managed a cordial smile and said, "We're happy for you, Your Grace."

Greg forced a smile of acknowledgment in return, still feeling the residual guilt of what he'd done to her. The fact that she could say something so diplomatic only made him feel worse. Greg would've never forgiven anyone who hurt him and the people he cared about, much like Christian.

Annie's eyes turned fierce when she locked gaze with her husband, linking, *'He's trying, Christian. We should be too. Control yourself.'*

The duke heaved a frustrated sigh and kissed her temple. *'As you wish, my duchess.'*

Greg's sights went to his cousin. "Well, what is that thing? I don't remember any fairy tales about a spooky room in an abandoned castle, so it has to be in some history textbook I burned after the school year."

Xandar and Lucy glanced at Enora, who sometimes got agitated if they spoke a little louder than usual, exactly what Greg was doing right now. But the baby seemed properly distracted.

Xandar rose from his squatting position as he admitted, "This wasn't in any history text that we studied. I have no idea what this is."

Pelly said, "No one does. What's strange is that my instincts gravitate toward this room and this particular sector of the circle." She walked over to the one with vampire fangs.

Lucy felt a pull too—like a thread beseeching her to close the distance, to reduce the tension that was straining both ends. Following her instincts, she came to the sector with the lycan print. Kneeling there and feeling the earlier tension reduced, her animal's hand pushed forward, and they found her hand fit perfectly into the depression.

An idea came to Xandar. "How about you try channeling your Authority and see what happens, Lucy?"

Her eyes turned blue, and her power radiated, making the print and the lines that formed her sector glow in faint blue.

Like a calling, Pelly naturally emitted her own Authority. The fang marks glowed in faint green alongside the lines that form her sector. The two realized they felt an emptiness that should have been filled by the other three creatures destined to be in the three remaining sectors.

Christian muttered, "I wonder who the other three are."

Staring at dormant sectors, they were disappointed that this wasn't a day for complete closure. It might take years or decades before they would know.

Xandar's voice permeated through the silence, "Whoever they are, Lucy and Pelly should be able to mind-link them without forming a link the old-fashioned way. These five share a connection that we don't understand yet."

Octavia mentioned in worry, "The question is: what is it for? There was never anything like this in the past. Why the sudden need for five creatures of different species to form this sort of . . . predetermined connection?"

As Xandar drew circles on Lucy's shoulder, he replied, "I wish I had the answers, Octavia, but I'm afraid I don't. The reason none of the experts could find anything is probably because there isn't anything to find. Our generation might be the first to witness something like this."

Octavia then asked what she really wanted to ask, "Should we be worried about a war breaking out, where these creatures are needed?"

Knowing that it was a possibility, Xandar's brows knitted, but his voice still carried confidence when he declared, "If that ever happens, we'll be ready."

"Yes, we will be," Pelly uttered in ominous agreement.

A servant came to remind the royal families that the ceremony was due to start in twenty minutes. They left the room and entered the grand hall, where the ministers, friends, and families were already gathered.

###

The rulers stood on a makeshift stage, facing the audience as Pelly's voice boomed through the speakers, "For more than a millennium, the kingdom and the empire had been at war. Two hundred five years ago, my late father and the late Lycan King Lucas declared a truce. Even then, our species had never seen eye to eye. Territorial lines drawn in the years of war were never erased and never allowed to be crossed. Integration was a wishful dream, and only the mentally ill would've dared suggest we could achieve something beyond peace with the lycans and werewolves."

Turning to Lucy, who met her smiling eyes, the empress took her hand like she did with Rosalie when she faced the audience again. "When our people were abducted in Falling Vines and Saber Vagary, leaving misleading scents of the species found in the kingdom, we reached out to the lycan king and queen of today, who had been nothing but gracious in lending us a hand, alleviating our plight like it was their own. Their humility and diplomacy are unmatched by predecessors, their skills and character are the epitome of true leaders, and their nobility and ferocity go beyond protecting their own people. They lead with a government that shares the same intentions and virtues, whose members exhibit equally strong and noble characters.

"Apart from them, let's not forget those who've come out of the shadows to assist us, showing us that it is possible for help to come from the most unlikely of places." The rulers looked toward Greg and his mavericks with appreciative smiles, who were touched that their contribution was acknowledged.

Greg whispered to Enora, who he held on his lap, "The ones up there are your mama and daddy's bloodsucker friends. They are safe. Your Uncle and Aunt Blackfur in the next row are safe too. They're just boring, not dangerous. Go easy on them, will you, sweetheart? And do you see that old man over there, the one looking at us like a creep? He's a shady liar. Stay away from him, Enora."

The creep was Maddock. And to be fair, everyone was looking at Greg because that was where the rulers' sights landed. It so happened that most of them couldn't help but see the princess on the duke's lap when their intention was simply to look at the mavericks and their leader.

Pelly's voice brought the attention back to her when she continued, "On behalf of our people, my consort and I convey our highest gratitude to them, their government, and their allies. It was an esteemed pleasure to work with them, and it is our honor to be the ones to return the Crown Jewels to their rightful owners."

Two vampires brought out the royal scepter and brooches on dark green velvet pillows. Pelly took the lycan queen's brooch and pinned it onto Lucy's blouse. Octavia pinned the lycan king's brooch on Xandar's blazer jacket, shaking his hand with a warm smile right after. The empress and consort then handed the king and queen the royal scepter together.

The vampire rulers took a step back as Lucy and Xandar held the scepter facing the audience before Pelly and Octavia offered a bow and uttered in unison, "Your Majesties."

Every werewolf, lycan, vampire, and hybrid in the room got down on one knee as they repeated, "Your Majesties."

The two bowed in return, and as everyone rose to their feet once more, Xandar couldn't help but leave a kiss on Lucy's temple, making her softened eyes gaze into his blissful orbs as her hand gently touched his chest.

At the side, Octavia muttered to Pelly, "Would you look at that—a love as strong as two Rs."

AUTHOR'S NOTE

Dear readers,

Thank you for giving the sequel a chance. I hope the journey taken with the characters in *The Rogues Who Went Rogue* offered the escape you needed. Do spare a few minutes to leave a review on Goodreads and the site you've bought this from!

The title of this book was designed to carry the essence of the story in two ways: first, how the rogues' *pasts* tainted their prospects to the point that they went rogue; second, how their given chance offered them a better *future* after they went rogue against the unwritten rules of their own community, against their nature of never trusting or cooperating with the authorities.

It's a tale of second chances and taking risks, trusting the process while still being wary of pitfalls, and taking necessary precautions to safeguard the interests of those who matter most.

Like the first book, I hope this one offers laughter and strength whenever you may need a replenishment of either.

Here's some insight into the sequels to come: in book three, we'll be acquainted with hunters and a potential duchess; book four, witches and other magical beings; and book five, merfolk; and book six will be an integration of all the species.

We will see how each world collides with the lycans and werewolves, and whether creatures from two different backgrounds and cultures can ever attain peace and harmony.

As per book one, I'll leave you with the thought I kept at the back of my mind for book two:

i. In Margaret's situation: **no one chooses to be in pain, but we can—at our own pace—choose to heal, leave, and grow from it**; and
ii. In Greg and the mavericks' case: **no one wants to screw up, and those who work for a second chance *may* be worthy of that chance.**

Thank you Stacey (@grammargal on Fiverr), for editing and proofreading every line and punctuation; and Sam (@Psalmyy on Fiverr) for formatting this entire thing.

Have a spectacular day, everyone! See you in the next book!

Stina's Pen
AUTHOR

ABOUT THE AUTHOR

Stina's Pen is the pseudonym used by a young woman who has been fascinated by the idea of mate bonds and its corresponding concept of rejection and wanted to write up her own take on the idea. Therefore, she put pen to paper and wrote her first book— *The 5-Time Rejected Gamma & the Lycan King*, which led her to continue the journey with this sequel. Writing also works as her escape to help her manage her less-than-sunny days. She hopes to help readers take a vacation from their everyday lives and experience a whole new world.

When Stina is not writing, she can be found reading anything that piques her interest, accidentally buying books on accidental visits to bookstores despite the shelves of unread novels at home. Always a daydreamer, she often fantasizes about what could unravel if something that didn't happen happened. She is also prone to buying stickers and washi tapes (by complete accident) and then wondering what to do with them.

With a goal of inspiring others and hoping they draw strength from her characters, she wishes to write in a way that makes everyone's days a little brighter, that allows them to appreciate who they are and fall in love with the magic they add into the world.

IG: @stinaspen
Facebook: Stina's Pen
TikTok: @stinaspen

Printed in Great Britain
by Amazon

42337475R00290